EYES OF FAITH

A novel

By Terrance Johnson

7-Fold Publishing

7-Fold Publishing
7732 S. Cottage Grove Ave.
Suite 121
Chicago, IL. 60619
http://www.7foldpublishing.com
email: VIIfoldTerrance@aol.com

Library of Congress Catalog Card Number: 00-191544

ISBN: 0-9667938-2-X

Cover Models: Terrell Clayton and Natasha Hampton
Cover Illustration: Justin Jordan Photography and Digital Imaging
Web Page Designer: electronicmediafactory.com

Dedication

It's an honor to show appreciation to someone when she can see it; give flowers when she can smell them; give praise when she can hear it; give sugar when she can taste it; give love when she can feel it.

It is much more gratifying to give flowers to a beautiful soul while that soul is present to experience it and you can witness their reaction to receiving them. Ma, this is a small flower—a minor token for the many ways you have touched, influenced, inspired, encouraged, loved, and nurtured me. Out of the many examples in humanity, your love for your sometimes scandalous children is one of the closest illustrations of God's unconditional love for us. Your love for us never fails and your arms are always open and willing to embrace us, despite ourselves. May our Lord Jesus continue to use you, and thanx for dedicating me to the Lord when the Lord gave you me. I love you.

Pushing up Daisy Johnson, my favorite flower.

ACKNOWLEDGMENTS

I first of all give thanx to the Author, Editor and Publisher of me, Jesus Christ. Lord, You write my life; when there are errors in me, you edit me; and when I'm ready, you publish me, so I can bring glory and honor to the greatest writer. For rewriting a brother like me—who used to raise the white flags of defeat in the classroom (Lord, remember when I made straight F's that semester)—and giving me the juice to make the Dean's list, I gotta give the highest praise up to You. Hallelujah. Glory to Jesus Christ, for though You have allowed me to memorize Your Word, You have given me my own, personal testimony. I don't have to boast of the miracles you performed for the saints of old, but I can testify of how you gave me an abundance of strength to withstand and overcome the opposition, and wisdom to discern Your righteousness; parted my seas and taken the heat out of my furnaces; fed me when there wasn't food available, shielded me in the presence of my enemies and gave me favor in the face of danger. It is an awesome thing when You just make a door of opportunity when I'm walled in on all sides. I love You, Jesus.

Thanx to the Johnson Five: Travis, Darnell, Lyonel, Bertram (See you in Baptism of Fire, Slick) and Trent (U're gonna have to get on your piano game, 'cause Zac is bad in "Melody in the Midnight Hour" and God has gifted you for a purpose). Kenny "Top Cat" Brock (Jesus has given you a 9-lives testimony...go tell it TC). Albreta (I'm still trying to make it to Dallas ☺) and Spring (I'm gonna use your name, Sis...thanx for proofing me again). It's good to have you all as my older siblings. Thanx Aunt Rose for the encouragement and the publicity. Thanx Aunt Ceuse for the encouragement. ☺

Thanx to all of my writing influences and mentors: Walter Perkins, Derrick Baker, Bernice Williams, George Williams, Sam Henderson, Susan Blakes, John Hector, Tony Baranek, Marilyn Olson, E. Greer (one of the best language technicians ever).

Thanx to the rockers that took the time out to talk to me: Terry Cummings, Craig Hodges, Sherrell Ford, Bryant and Clarence Notree, Hersey Hawkins, Michael Ingram, Tim Bankston, Deon Thomas, David Knight, Nick Anderson, Mario Bailey, Coach Bob Hambric. Also Chris Zorich, my first professional interview. The players behind the players: Norm Nixon, William Strickland, David Ware. Also, a special thanx to

Ben Wilson (the greatest baller to ever step on the court), Mary Wilson, and Jeffery Wilson. My life has truly been touched by you all and I hope that this book does my experiences with you justice.
Special Thanx to my Gospel mentors: Reverend Dr. J. E. Hopkins (a preaching warrior) and my New Nazareth Baptist Church family, for laying the Good News Foundation and for being behind me all of the way; Reverend Leon Edwards and the Southwestern Baptist Church extended family, for building on it and getting the growth process started; Pastor Dwight Craig, for bringing me to maturity, being a Father to me in the ministry (even though you're not elderly), and for being one of my favorite living epistles to read; Pastor Dr. Donald L. Parson, one of the best preachers of the new testament and my new millennium undershepherd, and my new family at Logos Baptist Assembly; Reverend George Cooper (a hard, powerful preaching teacher), Dr. Louis A Barbieri (that Daniel and Revelation class was too enlightening); Evangelist Vincent Craig, my big brother and mentor. The Word that God spoke through you to me in 1997 is coming to pass (but of course, it came from the Lord). Now spit 'em out Vince, this is only practice; Pastor Jacob Pickett, my soul winning general and trainer, and a key player in the demolition of denominational walls.
My fellow Saints that I've met along the way while writing this novel: Ellen Green, a human seraph, true encourager and one of God's powerful Evangelists (I know you don't emphasize the title, but Father called you out like that), Pastors Tony and Lavern Sparks, a power packed team; Terry Jackson, Pastor Dorothy Bledsoe and the whole Walk In Prayer Mission Church of God In Christ. Deirdre Beaver (What a powerful testimony you and your family have. Your humility is amazing and your humor is refreshing); Rasheeda the sensational one, too, for reading the manuscript and encouraging me; Felecia "Fefe" Thompson, thanx for reading the script and giving me your input. Romans 8:2-3 was da apologetic bomb—literally and figuratively speaking. Hurry up and pour out your creative juices. Hey Dove. I'm still considering using your poem ☺ Greetings and much love Eva ☺ Hey Lil'Donna, can't wait for you to pen your book. I hope your narrator is as sassy as you are. Thanx for the vote of confidence Damita. Thanx for the support Jennifer. It's here Ernestine. Thanx for the publicity, my Afrocentric Sister. THIS IS GWEN/LYNN ☺ (I know how to spell your name Gwen). Our meeting is what novels are made of. It was one of the greatest

honors in my writing career to spot you reading my work even before we met. Your captivating looks and resemblance to Faith were big bonuses. Pat "the Cat" Hill. And what a roar you have, Sister ☺ You'll love this one Linda "Sister Saint" Murphy. God bless you Katherine Bush. Here's number two, Sherry G. Hey Katherine Bell, it's finally here. Hurry up Andrea. Thanx for the support, Gail "Gaily" Jones. See you on the Moody's Campus Rev. Donald Fly. Debra Moore, where are you? Stop freaking out Ernie. We'll break bread and a wishbone from Harold's my covenant brother ☺ I'll see you on the east coast Patricia Haley-Brown. "Nobody's Perfect" was all good. Thanx and double thanx for all of the insight, encouragement, and co-struggling in the genre Trevy McDonald, and I can't wait for your sequel ("Time Will Tell" if Mel and Rachel hook up. Sounds like a bestseller to me. See you at the top ☺). And W.L. Wesson, my fellow anointed pen servant who sharpens my countenance. I can't wait to read "Sleep" and "Snatchers", because "Judged" was da bomb.

Extra Special Thanx to Stacy Menefee for editing the first draft. I realize that the manuscript was in its rawest, most grueling form. You have truly elevated Eyes of Faith to Best Seller quality. The publishing houses in New York are not good enough for you. Can't wait to read your work. Peace and blessings Cuz. Also thanx to cover models Natasha Hampton and Terrell Clayton. Much thanx to Rosaline Joshua for helping me with the Yoruba language. May God bless you abundantly for being such a gracious saint. Laura Mayoral, thanx for helping me with the Spanish. Can u match the royal purple on the cover ☺ Thanx Margaret Rivera. Thanx Nicole Abusharif for the Arabic translations. Thanx Tempo Editor Danielle Duncan for the authorization. Once again, Justin Jordan, you hooked the cover up big time. Big ups brother. I look forward to the next two covers. And Eric Johnson, much thanx for creating my website with more flair and care than I could have imagined or dreamed. May God bless you richly, for you have done me a great favor.

Last, but always First, I thank my Father, Brother and Friend; King, Lord and Savior, Jesus Christ. The revealer and fulfiller of dreams and visions. There was a time when I couldn't see my purpose. Society appraised me as something of little value, and that's what I saw. The images and illusions that were presented to me; My surroundings and situations; stresses and struggles seemed to support and reinforce that myopic view. But I'm thankful for hindsight. When I look back at that bad day in which I lost my job, went into foreclosure with my house, had my phone cut off, and had my last $20 ripped off—all on a Friday—I can see clearly through the eyes of faith how You were showing out on my behalf. It was You that turned that bad situation into a liberating testimony and a plush vacation. Lord, I never missed a meal during that period, I didn't make a mortgage payment for the year, I didn't lose my home, and I didn't get an ulcer. Thank You Jesus, it was an amazing ride. I thank You for the personal revelation of the power of prayer, even though I had to break a leg and lay up on my back for a whole summer to get that understanding ☺ Your grace is more than sufficient, for I'm on my feet again, walking by faith (Thank You for the healing touch, Daddy). Just as important as the manifestation of the power and result of prayer, is the answer from You. When I asked You "What do You love about me the most", You replied "Your potential." I know that I have grown because of Your nurturing, but I know that I'm not the most lovable person, so Your answer was a blessed assurance for me. Thank You for not giving up on me when I seemed like a hopeless soul. I don't know what I will become by Your hands, but I do know that you don't half step or give up, and your creativity is extravagant. Even though the picture isn't that attractive, I thank You, for through the eyes of faith I can see the end—which allows me to scorn the current image. Blessing, and glory, and wisdom, and thanksgiving, and honor, and power, and might, be unto my God for ever and ever. Amen.

The steps of a *good* man are ordered by the Lord.—Psalm 37:23

For we walk by faith, not by sight.—2 Corinthians 5:7

Now faith is the substance of things hoped for, the evidence of things not seen.—Hebrews 11:1

PROLOGUE

What I do, say, and think is in the name of the Lord. I'm not an overzealous, self-righteous soul walking on water. I just love the Lord, and I'm not ashamed of loving Him with all of my heart, soul, and mind. He's the reason why I lead the junior church choir—to give praise. He's the reason why I preach the Gospel—to spread the good news to the nations. He's the reason why I wear Jesus memorabilia—to remind others of the Lord's goodness. And He's the reason why I bought this button with the letters GD in caps and the statement "ask me" in lower case, just below it—so when people ask me what GD stands for, I can tell them "I'm God's Disciple." I'm not naive. That letter combination in the wrong place around the wrong person can bring on a world of problems, including death. GD are the initials for the Gangster Disciples, better known as Folks. Their code name is growth and development, as in the growth and development of young drug entrepreneurs. They're the largest of several street gangs in Chicago. Folks is a term of endearment from fellow gangsters and a mockery from their rivals, the Black Stone Rangers, a.k.a. Brothers.

The dealings of the "Brothers" are a contradiction to their nickname. Their activities include robbery, assault, rape and homicide in the name of their gang (just as the Folks do), and that includes their comrades, not to mention innocent children who may happen to be in their way. They're the nations that I want to reach. I want them to "ask me." The button is the knob to open the Door. Every neighborhood is the Lord's territory: ***The earth is the Lord's, and the fullness thereof; the world, and they that dwell therein.*** Most fade away like the color on a bleached garment when I tell them Who I represent. A few listen intently to what the Lord puts in my mouth. They respect God's servants when they stick to their convictions and show respect and concern for people. Often, they claim to know something about God and would consider going to church to join His gang. It's encouraging when they allow me to intercede for them. That alone is worth the risks. As a result of my God-ordained crusade, several young men know the Lord as their Savior, many weak Christians are stronger, and a multitude have seeds planted in their souls.

"I wish you would give the button a rest," Malcolm pleads to me as I pull into the currency exchange parking lot on 75th and Exchange. Anointed's "Spiritual Love Affair" CD plays a soul inspiration, but it doesn't saturate Malcolm's mood like it should.

I smile at the opportunity to preach to my weaker brother and best friend. "Oh brother of little faith, don't you realize *that the battle is not yours, but God's?*"

"Who's to say that the Brothers are going to be curious enough to ask?"

"The way I look at it, *if God is for me, who can be against me?*"

"You know some believe in shooting first, asking later."

"You know from experience that *no weapon that is formed against thee shall prosper,*" I claim, pocketing the keys.

"I also know that *that's* a death wish over in this area."

"I'm like Job: *though He slay me, yet will I trust in him.*"

"C'mon Dex, you know I don't want to see you get taken out."

"I know you don't, but I also know that Jesus loves me and *neither death, nor life, nor angels, nor principalities, nor powers, nor things present, nor things to come, nor height, nor depth, nor any creature, shall be able to separate me from the love of God.*"

"Well," he pauses as we step out, continuing, "if something happens to you, I can't be held responsible for my actions."

"And I can't be held responsible for God's actions...*vengeance is His.*"

"I can't win," Mal says as he throws his hands up to the side.

"Sure you can. God has made you *more than a conqueror,*" I mention as I open the door.

A tall, gaunt guy with a black Sox hat cocked to the left is standing in the doorway, as if filtering the unwelcome out. I greet him with a nod and "what's up" as he glares coldly through my forehead as though he was looking at a bull's-eye through the scope of a rifle. He doesn't utter a word as he eases out, warily tracking me with his predatory eyes. That is as icy a reception as I've gotten out here, but I'm used to it. Too many preachers are comfortable speaking exclusively to church folks from the pulpit. Every Christian has the divine obligation to be missionaries. Although I love bringing the message from the pulpit, there is a greater joy in being out here. The Word is like fire in my bones and I feel ready to erupt, like a volcano. I'm inviting, but I never force the Good News on anyone. When people come to me, I boldly—not confrontationally or condemningly—speak the Gospel.

"Looks like your lure has his attention," Malcolm comments as we proceed to the line.

"He's not bold enough to bite it when he's alone. If he had the backing of his homeys, I would be reeling him in at this very moment."

"I hope he doesn't bring back a legion of thugs. I get uneasy when you try to talk to a bunch of them like that. All it takes is one loose cannon to draw blood and set the whole group into a feeding frenzy like a pack of sharks."

"I hope he brings every wanna-be gangster in the city to me. *One man of you shall chase a thousand: for the Lord your God, he it is that fighteth for you, as he hath promised you,*" I reply with spiritual confidence. "You won't be fearful if you truly trust God. Look at it this way, unless the Lord gives His consent, no harm can come to you."

"That's what I'm afraid of: He'll consent to me getting jacked up," he jokes.

I chuckle along with him. "With the way He reveals things to you, I wouldn't worry about that right now. You have a powerful anointing and you haven't even begun your ministry. So until you proclaim the message He wants you to proclaim—until you hear the message He wants you to deliver—I don't think you have to worry about your life."

"If you say so."

"Just kicking scripture, brother. Just the Word."

"As much Word as you kick, I'm surprised you're not studying theology."

"That's a given. The Gospel is my life. If I don't make a living from preaching the gospel, I'll make it in my Psychology career."

"I don't know," Mal ponders. "The social sciences and the Bible are a strange mix on the mind, wouldn't you say? I mean they say that most psychologists are crazy anyway, and everybody knows that you're a lunatic...after all, you walk around the 'hood with this 'slap me'—I mean 'ask me'—button on."

We both laugh as I step up to the window. "Listen to this slam," I insist as the teller steps away from the window.

"Her charity spares the fool
Who's off to the tort school
Balaam, stop conversing with that mule
She is a Nay answer to a death wish under duress

An emotional bluff is a root of all kinds of mess
I can better you Elijah, enter into eternal rest
Her smile is sunshine on the blind
Everyone has a 20/20 mind
My good son, you left the other nine lepers behind
She opens evil eyes
Waking to the sight of forbidden thighs
Because you see sin like I, David you shall be a child of the Most High
Her nursing hand brings in the birth of a healthy bastard
Deliverance is a breathing word
Solomon heard wisdom gird
She discards high debt
Acceptance of the master plan is a sure bet
I promise that from this day on, my fellow cross bearer, you will be kept
Her love is present at the start of another day of a reckless life
The soul is precious even though it holds iniquity nigh
Protocol son, you were the world's, but now you are Mine
She grants leniency of a capital offense
Unlimited is the charge of penitence
Moses, I will show you deliverance"

He holds his fist out and claims, "I like it" as he grins at me. "It's tight."

I pound him and note, "It's titled 'Twin Sisters of Divinity'."

"It fits," he nods. "The message is clear, because some of those other poets talk like they smoke heroin."

Some of the work that I've heard is like a foreign language or a fragmented concept from a mentally challenged child. "You're a nut," I laugh out as the cashier returns to the window.

The winning prize money for the open mic contest at The Green Door will come in handy at this time, and I'm already claiming the victory. My Uncle Freddie in Atlanta wired some money to me as a Christmas present, which will make the season very merry. Every now and then, he supplements my scholarships and grants to offset my expenses, since I have a family of three to feed and a $20,000 education to get. Uncle Freddie is always on time, because I'm barely making ends meet. I inform the cashier of the wire request as I reach into my pocket for my wallet. That's when I remember that I left my license in the ashtray after the police pulled me over.

"I need to get my ID out of the car," I inform her, darting out the door. Once I get out, I hear "Aiight now Folks" announced from behind.

By reflex, I turn around, not realizing that it's directed at me. The dude that we walked passed on the way in, is trotting towards me with two other dudes. He's ready to "ask me". In slow motion—just as I pull out my sword (better known as the Bible) and open my mouth to greet them in the name of God—he pulls out a gat. The stale pop isn't deafening at all and the fire from the barrel is like a camera flash, but doesn't blind me. He was at point blank range, so I assume that I'm hit, because I'm stumbling to the Currency Exchange door. My senses are going berserk as I hit the ground face up: the sounds around me are choppy and muffled; my body is numb and hot; my vision is tunneled and red. Breathing is difficult and my mouth is like cotton. The sky turns gray and it seems like the sun is eclipsed. Now I'm frigid. Malcolm is in my thin, straight line of vision. His lips are moving, but no sound is coming out. I open my mouth to talk—to tell him it's all right—and I taste liquid rust. My lens closes up some more and the lights dim as the scenes play out: the birth of my son; me and my wife on our wedding day; my classes at DePaul; me and the youth church; my Lord and Savior. My vision spirals shut as I drift into a zionic darkness. When I open my eyes, there's a glorious light and I can hear my favorite song:

O Hap - py day, O hap - py day,
When Je - sus washed my sins a - way!
He taught me how to watch and pray
And live re - joic - ing ev - 'ry day;
O Hap - py day, O hap - py day,
When Je - sus washed my sins a - way!
O hap - py day that fixed my choice
On Thee, my Sav - ior and my God!
Well may this glow - ing heart re - joice
And tell its rap - tures all a - broad.
O hap - py bond that seals my vows
To Him who mer - its all my love!
Let cheer - ful an - thems fill His house,
While to that sa - cred shrine I move.

1

Tis done, the great trans - action's done—
I am my Lord's and He is mine;
He drew me, and I fol - lowed on,
Charmed to con - fess the voice di - vine.
Now rest, my long - di - vid - ed heart,
Fixed on this bliss - ful cen - ter, rest;
Nor ev - er from my Lord de - part,
With Him of ev - 'ry good pos - sessed.
O Hap - py day, O hap - py day,
When Je - sus washed my sins a - way!
He taught me how to watch and pray
And live re - joic - ing ev - 'ry day;
O Hap - py day, O hap - py day,
When Je - sus washed my sins a - way!

You never knew the lyrics to that song. The chorus is catchy and up until Monday afternoon, you didn't know there were any other words to it. The purple overlayed junior choir, over which Dexter presided, only vitalized the song that's been ringing in your mind's ear for five days. Unfortunately, the eternal echo of the door-dulled pop is not drowned out. It's amazing how such a powerful, consoling message in music can dilute and sugar-coat with Nutrasweet the bitter reality of the setting dawn—a dawn that you watched as the storm clouds eclipsed and dusked it out. The sun will rise tomorrow, but you will never see that day again. Tragedy is the fertilizer to creativity, so you write your mind:

Although Black is beautiful, there are some ugly shades.
The hue is always in the negative light, though.
Shadows consume each other. The reflection of luminosity.
First there was black. The source of white. The source of sight.
When illumination infiltrates the dark, blackness leaves faster than the speed of light.
But what happens when you snuff out the light?
White light is replaced by total blackness and you shall see no evil.

You let your pen fall in the crease of your burgundy daily minder and slowly close it as you stare out of the window in the back of the limousine. A dry, grainy snow is blowing impatiently. It's a quarter after 11 in the morning and the sun still hasn't made an appearance. If there weren't a cloud in the sky, it would still be a gloomy day. The wind chill is driving away from the grave-sight the few people who came out. It wasn't the Chicago hawk that drove you in. You didn't even feel it since you were already numb before you stepped out into the nippy air. Shock has a tendency to deaden the nerves and repetition has a conditioning effect. It's too bad it doesn't apply to your heart. It feels like somebody caved your chest in with a battering ram. Where's the anesthesia? You've felt this before, but no matter how many times you feel it, your heart can't get used to it. Otherwise, you might have been able to watch as they lowered Dexter Lewis into the ground.

Dexter's wife emerges from the far side of the hill with their son Dexter Jr. being towed by the hand as she rests her head on Uncle JoJo's chest. He offers her the solace of scriptures and blessed assurances as he escorts her down the hill, his arm around her. Perhaps she's taking it the hardest of everybody that knew him. There's no way to gauge grief, so the only indication of the heartache is the ostensible manifestation. By those standards, you're fairing quite well.

You take a deep breath and bury your head into the palms of your hands, contemplating what two-dimensional words you can say to her that haven't already been said and re-said. Words are weak if actions aren't speaking. What would you want to hear? *Get up Dexter...*And of course, you would want to see Dexter rise with that command. But it's not happening on this side. Your best friend is gone, shot dead like public enemy number one; like big game in Saint season. Another gun crime stat. The second senseless death in five years that has had a direct hit on your heart. The wounds hurt worse with every friend that perishes. This is becoming so common in your realm, that you've started wondering when it will be your turn.

Five summers ago, life reached an all-time, tenebrific low. You, Dexter and your first cousin, Raymond (the Three Musketeers, as we called ourselves, since back in the day we were inseparable, doing everything together from backsliding into iniquity to trekking the path of righteousness) were eagerly anticipating the end of the school year, b-ball in the park and girls in biker shorts. Puberty and summer both checked in with a bang. There were already three 90-degree days in the first week of June, so you took it for granted that we got a sneak peak of things to come.

The last day of school came and we celebrated by going to see "School Daze" at the Evergreen Plaza. It was entertaining and funny, even though we didn't get it when Laurence Fishburne said "Wake up" at the end. His roles are some of the most profound, but at that time his character was too deep for us. We tripped on it all the way to the 95th Street stop and mocked it with the rest of the youngsters who had gathered at the back of the bus. We all tried to tell our own version of the movie simultaneously. It was festive until the bus passed the tracks at Vincennes. One of the dudes in the back of the bus near us threw his hand up at some guys on the outside as the bus passed them. He was hardly waving good-bye: he threw up a 'five' (a gang sign people don't flash in that neighborhood, unless they are ready to be embalmed with lead). You doubt if the guy was actually in a gang, let alone ready to duck, but the thugs outside took him literally. No one had a chance to take cover. One shot was fired through the back window and into the right temple of Raymond. Blood sprayed everything and everyone to his right, including Dexter, who passed out as if he had taken the lead. Raymond sat just to your right, but in a twinkle, he departed like a raptured saint—blinking in this realm and awakening in glory.

It was an awakening for you, too. Your eyes were suddenly opened to the realization that life shouldn't be taken for granted. Despite the promise of a cycle of goodness, fate reneged. One's existence could cease before conception in a mother's womb or decease at 120. But who controls destiny? You're tempted to test the architect of life and conclude your short story. It's a bluff that you're afraid will be called. Raymond turned 11 three weeks prior to his death. That summer turned out to be one of the hottest and most eventful in Chicago, but you missed it all while mourning in private. In retrospect, the only thing worthwhile that you missed, was Raymond. There came a point in that season when people couldn't tell if you were sweating or crying, becoming involuntary witnesses to your last recollection of the watery release. Even on this record-tying day of desolation, the clouds are dark and full of the promise of water, but the water doesn't fall. Memories are like two-edged swords: one end is a blessed protection; the other is a self-cutting curse. After a year had passed, you still felt that getting over it was an impossibility, although life had progressed like a glacier. You slowly realized the grief wouldn't kill you, and for that you didn't know whether to be thankful or regretful. Dexter is now buried about thirty yards away from Raymond. You will never be the same until the Three Musketeers meet up again in the afterlife—if we ever meet again—and even then, you will be changed.

We did everything together. When we fought against each other, we were still allies. Our conflicts were never more than empty threats or half-hearted shoves. No matter what the squabble, the sun never set on our unresolved differences. However, let one of us get into it with someone else. We would be on him like a pack of piranhas. Whoever was against one of us, had to deal with all three of us. Even if we were outnumbered 100 to 3 (10 to 3 in the case of our run in with some Disciples around the church), we took a beating together if we all couldn't get away. That's what we were about: Three-in-one and one-in-three, just like the Trinity—Brothers willing to die for one another.

You lean back and tuck your minder in-between your legs on the floor as they reach the limo. The door opens gently and Dexter Junior climbs in and crawls onto your lap, oblivious to the solemn mood. The door remains ajar as Uncle JoJo and Angela linger outside. You look at Junior, force a half-smirk and ask, "How's my homey?"

"Fine," he responds.

"You gonna throw me an alley-oop?"

He excitedly responds, "Ollyoop. Ollyoop."

"Gimme a pound," you say, sticking your fist out for Junior to hit. He obliges so you shoot, "Right back at you." Jr. sticks his fist out and you gently tap the tiny fist with your fist. "Let's bring it home Dex-in-effect," you say, extending your hand for him to clasp. You pull it away simultaneously with Jr. and our hands make a snap to the delight of little Dexter.

Junior quickly calms down and grows quiet for a swift second, as if he is deep into his own little innocent world. His attention seems to be focused on the falling snow on the outside as he gapes out the window. As if in a trance, he monotonously asks, "Can we go shoot?"

"A little later, Buddy. A little later," you answer, absently rubbing his head.

Your smile fades and you brace yourself when you sense a more serious question coming. Junior's face reveals that he's brainstorming and something is definitely troubling him. Dexter would go into the same type of daydream before he would ask a blunt question. He turns and focuses on your face, searching. "Why daddy won't wake up?" he queries intently, expecting an answer.

You look him in the eyes for a moment that lasts forever, before quickly turning away and rapidly blinking back unexpected tears. Why did they let him see that? If an adult can't handle the finality of the end, how can you explain it to a three-year-old?

"Because..." you attempt to give him an answer, but choke on volcanic grief and despair. You take a deep breath and swallow, trying to regain your composure. Somebody has to initiate the healing process with Junior, even if he doesn't perceive his injury. "Because he's very tired," you reply.

"Is he coming back?" he shoots.

You gaze at him and pause, because you realize you can't feed him any manure this time. It's a delicate situation and you know you have to make it as good as possible. "No...But when he wakes up, he'll be in Heaven with God and he'll be waiting there for you."

Junior looks intently at you, watching the words spill from your mouth. When he's satisfied that you've finished answering, he asks you "Where is Heaven?"

You knew this was coming. "Heaven is...way up in the sky—past the clouds, past the stars and even past the sun. Airplanes and rocket ships can't even get there. Only the wings of an angel are strong enough to make it. It's a looonnng way from here, because that's where all the good people go to live when they take their long nap. It's far, far away from everything bad. When we take our long nap, we'll wake up in Heaven, too...with Daddy."

You know what the next question is going to be and you almost answer it before he asks, "Why they put him in ground?"

"So Daddy can grow his wings. When you put things in the ground, they go through a change. When you plant a small seed, it grows into a big, strong, beautiful flower. Daddy is going through his change now."

Complicated explanations are not necessary. It would confuse you and the kid. Either Junior is so mesmerized by the revelation that he's satisfied or he's so confused that he doesn't know what to ask next. At least you were honest without being blunt. So you paralleled the wing story with the Apostle Paul's explanation in 1st Corinthians 15—it fits for now. No one has all the answers at the moment.

Junior turns to look outside the window at his mother, and asks, "Why Mommy crying?"

"People—especially ladies—cry for different reasons. They cry because they are sad. They cry when they are happy. Mommy is crying because she's happy that Daddy is going home to be with the Lord, and she's sad because she's going to miss him."

"I'm going to miss him too, and I can't wait to see him again."

"I can't either, Buddy," you say, palming his head. Your eyes get dewy, but you're not about to let yourself cry. There's something in the car that's making you sniffle—something that you're allergic to. Right now, Junior is the only glimmer of daylight. You feel good that you briefed him on Heaven, even though you yourself have a lot of unanswered questions.

All of your life you were taught the Bible. It was the law of the house. Uncle JoJo (Deacon Joseph Johnson to the congregation) ran a tight ship. He knows his Bible inside and out, and even knows a little bit about the other main doctrines of the world. The Watchtower Society (as he calls them, claiming that he's a real Jehovah's Witness) is at the top of his food chain. They usually come to him in a group of three, with one spokesperson. It's an amusing, yet sad, sight to see him salivate, bait, trap, skin, wash, engulf, chew, swallow, indigest, digest, fart and defecate the JW's and their literature before the two pupil's very eyes. He does this without being affected, infected or neglected by the doctrine he calls 'spiritual poison', presenting it back to them on a silver platter, along with the unadulterated Gospel and all of the epistle trimmings. He's never mean, confrontational, antagonistic, or patronizing. Often, they would flee spiritually wounded, naked and defeated; other times they would start a side argument (usually losing that one, too); occasionally, they would play the dumb, brainwashed, non-thinking androidic follower who "can't compute simple logic" role. When all is said and done, the Watchtower Society can't stomach their own by-product. When it comes to religious debates, Uncle JoJo is seemingly untouchable. He can convince almost any faithful, open-minded non-Christian that his faith was crap. Like you, he has the perfect foundation for an exceptional lawyer.

In Uncle JoJo's house, you ate, slept, and drank Jesus—everyday and every night. He made sure you knew the account of Joseph—the favorite son of Jacob—and Joseph—the husband of Mary and earthly father of Jesus. He never tired of telling you about their dreams and reminding you that he is their namesake. By the fourth grade, you knew and pretty much lived by the Ten Commandments. Of course you've fibbed here and borrowed there without asking, but you've never killed anybody, blasphemed against the Holy Ghost or worshipped another god. By the sixth grade, you knew every book of the Bible. You even finished reading the whole thing from Genesis 1 and 1 to Revelations 22 and 21 in just under three years, and believed what you consumed—still do...for the most part.

No matter what happened, you had to glorify God. If times were good, you praised the Lord; If times were bad, you still worshipped Him because all happenings were in His perfect will. You're not throwing away everything you were brought up on—that which you are made of—but your faith has taken a heavy blow below the belt. You feel that your spiritual foundation is cracked. It was you who was supposed to give remarks during the service. The Jesus speech was well penned, but your faith felt shattered and grief gripped your larynx just as you stepped in front of the mic. You feel justified in your silence, because Jesus' followers were melancholy while Jesus was in the grave. It wasn't until they saw Him alive again that they were encouraged. Do you have to wait until you enter eternity to once again be heartened?

Of course, the question of "Why?" lingers around your soul like a foul odor. You have started questioning everything about the Word. It made sense when the characters in the Bible had their peaks and valleys to travel, but when you are faced with this adversity, you can find no mitigation or understanding in the scriptures. You could handle other trials and tribulations (even the wound from the first loss closed into a scar), but this is too overwhelming. You are so traumatized that you can't even cry if you wanted to...just moan. This is pain beyond your imaginable threshold. You didn't know you could hurt this bad and still be alive, though you're so numb you don't know if you are alive. Perhaps this is just the long, painful process of dying. And the worst thing is knowing that you have to forgive the bastard who pulled the trigger. Scripture states, ***"For if ye forgive men their trespasses, your heavenly Father will also forgive you: But if ye forgive not men their trespasses, neither will your Father forgive your trespasses."***

With you fatefully absorbing the news firsthand, the unmerited privilege to phone Dexter's mother in the midnight hour and inform her that her baby went home, but wasn't coming home, fell hard on you. She could only wail the keening song of a heart tortured beyond comprehensive endurance. It was Ms. Lewis who plodded to the podium after he was eulogized as a martyr, and beseeched the congregation to pardon the triggerman, who was picked up on a corner two blocks away and two hours after, kicking it with his boys and smoking a joint for the road with the same indifference that he smoked Dexter. He didn't even hide out. You tell yourself that you will eventually pardon him, but right now, you want to drive a stake through Kenny Reed's black-ass heart.

The door opens slowly and Angela steps in. She moves like a zombie. Her eyes are naturally big, but they are puffy, red, bloodshot, and swollen like a defeated prizefighter's. She looks straight ahead, as if in a daze...as if in a nightmare. Of course she's been crying for days. Her body is probably sapped of most fluids. You reach over and pull her close to you, assuring her "I'm here with you." She buries her head in your chest and starts sobbing. There's nothing that can be said or done to ease her pain. Time is the best healer. Unfortunately, it has stopped right now. The only thing that you can do is support her...spend time and cope with her, which is good therapy for you, too. In tragic times like these, real friends step up.

You lay trance-like on the bench in the locker room, dripping wet with a towel wrapped around your waist and your hands folded across your chest. Shaq's cut "I Know I Got Skillz" plays on the team boom box, drowning out the echoing whistles and bouncing ball. A vaporish climate blankets you. The steam is dense enough to drink with a deep breath. Your team is still on the court blowing South Suburban out, but you were sent to the showers early. You're replaying the whole first half that you did play in your head over and over, just like an action scene from a movie. When you heard that Greg Byrne was going to ref the game, you knew you were in for a long evening, although it was cut short.

Not once was South Suburban whistled for fouling you. They were playing Rugby. The game turned into a battle royal, with you and your teammates on the receiving end of clotheslines, elbows, and forearms. You even absorbed a punch to the face, as evidenced by a busted lip. Ironically, every breath you exhaled and every drop of perspiration you released seemed to be interpreted as a foul against South Suburban. However, the one thing that pissed you off to the third power occurred when you played defense against their top scorer, Tom Dubinski. Every time you were in front of him with good position, he would stomp on your foot and run you over—an obvious charge, even to a one-eye bat with a cloudy cataract, but a no-call to your good buddy Greg Byrne—and drive in for a lay-up. Not only did you end up on your back looking at the bottom of his Reeboks, but those size 15's put blisters on your foot. It happened twice and you were waiting for it to happen again; all you needed was three steps and Tom would be out like a light.

South Suburban was shooting two free throws with two minutes left in the half and you were lined up next to Tom in the shooting lane. Just before the first shot, you leaned forward with your knees bent and hands clasping the bottom of your shorts and gave him a warning straight from the ghetto: "You step on my foot again and I'ma drop you." Tom heard you loud and clear and knew where you were coming from, because without even looking at you, he placidly responded "Alright" as if it was only a bluff.

Sure enough, on their next possession he was dribbling down with his body protecting the ball. When you came up close to him, he stomped on your foot and thought he was going in for an easy crip, but you grabbed the shoulder straps of his jersey with your left hand—pulling him to you—and let a right cross fly to his nose that staggered him back like a punch-drunk heavyweight. That snout will never be the same. It was definitely a knockout punch. Not even the roaring crowd could muffle out the echo of the missile hitting its target. It made a "CRACK SNAPPLE POP!" sound, like the combination of a raw egg hitting the ground and hands clapping. Tom—about twenty feet away then and out of arms reach—just glared at you, visibly startled, with blood dripping from his beak. He didn't believe that dog dung stank, so he had it smeared all over his face. Even if both benches hadn't cleared and the refs hadn't come between us, he didn't want any more. And that ended your Christmas Tournament. You close your eyes and smile as you reflect on what happened about forty minutes ago.

Regrets are one thing you don't believe in. So what if there were talent scouts crawling all over the building; So what if the fight only fortified the reports that had spread throughout the high school basketball community that the 'M' in Malcolm stood for Maker: Maker of Trouble. There is no sweat in your palms.

As one of the top guard prospects in Illinois, all facets of your game are solid: White boys envy your range; you can keep the defense posted; the lane is yours when you want it; the vertical is 48 inches and rising like yeast; your handles are tight (although you're not a point guard); only smoke from burning rubber comes close to the density of the D. At 6'4" (6'5 1/2" with shoes on), you can even play small forward, and your name has been mentioned in the same commentary as the best to come out of Illinois. The comparisons to Nick Anderson with handles and Hersey Hawkins with a smile are incessant. But the main thing that made you top grade meat and every college coaches dream, was that not only could you play—it was natural to you—but you *would be able* to play: 33 on the ACT; 3.98 cumulative GPA; top three ranking in a class of 500. With credentials like that, most coaches will find a way to justify you going on a killing spree, but the "smart-ass with a bad attitude" tag spooks the recruiters who expect a humble indentured servant. It's all about perceptions: "Smart" you earned and wear well; "Ass" is a hoofed *animal* that resembles a horse (you're 100%—not 1/3, not 2/3, but 100%—hu*man*); "Bad" is an adjective to describe how good you are; "Attitude" is subjective to several variables, but yes, you do have one that is often misunderstood.

When you were picked up for violating the 11 p.m. curfew, it was news that the public could use. No doubt about it, a high school sophomore has no business out at two in the morning. Adults really shouldn't be out unless it's for legitimate employment purposes. Perhaps in the distant future people will look back and say that it was to enhance your career (if you go pro). You had studied for your second Biology test all day and into the night. The first test score was a disappointing high "C", so a redemptive "A" was the motivation. It wasn't your rigid routine of exercising for an hour a night that brought you out. In order to retain heaps of mental food for long and short rang recollection, you have to get your circulation going. That's the only way to an "A". Otherwise, you would've wasted six hours of your life reading about biological order, regulation, and homeostasis. It was on the last block of the one-mile run on 82nd and Yates that the brave officers took a bite out of crime. You were 50 yards from your home when they rolled up beside you. If you had known that they were going to "do their job," you would have kept running. Instead of seeing you home, they loaded you in the back seat, filled out the tedious paperwork, and leaked the offense to the press, as if they picked up one of America's Most Wanted fugitives. The demigods of the media had a field day commentating on morals and the good old days. To let them tell it, criminals always start off with curfew offenses and graduate to acts of terrorism, mayhem and murder. You vowed to do a drive-by the next time and really earn your bad rap.

Your next transgression came a year later, and the death penalty seemed to be the only satisfactory remedy. Deadly sin: You "hopped" the 79th Street bus. Fare jumping was the legal lingo they used. What was the world coming to? It had to be a sign of the last days. Forget the blood of Jesus, the heroic detectives purged the world of sin by taking you to the station for "stealing" a bus ride. Never mind the drug trade that was—and still is—as covert as a nuclear explosion; Forget about the mounting homicides that were—and still are—making millionaires out of morticians; Don't worry about the sexual assailants that had—and still have—canines watching their tails and taking cover. Arrest the desperado for trying to get out of paying a buck and there is world peace. It's Miller time. The media made you an icon for Generation X...a symbol for all that's wrong with today's youth. It amused you to no end and there were more publicized "run-ins" to come.

The final buzzer rings out, so you sit up and stretch in anticipation of your celebrating comrades. After about five minutes, the roar of the victors races down the hallway just before they bust through the door, wolfing it up with the trophy being carried by two players. The team immediately comes over to give you high five's for the TKO and the championship. Chuck Duncan (a.k.a. Chuck D because of his tight D), the point man, comes over to shake hands, and we snap our fingers as we break the clasp. Then he palms your bare head with his hot, massive hands.

"Yeah Dawg. You served his ass well. I was waiting for another honky to jump. We would've tore this mother down. They would've had to call the National Guard in on us. Next week I'm going to have 'M TKO J' etched in my head," he says with great enthusiasm. Chuck is always getting symbols and messages cut into his close cropped head. The Knicks emblem in the back has almost faded away.

Then the center, Mitch Harper, yells out "He looked like the Scorpion from Mortal Combat when he pulled him by the shirt and knocked blood from him. How you say it X: *'Get over here!' BOOMSHACKALACK!* I was waiting for the chance to take his head off myself, since he messed up my do," he notes, patting his short afro that adds an inch to his 6'7" frame. He pokes out his mouth to illustrate "He busted my lip, too," as if those inner tubes weren't inflated enough.

Coach Wade comes over to you and puts his fat, stubby hands on your shoulders. "I'm not going to chastise you because I know they were playing bullshit ball and the refs weren't going to give us any calls. It was a good shot, though, but next time try to keep your cool. We need our top gun available when we're on the battlefield," he says as he squeezes your arm and baby slaps you on the cheek.

"Next time I'll just switch men with Chuck D and let him get thrown out," you joke with a half-smile.

"You must've been doing some serious bench pressing before the season. Tyson would've been proud of that KO," Mitch says as he walks up and play punches you in the arm.

"I haven't touched a weight in six months."

"Then how did you get that definition in your arms? You ain't on steroids are you? Hey y'all—X been using steroids. We gonna have to forfeit the game and give the trophy back," he jokes.

"Then I'll have to rip their spines out." Mitch calls you X in reference to Professor Xavier of the mutant comic book heroes from Marvel. He christened you that since you're "stupid-smart" and clean-shaven. Today, Wolverine would've been a more appropriate dub.

"Damn. You are kinda on the bigger side. What's up with that? You wasn't this big last season and I know it didn't come from eating red meat and potatoes," Chuck D declares, grabbing your biceps.

"I bet he can't get through the key hole now," seventh-string center Deon Harris jokes.

"All of y'all just line up for a complementary bloody nose," you offer. "Don't envy me for my fat-burning abilities."

You loathe the way your system burns up calories. If you could carry weight, you would gladly carry about 200 pounds. You've tried both extremes of adding mass: Working out and sucking down all the calories you could pack into your belly. When eating three full meals a day amounted to no ounces gained, you tried drinking those high calorie milkshakes that went down like stale oatmeal. For a few hours, you would be about five pounds heavier, but then your body would send it out of your rear, ears, mouth, nose, and pores. That was a serious case of acne, and it didn't give you a rush, even though it was sweeter than molasses. Your reflexes were shot while on that diet. While playing defense, it seemed like you had a gorilla on your back and iron shackles on your feet, so needless to say, Heavy D could've beaten you off the dribble. On a couple of occasions, ingesting it was more strenuous than the actual workout that usually followed. After the bloody bowel moving muscle-enhancing pills failed to turn you into a hulking swingman, you resolved to count the blessing of high metabolism and accept your life as a stick character.

"RPS man," Mitch suggests. "That'll put some mass on you while you earn some money. When I worked for them during the school strike, they had me lifting those heavy boxes for four hours a day. It was like lifting weights."

"Sorry man. I ain't interested in my nights turning into mornings on a rigid quota system at the conveyor belt. I'll just stay slim," you declare as the Daily Southtown reporter that covers your school approaches you. Of course, the press is your nemesis, and you're reluctant to talk to them. At the same time, you are a by-line-credited member of the fourth estate yourself. In fact, your writing credit came in the form of an editorial, in response to a biased account of another brush with the law that you didn't think the Sun-Times would print.

After a blowout victory (90-55) over a scrappy, top-ten rated Buckland Bison team in the Thanksgiving Tournament of 1992, you were in the corridor of the school for a drink of water. It was a highlight game for you: 28 points, 4 spectacular, home-crowd silencing dunks, 5 steals, 3 blocks, 8 assists and 10 boards. You shutout their top threat, Dan Chapman, before he fouled out, which really disappointed their fans.

An overzealous Bison devotee full of brew-fueled bravado, stupidity and prejudice got in your face as two of his less boisterous buddies stood back. You ignored him and stepped around him, not that you were afraid (you knew that it was more potential negative publicity that you were growing weary of). What did Joe fan do? He got up beside you as you headed back to the gymnasium and started calling you all kinds of nigger SOB's. You've been called worse by better, so you played him like the tongue-tied invisible man. He took your long-suffering poise as fear and got in front of the door before you went in. Not only did he spew verbal venom, but hot, sour saliva, which made you snap like an overstretched rubber band. You were in the last stages of a head and chest cold, so you coughed up the remnants of the germs from your chest, sucked a big, slimy mucus ball from your nasal passage, and shot the gold concoction right in between his eyes. It stuck there and stretched down to the floor like mozzarella cheese. You proceeded to grab him by the hair and deliver a wicked uppercut as his comrades interceded, adding momentum to the tussle as you all spilled onto the gym floor.

The press went into a frenzy, but what vexed you into action was a comment about your upbringing. Your home training has nothing to do with outside, controllable elements, although your momma told you that if a person spits in your face, that he has given up his human rights to live and to... The only thing that kept you from going to jail (a la Allen Iverson in Virginia earlier in the fall) is video cameras in the hallway that caught the whole thing on tape.

All along you knew you could write "A" compositions and research papers, but you never knew or appreciated the power of your written word...that is, until you saw your editorial appear in the daily paper for millions to read. It was terse and potent. You aspired to be a lawyer, and you will eventually end up in law school, but writing is something that you can do on or off the job, with or without an advanced education. A legal foundation and your communication gift will only compliment each other. God anointed your pen as follows:

> **Not only was the account in the editorial blatantly biased, but it was laced with hypocrisy. It is amazing how the media will implicitly place athletes like me on a godly pedestal while in its heart is a total disdain for my race. You judge us by rigorous standards, and you have fallen short on your own objective pledge. You deem every shortcoming and mistake from an individual as an affirmation of innate evil. You have perpetrated greater transgressions on a sanctimonious scale against the people of my race.**
>
> **I can't walk on water, raise the dead, heal the sick or conquer death. Often people cloak their transgressions**

behind the sacred principle "He who is without sin cast the first stone". I am full of faults. I'm not proud of them, but I'm aware of and acknowledge them.

Several writers have prospered by slandering me. My family has been accused of being irresponsible. It is such a strong axiom, that several of my "colleagues" have written personal things about me without as much as saying hi or bye. Until you actually walk in my shoes, walk the same road, walk with me, or at least talk with me, your articles will only serve as fertilizer for racism, and eventually there will be a harvest for you to reap.

That gave them a severe case of writer's block concerning you, and it earned you the nickname in the media circle, of X—as in Malcolm "What will he do next?" X: the man of mysterious means and a mind of maximum magnitude. The praise for the article meant more than the glory from the court. Of course, you would rather write commentaries on your point of view or editorialize a neutral subject, but you're not bashful or reticent with reporters. Todd was the first reporter that actually did an in-depth, flattering feature on you after the liberation letter. His story will be juicy today, since you're emotionally charged and full of insight. If you were in the NBA, you would get fined dry for some of the things you're about to say. However, you'll spare Todd's white ears the racial epithets that taint your tongue.

Todd comes up and nervously says, "Sorry the game didn't go well."

"Apology unnecessary. We won the game anyway."

"Do you feel that the officials called a good game?" he questions, as if reciting from a standard questionnaire.

"Absolutely not. I think they were very biased, prejudiced, racist—however you want to put it. Every time Byrne calls one of our games or any other public league team, he suddenly goes blind when it comes to making calls on the other team. Granted, they call the game differently in the suburbs, but a punch in the face is a foul anywhere. It was obvious he wasn't inclined to call it," you state precisely, without any possible misinterpretations as Todd holds his recorder a few feet from your mouth.

"So do you feel that their lack of calls in your favor caused tempers to flare?"

"Definitely. The refs should have stepped in when their players were making every illegal wrestling move in the book. But the way I feel, it didn't matter. They knew better than to strike the face in the name of winning. I took it real personally, because they made it a personal attack. Regardless of whether the refs call it or not, you should expect to get into a fight when you play dirty like that. And they were sure playing dirty."

"You still ended up with 20 points, even though you only played the first half. How did their style of play effect your game—if at all?"

"They shut me out in the second half," you joke. "But seriously, it made me mad. When I was bridged in the first two minutes, that set the tone. When I get mad, my game goes to another level. I can play effectively with anger. If I would've played the second half, I would've probably ended up with 100 points. I'm used to playground ball...that's where I'm at my best. And on the playground, if you play you pay. They played dirty, so they had to pay," you claim as Todd listens intently and nods his head in agreement.

"Do you worry that the fight will scare some recruiters off? I hear there were supposed to be a lot of scouts..."

"Not at all," you answer before Todd can finish the comment. "This isn't the first time I did something considered bad for a basketball player trying to get into a Division I school on scholarship. I'm a person before I'm a player, and there's only so far I—or anyone else, as far as this matter is concerned—can be pushed before I push back. In this case, it was a punch. I believe my skills speak for themselves. The way I see it, if a college doesn't want me because of this, I don't want them. One way or another, I'll end up at somebody's university, and I'll play ball next season, too. If I don't get a basketball scholarship, I will get an academic scholarship. There's more to my life than basketball. I'm going to college to get an education and help my community, not to play basketball and make somebody's program look good and earn money. I'm at no man's mercy and no man is at my mercy," you state as Todd starts getting a little uneasy.

"One more question...you lost your best friend earlier this week. How did that affect your game and your life?"

You pause, drop your smile and look at the white wristband on your right forearm as your heart smarts at the thought. Dexter wore the arm piece during his tennis matches and it still has his light, metallic scent in it.

"How did it affect my game and my life," you recite. It truly has turned your world upside down. You want to know the reason behind God's season for the angel of death to reap his soul. And if He did give you a reason, you would still ask why. Why now? Why him? If the Lord gives you an audible answer, you wouldn't be able to comprehend it with your finite mind. "From this day forth, I do every thing in remembrance to him. My career—both basketball and otherwise—is dedicated to him," you claim with finality.

"Well...that's all for now," he says as he turns his recorder off. "I'm gonna let you go now. Sorry about your friend, and thanks for talking with me," he says as he extends his hand.

"Thank you. See you at the next game," you say as you give him a firm handshake. "Have a Merry Christmas."

An hour later, you find yourself home...alone. Mitch had a girlfriend waiting in her ride, while Chuck D's grandfather dropped you off from the school after the bus let you out in the parking lot. Ma is at work (she works the night shift at Mercy Hospital) and Uncle JoJo left for a visit to Christ Tabernacle Apostolic Church in Gary, Indiana with the Walk of Faith congregation. Usually you savor the solitude of an empty house, but now it only highlights the fact that you're not only alone, but lonely in the worst way. Two components made up your inner circle of friends: Dexter Lewis and Raymond Johnson. Your sanctity went to the grave with them. There are several people to talk to, but what you want to express is sacred and privileged emotions, which were kept in the triangle. Now the feelings are internalized until eternity.

Under the dim lamp and under the bed covers, you peruse the obituary, reading the scripture that gave Dexter so much inspiration and comfort, searching for a hint of God.

The disciple is not above his master, nor the servant above his lord. It is enough for the disciple that he be as his master, and the servant as his lord. If they have called the master of the house Beelzebub, how much more shall they call them of his household? Fear them not therefore: for there is nothing covered, that shall not be revealed; and hid, that shall not be known. What I tell you in darkness, that speak ye in light: and what ye hear in the ear, that preach ye upon the housetops. And fear not them which kill the

> *body, but are not able to kill the soul: but rather fear him which is able to destroy both soul and body in hell. Are not two sparrows sold for a farthing? and one of them shall not fall on the ground without your Father. But the very hairs of your head are all numbered. Fear ye not therefore, ye are of more value than many sparrows. Whosoever therefore shall confess me before men, him will I confess also before my Father which is in heaven. But whosoever shall deny me before men, him will I also deny before my Father which is in heaven.*

Nothing. You can't feel God in Jesus' promise of worth in His sight. His life line of 1975-1993 on the front seems to contradict that scripture. You place the obituary on the nightstand and turn the light off as you lay on your back and stare up into the darkness. Without saying a prayer, you close your eyes...*just as Dexter reaches the splendid form on the mountain peak. The journey was long and treacherous; his body was worn and battered. However, the expedition has concluded, his person is rejuvenated, and he has his reward. His body and countenance beam with peace and love as he fades behind the silhouette of light. He enunciates, "It's okay." You're left looking up from the valley of woe...alone. The mountain is too high and too steep to climb. Grief grips you as you weep. He urges you to come. You don't question Him as you step to the base and start your ascent, determined to get over the mound of resistance. The sky blackens, the earth trembles and the mountain opposes you with an avalanche. The ground splits with each step; boulders fly past your head with evil intent, but you don't flinch or stumble and He doesn't move as the volcano erupts with a sonic boom that tranquilizes the atmosphere. The land stops sliding and the earth stops quaking as you peek at the rifts all around you. The ground opens up beneath your feet as you lose your balance, and you're sucked into the lava. Starting with your spirit, you vaporize from the intense heat. Your soul disintegrates as you descend. Just as you reach the molten rock to complete the final phase of the destruction of your whole being—the killing of the body—*you wake up broiled and airless. That's not the answer you're looking for.

2

Just as your eyes shut...Raymond reached the lustrous figure in the clouds. Raymond was radiant too, as he gave you an approving smile. "It's okay," he said as he disappeared behind the glorious being. There was no ground between you...just air. You looked on in sadness as He gestured for you to come. Excitedly, just as you started walking His way, the tempests raged on both sides of you, but you boldly pressed on and sidestepped them. That was hang time in overdrive. With each zephyr step came divine power. That was a walk of faith, but your focus was the key. Debris filled winds beat against your body as the vortex came in your path. Your vision still wasn't obstructed as His glory shined through. As you entered the eye of the storm there was serenity, so you reluctantly glanced to the side. A gust picked you up and tossed you about with such force that it seemed like your limbs were being ripped off as your lungs deflated. You willed yourself awake, hyperventilating and sweat wet. That wasn't the answer you were looking for. June 24, June 29, June 30, July 3, July 7, July 8, July 12, 1988. "It's Gonna Rain".

It's intriguing how your supernatural dreams have a stereo soundtrack to them, like the musical backdrop of a movie. The chorus "Can't you see the clouds gathering" gave it a negative meaning, but the actual visuals are too abstract for your mortal mind. It's been raining for five years and an earthquake has been added to the forecast. "I'm Going Away" was the theme song for your latest series of premonitory nightmares. The lyrics are as clear as tap water, but the message is murkier than mud. Obviously, you have other family, friends and associates, but the inner circle...

"Still having dreams?" It's Ma in the doorway in her gray sweat suit and baby blue-trim Reeboks.

"A knock before coming in would certainly keep me from having a heart attack, Ma," you chaff.

"Did I scare you?"

"Almost to death," you inform as you set the journal down and turn to face her. She's off tonight, which means she's early to rise.

"Your light instinctively woke me up. I almost 'cockadoodledooed'."

"And yes, I had another dream tonight, but I don't think you have to worry about me waking up at four in the morning anymore."

"Do you want to talk about it?" she fishes with motherly concern.

"There's nothing to talk about: He's dead; I'm hurt; This morbid life goes on."

She walks over and gently places her hand on your head. "Maybe you should open up and have a good cry."

You take a deep breath and exhale slowly. "That's not how I grieve," you respond despondently as you look at the floor. "We shared something more than a friendship...stronger than a brotherhood. It was sacred and silent...sealed with the sleep of death."

Ma takes a seat on the edge of the bed.

"We walked through the fire together, Ma," you explain, going back to the initiatory furnace.

Uncle JoJo compared us to Shadrach, Meshach, and Abednego in the book of Daniel in the Bible. But then again, it seemed like Uncle JoJo associated everything with the Bible. When we were seven, eight, and nine, he was about to take us home from a church skating trip. Everybody had left except for us and he locked up the church while we waited in the car. Out of nowhere, two dope addicts jumped in the car and drove off. You didn't see them coming, not that we could have stopped them since they were armed and trigger-happy. Both of them were crack crazy with the mephitis of death. The chemicals in their brains just made them more insane. The ugly one with black teeth in the passenger seat kept threatening us with what looked like a canon. It was a very big .357 that looked like it could do some serious damage.

Our calmness during the ordeal was miraculous. Everything hit the fan when that guy threatened to stick Dexter with a hypodermic needle. Why was Dexter terrified of all needles? He gave us all a choice of a shot of dope or a shot from the glock. Dexter went berserk and choose the bullet. We knew he would and we would have too, because the week before during a seminar at church we made a promise to ourselves, to the congregation, and—most importantly—to God that we wouldn't have anything to do with drugs, no matter what the temptation was. We didn't expect this type of inducement, though. It was our first leap of faith. We all vowed not to do it, so what else could we do but back him up.

You tried to grab the gun, but it exploded in his hand. His buddy got burned by some of the fragments and swerved into the lagoon by the Museum of Science and Industry. The impact caused the steering wheel to crush his chest. He was killed instantly. His partner drowned. We could swim like anchors, so the Proverb "God takes care of fools and babies" became a partial reality. We were glad to fit into both classifications. Somehow, we were able to get the back door open (despite all of the water pressure) and make it to shore in the dense midnight air. That was the first power move of God that you experienced.

Throughout your life you always observed the little things that God did that people take for granted: the sun everyday; the ability to go into a deep sleep, not feel a thing and wake up with a good or bad feeling; life in the smallest visible animal to the naked eye—the ant. That incident was major. At that point, you thought that you and your friends were invincible. Your faith was fire tested and firm. It turned out that those dudes just got through killing two families with the same gun that malfunctioned. Seven kids your age or younger ended up with bullets in their heads. Death has been on your heels ever since.

"The Lord's will is perfectly confusing," you resolve. "Why would he call a soul-winning, ordained preacher like Dex home so early in his ministry?" you question her. There are not too many called vessels that will minister to the scum of the earth. Even those who get a calling to the gutter don't answer. Dex answered and went with no questions asked, and he went with a smile. "Do you remember when James Brock joined the church?"

She nods. "Always ready to fight...and his mouth was contaminated. God did some serious converting. If He can turn Saul into Paul—one of the greatest preachers ever—he can turn JB out," she reasons, adding, "And He did."

"There's a testimony behind that story that's just as sensational as his conversion. Getting him into the church was easy for Dex; getting him out of the Gangster Disciples was impossible on eye level. JB asked Dexter about the button, and, of course, Dex preached the Word to him right on 79th and Cregier...with his boys watching and listening. I was right by him, holding his Bible and praying. One question led to JB's deliverance from weed and a volatile spirit when Dex laid hands on and prayed for him. However, there's a drawback to leaving the gang cold turkey: a bullet in the head," you state solemnly.

She looks on intently as her brow wrinkles.

"They started harassing him whenever he couldn't dodge them, and they promised that he wouldn't see the next season. Well Dex didn't witness to him and then leave him hanging. No. He confronted all of them—including the so-called general, who probably couldn't spell Disciple. He tried to reason with them, but they got real nasty—going as far as sticking a gun in his face. Dex didn't blink...he just spat out Romans 8:31-39 without stuttering. And if I didn't know him, I would have sworn that there was a trace of venom in his words. Finally, Dex spoke into gun: 'THE LORD MY GOD SAYS *LET MY BROTHER GO!*' The guy guffawed at him and assured that after he smoked JB, there would be a bullet left for him and his God. It was powerful, but part of me thought Dex was crazy. Before the sun set, two of the enforcers were mowed down in a drive-by; before the week was out, I bet that general was in federal prison for drug trafficking; a war for power erupted within the ranks and GD's were piling high at the funeral homes. Dex and JB were a non-issue for the gang. Needless to say, that general is still locked up and will be caged up for a loooonnnnng time," you emphasize. "The community needed an evangelist like that. Why would God leave all the thugs preacherless?"

Ma closes her eyes as if she's sending up a prayer, and exhales rather loudly through her nose. Naturally tacit, she's outspoken when it comes to the scriptures. She gazes at you intensely through her warm grin and explains, "God never leaves us or anyone hanging without His Word. Notice that when the Lord called Moses home, he raised up Joshua to lead the children of Israel into the Promised Land; When Elijah was carried into heaven, Elisha stepped in his shoes and performed twice as many miracles; John the Baptist's ministry didn't compete with or overlap the earthly ministry of Jesus Christ; and once our Savior ascended to heaven, the Holy Spirit came to minister to *ALL* believers. So you see," she pauses, completing, "God never leaves us nor forsakes us. Understand, He loves the gangbangers, too. He'll raise up another witness for them that will probably preach with more Holy Ghost fire than Dexter."

"Why couldn't they both have worked together? Don't you think that would have been a more effective ministry?"

She humps her shoulders and insists, "I can't answer that, but I do have a suggestion for you."

You don't look at her with your eyes, but your ears are all over her.

"Rejoice that Dexter is home at rest. One day we will meet again and it will be a glorious time indeed. So let's live for the Lord in hope of that beautiful day."

"Part of me hopes that that day is soon," you muse.

Ma doesn't say anything as you peer at her reflection in the desk mirror. The pinpoint freckles on her nose and cheeks seem to dance about, as if the angels are in a kissing frenzy with her face.

"What angel has been kissing on you?" she questions.

You smirk slightly at the pseudo-telepathic connection. You were self-conscious of your genetic inheritance from her when you were a child. They reminded you of a dreaded skin disease. Your face looks like toffee with sprinkles of tiny almonds, and you hate nuts. When you looked at your reflection, you imagined one of those ugly bananas with the dark brown spots on them, and you hate bananas, too. Somehow, she managed to convince you that the dots were seraphim marks.

"Well it wasn't Charlotte. I'm probably in her dog house since I haven't spent any time with her."

Ma just rolls her eyes and half simpers, since Charlotte isn't one of her favorite individuals and absent from her list of worthy brides. From the start, she stated that she was too old (20) and too possessive. After she stated her case, she rested it and doesn't ever comment about her.

"I'm going to visit DePaul in a couple of weeks," you offer.

"Still intent on staying close to home."

"It'll make it much easier for me to get money from you."

"I'll pay you to leave," she jokes. "The farther away, the more I'll pay."

"Well then I'm at Columbia in New York," you concede. "Better yet, I'll study in Europe."

"I'll pack your bags," she laughs.

"Europe probably won't even allow me to set foot on the soil. Do you think that all of the bad publicity will catch up to me eventually? Of course the press made me out to be Satan incarnate, again. I must say that the photographer snapped a good shot of my fist connecting to Tom's nose."

"You can walk to your destiny with your dignity intact, or you can get walked over all of your life and not reach the Promised Land," Uncle JoJo interjects as he stands beaming proudly in the doorway wearing his dingy pajamas. "Good morning. I see everyone is outrising the sun."

"Good morning, Uncle JoJo. Sorry for waking you up."

"That's okay. I had to go to the outhouse anyway," he justifies. "God talking to you again?"

"You can say. What language He's speaking is the real question."

"Ask for discernment, Malcolm," Ma interjects.

"Yeah. The Lord doesn't tell you something and leave you clueless. Didn't Zechariah ask for a sign to the simple message that his wife, Elizabeth, was going to give birth to a son? Didn't the virgin Mary ask how will she know that what Gabriel told her would come to pass? And of course, we can't forget about the dreaming Joseph's in both Genesis and the Gospel accounts. Both of them got divine revelations from God. *I* should know," he says sarcastically.

"I understand that, but it would be nice if He told me what he was trying to tell me in simple English without all of the dramatic visions that keep me up at all times of the morning."

"Maybe the message isn't simple."

You can't argue.

From the start, the messages have been anything but modest. The dreams started soon after Uncle JoJo anointed our heads with oil. It was like he gave us all a portion of his spirit. Uncle JoJo's birth name is Joseph: May God Add in Hebrew. One of his gifts is prophecy, in the form of visions and dreams. Unlike yours, his is accompanied by the gift of interpretation. It's eerie. Once upon a long time ago, the church had a basketball team. We used to play in the denominational tournament every summer. After the last game of the season, Albert Baker's mother wasn't there to pick him up (she overslept and didn't hear the phone ringing), so Uncle JoJo gave him a ride out of good faith and Christian duty since it was late. A block away from his home, a van slammed into the back of us. Everyone was okay except Albert. His back was jacked, but he would recover. A shyster put a bug in Ms. Baker's ear to sue Uncle JoJo and the church, and she gave in, a la Judas Iscariot.

There's nothing more ominous than a prophet giving an ambiguous, apocalyptic message. When he confronted her, he was brief and melancholy when he said "The devil is a liar and a lie will not live." She ignored him. The irony is that the papers for the suit hadn't gone out and nobody knew about it except the lawyer, Ms. Baker and—through the Holy Spirit—Uncle JoJo. Two weeks later, the papers arrived and the phone call came from the lawyer. A week prior, Ms. Baker was buried at Oak Wood cemetery.

You dreamed of an exploding gun pointed at you seven times before you were kidnapped. It wasn't until you learned of the seven children that perished that you understood that the dream represented the end of a reign of terror (seven shots for seven lives). You're still trying to figure the other two dreams out.

Ma rises and announces, "I'm going to fix some eggs and bacon. Would you like some?"

You nod as you sit quietly.

She starts crooning "Because He Lives," as she exits. Uncle JoJo ducks under the basketball net and follows her out, which pleases you. Ma's voice is mellow and mesmerizing, and Uncle JoJo's testimonies are full of life, but you're not in the mood for any more inspiring biblical stories or songs. You walk over to the door and study the obituary of Raymond, which is tacked to the backboard that's posted above the doorway. Dexter's biography is right next to it. *Raymond Johnson 1977-1988.* You wonder what he would look like if he were still alive today. Would he have a mustache? How would he wear his hair? Would he be buffed? The photo captured his chubby, cherubic face. His eyes seem to be looking past you—not directly at you.

Raymond was a year younger than you (two years younger than Dex, since Dex started school late and ended up doubling to catch up with his class in high school). He was also about 20 pounds heavier, an hour slower (when it came to racing), a couple of grades smarter, and about a generation wiser.

You and Dex envied his intellect. Not only was he in the same class, but he was working a minimum of two grade levels ahead, so we got an eyewitness account of a genius in action. "The Head" was gobbling up Trig in sixth grade. That's why "The Head" was headed to the Chicago High School for Agricultural Sciences that August before he was gunned down. He sure wasn't going to play ball, although he would have made a decent guard (on the offensive line of scrimmage) with his girth. He was always on guard for God. Not that he was perfect, but when we were collectively engaged in sin, he was always the first to repent. He couldn't even tell a white lie. Once we had to stay after school for blabbering too much, so, of course, we were late getting home. Our plan was to be as vague as possible, explaining that we got tied up. Uncle JoJo casually asked what were we doing, and we told him that we were playing together. It was working too, until Ray gave him the other half of the truth, which cost us a behind whipping and a month without television.

It was ironic that Ray didn't regret it. He explained that a white lie isn't pure. "If we went along with the story, we may have had to tell another lie to stay out of trouble. Pretty soon, lying would become comfortable, which would make us ignorant to the truth. We would get to the point of believing our own lies and even going to the extreme of murder if it meant keeping a lie going and staying out of trouble. Sin is sin in God's sight," he reasoned to your dismay. Sometimes he got on your last nerve with his saintly deliberations. Sometimes you were just itching to roll around in sin, but he was like an amplified conscious.

You perpetrate one of the greatest oxymoron's: a sorrowful smile. However, it doesn't even come close to his contradictory demeanor: humble intellectual. Raymond reminds you of God in the flesh. On eye level, his potential stretched past the horizon: Nuclear Physicist? President? Apostle? In sixth grade, his science project was on the working atom. IN SIXTH GRADE! With all of his gifts and prestige, he wasn't big on himself. He rarely talked about it. Rather, he was concerned about his two best friends...his brothers whom he loved dearly. You're blessed with a prophetic gift; Dexter was endowed with a boldness to speak divine messages. Ray had a less spectacular, yet more important present: the wisdom of love. You would love what he had; you would love to be where he is. You're full of contradictions: love isn't envious.

"It's a shame to go the holidays without seeing my man," Charlotte huffs.

You stay calm as you zip her Probe down 79th Street. "Next time I'll tell my friends not to get shot during the holiday season," you promise. "Actually, since I lost my last friend, you shouldn't be inconvenienced anymore," you assure.

"People make time for the things they love," she retorts.

You look at her, trying to figure out where her mind could have gone. "I think there's a better way to say 'I miss you', but maybe it's just me."

"How's this," she says, leaning over and pecking you on the cheek as the Chanté Moore cassette hums through the speakers.

"That's much better," you claim as your glow brightens.

"I'm sorry, Mal. It's just that it's hard to go so long without seeing you," she insists. "This time of year is always cold and blue for me and I wanted you to warm and brighten it for me."

It's ten o'clock on a quarter moon night and the wind-chill makes it dangerous even for Eskimos, but your internal thermostat was just cranked up 200 degrees and the light radiating from within you makes it impossible for anyone to look your way as you pull in front of your house. Originally, you wanted to either go bowling or stay home—alone. However, Charlotte has a way of turning you OFF and ON with the ease of flicking on a light switch. She has you ON right now, although she was on the verge of blowing a fuse. You're not thrilled about watching "Juice" over pizza and pop, but it is good to see her. It's always good to see her. Her mouth sometimes leaves you longing for a volume knob, though.

Most of the time she is as sweet as perfume, but when she's at the sour extreme, her mouth is in violation of many health codes. Words are very powerful elements, and no one appreciates a well-placed word more than you do. From a creative standpoint, you have been on the receiving end of some potent inspiration from her mouth. Unfortunately, she has also jacked up your mood with ignorance flowing across her lips too many times to mention. Charlotte likes to sit at home, watch movies and talk. That's it, in reverse order. Anything that requires physical exertion, even walking in the park, is out of the question. She has a chameleon like profile. Often, she can be mistaken for a Latin lady. Other times she can pass for a Caribbean queen. She has a polished, batter-brown skin tone with a golden tint and these exquisite black eyes that could charm a snake. When you first met her, she had back-length, streaky, mahogany/dark brown hair. Now it's jet black and close on the sides with a V-line in the back (your preference by a slight edge).

You come to a stop, grab the Reggio's pizza and let her out. Ma has left for work already, Uncle JoJo doesn't get off for another two hours, Charlotte is due back on Circle Campus in three weeks and you go back to school in two days, so the time that's left is valuable. We hold idle conversation and devour the Italian pie while the film flashes. Before the movie that neither one of us is following reaches the midway point, she's on your lap and in and out of your mouth, intoxicating you with her passion. When the closing credits start floating up on the screen, she gets audacious and goes into your pants.

You disengage your tongue and re-inform with a hushed "Not here," as you grab her wrist that's in the jewelry box with a grip on your life-giving, precious, black birthday pearls.

She clicks her lips and begs, "C'mon Mal...Why not?"

There won't be a dumber question this year. "We have to respect my Uncle's house."

"Mal, don't do this to me," she breathlessly whines. "I want you so bad."

As if she isn't the woman that Uncle JoJo caught you with in the basement five months ago, prancing around like the pre-fall Adam and Eve. You were supposed to be in school and he was supposed to be at work. However, we both got home early. He said if it ever happened again, he would throw us out without any fig leafs and banish you forever.

"Let me get this straight: you're willing to estrange me from my Uncle—who graciously let's me live here—for a moment of fiery desire? Sorry Charlotte, but the thought alone cools me off and shrivels me up. Don't you realize how cold it is out there?"

"Please Mal. All I want is a quickie."

"No. All you want is a dummy, and I ain't the one."

She soughs as she pushes herself up and away from you, flopping down miles away on the other end of the sofa. You shake your head at her gall as you collect the cups and pizza board.

Your phone rings when you get to the kitchen, so you answer it in order to be away from Miss Thang for a while. It's Angela and it doesn't surprise you that she's crying and in a melancholy mood (it's only been two weeks).

"How you doing, Angie?"

"Not too good," she sobs. "I feel my heart breaking all over again."

"What's wrong?"

"I just found a letter from Dexter," she confides as she goes on to explain how they had a little tiff over him leaving his clothes all over the place the day before he was killed. They made up before they went to sleep, but he went a step further and placed a rose, necklace with a heart-shape charm containing an angel in the center, and note in the clothes hamper. She reads the note to you:

"Like the Sun of Righteousness
My Angel is true
Like the Wonderful Counselor
My Angel is nice
Like the Advocate
My Angel is gracious
Like the Dayspring
My Angel is ravishing

From afar
She speaks His will
As bright as a star
Yet as common as a lily
My Angel didn't fall from grace
She descended to bless
Even at my point of base
Her wings engulf me like a crest
Love in action
Is how my Angel is defined
Always providing satisfaction
Forever you are mine

Homes are made by the wisdom of women, but are destroyed by foolishness.—Proverbs 14:1. Not even my foolishness will overcome your wisdom. Sometimes when I'm alone I like to say your name: Angel. Often, when we disagree I ponder the reason and the blame usually shifts to me. You're too sweet to curse me and hold it against me. Instead, you bless my whole being: body, soul and spirit. Jacob wrestled with the Angel, and wouldn't leave until he blessed him. You have blessed me so that I feel like I'm in heaven. Many women are good wives, but you are the best of them all. Hallelujah. Thank you Jesus. And thank you Angel. Love Dex."

You are touched to the point of tears that don't fall. It is like a last testament. She was crying because the rose was dead; the angel was descriptive of him and not her; the note had Eternity—her favorite cologne—sprayed on it; and she couldn't hug him anymore. She weeps on your mental shoulder for a while before she thanks you and tells you she loves you.

"I love you, too," you return and you hang up as Charlotte the Hornet enters the room.

"As I stated before, people make time for the things they love," she subtly spews.

"She's grieving and you're griefing," you shoot with caveatous intentions.

"You must be screwing her since you don't want to screw me," she murmurs under her breath.

"Check this out: I'm going to the bathroom, and when I come back I expect you—whoever you are—to be past tense and Charlotte to be here," you advise and head out. You're a little pissed and wish that you could release that emotion in the toilet. Hopefully that insect is gone, otherwise you may have to exterminate.

As you walk into your bedroom, you discover that she's still buzzing around as she flips through your minder that was *in your* drawer.

"These are interesting entries: Nicole Hardy—555-2583, 8068 S. Paxton—that's real convenient. I bet you were probably over her house before I arrived," she announces as she rips the page out and tosses it over her head. "Traci Dawson—555-7659," she reads as she rives that page out. "Oh: here's one with a star next to it. Desireé Watts—555-1829—8570 South Rhodes. You must be fucking Desireé. Or perhaps you have a *desire* to fuck Desireé," she assumes as she tears that page out.

You find out something about yourself at the moment: you have three levels of rage. Each cleave sent it to the next notch. The last page (with Desireé's name on it, who happens to be an editor for a newspaper in which she promised you some freelance assignments) is the rend that breaks your tolerance. You charge her with steam coming through your gritted teeth and seize the minder—your sacred feelings—from her with force overdrive, almost taking her arm with it. It is the restraining ministry of the Spirit that keeps you from decking her or yelling like a mad man.

"Close the door behind you," you demand with the calmness of the eye of a hurricane.

She shoves past you, snatches her coat and slams the door behind her without another peep.

You rush to open the door and sling her keys past Uncle JoJo's face to the street. "Don't call me, 'cause I'm definitely not going to call you," you request/promise as you slam the door again, rattling the crystal in the dining room.

"Trouble in paradise," he casually questions without looking at you as he heads to the kitchen.

"Just driving the serpent out."

"Um," is all he mutters.

3

"Twenty—count 'em: Not one, not five, not ten, but twenty long, maniacal messages. I kid you not, Nick," you shout over the lunchroom chatter, shaking your head in disbelief as you take a sip of your Grape-Strawberry Mystic. "Some were desperate pleas for me to pick the phone up; then she got angry and accused me of not being perfect in the relationship—which is true; then there were the self-pitying, sob recordings; and finally the calm resolve of the end...then she repeated the whole, insane process over again."

"Sounds like you're driving her a little crazy," Nick comments.

"Driving *her* crazy?" you guffaw. "I got two hours of sleep because the answering machine didn't stop clicking until four in the morning. If I had listened, I would've been carried out of my house in a straightjacket. I kid you not, Nick. I felt nauseous when I listened to all of those messages this morning. I mean, I wanted to jump out of a window...first floor of course."

"She's madly in love with you and a little insecure with herself and without you," Nick states assuredly.

"Mad is correct. Don't get me wrong: she has a good heart and I think her intentions are good. She always takes time out of her busy study schedule to come all the way to my house and chauffeur me around—without as much as a single gripe."

"Sounds like you're still in love with her."

"In love with her? What is this, a psychiatric evaluation? I feel like I'm being marriage-counseled. Why do you say that?"

"You follow every negative statement with a positive, justifiable comment, which is admirable. Most people would trash just their ex."

"I'm just being honest."

"Yep. You're in love," Nick diagnosis.

"Did somebody say love?" Deon pries as he plops all 6 feet 8 inches down next to you. "What up, Mal? How you doing Nicole?"

"Nothing much."

"I'm fine," Nick replies. "Thank you."

Deon nods with a haughty smile.

"Guess what, Malcolm?" Nick fishes.

"Are there any other choices?"

She forces a smirk and announces, "Pastor Wells asked me to teach the junior class."

"Dexter's class?" you verify, pleasantly surprised.

She nods.

"That's good, Nick. Did you accept?"

"I told him that I would think about it," she says dubiously.

"What's to think about?" you question.

"I'm saying," Deon seconds. "You will never be another Dexter, but you'll be a great Nicole."

"You think so?" she asks sheepishly, her face flushing over.

"Of course. Good students make excellent teachers," he insists.

Nicole sits, tacitly flattered. "I don't know if I'm ready," she says humbly, suggesting, "Maybe I should go to Bible school before I do something like that."

"He—*or she*—that observeth the wind shall not sow; and he that regardeth the clouds shall not reap," he waxes divinely.

"Is that scripture?" you question, as his Shakespearean proverb pricks your mind.

"Ecclesiastes 11:4," Nick confirms dreamily as her eyes lock on him.

"My mother used to tell me that if I waited for the right time for everything, I would go to the grave without accomplishing a thing," he explains as he sucks down the last of his hamburger with the smooth ease of a Hoover. "Seize the moment, Nicole," he encourages in the manner of an old wise man as he glances unassumably at her.

The statement echoes for an eternity as our minds chew on it.

"Y'all ready for that Lit test?" he queries, forcing the simple, yet rubbery, concept down our throats while he slurps on his punch.

"I'm ready for it to be over with."

"You can say that again," Nick seconds, breaking the trance and rising from her chair. "Which reminds me, I need to go over my notes one more time. I'll talk to you Malcolm. See you Deon."

"Aiight, later Nick."

"Bye-bye Nicole," Deon croons, careening his neck to follow her retreat all the way out the door, before turning back to you and inquiring, "What's up with y'all?"

"That's my girl. We go back to seventh grade."

"I mean are you hitting it?"

You cut him an "off limits" look. His pager—which is in violation of school policy—rings and he checks it. "Don't forget the milk...and tell Moms I said hi," you pun.

He ignores you. "Seriously man. Did you see her in that skirt?"

"I bought her the whole outfit for Christmas," you confide, recalling the burgundy, wool, wrap-around skirt, black, top-hugging turtleneck pullover, and black, leather riding-boots. You also remember the thin gold rope with diamond-studded stick-cross she bought you. "Did you get a whiff of the Poison?"

His mouth hits the floor. "So you are tagging that," he assumes.

"No, not at all. She's one of my closest friends, and I'm losing them rapidly."

"Friendship aside, how can you look at her and not want to lay with her?"

"She's like a sister," you casually affirm as you gulp down the last of your drink. "Didn't you just spit out a scripture?" you ask incredulously.

"Yeah. Why?"

"It amazes me how brothers can shroud a game behind the Bible. I mean, how can you cloak lasciviousness with the Word of God?" you ask, knowing the question you'll get as an answer.

"What does *lasivness* mean?"

"Lasciviousness," you correct, explaining, "You had me fooled for a split second, but the smell of fertilizer gave you away."

"Well, do you mind if I talk to your *sister*?"

You glare at him like he has pink hair and a third eye in the middle of his forehead.

"Seriously man...if you're not messing around with her, I want to see if I can get with her."

"Well, truthfully I don't want you within ten miles of her," you protest. "Besides, you're not her type: she's allergic to Bible verse dropping, hypocritical jocks."

"I bet I get her," he challenges.

"I wouldn't make a bet like that, although I know you would have a better chance of schooling me...on the court or in the classroom."

"Well then my chances are pretty good."

"Keep wishing upon that star," you encourage as the bell sounds, ending lunch and starting Chemistry class.

You struggled to keep your eyes open during class as Mr. Richard lectured away about nuclear fusion. When you got to study hall, you didn't keep your nap waiting. The 45 minutes felt like a good night.

Deon's observations about Nick ring in your head as the Lit class tests. You find yourself entranced by your unwitting friend as she writes her essay. She is very cute—even for a friend. She's a cinnamon shade of brown with processed, shoulder length hair, which she usually wears in a ponytail and a front bang hanging just over her right eye. What you find most charming is her two oversized front teeth, which make her look like a comely little rodent. She has come a long way from the tomboy that challenged you at Eckersal Park six years ago. You barely won, and you weren't slacking up on her because she was a female. She was a hard, compact, thick country-girl from Mississippi. You immediately took a liking to her and her laid-back spirit, naiveté to big city culture and southern accent.

Six years later, she still has her southern hospitality intact and is still thick like most brothers appreciate, but she's soft and conservative both in her dress and demeanor. Her chest sticks out with pride and her round hips protrude out from her modest waist, giving her the look of a comic book super-heroine. Today she's a burgundy bunny: beacon to a generation in darkness; empowered with the grace and charm to touch hearts without physical contact; inner strength to resist sexual temptation and remain pure in an immoral environment; beauty that appeals to the eyes, ears, and heart.

You look at her mouth and imagine what her red lips taste like. Surely, they're sweeter than strawberries. After all, the bitter truth has a way of oozing out honey thick and sweet from that opening. Are those cross earrings, filters? Do they keep whispers from her? If she hears a lot of anything, it is assumed that she's not deaf, yet she's never judgmental. Would it be good luck to rub her foot? You chuckle at the thought of getting romantic with her, just as Mrs. Harper catches you gazing at her, when you really should be concentrating on the Macbeth test.

"Is there a problem, Malcolm?" she queries.

As you snap out of the reflective realm, Nick catches your eyes. For the split moment between the dreamy and reality dimension, you got a glimpse of her soul through the deep brown windows of her eyes. You tersely reply, "There's no problem" while watching Nick beam and blushingly turn away.

"Well then, perhaps you should keep your eyes on your paper and concentrate on finishing the test."

You just nod in agreement as you commence to ace the test.

The bell rings, punctuating the day, just as you put the period on the last answer. As you exit the classroom and proceed to your locker, you remember there is no practice today, and you thank God for that. You hurry down the stairs to catch up with..."Nicole." The name involuntarily glided over your tongue, past your teeth, and over your lips.

She pauses in her tracks and turns to verify the source, a puzzled expression clouding her angelic face.

"Would you rather be called that?" you question sheepishly.

"Don't be silly," she giggles. "Why do you ask?"

"Well, I guess it has a more feminine ring to it than Nick. I mean there's Nick Anderson and Nick Nolte: two guys," you stammer.

"Whatever you're comfortable with," she assures. "My friends and family all call me Nick, if that's what you want to hear."

"I'll continue to call you Nick," you promise as you grin nervously at her. She gazes back at you, mentally inebriating you as you suggest, "You want to see a movie?"

"Now?" she questions with raised eyebrows as we stop just outside the door.

"Yeah."

"Well, it sounds good except for one thing."

"What?"

"Charlotte probably has other plans for you."

You wrinkle your brow as a question mark blinks in the middle of your forehead.

"She's waiting for you at the car over there," she informs as she tilts her head slightly in the direction.

You look out to the curb where Charlotte is standing by her car with sorrowful, expectant eyes. Elation and frustration jolts your belly as you regretfully turn back to Nick.

"I told you she has it bad for you. Never keep a woman waiting," she advises with a smile. "I'll see you tomorrow," she promises, strutting away.

Seeing her is no consolation and tomorrow isn't soon enough.

As you make your way to Charlotte, she rushes up without saying a word and engages you in a neck embrace tight enough to strangle a gorilla. You disengage yourself from the chokehold and greet her with a distant "What's up?"

She anxiously says, "Let's ride." We climb into the car and she peels out before you are buckled in. You thought of tuning in to WGCI to sedate the tension, but she kills that idea by covering your hand with hers. "We need to talk," she suggests.

In the car she spoke with a disciplined equanimity while apologizing. You even found yourself begging her pardon for your role (whatever it was) as we ended up at the Oasis Motel on Stoney Island. That evening the hurt feelings were soothed over and your body was worked like a thoroughbred. Basketball practice wouldn't have been that intense and draining. All of the fights and harsh words were forgotten; every flaw was overlooked; the differences were compromised. Lovemaking covered the stench of her transgressions with the funky-fresh floral scent of a black rose.

Chuck D rips Kenny as he tries to drive, and pushes the ball up the court with Deon in hot pursuit. Chuck D fakes a drive and feeds you well as you fill the lane from the wing. You go for a reverse jam, only to get your head knocked into the stands by Deon. "Damn. What's with that, man!" you shout from your back, rubbing your cranium.

"Stop acting like a *gal*, Mal," he retorts, to your dismay, as he starts away.

Before you can react, Chuck D intercedes. "You damn near decapitated him, with your Baby Huey ass."

"Shut up, Chick," he bastardizes.

"Chick?" he questions. "At least I don't sound like a chick," he declares, mocking Deon's high-pitched voice.

"Okay Dionne. Come off that psychic line," Mitch interjects.

"That's why you're making me rich, Bitch. Now go stand on your corner."

"Is that the best you can do," you question as you get up in his face.

Deon shoves you away as he declares, "That's why I'm going to bone your girl and send her back to you in her wrinkled outfit."

You charge at him with the intention of putting the tooth fairy to good work, only to have Mitch grab you. "Keep dreaming, big guy. She wouldn't even try to pry you from your pine," you avouch.

"Why don't you chill, Deon," small forward Dennis Meachum pleads.

"That was an unnecessary foul, Dawg," power forward Jayson Reed seconds.

"Mind your own business, Denise," Deon insults. "What is this: a basketBALL-LESS team? Mal the gal, my bitch Mitch, Chuck the chick, Denise, and Gay Jay. Is it that time of the month for y'all?"

"Give me twenty laps and call it the day," Coach Wade announces to the team's dismay. We had already run five miles and had a playoff-charged practice to make up for the previous day off. Afterward, everybody avoided the 300-pound annoyance in the locker room as we got dressed.

The Jeffery bus ride is long and quiet as you, Mitch and Chuck D relax our minds and bodies that have been tested. Mitch would normally have a ride reserved for us with one of his many girls, but three of them discovered that they were limo competitors and went on strike. You bid them "Later," as the bus approaches your stop. Their stop is all the way in the Jeffery Manor. The 79th Street bus is nowhere in sight when you exit, so you tread the six blocks in the Arctic elements until you arrive on your porch, too numb to get your keys out and too anxious to notice Uncle Ben's black Blazer. Before you can reach up and ring the bell, the door swings open. You're immediately greeted by a blast of warmth.

"What up Snake," Ben says enthusiastically as he clasps your hand and embraces you. He dubbed you Snake on the basketball court too long ago to remember. It isn't because you crawl on your belly or smell with a forked tongue, but due to your physique and highly honed skills. You're rail thin and move cleverly and cunningly: slipping, sliding and slithering all over the court with or without the ball. And you have come to love the moniker.

"Nothing much," you declare gleefully.

Ben is more like your big brother than your uncle. Dad renounced his Christianity and converted to Islam in 1969, which—according to Ma and Uncle JoJo (Uncle Ben's and Dad's natural uncle and surrogate father)—made them unequally yoked, even though they initially stayed together. Dad was 18 and Ma was 16 when they eloped in 1968, so they had only been married for a year. In 1977, Dad decided to forsake all for the sake of Allah. Uncle JoJo was devastated when he found out his oldest nephew, who he endearingly saw as a son, changed faiths. Although the divorce wasn't messy, Ma was left with a one-year-old toddler and in an economic Hades. Uncle JoJo embraced her and welcomed you two into his home while Ma earned her nursing degree. As a result of losing your daddy, you gained the older sibling you never had.

Ben is eight years up on you, and for the longest time seemed a couple of stories up, too. Four years ago, you sprouted like a weed and surpassed the six-foot Benjamin tower. It wasn't until two years ago that you reached the milestone of a b-ball victory over him. It was the most rewarding 2-point win you have ever experienced. After twelve years of watching in awe as he rocked with Tim Hardaway, getting blown out by ridiculous scores like 32-4, and his sound instructions on jump shooting and defense, you finally got over the hump. Ben was probably more pleased than you. After that game, he bought you some new Reeboks and a Lakers' warm-up. You haven't even worn them, because they are a sacred reminder you keep hanging on your wall.

"How was Japan?" you ask of his two-week, job-related trip. He is an account executive for a computer firm and they sent him there to learn about some of the latest technology.

"It's a nice place to visit, but I wouldn't want to live there—too many short people," he says, shutting the door. "More importantly, how are you hanging?"

"I'm adjusting," you assure, in reference to Dexter. "I got some more bad press."

"I heard you swung on somebody in the championship game. Doing your best to scare the scouts, huh?" he jokes. "I hear you're considering Chicago State?"

"You can say that I just want to get out of class for the campus visit," you rationalize.

"If you say so, but I'm telling you, U.I.C. is the place for you. You and Sherrell Ford will do Coach Hallberg and this city proud. Y'all will blow DePaul off the map. Didn't you like his game? 29 points and 10 boards ain't bad."

"He has game, but they got *flame*-broiled 101-80—no pun intended," you mention of the game at Illinois that you rode down with him to see.

"The Illini had a bigger gun, that's all," he justifies. "Besides, they had Mario Bailey playing Deon Thomas in the pivot. Bailey is good, but he's a power forward at best; a swing-man by nature. He was giving up too much beef in the paint."

"I hear you, but if I go there, somebody is going to have to compromise on 25, and it's not me," you joke.

"Unless you red-shirt, I don't think Bailey is coming off of the number."

"If I red-shirt I'll have too much time to spend with Charlotte," you mention, walking back to your room.

"You still kicking it with her? What, has it been four years?"

"It feels like it sometimes," you testify, dropping your bags on the floor and throwing your coat in the closet. You met Charlotte last year at the U.I.C./Chicago State game on 95th Street and King Drive. You didn't have the intentions of meeting a girl that day, but she was flirting with undeniable determination. You thought you were getting into a mature relationship just because she is three years older than you. You've been tempted to check her birth certificate. "If we make it to March, it'll be one year."

"You're a good one," he says as he parks at your desk. "Any other interests'?"

"Well," you beam as you take a seat on your bed. "I don't care what nobody says, Ricky Byrdsong is a good coach and Northwestern's exposure in the Big Ten isn't all that bad."

"And then he's a brother."

"And then he's a brother," you second. "Unless it's Dean Smith, I want to play for a black man, even if he does walk on the wild side. He's a saint compared to Bobby Knight...he'd make the mistake of breathing on me too hard and I'd sling him across the court like he slings chairs."

"Well, you couldn't lose at Northwestern since their journalism program is one of the best in the nation," he asserts, pausing to marvel at all of the basketball and black pride memorabilia on your wall. His eyes wander from the "Highlight Zone" poster of Dominique to Barkley's "Get Off My Backboard" pose. In a revolution, he covers all of his favorite players—including Magic (your favorite player of all time), Bird (the most respectable white player alive), James Worthy, and Spud Webb—a life size cut out of Patrick Ewing, your press clippings, a couple of plaques and trophies, a Jason from "Friday the 13th" hockey mask, your $175 plus Reebok pumps, your first number 25 jersey, the all-Illinois wall (Nick Anderson, Tim Hardaway, LaPhonso Ellis, Zeke, Terry Cummings, Mo Cheeks, Hersey Hawkins, Mark Aguirre, Ron Anderson, Kendall Gill, Craig Hodges, Marcus Liberty, Doc Rivers, Jeff Hornacek, Kevin Duckworth, Randy Brown and the legendary Ben Wilson) and other tid-bits that were passed down from him to you. With a few exceptions and compromises, it is all intact.

"You really need to air this room out before you suffocate."

"Sorry, but this room will remain airtight as long as I occupy it," you claim with conviction.

"Still don't want to be like Mike?"

"You know where I stand."

"Give him a break."

"I'm not doing anything to him and I don't have anything against him."

"You don't have anything against him, yet you have everybody's mug shot on your wall except the greatest player ever."

"Don't you see Magic up there?" you quiz, pointing to him reversing on McHale in the 1985 finals.

"What's up Snake—Did Jordan throw your stuff in the bleachers or dunk on you or something?"

"Outside of him being a shot gun, too politically correct, and taking a fall—not a stand—on the apartheid issue with Nike, I don't have anything against the man. He's cool as far as I'm concerned. I don't even hold his golf playing against him. I'll give him his props as the second best basketball player."

"The X-man speaketh," he teases with a chortle in reference to your militant stance on black/white issues, a la the deceased Civil Rights icon with the same first name. He's one of your favored historic figures and his autobiography ranks in the top five inspirational pieces you've read, so Ben's light baiting doesn't bother you.

"Seriously Snake, you need to ease up off of him and that apartheid issue."

"Why should I?" you question defensively. "I idolized him until he choked in the clutch."

"For the sake of argument, let's say that the apartheid stance was as monumental to his character as a man as you make it out to be. How would you respond to the issue in *the clutch*?"

"I would like to think that I would have taken a stand for what was right," you huff.

"You 'would like to *think'* is right," he antagonizes. "But in reality, you don't know what you would have done, because *you* weren't put on the spot. And you don't know if it was right for him or not."

"Yeah, whatever," you blurt with attitude.

"Sounds like it's something deeper than a stance that a man took. If I didn't know any better, I would swear that you were jealous of his star and his so-called stance is an excuse to player hate."

You look up in disbelief and roll your eyes at him.

"Let me put it to you this way, the media has placed him on a pedestal he didn't ask for. Personally, I think he carries himself with a lot of class, considering all the scrutinizing eyes that are on him. As much as they watch him, do you think that they record every philanthropic deed he does like they catch every so-called slip? Of course not, and I have more respect for him because of his good work done in secret; I admire him for keeping his personal life under cover. To me that illustrates sincerity as opposed to a show. If it was me, they would have a lot of negative things to say about me and I would try to get on camera every time I gave a buck to a bum. The man can't even go to the bathroom without the press over-analyzing his shit—excuse the French."

"Fine," you resolve. "I'll plaster Jordan all over my wall."

"You don't have to if you don't want to. What I'm trying to say is disliking someone that you really don't know for something trivial is an indication of a bigger problem and that in the end, it will have a negative effect on you. Lighten up on the Black Nationalism, otherwise your faith will fade and you will lose your way and miss out on life."

You take a deep, silent breath and determine that Ben is right: *your demons have nothing to do with Jordan and what he does, personally. Yes, you envy his game to a degree, which, in itself, is fuel for self-improvement. There will never be anyone that can exceed what he is. In your heart, you admire him. You hate that he and other stars are embraced by a mainstream America that kicks poor black folks to the gutter like snot-smeared tissue. Jordan is your philosophical scapegoat, representing half of an oxymoronic media message: On the ten o'clock news you have Theodore Thug smoking Tyrone Blow to the admonishment of the system, and Miracle Michael smoking Greg Anthony to the admiration of society. On one hand, black men get resisted, roasted and razed like a ragging rash, yet Jordan (professional athletes in general) are sentimentalized, showcased, and celebrated as heroes that break the color barrier. Axiomatic-like negativity presents African-Americans as lepers, while cross-cultural acceptance paradoxically project black athletes as transparent, acceptable exceptions to their race.*

To put it in perspective, athletes didn't necessarily ask for the role of societal or race leader; they just want to play ball and get rich. At the same time, many daddies didn't ask to be fathers; they just wanted to philander around and lady-kill. However, the wish doesn't negate the responsibility of the lot. You couldn't stay mum if the government set you up in a fat house with cash at your disposal, while your family lived in poverty. Instead of living large under the banner of a tyranny, you would rather live poor with your people. The Chicago Stadium is right smack in the heart of the ghetto, yet most of the youngsters that look up to the predominately black stars have never seen them play in person. And the players don't even whisper a serious word about it. They don't realize that NBA stands for Negro Basketball Association; they don't realize that freedom is theirs if they want it, but security is more important to them. Yes, you resent them for being silent on the worldly platform.

Your demons are an inheritance that you hold on dearly to. Your elders' scars are your scars; your elders' ghosts are your ghosts: black men getting castrated, hung and dragged to death in the south; African-American women getting raped; human rights and recognition being denied on the bases of dark complexion. You weren't even thought of during the peak of lynching season, but your heart aches from the injustice of it just as if it was perpetrated directly against you. The devil isn't red and evil isn't black. Ash white is the color of curse. When you see white, you see red. Dad was so consumed with the struggle that he's on the extreme level. If others (including his blood) aren't down with his way of thinking, then they're against him. That's part of your inheritance from him. The strength of the gene pull has yet to be determined.

Dad has been underground for almost 17 years. You haven't heard from him in about a year, and the last time he saw you was when you were seven months old. Are you capable of going the distance that he's gone? Can you snuff out the life of someone you don't know? Is it in you to cut family ties—to turn your back on a father and a son for a cause? How deep are your spiritual roots? You've had dreams and fellowship with God, but you're not sure what it means—what you believe. If a fall is in your forecast, will you rise again? Will God be willing to forgive you? Would it have been best if you weren't born? What's the purpose of this life? If you stray, will you rediscover the path of righteousness? From deep within yourself, you long for the fellowship of both your natural father and your Heavenly Father.

"You think my dad will ever find his way back?" you ponder aloud.

Ben shakes his head and humps his shoulders. "I don't know," he murmurs.

"You think Jordan will make a comeback?"

He humps his shoulders and shakes his head.

Usually he has a solution for everything. His lack of answers makes your outlook seem so uncertain. However, there's a time to sweat, and there's a time to chill.

"When you enter this room, take your shoes off," you order gravely, adding, "you're on sacred ground."

His eyebrows rise slightly as he peers inquisitively around the room.

*"He arranged the wood, cut the bull into pieces and laid it on the wood...Then the fire of the Lord fell and burned up the sacrifice...*So there you have it: even the Lord hates the Bulls, according to 1 Kings."

"So you're on this Lakers/Bulls trip again," he observes, shaking his head. "Run with the Bulls, or let the Bulls run."

"It was Oleary's Bull—I mean Cow—that burned the city down a century ago."

"If I'm not mistaken, didn't the Bulls stampede the Lakers back in 1991? Maybe I dreamed it."

"That's okay," you concede. "If there was one thing proven, which I already knew, it's that Jordan couldn't do nothing with Magic. He kept Jordan posted, didn't he?"

"Aiight, that's true, but at Bull Run, Magic got ran over and was talking—wait a minute—he actually did retire after the season. It wasn't AIDS: He couldn't handle Jordan."

"Wasn't a purple rob placed on Jesus—symbolic of royalty?"

"Perhaps you should read the gospel according to Matthew, which says that it was scarlet."

"Sorry, but there are two witnesses that say it was purple: Mark and John," you state emphatically. "And another thing: you know where all non-Lakers go, don't you?"

"To the championship?"

"To the *Lake* of Fire."

"You're too young to be on that old-school, outdated Lakers' bandwagon."

"I'm just down with the best team, EVER, which boasted the best player, EVER. All five positions and five rings to show for it, Ben. Not two or three, but all five. Count 'em Jordan. Oops. He can count to a maximum of three, as in three rings and a position limit of small forward."

Ben chuckles as he encourages you to "Make sure you have a *magical* game tomorrow, 'cause if you get embarrassed, I'm going to play like I don't know you."

"You're gonna to get a glimpse of Show-time tomorrow...90's style," you promise, beaming at the prospect.

You go up for your seventh board when you feel a powerful force come over your back, coupled with the whisper "I'll take that" as you almost wind up on your face. Mitch forces him to bring it back out as you peek over in the stands at Ben, who's giggling at you. You return a plastic smirk. Brian Meeks has been jawing all game. He's two inches taller, about 40 pounds heavier and you wish that he was playing his natural power forward spot. Crawford Academy went big, because we were collecting every misfire. Now they have a redwood tree planted in the middle that's taking up a lot of space.

Their team sets up with Meeks dribbling at the top, so you turn the D up and get under his shirt. For a split second he takes his eyes off of you, which is all it takes for you to tell him "I'll take this" as you swipe it away and race down court. You give him a chance to catch up. He gets three paces from you when you reach the lane, just under the basket.

Just as he takes off, you blast off from both feet, cock the ball behind your head, watch him fly by with his arm extended, and throw it through the rim—bouncing it off of his back as you claim, "You'll take that." Joe Louis Magnet up two with a minute and a half remaining.

He glares at you as he takes the ball out. Their playmaker brings the ball up as Meeks takes you down to the box and gets the ball. "Don't put you hands up there when I take you, because you'll get your fingers broke off on the rim and your season will be over," he expresses. He leans against you, knocking you off balance with a shoulder to the chest and charges to the rim. Like a fool looking for a bad rep and a spot on the wrong side of a highlight film, you jump and extend your hand up—drawing it back a nanosecond before he jams it home. "Smart kid," he encourages. Tie game. A minute left.

Jay takes the ball out, passing it to you at your urging. Brian picks you up at the top as you bark out a play that will not be run. You address him with "This move is called a crossover, made famous by Tim Hardaway; perfected by Malcolm Johnson. I'm going to dribble it through my leg, to my left hand and then crossover to the right for an easy finger-roll over your 7-footer that can't jump over paper. On three, okay," you verify. He nods as you start counting to him and take him just as you tele-choreographed. "Told you," you boast as you run back down court. Bombers up two with 45 seconds in the game.

Again, he goes down low and gets the ball, asking, "Is the bank open" as he leans into your chest again and fades away as Mitch comes over, kissing it in off of the glass. "I would say the bank is open, Mal," he jokes as he runs back down court. Knotted up again with 20 seconds to go.

No time-out is called, so you bring the ball up the court again. "Your fans are going to be talking about number 25 in bomber brown and black in school tomorrow," you promise as they start counting down from ten. You dribble at the top of the key. "Now I hope you learned your lesson the last time, because I'm going to show you the same thing. On the count of three," you announce as the crowd gets to five. On two you crossover, stop and pull up as the center comes out and trips Brian up. The ball pops through the net as the buzzer goes off. You inform a dazed Brian "I lied," as you stroll past to the embraces and high five's of your teammates. Louis 70. Crawford 68.

It's the same story every time we play the Panthers: Feces coming from everybody. The lines change slightly, but whenever we take the same court, there's high drama and spicy dialogue. In the four-year rivalry, we're 4-3 against them in the regular season and always manage to miss each other in the playoffs. If our games weren't close, the level of play would drop like mercury on a sub-zero day. The liplash makes it fun and adds sound to the action movie. Every thing is cool after the games and we often chill out together in the summer. Today, however, the dung continues to fly in the locker room.

"Why were you out there imitating a can of dog food, *gal*?" Deon queries between sneezes.

"Excuse me, can somebody bring in the box scores for number *DOUBLE ZERO* here," you request as Chuck D gladly obliges. "Let's see: Double Zero had ZERO points, ZERO boards, and approximately...ZERO STATISTICS. Oh my. At least you collected 20 splinters: your average for the season. Good game, D."

He sneezes again before he reasons, "That's okay. You need to come off that hunger strike so you can have the strength to stand up and play defense."

"Well at least we know you can shoot your mouth," you comment.

"And he knows how to sweat in practice without actually working," Chuck D adds.

"Maybe you should hang up your jersey and try golf, you big DOUBLE ZERO under par," Mitch interjects.

He sticks his middle finger up as he sneezes in machine gun succession.

"They say that you lose a brain cell every time you sneeze, so since you just sneezed ten times you have about one brain cell left," Mitch informs.

"That ain't good for a brother who's ranked 501 in a class of 500. That girl that doesn't even come to school is rated higher than you, so you might as well stay home to improve your ranking," you note.

Deon sneezes three more times.

"Uh oh. That leaves you with minus two cells, which means that you're officially mentally retarded and qualified for SSI," Chuck D states.

"A corpse has a higher IQ than you," Mitch informs.

"Spell box," you challenge.

"Okay, so the bitches with dicks are going to gang up on me. That's cool. But check this out Gal: I bet I can score on this court," he challenges as he pulls out a sheet of paper with Nick's name and number scribbled on it in her handwriting and red felt ink she uses when she tutors.

What is he doing with Nick's number? Did he steal it from somebody? It doesn't mean a thing, but it does surprise you that he got that far. "That's okay. What's a phone number?"

"I'll be sure to show you the blood stained panties," he vows. "Better yet, I'll show you the whole outfit."

You wave your hand at him as you turn your back to him and the smell of his bowels. He proceeds to yack as you grab your bag and exit into the hallway of Crawford, where Brian is listening to an intense Khalid Muhammad, who's wearing a gold on black dashiki, sporting a fresh, blade-lined, close hair-cut and the trademark Nation of Islam countenance of solemnity. Never have you seen a black Muslim smile. You went up against Muhammad—a wing forward from Chatham Career Academy with the quickest first step this side of James Worthy and range and accuracy comparable to yours—in the summer league two years ago. He doesn't talk on the court with his mouth, but his game is outspoken. Brian spots you and nods his head up as you proceed to join them.

"Malcolm X: the Second Coming," Khalid announces. Everyone wants to make you and your ways so mystical. "What up black man?" he asks, extending his hand for a firm, gimickless handshake.

"I'm living."

"That's a blessing in itself."

"Payback is coming to you in February," Brian announces of our meeting. "You got me with a good shot at the end, but next time I'll be ready."

"We'll be 5-3 against y'all."

"I would say that I was taking it easy because of your friend, but I would be lying," he states in reference to Dexter. You have his name on the wristband. "I hope they fry them jokers."

You disagree with that statement, but not for the reasons that Khalid interjects: "Some of us don't know where we came from, so we really don't have a clue as to where we are going. Those brothers did a terrible thing, but we really have to be tolerant of each other until the day that we wake up out of this deep sleep that we're in. It's a process that doesn't happen over night. Almighty Allah will appoint the time."

The lawyer in you peeks out. "With all due respect, I don't consider Allah God. I'm a Christian that prays to Jesus," you point out.

"I'm a Christian too, brother," he retorts.

"Didn't you just mention Allah? You *are* a Muslim, aren't you?"

"Yes I am: I'm a Jesus believing Muslim," he states to your surprise. You've never heard that before. He elaborates: "I believe that Jesus was the son of God, and there is only One God."

It makes sense, but then again, you weren't expecting to hear that come out of his mouth. The last phone conversation you had with Dad, he insisted that Allah had no son and you understood that to be Islamic dogma.

With nothing else to say, you query with intrigue, "Don't you go by the Qur'an?"

"Yes I read the Qur'an daily, and the Qur'an recognizes Jesus," he testifies. "And I also read the Holy Bible, too."

You twist your mouth at this new revelation.

"The white man would have you believe that Islam means anti-Jesus, which is an absolute lie. The way the White devil has twisted the scripture has brainwashed the Black man into thinking that God ordains slavery and that Black people are cursed. I'm here to tell you don't believe the hype. What do you know about Islam, Black man?"

"Obviously, not much," you concede.

"My point exactly. The only thing that you know is what the racist media has shown you: Islam is a terrorist religion; the Nation of Islam promotes racism. I ask you: how can a Black man be a racist? Racism is about racial control and domination. A Black man can't be a racist in America, because we have no control over anything."

You nod in agreement at his verbal thesis.

"Take the athletic industry for example. Jordan can make a 100 million, which is superficially good, but if you examine it closely, how much control does he have? First of all, he has White representation, he promotes White companies, and he only makes a fraction of the billions the NBA makes off of him. Let's take it a step further: How many young brothers are going to make it in professional sports? About one in every million or so high school athletes? Yet the images that you see on television and billboards is this glamorous lifestyle of riches and respect."

"And then they try to keep us from playing in college by requiring us to pass a biased test," Brian adds.

"That's what I'm trying to tell you, Black man."

"I think I'm going to skip college and try out overseas," he ponders.

"You need to load up on knowledge, brother," Khalid encourages. "Don't let the White man keep you from your mental food. He would have you believe that you can't do it, but with Allah on your side, no one can stop you."

You cringe every time he acknowledges Allah, but you start wondering if there's any truth to what he says. After all, you know firsthand that the media has spread lies about Black people—you in particular—to the point where African-Americans are in a perpetual state of infighting. You really don't know much about Islam. Does Islam worship the same God, just calling Him a different name? Is that His real name that has been hidden from us by White Christianity? After all, Khalid did acknowledge Jesus.

"I can help you study for the ACT Brian," you offer.

"That's what I mean: Brothers helping brothers," Khalid shoots.

"What did you get the last time you took it?" you query.

"I got a 15...two points short."

"I'm best at English and Math," you inform.

"And I'm good at Science and History," Khalid interjects. "With a little from both of us, you may score higher than both of us."

We all laugh at that, although the unity scheme for Brian's mental edification is earnest. We exchange numbers and plan on getting together Saturday.

"So you're still going to come down to the Mosque Sunday," Khalid confirms with Brian.

Brian nods his head. "Yeah, I'll be there."

"What about you, Malcolm? You're invited to come out and hear Minister Abdul Allah Muhammad speak."

Without weighing it or extending him a similar bid, you promise, "I'll come out" as you ponder the unfair racist tag Minister Muhammad has. You actually like what he has to say when people label him a bigot. However, your body fells deadened with that announcement.

"It's good to have you come out," Khalid declares with a hint of a grin. "You will not be disappointed at this powerful speaker."

"I'm sure I won't," you assure with your mouth. Your heart is mum.

"As-Salaam-Alaikum," Khalid bids as he starts off.

You nod your head slightly.

Nick persuaded you to go to Sunday school for her inaugural lesson. It would've been an easier task to stop a speeding locomotive in its tracks. She could barely wait to get home to call Pastor Wells to announce her acceptance of the class after the vote of confidence she received from you and Deon, mostly Deon. It's a special moment that shouldn't be missed. She's so quickened that she's a blurred blur. The days leading up to it tickled you as she miraculously managed to keep from bursting a vein in her head. Despite your reluctance to step within smelling radius of Walk of Faith (W.O.F.), you find yourself sitting at the back of the class in the basement as Nick sets the Dunkin' Donuts out, organizes her presentation papers and fiddles with everything. If you didn't know better, you would swear that she is preparing to address the United Nations for a three-hour meeting instead of teaching the school kids for 30 minutes.

You elect to stay downstairs during the brief devotion and peer at the bulletin board announcing the coming events. The Scouts are planning a hiking trip to the Grand Canyon during Spring Break. Membership and participation are up in the Boy and Girl Scout chapters here.

When it started up three years ago, everybody and their momma joined, but it tapered off after a year of no actual scouting. Meetings every Saturday decked out in the seaweed green uniforms, learning the promises and motto, and reading the code book can merit only so many badges and hold the attention of adolescent boys for so long. Elder Nathan and his wife can do so much at 86 and 83 respectively. It's good that they can get around without any assistance, but expecting them to take 30 kids out in the wilderness with no difficulties is like running through an obstacle course with no vision.

They attempted a field trip to the Museum of Natural history. After an hour, they detoured to the emergency room and damn near the nursing home. Then along came Brother Ernie Wheaton, a Bill Dukes caricature with these bulging eyes that look like he opened them up to death. They're a hard speed bump away from popping out. He's a nice guy, but a little too intense for even a drill sergeant. You can't tell if the children fear him or respect him, but whatever it is, they seem to love the Scouts. And they have fun without endangering or excluding the Nathan's. In fact, it seems to have invigorated them. You wish they would have had Brother Wheaton and the Scouts when you were younger. Camping in the forest would have been a nice change from the riskier concrete jungle.

A skating social by the Junior Usher Board, of which you're an AWOL member, is scheduled in two Saturdays at the Rink on 87th Street. You're tempted to make an appearance. W.O.F. knows how to throw a skating party.

Even though they forsook Markham Roller Rink and the secular music for the conveniently located Rink on Gospel night, it still makes for an exciting night out. It was Dexter's idea to have "Skating For the Lord" five years ago. He insisted that it was a contradiction for a congregation to partake in the worldly music and dancing. "If anything, they should yield to us," he urged. He had a point that was well taken since gangbanging, drug dealing/using and liquor elements were present. The church has been sponsoring gospel skating affairs ever since. The invitations are open to all churches in the city and abroad, and especially to the non-church goers. There were always several worthwhile representatives (women) from several of the area congregations and from assemblies as far away as Gary. WYCA, WGCI (on the Music of Love and Inspiration with Jackie Haselrig on Sunday) and WKKC (on the Morning Gospel Drive and Thursday Inspirations with Reggie Miles) would announce it a month in advance. There was food, catchy spiritual tunes, and joy for ages ranging from fetus to 120. Absent was the heathenistic hedonism. However, you decide against showing up, because you'll be pressed back into active Sabbath duties.

There is a huge poster board announcing the Angelic Choir's 30th anniversary concert. As if the black and gold streamers, tablecloths and napkins draped all over the kitchen weren't a big enough hint. You saw a couple of the members decked out in their gold tops and black bottoms. It promises to be an electrifying event, with people jumping, running, shouting and dancing all over the place. They're good enough for prime time records. However, you opt to stay home, because the devil sings in the choir and "Rejoice" from the Tabernacle Church of God in Christ is the guest choir, featuring Joyce Akins (your first love).

Whenever you know she's going to be in a certain place, you try to stay a time zone away and out of any possible routes that she may take to get there. It's ironic that the usher board's skating trip to the Rink is advertised next to the concert. It was at one of the skating socials that you met her and made your ascent from despised innocence to pleasurable corruption.

The abundant queries to the "Hallowed Be Thy Name in 1990" caused the anticipation to ferment like old grapes. The outing was a trick-or-treating alternative, since W.O.F. was part of the anti-Halloween Movement. It was truly a treat. You were shooting the breeze with Nick and Dexter, watching the skaters zoom by and admiring the gracious representatives, when Joyce floated in your line of view with the intention of threading your eyes with a web of inveiglement. She kept rolling by, wiggling her hips, spinning her body, bouncing her chest, bobbing her head and batting her eyes to the rhythm as she lip-synched to Commissioned's "King of Glory". With every revolution, she looked a degree more enticing. Each time she glided past, she would glance out the corner of her eyes and then spin around to face you as if she knew you were watching. You sloughed Nick and Dexter off like a muddy suit and went to the edge of the rink. She rolled so close to you that her momentum almost whisked you up and along for the ride as she ordered "Come on out" in an alluring murmur. She barely completed another circuit before you jumped in some ugly, paper-bag brown rent-a-skates and clumsily tailed her as if she was dragging a can on a string.

She was wearing a red, Illinois State, hooded sweatshirt, black skates with crimson tinted wheels and faded, torn Levi's with pink spandex leggings beneath that hugged her svelte, curvaceous thighs. The song was fast and the other skaters were flowing with it, but she seemed to glissade in slow motion as you chugged awkwardly along, admiring her rope-like braids that seemed combed in place down her shoulders. Skating wasn't and isn't your forte or joyride. As you probed her background, she didn't utter anything audible except her name. Everything else was acknowledged with the smiley-masked grunt "Um hmm."

When the five-minute song ended, it felt like you had been hiking in the Grand Canyon for a week. She picked up on it and escorted you by the hand to the food court, where we dined on sausage pizza. It was over the din of constant chatter and booming music that the rare moment of disclosure was exploited. Seldom are mutual confidentialities bartered in rapid-fire successions with no tricks attached. All of the vitals were swapped, from the Zodiac signs (she was an Aquarius and you're a Gemini, which made you astrologically compatible) to our deepest dreams. She fantasized of living on a deserted tropical island with a tall, brown, slender man—a flattering allusion to you—in order to replenish the island with descendants; You half-lied and confessed you longed to walk the dark corridor of life, get a glimmer in the form of an enduring woman, take that glimmer by the hand and walk together through the darkness to the light at the end. While there was truth to it, your heart really hankered a quick tryst with her in the bathroom. We connected like puzzle pieces and were floating on emotions, so you weren't trying to jack it up with the brutal truth.

"It's Okay" by the Winans came on, and without making physical contact or conversation, we touched and agreed into a consummatory roll, since it was the couples-only set. You clutched her gently from behind and, surprisingly, sluiced cursively with her like a master psalmist with a feather pen and a cup overflowing with passion. Heaven and earth passed away and there was just you and Joyce—floating against the backdrop of time. You closed your eyes and realized you were treading that dark tunnel. Later she confessed that her eyes were closed, too. The everlasting song was four minutes, which was too brief for a walk through paradise. The end of that song signified the beginning of the age of accountability and the end of the age of innocence. Halloween 1990 marked the first sighting of the sooty rose, but you dismissed it as a product of your imagination. It wasn't until later that you perceived that there was an esoteric correlation between the flower and divinely verboten intimacy.

There is no remembrance of removing your skates. Sometimes you wonder if you even took them off that night. We were on the same cloud when we exited the rink and were sucked out by dual concupiscence. On a night that we were supposed to be shaming Satan and having a good time in the Lord, we reversed by grieving Jesus and making the Devil proud in the back seat of her Skylark. Your eyes were open and she was a remarkable sight. Guilt was gratifying.

The cherished recollection brings a doting smirk to your face as Ms. Davis (the Devil's grandmother) walks up, startling you back into the dreadfully real present. "Hi, Malcolm," she ardently greets as she embraces you and holds her cheek up to be pecked.

You oblige, because she is as venerable as any saint is. "How are you Ms. Davis?" you question as she puts a glow in your smile like only a sweet mother could.

"Fine Baby. It's good to see you."

"It's good to see you, too," you comment as Penny turns the corner and displays a jolted expression that quickly spreads into a sardonic grin.

Your smile drops and the glow obfuscates like a black cloud dims a sunny day.

She asks her grandmother for the keys to the car to retrieve the cake that she left in there, her eyes and smile staying glued to your antithetical scowl. Her muzzle is made up like a peanut butter and jelly sandwich. Ms. Davis discerns your ire and quickly hands her the keys, shooing her off. She leaves the stench of rotting corpses in her trail as she trots up the stairs, through the vestibule and out of the door.

Only dead people are soulless and icy like Penny. Though she's physically out of your presence, her spirit lingers and haunts you. Apparently, it's written in bold black letters across your face, because Ms. Davis encourages, "Don't let anyone steal your joy, baby" as the class gathers and Nick opens with a prayer. It would probably be easier to resist a robber with a bazooka pointed at your chest, than to recapture your happiness after spotting Penny. You stand mute and focused on bitterness as Nick pleads to God to bless the lesson.

It was two years ago that Penny ripped into your bosom with her talons and baptized you in a truculent tub of disgrace. When you needed time to adjust to yourself and the reality of a failed love, you exchanged mutual happiness for the security of her sultry body. At the time, you didn't know what you wanted, let alone what you needed. She was the rebound of a game winning shot. You missed at love, but she was right there when you couldn't distinguish night from day. Everything she said sounded good; her appearance was magnetic; her aroma was fresher than a lakefront breeze. You never imagined a demon masquerading as a big butt and a pretty smile. Penny is a melting pot of the most exotic features that make her one of a kind: wool-like Native-

American hair; an olive, Italian complexion that was as flawless as a newborn lamb; black, crystallized, Arabian eyes; scarlet lips full of the Motherland. As scrumptious to you as a candle is to a moth in a dark cave, she was just as pestilent. You were consumed briefly, but her flame on you was inextinguishable as you vaporized from the touch of her Pluto-imported, dry ice heart. Ma's constant prodding about her five-year seniority and your depleted soul enabled you to grudgingly walk away cold turkey, when the game was over.

If there was an escape from knowing her, it was too narrow to see. One burn is all it took to addict and scar you. For eight months, all was well while you thought you got to know yourself again. Then she tore the scab off: "You're the father." She claimed that she knew only you when you queried, and you took her word. Even though you smelled the roses of conviction, you didn't repent, so a fall was in your forecast. Financial support wasn't a remote issue; marriage was the dilemma—for her. After Edwin arrived, you were ready to elope, but she insisted on waiting two years for you to graduate from high school. You didn't hesitate to shell out $200 of your weekly $300 take-home to them from Regency Communications. You didn't have a car note, rent, utilities or credit cards to pay...just transportation, clothing and lunch expenses. The arrangement seemed acceptable. In the meantime, you were a step away from walking away from b-ball when the seeds of deceit started yielding the crop of lies.

You answered the phone when Ms. Davis (bless her heart) called your mother. The family was just finishing a joyous dinner, when you observed how the ominous, 45-minute conversation shriveled up your mother's brow as she cut her eyes at you with each confirming, "Uh huh." She passed you the telephone and left the kitchen as Ms. Davis gave you an abbreviated account. You edited it down to "Penny is getting financial child support from another man that she is involved with." The paternity test Penny suggested was a farce: 99% unlikely that you were the man. She knew it, but she wanted to prolong the stratagem. You, on the other hand, wanted to kill her, serve a life sentence and die in a cage. Although there's no enmity between you and the actual man, that sorry gump stayed involved with her until she got tired of toying with him.

In a three-way phone conversation via Ms. Davis, the mediator, you found out that he was 25 (she screwed the best of the generation), he worked as a computer programmer (she likes them book smart), lived five blocks from you (she likes brothers from the South Shore area) and he was planning to move in with her (she likes living dangerous, since she suggested shacking up with you, but you declined). It would've been interesting to see how she would've pulled that off if her grandmother hadn't exposed her game. It never dawned on you that something was going on when your visits were restricted to bi-weekends. You were too busy telephone selling five hours a day after school in order to provide financial support to her and the baby to take notice. Penny told you that she was taking Edwin to see his maternal grandmother. Ms. Davis became suspicious when both of us became too affectionate with Edwin. Penny denied running a game, but Ms. Davis overheard the conversations that said otherwise.

What was worse than the deed was the pride behind the deed. It was all a game to her. Never mind the bond between man and child that had developed; she wasn't even ashamed. Not only was she non-repentant, but she bragged about it around the church, as if she reached some type of milestone in her life. That's when you left the W.O.F. God's Word started contradicting itself: A spring shouldn't produce sweet and bitter water. How is it that a priceless soul like Ms. Davis could produce something remotely close to Penny?

You're thankful that Nick is closing out the lesson concerning the two youngest kings of Judah, Manasseh and Josiah. Her main focus was King Josiah—the youngest King in the history of Judah at eight years of age—and the righteous reforms he instituted as contrasted with Manasseh's (12 years old) idolatrous practices. From the few moments that you observed, her presentation explained the background, accurately interpreted the passage, and applied it to the individuals in the class. However, you were distracted and it was grueling to be there. When she asks, "Are there any questions; comments; clarifications; points of disagreements," you dismiss yourself.

You make it up the stairs and to the front door, only to come face to face with the Devil as she walks in with Edwin. The temperature rises 500 degrees. It drops a degree when you behold Edwin through the exploding silence.

"Don't hate me because I'm beautiful," she mocks through the tense partition.

You can't resist dignifying, even though she or the statement aren't worth the carbon monoxide. "People who use kids to run unnecessary game, are as far from beautiful as the east is from the west," you declare through strained restraint, recalling a scripture from the Anti-Halloween movement in Exodus 22:18, adding, "I agree with Moses when he said 'Thou shalt not suffer a witch to live.' Bitches included."

"I see you've added a new word to your vocabulary," she teases. "I didn't know you had profanity in you."

"Some people bring out the best in me; you have the ability to cast the devil out of me," you claim.

"You're always welcome, Malley Mal," she croons as she attempts to caress your face.

You snatch her arm and grip it as you charge, "Don't give me a reason to rip your throat out." You shove her arm back as she sniggers to your dismay.

"Nobody told you to fall in love with me...only fools fall in love."

"Don't flatter yourself," you retort with an uncontrollable chuckle. "You just happened to step on an already shattered heart...like tearing the wings off of a dead fly."

"You want another sip of the juice."

"What I really desire is to douse your face with paint remover so I can scrape a few layers of makeup off of your irritating mug with a flat-head screwdriver."

"Do you think you'll ever get over me?"

"I never got started with you."

"Why do you avoid me then?"

"Let's see," you start, measuring her up to break her down. "My four reasons coincide with my four senses: I can't stand the sight of death; I can't stand the smell of death; I can't stand the sound of death; I can't stand the touch of death. The body without the soul is dead. Vultures even avoid you. You have no heart and you seem to be brain-dead, so you need to pay the Wizard a visit for a double dose of his benevolence, you foul-mouth, fickle-minded, foolishly frolicking, fake fly-girl trying to find her way back from Fantasy Island."

"Can you give me a piece of yours? I'll refund the 4,000 sweaty dollars you gave me."

That comment hits a nerve, causing your right eye and fist to twitch, as you brush past her.

She laughs at you, not realizing how close she was to a cracked cranium.

Your curiosity won't be satisfied today. You wanted to see what the inside of the Mosque is like, but it is filled to capacity, so you have to hear/watch the sermon on close circuit television in the gymnasium of the Muhammad University of Islam. The bow-tied security detail thoroughly pats you down to the borderline of discomfort, getting real close to the zone that's reserved exclusively for women. Chicago's finest aren't this particular. However, you don't take it personal since they show the utmost respect to you. You are running a bit late because you took a catnap that turned into a four-hour slumber.

A brother with a strong Motherland (there's no way to distinguish the tongue, with there being so many) accent is introducing another Muslim with the common Arabic Muhammad surname when you walk in. There is no need in searching for Khalid, since everyone is uniformly dressed, groomed and mannered. Two rows of folding chairs with several compact aisles extending back to the exit face a stage with a giant screen television. Men are seated on the left, while the women are to the right. As you're ushered into a row in the middle of the gym floor, the Muhammad brother goes through a few current ills, such as the Nancy Kerrigan assault and the kindergartner who brought a loaded gun to school the previous week, to qualify the check in procedure. He loosens things up with a bit of humor as he explains the separation of males and females within the Mosque, before he introduces the editor of the Final Call.

The editor goes through the routine greeting and creed: "As-Salaam-Alaikum. In the name of Allah: the beneficent, the merciful. I bear witness that there is no god but Allah, who came in the person of Master Fard Muhammad, and I bear witness the Honorable Elijah Muhammad is his exalted Christ, and Minister Louis Farrakhan is the word of god among us at this present moment," just as a speaker in the church would greet "First giving honor to God." It's a cool mouthful before he details more current events, starting with the fulfillment of some weather prophecies that Minister Farrakhan made.

You study the gym while the health minister takes the podium and addresses the issue of going to the devil for vaccination. A gigantic picture of Elijah Muhammad hangs on the stage behind the TV, and a school bookstore is situated just to the right of the stage. A flag of the Islamic crescent moon and star hangs above each basketball goal. To your left hangs three banners, which read from front to back: Cultivating new minds with a new education for developing a better future; Mosque Maryam loves and supports Minister Louis Farrakhan; Muhammad University of Islam in pursuit of excellence. The restrooms to the right are labeled Brothers and Sisters—how appropriate; how welcoming; how comfortable. As you scan the audience of brothers—Christian, Muslim, faithless; light, dark, in-between; educated, ignorant, learning; chic, casual, hoboish—a satisfied smile erupts from within your heart. So different, but so alike we all are. Walk of Faith wishes they could gather this diversity of brothers on a given Sunday.

The health minister finally introduces the speaker, Abdul Allah Muhammad, to the ovation of the assembly. You cringe as he unnecessarily, degrades Malcolm X to lift up Muhammad. Some stand, others sit and clap; you eagerly anticipate. He doesn't disappoint as he delivers his message titled "Farrakhan: the Revolutionary."

His voice is deep and prudish and his stage presence is free-spirited. He drops a savory sound-bit that satisfies your appetite for the truth: *The Black man can't be happy in America unless he's dead* (one of your favorite philosophical morsels, served up well-done and specially seasoned with Muhammad's personal spice). He affirms that the Black-on-Black violence that filters into the White community is self-destructive, even though Whites are being destroyed in the process. The notion is reinforced with the catch phrase "Strength without vision is not going to get you out of hell" and biblically illustrated with the story of Samson regaining his strength, but not his sight, and then killing the Philistines—and himself.

Muhammad rhetorically questions the Christian listeners on whether Jesus supported the Roman government and if he got permission from them to preach. Then he attests that the licensed preachers are representing the licensee who, in turn, are their gods. That stings you while the crowd applauds. He follows up by affirming that the Nation wouldn't ask for government assistance, because the Nation is preaching their doom, satirically comparing itself to Jesus asking the Roman government for money when Jesus was prophesying how His Father's kingdom would be taking over.

Muhammad's testimony that he was once a Christian surprises you. He playfully recalls how he saved a picture from Sunday school of Jesus whipping the moneychangers out of the Temple. Out of all of the preachers you've heard, none come close to skillfully quoting the scriptures like Muhammad. So far, his source of divine reference is the Bible and his main character illustration is Jesus. He quotes Jesus from a scripture: "Father, I pray not for this world, but for those you have given me out of this world." You make a mental note to check up on that, because Muhammad indicates that Jesus didn't pray for the world, but for believers only.

The names that White folks gave Blacks is his next topic. He's good. His take on why blacks don't want to be called black: It's opposite of white, which is opposed to white. Whites and Blacks are natural enemies, like dogs and cats are natural enemies. However, a dog and cat raised together from puppy and kitten will play and not fight for a generation. Blacks have been living with whites for several generations and still don't get along. On the tag African-American: Moses never said that he's an Israelite-Egyptian; I'm an Egyptian of Hebrew descent. *You're black to the bone and tempted to change your name.*

Abdul Allah Muhammad appeals to your soul. You're absorbing every point like a fresh sponge absorbs water. The message has you fired up and hungry for more. It takes a special person to uplift you with words. At the same time, he humbles you like a barren woman in a maternity ward. You have always prided yourself on the knowledge that you have gained throughout the years. He serves up a couple of ethnic dishes in addition to the Word, which make it clear that you are lacking. The concept of First, Second and Third World comes from the Talmud—a Rabbinic training manual. He cites the contents of a tri-world humanity. The First World is composed of the top intellects; the powers that be; the knowledge giants who can actually become god. The Second World is made up of the mass of humanity that struggles with divine intelligence and animal instincts. The Third World consists of animals walking upright in human bodies.

That was sea deep and shit insulting. You're going to pick up a copy of the Qur'an and the Layman's Parallel Bible with four translations across—to which Muhammad refers. He takes your religion to task when he explains that Genesis 1 and Genesis 2 talk about two different Adams, backing up his hypothesis with 1 Corinthians 15:45, even going as far as to spell out contrasting chronologies of the first and second chapter. You didn't realize that it was a fish—not a whale as some attribute to the Bible—that swallowed Jonah. You have a lot of examination of faith ahead of you.

Before he delivered his message, you took a personal liking to him, since White folks despise him and he speaks to get them to loathe him the more. You could relate to his testimony of how a White cop, William H. Parker, had vowed to kill him before he died. Muhammad relates how Parker, during a police awards ceremony, dropped dead of a heart attack while en route to his seat after accepting his award for being the top cop. This is something to shout about. In closing, he encourages everyone to read and research the message and scriptures for themselves before he begins his invitation to Islam.

Of the bits and pieces that Khalid gave you of the Islamic doctrine—combined with Muhammad's message—you can't see much of a difference between it and Christianity. The main difference in the services is the singing—or lack thereof at the Mosque. With the exception of calling God Allah and the discipline, which the Christian church should make note of, it's all good. Brotherly love is flowing freely at the Mosque. People actually speak to you and seem genuinely glad to see you. At Walk of Faith, it's not uncommon for the so-called saints to superciliously or vindictively play you like an ugly mannequin. Schisms can linger until the millennium and some members carry them to their graves. Based on their thinking, you can imagine some of them feuding in heaven.

The brothers are all clean-cut and studious; the women are modest in dress and well-spoken. They all have knowledge to kick around; a message to give; scriptures to back up their faith. Most of the Christians you know retain only what was taught to them in preschool Sunday school class, and probably don't even know where to find 'Jesus wept' in the Bible. You really don't hear many Baptist preachers truly addressing racism and calling the White man by his name: devil with a deep, lowercase d. If you take the D away, they're still as evil as hell. They're so stuck on their misunderstanding of what *turn the other cheek* means that, in essence, they teach a doctrine on punkology—as if it is in God's will for Black folks to just take beatings like it is our special calling. Jesus sure didn't take no whipping from Satan. It seems like the Christian ministers are oblivious to the problems that Black folks have in

America; big offerings seem to be their only concern. Personally, you're tired of those "I have a dream" sermons. You're ready for a black reality, as opposed to an American nightmare.

Instead of waiting for things to get better, which too often the church emphasizes, the Nation of Islam seems to have a proactive walk to back up the talk. They have the newspapers, businesses and unity. You haven't taken notice of much unity in the Christian community. Otherwise, all of the self-professing Christians would do a better job of networking and helping each other and the community. Your theory is that many are Christians by confession, not in heart. Outreach is terrible. The divers denominations that know Jesus in the same way constantly condemn each other. There is no Christian visibility in the 'hood, with the exception of the many immaculate church buildings. Yet, they're quick to verbally cut down "cults" like the Watchtower Society, who get out, recruit and spread their doctrine. The Nation is out selling newspapers, running businesses, and promoting self-sufficiency. Although you're not going to claim Islam as your faith just yet (you have the bold desire to walk the Islamic aisle, but something from within has you immobilized in your seat), you like what you see, hear, and feel and you're open to study it.

Traci Dawson: the hemorrhoid in your anus. Those feelings accrue with every piece of writing she does. Her views are overdosed with conservative, political correctness. You don't hate her, but you can't stand to be around her. Unfortunately, you're in the same major. You've had the same writing classes with her, and participate on the school newspaper together as Joint Editors in Chief (that was her equal-opportunity, feminist idea after you were nominated unanimously by the majority student body). We're neck-and-neck at the top of the class, and with her summer cotillion, she has an edge in scholarship and award money so far. You were reluctant to ride with her to another Chicago Association of Black Journalists meeting. One of her mentors, BJ Thomas, is supposed to be starting a project for high schoolers aspiring for careers in journalism. It would allow students to get internships, scholarships, professional mentoring, and opportunities to write, edit and publish a newspaper. Last month, he got called on an assignment at the last minute and couldn't keep the appointment, so you were annoyed by Traci for nothing. Sometimes business can get personal, so you put your tongue in check to avoid any topics that can generate a debate, and politely go along with the mechanic conversation that Traci is directing.

"The Real World" was one of the favorite topics in the entertainment section of the school paper. The second season episode, in which David was evicted for pulling some covers off of Tami (one of his three female roommates, which included Beth), typified the differences of opinion. Initially, Tami, Beth and the whole crew were laughing hysterically as David tugged at them, but when it was over, she was tearful. At Beth's goading, it wasn't long before Tami was seething. While it is clear that the incident started off as mutual horseplay, the issue of when the mood took a no-nonsense twist, was the source of the debate. The lines were simple: Pro-David/Anti-Beth or Pro-Tami. The arguments got complex with the battle lines being drawn based on gender—with a racial undercurrent—since the incident involved a Black man (David) and a Black woman (Tami), yet the controversy was kindled by a White woman (Beth).

You and Traci were in charge of presenting the Pro/Con arguments, which was a compilation of student's opinions and personal commentary. Of course, your position was in favor of David, although you thought that he was generally a boisterous clown. You believed, nevertheless, that the circumstances didn't warrant an eviction. The bottom line: Tami was a little embarrassed and highly peeved to be seen in her underwear, and Beth had a vendetta against David (from a previous disagreement), so she instigated an unnecessary civil war.

Your nemesis felt that criminal charges should have been brought against him, echoing the cliche'ish sentiment that "NO MEANS NO" recited by Beth. She felt a sexual assault took place. It was almost as if we had watched different versions of the show, and you had to strain to keep the commentary focused on the show and not Traci. Traci loves to squabble a point that is arrantly erroneous. As opposed to finding the truth, it was a debate. You love to dispute issues for the sake of winning, even at the cost of reaching a righteous medium. It's when you go against someone who's just as determined—and wrong in the process—that your patience gets frustrated. You can't deal with someone like you. After her contrary commentary, you've avoided unnecessary communication with her. The only time we talk is when it's totally necessary; exchanging ideas is counterproductive.

She backs her mother's Sentra into a parking space on underground Wacker Drive, while the Jade tape plays low. A pariah stirs in his cement bed, right behind her space, prompting her to nervously state, "Maybe I should park somewhere else," as she peers at him in her rearview mirror.

She has a way of tickling the demons within, so you acerbically attest, "He sure looks threatening welding that raggedy blanket."

She doesn't respond or seem to get it as she restarts the car and peels out, just as a space on the other side becomes available. She goes all the way to the end of the block to the Stop light and U-turns as the light turns green, barely beating someone else to the space.

"Hopefully he won't come to this side," she mentions to herself as she let's herself out.

All you can do is shake your head and hold your peace as you stroll over to him and drop a dollar bill in his paper cup. A smile shines through his soiled face as he hoarsely thanks you and holds up a disfigured hand. You nod and "God bless" him.

On your way back across the barrier, Traci seems oblivious to and unimpressed by the act of benevolence as she impatiently glances at her watch. "We don't have all day," she reprimands as she starts off before you get to her.

"They're not going anywhere," you assure.

"Neither is he and the rest of his bum associates," she cuts, nodding her head back in his direction. "You could've given it to him when you got back."

"Just like you could've stayed in your original parking space and saved three minutes, Mother Time."

"Someone that's too lazy to work isn't worth my time," she huffs. "If you want to concern yourself with slouches, that's your business, but don't hold me up while you're doing it."

"You know, if I had realized I had a leash on you, I would've tied you to the steering wheel. Tell me: Do I have a muzzle for your mouth, too?"

"Why don't you open up an outcast shelter in your house," she urges. "Oops, I'm sorry, you don't have a home of your own, Mister Crusader."

"Why don't you go get a heart transplant, because the one you have ain't working."

"Do you have to always start with me?"

"We'll be okay once you realize I'm right and you're wrong."

"Whatever," she blurts condescendingly.

Growth is a part of human nature. Some grow in to six- or seven-foot giants; others inflate into superior intellects; many increase in charitable inclinations. Often, mankind grows in all areas. In the case of the vexation incarnate walking with you, she has grown maybe two inches since the sixth grade, and most definitely she's become a mental Goliath within a short amount of time, but she lacks a spiritual conscious. Traci was always the tall, arrogant, class smart aleck, voted most likely to grow old alone in a nursing home. Biases and contempt aside, she is striking and she knows it. Without opening her mouth, her disposition tells everyone to revere her 14-karat gold skin-tone and look up to her—literally and figuratively speaking. Unfortunately, she's gold plated; fortunately at 6'1", she doesn't tower over everyone, although she perceives such, since her nose is always pointed to the heavens and her line of vision deceives her into thinking that the horizon is beneath her. She has a good grade of over-moosed hair that curtains her shoulders. Her quarter-moon shaped eyes make her one of the biggest contradictions in creation: Pretty Ugly.

When we get to the building, we elevate to the third floor. When we step off the elevator, there's a crowd of professionals and wannabe's socializing and eating Giordano's pizza, chatting away about this and that in the business. A lot of them are dressed in their on-air best: gentlemen in smooth blazers and crisp slacks, ladies in skirt or pants suits. Traci is a natural in her black, sub-knee skirt, gray jacket, white blouse and blabbermouth. You follow her through the sea of people as she makes a beeline to a short fellow (about four inches shorter than Traci, who's wearing flats) with a canary yellow face and a heart-shaped hairline, who's chattering with a few other young folks. She touches his shoulder, breaking him away from his conversation. He gleefully grins and enthusiastically shakes her hand.

"This is Malcolm Johnson," she introduces. "Malcolm, this is BJ Thomas."

"I know," he says, extending his hand. "I read the papers from the sports section to the front," he testifies.

That brings a smile to your face as you greet, "How you doing, BJ" and wring his hand.

"I'm living, bro. How about yourself?"

"Well, I haven't gotten any negative press today, so I would say that I'm doing pretty good."

"I hear you," he agrees. "I'm just taking the names and numbers of those interested in the project, so go help yourself to the pizza and pop," he encourages.

You oblige as Traci stays behind and talks. Everyone looks familiar and important. You maneuver your way through the swarm of eloquent professionals, balancing a plate in each hand. BJ has herded the preppies to one side. You offer one of the plates to Traci and she thanks you as BJ starts addressing us. Most of the students sit excitedly silent, while others attentively jot down notes.

"In thirty days, we—YOU—will have a finished product. Your deadline is February 11th at 21:00 hours: nine o'clock for those not familiar with military time," he says with a chuckle. "And on Valentines Day, the completed product—Volume 1/Issue 1 of the CABJ Testimony—will be in circulation."

Traci raises her hand and he recognizes her. "Does the newspaper have a theme?"

"It will, once you all come up with one," he states. "I'm overseeing the production of the paper, not writing. You will decide the topics—of course, I have to approve them. You will be doing all of the writing, proofreading, editing, and layout. Production is on you from beginning to end."

"What is the circulation?" you query between bites of your sausage and cheese slice.

"Good question, Malcolm," he compliments. "Circulation will be 10,000 copies to start. To give you an idea, it will be an insert in the Chicago Defender, so you will have a lot of exposure. That's why you have to take it serious."

"How will the work be allocated," Traci questions.

"Another good question. There will be no titles such as editor in chief and managing editor. There will be specific departments, but you won't be restricted to any one particular area. So if you want to work on a political story, you can. If you want to cover sports next time, you're free to do that," he assures. "Depending on your strength and discipline, some may do more editing and layout than writing. However, I want everybody to be involved in the editing and layout process. For this initial year, it will be a bi-monthly, eight-page supplement with issues coming out in February, April—and June will be the last issue of the school year, with a possible summer issue."

It all sounds good to you as he announces the meeting for Saturday at the Woodson Library on 95th and Halsted. You tentatively sign up to do a sports article for the first issue, although you have no idea what you will write.

As we enter the general CABJ meeting, he encourages everyone to brainstorm. After the meeting, which was held on the set of the Jenny Jones Show, he pulls you to the side for a little pep talk.

"That editorial you wrote to the Sun-Times a year ago was riveting and powerful," he insists. "Your language and writing skills are on an advanced level."

You smile with pride and humbly thank him. "I can put out when I'm emotionally charged-up."

"That's the fuel for good writing. All of the good writers put out their best work when they feel strong about something they're conveying," he insists. "That's why I would like you to do a commentary for the first issue to set the tone for the paper in February: Black History Month."

Your eyebrows hop like Shawn Kemp, which distorts the honor that rushes through your heart.

"You have a strong voice, but no mouth for it to be heard. This is the mouth."

A smile spreads across your face and overlaps the lobby as you nod in agreement.

"The press never hesitates to trump up your rep without your side of the story, conveniently omitting your classroom accomplishments. A number three ranking out of a class of 500 and a 33 on the ACT test? A lot of them can't even score a 15."

"Now I can write like a man possessed on that topic," you assure with a guffaw.

"That's what I'm talking about: a Revolutionary voice. Everybody's talking about Generation X is lost and out of control. A lot of the things that are happening now, happened in the past two generations, and look at us...we're still not that much better off than our grandparents. As quiet as it's kept, we're not doing all that well in the sports industry."

"I know what you mean," you second. "The ratio of black management to athletes is a big joke, even if the 'super stars' are making

100 million a year. The owners are making billions, so what the players make is nothing to get excited over," you testify intensely.

Now BJ is grinning from coast-to-coast.

"What's up?" you query.

"That's exactly what I'm talking about," he says with a knowing nod. "I hit a nerve."

"What do you mean?"

"That's the topic of your first commentary."

You connect with him and we both smile mischievously. He glances to the side and spots someone else that he needs to talk to, excusing himself with "We'll talk about it some more at Saturday's meeting. Is there anyway I can get you a tape before the meeting?"

"Drop it off at my house or school."

"I'll leave it in your mailbox tomorrow."

"Sure thing," you say excitedly as we shake hands and part company.

4

"Have you ever had the feeling you were being watched?" you inquire of Chuck D and Mitch as we all examine the computer systems in the electronics section. We decided to stop at Elite's in the South Chicago Mall before we head to the Mount Carmel/St. Francis de Sales game. Practice was postponed because of a death in Coach Wade's family. You decided to go along with CD and Mitch at the last minute in order to unwind from a long week. Tomorrow you plan to spend the day writing the commentary for the CABJ Testimony, so this is your weekend.

"Yeah, I've had that feeling before," Mitch confirms, adding, "I've also felt like I was being followed."

"What ever do you mean?" Chuck D questions in mock naiveté.

"What I'm talking about is that *TOY COP* down there perpetrating like he's reading the CD," you broadcast of the of the uncovered undercover store security guard. "He can't read rap, so I don't know why he's fronting," you announce loud enough for the middle-aged, Mel Gibson caricature to hear.

"C'mon Dawg, Robocop can be into LL Cool J," Chuck D justifies.

"Yeah...and I'm into the Beetles," you agree.

"Personally I wish he would get out of our asses. What is he gay or something? Does he want to strip search us?" Mitch mulls. "WE HAVE MONEY. WE'RE NOT HERE TO SHOP-LIFT, MISTER OFFICER," he blurts, as we leave Officer Friendly to play it off.

Chuck D nudges you and Mitch, and wonders, "You think we're gonna be on COPS?" as he points up to the mirror dome that houses the camera.

"BAD BOY BAD BOY," Mitch sings with a complimentary middle finger directed to the people in surveillance land and dances out the door as we all chime in "WATCHA GONNA DO, WATCHA GONNA DO WHEN WE COME FOR YOU. BAD BOY BAD BOY."

"What would you do if he came for you?" you question.

"I'd give him a prime time, nationally-televised beat down...Jeffrey Manor style," Mitch assures as we exit. "Then I'd throw his ass in a dumpster and roll it into Lake Michigan."

"He would've been screaming 'CUT THE CAMERA...I NEED BACKUP--COMMERCIAL BREAK...WHO FLIPPED THE SCRIPT...THESE NIGGERS HIT BACK' as he had *real* bottles broken across his head and kicks to the face that weren't pulled," Chuck jokes.

"Then you would be the featured fugitive on *America's Most Wanted,*" you assure.

"At least I would get some press," he says as we make it to his sister's 1988 Ford Escort, adding, "Chicago State Penitentiary will be throwing themselves at me."

You fold your 76-inch frame in the front passenger seat, Chuck spreads his body across the back seat, and Mitch reclines almost in a lateral position as he inserts the Notorious B.I.G. cassette and peels off in the boom-box on wheels.

"Eh Dawg," Chuck shouts over the thumping bass. "Whatcha think about what Ken said yesterday?"

Mitch turns the volume down to backdrop level, awaiting your answer.

You peer out the window, recalling yesterday when Dexter Jr. mentioned how his father used to come home and watch the Cartoon Network with him; how the whole family would go out every other weekend. His reality is distorted like a television's reception without an antenna. While you were over there, he was anticipating his father walking through the door with every passing moment. He slipped into an insistent slumber replete with dreams unfulfilled. You vow to do any and everything in your power to keep Junior from knowing about Kenny Reed: the triggerman.

"I don't think anything of it, because I don't know what he said," you respond absently, not taking your eyes off the passing street.

"That motherfucker said that he didn't mean to shoot...said his finger slipped," Mitch venomously interjects. "I want to slip my foot up his dumb ass."

"I want to see the switch slip just as the governor brings in a pardon," Chuck asserts.

"That's too good for him. They oughta turn him over to the loved ones."

"On TV. Let any other punk that's thinking about shooting somebody see what an angry relative can do to the human body."

"All I need is two minutes...just lock me up with him for two minutes...."

"I really don't want to hear this," you murmur solemnly, your eyes still focused on the window, seeing nothing in particular. They're surprised into a verbal and motion pause. "No disrespect fella's, but this is how I'm dealing with it: giving Kenny as little thought as possible when it comes to Dexter's memory. His life was much more than Kenny."

There's an awkward moment of muteness, as they gauge your temperament with their eyes.

"I'm cool Mitch, so you can watch the road," you assure as he screeches a bad inch away from the rear of the dope man's gold Lexus. An eyelash separates the front bumper and the vanity plate that reads "HI ROLLR". You could actually smell the weed-tainted exhaust. The car jerks back to a stop as our pulse, breathing, and heartbeat freezes.

"And he's thrown out at second," Chuck jokes, shattering the stillness.

"SSSTOOOPID!" Mitch vents, throwing his hands up to the side. "Why did he stop all the way back here, anyway?"

"Maybe because the light is red and the line is right in front of him," you reason. "And you know he's not trying to end up on COPS, like us."

"Speaking of dope, you know Deon call himself selling that rock," Mitch informs.

You glance over at him. "He's the brokest dealer I've ever seen."

"He's just that dumb," Chuck D states. "Can't even make a profit dealing drugs. He was born to lose."

"I know he lost that fight, too," Mitch drops.

"That slam registered ten on the Richter scale," Chuck D states.

"He got into a fight? With who?" you question.

"He was cussing his mother out and stepped to her like he was going to smoke her, when his older, smaller brother came and planted him so hard, it left a canyon scattered with his body parts," Chuck D informs.

"And all the king's horses and all the king's men had a job putting him back together again," Mitch says, shaking his head. "I heard she was getting on him for taking the car. The cops pulled him over for going down a one way, and since he didn't have his license, guess who had to come down to the station to get him?"

"He pulled one of your numbers, huh?" CD jokes.

"At least he didn't crash into a light pole," you guffaw.

Last year, Mitch snuck out of the house at midnight to go joyriding in his momma's Cadillac. He scooped you and CD up and we headed down to Rush Street to cruise the north side. All went well: we got a few numbers, had a greasy meal and avoided all the drama from the cops. On the way back, he gawked at the biggest butt on 87th street too long and killed the street lamp. And he managed to scare about 40 years off our lives. After he leveled it, he proceeded as if nothing happened and dropped us off. You and CD offered to stand before his momma with him, but he insisted on us going home, assuring, "I can handle it." Well, he apparently said all of the right things, because we were kicking it the next day, which was Saturday. You couldn't imagine what outlandish story he could've told her, so you assume that he came clean and got off with a lecture.

"That pole shouldn't've been in the way," he dismisses with a mischievous smirk as he cranks the volume back up and proceeds down Ewing after the light changes.

After two blocks, Mitch takes the bass out of "Warning" and pleads, "You're going to have put a good word in to Traci for me, X" while playing with the cleft in his chin.

You cut your eyes at him and huff, "I can't get a letter in with her, let alone a full word."

"Why you sweating that high altitude chick anyway?" Chuck questions. "Are you planning on going one-on-one with her? I got ten on Traci."

"He has a craving for giraffes," you comment sarcastically.

"Outside of the fact that she's fine—not to mention her abundance of brain power and proficiency in Trigonometry—she would be healthy for me."

You and Chuck cut him a look that coincides with the last statement that came out of the side of his neck.

"Yo...with an average size woman—between 5'3" and 5'8"—I have to bend over to kiss them and careen my neck on a 90 degree angle to hear what they're saying. Over a period of time, that puts stress on my spine. And when my back is out of whack, there goes my hoopin' career," he explains, pulling into a parking space at the corner of 102nd Street and Ewing. One limb at a time, you all exit the matchbook car and collectively stretch out like a fragmented snake as the Southeast-side chill slices through your school jacket, warm-ups, long johns, epidermis and ribcage, and comes out on the other side. "When you see her again, tell her that I'll give up all of my freaks if she'll sing for me like she did when she turned the school out at the talent show last year," he yawns, bending backwards to stretch his back.

You don't dignify that idiotic comment with a response, but Chuck cuts in "I don't get it: you're willing to ditch a privileged life of ho's and favors for a seven-foot load with baggage..."

"She's six-one," he corrects.

"Whatever. I can't get with the idea of you settling down with a ready-made family."

"Ain't nothing to it," he shrugs.

"So you're gonna go from Big Mitch and M-Dawg to Mister Mitch, Dad and honey?" you query. "I'm with Chuck: that script is as phony as professional wrestling."

"And you're doing a good job macking her down. Here we are up at St. Francis...not to watch Antoine Walker school these boyz, but to fill the pages in your black book."

"I'm just staying occupied until we hook up," he says as he comes to an abrupt halt ten feet from the door. He focuses on the ground—as if he left his money in the car. You and Chuck look at him quizzically. He somberly peers at you as he raises his leg slightly to the side and releases gas to the lake effect winds with a butt-clapping fart. "Thank you, gentlemen. Thank you very much," he says, taking a bow.

You scowl at him and rebuke, "When that wind strips someone's flesh off and scrapes the paint off of a few cars, they'll be able to trace the DNA back to you. Don't ask me to hide you out."

"White Castles and gastric juices is like radiation," Chuck notes. "Just make sure you don't clear the gym out. Remember, you're trying to make a *good* first impression."

We make our way up to the second floor gym where the second quarter of the game is under way. You're surprised that the Pioneers are within single digits of the Caravan at 27-24. The atmosphere in the gym is charged and provides you with a unique point of view of prep hoops. During the course of watching the game, you're desensitized by the cheering, but you know that the noise is the catalyst for the players' adrenaline. Every dunk, steal, blocked shot, three-pointer, rebound, statistic, chest-thump, fist-pump, emotional outburst, or expression of excitement stimulates the crowd like a spark ignites gasoline. The enthusiasm surges through you like a subtle narcotic with the potent effect of gamma rays on Bruce Banner. Antoine Walker pops a three from the corner, a few strides away from your seat, and winks at you as he glides by. The noise—already at a deafening level—rises an octave, causing you to get jittery.

Mount Carmel is one of the primetime teams in the state, with a highflying roster that includes the hilarious, trash-talking, state-champion quarterbacking Donovan McNabb and the pseudo-intimidating Willie Jones. People come to see them, because not only do they come to run and gun, but they also make noise and have a lot of fun doing it. Weak teams get strong when they know the Caravan is coming to their town. You balled against them during the summer at Kennedy King College and a few other tournaments. You were matched up against Antoine and he played as if he was putting together a highlight film for the scouts. While he was shooting the lights out to the tune of 50 points (including a wide array of monster jams), he was shooting the breeze with you—complimenting you on a couple of treys and mentioning your article in the Sun-Times. Even though you or the team couldn't stop him, we did manage to beat them two out of three games. Walker reminds you of Dominique Wilkins with handles. He's considering Kentucky, UNLV and Illinois, but he really shouldn't waste his time with college ball. A summer in the weight room is all that separates his game from Scottie Pippen's level.

We watch the second quarter on floor level as Mount Carmel goes into the locker room with a 46-37 advantage. After Mitch scans the stands, he spots his prize just when the third quarter gets under way. You follow his lead as he slithers his way up through the stands to three of the IHSA's finest. Mitch didn't tell you that there would be three babes waiting! You have a first lady who doesn't leave you with any playing time for a second stringer, and even if she did, you would never get into *that* mating game. After all his preaching about the advantages of tall women, Mitch fondly embraces the girl with the all-state 36-24-36 body who barely comes past his knees. CD greets the anorexic bleach-blond cutie with tight jeans and brown work boots. A quick take of the remaining dove reveals a smooth, batter-toned face with a complimentary Hallé hairstyle.

As you turn back to the game, playing off her presence and their rudeness, you take mental note of her wine-colored, glossed lips that look like an M/W encounter and the kissing cousin to the extinct MAGIKIST neon sign on the Dan Ryan. You imagine those lips caressing your chest and sucking the freckles from your face, one-by-one, propelling you to cloud heights. Then you see Charlotte's lips lashing and chastening you for your wandering mind, sending you crashing down to a concrete reality, just as Antoine throws down a tomahawk, once again sending St. Francis' crowd into a frenzy.

"X," Mitch calls as he, his girl and your fellow stag-mate bear down on you. "This is Patricia; Patricia, this is Mal," he says, introducing you to the dwarf with giant body parts, and continuing, "Mal this is Sharlene; Sharlene, this is Mal."

A laugh begins to erupt, but catches in your throat as you toy with the homonymism of Sharlene/Charlotte in your head. Addressing them by name would require too much thought. You cover the guffaw with a smile, extend your hand, and greet, "Nice to meet you Sharlene," extremely careful not to let the name Charlotte slip through your teeth.

"Nice to meet you, too," she returns with a gratuitous, sparkling smile with the whitest, straightest teeth you have ever seen. The top row looks like a long stick of chalk.

"Sharlene writes for her school newspaper," Mitch offers.

"Is that right?" you ask.

She nods, still grinning slightly.

"I do a little writing, too."

"I know," she testifies. "I've read your piece in the Sun-Times."

"Really," you say, nodding. "You like?"

"Um-hm," she says as we both instinctively turn to the game when the crowd erupts. Donovan McNabb just finished a fast break and blatantly snickers at the fellow that tried to block his shot.

You take a seat next to her, focusing on the game and harking to her words. "Do you have an area that you specialize in?"

"I usually write commentaries on social issues."

"Issues such as 'Save the Whales' and 'Preserve the Rainforests'?" you chide.

"No," she giggles. "Things closer to the 'hood, such as 'Just Say No', 'Find Tyree a Job', 'Stop the Violence' and 'Why is Shanaenay Having Her Third Baby Before the Age of 18!"

"I hear you," you respond with a chuckle as she agrees and laughs with you. The crowd reacts when Antoine gets fouled hard and starts after the offender, as if he's going to swing on him. Vintage Caravan. "Everybody likes to talk shit," you Freudian slip. You casually turn and see her startled expression. "Oops...I mean everybody likes to commentate," you correct.

She just laughs.

There are a few other tongue trips during the remainder of the game, but not once do you call her Charlotte. In the last four minutes of play, Mount Carmel goes ballistic. After their top gun, Lee Lampley, fouls out, the Pioneers start shooting blanks, while the Caravan unloads their Uzzies into the basket. When you turn to talk to Sharlene, it is a tight 11-point lead; after you turn back to the game, it is a gapping 23-point route.

After the game, you hang out with Sharlene, discussing life in general and the journalistic angle in particular while the crowd lingers on the floor. After a while, the players emerge from the locker room. You make eye contact with Antoine as he talks with Kenny McReynolds. He throws up his fist at you.

You mouth, "Later", and he confirms with a nod of his head.

You run out of conversation with Sharlene while waiting by the door for Mitch and CD to commence their after-game analysis with Donovan and Willie.

There's no mistaking her honey heart that pumps maple syrup. She mentions that she volunteers as a tutor at a community center for troubled youths and often serves as a chaperon on their field trips. Yes, she has a profile to drool over. Her eyes twinkle, and when her lips are not smiling, her eyes seem to smile on their own, projecting "Welcome" and possessing the potential to invoke a beam from an ancient sculpture. She has knowledge to kick around. With journalism aspirations, she has to be on top of her game. We both pulled out our dictionary during the discussion to verify the correctness of some words the other had used. However, outside of our mutual career aspiration and patterning our writing styles after famous commentators (Carl Rowan, Ronald Childs, Vernon Jarrett and Derrick Baker), there's nothing else to talk about.

After squeezing out the last bit of courteous script, which left the impression of a grueling interview with a non-cooperative interviewee, there is nothing left but the murmur of background noise. Perhaps it's because she has a reserved, soft-spoken demeanor. Then again, it could be your woman with the similar name that discourages your interest. Whatever the case, you stand comfortably mute beside her while your boys wrap up their shoptalk.

They conspire to catch a movie, but you opt for an early evening. Chuck hitches a ride with Heather, his slim friend who drove. You bid Sharlene a formal adieu and fold yourself into the back seat of the Escort, leaving no room for even a single, slippery sardine. Everyone else is left awkwardly guessing like a Jeopardy contestant without a clue. Although your actions weren't intended to magnify the wind-chill, you could tell that Sharlene is frostbitten as she slinks into the back seat of Heather's Tracker.

After everyone has loaded into the vehicles and is prepared to roll out, CD jumps out and runs up to the Escort window. To your annoyance, Patricia lets the window down and the hawk in.

"Mal?" he bullishly asks, "Aren't you going to give her the digits?"

You shake your head ruefully as everyone seems surprised.

He hesitates before asking, "Do you want hers?"

"Not really," you flatly reply.

You did mention your girlfriend to her during the conversation, so it is very necessary to stand on your word. She knows. Mitch knows. CD knows. Since they all knew that ice was in the forecast, they shouldn't have exposed themselves. Now you seem like a snob for declining any further acquaintance.

CD's face breaks in sympathy for Sharlene. "Aiight," he confirms and trots back to the Tracker. No one in their car looks your way as Mitch cranks up the volume and pulls off.

An elderly woman with a head covering methodically and wisely answers the question from the study guide. *"Do you agree that most women seem to need the approval of a man in order to feel special to themselves? Why or why not? If you agree, to what do you attribute this apparent need?"* That's only the second of 12 questions and about half of the 30 or so people in the circle have commented on it.

Khalid was on the phone when you got in from the game and he invited you to the Friday night study group at the Mosque. He mentioned it before, but you had totally forgotten about it, although you promised that you would try to make it. You agreed to go tonight because your creative juices were frozen and your desire for television was nullified like a raindrop in the desert. Their topic is taken from a sermon by Minister Farrakhan, with references from both the Bible and the Qur'an. There's another group gathered in a circle a few feet away discussing the same issue, in the gymnasium of the Muhammad University.

You are more awed by the oratory skills of the respondents than with the message. From the youngest to the oldest, the Black Muslims know they can creatively and metaphorically express themselves. It's not beyond the realm of thought that if they were asked to deliver a sermon, they could do so without any exhaustive preparation. The discussion utilizes real life examples to make the spiritual and moral point. You're impressed with the format. As opposed to a minister teaching, the minister just directs the discussion. Everybody fires out their views. Either you're coming down with something or it's a full moon, because you suddenly bottle your thoughts and bridle your tongue. You begin to feel that they have dwelt on the same question too long, and the responsive opinions and answers are beginning to sound regurgitated to you.

After the two hours are up, the groups turn the chairs toward the stage and the presiding minister recaps the topic. He's even more eloquent than all of them put together, as he speaks without any notes. In all honesty, you're more interested in talking to Khalid one-on-one about the faith. When he finishes his speech and dismisses the congregation, you question Khalid in the parking lot.

"If God is everywhere, why do Muslims pray towards Mecca?"

"It's symbolic of the people of God being on one accord. In 1st Kings the 8th chapter, Solomon prayed that when the people turn to the temple to pray, that God would hear them. Of course Allah is everywhere, but when we pray to the east, it's symbolic of unity."

It makes sense, so you nod in agreement.

You're looking to expose holes in Islam, but so far, you haven't been able to penetrate. There are so many parallels to Christianity that the names are starting to be the only recognizable difference. The

Qur'an you bought last week has only been skimmed through, however, you did take note of the account of how God saved Noah and his whole family.

"I have a question for you," he warns. When he says that, usually it's not good from a Christian knowledge perspective. "Why do Christians insist that Jesus was God when Jesus denied it...even in the Bible?"

You don't respond, as the mind virus spreads quickly. It germinates into doubt, producing an anxiety that surges to your belly, and prompts questions galore that cripple your natural thought processes.

He has dropped several bombs that have been growing in your soul like cancer: *Where does it say that Jesus forgives sins? If others were called the sons of God, what makes Jesus unique in that sense? Since Jesus was the Son of Man, doesn't that make God a man?* Then there was the list of biblical "errors" he furnished you with—from the number of chariots in King Solomon's stable, to the narrative voice of Matthew (written in third person as opposed to first person)—and his etymological reasoning that he used to back up his stance, which justified studying the Qur'an.

"Think about it, research it, and get back to me, Black man," he encourages. "As Salaam Alaikum."

"Wa-Alaikum-Salaam."

"555-9983," you spit as Sharlene scribbles it in her 3x5 memo book. "Of course, if I'm not in, kindly leave a message after the beep."

"You know I will," she suggests suggestively as she flashes a wily smile.

When you arrived five minutes late for the meeting, who was sitting in the front row with a big, expectant, irritatingly chipper grin? Sharlene. It almost seems like you didn't leave her. To make the scenario humorously annoying, BJ teamed you up with her. You, Traci and Sharlene will work as a team on the article. You will do the writing, Traci will do the research and editing and Sharlene will concentrate on the photos and layout. BJ insisted that we all exchange numbers, to your secret ire and her visible mirth.

You wasted no time in viewing the tape BJ dropped off Thursday titled "Outside The Lines: Portraits In Black & White" from ESPN. The piece was well researched and educational, not to mention provocative. It's going to be hard to decide between the many quotes and sound-bites. You already have a title for your commentary. After you got back from the study group at the Mosque, you were sleepless, so you popped it in and got aroused. It promises to be an easy write and a powerful message.

5

OFF TO THE RACISTS

By Malcolm Johnson

February signifies Black History Month. It is a time to reflect on the culture, struggles, and accomplishments of our ancestors in society in general, and the world of sports in particular. We, as a community, reminisce about past athletic pioneers and great leaders, and the sacrifices they made toward progress in a country that's bent on oppressing the descendants of Africans. When I look back on the recent history of Blacks in America, it seemed as if we were on our way to the championship, but after pondering over the present state of the race, it seems as though greed, deception, and separation amongst ourselves, and biased officiating from the system will cost us the victory. It is one thing to lose because of inferior ability, but it is another to lose because of infighting and bad calls from the referees.

Black people are blessed to be top physical specimens. As a race, we add creativity and style to major sports with the natural ease of simultaneously breathing and walking. In the sports of basketball and football, Blacks account for 75% and 62% of all athletes, respectively. If one looks quickly at those statistics, it would seem impressive, but a closer look reveals that Blacks only make up 8% of head coaches, 16% of general managers, and 15% of executive positions in the NBA and 7%, 0%, and 9% in the NFL.

The racial make-up of the front office gives a whole new meaning to the term "white collar position". Although there have been huge athletic advances since Jackie Robinson broke the color barrier in 1947, it is obvious that we are still in the field picking cotton. The Black community could easily mimic the statistic's cry of racism, but why waste breath when there are enough high profile bigots to sing that song.

Al Campanis's comment echoed in 1987 of "Blacks don't have the mental necessities to handle the white collar positions in a sports organization" gives an explanation to this lopsided ratio. However, that statement is a slap-in-the-face, kick-in-the-rear insult to anyone of African descent born of a woman. Judging by the actions of today's sports owners, they still hold that sentiment to be true.

When Marge Schott referred to one of the Black players on the Red Sox as her "million dollar nigger," she seemed to have reflected the disposition of all or most of her fellow owners and of society. In other words, a Black athlete is another word for an indentured servant, which is an evolutionized slave.

Jimmy "The Greek" showed his and all racist's color, which is ghost white, when he said: "If you give Blacks those positions, there will be no jobs for Whites." In essence, he and other racists feel that after 400 years of oppression, if Afro-Americans were to get prestigious positions, we would turn the tables and oppress our Caucasian counterparts. Feet seem to be on the dining menu judging from all of these Freudian slips.

Sports opens up doors for education and white-collar jobs, not just in the world of athletics, but also in the corporate and real world, since sporting institutions are businesses. Waiting on prejudiced owners to give a break to Black people is not the answer to solving the problem of discrimination. Part of the answer lies in the brothers who have made it. Let's face it, when people crowd basketball arenas all over the country, they don't come to see John Paxson or Will Perdue, they come to see Michael Jordan and Scottie Pippen. Black professional athletes should realize that sports organizations need them to make money. It's like a circus marketing a sideshow freak to attract a crowd.

Black athletes should fight for their fellow African Americans and demand that the owners stop messing over qualified black candidates for the top positions. There is more to being a role model and supporting your community than giving money to charities and offering motivational speeches.

So many Black athletes are cast as the "ultimate role models" by White society. They always show how glamorous it is and how much respect they get from all races. The racist institutions show this image of a black man getting riches and respect because they know, that of the thousands of black kids setting their only sights on making it into professional sports, only a small fraction of them will make it to those heights, and the majority will fail, not just athletically, but in life.

Some Black sportsmen may argue that they don't go out of their way to help just the Black community, but they try to help all communities. Well, there are two reasons why that attitude is bogus: 1) The system goes out of its way to knock us down, and 2) Black people need the most help. A person who is having a heart attack would take precedence over someone with a paper cut in an emergency room, and Blacks are definitely in cardiac arrest.

Last summer, after Craig Hodges displayed his Afrocentricism to other Black players and advised them not to forget the Black community, he was discarded like spoiled milk. Could that have been a warning to other players about expressing self-pride?

Racial discrimination is present all over the workplace, not just in the sports world. There are no Black top executives in the sports media or on national publications, and of the 1,550 sports editors for major newspapers, only three are black. Those statistics indicate that despite being qualified, me and other aspiring Black sports editors may never have a position of power. Although my assessment of where Blacks stand in society is enough to make me militant, I will not label

every Caucasian a racist. Even though there are not enough successful brothers speaking up for their race, I am not chastising and putting the whole load on them, because it is too much for man bear. However, I do speak for Black people when I challenge the sporting institutions to back up all of their shucking and jiving about race not being an issue and give Afro-Americans a sporting chance, and for the successful Black athletes to demand better treatment for your brothers, not just a big salary for yourselves, otherwise Blacks will be history.

A self-satisfied grin strains to spread as you finish reading your published article on the crowded Halsted bus, but you check it with a bite of the lower lip. You're pleased with the angry tone of the commentary, but it doesn't quite bring you happiness. Deon has been letting you have it over his conquest of Nick. You don't know who you despise more between the two: Deon for being a big, stupid Great Dane, or Nick for giving it up to something as goofy as Marmaduke. Nick probably feels the blunt of your malevolence since Deon has always been in the doghouse. For a good two weeks, you have managed to avoid any verbal contact with her, but today she confronted you at the front door after school and asked if you wanted a ride. You gave her a gruff "Naw" as you brushed passed her without eye contact. If you were dehydrated from trekking 40 years through the Sahara with two broken legs, you would've blurted the same response if she were driving an ice cream truck.

As the bus pulls into Jew Town, the buzz of grilled onions triggers your taste buds and prompts you to jump off five blocks from your stop and get three polishes: one for you and two for Charlotte, since it's one of her favorite meals. You decided to pay her a surprise visit, since you haven't seen her in about a week due to full, conflicting school schedules. Besides, you miss her. One thing is for sure: there will be no kissing tonight, since she likes hers heavy with onions and mustard.

The schism between you and Nick has left your affections void of a neutral, verbal outlet; they are like ticks without a dog. However, it will take more than a little pettiness on your part and bad judgment on Nick's to destroy the seven-year foundation your friendship rests on; the fault will mend soon enough.

With all due respect, Charlotte is your love. She's always there for you, providing all the things a good girlfriend should give, such as cards, calls, concern and caresses. She has an innate ability to stroke you at the right time. If you're miffed about a game, down about the grades, or even in one of the melancholic moods of indecisiveness concerning tomorrow, she convinces you that everything is going to be all right. There's no mind as independent as hers; not only does she not let her peers influence her, but her girlfriends are secondary to you. When push comes to shove, she'll dump them in the trash in a New York second for you...and vice versa. She has lost so-called friends on your account. That's one of the reasons she doesn't have many female associates. The lateral line to that positive is that she feels that you shouldn't have any contact with any females, with the obvious exception of your mother. That issue is the main source of many disagreements. Past pain has conditioned her to expect the worst from men—her last two boyfriends put her through the meat grinder and ended up hooking up with their platonic friends. Because of this, she feels justified in her "female prohibition" and strictly enforces it by occasional surprise checks and interrogations. Sometimes you are sympathetic; most of the time you reason that she has only gone through the same agony of infidelity that is as commonplace in America as sex during courtship. In other words, she needs to get over it quick, fast and in a hurry, because you ain't the one to be monitored.

You sail noncognizantly through the sea of students in the food court, with a vague grin on your face as you collect some straws for the Pepsi. As you turn toward the elevator, you are smote stupid by a point-blank line of vision when the doors open. There is no chance to duck or run; you can't play it off or grow ignorant. You're exposed like a bushman in Alaska; like a hooper with wet, oversized shorts and hydraulic hops. A look of regret spreads over her face, like a hunter that has second thoughts about gunning down a nursing doe. Fate: the blink of an eye can blow one's witness account; a single number can make a man a lottery millionaire or keep him in the gutter; inches separate the wrong place; seconds are the boundary of the wrong time. Was it fate or laziness that lead you down the path leading to Joyce Atkins? You could've/should've taken the stairs and you would've if you had known. "Rejoice, Ye Pure in Heart" harmonizes in your mind's ears. There she is, but there's no reason to rejoice. How can you dread seeing someone that you loved with an overflowing, overwhelming passion?

"Hello," she greets reluctantly through the constipated pause in life, as if she's asking a question. Her reconnaissant speech with the potent pitch always charmed you. It was during an awkward silence following your first night of passion with her that she said, "I Love You" in the same delving manner.

You answer with a mute, open-arm plea for an embrace, and she obliges with a tight squeeze.

Spreading her contagious smile, she asks, "How have you been, Malcolm?"

What an unfair question, since she killed you three years ago! Right now, you're an apparition staring your beautiful assassin in the eyes. She's an engineering major, yet she resembles a businesswoman in her checkered gray slacks and jacket with white blouse. Seeing her raven, feathered hair, globular, cherry-tone face, and full hips is almost worth the price of the funeral.

"Well, considering you put a fatal shot through my heart, I'm doing as good as can be expected for a corpse," you inform her with serious conviction, although it's difficult to restrain your elated smile.

She let's out a dominoing guffaw that shatters your somber countenance. "For a corpse you sure can jump mighty high," she jokes. "And I've never known a cadaver to make the all-section basketball team."

"I'm serious," your mouth pleads, in contradiction to your facial expression.

She hushes up and turns staid. "I know you're serious," she assures, dropping her head and eyes slightly, adding, "It was something that I had to do, even though I didn't want to."

"Okay, let me hear your account of this mercy killing so I can be buried," you antagonize.

"C'mon Mal," she snaps, shifting to the side. "I told you that the distance was too great for us to survive."

She never snapped. She was always straightforward and even-keeled, which contrasted well with your sometimes abrupt, often fiery, always unpredictable nature. She's out of character, but you don't disappoint.

"Speak in singular terms, because I was willing and able," you cut in, your voice rising an octave higher than hers.

"We were growing apart, Malcolm," she replies, a level below a mousy shout.

You inhale deeply and explode: "You're still grammatically incorrect, so allow me to speak for you: You—not we—were lacking faith, hope and love: the greatest deficiency being love. You—not we—had myopic faith in me and us: as long as you could see me, you could see us. You—not we—had no hope in our future, so you sabotaged it; and you—not we—lacked a true love for me—love conquers all, including a 200-mile drive—otherwise you wouldn't have dropped me with such an easy finality. When I entered the relationship, my heart was an empty house with an open door of high expectations...expectations of being furnished with good love, good times and good memories. When the relationship was over, my heart was abandoned, vandalized, and razed. Thank you very much."

She glares through glazed eyes at that lie as her face puckers into a frown and her breathing grows deep and rapid. You're in the presence of a stranger; a new creature. *Raining tears of happiness was the norm for her, but during our season of heat, there was never any signs of clouds. She flooded your suit at her graduation; after the birth of her niece, you thought someone had died; you laughed and yucked it up when you helped your team win a summer tournament, while she boohooed. She was deathly precise, bone dry and uncomfortably siren when she kissed you good-bye on the way to Illinois State; when you were torn up about the retirement of Magic Johnson, she was irritatingly stoic (that moment went down as one of the all-time tragedies in your life outside of the death of loved ones). You went crazy with grief while she walked away from you and moved seemingly happily on with her life.* You don't know what to think of her now.

"I would have never pulled the trigger and shot the relationship dead like that," you insist in a confidential tone, quenching the fire of the moment that you nightmared about ever since she wrote the "Dear Mal" letter.

She sighs and concedes in a whisper "You're right," as she closes her strained eyes, opening the dam. "Can we go somewhere to talk?"

You hand her a napkin, and without verbalizing it, you move to follow her. By the time we make it to a secluded table at the far side of the dining room of the dorm, she has regained her grip on her composure.

"So what brings you up here?" she queries with the intention of diluting the tension, as she sets her attaché case on the table.

You take a seat on the edge of the chair and confess, "I'm paying my lady friend a visit," although you don't feel convinced by your own words.

"You still like them older," she jokes in reference to the age difference between you and her, but you're too caught up in the moment of truth to laugh. "What's her name?"

"Charlotte," you answer, sitting back in an attempt to chill.

She rolls her eyes up in search of the Charlotte file and comes up empty.

You shift the subject indicator back to her, commenting, "I see you've forsaken the braids."

"Last year," she mentions, fluffing her do up. "They were taking my hair out."

"It looks nice."

"Thank you."

Silence. Eye probing. Flushing faces. A glimmer of light.

The moment has the inebriating effect a case of brew would have on a choirboy, as her aching smile addles you. Her smirk stiffens straight when your loss of equilibrium becomes apparent by your wavering head.

"Well," she starts as she looks to the side, resolving, "I guess an explanation is in order."

You fold your hands across your torso and recline back as she methodically details how she was told by God to separate herself from and part ways with things that hindered her relationship with Him, including, but not limited to, you.

She was down there a full semester before she visited Bride of Christ Church of God In Christ. It was a small house-like church that could rock a cappella when the piano man wasn't around. They were having revival in early February when she commenced to taking her semester lumps and getting dragged through a bout of homesickness. There were three exams to prepare for and a rough work schedule to rest up for at Carroll's Grill, when she just got up, put on her boots and coat, and headed out. Her books were left open and the lights on. Without a set destination, she found herself on the back pew of the church as the evangelist was bringing the electrifying message. His text was taken from the Gospel of Matthew, and the title was "Come as You Are." He was talking to her, because she was in her jeans and school sweatshirt. The subject was how God can use who or what he wants to carry out His will. She will never forget the reference to Amos and how He used a herdsman and fig tree caretaker to speak His word. The talking ass in Numbers was the humorous illustration he used to wrap-up the message.

Before he extended the invitation, she had settled on making Bride her church home away from home the following Sunday. Several months away had her spiritually malnourished and on the verge of withering away. The argument that she was a spiritual anorexic anyway, was strong. God had a hot, gourmet, seven-course meal prepared for her at that moment, though. Evangelist Rashawn Booker was facing the back, but she didn't realize his lenses were directly on her, and God was looking through them. The Lord had never revealed a promise to her with such a dramatic manifestation as when He spoke through Evangelist Booker: "Your voice is anointed by God to rejoice," he proclaimed.

"Malcolm, you know how inhibited I was when it came to singing," she insists to you as felicity emits from her being and she details her calling.

Her naturally grainy voice is waxed smooth and her speech is inspired by memory. Cranberry juice is the craving that her inflexion conjured up. You knew that her breath was consecrated when you first heard it, but she relegated herself to background singing in the choir and waggishly crooning solos in your ear. You insisted that her voice could and should chant alone; her family encouraged her to consider stepping to the forefront with her talent; the birds would chirp that she should be leading them in song.

Unfortunately, she listened to the wrong person: the choir director at her church. Ramona Long was highly esteemed in Joyce's eyes because she had a platform to vocalize on. At best, she could blend with the rest of the choir members, but the power of royalty is what lifted her up on the stage, not her talents. Not that Pastor Herbert Long (her grandfather) was corrupt or advocated nepotism in the church offices, he was just deaf, dumb, and blind in his old age. Every major board was "controlled" by one of his evil descendants, including the pulpit and the deacon board. You visited her church and before she mentioned the

Long lineage, you discerned the Nimrodian spirit, especially concerning Ramona. She directed, led and soloed in the choir. Even her robe was peculiar with garish tassels and a tacky overlay. She was a hard love that reeked spitefulness. How could a person tell a child that her voice is too funny to lead? Joyce believed that lie as if it was the gospel according to Jesus.

"I remember," you agree with a nod. "And look at you now...what a difference two years can make."

"The Lord liberated me," she claims with conviction.

When Evangelist Booker prophesied to her, she was in the middle of a pleasant daydream and didn't realize she was being addressed. "The Lord has called you to make a joyful noise," he announced. Instantly she came back to Bride of Christ and met his eyes. "You, young lady," he addressed her conscience as it questioned 'Is he talking to me?' "The Lord is going to use your voice to rejoice in His glory."

She grew reticent: she had become the center of attention of the modest assembly that increased into a magnificent multitude in a millisecond; it felt like heaven was looking down at her through a giant microscope. Her eyes swelled like water balloons as he drew near her. When he stood over her, assuring her that "The Lord has declared your voice sanctified to sing praises", she focused on how Goliathian his 5'10" posture seemed at the time and couldn't rejoice in the message. Even if she wanted to resist his hand in prayer, she couldn't. There was nothing but the Lord and her being. God's vessel anointed her head with oil and prayed over her. She passed out during the prayer in which he laid his heavy hands on her head and later realized that she was slain in the spirit. Her cup overflowed with the Holy Ghost and He has spilled out of her mouth ever since. But there was a pledge of allegiance to make before the fullness of the prophecy was realized.

"I pulled an Eve in regards to understanding the prophecy," she explains in reference to Mother Living's addition "Neither shall ye touch it" to the Almighty's garden ordinance.

After the revival, she was intrigued and drawn by the message and wanted to hear more of what 'thus said the Lord', so she took off after Evangelist Booker and wound up at New Revelation Church of God in Christ in Lubbuck, Texas. She was straightforward with God: "What does the Lord want me to do?" God was straightforward with her: "Cut off all things that keep you from loving the Lord thy God with all of your heart, with all of your soul and with all of your might. Cast down anything that you have exalted above the Lord thy God." She had a clue, but wasn't sure, so she asked, "Is there anything in my life that I have put above You?" His answer was direct: "The source of your idolatry is THAT man in your life."

"You weren't named, but I knew you were my idol," she confesses.

It's a good thing that you're sitting down, because your body feels like it was thrown down 100 flights of stairs; your soul feels like it was spooked, and your spirit feels like it was hexed. Then you go on the defensive and privately critique the "prophesy" from the "fortuneteller". *THAT MAN* seems like an easy answer. The source of a woman's problems is always some woeful man. Never mind the drugs and poverty—it's the man's fault. Forget about the woman's bad decision making—blame it on the man. If the woman goes to hell, the man sent her there. At the moment, you believe that the evangelist took a wild guess and placed blame on the shibbolethic scapegoat. Before you can justify yourself, she modestly admits the folly of her initial interpretation.

"I basically plucked my eyes out with the intention of removing the sin, not realizing that the change was to take place in here," she says, placing her right hand on her left breast.

She visited Evangelist Booker a few months later and told him that she swept that man completely out of her life. That's when he told her that it wasn't him that needed dusting, but her that needed a vacuuming. But it was too late. She cut you off cold turkey and when she came back around, you wanted all parts of her, but you weren't going to put your soul on the line. You didn't return her phone calls wrought with pleas for a chance to explain, you didn't answer the door when she paid a few surprise visits, and you put everybody on notice to not disturb you when it came to her, even when you were collecting dust on the couch. You were lifeless thanks to her and you really didn't want to hear what she had to say.

"Is your ship still floating," she queries through a captivating simper, interrupting the calling recall as she pulls out a sheet of folded filler paper from her purse and starts reading the contents:

"There is no fine print to read
There is no written contract to save

No need to notarize my actions
With no obligation I gave

Sometimes it may be so obvious
Other moments you don't know what to think

By relation or as a friend
My ship will never sink

The signs will be dense
Affection will not always rinse

Whether I'm gazing, tasting, smelling, touching or hearing
My heart beating is not contingent on my sensing

When the weather is warm enough to shed our clothes
And when the season is dark and cold

I can come through the eye of the storm
And our picnic will not be on hold

The sands of your hourglass are short term
So the statue of limitations is a lifetime guarantee

I can't put limitations on love
I'm in unconditionally"

She grins at you when she finishes and comments, "I knew you had the gift of gab and aspiration of becoming an attorney after that business law class, but I didn't realize you were a poet," as she puts it back in her purse.

That poem was a glimpse of the gift that was opened last Christmas. Dexter assisted you in pouring out your feelings. Truthfully, he was your editor, co-author and creative motivator of the ode. In hearing it again, you consider it one of your best pieces of any genre. The inspiration behind it was profound. It's the same motivation that a mother has to save her child that's in danger, even if it means putting her own life on the line. The love of your life was at stake and you would've swam across Lake Michigan to save the relationship—and you float like a rock. Never have you exposed your soul to a woman like you did with Joyce. It made you feel...vulnerable.

"I didn't know I was a poet either," you agree.

You sent it in faith. The six letters you mailed her came back stamped "RETURN TO SENDER". When you penned it, you did it for your own closure. Your feelings had to egress from your heart, even if they weren't going to cultivate the garden of your desire. The reasoning was that the wind would catch the seed and plant it somewhere else. Keeping it to yourself was only a disadvantage. You didn't even realize that it wasn't returned with the rest of them.

"I didn't know you read it."

"It got overlooked during my cleaning stage, and it miraculously reappeared after I talked to Evangelist Booker for the third and last time."

More silence. More eye probing. More flushing faces. Another glimmer of light.

The moment of reminiscing has a sobering effect as you douse the flare, blend in with the indifferent temperature and view her through the eyes of bitterness, smashing the silence.

"It's too bad I didn't miraculously resurrect," you cut. "Instead, I've been kicked out of the heavenly bliss and cast into romantic hell."

Her lips are still frozen in a grin, but her eyes are downcast as she rolls around in her old disposition. No tears, fire and brimstone. Still more silence. Still more eye probing. Still more flushing faces. Yet another glimmer of light. She touches your heart, but she isn't the owner of it.

"To answer your question, the ship is still afloat."

Her eyes smile. "I would love to eventually marry you, but I realize the bridge is burned and there's somebody else on the boat...I respect that," she insists, adding, "But I'm honored that you're willing to even talk to me after the way I handled the situation."

You nod, consolation that it's okay.

"Do you think that we can ever get back to that point of intimacy again..." she slips.

"Tomorrow isn't promised to you or me, but the answer right now is no," you conclude. "However, if we get to that bridge again, maybe the waters won't be too deep and maybe we can tread the water together."

Final silence. Final eye probing. Final flushing faces. Glimmer of light fades into twilight.

After microwaving the polishes, you resume preparation for the surprise visit. With two knocks, the door swings open and a gust of heat charbroils you. Charlotte stands in the doorway with her hand on the knob, seemingly ready and waiting to slam, and questions, "Yeah?"

"I was in the 'hood and picked up some Jew Towns to go with those pretty, red roses on the bookcase over there," you announce through a proud smirk.

"I'm not hungry," she blurts.

"Okay," you yield. "Nice shirt," you comment of your black and brown school sweatshirt that she's wearing. "Can I come in?"

She doesn't say anything as she turns and walks to her bed.

"Are you okay?"

Apparently, she doesn't hear you as she parks on her comforter and gets buried in a romance novel. This may be a good time to walk out, but you don't. Instead, you aversely settle next to her and stare pensively at her, hoping to make a connection or break down the wall of isolation. You are not even present in her eyes. You pull the paperback down and her expression hisses like an alley cat as she snatches it away, springs up and stomps to her desk. You can take a hint.

"I'll leave your polishes on the bookcase," you affirm, starting for the door.

"Don't you go nowhere, Mister Loverman," she growls, jumping in your path. "I saw you getting close and personal with that choir bitch," she accuses.

The denouncement almost induces an aneurysm. Instead of brushing past her, you get stubborn and spray lighter fluid on her flame. "My gosh...you didn't see us tonguing, did you?!"

"I don't think that's funny," she huffs, folding her arms.

"I'm not laughing," you say, waving her off and turning your back on her.

"Who was she?" she grills, following behind you.

"You know, you come incorrect every time around. First the accusation; then the interrogation. Use your imagination to answer that. I ain't thinking about you."

"Get your shit out of here and don't call me no more. I mean it Malcolm," she orders as she rips the shirt off.

"What did I do to gain your favor?" you ask, collecting it.

"Have the nerve to fool around with somebody in the same dorm."

"Nothing like being a player in a whorehouse."

"All you nigga's are dogs."

You cringe slightly at the peeving N-word and sink to her level. "Well that means a bitch is a bitch, bitch."

"I hope you catch AIDS and die."

"Death doesn't sound too bad if it means getting away from you."

"I can't stand you."

"Well then, take a seat for a better point of view."

With that, she snatches all 12 Valentine roses that you sent the day before from the vase—tipping it over and shattering it on the floor—and slings them at you. She grabs the polishes from the bookcase and hurls them your way as well.

"Good, pork isn't good for..." Before you can finish the wit; with the quickness of a twinkle and the crispness of a whisper, her palm slices sparks from your cheek like she was striking a match. You saw it coming in slow motion, but the reflex to duck or block was constipated. The impact made both ears burn as if they were shooting acid out; the sound was of a firecracker at close range. It's debatable what's blazing more: your face or your rage. Charlotte has a strong argument that your wrath is hellified as you impulsively send the wanton whirlwind back to the sower of the brazen breeze. Her face does an exorcist-like 720 on her idle body, making her countenance helter-skelter, with an eye in her cheek, her teeth in an ear lob, her nose in her temple, and the bottom lip on her forehead. Her knees buckle slightly...not a stagger or a collapse, just a half-squat. We both have flaring faces and ignited hands. The claps still echo around the compact room that now seems to be spinning.

You stand in stationary silence, not knowing an appropriate transition from the restive moment. Gloat and regret are engaged in a bloody battle in your bosom like Greek gladiators in the Coliseum before Caesar. Part of you feels justified—almost pleased—at unleashing on her, for all of her transgressions in the relationship. The wages of sin is death. But her blaring, sizzling tears rip into your belly like a white-hot dagger. Satisfaction gets the thumbs down. However, the exchanged blows have knocked your instincts out of alignment as you stand paralyzed in front of your grieving woman. Not that it was done purposely, but Peggy, her roommate, comes in and recharges the stale electricity.

"What's going on?" she queries as Charlotte's scorched face cries out and your scarlet hand incriminates you. Let the long night begin.

Theoretically, five gallons of nitrogen can't be condensed into a one-liter container, but that's the state that you're in: Pressed like a handleless backcourt in a Knick trap. The nerves in your cheek are still screaming, but that's minor compared to the war-zone that used to be your soul. Everything that you believed in is in jeopardy while it goes through the Islamic litmus test. What if your "Lord and Savior" was only a prophet? He did do everything in the name of the Father. Elijah and Elisha performed the same resurrection miracles. He never explicitly claimed that he is God. Islam sounds true at the moment, but you would rather not deal with it right now, especially in light of the suspicious dismissal of Farrakhan's national spokesman, Khalid Abdul Muhammad, two weeks ago. Is the Nation of Islam loyal to their brothers when they are under fire, or do they cut them loose when they step out of line? An easier issue to tackle is the stupidity of Nick.

She answers the door before the bell stops echoing. She's wearing white sweat pants, a plain white V-neck T-shirt, and white footies. Who does she think she is: The Virgin Mary? Not hardly.

"Hey Mal," she greets, too cheerfully for your liking as you brush past her without saying a word. "You've been a hard one to catch," she comments as you flop down on the sofa and stare at the TV.

"I've been busy," you remark curtly.

"I figured," she assures, as she takes a seat next to you and folds her legs like we used to do in kindergarten.

The news is on, but you can't really focus on it while we sit in silence for an everlasting moment. You have a lot of venom on the tip of your tongue that you're hurting to spit out, but you're waiting for the right opening.

"How did you do on the last Lit test?"

"I got an A," you blurt with finality before she can get the whole question out.

"I got a B," she offers, as if you asked. "I didn't study that hard for it and it showed. I didn't even read over the part about 'no man being born of a woman's womb.'"

"Um," is all you can grunt as she flashes a curious glance your way that you don't return.

"That Sunday school class is something else," she claims excitedly. "I love it, but I don't see how Dexter was able to handle them all this time. It's going to take some time to get used to them."

"I'm sure," you remark, nipping the subject just as it sprouts.

She goes along with it without resistance and asks, "Are you ready for the playoffs?"

Is this an interview for Sports Illustrated or something? "I'll know when I play," you snip.

She peers intently at you as you continue to glare at the television. "Are you okay?"

"I'm fine."

She looks away and asks, "Do you think that you can contend with Simeon or King?"

"Well, I won't be playing a one on five," you snap. "Remember, Chuck D, Mitch, Dennis and Jayson are part of the starting five. Why don't you try asking them if they think we can handle them."

She looks baffled as you cut your eyes at her.

"Deon seems to be in good spirits. You may be able to get a good forecast out of him," you conjecture. "I hear you're real close to him any way."

She clicks her tongue and snaps, "Do you have a problem with me going out with him two weeks ago?"

You peer nonchalantly at her and assure, "I don't have a problem with you going out with him," as you turn back to the news and pause as the silence stretches and the poisonous thoughts get too potent to hold. "I just didn't think that you would drop your pants on the first date."

You don't look at her, but you can tell her mouth is on the floor as she gazes at you. "That wasn't called for, Malcolm," she protests.

"And I suppose a tryst with the dumbest, weakest, biggest, smelliest, non-playingest, trash-talkingest jock on the team was called for?" you cut. "If you just needed some, you could've at least given it up to one of the starters that doesn't have a cloud of dust hovering him."

She calmly rises and treads to her bedroom as the statements bounce around in the universe.

Just as quick as they came out, regret sets in. You wish that you could catch them, put them back in your mouth and send them out of the other end into the toilet. The news goes off a few minutes later and you head to her room, not knowing what you can do that will propitiate your folly. You stop just inside the doorway and observe her sitting on the floor with her back against the bed playing a game of Solitaire while "His Eye Is On The Sparrow" plays softly on her CD player. You watch a single tear streaming down her cheek to the tip of her chin, where it takes a dive into her lap. This *first* pierces your heart.

In one of our famous one-on-one's at the park, there was an intense regulation whole court with the men going on simultaneously. The courts criss-crossed and often the half-courters had to step out of the way of fast-breaking freight trains as they maneuvered around us bugs. Occasionally, they left road-kill behind before flying in for a lay-up. You've had a few head-on collisions and usually you didn't know what hit you when you ended up on your back, facing a tear-blurred sky. Often times, you would be left with a bruised body, scraped elbow or lumped head. Most of the time, you would go home crying. Sometimes you stayed and resumed after the shock subsided and the tears dried. Once, Nick was body blocked in mid-air and landed face down on the cement. She sat there for a few moments to get her wind. Not a whimper; not a teardrop. Then she would rise and play harder. Once, a tank-built man landed square on her on the asphalt, almost flattening her. She ended up with a bloody nose and a couple of cracked ribs. Not a whimper; again, not a teardrop. It was obvious that she had a high threshold of pain; however, it transcended the physical into the emotional.

Just before we started high school, she lost her older brother, Leon. He suffered from severe asthma. Their family took a trip to Detroit as a dual graduation present/vacation (he graduated from high school that same year). The second he arrived, the Motor City air clogged him up and he was dead within two hours. They loved each other more than their own lives. He taught her how to play basketball and to defend herself, although he was always gentle with her. She always talks about his accomplishments and the things he did for her, always insisting that she wanted to be just like him.

When you found out from your mother what happened, you immediately went to her house. She opened the door as if all was well and held up both ends of the conversation. At first, you thought the suddenness sent her to the Land of Denial, but she swore that she understood what happened and reasoned that he was in a better place. Not once did you see any hint of moisture in her eyes; perhaps she wept in private. She never showed you that side, which surprised you since she wasn't hard and callous. The kids at the church flock to her like mosquitoes at a picnic. She always makes the time to pick them up and hug them. She came to comfort you that night when she found out about Dexter, holding you until the break of dawn. She's part of the deterrent that keeps you from tearing. What does this unseen side mean? What have you done?

You hesitantly approach and take a seat next to her. Seemingly oblivious to your presence, she concentrates on winning the game. Another teardrop leaves a wider dark spot in her pants. "I'm sorry," you offer in a confidential tone. She turns a card over and lines the 2 of hearts up with the 3 of spades. The puddle widens with two back-to-back drips. "Do you forgive me?"

She sets the Queen of diamonds up with the King of clubs. Her face is pleasant, yet stone-set, like a weeping statue. Three more globules fall and the waters pour from the opposite eye to form a parallel river that spills over on the other thigh as her CD clicks to an end. After playing to an impasse, she stacks the cards up and places them to the side. You peer at her as she gazes toward the wall. You count 200 blinks and then give up on willing her to talk to you, so you lay your head back against the mattress. Just as your eyes shut, she gently rests her head on your shoulder.

"He hasn't called me since that night, which was two weeks ago," she comments, cracking the silence. Your eyes open and you raise your head. Of course she can wait until the next millennium and she still won't get a call from him, but instead of verbalizing it, you embrace her. "When I was growing up in Mississippi, people would twang my name so that Nick was stressed: NICKle is how it sounded coming out of their mouths. I hated it," she says solemnly as she turns to face you. "It was the same story when we moved up north. Remember when they used to throw nickels at me in the seventh grade," she recalls as she twists the left side of her cheek into a plastic grin.

You nod once.

It was so ridiculous that you came to blows with the ringleader of the Nickel Crew: Russell Pitts. Russell ragged on everybody, but he had his choice butts: You and Nick. He gave you the moniker Manute Bol and insisted that a sesame seed could fill you up. You were slim, but had a brick epidermis when it came to thin jokes. It was the truth and you were used to it, although the Ethiopian analogy that has lingered ever since is not appreciated. He was particularly cruel to Nick from the first day she came to the school. To say Nick struggled when it came to the books is more understated than mentioning Dennis Rodman is not cute. It wasn't until the summer before eighth grade that she was diagnosed with dyslexia. Russell fed on the weaknesses of others, and that was sad, not hilarious. However, bad kids will be roguish and stanky assholes will be shitty. A sample of his favorite punch lines: Nick's IQ is so low that she puts a class that has an average of 100 percent below zero; If Nick doesn't come to school, her grade point average would be much higher; Nick doesn't have a nickel's worth of brains in her head. That's when the nickels started flying her way. He urged her to put them in her memory bank, but not to try to add them up because it would break her bank. The irony is that Russell wasn't swift either. He spelled fool with a PH. Reciprocity was bitter-sweet when the script flipped on them: Russell went on to struggle in all of his freshmen classes, earning flags in every subject except gym, before he dropped out; Nick endured and labored like a construction worker to make the honor roll every high school semester.

Never did Nick shed a tear or hint at being fazed. When he would boisterously crack on her, she would persist with what she was involved in—as if she was the only person in creation—which didn't set too well with Russell, who wouldn't settle for nothing less than blood and tears from her. For that, you were waiting for a good reason to see him after school. It took him almost two years to finally come through. You were lunching a Spring Thursday with Nick in the school cafeteria, when he rained 20 nickels on her. One of them happened to touch you. Without a word to utter or the patience to wait for the end of the day, you gathered the coins up one-by-one, with your ire rising a power with each financial appreciation of your hand. When you had a dollar to ball your fist up tight around, you were furious[20]*. Russell had an extremely long, pointed nose. He also had the body of a man among boys, so when you* *popped him flush on the snout—almost driving your fist through his nostrils and into the spot where the brain would be, making his muzzle a perfectly level plain—he commenced to mop the cafeteria floor with you. From the moment you gave him the bad nose job on, he didn't look our way. The thrashing, 10-day suspension, and flogging (by Ma and Uncle JoJo when you got home early) was well worth it. Nick didn't deserve to be hazed for two years by that 140-pound gnat. Under normal circumstances, you won't trade shots with a bigger gun, but when you fight for the honor of a loved one, you're willing to offer your body as a sacrifice or dish out some punishment.*

"I made a mental list of every single person that hit me with the nickels, and you and Dexter were the only two out of the class that were absent from the list. For that, you were always special to me—you were on my buddy list. Those nickels could've made me wealthy if I wasn't too insulted to pick them up," she reasons with a chuckle. "That's how I got the nickname Nick—no pun intended. Nick always had an androgynous ring to it, which was better than having coins tossed at me," she reasons, intimating, "Deon was the first person to make my name sound pretty, and that's how he got to me."

You rub her back and promise in her ear "It's going to be okay...Nicole." You're surprised that you enunciated it correctly. She seems to warm over in your bosom.

"There's something that I'm ordained to do, but it isn't what I really want. I was actually running from the call when I had the encounter with the whale," she jokes, bringing a smile to your face and a surge of life in your enfold.

"Imagine a dumb ass talking to one of God's own in 1994," you add as she chuckles out.

"I never would've imagined that in '94...and I never wanted to teach...I would rather listen, like a good psychologist is supposed to do. I resolved to teach though, especially when Moby Dick was swallowing me up. But He told me that there's more to it. The harvest truly is great, and it's beyond the walls of Walk of Faith, which is where my comfort zone is. I'm not into street evangelism."

There's no need to question her, although you are dying for quick clarity of the revelation.

"I just want to go to Howard and get my degree in Psychology and help people that way. I don't want to be preaching on the corner," she whines.

You can't hold yourself, which is an area in your life that needs serious correction. "What are you talking about, Nicole? How come you can't go to Howard and why is it that you have to preach on the corner?"

Instead of responding, she opts to play with the cards. After she once again gets to the point of no-win, she reshuffles and narrates her ambiguous soul story.

"When I was little I would hide in my closet if I was upset and talk to—I thought—myself. When my brother didn't have time to play with me, I slammed the door shut; After I got chastised, I found my way to that secret place; Following each math test, I migrated to my closet," she says as she abruptly halts her explanation and card game, seemingly struck with enlightenment. "You know, I was in that closet when I was happy, too. When I wanted to talk to myself about the good things that were going on, I was in that closet, so as you can imagine, I was in there a lot," she declares, resuming the card game.

"So you're saying that you're a little schizophrenic and that you're a few brain cells from a straight jacket," you banter as you squeeze her.

She smirks through the interruption. "To my knowledge, no one has ever heard me, but then again the door was closed," she plays along. "Before I started having those talks with myself I had a generic, constrained belief in God. To be honest, I don't recall not knowing of Him, even in the way that I limited Him. It's almost as if God was man-made and that His thoughts and actions were dictated by us. It didn't take long for me to shed that weak theology.

"I came home one day after going 0-for-10 on the fraction test and went to my closet. There, I bitterly wished out aloud for a new home...a new set of friends. No sooner than the words left my mouth, the Lord showed me Chicago, specifically Ekersal Stadium and a boy on the court with freckles and purple and gold Converse Weapons on his feet."

You were listening intently, maybe too intently, because it takes a few moments for the statement to register. "You saw me?" you question with incredulity as you draw back from her slightly. "You had a prophetic vision?" you question/confirm.

"Why do you think that out of all of the boys our age up there, I challenged you? I could've played someone shorter and won. He showed me a vivid image of you and those freckles."

"Angel kisses."

"Angel kisses," she restates as she goes into this vision.

How quickly one forgets about the Islamic god, who you can't recall by name. Your heart revs with adrenaline as she testifies how the Lord divulged how we are 'fraternal soul twins' with a similar—not identical—relationship with the Lord. Although you believed that she had foretelling visions, you found it unbelievable. Her gift truly mirrors yours, like Eve resembled Adam, although you were somewhat envious of the clarity and beauty of her talent. The messages seem a bit murky in your sleep. Now, you see Nicole in a totally different light. It's as if she's incandescent. Never would you have imagined her with that type of anointing. She always seemed like the meek usher that she is. That's it.

"How come you never shared this?" you question, slightly disappointed, although you're happy to have another spiritual sibling.

"You never asked."

"How was I supposed to know what to ask?"

"You never shared the intimate details of your communication with God. If you had, then it would have come up."

She has a point as she zips your lips.

Your Spiritual encounters were kept in the inner circle. It's apparent that she's a part of that inner circle that you've neglected, so you swap testaments with her that have a Spiritual Friends Network ring to them. The conversation actually unveils a mysterious dimension of the mountain ascent dream you had after Dexter passed: "You're Never Alone" because God has blessed you with Nicole. It's ironic how Nick stepped into your life when Ray stepped into the presence of God. The conversation sways back into the secular as you explain what happened at the dorm and she details the account of spending time in the belly of the big fish.

"Between me and you, from a carnal standpoint, he doesn't have to worry about someone chasing after him."

"So what are you saying: he came up short and he needs to work on his game?" you pry, seeking an angle to throw in his face.

"I'm saying that if he lives a compassionate game—instead of playing, if he was just playing—he could get further with a lady than relying on his sexuality."

"So he is weak in the bedroom," you bait. "He made you regret not waiting for the honeymoon, huh?"

She let's out a jubilant giggle and drops a bomb on you: "I'm sorry to tell you that he wasn't the one that made me wish that I remained pure until marriage...and it wasn't because it was lacking pleasure either."

You throw your head back and wrinkle your brow. What is she saying? Deon was her first encounter.

"I'm not bragging, but once upon a time before Minister Walker was spreading the Word, he was good to go," she proclaims in an arrant tone.

Your freckles start sweating as you drop your head, fixing your questioning eyes on her.

Oscar Walker is a twenty-something ball of extravagant energy. Before he announced his calling into the ministry, he was the high profile choir director. He was fervent about gospel music in the church, and often the congregation would feed off his enthusiasm. He shouted the loudest when the songs would set the church on fire. And he ran around the sanctuary like his clothes were on fire. You couldn't discern whether he was putting on a Phariseedal act or if he had a higher dosage of Holy Ghost. Even Dexter commented that he was charged up like the Energizer Bunny when it seemed appropriate for the switch to be turned off. Scripture states that Christians are supposed to be a peculiar people. To call Oscar quaint is like calling Magic Johnson talented. There was something about the way he walked and talked that made the congregation let out a collective "hmmmm."

"I thought Oscar was a little sweet," you mention.

"He *is*," she attests, adding, "He could've been the sugar fix for quite a few women if the Holy Spirit didn't grab hold of him. Don't believe that other hype, because if he allowed the devil to captain his vessel, he could've enticed shiploads of ladies to hell. Instead, he taught me how to defend my faith and he turned out to be one of the best mentors I could imagine, in spite of our stupid mistake."

The smirk you're sporting is a covert lie. Your heart is burning with jealous hypocrisy. Part of you wants to know the what, when, where, why and how, but you've already dealt your tasteless card for the year. You have no more stupidity to spit out, which you're thankful for. There's nothing like vitriolic and sugary expressions coming out of the same mouth.

"Oh Malcolm," she sighs as she places her hand on your knee and her head back on your shoulder, and musing, "I wish I did wait for my honeymoon."

You hear yourself agree, "Don't we all," as you plant your chin on the dome of her head and close your eyes for...*a utopian trip to the spiritual theater.*

The screen is bright and presents the dejavuish image of a sparkling, blossoming, black rose in all of its splendor. Your nature rises on conditioned cue as you come to the crossroads of slumber and functions. There's a possibility in that reality that could turn out to be destiny, but the rose has something to expose that has never been perceived with natural or spiritual eyes. You're torn between terrains...between the anticipation of goodness. There is only one right answer...one door to go through. The sounds of R. Kelly's "Your Body's Calling" blasts into the indecisive ambit and yanks you into the resoluteness of actuality. (Nicole usually wakes up to Gospel Drive on WKKC and switches to the all-Christian station in the evening, since WKKC plays secular songs around this time.) Your eyes pop open to the surprised, freshly awakened eyes of Nicole. The smell of roses emboldens you to act on the lot that you are given. She cooperates as you mutually osculate once and then embrace. It feels right; she feels good, but she releases and gently pushes away from you. You ask, "Why" with your eyes.

"I know what my heart and body are saying, but God has already told me not to touch you, and woe unto me if I go with my own program," she announces as she rises.

"What?" you exasperate as you spring up and block her way.

"I'm sorry, Malcolm," she apologizes as she peers up at you through glazed eyes. She wraps her arms around you and explains just as the chorus "I'm listening baby; I hear you calling" echoes from her clock radio: "For as long as I knew you I desired you with my whole being, but the Lord has always contended that He has something else in store for you and me. I've always questioned why God would put the Tree of the Knowledge of Good and Evil in the Garden if its fruit weren't for consumption; and I've always questioned why He would bless my life with such a beautiful person if I was forbidden to have him. I haven't gotten an answer to either, but God is still good."

The rose fragrance is gone, the song ends, your manhood deflates and you're totally flabbergasted, which explains why "Maybe you should listen to another god" foolishly falls out of your mouth, followed by a hollow "As-Salaam-Alaikum," as you pull away from her clutch and out of her house without another utterance. You thought you emptied all of the ignorance.

Louis Guard assaults U.I.C. student
By Jason Smith
Tumultuous Louis guard Malcolm Johnson was detained by Illinois-Chicago police after striking a U.I.C. coed. When police arrived to the scene, Johnson was being restrained from another female student.

According to witnesses, Johnson, 17, attacked a female acquaintance in her dorm room. The student sustained facial bruises as a result of the attack, but refused medical treatment.

"When I came into the room, I had to separate him from her," said Peggy Ramsey, who is the roommate of the victim. "I thought that he was going to attack me, too."

Although the victim refused to press charges or fill out a report, Johnson will be restricted from campus. "It's not necessary for the victim to sign the complaint for the University to take its own action," according to Residence Hall Director Lynn Whitman. "If an incident takes place on campus involving a student and non-student, the University can forbid the non-student from coming on the premises."

The incident follows a long list of transgressions that have plagued the high school career of the All-City guard. In 1991, he was picked up for curfew violation when police noticed him roaming the streets at two in the morning. The following year, he was arrested for theft of

services. In his junior year, charges of crack possession were filed, but later dropped.

Area colleges are reluctant to recruit him even though he is an academic qualifier. Reports are that he is leaning towards Chicago State, Northwestern, and Illinois-Chicago. Campus officials indicated that the incident has doused their interest in him and have hurt his admission chances.

This season, Johnson is leading the 15-1 Bomber's in scoring at 21-points per game and second in rebounds and assist at 8.5 and five respectively.

Neither Bomber Coach Bobby Wade nor Johnson would comment.

Your comment wasn't requested. The only consolation is that it wasn't on the front page. You fold the evening edition of the Windy-City Daily shut and recline back on Traci's living room sofa, as she prepares to go to the CABJ Testimony staff meeting. She offers you some fried chicken while she waits for her daughter, Brittany, to finish her supper. Your stomach seems to have inflated with helium when you read every slanderous word of the article, and that poisonous balloon now rests in your bosom, so you decline. Uncle Ben informed you that the story—which must have missed the deadline for the early morning edition that we have delivered—was on the afternoon news. Before practice was over, a couple of people asked if "you beat up your girlfriend last night?" It shouldn't surprise you that the story leaked out, but the celerity of the report caught you off guard. You're glad that you made it out of school without having to answer every person you passed in the hallway. It is ironic that the story of Kenny Reed and Matthew Barker being sentenced to life and 70 years respectively—which you by-passed all together, although the headline snagged your eyes for a moment—was on the opposite end of the paper.

There should be a criminal law against character assassination. Correspondent Jason Smith would have been tried, convicted and sentenced a long time ago. You imagine how he would react with his name before the firing squad. There would be so many holes in his persona, that he would fall dead before the first accusation is shot. His sole reason for existing seems to be to wipe your reputation in the deep crevice of his ass, and then smearing it in the media, like graffiti on the outside walls of City Hall. Although you will never give Jason the satisfaction of knowing that his smudge campaign fades you one iota, the vilification stings like an acid bath after a full body shave. Your psyche feels like it was injected with cyanide as your body reacts by quaking. You may ditch school tomorrow and Friday rather than deal with the press conference-like queries throughout the day. Charlotte called this afternoon to put a peaceful closure to us. After we exchanged apologies and well wishes, we officially parted on good terms.

Miss Dawson marches her thick, stately, six-foot frame in chest first and trumpets, "It's not polite to keep your guest waiting, Traci", prompting you to adjust your sitting posture and clear your throat.

"I'll be ready in a minute, Mother," Traci insists from the kitchen with a bit of edge, without crossing the borderline to slap city. Miss Dawson don't play that.

"You should have been ready," she retorts as she takes a step to the edge, pulling her balled fists from her housecoat pockets. Traci wisely gives her the last word as you can picture her exasperated expression beyond the walls of the house. "Please excuse that trifling girl," she pleads. "She just has trouble getting herself together sometimes."

"That's okay," you grin with a touch of excitement.

In her business suits, Miss Dawson has a shrewd, cold air like someone who would boldly take your money and dare you to complain. In her housecoat, she has the appearance of a woman ready to throw down when the doorbell rings. She speaks with authority, often thundering her mind, but she is really a nice, grounded woman. Vice-President of Finance at First Federal is a natural fit. She rose through the ranks from the teller level through loan officer, business accounts manager, and branch manager all the way to VP like a seed grows into a beanstalk. There was no glass ceiling strong enough to withstand her will. Several white boys answer to her, rarely questioning her; never challenging her, since she could terminate them with a stroke of a pen and then take them outside and spank that behind if they had a personal problem with her.

"How are you, Mister Johnson?" she asks as she takes a seat down next to you, causing you to sink towards her.

Those were the first words uttered over the phone to you that struck anxiety in your heart. The query had an "If you're doing good, you're about to do bad; if you're doing bad, you're about to do worse" tone to it. You had never seen her and dreaded the inevitable (literal/figurative) face-to-face encounter. You're still nervous in her presence, but it's a venerable nervousness, not a fearful nervousness.

"Pretty good."

"You keeping the grades up?"

"If I was in college, I would be on the Dean's List for the fifth semester in the row," you boast.

"Still considering U.I.C.? I think you would look good alongside Sherrell Ford," she comments in rapid-fire succession. She loves college basketball and she loves her undergraduate alma mater: The University of Illinois at Chicago.

You hesitate before answering, wondering if she's read in her newspaper that the latest casualty in recruiting you is U.I.C. "I'm leaning more towards Northwestern and DePaul, with a 'Clippers-chance-of-going-to-the-championship' possibility of Chicago State."

"What's wrong with the Flames," she interrogates in mock seriousness.

"Nothing at all," you assure. "I'm just more interested in those other schools at the moment, although my uncle holds your same position."

"Well," she laments, continuing, "Northwestern does have an excellent journalism program. I just hope that if you do decide on the Wildcats, you don't let Traci have too much of a negative impact on you," she jokes to Traci's dismay.

"Mother," she shouts.

"I'm just messing with you Traci," she insists with a chuckle. "Don't have another baby."

Miss Dawson can go from dead serious to silly putty in a blink, which has a way of releasing the tension in the house.

"How are things going with you and the bank, Miss Dawson?"

"Things are going great: there's no blatant power struggles in the hierarchy; the number of student loan defaults is down 15 percent; First Federal is financing the new, 33-acre building project for New Liberty Baptist Church," she claims proudly as Brittany trots in, adding, "and Precious just brought sunshine into the room. Hey Precious," she coos as she opens her arms up like double doors and closes them shut behind her. "It doesn't get much better than this, Malcolm."

"I hear you," you affirm as you pinch Brittany's cleft chin, which elicits a big, dimpled smile. The gaps in her face form a triangle, which only outlines the prettiest simper you've ever seen.

"Just like Traci, Precious is more advanced than her mother was at this age...which is no menial accomplishment. Traci was a borderline genius growing up, and still is super smart. It's just that she gets a little cocky and lax when it comes to school sometimes. Now is a prime example. *TRACI!*" she yells. "IT WOULD BE NICE IF YOU MADE IT OUT BEFORE PRECIOUS TURNS TWO."

"I'M COMING!" she yells, careful not to cross the thin line between raising her voice to be heard and snapping at her mother only to be smacked.

"As I was saying, her attitude will be her downfall—if she lets it. Her potential is unlimited. I had to forsake extracurricular activities and study thrice as hard as she did just to make B's, when she can make straight A's with no real mental effort and still participate in the gospel choir, dance, French, Spanish, the paper, church and all the other things that I can't even keep up with," she testifies as she balances Brittany on her lap. "Precious has a hunger for knowledge and a sweet disposition. Traci seemed to always be arrogant, and although she acted nasty when she was younger, she was really nice," she notes as Traci walks in ready to go, sporting her red riding boots, black form-fitting, pocketless cords, black cashmere sweater, crimson lipstick and yuck face. "It's about time."

Traci doesn't dignify that response, but instead, asks, "Can I borrow your Carson's charge plate?"

"What do you need it for? Or should I say, what do you want it for?"

"My attaché case is torn," she mentions, holding it up.

"So you want another one?"

"Yeah, whatever," she says, leaning to the side.

"I'll give it to you tomorrow morning," she promises as you rise. "Take it easy, Malcolm. Bye-bye Sugar."

"You too," you return.

"Bye Mother," she says as she gives Brittany a kiss and proceeds out the door.

Traci has to be the only black person that calls their mother "Mother". You're thankful to finally get going and even more grateful that she doesn't bring up the article. The initial 20 minutes of the ride is limited in dialogue to a melancholy greeting/response. Her valley seems to be deeper than yours, so you knock the partition of silence down and note, "Mitch still loves you."

She half smirks as she peers out of the window. If she weren't too callous, she would probably cry for whatever it is that's bothering her. She would snap on somebody—innocent or guilty—before she would weep, so you're careful about how you tease her.

"What's up, Traci?"

She shifts hard in her seat and lets out a strident sigh. "Aside from my mother aggravating me, everything is fine."

"Perhaps you should boycott using her credit card."

She ignores the antagonism and states, "I can't wait to graduate and move on campus. I oughta go to New York U to get as far away as possible. If it wasn't for..." she stops before she denounces the Brittany blessing, reflecting on what could've been done. "You know," she starts, commencing, "if I had it to do over again, I would have put her up for adoption." She doesn't mean that, and plays it off with a chuckle. "If I had it to do over again, I wouldn't have gone to that party." She thinks about it and gets a bit crazy. "Maybe I would've gone...I just wouldn't have gotten as toasted. I hear it was pretty live." She pauses and gets a little serious. "I wonder if the father is someone that I like; if he's someone that I actually know." She shifts emotional gears again and ponders with a laugh, "I wonder if I would've enjoyed it if I wasn't knocked out."

It feels like a 600-pound ape is in your lap. She's not looking for an answer or a commentary, just a listening ear. You oblige, which is the minimum that you can do. You want to tell her, but shame has a vice grip on your throat.

1991. It was the start of the Christmas holiday. Word of a house party a few blocks from your home spread through your school. You don't even know the guy's name or where he was from, but it was supposed to be the place to be. When you arrived, there were people hanging out of the windows, music bouncing off the walls and liquor flowing like a Magic-led Lakers' break. Even though you saw some familiar faces in the crowd (Chuck D, Deon, Mitch, and even Traci was a welcome sight in her red, short, body-hugging dress, revealing so much woman that day), you couldn't find your comfort zone in there. You *never were a person for parties. Instead of wasting the $5 admission by walking right back out, you decided to stay for a couple of hours. Two-fifty an hour isn't such a waste. By the end of the first hour, you had three Wine Coolers and a small cup of a potent mystery drink tainted with Vodka—your first and last experience with alcohol. You underestimated the strength of the imp that you gulped into your soul. Amazingly, you had actually gotten a little past tipsy and bold and stupid and goofy and dizzy, which wasn't quite as bad as the rest of the revelers, especially Traci.*

She was so out of it that she found you irresistible. In the ten years we had known each other, she had never ever hinted at being the least bit attracted to you. It's amazing what booze can do to a person's outlook. Either she was out of her mind or her mind was coming out, because she was literally ripping your clothes off. You told Ma that you tore your jacket hopping a fence. Even under the influence of alcohol and the pressure of peers, you didn't want any part of her. After fighting her off for the duration, your anger and flesh got aroused, so you dragged her into one of the vacant rooms. You shoved her to the bed and snatched her panties from beneath her dress, then proceeded to thrust yourself into her. Upon entry, you sobered up enough to get some of your wits, and pulled out like an enlightened saint coming out of the Great Whore of Babylon. Even if she didn't insult your drunk manhood by passing out, there was no way that you could go through with it.

Come to find out, the home the party was in belonged to a pastor, and the bedroom that you were attempting to fornicate in was that of the pastor and his wife. Before you noticed the picture of Jesus just above the bed; the angel figurines posted on the headboard; the praying hands statue on the chest of drawers; the anointing oil on the night stand next to the giant sized Bible and the pastors' plaque with his picture in it, you smelled the roses. You thought it was perfume in the pillow, until you saw the black petals closing up. The uncanny element to the flower was that your eyes were still closed, but it was as vivid as ever.

You got dressed in a record five seconds and you fled the house as if it was on fire. You made it a point to cover Traci up and lock the bedroom door behind you, however that didn't prevent her from being the main stop on an express freight train. Unfortunately, the engine tag hangs over you like a bad day. To add conviction to the guilt, they threw her out in the cold after they finished with her. How she made it home is a bigger mystery than the man behind the seed. It could be anybody. You can't help but imagine that it's a combination of cars, although the law of reproduction denies that possibility.

"I was so drunk, but not too drunk to not feel that extension cord all over my body. My mother beat me into sobriety," she recalls in awe. "I've never gotten a beaten like that. She left so many welts on me that I looked like a tigress," she mentions with a guffaw. "That's the only thing I remember about that night: the beating."

You cringe at the thought, wondering if her mother can do that to her own flesh and blood, to what extreme would she go to a man who violated her daughter.

Traci's mother figured out that she was pregnant after two months and grilled her about her sexual activity. Traci insisted that she was a virgin before that night and nothing else happened since then. She mentioned that she thought she remembered seeing you at the party. Miss Dawson called you up and over to her home for interrogation. Of course, you didn't tell her everything. Your testimony was that you left before it happened, which is a half-truth. After a fruitless self-investigation, Traci and Miss Dawson came to grips with not knowing. You want to tell her.

The meeting went fast and smooth. For the next issue, BJ encouraged you to do some editing and layout in order to be well-rounded before college, noting that your writing skills are advanced. He informed you that there was a lot of positive response to the "Off to the Racists" piece and that he would see about setting you up with a couple of celebrity interviews for the June issue, and possibly the August issue. He pulled you to the side after the meeting adjourned. Not only did he see the news account of the slapping, but he also read the story in the Windy-City Daily. Surprisingly, he didn't pass judgment or blindly defend you. You explained how the campus police filled out a report and the Director of Housing questioned you thoroughly before banning you from the campus. She didn't fold under the pressure from Peggy (who wanted you to go to jail) and the police (who were itching to lock a nigga up). Instead, she took into account that Charlotte declined when asked if she wanted to press charges. She didn't even sign the report. Ms. Brown seemed to be exceptionally objective and only "followed the rules" in prohibiting you from the campus.

BJ informed you that the newspaper was a good illustration of "yellow journalism." Up until that point, you never heard the term before, but you discerned that it had to do with exploitation and reporting without objectivity. He said he has crossed paths with Jason and exchanged unpleasant pleasantries with him on more than one occasion. "Just one of many adversaries in the business," he declared. You cringed when he told you to "Lean on the Lord." It shouldn't have, but that statement jacked up the whole pep/consolation speech.

"I also want you to follow Sharlene on a couple of photo shoots and go to the dark room with her so she can walk you through the development process a couple of times," he says, putting on his coat and gathering his things.

"That's cool," you say with a nod as Traci checks her watch—a gesture to wrap it up.

BJ announces, as if on cue, "Let me get out of here," extending his hand.

"As-Salaam-Alaikum," you bid, catching him a bit off guard.

"What?" he questions, his forehead wrinkling up.

"As-Salaam-Alaikum," you reiterate, explaining, "That's *peace be unto you* in Arabic."

"I've heard Muslims use that greeting, but I haven't taken Arabic," he notes, adding condescendingly, "and the Holy Ghost hasn't given me discernment of or utterance in Arabic."

"That's funny black man, but I can't imagine you quoting a white God and a white *'Holy Ghost'*. Does this *'Holy Ghost'* wear a white sheet a la the Ku Klux Klan? Any relation to Casper the Friendly Ghost?" you spit as your grip tightens up with your rising temperature. "Is that what you call select, religious uncle-Tomming?"

His grin spreads and his grip stiffens as he announces, "I see," with even more potent mockery. "You're on a pro-black spiritual trip and Christianity is a *white* man's religion, while Islam is the native religion of Africa. I've been there, done that and got the pieces of a broken coffee mug to prove it, but you've been bought with a price, so this will pass: Heaven and earth—just like religion and works; misguided Afrocentricity and color barriers—will pass away, but the Word will remain. Don't sweat though, because your understanding won't always be callow...raw...immature," he says with finality, imputing callow into your lexicon in the most unpleasant, patronizing way. He adds, "It is scary when the Holy Ghost hits them church folks and they start doing the headless funky chicken, ain't it? Boo. If I really knew what Wa-Alaikum-Salaam meant, I would say it. It could actually be a curse of God in another language, so May *'the grace of the Lord Jesus Christ, and the love of God, and the sweet communion of the Holy Ghost, be with you'.*"

Your grip and tongue go limp as he disengages his hand and saunters away with too much pep. The feeling that you were just cussed out weighs on your pride. Getting bricked in the face would probably be more soothing than the verbal foot in the ass you just took. The power of the spoken word...BJ is very skilled at it. Not once did his peevingly pleasant expression shift; his devilishly delightful demeanor was stationary. Unminced words can muzzle a mad mouth and trim a tight tongue. That oral thrashing has your mind flooded with grammatically incorrect adjectives. Wa-Alaikum-Salaam indeed.

The brusqueness is buried beneath your bromidic beam on the way home. Traci doesn't pick up on it...perhaps she doesn't care. Or maybe she's concentrating on her own concerns. When you reach her house, she notes the living room lights are on.

"She's waiting up to annoy me," she ruefully remarks as she sits, staring there longer than you care to wait, since you need to go fill Ben's Blazer up in Indiana.

Without even informing her, you pull off and set out for the gas station. She doesn't even ask as she gives her eyes a break from the gloomy gray night. As Indianapolis Boulevard comes up "I Never Should Have Let You Go" by Hi Five is just ending on WGCI and Traci is coming back to life.

"So why did you *assault* Charlotte?" she impassively queries out of the deep blue sea.

You glance at her and question, "How did you know" with your countenance.

"My mother showed it to me in the paper."

You hesitate, take a deep breath and blurt, "She smacked me; I smacked her back; her roommate called the campus police and the whole thing was blown out of proportion and whispered to the media" with finality.

"I'm glad I'm not you, because the press seems to have it in for you," she notes, to your ire.

"Are you trying to be caustic?" you question with an edge, hyperbolically adding, "If so, now is a good time to back up, because I'm not in the mood for it and I'll be on the news for abandoning you in Indiana."

She chuckles, further ticking you off, because she knows that it was a vacuous threat. "I'm serious, Malcolm," she justifies. "Me and Mother noticed how the same reporter is always ripping you and she concluded that his articles are slanted because you're never quoted. Mother defended you and dismissed it as garbage."

"Really?" That's a big, pleasant surprise. "I didn't even know that you kept up with my basketball career."

"Of course I do," she insists. "How can I not follow my main competitor's out-of-classroom accomplishments as well as his scholarly achievements?"

You just shake your head and swallow your pride. "Sorry for tripping."

"I'm used to it."

With that comical statement, the tension in your body dissipates as you reach Gas City. You start out the door when she grabs your hand and forces a twenty dollar bill in it, stressing, "This is for fixing the flat and paying half of the gas the last time I drove, so don't even think about giving it back."

You hump your shoulders and "Thanks" her as you start out, only to be grabbed again.

"And could you get me a giant sized bag of Bar-B-Q flavored Jays? Please. Thank you," she says with a big Cheshire grin.

"I knew there was a catch," you joke as you go pay for the fill up first.

When the tank is $10 full, she states, "You should have paid for the chips first," as she rolls the window up.

There's an expedient line when you get back in and a short wait. "Change on eight," you announce as you hold up the giant sized Jays and request, "and take the cost out for these."

She punches in the pump number and hesitates as an ambiguous expression spreads across her face, making the pause seem like a lunch break.

"What pump did you say?" she questions, throwing her stringy, sandy hair back with a jerk of her neck.

"Pump eight," you clarify. "Right over there," you say, pointing out to where the Blazer is sitting in her line of vision.

"Was somebody else with you?"

What kind of question is that? "Yes, somebody *is* with me. Why?"

"I just gave your change to somebody else."

Yeah right. "You didn't give *my* change to somebody else," you correct.

"Did the person that's with you come in and get it?"

"No she hasn't," you answer as you start to get perturbed. "She's been in the car all of this time and if she were to come in, she would've came for these," you state, trying to deflate some of the tension.

She hesitates again before she comes incorrect again. "I gave your change to someone else."

"No you didn't," you assert as the line behind you grows and people start thinking so critically that you can almost hear their thoughts. "Maybe you gave *your* change away, but *mine* is still coming."

"I'm sorry, but the change was already handed out," she pathetically notes as her indifferent expression starts looking dumber and stupider by the moment.

You knock on the bulletproof glass and ask, "Is this thing on? Apparently you don't understand me, so I think you better get your manager."

Just as the manager walks his scarlet face in from the back with the redder cashier closely behind, Traci comes in and concurrently questions the situation with the manager.

"Your cashier doesn't understand that since *I* gave her a twenty and the gas was only ten less the $2.99 for these chips, that *I'm* supposed to get seven dollars and one penny back, and I was wondering if you could grasp that elementary concept so I can make it home before spring comes."

The cashier briefly explains to him that she gave *my* change away and he basically regurgitates the same rigmarole that you've been getting from the cashier for the last five minutes and counting.

You explain, "I didn't get my change, so why is it that you're insinuating—I say insinuating because I'm not leaving until I get it—insinuating that I'm out of luck, and seven dollars and a penny?"

The manager looks like a sufferer of Downs Syndrome as he tries to explain, "She said that she gave the change for pump number eight out already and it's no way that we can take cash out of the drawer for change again on that pump."

"You can't penalize the customer for the cashier's mistake," Traci dignifies before you could get ignorant.

"I'm sorry ma'am," he apologizes.

"So are you saying that I can't get my change?" you question as you turn to Traci and mumble, "This is what you get when you inbreed."

"I'm saying that we can't give you change from a pump that's already been changed."

"Let me speak to *your* manager then," Traci demands.

At that, the patrons behind us are grumbling and playing gas station jurors. You now come to the understanding of the purpose of the brick-thick glass that separates the customers and the cashier: to keep the customers for snatching the cashiers out when they don't want to give them their seven dollars and a penny back. Why does the manager say that she's the highest superior there, and if you want to speak to someone over his head, you would have to call back tomorrow. That snaps your tolerance threshold.

"Look, you poor, white, redneck, pig-of-the-earth hill-billy hick," you hiss, stating, "I'm not coming back tomorrow for what's mine, now it's about to get ugly up in here."

Of course, they call the Indiana Pigs and they come and question everyone involved. A report is filled out and it is noted that you "made a threat." As it turns out, you don't get your change and Traci doesn't get her chips.

"Now you see what I mean," you declare, pulling out of the gas station an hour and a half later. "Mother should be sleep by now," you note.

"Identify the unknowns as x and x + 3," you hint. "Then translate it and you will get your answer." The word problem is *One positive number is 3 more than another. Their product is 54. Find the numbers.* We decided to meet up at the Harold Washington Library on Congress Parkway and State. As Brian methodically works it out at a hesitant pace, you and Khalid patiently encourage him. It pays off, as he comes up with an answer of 6 and 9. You already gave him a grammar tutorial.

You found that the concept of prepositions is easier for you to apply than teach. Thankfully, he seemed to grasp it. Khalid gave him a crash course on atoms, which served as a chemistry and biology crossover lesson. Brian absorbed it. Some things were stubborn comprehensions; other concepts took root immediately. If he had any of the advanced classes such as Geometry, Trigonometry, Biology and Chemistry, he probably would have aced the test on the first try without the help of you and Khalid. He's a prime example of the biased foundation of Proposition 48. The sun seems to beam from within his face, illustrating the mental illumination. We let out a collective sigh as Brian stretches out in the wood chair.

"Did you get a chance to read it?" Khalid questions.

You nod.

At the last study session, he gave you and Brian a copy of "Message to the Black Man in America." Elijah Muhammad's writing style is persistently potent. With your editorial eye, the book could've been condensed to half of the 350 pages. At times, his relentless, repetitive, rhetorical writing gave off a desperate sales tone. You were intoxicated with rage and dizzy from revelation. His quick, precise words communicated his divine knowledge. However, he referenced a new understanding of scriptures. The Bible was cited more than the Qur'an, with the insistence that they agreed with each other. The serene tone tainted the black passion. Many of the points raised regarding Black/White relations seemed valid and choleric, however, he didn't advocate violence. It's like he heats you up, only to tell you to chill out and wait for Allah. His words are provocative enough to incite a race riot, yet just subtle as to simmer the wrath of his followers. After reading him, you're that much more impressed with the self-control of the Nation, because any less of a mind would be bent on the annihilation of white folks, even if it's not under the banner of Islam—which teaches that White people are the devil's descendants. Truthfully, this doctrine of rage is more appealing than Christianity, but there are still some questions that need to be answered before you are sold.

6

What a long night to be so young. Normally you would be out and about in a weird dream. After a long practice, the only thing left to do is sleep. But you can't sleep. Coach Wade worked everybody's body...especially your body. You are worn like canvas jumpers on the asphalt, yet it feels like your veins are hosting the Indianapolis 500. The anxiety is so intense that you're trembling, as if your body is having an earthquake.

"Regulators" by Warren G is playing on the BOX (low of course) and you can picture yourself jamming to the beat. Nothing like basketball inspired soundtracks. Tonight is the beginning of the end, as in goodbye Bob Gibbons/hello Dick Vital. Tomorrow is the first game of the city playoffs. In your eyes, the city is where the real champion is. Never mind the official championship down state; it doesn't matter that the city ambassadors usually get smoked by the second round in Urbana. The officiating slants against Chicago's best and the games are called in favor of the predetermined downstate winner. You know; the officials know; everybody knows that the real ballers are in the city. If you put a city all-star team together, it could compete with some of the expansion teams in the NBA. Excluding yourself, there is Bryant Notree, Michael Hermon, Mark Miller, Roy Majors, Damion Dantzler, Alvin Robertson, Antoine Walker, Jerry Gee, etc. City ballers are conditioned to ball in the NBA. Chicago isn't known for producing big men (Rashard Griffin, Juwan Howard and Deon Thomas being the recent exceptions), but when it comes to versatile guards and swing players, there is an abundance.

The basketball court is a very good chapter in your life that has yet to be completed. Of course, your long-shot goal is the NBA. If you don't make it, you'll still live happily ever after. You aspire to be a big, ambidextrous force. Instead of being known by a title or restricted to a by-line, you want to be a well-rounded, influential entity. You can't even imagine going through the same monotonous, 9-to-5 routine for your whole life. Even if your body doesn't wear out, you can't dream of playing ball for twenty or thirty years. You can't even fathom your by-line in a publication year in and year out until you croak. The deadlines and AP-style conformity would turn you into a writing corpse. And God forbid you should practice law until you're old and gray. It would be like sipping from the grail of death. Perhaps you will become an artist once you get tired of crusading. Or maybe a theology teacher. The presidency doesn't sound bad either.

You throw on a Lakers' sweatshirt and slip into your black Reebok cross-trainers. You're on your way to the courts since dreamland is closed and the sandman has the night off. It is so peaceful at this time of night—or rather morning, since it's a little past one. The perfect time and place to meditate and liberate your mind. At one-thirty, the court lights go out, so it's just you, the basket and your radar-guided jumper, which is how you perfected it for the daylight. You shoot by faith, not by sight. Every shot you take, you believe will go in. If there's a hand in your face, it's not good enough. There is no such thing as someone stopping it. If you miss, someone's prayer was answered.

You walk light-footed down to the basement, since uncle JoJo and Ma don't approve of you violating curfew, even if it is to go play ball a block away. They trust that you will avoid trouble—and you do—but they worry that trouble will not avoid you. They've caught you sneaking in and out a couple of times, but stopped sweating you after they realized that you were going to go even if they did whack you a couple of times with the belt or put you on punishment. The same instinct that draws birds south is what draws you to the court. They realized that you were serious about playing and that you were good enough to take it beyond the playground. Uncle JoJo—who was the one that usually caught you and always chastised you—could understand, because he was a football player and runner in high school. You don't know how many tales he's told you about his gridiron days. They were good stories, but they were old and tired and needed to be sent up to the front office. If he had gone pro—which he claimed he could, were it not for an injury—it would be daily, front-page news to him. Mom just wanted us both to be happy, so if Uncle JoJo ignored it, so did she. You often wonder if it was necessary to climb in and out of the window all those times.

You skip the last step at the bottom because it creeks, and ease your way to the basement door, trying to avoid tripping over a pail—as you've done on more than one occasion. You can shoot at night, but you can't run through an obstacle course of brooms, buckets, and crates in the dark. After feeling your way to the door, you grab the knob and lift up on it since it rubs the door panel. You push it up enough to keep the draft out and jump up the stairs. Feeling like you just escaped from prison, you breathe a sigh of relief. Out of courtesy, you resist the temptation to dribble down the street. Most people do sleep at this time, and if *you* were awakened by a basketball, you would shoot the ball (no pun intended) and the dribbler.

As you approach Yates Boulevard, you can see the basket on the south end of the court. It seems to glow, and even though it's about fifty yards away, it looks close enough score. The 40-degree air is clear and calm, and although your legs are exposed, it feels like nitrogen is circulating through your lower body. Without even realizing it, you jog across the street and start dribbling once you get to the other side, where your jog turns into a sprint through the grass. Your shot just before you get on pavement feels good, but it rims out as you chase it down and run to the other end to reverse dunk.

This is where it all began. The very court that Tim Hardaway used to turn it out. Ben started bringing you up here when you were five. All you could do was watch. Occasionally, he would let you shoot it when there wasn't a game going on. The ball was so heavy it wouldn't even reach the basket. He would have to hoist you over his shoulders so you could hit the backboard. You cherish those days. Within a year, you didn't need a boost to shoot. Not long after that, you could dribble with your right hand and by the age of eight, you could hit five free throws in a row. You got your first dunk when you were fourteen and all of 5'9".

You take a shot from the top of the key and it hits the bottom of the net as you trot to retrieve it. You shoot it from the corner and it barely touches the net. Again from the corner, and it bounces back toward you. Pretty soon, you hit ten in a row from beyond the imaginary three-point circle and you miss the eleventh. Catching the ball with a shout, you jam without dribbling. You run back to the other end and start popping from down there. This time you hit twelve in a row. You continue shooting and before you know it, beads of sweat are on your forehead. You pause and peak at your watch, noting that you've been out here for almost two hours. Since you *do* have to get up at seven, you decide to shoot about fifty more jumpers after you get a swallow of water from the fountain. They turned it on after the temps shot up to the seventies for a couple of days. It's been kind of cool ever since.

Just as you reach the fountain, a long, black car turns down the street. It looks like an early model Buick or Oldsmobile. Definitely a Duce. Dr. Dre is blasting from the kick drum as it slows down. It actually resembles the Bat-mobile. It's too dark to make out if it's somebody you know. You almost expect the Capped Crusader to jump out and start knocking knots upside your head. The windows are tinted smoke black. You're not in the mood for any of the neighborhood thugs tonight...if ever. Whoever it is, is probably drunk and/or high. You watch them as you lap up the water, prepared to run if necessary. Your breathing is labored and your heart thumps hard and fast from the workout and the anticipation of their next move. It doesn't take long.

Smoke and laughter pour out as the doors open. It's hard to believe anyone could breathe in there. Hook, Popeye, and two other hoodlums you don't recognize emerge from the car. You recognize the silhouette of Popeye's head as the street light hits it and nobody sounds like Hook...except maybe a preacher. The whole scene reminds you of a laser light show...or a horror flick...then again, "Boyz in the Hood." Just the people you *don't* want to see. They are cool with you, but they are too obnoxious and their ignorance is only magnified with the chemical factor. You'll shoot those last fifty during the warm-ups just before the game. You're still thirsty, but you've had enough water so you start walking away.

"Shorty!" Popeye yells out with a slight slur. "Shorty! Let me get a shot."

Oh great. Thug Life wants to play ball. Why don't they play without a ball? They're too high to know the difference. "I'm out, man."
"We just want a couple of shots, M-Dawg," Hook says as they get up to you.

"I gotta game tomorrow and I have to get some shut eyes," you insist as you peer from patch to patch. Between Popeye and Hook, they have a pair of left eyes left. Recently, Popeye played crazy with an apparent loaded lunatic on 79th and Essex and had his bluff called and his eye popped out. Hook had his shot out years ago by one of his delinquent hypes.

"I know. You going up against Englewood. We ain't gonna keep you, slick. We just want a couple of quick shots," he pleads, throwing his hands up to the side.

You eye them all and hesitate before saying, "Aiight...one varsity and I'm out."

"Shorty," Popeye slurs, giving you a pound.

This is just what you don't need. Things are going too good to be caught in the park at three o'clock with one of the south side's biggest drug dealers. You will make quick work of this.

You take the first shot from the free-throw line...and you miss. Damn. You're a 90 percent shooter from the line. One of the other thugs that you don't know that well name Nate is too clumsy and drunk to get control of the ball and kicks it all the way across the street. Popeye chases it down as you shake your head in disbelief. You try to watch who's in your presence...especially after curfew.

Mitch, Chuck D, and Jay are clean characters, and it was just after eight when Porky Pig picked the wrong brothers to set up. July 28, 1993, goes down as one of your most diabolical experiences. It was payday, your team smoked Shepherd for the Public South Summer Tournament Championship and you were kicking it with the fella's on Jay's side of town: the wild West side. Mitch edged us all out in the babe contest by two numbers. His dual dimples and cleft chin gave him a handsome advantage with the ladies while we walked through the Brickyard mall, hung out at North and Narragansett, turned Columbus Park out with a dunking convention, and chilled in Garfield Park before finally heading to Jay's house for some barbecue. Make no mistake about it, the 10-mile radius of Jay's house is an ideal narcotic's market, with the equilibrium fluctuating slightly when a corner runner gets taken out or a hype overdoses. This is how you were able to grasp Macroeconomics in summer school: by observing that microcosm.

We were strolling past Roosevelt Road down Keeler when "One Time" swooped down on us like a colony of pigeons on an open new car lot. Did they drop some shit? Collectively, the crew never even as much as smoked a joint, let alone sold one, yet there were four bulletproof, trigger-ready, frisky cops for each of you. We all managed to stay clean after the game up until that point, when the friendly officers dropped you all to the gravely ground. No sweat. No one was stashing dope or packing a pistol, so the knees in the back were unnecessary. After they scrutinized those facts, we were cuffed and subjected to interrogation/accusation/trial/condemnation in the back seat.

We all had identification (that the officers had in their possession), which was to your disadvantage. After your name was put in the computer, they put it together that you were a "troubled" ball player and figured more trouble would do you good. They threw several insults your way as Mitch was on the verge of cardiac arrest. You remained calm when they demanded a gun, as if they didn't have access to a gun shop. You didn't blink when they remarked that your $400 bankroll seemed like a lot for a teen. A $400 payday won't hold you over for a week, let alone two weeks. You didn't even lose it when the extortionist pocketed $200 of your legitimate ducks. That's just one less outfit that you would have. However, you became enraged enough to kill a cop when he announced that we could get five to ten years for five ounces of crack cocaine as he held up a sack of rocks and the other officer proceeded to take you down to the station. You bitterly pondered the number of brothers that are wasting away in a cage because of a stereotypic quota. You didn't want to know how many black men have been fried for the sake of closing a fucking case.

Four hours wasted away before Uncle JoJo came down with a lawyer to bail you out. You're grateful for attorney Stanley Tyson's diligence, but what pleased you more than getting out of jail, was how Uncle JoJo declared you innocent before even talking to you. He knew that you were in jail for no reason and he didn't even question you about the matter. The media, on the other hand, had a field day castigating you.

There was an article on the front page of the Windy-City Daily and several excoriating editorials in the other papers. Thank God the devil is a liar. Our alibis held up; our records spoke for themselves; there were credible witnesses to the incident that came forth (a minister and a white sales woman happened to observe us walking down the street); and the police reports contradicted each other (as it turns out, the devil didn't consult with the three black officers, who told the truth). The charges disappeared like a chicken in a lion's den, your $200 reappeared like the memory of a first kiss, and the case fell shorter going to trial than a Mugsy Bogues' monster jam attempt on Shaq...all to the dismay of the press. A two-sentence press release was devoted to exonerating you and expunging your bad reputation.

And here you are with Chicago-style Nino Brown, a crack smoking cartoon character, and Nate the nocturnal. You have never seen Nate in the daytime and you wonder if he's a vampire. You don't even know what his complexion is after all of these years of seeing him. He's just a shadow—a shade of black.

Hook shoots from the free-throw line and you anticipate a miss, so you leap up just before it hits the rim. Sure enough, it bounces off and you catch—almost palming it—and hammer it through like the rim was your enemy. Popeye and the dude they call Ray Ray "Ohhh" it up as you keep a straight face and strictly business demeanor on the way to the free-throw line. You hit three in a row and take it out at the top. With token defense from Popeye, you hit a long-range jumper. After shooting the first free throw, you watch Dick Tracey slowly turn the corner in his sky-blue Caprice Classic with the plain, round, stainless steel hubcaps. He's one of the area's most notorious detectives. Many "brothers" have taken a drubbing at his hands. It's best not to cross his path, even if you're innocent.

"Don't sweat him, Shorty," Hook assures as he comes to a stop parallel to the Bat-mobile.

You're ready to run like a deer as you hold the ball in a cocked free-throw position, waiting on Tracey's cue. After a ten-second observation, he slowly pulls away, and you follow suit with "As-Salaam-Alaikum," as you start off without explanation.

"Awe Shorty," Hook starts as you stop in your tracks and cut him short.

"I'm laying it on the line just being out here, and then my company isn't too positive in the eyes of the powers that be," you state, continuing, "I'm a non-conformer, but I'm not a fool. If you want to finish this, look me up in two days before sun-down."

They remain mute as you trot across the park and across the street. You get halfway down the block when you take note of the squad cars swarming down on the bat car. You don't even stay to watch as you count your blessings of common sense and good timing.

What a perfect time to be in a dry spell. You don't have an answer for your shooting woes. 3-for-17. You sucked, as Beavis and Butthead would say. You sucked to the utmost. It appeared to be the start of a career showing after you opened the game with a 3-point dunk. You ended up with eight ugly points. You almost grabbed as many rebounds with six. Bad games are going to happen. The best players have the worst games. You understand that. But why did yours have to come in the third round of the playoffs? It wouldn't be so bad if your team won. To add insult to a humiliating day, we lost by one point. 51-50. One lousy, funky point. The point you could have scored at the free throw line with 42 seconds left. You were shooting the front end of a one-in-one, and when you released the ball, you knew it was a brick like the rest of your shots. In the end, you had enough to build a well-fortified tower. It missed by a mile to the left and you damn near broke the backboard. Triton Magnet got the rebound and nobody else scored the rest of the way, so the second free throw could have won it.

You feel so bad that you don't know if you want to play in college. Hell, you don't know if you want to play organized ball again. Maybe the playground is where your skills belong, and perhaps you should focus on a career in journalism. If you can't come through in the big game—and this game was the biggest—why bother dreaming the NBA dream? This year's team was the best out of the four years. We had size, speed and experience. Three players on your team are ranked in the top fifty in the city. Throughout the season, we were ranked in the top ten, which is no small feat. Handling all the hype apparently was a big feat for you. You will have nightmares about this day for a long time, which beats what was playing in your head last night by a long shot.

If you were any less of a man, you would attribute the bad day to the bad night. Prevarication isn't an option, since you had the same *night* the nights before the first two playoff games in which you were on fire. Last night was just that: NIGHT.

The image was like a television with no reception. That slumber was a death-like, dismally dark abyss. If that was remotely what death is like, it sure broke down one stereotype: Rest In Peace. According to secular thinking, death is the absolute cessation of life, as in the end of consciousness and perception. In other words, a permanent nap with no dreams or feelings. You were aware of every constipated moment. In fact, it was like being stuck in an elephant's alimentary canal. You felt cramped to the point of suffocation and anxiety; when you were able to get a breath, it was as malodorous as a dead skunk; your mouth was dryer than salt; you were auditorally muffled like your ears were clogged with cement; and through your eyes you saw nothing but soot. That was like a preview of hell without the fire, because you didn't get any rest whatsoever...and you didn't sense any evidence of God. Normally, in your good dreams you could see the bright colors of flowers and rainbows, feel the summer breeze blowing across your face, hear the lyrics of bird songs, taste buttermilk pancakes and smell fresh coffee. Now all you have is deep space. If you weren't so exhausted, you would've labeled it an out-of-body experience. No excuses though.

You're irked more than embarrassed. Minus Ma—who stopped coming to your games after she almost came to blows with an over-critical fan in your sophomore year—the family was all there. You didn't feel like having Uncle JoJo try to cheer you up, and you didn't feel like explaining your bad day to Dexter Junior. You would rather be peeved in peace, so you hitched a ride home with Ben. He understands you better than you understand yourself sometimes, and you admire him for that, because you can be a strange animal sometimes. He knows when and how to talk to you in every situation and he knows how to let you be, just like in this situation. He let you drive the Blazer, because he knows you love to drive his car, even though you can tell he doesn't trust your driving. Not only does he fasten his seat belt, but he also insists on you putting on yours or being taxied. The nerve. So you're tucked in nice and cozy and belted like a lunatic in a straitjacket, and he still has the audacity to be nervous. He's clutching the door handle as you roll down 83rd Street.

The light is green as you approach Cottage Grove. Three cars ahead of you are trying to *miss* the light. "C'mon!" you yell, punching the horn as the light turns yellow. "Is this a turtle convention!" The light turns red and so do you as you come to a stop and the cars ahead of you speed up, making it across. You're fuming.

"Damn!" you yell as you draw up like you're going to throw a punch at them. "This is the source of high blood pressure."

You turn to Ben, who is still clutching the panel as he looks straight ahead with an expression that hints that he's biting his lip to keep from laughing. "Turn that door loose," you order as you snatch his arm. He starts cackling. "And shut up." You start laughing too, even though you don't want to, which makes the whole thing funnier.

"Easy now. Take a deep breath and count to ten. There'll be another light five seconds later, Snake" he teases.

"There's no remedy for that type of stupidity," you note, pausing to watch the cars go by.

Now that some of the tension is gone, you reflect on the game—you confront it and break your post-game silence by asking, "Was that my worse game ever, or what?"

"It wasn't that bad," he says like he's been itching to say it for the longest, but was waiting for you to bring it up. "I used to beat you worse before you grew taller than me. You could've been held scoreless like I used to do. Seven points isn't bad."

"Eight. That long jumper was a three," you correct him. "What hurts more than losing and playing like Danny Ferry was that it happened at Simeon...in the Ben Wilson gym. I felt like I was on sacred ground. I feel like I've sinned...like I desecrated the place and disgraced the number 25. I'm so ashamed," you say with a touch of sarcasm, but in your heart, you're serious.

"Don't sweat it. I'm sure he would forgive you."

"Have you ever just felt that your talent was depleted and obsolete after playing?"

"That day Robert Shepherd from Bowen came up to Ekersal and broke my ankles with his cross-over, is the closest I came to feeling like a chump. I ain't never got clowned so bad, but then again, Rob was a straight joker with the rock. Probably the best ball-handler I've faced...even better than Hardaway. I'm surprised he didn't get drafted out of Arkansas last year. But when it's all said and done, my best days had passed and he gave me that wake-up call. Your best days are still ahead, so don't wake up from your dream, Snake."

You nod at his encouragement. "If I didn't take all those bad shots and miss all those bad shots, we would've won. Ben wasn't selfish...I was," you state as the light turns green and you pull off.

That game meant more to you than advancing to the next round. You finally got to play at Simeon, which is where you wanted to go. It was your top choice when you were coming out of eighth grade. Unfortunately, your choice didn't matter. Momma sent you to Louis Magnet. She claimed that the academics are better. Maybe it's a good thing you didn't go, because you might not have made the team if you had a day like this at the tryouts.

As you approach Stoney Island, the three cars that gave you a stroke five minutes ago, are still putting along. "Hurry up!" you shout as you press the horn. The light turns yellow, but you're not missing it even if you have to ram them from behind and push them along. They accelerate, and so do you as the light turns red when you get to the intersection. "I thought y'all would see it my way," you say, cruising on through.

Three blocks down, you feel flashing lights in your rear view mirror and on the back of your neck. "Damn. Go raid a Dunkin' Donuts and leave me alone." Now you're really frustrated as you slowly pull to the curb, hoping they pass you up. The squad car slows down and pulls right behind you. Yep. They're gonna get you for running the light. A Tribe Called Quest is thumping on the radio, so you turn it down.

You don't hate white people and you don't hate cops, but you know that Caucasian and authority is a bad combination that has spelled racism in your experience. Your first taste of that bitter reality came in 1983. The White Sox were in the middle of an amazing season and on their way to clinching the Central Division title. Ben allowed you to accompany him and four of his neighborhood buddies to experience history in the making. The Sox were bad hosts to the Minnesota Twins, sending them back to the land of 1,000 lakes with a 7-1 loss. As high up as our seats were, it didn't diminish the magic of being there. You determined that television didn't do baseball justice, because the box couldn't capture all of the excitement of a free roaming eye.

When we left the park, you discovered that it was raining from the ceiling of the overshadowing steps. The drops that hit your arm were hot and hateful. Ben got a look at the clouds before you even knew the forecast. All you knew is that he was intent on lingering around without an umbrella.

After patrolling the parameter of the exits, he came to an abrupt stop, pointing out a group of white boys his age who were leaving the confines of Comiskey. They stopped under the scrutinizing eyes of your livid uncle, and then took off. Ben and Felix—his fast friend—went after them, with the rest of us following suit. You had the advantage of piggybacking on Roy's back, because it was no way you were going to keep up. The chase was bumpy, yet exciting. You thought it was child's play—a game. Ben and Felix caught three of them a half-block under the viaduct—on the outskirts of Bridgeport and a few steps away from the police station—and when the rest of us reached them, you discovered that it was quite serious.

Your uncle had a blond boy on the ground nailing his head into the pavement, while Felix had the other two by the shirt collar. Just as we surrounded them, their white friends came back...with the white police. Of course everyone froze, without the oral command. The white boys were pointing us out as troublemakers—it didn't help that Ben was caught red handed reddening the face of one of them—and we were pleading our case, calling them the rainmakers. Although we were talking just as loud, the officers weren't hearing us. When Ben perceived that they were buying into their tale, he got just a little closer and spoke just a little louder. However, the verdict was already in and injustice needed to be served.

While Ben was explaining, the cop came all the way from California and slapped Ben's explanation all the way to New York. Everybody shutup. You realized at the tender age of seven that the testimony of a black person to a white mediator has no credibility when going against a white person's lie. The officer proceeded to hustle us into the squad car, send the white boys home, and take us to the station. This is why someone's spit on you insults you so. On the way there, they made the word Nigger sound so ugly. You had heard it before, but it didn't have the same sting that it had coming from their mouths in reference to us. To this day, the aftertaste remains and Ben has yet to find those words.

Red and glowing as if he swallowed a lantern, the driver slowly steps out of the car and cups the gun in his holster. It's amazing how a routine stop can get extreme. It's as if you're an allusive, armed fugitive. He's probably straight from Bridgeport, whose slogan is "Niggers Beware". Talk about fighting Irish. After the citizens of that infamous neighborhood give you a Jim Crow simulation, the cops will come and give you triple jeopardy in the form of a night stick across the head and a booking for being the wrong color in the wrong neighborhood. It's hard to believe that Bridgeport is on the predominately black south side of town—just a viaduct and expressway across from the projects. It's always open season there on the pigmented.

The driver is about fifty with a stomach full of booze, coffee and doughnuts. Santa Claus ain't got nothing on officer unfriendly. You observe him pull his pants up as he walks toward you. Those sandy-brown, Elvis Presley sideburns growing down from his long, thick, gray hair makes him look like a Leprechaun on the brink of retirement. His eyebrows are thick enough to smuggle an extra gun or even an army. Those bushes have the gall to graft right above his big hunkity-hunk nose, a la Ernie's. That snout could do Bazooka damage if he sneezes when he's congested.

His raven-haired partner is taking his time getting out. He's a shrimp, and without his gun he's even smaller. You could grab him by his thick mustache, that matches his straight, jet-black hair, and sling him in the bushes on his partner's face. As he strolls out, he takes a peek at the license plate with his dreamy eyes. You perceive their prejudices, so you tell Ben to "Get ready. I'll take the big, ugly, Lucky-charm imitation and you take the midget" as you roll the window down.

"Don't do or say anything that'll get you crowned like a 'King'," he warns, just as the big one makes it to you.

"Can you step out of the car," he demands more than asks in his baritone voice. "Slowly," he adds.

"Good grief," you mumble under your breath with a slight attitude, knowing that they're going to pat you down and start tripping. What happened to 'Can I see your license and registration?' You should have let Ben taxi you home.

"Is there a problem officer?" Ben foolishly asks in a friendly tone, as if he flunked the racism exam from 1983.

"There will be if you don't step out of the car like he said," the little one calmly threatens with an Italian edge. Sounds like one of the Good Fellas and you immediately think you smell garlic coming from his direction. What nerve. He's about as intimidating as a butterfly. Unfortunately, this butterfly has a badge and a gun.

Ben hesitates as his poker expression hints that he's weighing his options. You both oblige at the same time.

"Put your hands on the hood and spread your legs," he commands. Why doesn't he just tell you to heel, sit and roll over? You want to question why you're getting the third degree over a traffic violation, but it would only be used against you. Why not tally up another ticket and be done with it in order to get back to meeting that quota? Your face is tight from the frown and your jaws are locked shut like a pit bulls as you breathe hard and fast. You can feel the intense anger rising in Ben.

"Do you have a license and registration," the big one finally questions as he goes through your pockets and pulls your wallet out of your back pocket.

"It's in there," you mention.

Ben informs him that the insurance and registration papers are in the glove compartment.

Satisfied that you're harmless, he inspects it before he reminds you "The light back there was red and this is a no flying zone," as he goes back to his car to no doubt run your name and write the tickets.

Maybe he'll come back with a funnier witticism. At least you didn't get pinned on the ground. You and Ben sit on the hood while they take their time writing the tickets out. Ben says a few unmentionables as you remain tight-lipped, wondering what are they going to try. Of course, they disappoint: a ticket for running the light; a speeding ticket; a ticket for not wearing the seat belt (you had it on when they pulled you over, but you didn't have it on as you waited outside. He still needs a few lessons in comedy, because he is weak); a ticket for not having insurance (which you'll have to waste three hours of your life going to court for). As a parting shot, he notes that there should be a law against basketball players with bad attitudes, and that if you were any good, he would've let you go. Perhaps you should stop yielding to cops, because nothing good happens when you do.

You feel awkward standing up as the gentleman leads the gathering in prayer. Although your mind isn't focused on the words, your body is conformed with all the Muslims paying homage to Allah. In your age of innocence, Jesus was the only thing you stood for. For the past two months, you haven't been able to discern the difference between innocence and ignorance. All you know is what you don't know, and that's what you stand for.

Last Sunday you missed the first part of Saviors' Day, and Khalid assured you that you didn't want to miss this message. In light of the controversy that Farrakhan's appearance on the Arsenio Hall Show caused last Friday, you're eager to hear what all of the noise is about. Who is the man behind the myth? So, here you are in Mosque Maryam for the first time, about to hear your first live sermon by Minister Farrakhan. You're hurting for some uplifting. Apparently, the hundreds of other brothers that lined up for about 30 minutes outside to get a choice seat beyond the rigid security point, are here for a therapeutic word also.

You tried to get into the Holy Qur'an, but its historical accounts differed from what you learned in the Bible, and that only confused and frustrated you into an anxious sleep. Imagine calling it the night at eight in the evening. It's ironic that you never fell asleep reading the Bible. In fact, you felt vigorous and lively after mentally gobbling up the scriptures.

When the prayer finishes, you sink into a gold, theater-like seat with the gold dedication plastered on the back. Although armrests separate them, it still feels like you're shoulder to shoulder with the brothers on your sides. As one of the young sisters presents awards, you case the sanctuary.

The gold carpeting that stretches up to the pulpit, sparkling whitewashed walls, and gold trim columns and posts purifies the aura. The brightness alone can raise a bad mood a notch out of the pit of despair. Light beams in from the windows of the dome at the top, seemingly sanctifying the shrine with a spiritual presence. An octagram is situated in the center of the ceiling with a circular symbol in the middle. Flowers line the podium and cameras are stationed in out-of-the-way corners and on the balcony. The rest room (that you visited before taking your seat) is even cleaner than a bottle of disinfectant. Every inch of the place radiates as if it was polished with a toothbrush. Being here pleases your senses, however...it doesn't put your soul at ease one iota. Maybe your religious pride is beaten down; perhaps it's going against the acceptable grain, even though that hasn't discouraged you in the past. An inspirational song, which ain't happening here, would soothe your spirit. You could stay home and watch the news to get mad. A religious service shouldn't be emotionally one-dimensional. It's possible to put your rabid feelings to sleep with a credible word.

A Mother Muslim is speaking on the ways to good physical health. Three statuesque sentries—better known as the Fruit of Islam—are situated in front of the stage and react to the crowd's applause. Whenever there is a standing ovation, they rise from their seats and stand in a defensive posture like well-trained attack dogs. Two FOI are always posted on each side of the speaker at the podium. Personally, they would be a big distraction to you, but since there's a threat of attack to the Islamic dignitaries, you can justify it. Since they don't carry weapons (at least they're not supposed to), it's a matter of trust, since you assume that in case of gun fire, they would act as a shield. Most of the military attired Fruit remain outside. You didn't understand the color rank of the brazen brown with gold strip and midnight blue clad FOI. The happy blue/violet donned females intrigued you, since it was your understanding that only brothers were allowed in FOI.

After a few more minutes of filler, pro-black/anti-white speaking by the Assistant Minister to Farrakhan, he goes into a long introduction of Minister Farrakhan as two followers prepare to open the door for his entrance. When he emerges through the doors, he gets a strong, standing ovation. Wearing a well tailored, grim-green suit, smoked shades and a trademark playboyish bow-tie, he bows to the followers on stage and greets the audience with the Nation's statement of faith. You didn't realize he is that short. He has to be only a head higher than Bushwick Bill.

After he announces that he has another engagement following this sermon, he jumps right into his message by eloquently recounting the Passion of Christ with precise, prudent prose. After he finishes the account without error, he goes into the relevance of it to Saviors' Day and black people today. Just before he gets into it, you step over that thin line that separates the sane from the lunatics, because you hear a voice calling you. You turn around, peek to both sides and glance up, but you can't spot anyone that owns up to the call.

Farrakhan proceeds to reinterpret the Gospel message by paralleling Fard Muhammad to God the Father and Elijah Muhammad to Jesus, going as far as saying that Elijah was *the* Savior, emphasizing not *a* Savior, but *the* Savior.

You hear the voice in a whisper again, and you turn all about. Everyone is focused on the speaker, gobbling up and agreeing with his thesis. He commences to debauch the traditional Good News translation by comparing Elijah Muhammad's escape from a death plot to Jesus' escape from the crucifixion. He backs up that argument by citing Jesus' petition in the Garden of Gethsemane for the Father to take the cup of suffering away, to which "God heard him."

You're not sure if "God heard him" as he quotes, but you are sure that the voice gets louder when you wonder if the whole world was deceived into believing that Jesus had died.

He smirks and scratches his head condescendingly as he states that Christians are waiting for his return 2000 years after the fact. Jesus' resurrection wasn't literal—according to Farrakhan and the applauding audience—but an allegory for how the knowledge, wisdom and power of

God will be seen in the black people who are mentally, morally, spiritually, socially, economically, and politically dead.

Although you still find yourself questioning whether the Jesus who died—or didn't die—was the Jesus that is coming back—or has risen from black folks or was Muhammad—the self-query jolts your conscience like a stun gun. It is perplexingly deja vuish when he notes that Elijah's word has life and that the world hated Elijah without reason.

He quotes Elijah Muhammad telling an audience of black preachers that he is the Jesus that they've been looking for, then cleverly mocks their mind-set of acceptance of a white Jesus only. The crowd absorbs that testimony as he goes on to call Elijah his and everyone's father—as in our Father, who art in heaven—that he was a mighty man and a mighty god born of a woman, citing the scripture "Ye are all gods, children of the most high god."

You devilishly play with the Elijah Christ concept in muted laughter: *If Elijah was/is Jesus, when he committed adultery, was that metaphorical masturbation or a holy blowjob, since Christ is the head and the Church is the body?* Any Christ less than Jesus is a blatant perversion of the righteous title; a disgrace to the purpose of soul salvation, rendering the oil of the anointing dead sewage. Not that you're condemning Elijah Muhammad, but it seems like you're the only person present that recognizes that he was a sinner just as every individual that has breathed...except Jesus. This message is sending all types of vibes through your bosom, but you still don't know what you believe.

Farrakhan continues to clear up/corrupt the Jesus concept by explaining his anointing wasn't to crush the wicked, but to teach the poor. He then factors himself into the deitized analogy by calling himself the Comforter that Elijah Muhammad sent, as written in the scriptures.

As he mentions the first thing concerning Islamic teaching (how Jesus and Mahdi—God the Father—are coming back in judgment), you yearn for your Bible so you can verify some of his quotes. You're not sure which one's he misstated and which one's he used correctly, but you are sure that Philippians 2:10 and 11 states: "That at the name of Jesus every knee should bow, of things in heaven, and things in earth, and things under the earth; And that every tongue should confess that Jesus Christ is Lord, to the glory of God the Father."

Just before Farrakhan launches into his death plot conspiracy, he vies for the title of Master of Misquotation by twisting that scripture, stating that "Every knee will bow and every tongue will be forced to confess that he [Allah] is god." You have heard enough.

Tears well up in your eyes as you make your way to the center aisle and towards the back exit, knowing that you won't be returning to the Mosque. At the same time, you don't know exactly where you are going. This message is worse than the last gospel message you heard at your church before your hiatus.

Walk of Faith was celebrating it's 24th year anniversary. The theme was "Unity in the 92" and they brought in a w-w-white evangelist to bring the message on the first night. In your heart, you felt that he was a dynamic speaker. From what you heard, he also knew the Word. However his message... It was taken from James 2:1 and titled "Take off the Shades to see the Rainbow." The long and short of his sermon was "Prejudice is stupid", which he kept emphasizing. While that is true, you felt that he should've preached that to a different audience. How in the hell was he going to come up in a black church in the ghetto denouncing prejudice? It's like preaching a sermon on salvation to the angels in heaven. In your eyes, it was a cowardly speech. Your thinking was 'Let him go to a Klan rally where the members are part of the clergy and deliver that message; write that sermon to the Racists' politicians; teach that lesson to his own congregation'. He reeked of hypocrisy for telling African-Americans not to prejudge people that have oppressed, degraded and mistreated them for 400 years and counting. Black people know it's stupid to be discriminated against and beaten down physically and spiritually because of their color. You never had a problem with the Word itself, just with the speaker's timing and audience.

The message you have just endured lacked substance, and depreciated of credibility with every utterance. What a shame, because you like Farrakhan. However, the speech supersedes the speaker like a Benz would outclass a minimum wage porter. You love the pro-black stance the Nation takes. You can understand their detestation of white folks. However, you can't follow someone that misuses words to influence his followers. For some odd reason, you feel that they have some of the truth, but it's hard to pick it out from the lies. You're not even sure if he realizes his errors (which would make him a false prophet that scripture warns about), or is ignorant of his folly.

Let the shit fly. Simeon and King. King and Simeon. According to Ben, that rivalry goes back to 1983, when King allegedly recruited one of Simeon's players. The next season, Simeon beat King in the quarterfinals and went on to take state. 1994. The stakes aren't as high and the grudge isn't as intense, but the talk is just as provocative. Michael Herman wants to prove who the best two-guard in the city is; your boy, Bryant Notree, is licking his chops, hoping that they can go one-on-one so he can isolate, expose and dissect Herman like a mad scientist would butcher a carcass. Your prediction: Notree will win the individual battle; King will win the war. Herman is a touch quicker, but Notree is two degrees stronger and twice as versatile. Simeon has an ace marksman in Kevin Turner, but King is stacked at every position, as usual.

That's the game you want to see, but Sharlene insisted on watching her school (Carver) beat Hubbard. The Greyhounds might as well stay home. Roy Majors has the deadliest crossover this side of Tim Hardaway. When you faced him at Cole Park last summer, you dubbed it "Crossover: The Second Coming." To put his game in perspective, last summer he was playing in a tournament with a collection of college ballers, high school notables, and playground legends. His team only dressed four and one of them fouled out before the half. With the score tied at 40 going into the third quarter and his team outnumbered five (not including the bench) to three, Majors mutated into a trigger-happy, shooting, power-center. It seemed like he had four hands, the way he was handling the ball. Not once was he ripped. The other team had to put three people on him—and that still wasn't enough to stop him. Even though he put on one of the best clinics on patting and perimeter you have witnessed, his team lost by four. You're glad that you weren't on the other side. You're already looking forward to the Carver game against Westinghouse. Mark Miller and Roy Majors. Damion Dantzler and Alvin Robertson. West Side and South Side. That's going to be good.

After Saviors' Day, you caught a little bug that developed into an alien. The hot tea, Sudafed and NyQuil strengthened and mutated it. It outgrew your head by a gallon, flooded your chest like a clogged toilet, and oozed out of every cavity and pore in your body. There's no misery like a simultaneous head and chest cold. Last night, your nose was like rush hour traffic during a rainstorm, so Ma took you to the emergency room for some antibiotics. Thankfully, it kicked in hard and effective. What's the use of going out if you can't breathe?

You walk up to the door of the three flat and can barely make out the last names on the bells. Assuming that the P in Parker got lost, you ring the second one that reads J. arker. It's breezy, so you pocket your hands in your jacket and turn your back to the wind as you peer down the street. The anxiety climaxes when she comes running down with a reluctant package. You must be special. As she drags her mother out by the arm, you notice that their expressions are like sugar and sin: Sharlene is sun saturated like a daisy in the spring, but mom looks like death in the morning before her coffee. Sharlene goes through the formal introduction, stands beside you and latches on your arm as if to claim ownership.

"How you doing, Miss Parker? I could've came up," you state with sincerity.

"I needed to get some cigarettes out of the car anyway," she blurts out, sounding like she's in the mood to flail somebody.

"You ought to see the article he wrote," Sharlene says with excitement. "It has a Vernon Jarrett tone to it."

"Oh really. What was it about?" she scrutinizes.

"It criticized the disparity of black managers to black athletes," you proudly utter, adding, "and how the seemingly ideal sports world mirrors the ills of society."

"Oh really," she questions without even trying to hide her cynicism. "Is there any objectivity, or is it a hypocritical editorial that doesn't hold people responsible for their own actions?"

She really does need a cigarette. Throw in a gallon of coffee, too. "It said what I wanted it to say—with an exclamation point—but it was objective in that the statistics and the quotes I used announced the theme, which is 'there's racism in sports.'"

"Uh huh. So..." she says, seemingly searching for something negative to insinuate. "Are you going to commentate on how athletes such as yourself get in trouble with drugs?"

"Mom!" Sharlene pleads through clinched teeth, clearly embarrassed.

You pause, smiling uncomfortably and retort, "That would be an excellent topic to editorialize: how the media blacklists young black athletes and the negative stereotypes it leaves with society."

You wonder if you can stay dignified while she keeps sinking in ignorance. Wrong assumptions vex you like water irks a cat, but you won't call her an asinine anus out of respect for Sharlene—even if your level *could* go that low.

She shakes off the response and grills, "So what's your excuse for beating the hell out of your girlfriend—were you a victim in that case also?"

"Mom!" Sharlene starts again as she is caught almost as off guard as you, but you cut in before she can chastise her.

"It seems that you know a lot about me," you verify, restraining your rage. Miss Parker to you is like a bucket of beer to a bladder: She pisses you the fuck off with the super quickness. "I'm sure that you've talked to Sharlene about me and she relayed my account to you, and if she didn't, you wouldn't believe what I have to say anyway, so is this press conference really necessary?"

"I'm gonna get my cigarettes. Don't be out all night Sharlene," she says, brushing in between the two of us without even excusing herself, and turns around to you, adding in a grainy tone, "And don't you put your hands on my daughter."

You were already hand-in-hand with Sharlene. "As-Salaam-Alaikum," you wit out of habit as she walks away. She doesn't respond.

"So you let Mike send you on vacation, huh?" you greet/query as you casually flip through your dictionary.

You got word shortly after you got home from the outing with Sharlene. With Roy ringing in 21, of course Carver won 60-51. He looked like Tim Hardaway out there. Simeon lost big, 86-63.

"Man," Notree starts. "He couldn't stop me. I'm just telling it like it is," he notes of the match-up with Michael Herman. "The first play of the game, I posted him up and it was a three-point play."

"So I take it you're going to follow in the steps of Nick [Anderson] and Deon [Thomas]?"

"You know that's right."

"That's a big surprise," you wit. "Well I guess that means that eliminates the Illini for me," you state, adding, "'cause I know you ain't coming off of the 25."

"It's a Simeon legacy and you know I'm holding it up."

"You and Kiwane [Garris] are going to be tight," you confirm as you ponder your college choice that is as uncertain as a Shaq free throw.

You never seriously considered Illinois, and now you sure won't find yourself on a guard-dominated squad. Confiding that if you weren't banned from U.I.C. that you might have played for them, he notes that Mark Miller (from Westinghouse) is leaning towards the Flames. You're happy for Bryant. His inspiration parallels yours. He lost a cousin when he was twelve. That was the catalyst for his dominance on the court. You reminisce with him about the three times you officially faced each other throughout the years in various tournaments. This season he stood you up on the fourth game of the season. The IHSA suspended him and super-soph Ronnie Fields for the first four games of the year for playing in an all-star game and accepting merchandise from Nike. He had you down two-to-one and you were looking forward to evening things out. You wish him peace and are surprised when he responds, "Wa-Alaikum-Salaam", considering he's not a Muslim. At least he's opened-minded with the greeting.

7

"After we pulled off, she told me that I have to ignore her sometimes because she can be a trip. A journey to the far side is more like it. We went to the game, then the show, and afterwards I took her to Red Lobster. I was trying to impress, but more than anything, I had the taste for real seafood and I thought she could handle it. So much for that theory. Not only did she act like she was used to it and expected it, but she ordered one of the most sizable dishes on the menu and had the nerve not to finish it and ask for a doggy bag. She was starting to look like a Hippo-swine. I didn't sweat it, because she was good company and I figured it might actually lead to something like a prom date, a good wife or a good night...you didn't hear that. After we got back to her house, she invited me up. Great. I had to deal with Momma Bear again.

"When we got upstairs, Sharlene led me past her mother's bedroom, where she was laying up with her 11-year-old son watching television. It almost looked kinda perverted, but I knew better since I used to sleep in the bed with you when I was younger. Nothing like young Negroes with Oedipus complexes. Sharlene led me down a hallway to the kitchen where she put her leftovers in the refrigerator. I then followed her back to the front where she had to ask her mother something. Before she could question her, Ma asked 'Where is he?' in an even snottier growl than earlier, as if I had Velcro hands. Maybe she needed a joint.

Sharlene said 'He's right here.' Her mother didn't say a thing, and after Sharlene asked her where the hair spray was, she went to the bathroom and proceeded to drown her hair in that stuff. She let me touch it and it felt like over-processed, freezer-dried seaweed. About five minutes later, her mother came back and she was still on a roll, saying 'It's time for visitors to leave' without looking at me, although I was right there. 'Especially out of the bathroom,' she said as she walked up to me and glared into my eyes, as if she was going to gouge them out.

"It was her house, so what else could I say besides 'As-Salaam-Alaikum.' Once again Sharlene was embarrassed by her mother's ignorance and she promised 'I'll call you tomorrow' as I left out the door. I started smelling my underarms as I walked down the stairs, wondering if it was my personal hygiene. Three days came and went and I didn't get a call from her, so I called her on Wednesday night, which meant that she would be home. But when a lady answered, assumably her mother, she asked 'who's calling?' When I identified myself, she abruptly said 'she's not here' and hung up. Three days later, I was driving to the post office and I spotted her walking from the bus stop. When I blew the horn, she looked surprised, turned her head real quickly, and kept walking. I couldn't stop because there was traffic behind me, so I went around the block, but she was long gone when I got back. There was no way she could disappear into thin air unless she was avoiding me. So as soon as I got home I called her and she answered. I asked why she was avoiding me, and she acquainted me to the click. As if her mother hadn't introduced me already.

"So much for another date. What a simple anus, which I attribute to a strong gene pull. She had good potential, but a bad coach. What's y'all's take on this, because I don't want to jump to conclusions," you query Ma and Uncle JoJo.

You came straight home with the purpose of having a family talk around the kitchen table. Today's Literature test B set the melancholy mood for you. The smell of Ma's hamburgers and hash browns combined with the soothing, old-school gospel sound of Albertina Walker blanketed your ill feelings as soon as you stepped through the door. When you finished pigging, you were able to put it in a humorous perspective.

"It could be a number of reasons why she took such a disliking of you," Ma concludes. "It could've been the way you smelled or looked, but she probably pegged you as a typical pretty boy athlete and made her daughter stay away from you."

"Your reputation probably didn't help, even though it's not valid," Uncle JoJo notes.

"The best thing to do is cut your losses and move on. It's not the first time and it probably won't be the last time a courtship doesn't work. She was wrong for not giving you the benefit of the doubt, but, oh well, it's her daughter's loss in the long run," Ma flatters

"Although she forfeited the game, I feel like I lost. At this point, I've lost all respect for unproven talent. That's the last time I play with rookies. From now on, I'm playing with the experienced veterans," you declare, shaking your head.

"If I'm not mistaken, haven't you had a couple of older girlfriends," Uncle JoJo verifies.

"Yeah, but they didn't come close to this level of stupidity. Sharlene has as much substance as smoke."

"On the bright side, you won't have Ms. Parker for a mother-in-law," Uncle JoJo consoles with a hearty guffaw which tickles you slightly and brings a big grin to your countenance.

"My short-term goal is a prom date. She can take a hike after that for all I care," you ponder.

"That's the least of your worries," Ma insists. "Keeping the grades up for the stretch run won't be easy with that job."

"What's my name?" you question confidently as you lean back in the chair.

BJ gave you a job lead before it was posted in the CABJ job bank. Starlin Media Services was looking for an editorial assistant to proofread, file, fact check, write (occasionally) and type. He encouraged you to call them immediately. You were off the phone with BJ a good two minutes when you had an interview set up. Your academic record, professional references and by-lines sealed the position for you. Walter Logan (the department manager) said you will start at the end of April at $10 an hour. You almost did flips out of the office. You owe BJ big time.

"Have you gotten in contact with the Chris Zorich guy?" Uncle JoJo questions. "I want to get his autograph."

"Yeah, I caught up with him the day before. He said that he'll set something up for me."

After BJ suggested a piece on Zorich, you called Halas Hall and asked to speak to him. Of course he wasn't available, so you left your name and number without giving it a second thought. Two days later, a gentleman claiming to be his agent left a message on your machine, stating that Chris asked him to contact you. You called him back, left him a message and sent him your by-line, then he called you back and left you another message. After a week of telephone tag, you got him from school and informed him who you were and what you wanted to do, and he promised to hook you up. When you told BJ about it, he bust out in stitches. He couldn't believe that you set it up like that. He informed you that you got lucky. Usually celebrities pay no attention to messages like that. He assured you that any other star would've blown you off and that the way to set it up is through the agent. You will take heed to that advice.

We all listen in unison as the Queen of Gospel anoints your ears with "Your Grace."

"Believe it or not, I like the older spirituals better than the contemporary stuff," you note as it comes to an end.

"When I was carrying you that's all I listened to."

"And your father insisted on playing it softly and even crooning them when you were in the crib."

"So Dad used to like it, huh?"

"He was fanatical about the sound, even though he drifted away from the Gospel message," Ma states. "You picked up the passion for the sound from him."

"That's not the only thing I picked up from him."

"As a covenant child, we had to give our utmost love. After all, I was barren, but the Lord gave me a fallow womb and sowed a seed of faith when I promised to dedicate you to Him as a Nazirite for life. And I sung the Song of Hannah even before I physically conceived you, because I believed in Him. Your father was caught up in the miracle of your birth for a while, but then he hardened his heart. I gave the Lord my word that I would raise you righteously when you were born—even though your father insisted on bringing you up as a Muslim—and I'm trusting that He will keep you on the path of righteousness. God gave you to me and I gave you back to Him."

You've heard the story more than a million times—usually accompanied by a hymn sung gloriously by Ma—but this account is heavier. If uncut hair was a part of the deal, it would've been blown years ago. As it is, your fickle faith may have cut the ties.

"I haven't had a pleasant dream in three months," you mention casually. "It's like my mind is blacker than that Mississippi road at night we were on three years ago. Not just any kind of blackness, but a dense darkness that I'm totally aware and scared of. I don't know what to believe or what to do."

Ma's brow wrinkles up as she asks, "What did we teach you to do when you were unsure about something?"

"Pray," you blurt. "But I've been praying, and to be honest, I don't know who I'm praying to or who to pray to."

"Before you got into that Muslim stuff, *who* used to work on your behalf?" Uncle JoJo queries.

"Jesus."

"Well why not go back to Who and what used to work?"

"I tried praying in His name a few times, but I couldn't get a reception."

"When was the last time you fasted?"

"It had to have been before the first advent, when I had enough weight to sacrifice a meal."

"I'm serious," Uncle JoJo claims.

You can remember the first time very vividly. Pastor Wells suggested the church fast for a higher level of fellowship with the Lord. He was really addressing the older members, but you took his advice. Advising the membership to fast from something that meant a lot to them besides food, he listed television and radio as examples. You took it a step further: no playing outside and no reading inside (with the exception of the Bible), in addition to no food or TV. Well, midway through, you were hurting for a McDonalds' cheeseburger. Instead of feeding that desire, you opened the Bible to Daniel 3 and it just came to life. At that moment, you realized that in life and death, God had your back, front, top and bottom. Afterwards, you decided to lay down. That's when you had the first vision of the gun pointed at you but not harming you.

"It's too long ago to remember."

"Deny the flesh and cater to the Spirit," he orders. "Make your purpose a revelation of the Truth. Have you done your homework on them? I know you read Betty Shabazz's claim that Farrakhan had something to do with Malcolm X's death in last Sunday's paper. I can tell you some shady things about that organization, but I'll leave that up to God."

You sit in muted agreement as you silently declare a partial fast from the TV, telephone, food, homework, and driving, starting in 30 minutes. It will be five, so you'll be on for twelve hours—until the break of dawn. Thankfully, you only have Calculus homework to do.

You rise and announce, "I'll be in fellowship until the morning" as you head to the meeting place. Once in your room, you read Psalm 34 in silence, throw in a Mahalia Jackson tape, cut out the lights, turn the ringer off on the phone, crawl under the sheets and shut your eyes.

"The Spirit is back," you reveal to Nicole. "The glow was unmistakable...my body could feel His presence."

"Did He ever leave?" she queries. "The Lord says He will never leave you nor forsake you. Perhaps it was dormant for two months. Have you gone any length of time without a message in your sleep?"

You nod. "Several months at a time, but that was when I was younger."

"Okay Methuselah," she cracks as she shoots a free throw, adding, "Even though you're a Gospel renegade, I believe the Holy Ghost is after you like a bounty hunter."

"Good shot," you compliment after it pops the bottom of the net.

You decided to go up to the park, since you haven't hooped since being eliminated from the playoffs, and the sun cleared the court, bringing in the warmest day of the year at 80. Slipping on your school shorts, you brought Dexter along to help you enjoy the beautiful day. Although you've spoken with Nicole since you told her to find another god, you never formally apologized. The egg was on your face long enough, so you wiped it off before you came up here with her.

"The fellowship was more frequent when I got older. It hasn't been a long gap like that in at least two years."

She gives you a questioning glance before she rims her second free throw out.

"And you know," you start as you rip the rebound down and dribble to the top of the key. "It seems like He's mad at me," you confide timidly like a child that has a misbehaving note to bring home to his evil stepparents. As you pop a string note from the top, you elaborate on the ominous ambiance of your latest encounter.

You were in the dim dining hall of a restaurant. Except for your working vision, you could have ventured to say it was dark in the forlorn room, with two exceptions: You and Khalid. Enlightenment never comes while you are slumbering or in the supernatural realm. You have to wake up and usually wait awhile for an answer. You're still waiting to gain understanding of why the smiling Khalid was serving food to you on a platter. A bigger revelation will be why you knowingly ate it, realizing that the bottom of the tray was stamped with a skull and crossbones. You might as well have been wide awake, since you could feel your stomach churning as your body broke down. You woke up gagging as if you had something to throw up. Your mouth was dry and sour, just like the postlude of a vomit. You already dreamed it seven times. "Bread From Heaven" was the solemn soundtrack. The irony is that it happened in one night. Never has the cycle ended in one night. When you woke up, what lyric was Uncle JoJo humming? "Bread From Heaven, Feed me 'til I want no more" of course.

"Sounds like He's giving you a premonition," she remarks after she catches your seventh free throw from out of the rim. "Maybe He's reeling you back in."

"I wish I could say that too, but I still don't know what to believe," you ponder as you ring in your eighth. She bounces the ball to you, and you take longer than Karl Malone. "Nicole," you call as she flashes a slight smirk and listens with her eyes. "Can you pray for me?"

You both pause, suspended in time with the basketball tick-tocking the twilight away. She gravitates to you, gapes through your windows and examines your soul. Something in there causes her brow to crinkle up.

"If you don't know, you better ask somebody," she insists with conviction as she takes your hand, calls Dexter over and forces you to your knees. "Father, in the name of *JESUS* I bind up the spirit of confusion right now my Lord. Your Word says that whatsoever we bind on earth shall be bound in Heaven; and whatsoever we loose on earth shall be loosed in Heaven. So, in the name of *Jesus* I command Satan to take his hands off of Malcolm right now. I rebuke any false doctrine that doesn't lead to eternal life, because Satan is a liar, the author of confusion. Lord, I ask that You plant Your Word deep into Malcolm's heart so that it will be a reality in his life. Give him a strong Holy Spiritual presence my Lord, and reveal the undeniable Truth to him. You said in Your Word that You are the Way, the Truth and the Life because You are the one Way, Your Word is true, and You are the source of life. So Lord, in the name of Jesus, I ask that you overwhelm Malcolm with your peace and joy. Bless him with the wisdom to discern Your voice and Your message, so that he can rightly divide the word of truth..." She went on in power, sending you home with an injection of equanimity and confidence. Before we left, we decided on a daylong fast starting at eight, for the purpose of understanding. She noted that the answers should agree. Dexter is even participating. The anticipation of the revelation is a ton on your conscience.

You go to bed with a smile, expecting an answer, and when your head hits the pillow, Heaven bombards your soul. Understanding of the visions was always veiled in abstractions. This time, there is no room for ignorance as the Spirit announces in a loud whisper *"YOU WERE BOUGHT AT A PRICE,"* as the sullen image of the suffering servant comes into focus against a dismally black background. A voice rises to a thunderous octave and narrates:

"Behold, my servant shall deal prudently, he shall be exalted and extolled, and be very high. As many were astonished at thee; his visage was so marred more than any man, and his form more than the sons of men: So shall he sprinkle many nations; the kings shall shut their mouths at him: for that which had not been told them shall they see; and that which they had not heard shall they consider..."

You try to wake up but you are not in control this time as the whole account by Isaiah in the 52nd and 53rd chapter flashes through. Then it replays six more times, ending with the epilogue: *"YOU WERE BOUGHT AT A PRICE."*

THE hand with the nail hole just above the wrist, clutches a pen as it draws an image of a mortal. Every minute detail of that man is you, from the 6'5" pinstripe frame to all twenty-five blessed after-marks of the heavenly beings sprinkled on your nose and cheek. You're decked out in home white with the number 7 stamped in pure gold on your chest as the Author maps out your life, from the time you praised away the rabies from the German Shepherd that bit you in the second grade (you didn't even go to the hospital, but that dog sure went to the glue factory) to the time you sacrificed your own hunger and allowance money to feed the beggar his last meal (the Spirit allowed you see him praise the Lord after he took his last swallow and go home to glory).

But then you get puffed up with writer's pride. You grab the pen and try to finish your own life. Immediately, you have to try to scratch out the lies, sex, and videotapes of more lies and sex. You wind up with ink smeared all over you. You're sweating mud and blood. Not even a complete sentence before the Author finishes what he started, by drawing a living hologram of a Lion. Without even a blink, it morphs into a Lamb. You're right up on it, admiring the sparkling white wool and the innocence of its aquatic green eyes. Not even a hint of impurity or defect. However, you watch in horror as the sickle slashes His neck. You try to holler, but no sound comes out as the blood sprays you from head to toe. The Spirit whispers, ***"Behold, the Lamb of God, which taketh away sin of the world."***

You weep as the deep dark sky consumes you and eclipses your hope. Midnight is only a minute, but the Dayspring is eternal. The Sun of Righteousness shines on you, revealing that you have been washed clean with the blood. When you look back, the errors of your life have been whited out and the Lamb comes to life and assumes the image and role of Lion again. You look forward to your infinite written life. The details are unclear and the earthly chapter has an end, however, there is an eternal, glorious chapter that begins where it ends. Just as the Lion roars, the thunder in the natural cracks simultaneously as your eyes pop open to reveal an unobstructed view through your window of the Bright and Morning Star. Your clock radio as playing a Stephanie Mills sounding gospel cut with the refrain "Everybody Ought To Know." The lead singer rings off some of the names of Jesus as the background vocalists keep repeating the verse. Now you know.

"You look like a muffler that's been dragged from the bottom of a car," Nick testifies as she sits across from you in the school library.

The cold that took you all the way to the emergency room at three in the morning; that you took antibiotics for and thought you licked after the third day—so you stopped taking the medication—is back with an attitude. You started taking the medicine again, but it seems to energize the bug like vitamins. So yes, you look bad. Your head weighs a ton, your eyes are crying gold oatmeal, your chest is full of orange jelly, and your nose is flowing like Niagara Falls. You've been wiping with that 20-lb. bond paper that the school calls tissue and you've scraped a layer of your facial epidermis off.

"And I feel like a muffler that's dragging from the bottom of a car on a bumpy street," you attest. "But it's all good, 'cause the Lord spoke to me last night."

"I had no doubt," she says as she pulls out her Bible. "Sorry I'm late, but that meeting ran over," she mentions of a special meeting between the Meredith Corporation and a handful of the top students in the school. "And would you know that Traci showed out in your honor."

"What?"

"The reason you weren't included was because of your soiled reputation. Only model students were qualified for the scholarship."

"My reputation is just bad press," you defend.

"Traci tried to explain that, and since they weren't trying to hear it, she blew up and excluded herself. She defended you like her life depended on it and flew out with tears in her eyes. I followed suit. And let me tell you Mal, it was a lot of money."

"I guess that explains why she stormed past without speaking," you recall of the trail of smoke she left just as you entered the library. "I don't feel right about that."

"It'll all work out for the good, so don't sweat it."

"Thanks for taking a stand for me."

"Don't mention it," she says. "Did you hear how Deon's sister OD'd on his stuff?"

"Really?"

"Almost died. I hear he's pretty distraught over it."

"I can imagine," you empathize.

"I'm going to give him a call," she declares, and shifts to the offensive. "*And let me see if I can save him.*"

"Be it known unto you that by the name of Jesus Christ of Nazareth...neither is there salvation in any other: for there is none other name under heaven given among men, whereby we must be saved (Acts 4:10, 12)," you affirm through the power from on high.

Nick smiles and fires, "Only God can save...who died and made Jesus God" and waits for the Spirit of Truth to bring the Word to your remembrance as she takes you through an ordination like quiz.

He doesn't disappoint, bringing back scriptures that you haven't looked over in a couple of years. "In the beginning was the Word, and the Word was with God, and the Word was God...and the Word became flesh, and dwelt among us (John 1:1, 14)."

"So what makes you think that this God wants to save you?"

"For God so loved the world that He gave His only begotten son that whosoever belietheth in Him should not perish, but have everlasting life (John 3:16)."

"You gotta do better than that phony, luvydovy, New Testament scripture that you learned in preschool. You ain't read about no love coming from Allah in the Old Testament. Allah is *merciful.*"

"Contrary Satan, for Deuteronomy 4 and 37 says, '*And because he loved thy fathers, therefore he chose their seed after them, and brought thee out in his sight with his mighty power out of Egypt*', and the

Prophet Jeremiah says in the 31st chapter and 3rd verse, *'The Lord hath appeared of old unto me, saying, Yea, I have loved thee with an everlasting love: therefore with loving kindness have I drawn thee'*."

"What an uninformed fool you are—adopting a doctrine of love from the white devil who was created by Yakub the rebellious scientist."

"For the time will come when they will not endure sound doctrine; but after their own lusts shall they heap to themselves teachers, having itching ears; And they shall turn away their ears from the truth, and shall be turned unto fables (2 Timothy 4:3-4)."

"It's obvious you have too much chitterlings on the brain. You are what you eat, and since you eat swine, you're too filthy to know the truth from a fable."

"Now the Spirit speaketh expressly, that in the latter times some shall depart from the faith, giving heed to seducing spirits, and doctrines of devils; Speaking lies in hypocrisy; having their conscience seared with a hot iron; Forbidding to marry, and commanding to abstain from meats, which God hath created to be received with thanksgiving of them which believe and know the truth. For every creature of God is good, and nothing to be refused if it be received with thanksgiving: For it is sanctified by the word of God and prayer (1 Timothy 4:1-5)."

"Jesus didn't give the okay to eat any and everything."

"Jesus declared all foods clean when he said *'There is nothing from without a man, that entering into him can defile him: but the things which come out of him, those are they that defile the man; Because it entereth not into his heart, but into the belly, and goeth out into the draught, purging all meats (Mark 7:15, 19).'*"

"Muhammad was the most Holy prophet of Allah and explicitly denied Jesus as the Son of God or God in the flesh. If he recognized Jesus as only a prophet, you have to consider his words."

"Beloved, believe not every spirit, but try the spirits whether they are of God: because many false prophets are gone out into the world. Hereby know ye the Spirit of God: Every spirit that confesseth that Jesus Christ is come in the flesh is of God: And every spirit that confesseth not that Jesus Christ is come in the flesh is not of God: and this is that spirit of antichrist, whereof ye have heard that it should come; and even now already is it in the world (1 John 4:1-3)."

"Whatever. It was your own *Apostle* Paul who said no good thing dwells in the flesh, which makes your Jesus a pretty *bad* brother. I would say that he's a little unqualified to even be in the presence of God."

"Paul also said, *'For the law of the Spirit of life in Christ Jesus hath made me free from the law of sin and death. For what the law could not do, in that it was weak through the flesh, God sending his own Son in the likeness of sinful flesh, and for sin, condemned sin in the flesh (Romans 8:2-3),'* and *'Seeing then that we have a great high priest, that is passed into the heavens, Jesus the Son of God, let us hold fast our profession. For we have not a high priest which cannot be touched with the feeling of our infirmities; but was in all points tempted like as we are, yet without sin (Hebrews 4:14-15).'*"

"Chapter 55 of the Gospel of Barnabas states that *'Jesus cursed everyone who called Him the Son of God'*."

"But though we, or an angel from heaven, preach any other gospel unto you than that which we have preached unto you, let him be accursed. As we said before, so say I now again, If any man preach any other gospel unto you than that ye have received, let him be accursed (Galatians 1:8-9)."

"Spoken well by the great Apostle Paul. Barnabas was right when he said Paul has been deceived. No wonder he had a problem getting along with Barnabas. This same Paul asked, *'But if there be no resurrection of the dead, then is Christ not risen? And if Christ be not risen, then is our preaching in vain, and your faith is also in vain?'* in 1st Corinthians 15 and 13 through 14," she emphasizes as she slides the Bible to you. "Your boy sounds a little flaky and unsure about the resurrection."

"For context and clarification, verses 1 through 4 state, *'Moreover, brethren, I declare unto you the gospel which I preached unto you, which also ye have received, and wherein ye stand; By which also ye are saved, if ye keep in memory what I preached unto you, unless ye have believed in vain. For I delivered unto you first of all that which I also received, how that Christ died for our sins according to the scriptures; And that he was buried, and that he rose again the third day according to the scriptures,'*" you declare, pointing to the passage.

"How is Jesus going to die for you when Deuteronomy 24 and 16 states, *'The fathers shall not be put to death for the children, neither shall the children be put to death for the fathers: every man shall be put to death for his own sin?'*"

"For the life of the flesh is in the blood: and I have given it to you upon the altar to make an atonement for your souls: for it is the blood that maketh an atonement for the soul (Leviticus 17:11); But Christ being come a high priest of good things to come, by a greater and more perfect tabernacle, not made with hands, that is to say, not of this building; Neither the blood of goats and calves, but by his own blood he entered in once into the holy place, having obtained eternal redemption for us. For if the blood of bulls and of goats, and the ashes of a heifer sprinkling the unclean, sanctifieth to the purifying of the flesh: How much more shall the blood of Christ, who through the eternal Spirit offered himself without spot to God, purge your conscience from dead works to serve the living God? (Hebrews 9:11-14); And almost all things are by the law purged with blood; and without shedding of blood is no remission (Hebrews 9:22). And as it is appointed unto men once to die, but after this the judgment: So Christ was once offered to bear the sins of many; and unto them that look for him shall he appear the second time without sin unto salvation (Hebrews 9:27-28). ...Behold the Lamb of God, which taketh away the sin of the world (John 1:29b)."

You have no idea where she got all of that heresy from, but the simulation sounded religiously, dogmatically demonic. You couldn't have studied for that onslaught, but surely the Lord has prepared you.

She grins knowingly at you, and proclaims, "Apologetics accepted."

Angela agreed to take you to the doctor to get a different prescription of antibiotics. When she opens the door, you hear Dexter Junior rehearsing for a solo on Sunday. The lyrics start the healing process even before you set out for the hospital.

"I once was lost in sin
but Je - sus took me in,
And then a little light from heaven
filled my soul;
It bathed my heart in love
and wrote my name a - bove,
And just a lit - tle talk with Je - sus
made me whole.
Now let us
    Have a lit - tle talk with Je - sus

let us
tell Him all a - bout our trou - bles,
He will
Hear our faint - est cry,
and He will
an - swer by and by;
Now when you
Feel a lit - tle pray'r wheel turn - ing,
and you
know a lit - tle fire is burn - ing,
You will
Find a lit - tle talk with Je - sus makes it right
it makes it right."

Dex used to sing that hymn around the house. It struck you as odd that the choir never sung it up until today. That's a non-issue though, because his namesake was chanting it with cherubic passion, poetic rhythm, and polished tone. You could actually feel it in your bones, and not because the volume was too high, but the Spirit penetrated your body and confirmed, touched and agreed with everything that you've gotten to that point.

Khalid sat stoically with his arms folded, mouth poked out and eyes intense as he shifted with an attitude throughout the serenade. That pew must have had coals beneath it. The contemporary keyboarding couldn't break through his stony frown. He ached for some venom directed at the white society. Brian was clueless to and curious of the anointing as he lightly bobbed his head and an involuntary smirk formed on his face. You clapped and rocked jubilantly when DJ turned the church out. You extended an invitation to them with the bait "I've been to the Mosque, but you've never been to Walk of Faith." They couldn't argue, although they reluctantly agreed.

Either today is Khalid's day or the Lord decided to Word whoop him, because Pastor Wells preached the Gospel message—Jesus died, Jesus buried, Jesus resurrected—from 1 Corinthians 15:1-4. That was the backdrop to the message titled "Shades of Black." His text was taken from Jeremiah 13 and 23a (Can a black man change the color of his skin...Good News Translation) and Song of Solomon 1:5-6 (I am black, but comely, O ye daughters of Jerusalem, as the tents of Kedar, as the curtains of Solomon. Look not upon me, because I am black, because the sun hath looked upon me: my mother's children were angry with me; they made me the keeper of the vineyards, but mine own vineyard have I not kept). You assessed the message as the greatest you've heard preached by any minister. He expounded on the context—context being fundamental—of the verse in Jeremiah by explaining that the prophet was addressing the people of Jerusalem—who had become so accustomed to sin that it seemed nearly impossible to bring them to repentance—and predicting there divine punishment as a result of their apostasy. Though contextually it seems impractical for a black man to change his complexion, Pastor Wells answered the question with a resounding "YES", commenting that the grace of God is reflected in the skin tone of black folks. Going over to Genesis 11:1-9, he noted that the different races came about by the settling of mankind in different parts of the globe (The hotter the sun in a region, the darker the skin tone; the less intense the heat, the lighter the complexion), not because Noah had tri-colored seeds in his secrets.

He explained that the Shulamite woman in the Song of Solomon represents the church that has gone through ostracization and persecution and King Solomon represents Christ. He compared the Shulamite woman to African-Americans: Of course blackness is viewed as ugly—even by some of the non-coloreds who profess to be followers of Christ—but Jesus sees us as His beautiful bride; the adversity has given us a reputation and a more profound image; the country was built on the labor of Blacks without just compensation or equal opportunity while Africa was ravaged. "When one rejects you, they reject Jesus, and when one rejects Jesus, they reject you. When Miriam spoke against Moses, they included his Ethiopian wife. How are you going to love a woman's face and loathe her body, with all of its sagging fatness and cellulite? Likewise, if you're satisfied with the body but not the head, you can't put a bag over the face. You either love it all in the fullness of the ugliness or reject it all," he declared. Of course the church is going to be dissed if Christ—the Head of the church—was played like a peon. "But rest assured: you are precious in Jesus' sight," he concluded.

If Khalid was a lighter shade of black, he would've turned red. Instead, he sweated it out and almost combusted. During the invitation, he glared defiantly at the Pastor as he held his seat. Needless to say that he was the first one out after the benediction.

"That Negro was stuck on his white Jesus," Khalid spits, which you saw coming an hour ago.

You advise him "Let's not go there," without even giving him an acknowledging glance as we continue to stroll through the campus of Chicago State to the Library.

"Let's go there," he snaps. We all stop in the midst of the field of trees. "I wanted to go up there and tell him how foolish it was to have faith in a lie. Jesus gave up His life and took it back? FOOLISHNESS!"

You turn to his intense face and calmly ask, "Doesn't Jesus say in the scriptures that 'I am the Way, the *Truth* and the Life', meaning that faith in him is the only way to the Father, that he speaks the truth, and that a belief in Him is the source of life? And what about His proclamation of being the Resurrection?"

"It's all about understanding. Jesus never claimed to be Allah."

"Didn't the gospel of John quote Jesus as claiming, *'I and my Father are one,'* in addition to His references to being the Son of God?"

"One in purpose, not in deity. C'mon Black man. That's almost as ridiculous as a Tri-head God. God is one. One plus one plus one equals three. Three doesn't equal one. That defies all types of mathematical laws...it defies logic and common sense," he says condescendingly, which brings out the ignorant debater in you.

"What's ridiculous is that you revere a man as *the* Christ even though he was guilty of adultery. *Adultery!* From a spiritual standpoint of a supposed savior, that charge is too serious to wink at. If Jesus had slept with His followers, it would've been tantamount to spiritual bestiality since Christ is known as the Good Shepherd and his followers are the flock of sheep. That alone would kill Christ's credibility. Elijah didn't die a sinless life as Jesus did, so as good and great as he was, he wasn't *the* Savior. A sinner can't save a sinner. And contrary to your reasoning that things don't come in three's, just look at Mankind. According to 1st Thessalonians 5 and 23, he is body, soul and spirit. And take water: it comes in gas, liquid and solid forms. The gas being like the Father, Who is Spirit that can't be restricted by space; the liquid being like the Holy Ghost that fills the believer and is the Living Water that comes from Christ the Solid Rock, as in solid ice that is condensed into space. True, one plus one plus one equals three, but you need to expand your mathematical mind, Black man, because you're using the wrong formula. One times one times one equals one. I'm sure you could go for a glass of that water now."

Brian is stunned silent as we heat up.

"I see you're buying into the white way of thinking. After all of the revival efforts, you're still dead to that white lie about a white Jesus that died and rose again..."

"...died, buried, and resurrected," you correct.

"Jesus was a prophet of Allah..."

"...and the only Potentate, the King of Kings, Lord of Lords, *the* Messiah, *the* Savior, *the* Christ, Good Shepherd, Suffering Servant, Friend, Big Brother, Lamb of God, Lion from the Tribe of Judah, Wonderful Counselor, Mighty God, Everlasting Father, Prince of Peace, High Priest, the Temple of God, Bridegroom, Captain of our Salvation, Head of the Church, the Bread of Life—as in the manna bread from heaven that the Israelites ate in the wilderness, the Rock from whom the Spirit of Life flows—just as the Rock in the wilderness provided water for the children of Israel, the Word of God...take your pick," you fire without giving him a chance to answer any of the titles.

"White lies...Blacks were Muslims before they were Christians," he argues.

"Explain this to me, my brother: How is it that Blacks were so-called Muslims first, when the Bible clearly teaches that Christianity was in Africa 500 years before the prophet Muhammad founded Islam? The copyright of the Qur'an was 500 years after the Holy Scriptures, Khalid...How is Muhammad going to refute the testimony of all of those biblical witnesses of the Gospel of Jesus, when he came 25 generations after the fact? Even if the case was questionable, he wouldn't even be a credible witness in a court of law."

"That's according to your poisoned Bible."

"Poisoned Bible?" You guffaw at his hypocrisy. "It's amazing how well you quote and ascribe to that poison. I love pizza, but if I knew that some of the slices were contaminated with cyanide, I wouldn't touch any parts of it; if a drop of urine dropped in my glass of water, the whole cup is dirty. Basically, you're more ignorant than me—based on your reasoning—since you believe that the Bible has been tampered with, yet you still use it."

"I don't put my faith in it because I can discern the obvious errors and you're foolish because I've pointed out how 2nd Chronicles 9:25 and

1st Kings 4:26 give conflicting numbers for chariots for King Solomon. Yet, the Bible is your only reference."

"It's funny how you can make an issue of a numerical mistranslation that's based on a misplaced zero. One zero off. Logic will tell you that it has the same root. And since you're on this error trip, let's journey to the holy Qur'an. Sura 21 and 76 states that all of Noah's sons were saved from the flood, while Sura 11 and 43 states that one of them perished. Your issue is a numerical non-issue when it's all said and done, but this is an issue of life and death; salvation and damnation, and the Qur'an has a quicksand foundation when it comes to that."

He draws closer to your face with the intention of intimidation—you assume. "Allah will judge everyone accordingly. He knows who submits and who doesn't," he insists.

Brian comes close with the intention of separating us, if necessary.

"Let's say that Allah is God and that he judges fairly. Let's also assume that Allah is holy and can't fellowship with sin. If Allah is a holy, righteous judge, how are you going to stand in front of him with your own righteousness? My God will cast you in hell if you come to Him talking about how good you are. I have an Advocate in Jesus who pleads my case when Satan accuses me before the Righteous Judge, who is also Jesus. And since Jesus was fully man and fully God, He's my Mediator to God and God's Mediator to me," you boldly claim, adding with cool conviction, "I believe in the blood of Christ. I accept His sacrifice as my Propitiation."

"What a shame," he resolves as his fire quenches.

"I am not ashamed of the gospel of Christ: for it is the power of God unto salvation to every one that believeth."

We pause as Brian looks on in tense anticipation.

"Isn't it one god and doesn't Islam and Christianity serve him in different ways," Brian reasons/questions.

"No," you declare. "Jehovah and Allah have totally different plans of salvation, and let me tell you, one of those roads leads to damnation, and I can tell you with confidence that it's not the Way of Jesus."

"So that's how it's going to be?" Khalid verifies.

"By the grace of God, I am what I am, and that's how it is. Brothers are on the struggle, so you fight the war your way and I'll fight the war Christ's way."

He probes you earnestly and insists, "Let's help our brother get into Purdue," as he breaks the stare and reinitiates the trek towards the library.

The good news is that the medication killed the germs. All of the symptoms went south. The bad news is that the antibiotics are killing you hard. After two days of religiously taking it as instructed, you were feeling nauseous. Your chest tightened up in school, and at one point, your mouth dripped a river. And talk about the worst stomach cramps known to man. Nick often detailed the belly pains as a result of her monthly cycle and claimed that it was like medieval torture. You could actually understand her analogy. No one should hurt as bad as you did.

Today—the third day—you couldn't make it to school. Just before Ma got home, the queasy feeling came on strong, so you stood over the toilet. As water poured rapidly out of your mouth, your stomach buckled you over. If a man is too proud to pray, he will pray if he sensed the death angel patting him on the back. It wasn't fancy, articulate or wordy, but you prayed "Lord have mercy" as your face numbed up, your body chilled over and your vision tunneled in. And He answered affirmative. The medication-tainted sickness hurled out with gale force into the toilet, leaving a bitter after-taste similar to the dream's remnants. The sensation came back to your face, your body temperature rose and you spotted Ma out the corner of your eyes. Her prognosis was an allergic reaction to the drug, so she rushed you to Provident Hospital, although you felt better.

Your legs feel like melted ice cream as you get out of the car. After you manage to make it in unassisted, you lean against the Triage desk, pull out your medical card with your information and hand it to the red, dreaded nurse. Apparently, she can't read, because she snaps, "I don't need that" and proceeds to get the information orally from you. After she takes your vitals, she orders you to have a seat and assures, "You'll be called shortly."

Shortly lasts through three sitcoms as you shift every 30 seconds in the chair that was tailored for a stick character with no curves (You're a toothpick man with a shape). After managing to doze off, you go into a coma, die and enter into the glorious presence of the Lord. Four days later you are funeralized at Walk of Faith and buried at Oakwood Cemetery, a few feet from Mayor Harold Washington. After the new millennium, you decompose into dust—by which time the church is raptured, so you get your glorified body. Seven years later, the Lord comes back, you judge the world with Jesus, rein with Him for 1000 years, watch Satan get cast into the Lake of Fire, observe the fruition of the new heaven and the new earth, and they still haven't called you.

After Ma funks the waiting area up with complaints to three different employees, she ends up speaking to the intake nurse. The exchange is long and casually calm. Ma makes her way back to you and says, "Go talk to her before I throw her out of the window. She thinks you're too dumb to speak for yourself."

Your body and mind were sagging like a bag of broken glass up to this point. Now you have energy to burn, and burn is what you do. She *thinks* she has an attitude when you get up there. You don't give her a chance to signify. Standing over her, you grow stupid alliterate.

"You're a dreadful, dragon-dread doomed Doberman-bitch to the deepest degree in every despicable, degradable sense of the word for being so fucking ignorant, ignoble and intransigent. Firstly, it's obvious that I'm sick, otherwise why would I be here; secondly, as you can see, I don't need a mouthpiece...don't insult me. Being weak, I didn't feel like talking and you were too stupid and insensitive to even read the medical card. I hope you get your tongue ripped out and have an intake nurse just like yourself register you. And thirdly, my mother being a medical professional herself would know hospital procedures and how things should be prioritized. If I had a legal issue, I'm going to utilize a lawyer if I can; likewise, I have a medical administration issue, so I use my mother as a mouthpiece. Personally, you don't have to go to school to understand the concept of prioritizing sick folks. If I had known I was going to go six hours without seeing a doctor, I would have called my registration in or died in the comforts of my own home rather than come here to be patronized by a callous ass such as yourself," you growl as all of the steam is blown out.

Without giving her the honor of a response, you turn and pace to the bathroom. You're so worked up that you don't realize there is residual medicine in your belly. Without warning, your body discharges the remains, leaving your stomach totally empty and craving some real food. The rancorous after-thought to the tirade, coupled with the foul taste of the vomit elicits the realization of an unsanctified mouth.

"What's the matter?" Ma asks as you emerge with the spiritual taste slapped out of your mouth.

"The Holy Spirit just washed my mouth out with the blood of Jesus," you state as you head up to the Triage.

In like style as five minutes prior, you erupt. "I apologize for the terrible things I just said to you. I had no right and I ask that you forgive me."

She nods and says, "It's forgiven."

"God bless you," you say as you leave without seeing the doctor.

"Hello."

"Hi," Traci returns dryly as she welcomes you in without the formal rhetoric. You follow her to the living room couch where some Columbia College literature is spread out for consumption. "Can you believe I'm still undecided. It's only the most important decision of my short life. Things should be more simple."

"If it makes you feel better, I'm still undecided as well," you assure. "And I don't have many good choices outside of Northwestern, since Columbia doesn't have a basketball team."

"I like Columbia a lot, but there are a lot of colorful characters there."

"What...you're not into green dreads, throat piercing and black fingernails? It's a place where you can express yourself to the utmost. You can compete with the other gifted cuckoos."

"I would rather go to cartoon central, but at this point, I'm willing to go to junior college to get out of Louis. I'm so sick of high school, it makes me want to get high," she says exasperated.

You force an agreeing chuckle as you contemplate your purpose for the visit. "Listen," you start as she continues to mill through the information. "I heard about the stand you took on my behalf and I just want to say thank you."

She nods without looking up. "Phony money is of very little value to me," she huffs, pauses and shifts back to Columbia. "Every area on here is appealing. I love to dance, but I don't think I want a job that has to do with theatre. I wish I had the time and money to sample it all, from journalism—radio, print and broadcasting—management and marketing to art, film, and music," she says wistfully, flipping through the pages of the catalogue. "To tell you the truth, sometimes I question whether I want to be in the communications field, especially broadcasting. Have you noticed all of the snobs at the CABJ meetings? They act like you're too beneath them to even see you. They have an 'I, I, I' and 'me, me, me' air about themselves, which is totally nauseating."

You nod and explain, "You're going to have phoniness in every field and every organization from Real Estate to Religion; from the NAACP to the National Association of Street Cleaners. Superiority complexes are the nature of the beast known as mankind."

"Hmph," she ponders. "Maybe you're right."

"I know I am," you boast, joking, "Besides, you should fit right in with the snobs. You just happen to be a lower case I at the moment."

She whacks you with a brochure.

"But seriously, it would be a waste of skills for you to avoid the field because of some of the negative elements that plague all terrains."

She looks intently at you and nods her agreement. "You know Malcolm, you're okay, and if you were a little wider, I'd sell my soul to claim you as my own."

You guffaw at that confession from the blind side. Normally you're overly sensitive about skinny jokes, especially coming from women. Charlotte was good for degrading your legs, often comparing them to vulture-ravaged chicken drumsticks. Most of the time she was playing; other times she was being mean. Many days you sweated it out in warm-ups, rather than show her your calves. However, there are no hard feelings in Traci's joke. The insinuation almost sounded like a compliment.

"Well, you're all of that, too, except I like my women looking way up to me instead of staring me eye-to-eye."

We both roll over.

Then you switch back to the subject. "You should've taken the money. There wouldn't have been any hard feelings on this end. I would have been happy for you. After all, it would've put you in a position to pay me restitution," you insist.

"Malcolm," she calls, looking up and into your eyes. "The scholarship they offered me would've made things very comfortable for me and my daughter. I could've gone away and lived luxuriously during my college years. There would've been enough money for me to get into a new set of wheels. And that's not including the other scholarships and awards I have and will probably get. Right now, I'm at about the

$12,000 mark, which doesn't include the free ride I'm going to get once I decide on a school. But I don't regret it a bit for turning it down the way that I did. I know sometimes I'm a bitch with you—especially when it comes to the grades—but it's only because you make me work harder. If you weren't so close to me academically, I would've relaxed and put forth a half effort. It wasn't fair for them to exclude you for not being a model citizen, especially since I've witnessed first hand how you're treated unjustly by the media. My eyewitness account makes me want to break in and show an objective angle of the black community. And I will. Unfairness aside, I believe that friendship is priceless, and if the amount was doubled, I would've been cussing. Besides, you would've done the same, so there's nothing to it."

You smile, scoot over and embrace her as you choke up slightly.

Your gratitude is taken care of, now for the confession, which is going to be hard after that. "I have something to tell you," you state, gently pulling back. You drop the details of that night as you peer into her eyes. Throughout the account, she stares aimlessly through you. When the whole story is out, her eyes glaze over and she trembles slightly as she remains in the stationary position.

"I'm really sorry..."

"How could you?" She cuts in. Her eyes are focused just below and behind your face.

"I didn't mean for it to happen."

"You didn't even make sure I was safe. I would have never left you exposed like that."

"I didn't realize you were in harms way...I would've done things differently..."

"My mother beat the hell out me for that...I couldn't sit for a whole fuckin' month...I have a baby by a mystery man...I'll forever live with this. Mal...you've cut me to the bone...nobody has ever hurt me this bad, even my enemies who had evil intentions," she insists as her voice intensity rises a few octaves with each utterance. She takes a deep breath, but still refuses to look at you, and calmly claims, "I don't ever want to see you again."

"Traci..."

"GET OUT!" she shrills as the tears gush down her cheeks.

You collect your bag and let yourself out without another peep as she starts sobbing.

8

Surprisingly, you aren't the least bit nervous, and it has nothing to do with the athletic camaraderie. Of course, you are exploding with professional excitement, but the prospect of interviewing Chris Zorich sets you at ease. After all, there is enough neutral conversation to keep it loose.

He grew up in the same neighborhood as you, and when you were ten, Ben took you up in the stadium and you got a glimpse of him in his senior year at Chicago Vocational. Ben wasn't there for the game, but for the "game", as he put it. You were the perfect pawn and conversation piece. Once he scoped the stands, he set his sights on Tonya, a fudge-toned, baby-faced sophomore (her school jacket had her name and class of 1989) with breasts bigger than basketballs. As Ben eyed her, you thought he was going to go for a steal and dribble them out of the stadium. Although you enjoyed the games he took you to, it was more thrilling for him to send you in the direction of some unwitting female to play lost and be cute. How he discerned which women to play that game with remains a mystery. All you know is that he got the digits and she ended up mounted on his figurative wall of good fortune, with the rest of the his trophies. Ben has since settled down and gotten serious about his religious convictions.

You did all of the research on his career, from high school, through Notre Dame, and on to the Bears. His personal life adds several interview queries that just begs for quotes, like the bittersweet January that his mother died and he was drafted by the Bears, how he was bullied as a kid, and his well documented holiday benevolence.

Traci was the designated photographer for this assignment, but ever since you disclosed the actual event of that night, things haven't been picture-perfect between us. If she doesn't hate you, she's only a minute degree shy on the emotional thermometer. Photos aren't necessary, but illustrations attract readers and add authenticity to the story. Besides, you want more than an oral record as a memento of the interview. Instead of going to one of the other staff members, you decided to get the photo credits and practice. And you brought Angela and Dexter along to snap the shot of you and Chris together.

"Isn't it pretty out here, Dexter?" Angela queries. "When Mal makes the NBA, he's going to buy one of these big houses," she comments, winking at you.

"It'll be a weekend getaway for all of us. That way, when we want to go to Great America, we'll already be out this way. Does that tickle your fancy?"

Junior beams and nods.

"You and your vocabulary," Angela comments.

"What about it," you question. "Do I use too many big words?"

"Not at all. Dexter was always impressed with it and joked that someone could think that you were complimenting them, when you were actually scarifying them."

"Scarify," you repeat as you pull out your Franklin electronic dictionary. "Lacerate the feelings of," you read with one eye and watch the road with the other. "To assail with withering oral or written denunciation. Lambaste, blister, castigate, roast, scathe. I like that word, Angela."

"I knew you would. I found it in my thesaurus just for you."

"So you don't mind if I use it?"

"It's all yours," she assures. "Why do you use so many uncommon words?"

You chuckle a little and think about it briefly, although you know why. "It makes dialogue more interesting. I'm a writer and often everyday terms become trite."

"See what I mean," she cuts in.

"Words get overused and boring, so me and other writers try to think of more creative ways of saying something, so that we don't put our readers to sleep. I'll admit that sometimes my mind gets real active and manifests a lot of esoteric terms that make it seem like I'm speaking a foreign language, but that's me."

"Keep your mind active and stay true to you, because your vocabulary is fresh."

You smile your concordance as "New Life" marinates your mood for the second time as you turn off on and zip down Deerpath Road. Angela's "Kim McFarland" tape took you away from the South side snarl even before you hit Lake Shore Drive. Lake Forest chimes a different tune as you observe the lifestyle of the rich and famous houses. A lack of colored folks in the ratio is the only exception to the vivid backdrop.

Flourishing green, perfectly manicured lawns lay at the sides; rabbits, geese, raccoons and swans harmonize like characters in a Disney musical, caroling hap-hap-happy happy happy Oolalala; suburbanites ride their bicycles on rainbows; soggy dogs host swimming pool parties with chatty cats. There are welcome mats in front of open doors. Driveways showcase exotic wheels that are only common in big budget action movies or fantasy car magazines. The natives float nonchalantly down the street, oblivious to the wild under currents of the inner city on the outer limits of their world.

It's nice and must be nice to have the means. However, you're not envious. If you had the means, you would focus on developing your surroundings, as opposed to spiritually and temporally detaching yourself from your people. It's too easy to forget your roots when you don't see or hear them. Chris Zorich is an exception to that notion. He cribs in the burbs, but he hangs out all around the city. Wanting and having a nice house in a nice neighborhood isn't detestable. It's when a person closes his eyes to the disadvantaged, that scorn is deserved. There were sad clouds singing the grays when you left the city. The sun grins knowingly at you in Lake Forest.

The directions from PR man Doug Akins guide you through the front door without getting amended instructions from a gas station. A gentleman walking out as you are coming in informs you that the team is still practicing at the Bubble when you query him. Gracefully, he allows you to follow him out there. The distance is covered in five minutes. As you pull into the parking lot, the facility seems to blossom. The doom is too much to take in for Dexter's eyes as he gazes with an open mouth. "Don't forget: adjust the aperture for depth of field—for more distinct pictures; adjust shutter speed for action shots—to freeze motion and always..."

"Make sure the light meter needle is in the middle," we recite, exiting the car.

When you walk through the opening, you are met with a blitzing wall of wind that almost keeps you out. The gusty line of defense is all that separates you from the players as you find yourself on the opposite end of the practice field. Every Bear and wanna-be Bear seems to be drilling at the other end. You immediately spot Zorich in his number 97 jersey. It must be a light contact practice, because they're wearing helmets and no shoulder pads. You peer down the sideline at all of the photographers and spectators and excitedly start towards the action end, when some type of Bears' police in a blue windbreaker halts you and orders you to wait. You don't have a problem with it, but Angela clicks her lips and wanders down the sideline, snapping shots with the rest of the photographers.

That's why you liked Angela for Dexter: Whereas Dexter was God's compassionate voice of reason, Angela was the hand of God with a rod in it to exercise judgment. He wasn't henpecked out of his pants by no means. She honored the divine marriage order and wore well-fitted dresses. However, she kept things within the line of reason. They were a Sunday school teaching team. Whenever the kids would get out of hand, Dexter would patiently tell them to behave about 99 times. On the hundredth time, Angela would get her purse strap out. It didn't really physically hurt, but they feared it, so therefore respected it. Dexter agreed to everything from speaking engagements at different churches and bringing the Junior choir to sing a couple of selections at a musical to MCing the Fried Chicken in the Kitchen Club's 150th anniversary and leading a clothes drive. Often times, his commitments would overlap each other and he would end up canceling something. It got to the point where it took him far away from his family. Angela wasn't having it. To the dismay of the older deacons, she handled his schedule. He was never overloaded with church work (his kingdom work was spontaneous and Angela didn't restrict that) and had time for his family.

You reluctantly follow her lead. When she gets a quarter ways down, a short pass play is run to our side of the field. Although they're not tackling, they are running full speed and making heavy contact. Maurice Douglass and Joe Cain force the play out of bounds right in front of you as Angela just snaps away.

"Good shot," you encourage as the urge to bear hug her grows. You manage to make it all the way to the end of the field for a better view.

"Television sure makes them look like average size citizens," Angela notes.

"I know. It looks like some of them *are* wearing shoulder pads."

Some of the big names and big players are recognizable by number, such as Alonzo Spellman, James "Big Cat" Williams, Barry Minter, and Jim Flanigan. Even from a distance, they make you seem like a toy soldier in an old time Godzilla movie.

A few more plays are run before practice ends and the players start off the field. Before you can advise her, Angela is walking towards Chris and snapping his picture. He looks almost surprised as you walk up to him and introduce yourself. "I'm Malcolm Johnson," you declare, extending your hand.

"Oh okay," he says as a smile of relief spreads across his face. "*You* left me the message."

"That's me. And this is Dexter Junior, my assistant," you state as Dex gives him his hand.

"What's up, big Dexter," Chris greets as his hand almost swallows up Junior's whole arm. "Who's your favorite team?"

"The Bears," he says nervously.

"My man," he says as he pats him on the head. "We'll do the interview back at Halas Hall," he informs you.

"Okay...I'll see you then," you reply, heading off with the rest of the team.

Before you get to the exit, the security guy confronts you. "I told you to wait there. What if one of the players had crashed into you? We wouldn't have been liable."

"Well, that didn't happened, so everything is okay," Angela snaps.

"Please, the next time when I ask you to wait, wait."

You both nod to get him out of our faces.

We beat the team bus back to the facility and as the Bears pour in, you take notice of the attention Angela is getting, so you playfully nudge her on the arm. Surprisingly, she elbows you back and flashes a mischievous, agreeing grin. Zorich tells us that he will be out as soon as he showers and that we can wait in the media room just to the side of the entrance. There are spots for all of the major newspapers and television and radio stations. Just as you scope the Windy-City Daily's seat, you observe Jason Smith slithering through the door. An expectant, conniving grin spreads as your stomach rumbles. This must be your lucky day.

He walks obliviously past the media room and up the stairs. You rise and follow a few feet behind as he goes into a room and informs the guy that guided you to the bubble that he's here to interview Chris Zorich also. It's his first time at Halas Hall, because he asks where the restroom is, and is directed down the corridor. He dashes out without taking notice of you, starts in the opposite direction and enters the men's room. You chuckle and crack your knuckles as you follow him in. Your mind is cocked, your mouth is loaded and your tongue is itchy. There will be no blanks fired today. Your words are laced with exploding bullets.

He takes care of business in the urinal while you take a seat on the sink, which is separated by a partition. After flushing, he scurries around the corner without looking. His face cracks when he stops dead in his tracks, as if he hit a brick wall that is about a foot away from you.

"Pick your mouth up off of the floor," you urge, sliding down off of the sink. He starts blinking and you can feel the vibrations of his heart. "Nice haircut," you observe.

He was confident, objective and hairy when he profiled you for a Freshman Phenom feature for his paper. You can even go as far and call him a good interviewer, because he didn't have his questions written down and the interview flowed like an intimate conversation. The article was too complimentary to be about you. He dubbed you a "radical fundamentalist" because you stayed within the team concept and looked good doing it. That was his only by-line that actually made you look good. His hairline has since receded past his ears into an M delineation, and everything he's written about you after that first article has been strictly personal. Four frustrating years you've waited to free your mind, get stupid alliterate and possibly flush the albino dung down the toilet.

"I'm available for comments...do you want them? I'm glad you do, because I have much to say. For the record," you state as you pick his recorder up from the sink, fidget with the play button and lose your head.

"Your work is rain-water weak, whimsically witless, wackier than a wind-warped warlock, and wickedly written, you woeful...wise-ass...wretch. You're lower than the worms in a wildebeest carcass. And then you have bad breath and ring around the collar. Why do you keep fucking with me? You remind me of a fly, buzzing around all day pestering people and feeding on the feces of bigger, more productive animals of society. Here you've been covering high school sports forever and a day and you're just now getting to the point of talking to the professionals, where I'm starting. Any comments Mister Smith? I didn't think so. It's amazing that someone so venomous, vexing and vitriolic when it comes to commenting on human beings has nothing in defense of himself. Off the record," you state through clenched teeth as you slam his recorder back on the sink and come head-to-head with him. "I have the insatiable urge to kick the bark out of your puppet ass for every slanderous, status-scavenging, reputation-ravaging, character-scathing, society-supporting, stereotypical story bearing your by-line. Beating the albino ape shit out of you would be well worth the lawsuit. You would win a Pulitzer Prize for your first person account of a ghetto style beat-down. Every bone in your body would be broken, except your hands, 'cause I want you to continue with your career."

His eyes bulge and he tries to covertly swallow as he states, "I was just doing my job."

"Doing your job?!" you exclaim. "You're a pathetic, pitiful, repulsively pissy piece of a pussy," you growl as you raise your arm as if to send him through the floor.

He winces and jumps back to your amusement.

"Your job is to report on and write stories objectively, not tear people down for the sake of readership. You should've learned that in Reporting 101, but I guess you put too much focus on your racism electives. Whatever. Are there any other comments or questions, Mister Smith?"

He doesn't even respond, not that you would've given him the honor.

"Good," you say through a comically phony grin. "Thank you for your time and have a nice day. And by the way, you should probably brush your hair to the front or get a weave...no one will be able to tell the difference between the horse's hair and yours, anyway."

You exit, feeling like your mental bowels moved after years of constipation and that you exhausted your lexicon of all the negative P and W words that you've acquired over the years.

Chris is just walking in the pressroom when you get back. He's sporting a red, patterned bandanna, plain white T-shirt, Hawaiian-like workout pants and a black leather brief case.

"Thanks for talking with me," you state, taking a seat.

"My pleasure," he insists as he takes a load off.

You pull out your questionnaire and recorder, and ask, "Is it okay that I record it?"

"You're the man."

"Okay, let's get started," you say as you push record. And you launch into your two-page questionnaire. Angela snaps away, causing Chris to blink his reddish eyes 20 times per snap, so you hold your hand up. She slows down slightly, until she uses up 26 shots of the 36-exposure roll. The interview lasts at least an hour and half as you go through every question, with a little improvisation. He graciously elaborates on each query, no matter how redundant it is.

The interview ends, your first time butterflies flew south, and Chris takes several pictures with us. He passes some business cards and some literature on the Christopher Zorich Foundation along to you to help with your feature. Before you start the trek back south, some of the sound-bites hang heavily over your head. You already have the article written in your mind. The only thing left is inserting the quotes.

"I'm glad he's dealt with the loss of his mother. I'm sure that overshadowed the draft to a degree."

"I would imagine, but the paper said that he was smiling and consoling everyone at the funeral. He reasoned that she's in a better place."

"I'm surprised he didn't see a live Bears' game until he played as one," Angela observes.

"I know. You couldn't pick a better person to get drafted by the home team, and you couldn't pick a stronger person to be on your side in a fight," you mention with a chuckle.

"Bench pressing 500 pounds is amazing. Isn't that what a car weighs?"

"Almost."

"I'm like you though: I would've paid the bullies a visit and been like *'I've been drinking milk...lots of it...and I haven't had my Valium for the day because, well frankly, I don't like the way that it tastes. And you know something, you look just like the nurse's aide that administers it to me. And you wanna know something else? I don't like the way you or he looks, so I think I'm going to make a punk a burger out of you, since it's my lunch time.'* I would've forgiven them after I punished them."

"I hear you." And so does your conscience.

Before Dexter died, he often taught the students that Satan is the master of mind games. Recitation made up a large portion of his teaching repertoire. The Romans Road to Salvation (Romans 3:23; Romans 6:23;

Romans 5:8; Romans 10:9-10) was required learning and rehearsing. 1 John 1:9-2:2 was also emphasized, because he insisted that they were going to mess up and that the devil would try to make them think that their salvation is lost. Antonette's presence in the sanctuary amplifies the onus that you are ferrying around resulting from Traci's condemnation. You can barely bench press 160, so the 500 that Chris Zorich pumps is simply awesome. Your conscious is in the state of having that extra 340 added to its threshold just as the weight is lowered to its chest.

John, Tyrone, and Anthony—a.k.a. Moe Larry and Curly, The Three Blind Mice, and Gump, Lunatic and Retard—used to be tight with you and your crew. They were the answer to the Three Musketeers; Shadrach, Meshak and Abindigo: the anti-Malcolm, Raymond and Dexter. Perhaps we were the answer to them, since they range from one to two years older. They were cousins from the same gracious grandparents, who used to smoke them with a fresh switch from a tree every time they stepped out of line in church. They didn't need privacy either. You had to cover your eyes whenever Grandma Hopkins lit into them with a shoe, hanger, tree branch, or purse strap. It's amazing how the best can produce the worst. Calling them underachievers is a conservative statement. If they couldn't do any better in school, work, social relationships, spirituality, and hygiene, then it wouldn't be a screaming disgrace. Flunking out of high school, never working a job, getting women pregnant just because of an unwillingness to use birth control—let alone abstinence, disregarding God in every area, and walking around with bad breath are just a sampling of their shortcomings.

You were at church for an usher board meeting on a Friday. The junior choir practiced that day, too. After both auxiliaries were done, the youth gathered in the parking lot, playing, talking and eating. Ignorant, Idiot and Ignoble pulled you to the side to tell you their plot to get busy with Antonette in the nurses' room, where there's a bed and zero traffic on a Friday night. Due to youthful naiveté that goes with being a hot 14, Antonette unwittingly dallied with the boys, bordering a light tease label. They were charged up like energizer batteries, but you dismissed their plan as boiled over the brim bravado and went to the kitchen to get some fries.

As the Lord would have it, Mrs. Oscar sent you to the nurses' room for a bag of plates that she left in there. When you opened the door, there was Antonette, the Three Stooges, and the devil. Antonette was pinned bare-chest on the bed, Tyrone had her bound by the wrists, Anthony locked her legs in a cradle, John (the oldest at 17) was tugging at her skirt, and Satan (with a lower case s) urged you to join in the "fun" as they pressed you to shut the door. For that second, you obliged.

When you got up on them, Antonette's eyes indicated that she wasn't having fun and the rose redolence turned your hormones inside out, causing a nasty chemical reaction in your mind. She was too petrified to shout as she peered at you through the stagnant mist and silently pleaded for mercy. The "she wanted it" or "she had it coming" argument is on the same ridiculous, unacceptable level as the "if I don't sell dope to the folks in the 'hood that want it, the white man will" reasoning the drug dealers misuse. A brother raping a sister is worse—in your eyes—than a white man violating her. Trust is breached by the act like a jaw is broken by a flush uppercut. Their Christian siblinghood added to the atrocity of that case.

"Get up," you calmly commanded.

They were oblivious to the demand and blew you off with a "Chill out man". That's when you and they discovered that super human strength begins at the breaking point of restraint.

"I said GET UP," you growled as you ripped John up with both hands, slinging him across the room where he landed flat on his back. Their seniority was a non-factor. At that moment, they looked more terrified than Antonette. You could've killed them with your hands, but there was a steel walking cane in your sight that would've had their blood on it instead...if they didn't adhere. She ran out holding her clothes together, while the Three Stooges remained in stupid form by excusing their actions as child's play.

After they were reprimanded, Antonette stopped playing around, and John, Tyrone, and Anthony didn't have another word for you to your face. Of course, they had choice words to your back.

During altar call, you thank the Lord for the new job, which you start tomorrow, lay the burden of guilt down, pray for perfect peace of mind, plead for mercy on Deon (who was arrested for possession last week), intercede for Traci—hoping for a happy ending, praise God for

Magic's presence on the Lakers' bench as the head coach, and petition for a message of confirmation. Jesus answers, sending the word to Pastor Wells, who delivers it first class priority.

He prophesies from Zechariah 3:1-10: ***"And he showed me Joshua the high priest standing before the angel of the Lord, and Satan standing at his right hand to resist him. And the Lord said unto Satan, The Lord rebuke thee, O Satan; even the Lord that hath chosen Jerusalem rebuke thee: is not this a brand plucked out of the fire?..."*** *Verses* one and two is all you need to rejoice, but you let the whole message bless your soul. Pastor Wells notes that Jude 9 indicates that the devil even accused Moses and opposed Michael the Archangel, to which he advises that Michael rebuked Satan in the name of Jesus, and countered with Exodus 4:6-7 of how Moses' hands were sanctified and that the blood guilt was taken away. Then he flips to the Gospel of Matthew, where he references the 27th chapter and the 51st verse (the account of the veil being ripped in two from top to bottom).

"But ye are a chosen generation, a royal priesthood, a holy nation, a peculiar people; that ye should show forth the praises of him who hath called you out of the darkness into his marvelous light," he barks with emphasis before mentioning that if it wasn't for the blood of Jesus, we wouldn't have the unlimited access to the throne of grace. "Don't take for granted the unlimited access to the Lord. Under the Old Covenant, a high priest had to represent the nation once a year on the Day of Atonement, and if he went in there with something that he shouldn't, the glory of God would kill him and they would have to reel him out by the rope that was tied to his ankle." He then emphasizes that once you've laid it on the line, stand still and let God answer. And that's what you're doing.

The first day at Starlin came and went without drama. Elizabeth Sawyer is one of the associate editors, which is only a small step above your position. She volunteered to take you around. When you saw her, you immediately thought of Alice from the Brady Bunch. She introduced you to all of the nameless people, promising that after a few weeks, you will have the names remembered. You still have to get used to the other four associate editors in your own department, who all seem overly reserved for writers. After the tour, you filled out some tax and employment forms. Although your day is only about four hours of filing and clerical work, it seems like a full shift. When you graduate, the hours will be extended. Walter assured you that the second day would be the same routine, with the exception of the tour.

Your chest inflates as you step through the revolving doors, past the security desk and up the escalator. Although you never let your age justify an adolescent disposition, you knew that getting out and working for your own way would mentally categorize you as a man. Speaking to the other building employees that you pass in the hall, you float to your desk without taking inventory of the office. When you look up, you take notice of two things: your goofy, subconscious, self-satisfied simper and the seraphic sight across the room. Your smile remains while you struggle to simultaneously set up your desk and examine her. Her sable eyes are thin and radiant, complimenting her naturally warm expression. She glances over and catches you peering at her.

"Hello," she beams, prompting you to drop your file folders. Her voice is soft and sweet like strawberry cotton candy, which matches her girlish countenance.

You stumble over your wastebasket and trot over to her. "Hi. I'm Malcolm Johnson," you greet with an extended hand and a frantic grin. Not only is it good to have a sister working in the office with you, but it's a bonus to have one oh so—so—pretty. Her skin is the tone of a glazed doughnut and appears smoother than a still pond.

"Pleased to meet you, Malcolm," she returns, giving you her feather soft hand. "I'm Cynthia Sims." Her voice seems as innocent and naive as Little Red Riding Hood's. And in accordance with the script, your eyes grow and your mouth waters like the big bad wolf's. You place her age at 17, give or take two years.

"I didn't see you here yesterday." With the exception of Darrin "Australian accent" Pearson from finance, you only remember the names of the people in your department. You will certainly remember Cynthia.

"Today is my first day."

"Really? Welcome to Starlin. I started yesterday, so it feels good to be higher on the seniority totem pole than someone else."

She giggles like a cartoon character. "What position are you in?"

"I'm an editorial assistant," you boast. "What about you?"

"I'm an administrative assistant."

When it's all said and done, we're in the same position. "Well, I'm not going to keep you, I just wanted to introduce myself. Maybe we can have lunch or something."

"That'll be fine," she assures.

You grin.

She grins.

"Well, enjoy your day," you close out, heading breathlessly back to your seat with your underarms leaking from excitement.

You were already charged up for work, but she boosts your morale another notch as you breeze through your proofreading and editing work. Unfortunately, she was in the first day orientation, so we couldn't go to lunch together. She was allowed to leave an hour early, but the sunshine of her image remains. It is enough to get you home after the sun set.

The phone is ringing when you get in and the smile in your heart comes out in your voice when you melodically answer, "Hello."

"Hi Malcolm."

Your face still beams, but your heart stops. "How are you?" It's Traci.

"Fine and you?" she returns formally.

"Doing good. I'm doing real good."

The pause is awkwardly thick.

"I take it you're still celebrating the Razorbacks' win over Duke," she finally assumes.

"You know I'll be celebrating the death of the Blue Devils all year."

"How about Magic and your Lakers?"

What a cheap shot, but it's all good. "All I can say is I hope he returns to play again next year, since he won't be coaching."

"Have you decided on a school yet?"

"I've narrowed it down to the schools in the Chicago area," you note, adding, "which means that it'll either be NU, Loyola, DePaul, or—by a long shot—Chicago State."

"Uhm," she grunts.

"What about you?"

"Still undecided," she responds despondently as she takes a deep breath and blurts, "Malcolm, I know I said that I didn't want to ever see you again—among other terrible things—but I want you to know that I didn't mean it. I know you wouldn't let anything happen to me if you could help it, so I apologize for what I said."

"Apology accepted," you gladly concur.

She pauses again as she seems to struggle with words, which is a first for her. "I need a favor from you." Asking for help is a rarity as well.

"Anything."

"Do you think you could help me find out who else touched me that night?"

Your throat tightens. That'll be like guessing the lottery numbers. Maybe there's a prophet somewhere that can help out. "Sure," you hear yourself answer. "I'll help." But how? Do we send out a questionnaire or take out an ad in the newspaper or on a billboard? Maybe the host has an idea of who came.

"Another thing," she says, and strains to ask, "Could you take a paternity test...I don't believe it's you, but I want to eliminate all the possibilities."

"That's cool." And it is. "By the way," you start as you struggle with your question. "Is your mother mad at me?"

She lets out a long sigh as you hold your breath and cringe for the answer. "Initially, she was mad at the whole situation, not just at you in particular. In her eyes you could do no wrong, even though she would have liked you to come all the way out with what you knew."

"Really?"

"Yeah. She always insisted that you would be a good man for me, and she still feels that way."

You're honored, but you don't know how to respond to that. And as it stands, you don't dare ask Traci her thought on that prospect. Instead, you change the topic. "I started a new job."

"I heard about it. Nick told me it's an editorial position."

You confirm and she congratulates you. After a little more small talk, you assure her that you'll keep it covert and see what you can do.

9

Not Just Another Word

In a paragraph You stand out and proud
Like the blackest among the whitest

Without confusing me with amplified extreme
In my eyes You are the nicest

You are in italic
So You are saying something influential

Oh so bold
To me You are substantial

Not too common
But with me You are always contextual

With the world so diverse
You can not be one-dimensional

When You are not visible
You are loud

If You are unreadable
You are still sound

You are so abnormal
You are unique

With You I am intellectual
Without You I would be incomplete

You are so humble
When I am speechless

***I am so content
Because You never leave me Wordless***

When creativity calls, you write. You're sitting up in bed at four in the morning full of nervous excitement, depleted inspiration and an erection to the ceiling. It's the kind of distress a basketball player feels at the free throw line on the front end of a 1-in-1 with his team down by one and no seconds on the clock. At best, both will go in, but the first one is crucial. Of course, this isn't basketball. It's life. There is a decision that you have to make that will affect the rest of your life. Obviously, one choice is better, but your heart makes the decision very complicated. You have narrowed it down to two: Chicago State and Northwestern.

It's evident NU is the better academic institution, they have the better basketball team (imagine NU being better ballers than some other school) with more exposure, and their journalism program is one of the best in the nation, let alone in Chicago. Columbia and Roosevelt were non-options, since they don't have an athletic program, and Loyola and DePaul were eliminated, because you will only play for a brother. On paper and in a colorblind society, Northwestern would be the easy choice. The recent hiring of Craig Hodges as the CSU head coach raised their appeal that much more. You love his game and you love his pride. He spoke out against the oppressive American system, sported Afrocentric attire to the White House, and even urged other players to take a stand for the black community. His—and the community's—freedom was more important than the security of the NBA. In your eyes, his heart is more impressive than his shooting range. Unfortunately, the dream in all of its abstractions wasn't in favor of the Cougars.

With the college choice so dire, you wouldn't expect to have a wet dream. There is something about the voice of the Lord that can't be confused with coincidence or consciousness. Ball had nothing to do with the vision of you decked out in your favorite colors: Royal Purple and Gracious Black. You got a good look at yourself, and then you were in the land of reality. Three emotions accompany your entrance into the presence of the Lord: Fear, Serenity and Joy. A reverential fear that only a believer can understand...a fear of being before the Almighty. His presence is overwhelming.

The will of God is the safest place, so there's a peace that can't be defeated. Pressing bills, failed tests, lost love, and impending execution can't fade the divine tranquillity. Nothing else matters and nothing else exists when you stand before Him. And the joy...sex doesn't even come close, and you love the feeling of a juicy booty. It's an awesome feeling to know that the Almighty thinks enough of you—out of the trillions of people across the globe—to have friendly fellowship with you. That was the inspiration behind *"Not Just Another Word."* You recognize that He doesn't have to even look your way. There are many others who would merit that type of connection, based on human perspective, but He chooses to hook up with you. And for such a trivial matter as a college choice?

The day stretched, the classes annoyed and the Calculus test baffled. It seems gluttonous to even stay up at the school to study, since your mind is depleted. You took the day off and decided to go to the school library. Most of the students cleared out thirty minutes ago and a few others linger in the halls. As you turn the corner towards the exit, you have a head-on collision with Deon and you take the worse of it, almost ending up on the floor.

"C'mon man," you start as he keeps walking without saying a word.

His countenance is...possessed. Never have you read so many emotions in a poker expression, but you felt him like Braille. If the face could illustrate multiple moods at once, determination, distress and self-destruction would manifest in a rainbow-like coalition of cadaverous colors. You watch him as he wanders aimlessly down the corridor. When he gets a few feet down, you inquisitively trail him. He covers the length of the building at a glacier's pace before he fades into the men's room. You stop ten steps from the entrance and peer in as your brow wrinkles from a deranging intuition. The stench of death supersedes the dense smell of soaking defecation. There is no sound coming from inside and a landing feather in the hallway would disrupt the resounding flow of life coming from within the bowels of the building. However, you hear. You hear the destroyer creeping up on him. You take one hesitant step and stop.

"Help me, Lord," you plead. And He answers. Nick comes racing down the hall, clutching a sheet of paper.

"Have you seen Deon," she questions desperately as she strains to keep the tears from falling.

"He just walked in there," you motion with your head.

Before you can ask what's up, she shoots through the door shrilling his name. You rush in behind her with a strong dose of apprehension. Actually, you are outright fearful to what lies inside. Nick is standing just at the entrance of the last stall, appealing to Deon.

"Deon, don't do this," Nick pleads as the tears pour out, insisting, "We don't have to go out like this."

You walk up beside her and peer in, causing your heart to sink. Deon desultorily stares past you, Nick and the sink behind you as he sprawls out on the undersized toilet. A hypodermic needle rests in his vein where the left arm bends, and a small pistol is planted in his temple from his right hand. The syringe is full of a clear substance that could be water for all you knew, but you assume that it was something more potent, based on the grave tone of the one way discussion. It doesn't matter. The glock ain't empty and will kill all of the noise, speculation and pain.

"Let's talk, Deon," she beseeches. Desperation is absent in her tone, but a sense of urgency remains. "Can we talk, Deon? Just me and you over a Fishwhich at Dock's."

He says nothing as his left fist balls up and his right hand intensifies around the gun like an itchy trigger finger. His remote countenance indicates that he's under the spell of a little dope and void of most hope.

"Deon, I know things are rough now...we made a mistake...others were hurt as a result, but this is not the solution. There is redemption Deon...we can't go out like this...it'll only make things worse on other people," Nick desperately spiels.

"We? What does this have to do with you?" he questions impassively. "This has nothing to do with you."

"This has everything to do with me, because it has everything to do with my Father."

"Your father? I don't know your father," he distantly refutes.

"He knows you, and He loves you and that's all that matters," she assures as she draws closer to him and inclusively corrects, "We love you, Deon."

"I've done too much to be loved," he assumes monotonously.

"We've all done too much to be loved, but the love of Jesus knows no limits and isn't conditioned on how good or bad we are. Jesus died for you so that you could have life and that more abundantly. Each breath that you breathe is a blessing from above. Every day that you open your eyes is a gift...a gift that no one has earned," she declares as she gently envelopes his massive right hand with her two smaller hands—lowering it from his head and pointing it to the floor—and slowly unbuckles his fingers. "Remember when you encouraged me to accept that calling to teach Sunday school? The Lord used you as a messenger. If you weren't there to give me that Word, I would have gone with my own program and ended up out of the will of God. There are many more people that the Lord wants you to encourage."

"I did a good job of seducing you with scriptures and causing you to stumble. The Lord doesn't need anybody like me."

"I wasn't raped and nothing happened that I didn't want to happen. I'm not proud of it, but I take responsibility," she persuades as you slide in on the side of her, clutch the heavy metal from their hands and pluck the needle out of his arm. You place the piece on the floor out of eyeshot and discard the syringe into the trash. He seems oblivious to you. And although he appeared intent on going through with leaving this world, he didn't want to.

"In your letter which you intended for me to get tomorrow—but by the grace of God I came back up here to pick up a book right after you slipped it in my locker—you repented. Now, let's move on from here. Your sins are forgiven. If God wanted you to go to His presence right now, I would've gotten the note when it was too late. When it's all said and done, everybody comes from the dirt of the earth and don't deserve love, but Jesus loves us anyway. Can we walk together in that love?"

Deon breaks down like...a child. Nick embraces him and weeps with him as he details how his family's anger kindled against him; how he had to fight for his manhood in jail; how he felt that the Lord hates him; how he disrespected his mother; how mean he's been; how he's a sinner. Welcome to the all-inclusive club, Deon.

You come over, embrace them both and travail on his behalf. Before you finish, you can feel another set of arms wrapping around us in that tight stall. You gain a certain appreciation for Nick's ministering abilities, especially towards someone that wronged her. It wasn't her soothing words—although they were effective—but her soothing life that read well. You saw Jesus at work through her. Nick is pivotal in both of our lives. She was a tool for reclaiming us. Pity isn't what you have for Deon, because that's a supercilious attitude more than a sympathetic emotion. We are all woeful creatures without the grace and mercy of God. You could feel him as a brother under the blood. Different demons we battle, but they come from the same camp and produce the same result. You lost your will to live. You didn't think that God loved you. You thought that you had sinned to the point of no return. By the grace and love of God, we are still here.

After Ma's car stalled on 68th and Lake Shore Drive at two in the morning late last year, you realized just how vulnerable she was. A sky-high fever and spastic gut forced her home from work six hours early. The car was hurting for some winterization and a new battery, so at the worse possible time, it went on strike. You were up studying and Uncle JoJo was falling asleep in front of a M-A-S-H rerun fully dressed, when you took the call from her. The nearest phone was three long blocks away on 71st Street, an economically ironic area of high property value and high crime. Ma lacks the naiveté of Little Red Riding Hood skipping through the forest. She grew up in the gutter of the south, so she knew how to survey her surroundings, since evil is all the same.

Just before she got off the phone, she spotted the two night crawlers sizing her up, so she urged you to hurry up. You were there in a minute and thirty seconds flat, because emergencies make stop lights null and void. When you pulled up, she was just making it back to her car, and the two shadows were bearing down on her like an avalanche. They disintegrated like sun-exposed vampires when you came screeching up on her car. If you had arrived two seconds later, they would have been close enough for you to reduce to a puddle of blood. Twenty seconds later, and she could've been spilled all over the pavement. The nearest phone was too far away. A cell phone was the likeliest birthday/Mother's day present to get. It's something she and you can use. After all, in case you're hurting for cash, she can be reached any place/any time...better than Western Union.

Mother's day is just a formal, commercialized acknowledgment. You love Ma more than your own life, and everyday that we are both on this side of the grave is a blessing. It's not to say that every day is sitcom perfect. We have more than enough disagreements. But the bottom line is she shares the same unconditional, Christ-like love. Ma would battle nature on your behalf, if necessary. When you used to bump your head on the floor, she would come and punish the ground with a literal Big-Foot stomp. There was never any doubt and there are too many illustrations to recall. However, the one that dances in your mind and brings a smile to your face while you sit in a cube desk in the Woodson Library, is the episode of the sports fanatic that called you one too many dumb motherfucka's for Ma's liking at a home game. He sat just within earshot two rows up. Ma didn't believe she heard it the first time. The second time she didn't believe that he was talking about her son. Strike three and she had him by the collar. In retrospect, it was a bit embarrassing to have the game stopped, your Ma restrained and you escorted from the stands. At the time, you weren't aware of the 1,000 or so other people in the gym. The only two people that existed besides you, were Ma and the punk that kept calling you out. That thought is the shot of exhilaration your creativity needs to express itself in words, so you do.

Lily of Love
You are my Lily in the valley of life
Reflecting the gentleness of the Bridegroom
Epitomizing the quintessential wife

Through my mad schemes and wild adventures
You stood with me
Just as God is a Friend in a time of need, so you are sure

The character of your soul is a sweet fragrance
Emitting goodness, intelligence, self-control, patience, godliness, brotherly affection, and love
Your flowering heart led me to repentance

Centered in gold and adorned like royalty
With the Righteous Light burning from within
Your presence is an element of the reality of the Almighty

What do I call this living Dilly
Who goes by the diverse order of holy
To me she's Ma, to Malcolm she's Lily

You smile as you put the y at the end of Lily. Poetic inspiration is contagious and consuming. Although you penned this as a birthday card for Ma, it actually touches your heart and brings you just a little closer to God. A Mac Performa with graphics would make card writing easier. However, the hand is anointed with rhythm that can't be captured with a machine. The invitation will be a good sub for colorful pictures. Illustrations are more profound than letters, but words reinforce actions like a steel frame.

You sign the card "*I love you. Your beloved son, Mal*," and insert the tickets in them as you pack up your things.

"Thanks for telling me that Northwestern called," you say sarcastically to Ma. "If only everyday was Mother's Day." You've had an ill two days, and although you're trying to be funny and upbeat as you prepare to take Ma to the Regal to see David E. Talbert's "Lawd Ha' Mercy", your mood has swung to the opposite end of good.

"I'm sorry...I forgot. Good grief," she apologizes.

"Good grief," you playfully mock.

Outside of being prom dateless three weeks before the big dance, the end of the Arsenio Hall era (you were looking forward to appearing on his show once you made it), and the close call with Deon—which you're still reeling from—Friday, Mitch confided that he was the first brother to enter Traci after you left the party (a couple of weeks after you sought his help in finding out who was a part of the train). You couldn't believe it. That's rape. You blasted him with all kinds of ill alliterations that are not worth recalling. Talking to the party sponsor, David Adams, was totally unfruitful and unnecessary. He blessed you with a tense encounter, providing you with rude and allusive answers. The urge to make that pretty boy ugly and throw an air freshener in his reefer-reeked mouth was strong.

After you calmed down, you three-way called Traci—but didn't let her know that Mitch was on the line—and informed her of the revelation. She called him all kinds of bastards and promised to call you back after she chilled. While her ire was still high, she phoned him while he was on the line with you. She lit into him without mercy and threatened to press charges against him. His silence indicated that his feelings were hurt when he got back on the line with you. As sick as the act was, Mitch truly wanted Traci, not as a sexual release, but as a woman. When he urged you to get with her, he was actually projecting his own feelings. The moral of that story is "Say No To Wine", which you did the moment after.

Traci was in and out—mostly out—after you left. As if dialogue was necessary, Mitch talked his way in between her legs. By the time he finished, she went back to another world again. He insists that the liquor didn't mask the guilt (he had more servings of the punch than Traci drank and it drowned out his judgment, but not the conviction), so he left the party briefly to clear his head. When he came back, they were throwing Traci out and Chuck D informed him that the railroad ran its course. Instead of going back in among the revelers, he bundled her up and literally carried her to her front door. She was too out of it to get the key in the door, so he opened it for her and dashed behind her steps when he heard her mother coming. Moments later, he heard Traci shrilling in pain and begging for mercy as her mother seemed to be flaying her with a rusty razor. He didn't get a chance to tell her his story, and that's when you became a mediator between them. You told his side to her, and she said the bottom line is for him to get a paternity test. He was at the clinic that same day. Yours should be back in a couple more weeks, since it takes a good, long month. As a result of the disclosure, Traci's wrath against you has been rekindled and it made communication extremely tense.

"What if it just so happens that my seed seeped into her," you wonder as you let Ma out of the car.

"Much worse has happened to better people," she encourages. "If you are the father, which I doubt, you'll just have to adapt and make the necessary adjustments in your life."

"I just don't want any kids right now...if I could..."

"...go back and do it over again, you would, along with the rest of the population, but you can't, so stop worrying about. You're supposed to be showing me a good time, not hosting a 'woe is me based on possibility' party. Now chill."

You love it when Ma uses slang. "Aiight," you agree.

Ma loves Gospel musicals, and so do you. She was surprised when you presented her with the tickets for two when she woke up this morning. You told her to be ready at six-thirty and went as far as setting her lavender dress out that matches your collarless shirt. The welcomed heat prompted you to shed the jacket to the black suit. After we got in and settled before curtain time, you mentioned that you would be making a college decision this week, but you wouldn't tell her where. You hinted that you were dressed in the school's colors. She didn't have a clue, since she didn't follow college sports—not currently, anyway.

A bigger cue was the account of your CSU campus visit. Everything seemed okay. The comfort of being among your folks tempted you to step out of His perfect will. Then you overheard a conversation between a group of students from a writing class. They were debating the importance of grades when it comes to getting a job. To your disappointing surprise, all but one had entry-level, minimum wage mind-sets. Apparently, they had just gotten a test back and the majority of them ended up with C's. One gentleman correctly insisted that grades carried weight. He must've gotten a better grade, because the remaining six refuted that argument, like the fox labeled the grapes he couldn't get as sour. America believes that Black people are lazy and inferior. If a surveyor got a whiff of that discussion, he would have a strong supporting argument to that false hypothesis. The jocks at your school strive for the best grades, even if they don't achieve them. Never does anyone in your class scoff at the higher notch. Although you and Traci are dead even at the top, only a few percentage points separate us from about 35 other students. That dialogue turned you off and confirmed your decision.

Even though the singing was loud enough to induce a headache, we were well entertained. Edwin Hawkins put together an inspiring soundtrack that included a mixture of oldies such as "Eye on the Sparrow" and "Jesus on the Main Line" to some contemporary cuts like "Choose" and "Happier Pleasing You". Morris Day and Jerome Benton turned it out, and as promised to Ben, you collected their autographs.

"You know," you mention as you pull in front of the house. "If I can't get a prom date, will you go with me? Although you're a little senile at 42, you still look like a homecoming queen. I'm wearing this color anyway and that would save money and drama."

She rolls her eyes at you and laughs with you.

For some uncanny reason, you haven't gotten up the courage to ask Cynthia to go to the prom with you. You only have less than three weeks. We go to lunch and ride the bus home together every day, but you still haven't been able to get a good feel for her. *And you do want to feel her.* You can sense her presence without even knowing she's in the room. Everyday she walks in glowing with glee like a living love song. You can spend the day just goggling at her. However, as gorgeous as she is, you have yet to muster up the nerve to ask her.

"So, Mister Northwestern man," she accuses as she gathers her things to head on out. She is really wearing a scarlet skirt with a white blazer. Her hair is draped down her shoulders and her makeup is unnecessary, although it does enhance her striking profile.

"How did you know?" you ask humbly. You know the signing of the national letter of intent is publicized in today's paper, but you didn't think she saw it.

"I read it in the Sun-Times. I'm impressed. Can I have your autograph?"

She can have your Social Security number, bank card and—if she continues to charm you—your personal minder. You haven't even exchanged numbers with her yet.

"I'll go a step further: I'll take a picture with you," you bait.

"I'm not very photogenic," she insists.

"Get Out Of Here," you demand, slowly enunciating every word.

"Seriously," she says as she pulls her work ID and Driver's License out. "Look at these."

Either she lied or her perception is jacked up like a broken nose, because both pictures are dribble material. As you study the license, you covertly look at her stats: *Cynthia Sims, 8888 S. South St. Chicago, IL. 60600 Sex: Female* of course; *Ht: 5'3"* perfect; *Wt: 140* and looking too good; *Eyes: Brown* and beautiful; *Birth: 12/26/60* WHAT?! *Birth: 12/26/60.* She snatches it away and warns, "Stop looking at my weight."

Her phone rings, giving you a chance to recover from the shock and to try to remember how to do simple math. If she was born in 1960, she would have to be...GASP...33. That's 16 years difference between us! Twice as old as you thought. She could be your momma! Then your addition skills come rushing back. When you reach 34, she'll be 50; when you reach 50, she'll be 66; when you reach 66, she'll be 82. Good grief. At the end of the year, you'll be 18 and she'll be 34.

In the meantime, you accidentally pick up on her conversation with *Cedric.* Well, so much for asking her out. When she gets off you get straight to the point. "Boyfriend?"

"No, silly," she says as she rolls her eyes. "Cedric is my son."

The conversation sounded so mature. Cedric must be your age. "How old is he?" you fish.

She pulls out a baby photo and informs you "He's three."

There's some relief. You're curious as to what kind of expression you have. "Cool," you note, studying the distinct features that he definitely pulled from his momma. "My godson is three, too."

"Really? Maybe we can let them play together sometimes," she suggests.

That's not a concern. You want to play with her, even though she's beyond playing days. "Where's his father?" you pry.

"Forever locked in the doghouse. I haven't seen him in a year, which isn't long enough."

"Okay."

"So Malcolm," she starts as she rises with her things and we start towards the exit. "What are you going to study at Northwestern?"

"Journalism," you proclaim. "I'm going into print journalism."

She smiles. "That's good. I always dreamed of being a teacher."

"So what happened to that dream?"

On the way home she gives you her life story, starting after high school. Her father passed and her mother was terminally ill, so she had to start working to try and sustain herself and raise her 12-year old sister. After her mother passed, she married Cedric's father and moved to California. He was an aspiring actor, and once he got a few roles, his interest in family life declined, so they parted. You feel kinda funny telling her your life story, because based on the age difference, you haven't lived yet, so you stay on the topic of writing and some of the inspirations to your creativity.

When the bus approaches her stop, a melancholy feeling blankets you. You want this woman, but it feels like a forbidden desire. It stings to part from her, so out of desperation, you ask, "Can I call you?"

She chuckles, which brings an awkward smirk to your face. "I'm sorry, but I don't have a phone yet. My neighbor keeps Cedric while me and Crystal are out."

"Oh. Okay. See you tomorrow," is all you can dejectedly utter as she exits.

You finally found yourself back on the door: "You would rather be a gatekeeper in the house of your Lord than to dwell in the tents of the wicked." Ushering is your place in the church. Many have suggested a more glamorous position, such as choir member or junior deacon. The trustee chairman even approached you to join the board. However, you know your place. If God moves you later, so be it. Your job is to greet everyone with a smile, even Penny. Her devilish grin didn't cloud your sunshine one degree. You greeted her with a beam, good morning and God bless you just like every other parishioner. A smile is more powerful than a frown. People come to church for rejuvenation, not ugliness. The first impression when they enter the sanctuary can set a good tone or jack up the human spirit. Even when Lucifer tries to rear his horned head, love still must abound.

Your college choice was announced in morning service. To your chagrin, Pastor Wells instructed you to stand along with the other graduates in the church, from the kindergartners to the collegians. He was using the scholars as a prop for his message. Thankfully, he didn't keep us standing during his sermon, which was titled "Faith Working Today For Tomorrow" and taken from Hebrews 6:11-12. "Blessing the Children" was the theme, and you were impressed enough to take notes. Never have you taken sermon notes.

After he finished, Pastor Wells announced the start of a scholarship ministry in order to give the students of Walk of Faith financial assistance in the form of a $500 stipend for college students (that brought your award and scholarship total to $7,500, not including the full, four-year scholarship that NU was giving you, and your year-to-date tithes to $950, not including your salary from work). He noted that it wouldn't pay tuition, but it would be an encouraging token that could be used for books and/or other secondary expenses. The paper notes represented the formal annotations in your heart, because you found yourself pondering what you could do as a service to others. Ushering is good for service on Sunday, but the Lord has blessed you with much more to be pigeonholed as a doorkeeper once a week. In the name of Jesus, you want to go out and about with your talents.

While the Spirit of charity was overflowing like the fountain of life, Nick approached you after service and suggested starting a basketball team at the church. "It would be a good outlet for them this summer," she insisted, adding, "Sleeping during sermons and listening to old, fairy-tale like accounts of biblical characters is the only dimension of church that they get, which is not too appealing for a young mind."

Nick could sell a bridge if she put her mind to it. She often downplays the impact she has in the class, but her presentations are savory, digestible and nourishing for young minds...and old, crusty ethos'. Not that you needed convincing, but she observed how the youngsters love shooting, watching and talking rock, and that they admired you since you are on the path that they want to be treading. The adoration of the Lakers that two of her students possess was a personal incentive. "I'll pray over it," was your response, although you and God knew it was on. Two seconds into the house and you were on your knees. Two minutes later, you called Nick and the President of the Christian Education Department, informing them that you'll start putting something together and that an announcement should be made in church next Sunday.

The telephone trail includes New Covenant Missionary Baptist (Pastor Stephen Thurston) and Trinity United Church of Christ (Pastor Jeremiah Wright): two prominent churches, with all type of programs geared toward evangelism and fellowship. From those two calls, an interdenominational church league with the Catholic Youth Office was found. Money was set aside for the cost of uniforms and tournament expenses, and an announcement was read that following Sunday. Interest was so high across the board, that two teams were formed: a 15 and under and a 16 and over. Several names were taken for the youth team, while Ben committed to coach/play for the adults. As it stands, you are the coach by default for the youngsters. You decided to play with the church this summer as a way to sustain your timing and wind without such rigid competition. After getting five uniform quotes, you decided to go with Benji's in Oak Lawn. Although their price wasn't the lowest, the name was endearing and the service was sincere. Reserving a gym for one-day-a-week practices turned out to be an unfulfilled task. You're waiting to hear from a couple of parks with indoor facilities.

All of the running, researching and reaching out taxed you more than the stretch run in school, so Saturday is as welcome as a time-out for an evil step-mother in a room full of screaming BeBe's Kids. It has been months since you and Ben went at it, so he scooped you up early to hit the courts before the hacks and hoods arrive. The sun is happy and the wind is content, prompting the birds to sing and the dandelions to blossom. Nature is synchronized. You split a game with him, when two neighborhood teens turn up with no ball of their own. Out of courtesy, an all-inclusive varsity is started.

Ben treks home to make a call, which leaves you alone to teach the fundamentals of trey serving. Surprisingly, they hang with you from long range, which provokes some light trash talking. In the process, characters' vitalities are swapped. Chris, the runt of the two, is in his freshman year at South Shore, with an interest in architecture. Although he's chiseled beyond the 14 years, his 5'6" stature decreases his visibility on the court, so he didn't get a good look or a spot on the team. Terry is on the verge of graduating from eighth grade and plans to attend Kenwood Academy. He's already acquainted with the coach and insists that he has a fro-soph spot reserved at forward. 5'11" is tall for 13. When you tell them who you are, they seem surprised that Malcolm Johnson would be at the courts playing pickups with them. They dismiss your bad press, noting that the media is quite biased.

Since the Nation of Islam doesn't seem to advocate or favor tattoos or body piercing (Mosaic law—which has more credibility to Islam—prohibits them in Leviticus 19:28), you assume that they associate with the Black Stones, because they're each branded on the left forearm with a crescent moon and pentagon and pierced in the left lobe. You have the urge to tell them that Jesus is the Way, but you don't have the gumption to preach to them. Instead, you go with what is comfortable and exercise your appeal.

"My church is starting a team, and I'm going to be coaching," you mention as you bank in a three pointer from the right baseline, adding, "I can't offer you money, but I would love to have you play for me."

They both glance at each other, as if they're expecting to be rebuked. "Will they let us play if we don't go to your church?" Chris questions.

"I got you covered," you assure. "You'll also get a jersey."

"I'll play," Terry commits, on the condition "If I can get a ride."

"I got you covered there, too."

"Where's your church at?" Chris asks.

"It's on Jeffrey right off of 81st Street."

"I'll play too, but you're going to have to ask my mother," he mentions.

Gladly.

"Can you also tell my coach how good I am?" Chris requests.

You admire him for seeking a professional reference at an early age, promising him that you would put in a good word and even invite him to the games. After hitting the winning free throw, you take names and numbers and pass yours along, noting that you would need a consent form signed by their parent or guardian. You assure them a call to square things away as you start the next game, continuing to talk smack.

"Do y'all play for the Wolverines?" you question of the blue football jerseys with gold lettering they're each sporting.

"I was a running back," Chris proclaims.

"Cornerback," Terry notes.

"I used to play for Will," you testify, recalling your brief stint as a wide receiver for the former CVS standout who took it upon himself to introduce grade school kids to helmets and shoulder pads.

It was admirable of Will Creighton, since the park district wasn't too big on football at the grammar school level. Without donations or sponsors, he managed to organize a two-team league. The Park's Wolverines (a microcosm of northern, bourgeois blacks) were comprised of most of the kids who lived between 83rd and 79th, and the Lakefront to California; the Tray (a model of the working class southerners) consisted of kids from 83rd to 87th, and also Lake Michigan to the west coast. Of course, some of the kids jumped the imaginary boundaries. Allegiance was to the team, not the block.

For the first few weeks of practice you smoked at receiver and Will gave you constant praises. Anything in the air was as good as caught. Flies, planes and comets couldn't escape your hands. Then we suited up from head to toe with the equipment that he provided (helmet, shoulder pads, cup—of course—thigh, and knee pads). You found it kind of bulky and restrictive, but you still had your hands and speed. You scored the first touchdown in the scrimmage on a long bomb. After we got the ball back, they called another play for you up the middle. It seemed simple enough. When you made the cut to the heart of the defense, the ball was waiting for you...and so was safety Ken Little. Ken was built for the gridiron. He outweighed you by about 20 pounds (10 pounds was the least disadvantage you had with your peers), which was a lot, given your four-inch height advantage.

After you stretched out and caught the ball, you proceeded a half step and heard an explosion. It wasn't until you opened up your eyes to singing seraphim a la the prophet Isaiah a moment later that you realized that you had been popped in the head. That's when you knew that your first real contact would be your last. Everybody huddled over you to make sure you were okay. Amazingly, you held on to the ball. Ken was proud of that hit, which was clean and crisp. Unfortunately, it was a typical tackle and you couldn't get used to opening your eyes up to angels every time you got cracked. With the winged creatures flying around your head, you gathered your limbs that popped out of the torso sockets upon impact, removed the equipment piece by piece, announced your calling to play basketball and hiked home without another peep.

Midway through the third game of 21, Ben returns with Nick, three other lads step up, and an Ekersal old timer name John Gunn makes an appearance. Just as you win with a three, an imposing, bald 6'8"er comes on the scene with an air to turn the park out. A full court is suggested and you hit the free throw to choose first, followed by Gunn. He earned the birth moniker not because he shoots too much, but because he *can* shoot so well. To make it even, you bypass the big man, opting for your right hand man, Ben. When the sides are set, Nicole, and your two buddies are teamed with you and Ben. You find yourself gaping at the big guy. Yes, he looks like he could go with the best swing/power men, but an arcane aura more abstruse than hoop arrogance seems to overflow from his expression. He's oblivious to your gaze as he introduces himself to everyone as Simeon.

Nick comments, "Nice shirt" since they're both sporting "Salvation Express" T-shirts. He just nods with a smirk.

When he rounds up with you and Ben, you mention that Benjamin and Simeon are brothers and sons of Jacob.

"A Bible scholar," he modestly remarks. "Do you know who mothered them?"

"Simeon, the second child, was birthed by Leah..." you claim as Ben cuts in.

"And Benjamin was the youngest, born to Rachel."

"Very good," he compliments. "It's good to see brothers well Worded." You smile and nod as he announces, "Let's pray before we kick off."

Peculiar indeed. Without an oral disclosure, you can discern the Royal Priesthood and a ministerial office. There is a self-confident glow that God's messengers possess, and Simeon radiates like a Christmas tree on December 24th. Everyone obliges without a hint of discomfort or offense as you all gather at half court and form a circle. He petitions the throne of grace in an abbreviated manner, just as Nick did a couple of months ago. When he closes with "In the name of Jesus," everybody seems to possess a little more bounce and the illumination of the Holy Ghost.

Of course, the bigger man is your assignment. Although it doesn't cause you to stumble, his lighthearted trash talking surprises and amuses you. Simeon could light it up from the top of the key. For his 3-for-3, he commented, "Jesus loves you;" "Jesus died for your sins;" "Jesus is Alive."

You retorted with "I'm going easy on you, since you're God's anointed."

The game is tied at 30 and he takes a shot from the top that you swat to the other end, where you retrieve it under the basket to dunk the game winner.

"Prayer really does work, because I pleaded with God to allow me to engulf it without getting struck dead," you joke.

We all yuck it up as the game is run back. They blow your team out 24-16 in that game. Simeon showcased his inside game and utilized his 50-pound weight advantage with a couple of dunks and about 20 boards. To your credit, you blasted his stuff for 20-yard field goals on five separate occasions. After your team won the third game, Gunn and the three cousins that came together—Reggie, William, and Fred—cut out, leaving the rest of us parked on the bench for an intermission and class. This series marks one of the hardest, cleanest triple-headers ever on any level. In talking ball, you gain a deeper respect for Simeon when he declares Magic Johnson as the best ever. You can only dedicate your biggest grin to Ben. Chris and Terry cast their ballots for Jordan. Youngsters. Curiosity presses you into steering the conversation to religion.

"What kind of ministry are you into?"

He chuckles and asks, "How do you know that I'm in the ministry?"

"I could easily say that it was evident from the prayer; or the scriptures and 'God bless you's' you used to back up your game were indicative of evangelism. But I could see your light before you opened your mouth."

He nods as Chris and Terry seem a bit lost. "I'm actually in the pastoral stage of my ministry, although evangelism—a former exclusive title—is a big part of my function."

"What church do you pastor," Ben questions.

"Englewood Christian Center..." he mentions as Nick interjects.

"Elder Hall?"

He affirms with a smiling nod.

"I love the radio broadcast," she notes in awe. "I didn't put it together when you introduced yourself. I loved your message on Satan and his demons. You're one the best teachers I've heard."

"Praise God," he humbly encourages.

"Okay," Ben announces as if a bolt of lightning enlightened him. "You do stand up comedy."

"Not like I used to," he declares, mawkishly adding, "I'm starting to do sit-comedy."

"I saw your skit about Biblical punishment at All Jokes Aside. You had me rolling, and at the same time, it gave me a renewed appreciation for what Jesus went through. That was as powerful as any sermon I've heard," Ben passionately proclaims. "It was dramatic, but I knew those were real tears falling when you emphasized the torment the cross presented."

Simeon just coyly nods as he accounts how the Holy Spirit improvised during that skit, revealing how His innocence made the punishment that much more painful and that most men of the means of Jesus would've summoned a battalion of angels to smote mankind out. Simeon conveys that the physical phase was harsh, but the unbearable aspect of the crucifixion happened when the Father turned his back on Him. There's a wonderment pause as we all bask in the anointing that was just sprinkled from above and ponder the move of the Father.

Chris can't hold his queries as inquisitiveness bursts his bosom. "How do you tell the difference between real religion and the fake stuff...there's a lot of religions out there that claim to have the truth."

On cue, Nick pulls out her pocket NIV, flips to a passage and addresses him: "1 Kings 13 tells the story of how one of God's prophets was instructed by the Lord what to do and what not to do, but he listened to some old man that lied about how an angel told him to tell the prophet to do something contrary to what the Lord said," she starts, riffling through scriptures to reinforce her points. "You would think that angels have a lot of credibility, but the devil was once a glorious angel and, in fact, he still imitates them. He convinced a third of the angels to rebel, so his game was pretty tight. Galatians 1 and 8 states that 'even if we or an angel from heaven should preach a gospel other than the one we preached to you, let him be eternally condemned'...that means you tell him to go to hell. The gospel that they're talking about," she adds, flipping to 1 Corinthians 15:3-4, "is the death, burial and resurrection of Jesus, which is Good News for us. First John 4, 1 and 2 instructs us to try the spirits—or messages—to see if they're from God. If the message contradicts the Bible and the Gospel, that false prophet is teamed up with Satan."

"Why is it that a lot of people attack Farrakhan? He teaches from the Bible," Terry inputs. He's talking to you.

"Yes he teaches from the Bible," you agree, adding, "but it's what he teaches from the Bible *and* the Koran, which contradict each other. Islam downplays the significance of Jesus, mentioning that He was a good prophet. Yes He was a prophet, but to say that He was just a good prophet is one of the biggest insults to His deity. There are many titles and designations for Jesus, but I find that seven truths believed as a whole separate the enlightened and the lost: Jesus was and still is God; Jesus was born a man; Jesus lived a sinless life; Jesus died for our sins; Jesus was buried; Jesus is resurrected and is ascended where He intercedes for us; and Jesus is coming back. The Bible backs me up, and if anyone teaches otherwise or believes only parts of it, then they're walking in darkness.

"To use a little logic and common sense, if I spit on your plate of food, but the saliva only got on your salad as opposed to your steak, biscuit, potatoes and gravy, would you eat the rest of the food out of that plate?"

They shake their heads.

"Of course not, because not only does it spoil your appetite, but some of my germs could have actually contaminated the rest of the food. Likewise: people will say that some parts of the Bible are wrong, even though they live by other parts of it. A lot of cults go by some of the Scriptures but disregard others as inaccurate. I tell you, if any parts of the Bible are wrong, then the whole thing loses its credibility," you conclude.

"I guess a Christian preacher has automatic access to heaven, but what if a person is good, but doesn't believe in Jesus...will they go to Heaven?" Chris wonders.

Without skipping a beat or superseding one another, Simeon speaks: "You see that pile of dog dookie right there," he points out a few feet away.

They affirm with a giggle as he pulls a big, burgundy, leather Bible out of his bag, opens it up, hands it to Chris and instructs him to read "verses one through eleven" of the third chapter of Philipians.

He does and smiles as he reads the eighth verse. "Yeah doubtless, and I count all things but loss for the excellency of the knowledge of Christ Jesus my Lord: for whom I have suffered the loss of all things, and do count them but dung, that I may win Christ..."

"Do you know what dung is?" Simeon questions.

Chris flashes a timid smile at Terry and shakes his head.

"Dung is doodoo," he declares, adding, "What Paul is saying is that all of his religious qualities are like dung compared to the relationship he has with Christ" as he flips the Bible to "Isaiah 64 and 6" and instructs them to read.

They oblige and he gives them an illustrious answer to his assumption.

"Imagine eating a pot of hot chili, cheese fries sprinkled with Tabasco sauce, a chocolate milk shake, an egg sandwich with sardines and pickles, with a tomato pie for desert. Now imagine what condition your belly would be in afterwards."

Between the five of us, the smiles stretch the length of the court, with Chris and Terry covering most of the ground.

"Then to top it off, you wash the constipation and gas down with a laxative and a gallon of orange juice. Of course you would spend the week on the toilet. Now think about the end of the week when your bowels are empty...you're going to need fifty yards of toilet paper. Let's say that you only have one wad for one good wipe, so you get as much after dung out with the one wipe. Needless to say, the tissue would be well soiled, with enough crap to fertilize 40 acres of desert. That stained tissue is what my goodness and ministry title is to God," he declares.

Terry speaks for them both, indicating that the concept of salvation is as clear as mud. "How can anybody be saved?"

"I'm glad you asked me that, because I have an answer," Simeon utters. "It's the same principle as how can all be damned because of Adam. If you stole on somebody with your right hand and they died as a result of the blunt head trauma, would your hand be cut off and tried, or would you—along with your right hand; left hand; both legs; torso; head; hair; toe nails; teeth; spit and whole body—get arrested and tried? Of course your whole body would be fried. Now, assuming that your reproductive facilities are working, would your sperm be taken out of you before you're fried like hot wings? Of course not. Your sperm will perish with you, because your sperm was a part of you when you went upside somebody's head. If you ingested cyanide, you and your sperm would die. It may not sound fair, but that, in effect, is the result of what Adam did. He contaminated the human race with sin.

"Here's where it evens out a bit. Jesus—being fully God—humbled himself because He loved mankind and became a man while still being God. Whereas we are born into sin as a result of Adam's disobedience, we are born into everlasting life because of our belief in Christ's perfect life and sacrifice. To be born again is a spiritual rebirth, not physical. The Church is the body of Christ, just like we were a part of Adams body when he jacked things up. A lot of Christians would burn in hell if salvation was based on works, because I know many a Saint that committed more dirt than an actual heathen.

"How can that be, you ask," Simeon prophecies. "Well, there are many oxymorons in life—an oxymoron being two combined terms that contradict each other—such as the Walking Dead...unless you know Jesus as Lord and Savior, you are literally walking spiritually dead; Big Dwarf...a dwarf may seem big to a midget; Girlie Man...some boys do grow up to be women, which defies nature. The Gospel is full of oxymorons, such as the dark day when Jesus was crucified. Imagine it being *dark* from noon to 3 p.m. Servant King: Jesus was and is *the* King, but served us by giving His body as a living sacrifice; by praying for us. He was also a *condemned* judge...innocent, yet crucified; righteous in that He never sinned, so He alone can judge. If you owned all the property in the neighborhood and actually built it, would you not have a place to stay? Well Jesus owned and made the universe, but didn't have a home to sleep in when He walked the earth. Metaphorically, He was a Lion, which is symbolic of power and authority, and a Lamb, which is meek and used for sacrifice; In Heaven He was a Bright and Morning Star that descended to be a lowly Lily in this valley known as earth.

"Certain laws just can't be defied: You can't go without oxygen for a long period of time, otherwise you would suffer brain damage; You can't go without food and water, because you would turn into a skeleton that can't hold his own in the paint; and in a fair game, Magic Johnson can't be stopped."

Your smile doubles with that example.

"Jesus defied some laws that no other person could: He defied the law of Gnostics, which states that God can't dwell in flesh. I ask you, if God created flesh, how come He can't dwell in it? If you built a house, couldn't you live in it? If you bought a car, wouldn't you have a right to drive it? He defied the law of gravity. What goes up must come down, even if it's Jordan. But Jesus floated up up and away to Heaven and gravity couldn't say a thing. He made a mockery of the law of sin, which states that *all* have sinned and come short of perfection and that the penalty of sin is death. If that's true, how is it that someone who hasn't sinned, die? In giving up His life, he kicked death's butt all over hell...And then He came back to life," he concludes with a smile of confidence as Chris and Terry sit captivated and edified. He sure is a people's preacher. His appeal attracted about five other guys that came up for a game, but got a Gospel message instead.

Ben takes the baton and compliments what we all said: "You go buy a $500 dollar stereo on promise or credit, with the notion that you'll get an allowance and possibly a job. Unfortunately, Momma and Dad cut off the allowance and nobody hires you. The promissory note states that you go to jail a year for every dollar, which means that you'll be in there for the rest of your natural life and several hundred years after, so basically you won't even get a decent burial and just rot behind bars. Out of nowhere, Billionaire Bill writes the $500 check just before they throw you in the cell, and just *gives* you his blank check book—that's just his one and only check book fella's—letting you know you're going to incur much debt in your lifetime. He tells you that whenever you incur debt, just write the check and sign it—you have to sign it, otherwise the check is no good. Now you can live stupid phat and ghetto-large because you have the blank check book of a Billionaire.

"Now, you did a little dirt in your life—according to Romans 3 and 23—not much, to give you the benefit of the doubt, but the payment of sin is death, as Romans 6 and 23 states, and death is a three-fold curse: physical; spiritual—the separation from God, which Jesus experienced on the cross as a result of bearing the sins of the whole world, according to Matthew 27 and 46; and the second death—which is basically when you go to the Lake of Fire from hell. You tried to work off your sins by doing good things and honoring most of the commandments, and even getting certain titles and jobs in the church to show your good faith and intentions, but you still come up way too short, according to Isaiah 64 and 6 and Philipians 3 and 8. You're still dead meat and soul even though you've never killed anybody and the most dirt you've done is tell a few white lies. Romans 5 and 8 says that Christ came down from heaven, paid the sin debt for you, which is death, and covers any sins that you may do later on—if you allow Him, as stated in 1st John 1 and 9. If you don't confess your sins and ask Him to forgive you of your sins, it's really like an unsigned check, which can't be cashed. Now you can have eternal life, because Christ has paid the sin debt, and you have access to the Father as a believer according to Romans 10, 9 and 10; 1 Peter 2 and 9; and Matthew 18, 21 through 35."

In rapid, Holy Ghost fire succession, we each witness to the crowd of two that has grown to about twelve hungry souls. All in the area are not interested, as illustrated by the game that started a few minutes ago.

"If you confess with your mouth Jesus as Lord and Savior and believe in your heart that God has raised Him from the dead, you shall be saved," Nicole testifies.

"By grace are we saved through faith; not of your own power...salvation is the gift of God, not of works, so no one can boast," Ben adds.

"Sanctification isn't a religion, but the forgiveness from sin; a separation from sin, and the glorification after physically dying, which is done by God alone," you mention.

"You can be saved right now if You accept Him," Simeon declares, adding—to address their nonverbal concerns—"Don't worry about how imperfect you are...the Lord will take a lot of those urges and desires away, as Brother Malcolm stated."

They sit nodding as the eyes of some of them well up.

"It's the biggest step anyone can make, but you don't have to be afraid," he assures. He continues to address their concerns, even though they don't vocalize them. "The water baptism doesn't save you; the faith saves you. Baptism is an outward sign. I'm not trying to get you to come to my church, however, I will leave my card with you all," he says as he pulls a handful from his bag and hands one to everyone. "If you have any questions or if you want to visit, please feel free."

"How do I accept Him?" Terry questions for the group.

"Do you believe in Him?"

Terry nods.

When Simeon's eyes go to Chris, he nods also. Then he scans the crowd. Three of the dudes reluctantly fade off, but everyone else acknowledges their belief.

"Praise the Lord," Simeon jubilantly announces. "Half of the work is done, now all that's left is an oral confession. If you repeat after me, it'll be complete," he assures.

They oblige while we all join hands and bow our heads as he starts:

"Lord Jesus..."

"Lord Jesus..."

"I acknowledge that I'm a sinner..."

"I acknowledge that I'm a sinner..."

"and I realize that death is the result of sin..."

"and I realize that death is the result of sin..."

"I thank You Jesus...

"I thank You Jesus...

"for dying for me..."

"for dying for me..."

"and I ask that you forgive me of all the sins I have done..."

"and I ask that you forgive me of all the sins I have done..."

"I accept the sacrifice You made for me..."

"I accept the sacrifice You made for me..."

"and I give my life over to You..."

"and I give my life over to You..."

"Lord Jesus..."

"Lord Jesus..."

"Please come into my heart..."

"Please come into my heart..."

"and deliver me from things that are not pleasing to You..."

"and deliver me from things that are not pleasing to You..."

"Lord Jesus..."

"Lord Jesus..."

"I thank You for saving me..."

"I thank You for saving me..."

The Lord takes over Simeon's mouth as He commends their souls to the Father and declares them righteous; prays for His holy angels to be dispatched to watch over and protect them, and to begin the sanctification process, which will be completed in glory. When he concludes with an "In the name of Jesus," you and Ben are glowing, while others shed tears of joy.

"From this point on, you *are* saved, and no one or nothing can take your salvation," he declares. "Do you all have a Bible?"

"Nope," Chris admits. Terry shakes his head. Five of the men nod.

"Alright," Simeon resolves as he starts toward his Astrovan. He retrieves four KJ/NIV parallel Bibles, still in the wrapper, and hands them to them, encouraging, "Study it, and if you have any questions about anything, just call me or talk to one of your well-read siblings here."

You're surprised that Joyce answers the phone. You called the U.I.C. campus directory assistance first and they informed you that she doesn't stay in the dorms anymore. After digging in your old shoebox of business cards and phone numbers, you found the yellow strip of flyer that she scribbled her name and digits on at the skating party three years ago, and took a chance.

"How you doing?"

"Malcolm?"

"Um hm."

"I'm doing fine. It's nice to hear from you."

Truthfully, her voice is sweet to the ears, too. You small talk her briefly and catch up on everything before you get to the point: "I need a prom date and I was wondering if you would go with me."

Cynthia turned you down softly, only because there isn't an ignorant bone in her bewitching body. You came right out and asked her at the end of the day and she smiled sheepishly before stating, "I don't think so." Actually, it was a nice way of saying, "HELL NAW!" You weren't insulted by the decline, but it felt like she stuck a dagger in your gut, which totally superseded the relief you got a day prior from the negative paternity test.

Whereas you were sweating for fear of a positive reading, Mitch is praying for affirmative. He's confident that he's the man, noting that Brittany has his cleft and dimples. He actually got to see Brittany for the first time, and they seemed to bond at first sight, which is amazing since it usually takes her a while to get comfortable with strangers. To your surprise, Traci warmed up to Mitch in a short period of time. On paper, they read like a prizefight, since Traci can be callous and Mitch can be immature. She always said he was cute, but too silly, even though he got through her serious front and elicited laughter out of her. Outside of joking around with mutual friends (friend, as in you), they appeared to shy away from each other on a personal, one-on-one basis. However, you don't know what was said when she would tutor him in Trigonometry. In the past, they seemed to be nervous and giddy around each other, as if they had a secret. Now the awkwardness has blown over. They've actually been perpetrating like a couple and have almost been inseparable. Chuck D hinted that they're planning to go to prom together, which means that you're the only one out of the crew that's stag. Even Nick and Deon have made amends and will hook up. There are many more-than-willing jock-drawn mannequins on the dateless list, but you will stay home and watch rented movies over Wendy's before you go with a girl you don't like.

To your disconcertion, she snickers slightly, before quizzing you about your love death. After giving her the dismal details, she assumes, "So I guess we'll be wearing purple."

10

The posse came to your house first to take pictures, then we headed to Chuck D's, followed by Mitch's and then back to Traci's house, so Ms. Dawson could check Mitch. In other words, a "when-the-clock-strikes-twelve-she'll-be-looking-out-for-you-so-don't-get-any-honeymoonish-ideas" talk. We all picked up our dates first before hooking up. Cynthia monopolized your mind on the way to get Joyce. You are sorry to say, but if Cynthia had changed her mind on your way out the door, Joyce would've been a day late and a dollar short. It's hard for you to determine if you want her so bad because it's impractical or if you're overplaying her gentle disposition and fine face. All that's known is that the power of manipulation over you is in her hands.

When Joyce opened the door, Cynthia fled your head and you hit the floor without any vital signs, because she was drop-dead gorgeous in her passionate-purple, back-less, sleeve-less dress and petal-violet pumps that match your bow-tie and cummerbund. Her hair overlaid her head like a crown of frozen grace, partially veiling her left eye. The goodness of the Lord resurrected you to behold her for the rest of the evening. We talked several times since she agreed to go, flirting with the idea of getting back together. It was a mutual decision not to get physically intimate until marriage (you brought up the topic), that is if and when we get married. The talks were like old times, but you were void of those same lay-your-life-on-the-line-for-the-love-of-Joyce feelings from three years ago. You would be lying to say that you weren't tempted to make a beeline to city hall for a marriage license instead of going to the Sheraton for the prom.

Everyone dazzles like emeralds. The guys are groomed and freshly faded; the ladies are seraphically dolled up with new do's. You and the fella's have identical black, tailed tuxes. Mitch wears gold accessories, while Traci has on a gold, sequin-trimmed dress that outshines the sun; Chuck wears fuchsia accessories at Heather's urging, whose dress is conservative for such a loud color, but totally radical, hugging her svelte curves; Deon sports pink trimmings to match Nicole's pristine pink, cascading dress that turns her into an ebony, South-side Cinderella.

Now you realize how movie stars must feel on Emmy night, as your eyes adjust after the last shot from Ms. Dawson. It's not quite as packed as the Stadium, but there is a nice crowd that boosts your pride, puts a little more strut in your step, adds a degree of tilt to your head, and inflates your chest.

"Y'all are too sharp for words," Ms. Dawson insists. "I'm tempted to keep you here so I can just look at you."

Everyone already has grins plastered on, now a touch of crimson is added with no way to really respond to that as we—with the exception of Mitch—disperse to our vehicles. After you let Joyce in, Chuck creeps over and brings the discussion to your attention. You crack up as you dip on the sly. Mitch is an ugly combination of scarlet, gold and black as he sports a chagrinic grin and nods like a rear-window toy animal on a hydraulic truck. When her instructions conclude, you meet a dragging Mitch at his rent-a-Grand Am and ask, "So when's curfew," as you release your laughter with Chuck. He's especially tacit as he smiles and shakes his head.

"Man...She threatened to break my kneecaps if I get too close during the slow dance," he notes, gazing lustfully at the back of Traci's head. The test came back 99% probable that he is the father. It didn't matter, since he and Traci were kicking it hard and she decided not to pursue the identity if he wasn't.

"Is a good feel worth your career?" Chuck D jokes. "I guess she won't conceive any new additions to the family tonight."

"If it's any consolation, Deon will have Nick back before sun up and not long after the prom...there will be no boots knocking with them," you declare, adding, "and I'm not going to be out all night with Joyce, although she's tempting," as you peek over at her in the car.

"Yo Dawg, speak for yourself and Deon, but the D in Chuck D is for Doing the Do and doing it right...hopefully."

"I guess I don't have to worry about y'all drinking then."

Chuck shakes his head.

"Ms. Dawson took the taste away a few minutes ago," Mitch says.

"Okay folks...let's do this then."

The prom was an overrated waste of money. Even if you could dance, you still wouldn't have wanted to with Joyce. You were distant throughout the night as you tried to feed off of the class's enthusiasm, floating in and out of the different cliques, yucking it up with the thugs and jocks, and posing with the beauty queens and the scabs. It goes down as the weakest display of beatitude this side of Hollywood. The best part of the night came at the end. Instead of acting on your urge to dump her on the curb in front of her house, you endured her for a two-hour cruise with the rest of the class. Thankfully, a late night dinner was served on the ride, so you could kill two after-prom events with one stroke. You couldn't get to the car quick enough when the ship docked. Your head banged and your stomach churned while you longed for a good night's sleep. If it wasn't for your comrades, you would've been the single holder of the record for fastest, non-happeningest prom. Since they headed for the flat too, we all clocked in at 1:55 a.m.

Traci addresses the audience as the class president. With every ounce of intellectual juice and a touch of grace, you finished at the top of the class—in a tie with Traci. Instead of both of the Valedictorians giving a speech, she improvised since she was going to speak as the president. Ever since she hooked up with Mitch, she has mellowed out. Last year, she would've insisted on giving two speeches and her going first. She even conceded the soloing to Milton Anderson so as not to monopolize the program, even though every one wanted to hear her croon some inspiration. Your and Khalid's efforts with Brian paid big dividends: He smoked the ACT with a 22 and got the last scholarship to Purdue. More important than his first year eligibility, is his confidence. Not only is he cocky on the court, but now he believes that he can conquer the academic world as well.

A promise to Dexter was the only element that brought you out to Great America the morning after prom, and with Joyce, no doubt. The hairs on your arm didn't rise when she clasped your hand on the Demon. While she sat in your crotch during the ride on the Water Barrel, your flesh remained tile flat. Not even the drop on the American Eagle could give you or the day a rise. To bottom it out, your shot was broker than a bad joke on amateur night at the Apollo, as it took you ten tries to win a hand-size stuffed animal and $20 to win a prize for Joyce. How telling. Some mark, too young to drink and too stupid to hold it, hurled all over you on the Demon, of all rides. For the rest of the day, you had to walk around in a $30 Bugs Bunny T-shirt. To sum up the experience, the food poisoning from the pizza had you on the toilet for the three consecutive days that followed.

Through it all, Cynthia arrested your thoughts and provided a beam of sunshine on a gray day. When she gave you the graduation card on Wednesday, it wasn't a 'pat on the head' sentiment, she shared your victory. Cynthia isn't pleonastic or outgoing, but you found yourself gobbling up every word that fell from her luscious lips like it was sap dripping from a maple tree trunk. Without passing a hint or direct order, she shut your mouth and turned you on to listening for a change. The mere mentioning of her ushering duties at New Hebrews Baptist Church psyched you into believing our title camaraderie was a sign. Faith is an action, not a state or emotion. In studying the faith of the men in scripture, you discovered that they made seemingly foolish moves and were rewarded as a result. You weren't foolish in believing that anything would come of us, but hope fueled the resolve to level with Joyce and peacefully part from her yesterday. She took it well when you confided that you are drawn to an impossible dream and would rather stay asleep than make us a consoling awakening.

Milton Anderson finishes his solo "The Impossible Dream", which is your cue to speak on behalf of the class. It's amazing how many emotions your body can go through in the moment as you rise, starting with the paralyzing anxiety that strikes you every time you branch off outside of your comfort zone by verbally expressing your forte'—writing—in front of a multitude. The Holy adrenaline supplies you with an indifferent boldness as you step to the podium. A melancholy spirit blankets you as you note the empty seat in between Angela and Ms. Lewis, where Dexter would've been sitting. As you scan the crowd, looking past the class, your family and the other spectators, your soul is gripped with a gratuitous glee. You had the speech memorized and prioritized based on key points, but for the sake of peace of mind and security, you inconspicuously place it within reach on the podium. With Traci standing behind you just to your left, you take comfort in the reassuring pat on the back as you open your mouth and recite what's in your heart.

"Hebrews 11 lists some of the great men and women of old who are inducted into the heavenly hall of faith. A man who took to the task of building an Ark—without machinery mind you—and warning a society about a rain that had never happened previously; the Patriarch who left the comfort and security of a home without a map or destination; a woman who aligned herself with an enemy; a man of privilege who

renounced his wealth because his people were suffering. I would like to salute the present heroes and heroines of faith from Joe Louis, who went against the odds, evening things up for the disadvantaged; spit in the wind of adversity, not worrying about any backlash; stood strong on the front line, even though the system offered no support; mocked the impossible, realizing that all things are possible through Christ who strengthens us *and jumped from a plane with no parachute to the Promised Land, believing that their leap would not be in vain. This isn't a graduation ceremony, but a climax. What you are witnessing is the fruition of the collective faith of our community.*

"Society has all but given up on us, going as far as dubbing us the X generation. X represents the unknown in mathematical equations. Our methods are unknown; the dangers that we face in the wilderness of life are unknown; our destiny is unknown. The unknown is about not being able to perceive a thing, and that's when faith begins, for faith is the substance of things hoped for; the evidence of things not seen. *It was through your eyes of faith that we could see success,* for we walk by faith, not by sight. *If anyone knows first hand about the negative hype concerning us, it's me. I've been iconized THE X-Man. But I'm thankful for all of you, because it would've been easy to buy into all of that talk about a black out. On the contrary, we are lights in a dark world.* Your prayer of faith has produced a 500-fold blessing.

"It was faith that allowed you to face martyrdom. You were hosed, hung, dragged, shot, burned, beaten and castrated for us. Your tolerance of us alone is an exercise of faith. There were many reasons for you to have given up on us, but you've kept the faith in us. We've disrespected our elders, but you've kept the faith in us. We've smote our fellow humans, but you've kept the faith in us. We've rebelled against righteousness, but you've kept the faith in us. When we look at you, we see an aspect of God: FAITH. For Christ sacrificed His life for a sinful world, just like you've sacrificed for your rebellious children. God could've given up on us a long time ago, but He has kept the faith in us. Just as the just shall live by faith, we're the children of the just...living by faith. *So we're not gathered for our graduation, but for your induction into the hall of faith. Congratulations and Thank You so much."*

The powerful improvisations caught the audience and you off guard. The message serves as the perfect prelude to the class song: "I Believe" by the Sounds of Blackness. When the commencement exercises end, total strangers congratulate you, and many ask if you are a minister.

"Your head looks like a dandelion," you tease.

"If you sneeze you'll shed and be bald," Chuck D seconds.

"That's a lot of pollen."

You, Chuck D and Mitch came up to Ekersal Park just before dusk after the Knicks beat the Rockets in game two of the Finals. The remaining players were clearing out. We shot several games of varsity in the cool, crisp night until we couldn't stand. Then we collapsed on the bench and verbally battled like drunk comedians.

"That's okay Mal 'Watch-the-walking-stick-jump-through-this-keyhole' Johnson," Mitch jabs. "I've never seen anybody come in from a rainstorm totally dry. Must be nice to dodge the drops like that. I bet you can hang glide with a sheet of tissue."

"It looks like a canine started chewing on your head," you shoot at Chuck D.

"Like somebody started carving on it trying to make a Jack-O-Lantern," Mitch doubles.

"Doesn't Mal look like a Hobo with $100 jumpers on?" Chuck D questions in reference to your worn and wrinkled shorts converted from full length sweats and torn and faded tank top that used to be a $20 T-shirt. "Did you go into Footlocker and walk out without paying for them?"

"At least I don't look like a dust-devil, huh Mitch. Reminds me of Pigpen from Charlie Brown," you cut. While we were playing, Mitch tripped and slid into the dirt.

"That's okay though, at least my beak ain't a foot long," Mitch notes of your nose. "You look like a woodpecker...h-huh-h-huhhuh."

We all laugh.

"Check it out X...the teefis are six feet deep and Chuck D is only 6'1"."

"We'll call you Woodchuck with a wolverine haircut," you remark.

"Look at your lips though...you can scratch the top of your head, clean your ears out, and use them as a Jim-hat for your whole body.

Just call him whip-lips Mitch," Chuck D rags on Mitch as he swigs his fruity wine cooler. "You sure you don't want one, Dawg?"

You shake your head and declare, "You know I ain't with that."

Mitch bought a four-pack, one more than what you drank the first and last time you experimented with liquor. They both look at you as if you don't know what you're missing.

You explain what you're missing: "At that house party that Traci got pregnant at, I gulped down three coolers and that had me under the influence of the demon in that bottle. Even though I still had some of my wits about me, it messed with my will. I attempted to do something that I wouldn't have done with a clear mind. No telling what I would have done had I drank more of the stronger stuff. I never touched a woman that I didn't like; I never slept around with more than one at a time. That's an insult to my mother, who embodies the black woman—whether she respects herself or not. If my Ma was out of her mind, I wouldn't want any one messing her over. Period. Even if *they're* under the influence. My system can't handle it; my soul can't handle it. Three days later the wine coolers came out the other end and it felt like the Lake of Fire was pouring from there. The pain was almost as punishing as the guilt. I bet you I made a promise to God to never touch it again after begging on the toilet for mercy the whole day...and I haven't and won't."

Chuck D looks a little spooked and mentions, "I'm almost tempted to pour this out."

"What's up, X," Mitch says. "Why you gonna go deep and religious on us? You know we can't relate to that."

"I'm just being real with you, and you can relate if you seek God for yourself. I'm no better than you; I'm not perfect. I struggle with temptation just like the next brother out here. You've heard me cuss. You know about some of my sexual adventures. I still love to knock boots, but I have a love and reverence for Jesus that's so real and genuine that I'm making a special effort to not hit it again until it's my honeymoon."

They smirk and strain to contain their laughter.

"So you're going out like A.C. Green. Dawg, you know that he plays hyper because he has too much testosterone built up," Chuck D says.

"We can't play with you no more. You're liable to cripple a brother," Mitch seconds jokingly.

"Well, I guess I'll just hoop it up with the church folks, because I'm determined to do this the right way."

Mitch reflects and grows a little serious. "I can understand where you're going with that. We've been brainwashed into thinking that we can't live without a piece of ass, but when it's all said and done, the pleasure isn't worth the consequences that a lot of brothers are dealing with. To tell the truth, I don't really want to touch no one except Traci—and I haven't since we found out that I'm the father. I even burned my booty call list because the drama gets old. And on a deeper level, she showed me an attribute of God by truly forgiving me. It would've been one thing for her to pardon me and keep some distance, but she has embraced me totally after I violated her in the worst way. This experience has opened up my eyes to the Gospel message. I didn't understand the unlimited love Jesus has for the church until Traci opened up her heart to me."

"Not you too," Chuck D groans. "You should've gave me your black book, Dawg."

"Think about it CD. There's gotta be more to life than living for pleasure. We went through four years of school like four periods of study hall. Think about all of the brothers and sisters from our school that didn't make it...that dropped out, got dropped or couldn't keep the grades up. Shit, we should've been gone when Folks chased us from Washington Park because we looked like Black Stones."

"I didn't realize how far 59th was from 52nd. I ain't never ran like that before," Chuck D says.

"I didn't realize how ugly red was. I haven't worn that color since," you second.

"All 20 of them thugs couldn't stand red either, but to come at somebody with bats was a bit extreme," Chuck D notes. "We were lucky to have quick feet that day."

"It had nothing to do with luck and athleticism, CD. If it was luck, it would've ran out that day. When I went to church with Traci, the preacher said something that stuck with me: He said *'the strong don't always survive; the fast don't always win the race; the attractive don't always have company; the good don't always live long. The sun shines on the wicked just like on the righteous.'* No matter how good we are, we're not in control. You hear what I'm saying?" he questions with urgency. "That's the first time I actually paid attention to a preacher.

After he preached, he called Traci out of the audience to come and sing *'God So Loved the World.'* My girl tore me and that church up.

"When I used to go to Sunday school, God's grace and mercy didn't mean much to me. And I used to go to the Apostolic Church of God, and you know Bishop Brazier was kicking knowledge around. We weren't worthy to make it; we weren't better than those who didn't. I believe that there's more than what we see, and I tell you, my eyes are opening up to what the Man upstairs has to show and my ears are opening to what He has to say. What He's showing isn't visible to my physical eyes and what He's saying can't be heard with my natural ears. And since He's trying to get my attention, I don't ever want to be under the influence of this again," he concludes, emptying the contents of the bottle onto the dusty ground, causing it to fizzle.

You nod and confirm, "That's where faith begins: where physical sight and hearing ends. It's all about tapping into the wisdom of God; about living the now for our tomorrow. And you just took a big step of faith."

We sit back and reflect in silence for a moment.

"So what's next for you, Mitch?" Chuck D queries.

Mitch humps his shoulders and shakes his head. "I don't know. My main priority has shifted in a month's time from playing college ball to looking out for Precious. And you know...I think I want to raise her the right way...with a mother and a father in the house."

"Oh no," you jest. "Not the kid. You're not thinking about marrying Traci," you insinuate.

"Say it ain't so, Dawg," Chuck D pleads.

Mitch pleads the fifth, but his sly grin incriminates him.

"Are you still going to go to school," you ask.

"Oh yeah," he insists. "I'm going to look out for them, but it's not like I have to choose between them and self."

"Where do you think you're going?"

"I'm considering U.I.C. or Chicago State."

"That's where I'm going," Chuck D declares. "I already talked to coach Hodges about a scholarship."

"Cool," you and Mitch agree.

"Ms. Dawson is going to hook me up with a teller position at Citibank," Mitch notes. "She knows the Vice President and figures it's best that we don't mix business with our personal lives by me working at her bank."

"Cool...that's right up your alley since you're into that accounting and finance," you say.

"I'm going to be looking myself, but I'm in no hurry, Dawgs."

"Just don't ask us for any ducks," Mitch warns in jest. "But seriously guys, you know how folks fade after graduation...let's stay tight. We've been down for each other for the last four years, so nothing has to change."

"Even if one of us gets married," Chuck D hints.

We all laugh.

"But on the real, let's watch each other's backs like we've always done and stay away from golf courses."

"No joke," Chuck D mentions.

"Amen," you confirm as we triple pound and start back to your house.

"On a more serious note, how long will Michael Hermon last in Hoosier country?" Chuck D queries.

"About a day after practice starts," you predict.

"He should've just went through the Marines' boot camp," Mitch seconds as we continue to laugh it up. One full bottle remains on the bench.

"These are the dope," Mitch notes as he pulls out the black and blue L.A. Tech cross-trainers with the light in the heel that he bought from the FootLocker downtown.

"You can't be a part of the crew no more," Chuck D seconds as he pays his El fair. He bought an identical pair.

They each took advantage of the graduation money they got and went on a serious shopping spree. There wasn't a warm-up that was safe or a T-shirt to resist or dress slacks that wouldn't have an occasion or casual shoes to by-pass. They bought stuff that they probably didn't like, but loved the idea of spending money, so they went crazy. Mitch also sacrificed a pair of warm-ups to buy Precious three outfits that matched some of his, and a couple of toys. You opted to be ultra-conservative when we rushed the stores in the Loop and the Water Tower.

"Riding is better than walking any day," you assure, paying your fair at Chicago and State. "Hopefully I'll be rolling in that Firebird tomorrow."

"Hopefully we'll be rolling in this train today," Mitch eagerly notes as he boxes his jumpers up when the approaching El echoes through the subway.

"Hold the door," you order as you wait for your transfer.

Chuck D follows suit and dashes down the stairs to the subway. The ticket agent gives you the transfer just as the train comes to a complete stop, so you hop-skip down the stairs. Mitch rests against the second door two cars down, keeping it from closing. The doors shut just as you sprint through. You left your breath at the top of the steps. Coach Byrdsong would be nauseous if he observed your poor conditioning. You make your way to the next car and maneuver your way through a couple of standing passengers. Mitch and Chuck D are sitting in opposite side seats facing each other. An aisle seat by Mitch with a back sack resting in it is unavailable. That bag must've had a long day, but that's too bad since you're burned out too.

"Excuse me," you request, nudging the window passenger sporting the gigantic headphones with the headaching bass blasting a Reggae jungle beat through his ears.

He lowers the volume and nods his head down in your direction to peer over the top of his wire shade-frames. If you had breath, you might've just stood and marveled at his over-permed, long-overdue-for-a-touch-up, dirty, reddish hair with the part down the middle; nappy goatee; purple, unbuttoned flower shirt that reveals nappy chest hair and a black string necklace with some long canine fangs hanging from it, and the watch with the holster face-cover and bullet band. Instead, you bridle your laughter and ask, "Can I get this seat?"

Attitude permeates his pause as he grudgingly removes his bag and places it in between his legs. The nerve of you wanting to occupy the sack's seat. You could feel fervent fire coming from the character as you take a load off. He cranks the volume to an irritating level and starts bobbing his head so you can feel him. Although the bag is a decent size, he exaggerates the width by literally doing a split in the seat. Chuck D smirks when you glance at him, while Mitch looks knowingly ahead. You shake your head and try to settle in, although brother-man shifts every time you try to accommodate him. You have to almost turn around to keep his legs off of you. When his foot veers over on yours, that's when you've had enough of his ignorance.

"Can you give me a little more room?" you huff as he plays deaf. You nudge him with your elbow and lean forward to enter his peripheral line of vision.

He slides his glasses down, removes his headphones and turns to you, his countenance screaming, "WHAT!"

"Can I get a little room, man?"

His glare growls, "Eat shit and die motherfucker" before his mouth utters, "Take your ass somewhere else if you're not comfortable," as he adjusts his shades and slides his headphones back on.

You look at all the occupied seats and shake your head as you can feel Mitch and Chuck D biting their lips. This ain't funny and you fume as the urge to sling him to the other end of the train intensifies. It just so happens that his exit is Chinatown. When he rises and brushes pass you without an excuse, Mitch and Chuck D perpetrate like they're getting off too as they measure up all 68 inches of him from behind. When the doors open, you cringe as they simultaneously super kick, sending him flying face first almost to the train going in the opposite direction. He collects himself, rips his headphones off and charges the entrance just as the doors close. We all crack up as the train pulls off with him running alongside banging on the glass and screaming obscenities.

"He was hurting for a good ol' gang style beat down," Chuck D notes while the El zooms down the Dan Ryan.

"He was hurting for a good ol' bath," Mitch informs, adding, "I still have his odor on my shoes."

"That is exactly why I gotta get some wheels," you emphasize, assuring, "and that is exactly why I'm not going to wait until tomorrow," as you rise when the train pulls into the 87th Street stop and exit without giving your boys further explanation.

They're headed to the Plaza to commence their shopping, as you spontaneously trek out to South Chicago Dodge on 87th and Commercial. You called them this morning about the car that was advertised and promised Lonny the salesman that you would be out tomorrow. Tomorrow may never come and the car may be gone. Before you board the 87th street bus, you phone home and urge Ma to meet you over there. Although she advises against getting a used sports car, she did promise to co-sign if necessary. She told you that she's cooking a roast and waiting on the Sears repairman, but she would be over as soon as that is squared away. "Don't sign anything until I get there," she instructs just before you hang up.

When you arrive, Lonny is sitting around with all of the rest of the salesmen, seemingly waiting for a sucker. Without even asking, you go straight to him. Lonny doesn't look much older than you, and probably isn't four years out of high school. He eagerly greets you and asks in a heavy East Coast Italian accent, "You wanna take it for a spin, Mister Johnson?"

Your eager smile is telling enough.

After he retrieves the keys, he has a maintenance man bring the volt-wagon to charge the battery. When the car is charged up, you waste no time. You can feel the muscle while it roars with power when you start it. It almost gives you an erection when it shoots down Commercial after lightly accelerating. You didn't want to get out after the test drive and you tried to mask your grin with a somber, business expression.

"So did you wanna pay cash or finance?"

"I was considering financing."

"Okay," he notes, pulling out a credit application. "Fill this out so we can check your credit."

"What credit?" you question with a silent chuckle.

This is simple enough, so you oblige, even though Ma doesn't want you to do a thing until she arrives. He leaves you to salivate in silence for a good 15 minutes as you picture yourself pulling up in front of Mitch's house blasting the stereo. Gone are the days of dealing with CTA weirdo's and fat people that take up two seats on the bus. Today is your Independence Day.

Lonny returns with a "bad news" expression as he questions, "How much were you planning to put down?"

You have about $2,500 saved up, but you inform him "$1,500," as your heart anxiously races.

"Well, Mister Johnson..." he starts, pausing as his somber countenance cracks into a smile. "You've been approved."

You briefly go through a mute celebration as he pulls out a sheet of paper and jots down the figures $5,000 minus $1,500. Although the wrong price surprises you, his hesitancy in the simple subtraction stumps you. He literally freezes as he waxes over in stupefaction. It's a shame that the concept of borrowing is beating his brain into submissive mush. You hurt enough for him to cry and offer your tutorial services at no charge. However, the incorrect sales price kills your charitable urge. With the government misprioritizing their spending on space exploration and the wellbeing of other countries, they need to concentrate on their own home. As rich as the country is, nobody (black, white, yellow, red, or blue) should be without an education, shelter and food. It also angers you that there are degreed brothers on unemployment while this man with the correct color code works for a living. Oh well.

After the three-minute battle, he figures out that the difference is $3,500. "This will be the difference and your payments..." he starts as you cut in.

"The price is $3,995, right?"

He's still smiling as he notes, "It's actually $5,000, since you don't have any credit."

Damn. Why would he throw cold water on your wet dream? "The advertised price is $3,995" you inform, pulling out the ad in today's paper.

"I know, but that's the price for qualified credit applicants," he lies nervously. "Because you don't have a credit history, we have to charge you a first time buyer's fee."

Ma strolls in as your BS barometer (BS for Bovine Stool) registers a dunghill. "Have you heard of a $1,000 first time buyer's fee?" you question her sarcastically.

"Naw," she assures, her face crinkling up. "I've never heard of a first time buyer's fee at all."

We both look knowingly at each other. So the reputation of a used car salesman is real. "Maybe this is a good time for you to bring in the manager," Ma advises.

He obliges without another peep. The balding, blond manager comes in potbelly first and queries, "How can I help you, Mister Johnson?" as if he doesn't know the deal.

"I was trying to buy this automobile for the advertised price, but Lonny here wants to try and exploit my lack of credit by charging me a first time sucker's fee."

"It's not like that at all," he assures at warp speed. "We have to charge that fee because the finance company charges that for taking a risk on you."

"You can go fertilize your lot and reap a bountiful harvest, because that's some potent manure you're moving," Ma says with total calmness. It's been a long time since Ma was peeved enough to get country ghetto. "You're going to have to do better than that real soon, because I have important things to tend to besides getting hoodwinked." So that's where your sharp wit comes from.

"Ma'am, we didn't come up with that," Potbelly insists. Lonny nervously devours his gum as he continues to try to sell you a bridge, even going as far as sweetening the deal. "How about this: We'll cover half of the fee, which would bring the price to $4,500. That's what the price will be with tax anyway."

"How about you pay the whole thing and sell it to me for the advertised price?" you suggest. No. That was an ultimatum.

"We can't do that," he assures.

You and Ma glance at each other. With an offer like that, what could we say? "Well, you can let that car rust on the lot," you suggest as we rise and start out. "Have a nice day, Lonny," you bid, adding, "Thanks for wasting my time," as you let the glass door slam.

11

"It sure can be hard to come up with things to write sometimes, can't it?"

Lacy Banks—the Reverend Lacy Banks—is confirming one of the ills of the writing trade to you. He just finished preaching a dynamic message titled "With Friends Like Judas, Who Needs the Ku Klux Klan." You're surprised it wasn't a racially charged sermon, in light of the title and last Friday's OJ Simpson car chase. When he confessed his shortcomings—such as his taste in music and television programs—to illustrate salvation by faith alone, he seemed to humble some folks who boast about the good things they do and the bad things they don't do—as if their lives merit salvation. The church was in stitches when he noted that he couldn't guarantee that he would or could continue to turn the other cheek until someone's palm wore out from slapping him. After he concluded that salvation isn't forfeited because of lack of works, he could've stopped there, because you were well fed. Never mind the subject of the message, which pointed out the spirit of Judas at work in the people that we break bread and kick it with. You were already up on the many faces of deception. The Gospel stands alone.

Pastor Wells, who is a good friend of his, introduced us. However, you were well acquainted with him and his work. He is staffed with many dynamic writers in the Sun-Times' sports department. Each columnist has their own style, but of course Jay Mariotti (your favorite by a slight margin) probably gets the most attention, because he can be hilariously honest in one sentence and scathingly scandalous in the next phrase. Taylor Bell does an excellent job of objectively covering high school athletics. Even when the other writers from various papers were dogging you, he was objective enough to at least note your positive achievements when he wasn't able to reach you for his only article on you.

Lacy Banks. He is peculiar. His sanctification even comes out in his writing. If you never saw him or read that he is saved, the Holy Spirit is easily detectable. That doesn't mean that he's a dry, straight arrow writer. Actually, he's quite witty and dignified at the same time. Banks and Mariotti represent two contrasting, entertaining extremes of the sports staff. In nursing analogies, if a team suffers a debilitating, mortifying loss, Jay would rub the cuts with pure, unadulterated alcohol, ram your dislocated shoulder back in place without anesthesia or restraint, stick you in the butt with a big horse needle and inform you that "You sucked to the utmost"; Nurse Banks would soothe the open scars with ointment, put you under with anesthesia before popping your bones back in place, and tell you "You lost, but all is not lost; the next game can't be as bad. God bless you." It's an honor to meet him. Yes, your writing can go through periods of creative constipation, but your mouth has a strong argument for that right now.

Two whole weeks was the duration of your summer vacation. Evanston is as far as you got, and that marked the end of vacation and the beginning of college when you registered for summer school at Northwestern. The quarter ends in eight weeks, which will be the beginning of a real break. Today the class is abbreviated from the normal two hours, which is an excellent birthday present. After Professor Larkin passes out the syllabus and assigns the first book of six, he dismissed.

Ma dropped you and your bike off today, so after you pick up "The Bride Price" by Buchi Emecheta; you set out for a record timing of two hours on two manual wheels. Just on the border of the campus at Clark, you zip around the corner at warp speed in route to the store for fluids, and you seem to come to a freezing stop when your eyes get snatched out of the sockets by the apotheosis of Mother Africa, who cracks a glancing smirk at you. Even if you had the head on with the pickup truck that barely missed you when you came around the curve, you wouldn't have felt it, since you were tranquilized by her glorious countenance. Only by the grace of God are you allowed to be in her presence again. His love for you is evident: no distractions; no deadlines; no King on her arm; no fear. And then you have the luck of your birthday. She's wearing a shimmering gold, shoulderless dress that wraps around her neck and gives a tease of her cleavage, and matching head wear—fashionably different from the purple garment you originally saw her in, but equally glamorous.

Without letting her out of your sight as you fly past her, you do a 180 and zero in on her without a plan or a clue as to what to say. Perhaps bowing down would be in order. Maybe placing her on a chair and carrying her on your shoulder would be more appropriate.

Whatever you do, it has to count, because this is a once-in-a-life-time, Haley's Comet chance. Your vision is scoped in on her, your breathing stops and rigor mortis seems to set in when you roll up beside her at her casual ambulatory pace.

"Hello," you greet through a goofy grin as she peeks over at you and smirks from coast to coast. You almost fall off your bike. "I'm Malcolm," you introduce as she continues to look ahead. "Are you a student at Northwestern?" you probe as she halts to look.

"Emi ni (Yoruba: Yes I am)," she says. "Nje O gba Jesu Christi gbo (Yoruba: Are you a follower of Christ)?"

"Northwestern...are you studying at NU?"

"Tekekelena yeheywet menged Divine Vine weste ayetemarku new (Amharic: I'm studying righteousness at Divine Vine)," she says as she starts off again.

"What country are you from," you persist louder, with hopes of any discernible vitals gushing out like the blood of a fresh head wound.

"Ilu kanna ni lati wa (Yoruba: The same country as you)."

"Good grief, you're too gorgeous not to speak English," you comment dejectedly as you continue to roll beside her. "If I could speak in the language of angels, then we could have a conversation."

"Parlez avec votre coeur, et vos mots seront clair, car l'amour est plus grand que le don des langues (French: Speak with your heart, and your words will be clear, for love is greater than the gift of speaking in tongues)," she remarks enthusiastically as you struggle to keep from crying and laughing.

"Lord, this is a strong illustration of your sense of humor," you note, looking up to the sky.

She continues to maunder when we come up on Campus Florist. You take a deep breath and pray in silence as you stop. Gently grabbing her arm, you hold up your index finger and beg her to "Wait here," as you leave your bike in her hand.

She lets it lean against her in silent protestation as she favors her left side and folds her arms. You anxiously wait as the cashier seems to take a lifetime to get rid of the patron in front of you.

"Seven gold roses," you request as you peek out to make sure the cherub is still guarding your bike. You are relieved to note her checking her watch. You grab a card, pull out your pocket Bible and scribble, ***"Who is she that looketh forth as the morning, fair as the moon, clear as the sun, and***

terrible as an army with banners?—Song of Solomon 6:10. The king's daughter is all glorious within: her clothing is of wrought gold.—Psalm 45:13. If the Lord is gracious and willing, I have faith that we will meet and speak again on this side. If not, God is still great and worthy to be praised, and you are still as captivating as onyx. Malcolm."

After you pay the meager $20, you rush out to the watching and waiting stunner and hand her the gift. Her mouth opens up into a radiant smile, prompting her to lip off at a hundred foreign words a second.

"I know it's a bit extreme, but since I can't speak to you with words, I figured you could understand my heart," you gently explain. You show her the writing on the card and point to your Bible, noting, "If you have a Bible in your language, this is what it says."

"Delouty elbeak bekalem ya ighoua (Arabic: Now your heart is speaking loud, my Brother)," she says as she gives you a warm, brief hug, compelling you to embrace her. However, you resist because you don't know if you would let her go.

You nod as you take a good look and slowly wave. "Bye-bye," you sadly announce as you turn and start off, feeling like the faithful lottery player whose number comes up the day that he didn't play.

"Gracias Malcolm (Spanish: Thank you Malcolm)," she says, adding, "Son muy bonitas (They are very beautiful)."

Halting in midturn, you look over your shoulder and declare, "Cualquier tiempo...y no llegan a tu belleza (Any time...and they don't even come close to your beauty)" as you take off without looking back.

> ***Heaven On Earth October 12, 1993***
> ***Just as you stepped on the bus, she stole your attention like a camera flash. You were facing South, but your head mystically turned North like a compass needle. She had the most arresting onyx eyes that hijacked your soul. Her cherry-tinted walnut complexion gave the illusion of soot—as in blacker than a thousand midnights, yet more beautiful than a garden of daisies. She was clad like an African dignitary in a violet gown with matching head wrap. Long live the queen. She was somebody special...and you felt special too, because her eyes were on you for an eternal blink. Death is the expected result of peering at something so glorious. Just like the camera flash, she was gone.***

Photography is dependent on light and shutter speed. She provided enough brilliance in that moment to forever etch the negative on your inner screen. The moment made her seem like an apparition—just a beautiful shade of black. Can the umbra of heaven be seen with the naked eyes? Your day is made, but your life is incomplete.

The desire to live in this present age diminished considerably after another glimpse of Zion incarnate. You close up your minder, which you've stared wistfully at since you got in 30 minutes ago. Your countenance isn't supposed to be downcast on your birthday, but that's far from your mind. It would've been a different thing if she told you to "Step back with your weak game" in English. You don't know whether she told you to "Kiss my butt and go to hell" or if she said, "Thank you Malcolm, they're very beautiful." An understood rejection is very liberating. You can live with that. At the moment, it feels like your heart is being sucked into the abyss.

"Jesus loves you anyhow," Ma assures, catching you off guard as usual, adding, "and so do I."

"That goes without saying, especially today," you declare.

"What can I do to lift your spirits above ground level...you know that's the devil's territory."

"A genie? Great. All I want is one gold-clad, African-American princess that speaks eloquent English and is interested in a caramel slim with chocolate freckles, a fresh scalp and a bad attitude. You can keep the other two wishes."

"Well," she chuckles. "Here's what you wished for, young king to be," she notes, taking a seat on the bed next to you.

It's a little funny, but you don't even smirk because it hurts to feel good right now. Summer school is starting to seem like a dumb idea. You need a break from the mandatory books. Right now the only thing that you can seem to concentrate on is the empty side where a woman is supposed to be, and not Ma. It's not good or productive for Mal to be alone. At the moment, you want to resign from Starlin so you won't have to see Cynthia.

"Have you ever longed for the forbidden fruit?" you query as you focus on the image of Cynthia on the wall, which only you can see.

Ma gently rubs your back.

"There's this lady at work, Cynthia, that I can't have and it's killing me softly. I would move to Europe for her, but she won't give me a play. She's much older and I think the age difference is too much of a barrier for her. We get along and laugh together. And I believe she finds me as attractive as I find her, but her love has an age boundary."

"How old is she?" she casually asks.

You hesitate, because it's going to sound ridicules, but whatever. "Thirty-three."

"How many kids does she have?"

What does that have to do with anything? Whatever again, after all, there's nothing happening anyway. "One."

"Is she divorced yet?"

"No Ma," you answer testily. "How do you know she's married?"

"I just asked," she insists as the back rub ceases. In an ointment soothing tone, she explains, "She has more to consider than just getting involved with a gentleman. Whereas it would be boastful for you to hook up with an older woman, society would shame her. Then there's her child who complicates the equation. Maybe she's keeping your best interest at heart. She has more to consider than you do. As it stands now, you're in no position to financially or emotionally support a family of your own. Yes, she may be drawn to you, but sometimes the consequences of acting on those emotions are too great."

She pecks your forehead as you mull over it. She is right, but it tastes bad going down. Ma has a way of dealing with you that not only zips your lips in rumination, but also laces her loving advice with discipline. If it was a physical whooping, you would've thanked her for it. Although she's one of your closest friends, you know where the line is between authority and peer. Never do you cross it. Playful dialogue is one thing, but when it comes to the voice of authority, you're all ears. What makes it strange is that she has physically chastised you only once. Not saying that you were too good to get your butt beat—contrary, Uncle JoJo tore you up many days in your youth—but it didn't take all of that with her. She didn't sit you down and lay down an oral or written law. You conceived the understanding in the womb.

"Today I beheld the loveliest woman this side of humanity, and for a moment, I forgot all about Cynthia. She was like a dream; like a spiritual experience."

"It sounds like she was all of that and a bag of barbecue flavored chips with hot sauce."

"She was much more."

"Did you introduce yourself?"

"Ma, I bought her flowers and I don't even know her name."

"Whoa. That's an impression."

"That was the only way I could speak to her...she didn't speak English. If there was a time for the gift of speaking in and interpreting tongues, that was a golden opportunity in my eyes, but God knows best."

"Be of good cheer," Ma says through a forced smirk as she rubs your head, assuring, "I'm praying for you."

That's enough to tone down your depression.

The first time she promised intercession on your behalf, you made the basketball team at school. A week prior to the tryouts, you hyper extended your knee. You wanted to kill the brother that shouldered into your leg, and then die. The accident was avoidable. Why would anyone in his right mind dive for a loose ball on the asphalt? It's not that serious. There were no talent scouts out and no championships on the line. Not only were you limited to a two inch vertical, but you couldn't outrun the slowest competitor in the Snail Olympics. However, that didn't stop God's grace from raining on you as a result of believing. Ma told you that all you had to do was believe and show up, and the Lord would answer her call. Despite limited flexibility, you found yourself at the first day of tryouts with the other 200 hopefuls. You managed to jog through the drills and loosen up slightly. When it came time for the scrimmage to determine if the hopefuls could actually hit a shot, you found your range. In five minutes, you scored 12 points. You even hit a finger roll. The next day your name was at the top of the list of the 30 finalists. Practice was to resume that day, but a pipe broke in the building and flooded the gymnasium. That bought you four days of hot water therapy. When the tryouts resumed, you were at 80 percent, which topped everyone's 100 percent.

"Be sure to pray this dark cloud away."

"Why don't you come out into the dining room. I'm sure there's more sunshine out there."

"I'd rather not."

You adamantly forbade her from throwing you a graduation/birthday party, but this invitation has the sound of one. Ma is a creature of repetitive rhetoric. Those were her exact words when you graduated from grammar school. You detest parties, especially surprise parties, so she promised that she wouldn't throw you one. Why was it about 100 people crawling around the living room when Uncle JoJo brought you back from the library? Good grief. That's more than a 'little get together' for your friends, as she put it. You hate to admit it, but you actually had a good time and your enthusiasm testified to such.

If there are people here today and now, you will go jump in the Chicago River.

She closes her eyes and nods "Suit yourself...your caramel cake will be waiting," as she rises and exits.

If the 'sunshine' comes in, you and your darkness will exit. You lay back in anticipation. For five minutes it's dubiously quiet. Even with the door closed, you can hear her speaking in a clandestine tone and detect a light movement. Your temperature and irritability rise as you pick up on their soft steps to your door.

"Go away or I'll jump out the window," you shout with closed eyes.

They ignore you and shout, "SURPRISE" as they fling the door open and pour into your room.

"All I asked was for peace and solitude," you complain as you open your eyes to a small party of three grinning relatives. There are wrapped presents, but no crowd. "Sorry," you plead, sitting up and fading your frown.

"You're gonna be sorry if you continue to spoil the party," Uncle JoJo promises, shaking his fist at you. He can barely hold the box that's almost as wide as the door. Ben and Ma are holding oversized boxes, also.

"Maybe we should dump them on him and leave," Ben suggests.

"How about if I bake another cake and throw it in his face," Ma teases. They all squeeze you in. "You can start with Uncle JoJo's," she insists.

You shake your head and beam. "I just want y'all to know that you didn't have to do this and I love you very much."

"Awe shut up and open the presents, Snake," Ben urges. "Kill that sentimental speech."

In the box is a smaller, wrapped box. The package is small and sturdy. It doesn't take you long to strip away the wrapping paper and open the top of the box, revealing a black, leather Bible with your name imprinted in gold. Your face and your heart smile. "Thanks Uncle JoJo," you say gratefully.

"You have a Bible, fool, so you should know that's not all," Uncle JoJo insists.

You flash him a puzzled look as you hold the Bible and look inside the empty box.

"Open the Bible, Malcolm," he playfully urges in a testy tone. "Boy, if you want to keep things away from black folks, just put it in a Bible," he jokes.

You flip through the pages until it involuntarily stops at 892. A $7000 money order made out to you rests in between the pages. It doesn't take a second for you to spot Psalm 50 and 10. ***"For every beast of the forest is mine, and the cattle upon a thousand hills,"*** you conclude and look up. $7000 is a major, long-term sacrifice. This is the Macintosh Performa you've been hurting for and a down payment on a car. "You didn't have to do this Uncle JoJo," you insist as you rise and give him a firm hug. Is that the sting of stubborn tears you feel?

In jest, he rebukes you. "Remember who's your elder. Am I going to have to teach you a lesson on respect? Telling me what I don't have to do. Shut-up and open the rest of 'em."

You smile and shake your head as you commence to rip open the wrapping from Ben's heavier box. Before you get even one side of it off, you freeze and take note of the colorful apple icon.

"Oh my God," you gasp. You frantically tear through the paper and shout, "YES! YES! YES!" as the realization sinks in: Apple Macintosh Performa 6400; 200MHz; PowerPC 603e RISC Processor; Huge 2.4GB Hard Drive; 16MB RAM; 8X CD-ROM Drive; 16-bit SRS surround sound with subwoofer; 64-bit video architecture.

"You have all of the necessary software installed, with the modem, 16-inch color monitor and color StyleWriter waiting in the living room," he casually informs you.

You spring up and bear hug him off the ground.

"Did I mention that you got a bunch of CD-ROMs, too? You got the full hook-up, Snake."

You embrace him again.

"Now you know your mother is fragile and needs to be handled with care."

Ma's box is hollow, so there is no way that your first impression of a 20-inch television is accurate. It almost feels empty. They strain back smirks as you take the top off and dig out the confetti. Once you scoop out the shredded strips, your eyes zero in on the keys taped to the bottom. You peal them up and note the Eagle emblem.

"Ma?" you question with a gasp, flopping down on the bed to regain your composure. After bouncing back up, she lets her smile loose. *"MA!"* you yell as you grab her and spin her around. *"MA!"* you shout as you run out of the room and out of the front door. You stop ten yards from the curb and go into shock. Resting in front of the house in all of its glory is a brand-stanking new, black Eagle Talon. This can't be yours. You're not worthy. Ma, Uncle JoJo and Ben stop just behind you. You turn to Ma and ask her "Is it mine" with your eyes.

Allusively, she answers your query with a query. "Aren't you going to take us for a spin in your car?"

That sends you jubilantly into the air. Your vertical leap has to have peaked at 60 inches.

You were riding high at work the day following your birthday when Elizabeth sent you crashing in the valley of humility. When you got back from lunch, your desk and work-space was decorated with balloons and crepe paper, a birthday cake was ignited with candles and etched with your name, and the department was gathered around to sing to you. If your psyche is a house, it was made of straw, and Elizabeth was the big bad wolf blowing it down like you blew out the candles. Out of all of the people to remember your birthday, it was a middle-age white woman. She has a couple of nieces and nephews around your age; she loves animals and has a house full of birds, toy dogs and iguanas; every day she's chipper and talkative; Catholicism is her faith. You can't detect a controversial or evil bone in her being. Outside of sound-bites from her, you hadn't really listened to her, though you heard her every day. That had you re-examining your whole mind-set when it comes to white people, even though you weren't naive enough to think that all of them had the same heart. From that moment on, you saw her in deeper terms than complexion.

You were torn between toys. The smell of a new car is an aphrodisiac. Chuck D seconded that by proclaiming, "I could get high in here" as he marveled with you. Freedom to go and come as you please accompanied your new wheels. And the Talon allows you to fly in style. The looks you got made you blush with arrogance. Going to work and school made it that much more worthwhile and cut down on travel time by an hour. Of course, you showed the wheels off to Cynthia, and even gave her a ride home. If only you were as calm and confident as the car. You nervously chattered like a virgin teenager trying to run game on a Broadway diva.

The Performa makes writing more fun. Even when you're creatively constipated, you sit in front of the screen. Ben loaded you up with 15 CD-ROM's, of which only a couple were perused. Usually you go to America On-Line *and chat or research or explore. You smoked up the ten free hours on the first night. After only one day, you found yourself on an e-mailing list. You assume that the person with the screen name Carol was a sister, since she forwarded some information to you concerning imprisoned journalist Mumia Abu-Jamal. Since you had a writing assignment, you defaulted to the computer and had to concentrate on staying off-line long enough to finish. You scanned the Chris Zorich article on the hard drive before you started on your new assignment.*

Last week, BJ mentioned the black representation that Glenn "Big Dog" Robinson retained, which is a repeat of the stance of last year's top pick, Chris Webber. After discussing our feelings on the OJ drama, we talked casually about the sports agency field, which is white dominated but shifting in favor of blacks. With brothers making up the majority of the players in the NBA, the scales of racial equality are evening out when it comes to black representation. We both agreed that the only thing left for black athletes to do is leave the white women alone. Although it wasn't a formal meeting—just idle talk—you realized that BJ was getting you to brainstorm and consider a feature on that topic. He didn't have to pull your teeth. With the knowledge you had from the Chris Zorich adventure, you knew the steps to take. By the time you started writing the commentary, you had telephone interviews from William Strickland, Webber's proxy; David Ware, Barry Sanders' agent; Norm Nixon, Doug Edwards' representative. You kept the interviews brief and baited. They bit and you clip and saved some of the power quotes in your mental notebook and pasted it to your document.

Is the black choice among African-American athletes a matter of cultural pride?

"From (the) standpoint that there are young men—particularly here in the last several years—that have expressed a desire to work with black representation...and I think justifiably so because I feel that some are more sensitive to the issues and concerns that not only professional athletes have but black professional athletes have. And in that respect I can empathize with some of those issues."—William Strickland

Is there an advantage to being a black agent approaching a black player?

"It can be a disadvantage because he's black."—David Ware

"There are still those in our community who feel that white professionals are better than black professionals."—William Strickland

"It's (race) a disadvantage in certain cases because I think it's more difficult sometimes to get into basic college programs."—Norm Nixon

What about the advantage of former athletes becoming agents?

"I think it's an advantage that maybe the college guys don't understand yet. But eventually I think they will, because once they get in business with us versus some of the other agents, it will come to light at that time."—Norm Nixon

The backbone of the article consists of the quotes, which you built your research and commentary around. After you tack on your conclusion, you race out of the door to pick up Mitch and Deon, so we can watch the last game of the NBA championship at Chuck D's.

The latest adventure of Traci and Mitch was her much anticipated cotillion that he escorted her to. He noted that it was more formal and exciting than the prom, even though—again—nothing happened afterwards. Celibacy didn't seem like a trip rope for him. You were pleasantly surprised when Mitch informed you that he rejoined the Apostolic Church of God and recommitted his life to the Lord. That revelation set your mood so sure, that even if the Knicks lose, it's all good.

Mr. and Mrs. Duncan (Chuck D's grandparents/guardian angels) answer the door like Siamese twins. They are sweeter than grape Kool-Aid, but they don't do or say anything. They just smile all day, which is a docile characteristic from God's grab-bag of grace, and that has endure through the Jim Crow south. That's how they greet us...with a grin. They direct us to the den where Brian, Khalid, and Chuck D are already talking smack as the game is just under way and the recently delivered pizzas are laid out.

"All right people," you greet.

"What up, Black man," Khalid says.

"MJ in the house," Brian notes.

"Knicks in the house," Deon proclaims.

"I've been trying to tell 'em D," Chuck D seconds.

"I wouldn't put my money on them, Dawg," Mitch warns as we all give pounds and dig into the Reggio's.

You bow and briefly bless your food in silence. When you look up, Khalid has a critical eye on you. He glances away when he determines that you're not backing down from your convictions, and digs into his vegetable pizza. Khalid initially declined because the menu went against his food restrictions, but then you suggested a veggie pie and he was all good to go. The allegiance is split 3-3: Khalid, Brian and Mitch for the Rockets; You, Deon and Chuck D for the Knicks. For three hours, it's peacefully noisy as Houston goes on to capitalize off of a broke John Starks' jumper to win it in seven. We yuck it up as Chuck D pays Mitch the little wager. Chuck D is going to be starting his job at Carson Pirie Scott in the men's clothing depart next week, and his first paycheck is already reserved to pay off his debt to Brian. The post-game discussion is laced with harmless boasting, but then Khalid starts illin' by slinging Islamic insinuations and innuendoes at you.

"Brother Hakeem made his opponents his footstool," he notes with pride. "25 points, 10 boards, 7 heavenly assists and 3 blocks: tell me he wasn't called by Allah to dominate."

Whatever.

Although the statement wasn't specifically addressed to you, you knew it was for your ears. However, you won't give him the satisfaction of a religious debate. Just like the remarks roll off the others, you play his comments like muted noise. This is supposed to be an evening of kicking it over the game, and he's trying to shift it to a spiritual battleground. The news comes on and he still takes verbal snipes at you in regards to the Bosnian war. Everyone agrees in so many words that the U.S. should stop playing peacemaker and that the war seems unnecessary. Out of the four of us, he chooses to target you after several baited statements go undignified. "Black man: You said you're not for war...didn't your church sing a song titled 'I'm a Soldier in the Army of the Lord?'"

Every one falls silent and looks at you while you continue to stare in silence at the TV.

Since you've turned away from his faith, Khalid has tested you every chance he gets. In our last discussion, he echoed the sentiments of the esteemed leaders of the Nation. While you were in an indecisive mode, you checked up on the several scripture references that he reiterated to you from January and Saviors Day. After you illustrated an understanding of the interpretation of three in particular, he grew silent and left you for a season. John 17:21 stated that Jesus did pray for the world; Jesus noted in Matthew 12:40 that a whale swallowed Jonah (perhaps it was a whale shark, which would qualify as a fish and a whale); Genesis 1 and 2 spoke of the same creation of man: chapter one stated it and chapter two detailed it (1 Corinthians 15:45 spoke of Jesus being the second Adam in a spiritual sense). When he questioned where it says that Jesus can forgive sins, you quickly referenced the account in Mark of how he forgave the sins of the palsied man and healed him in the process after his friends exercised their faith by lowering him through a roof.

The devil is still a liar. You could call the loyalty and sanity of the Nation into question in light of last month's attempted assassination of excommunicated national spokesman Khalid Abdul Muhammad by another former follower of Farrakhan's, but it's a dead issue that has nothing to do with dealing with your comrade.

"The war we fight is not a carnal war, for we wrestle not against flesh and blood, but against principalities, against powers, against the rulers of the darkness of this world, against spiritual wickedness in high places."

That stuns and embarrasses him, but he doesn't cease. "So in other words, in the name of spiritual warfare, if I slap your left cheek, you'll turn your face so I can slap the right because it was a physical assault, and not spiritual? Deep," he mocks.

'Satan, get thee behind me' you rebuke in the spirit as Lacy Banks' sermon comes to your remembrance. "If you cross me the wrong way I'm not going to set out for revenge. Jesus denounced the eye-for-an-eye, tooth-for-a-tooth philosophy and stressed forgiveness. However, I will protect my body; this Temple of the Holy Ghost—especially if you

forecast an attack—for the scripture states that you should not tempt the Lord your God. There's a strong possibility that if you slap my cheek I'll blacken your eye and—religiously speaking—I could turn the other cheek and say that I didn't repay a slap with a slap, thereby, obeying the literal commandment."

He nods bitterly as everyone waits for the next round.

You shoot some friendly fire his way instead, to take the heat out of the moment. "I don't have anything personal against Elijah Muhammad, the Nation of Islam or Farrakhan. I don't know him to dislike him. Personally, he seems like a true gentleman. At the same time, his message and the Islamic doctrine on Jesus is a blatant insult to me and my faith, and he doesn't hesitate to openly criticize the Gospel and the Christian concept of Jesus. ***That's*** what I have a problem with—not the religion, and not the founder or leader. And you know I don't have a problem calling a lie, a lie. If my mother gave me the same message, I would still be in total disagreement.

"Christianity is like the spiritual litter box for most religions and society in general, but that's another song all together. Jesus has demonstrated how much he loves me many times throughout my life and I can't just sit mute when others belittle that love He has for me...and the whole world in general, including you. Khalid, you're a good man; your game is second to mine, and if we were on the same team, we would be an unstoppable one/two knock-out punch; there's no limiting your mind and we work well together when it comes to spreading our talents to our brothers. When we make it, if you ever get sued for medical malpractice, I'm your defender. We're cool Khalid, otherwise I wouldn't be kicking it with you. But I'm not backing down from my Jesus stance. And my belief is that you're going to hell if you ain't down with JC."

Khalid doesn't have anything left to say on the subject and switches to a more social disposition as Satan leaves for another season. "You're going to be an intense lawyer and journalist. It would be a shame if you don't go into broadcasting, because you're as quick-witted and strong-willed as anyone I've talked to, even though I don't agree with you," he compliments.

"And you're going to be one of the top MD's in the world, but since you'll be stressing me about a pork diet, I won't go to you," you joke, easing the tension in the room as the post-game gaieties continue well into the night.

"Let Deon start," you insist to Ben.

"But you're our best player, Snake," he notes.

"It doesn't matter. Let him start at center. That way Cody can switch over to power forward and Tommy can play the swing position. That'll leave more outside shots for you and Derrick." You didn't have to beg Deon to join the team. His enthusiasm peaked like the Gateway Arch in St. Louis. We were able to add him three games into the season, almost a month after the deadline.

Ben shrugs his shoulders as Deon looks on curiously. "Alright," he agrees and he nods to Deon, whose face immediately brightens.

They approach center court, where the other team is waiting and Deon takes it upon himself to say the opening prayer, which is short on words, yet full of sincerity. The church members showed up in large numbers. If it wasn't for the sweaty atmosphere and the picnic attire, you would've sworn they showed up for an actual Sabbath day program. Their mere presence boosts the ambiance a few notches, the humidity to aquatic levels and your pride to a heavenly height. Some of the church mothers even came, adding a good generational mixture. Ben is an excellent publicist. After three games, we've established ourselves as the team to beat, remaining the only undefeated team in a field of ten, with an average margin of victory of 19 points. Today's stepping stone are the Divine Trinity Baptist Church Trailblazers. This game starts off pretty tight and we can only establish a five-point lead on the Trailblazers. After everyone else has gotten some clock, you come in at the 12-minute mark for Deon.

"Number 20 is throwing some vicious elbows," he warns between breaths as we slap fives.

"Aiight, I'll watch him."

You are out there a good thirty seconds before you swallow, digest and defecate his elbow complete with forearm. It felt like a bronco kicked you in the face. Number 20 is playing the four spot, but his natural position is middle linebacker. He's a 6'2" mound of unrestrained, merciless muscle. The bald head he sports gives him an intimidating, Charles Barkley-type look. Unfortunately, he's your defensive assignment and he scores four quick points on you once you get in. When you look into the stands, you take note of John, Tyrone, and Anthony teasing you with their monkey can't see, monkey can't hear, and monkey can't taste imitation that you don't find funny.

You get the ball on the baseline, blow past "Unnecessary Roughness" and poke it on some simple Simon that wished upon a highlight poster. The next trip down, you blast "Mr. Football's" shot to half court, out-race everyone and retrieve it under the basket for an easy lay-up. You peek over at the Monkey see/Monkey do trio, cover your mouth, and raise your eyebrows, humbling them slightly.

After holding the opposition scoreless on their next three possessions, while scoring each time down the floor to take an 11-point lead, Ben forces their point guard into another bad shot. You spring with the intentions of an uncontested board, only to have your feet rise and head drop in seesaw fashion. You blink, and after you open your eyes, you're flat on your back under the basket looking up at the football player dunk with two hands. He resembles the faceless "And 1" icon with evil-Ernie eyebrows. That had to be pass interference or attempted manslaughter, but there's no whistle or sirens. You didn't see it, but based on the muted action—including the opposing team—he leveled a dirty tackle on you. You consider getting up and going after him, but he has a building wrecking body that makes being in a state of clipped more appealing.

As he trots gleefully stag down court, you peek up from the floor and observe Deon flying in from the sideline. Just when you thought that he isn't going to smash into him, he floors him with a shivering forearm. Of course, the benches clear. You even manage to pick yourself up and float over to the action. Deon and "Hackman" jostle like grizzly bears and it takes a good five minutes for the teams to separate them and restore order. The officials finally find their whistles and blow them to indicate that Deon is ejected, not only from the game, but from the building as well. What impresses you more than the stand Ben takes—promising that if Deon is gone after he stood up for you, that the whole team is gone for the rest of the season—is how the church backs us up and protests loudly enough to pressure them into rescinding the initial judgment and issuing a double technical. Walk of Faith was prepared to throw down as a whole and then vacate the premises. Even Mother Brown waved her cane at "Football", who should've been banned from basketball on any level or league.

With only three minutes remaining in the half, you opt to sit out until the second half. Even though Deon comes in for you and the guy that slammed you remains, peace prevails. They even shake hands. We go into the half with a 34-20 advantage.

After composing ourselves and watering up, you go out rejuvenated for the second half. On the initial possession, you rain a three. After they fail to capitalize on their ensuing possession, you repeat the three to put us up by twenty and in a collective zone. They try to pound it in to their "defensive back", but you bounce the ball off his head and into the hands of Ben. You trail him as he pushes it against the lone defender of a four-on-one break. Out of Ben's line of vision, you signal that "I'm on you, babe." After weaving and moving the ball too quick for the guy to conceive, it ends up back in Ben's hands, and he puts it high on the backboard, where you grab it with one hand from the side and slam it through. The crowd erupts.

Unfortunately, you're too winded to word a sub in as you hold your hand up to Deon and head to the sideline without even calling a time-out. Your strength seems to have deflated with that last jam, and the fatigue produces an unusual dizzy feeling. As you near the bench, you start stumbling like a man with two oversized, tied left feet and end up sliding face first into Deon's leg. Just before you hit the floor, it seems like you actually doze off and wake up after impact. That may explain why you don't hurt yourself. Then again, you managed to clasp onto Deon's jersey on the way down.

"You okay?" he asks, helping you up.

"I'm aiight," you think out loud as you collapse, bewildered and embarrassed on the bench.

It's odd, but it seems like no one really took notice; they seem more concerned with the game. A technical for an illegal substitution isn't even called. It doesn't matter, because the thinness of your head and sprinting of your heart startles you. Your team is oblivious to your woes as they commence to obliterate the opposition by 40. By the time the game ends, you're composed and energized. However, the experience has created an anxiety that moves and grows within you like a landslide.

After arriving at Deon's house, you sit in your ride and chat with him about life after high school. He's considering attending one of the junior colleges, even though his experiences with school haven't been that good. Although he hasn't declared a major, he says that he's interested in business and realizes that higher education is a necessity. He confides that he wants to run his own sporting goods store. You make him promise to hook you up with a job when it comes to pass. If all goes well for him, he will be working in a couple of months. Once his system flushes out the narcotics, he'll start applying, since everyone is drug screening.

"I tried to take his head off," he declares, recalling the tussle. "That was the dirtiest hit I've ever seen in football. He could've broken your neck."

"Thank God he didn't," you respond despondently.

"Yeah...I know that's right. This Christianity thing can be a trip, I tell you."

You nod in agreement. "How's your family doing you?"

He chuckles slightly and humps his shoulders. "Better," he says with finality. You confirm with a silent nod as he peers wistfully at his home. "You want to come and meet them?"

You really don't want to, but you can't turn him down.

"That's my brother's car," he says gesturing his head towards a burgundy Town Car. "I hope he doesn't have his white girlfriend with him."

You wonder if he would believe that you are allergic to Caucasian hair. That will have to do as your excuse for an early departure. When we get to the door, a jazzy piano/spirited old-school alto concordance thumps through, provoking your curiosity.

"We're big on music," he explains as he turns the knob and welcomes you into the vestibule.

We ascend the plush, sky-blue carpeted stairs and into the matching pool-toned living room, even though the dense, staggered hum opposes you. Historic family portraits and religious artifacts line the wall and an occupied piano rests against the wall facing the doorway. A petite, raven-and-silver haired lady that's definitely a mother (and more than likely a young, grand one) is holding a heavy note for dear life while the pianist that is a smaller version of Deon backs her up with the refrain *"He's my Joy"* in thunderous tenor. They don't acknowledge or recognize us observing just inside the door as they stay in their closed-eyed zone. Her voice stammers smoothly to different pitches as she improvises *"Jesus is my Life"* and *"Jesus is my Lord"* and *"Jesus is my Health"* and *"Jesus is my Source"*. It sounds like she's taking the best from Albertina Walker, Mahalia Jackson, Billie Holiday, and Ella Fitzgerald. This isn't rehearsal or leisure: They're having church.

It feels like the tune is going through you like radiation and the medium pile carpet gives the effect of cloud floating. If you didn't know better, you would swear that your hair was falling out. You love the song. There is life in the words and notes. It just produces a weird effect that seems like the opposite side of nausea or dizziness. There are songs that minister to you and pull you out of depression. Other songs inspire you to take your writing or playing to a whole new level. Some songs put you deep into meditation about your testimonies. This song: it's like powerful medicine that tastes good; it's as if your soul is getting a steam bath.

Deon *must* be used to it. Singing and keyboarding has to be a repetitive aggravation, like eating graham crackers day in and day out, just as dogs and cats are on a perpetual nugget diet. Just when you feel the wick in your heart spark and your head get light from the altitude, Deon gently tugs you back down to the foot of the mountain and into the kitchen, blowing out the fresh flame and sending the smoke of frustration out of your ears as you loathsomely oblige.

The dense scent of Baptist church style pound cake masks over the aroma of the succulent pot roast, and the garden fresh cabbage is a welcome smack of planet Earth. When you walk through the doorway, you crack an unwinding smirk. The table is set for a Thanksgiving feast in June. You recognize the duck in the center of the table, since Ma acquainted you with her favorite bird as soon as you could quack. Two of his older siblings (Adam, his oldest brother and Zenobia, the middle sister) are setting the conference room-like table with all of the edibles. Here comes the lasagna and biscuits from scratch and string beans and oven fried chicken. And here comes your appetite. All of a sudden, you're feeling the full effect of the game.

You gather that Zenobia is the one that OD'd on Deon's stash, because her face is bromidic and thin, and her eyes are sunken and sullen. However, she's full of life, even if her physical body is worn down. Adam is pretty laid back and seems to possess a controlled glee. His staunch body contrasts well with the thinning top. While Zenobia takes most of the get-acquainted edge off with light humor about the constant music, Adam just wears a satisfactory smile and poses open-ended questions to you about school, sports and family. They explain that Zachary, the brother playing the piano like a hustler plays a sucker, is the only one that stuck with music from birth.

"I can still go on the clarinet...and I still know enough about the keyboards to put out some decent tunes, but Zac is the only one out of us all that really built on his gift. His stuff is powerful," Adam insists.

"I can play the drums," Deon brags.

"Yeah, but you don't," Zenobia corrects. "If the Lord is willing, I'll be singing again," she hopes, confirming, "Heavy doses of crack takes its toll on the vocal cords."

You nod as the conversation stalls at that affirmation. The singing and playing stops to break the monotonous silence as Momma Harris and Zachary emerge to rescue us from the awkward moment. Their skin is the only thing that shrouds the glory of God, because they walk in illuminated like hot coals.

"This is my Moms," Deon introduces as you stand from the table to greet her. "Moms, this is Malcolm."

"I know who he is," she assures, approaching you with an extended hand, noting, "That was a powerful graduation speech."

"Thank you," you beam with elation as you take her sturdy hand, asking, "How you doing, Mrs. Harris?"

"I'm blessed, baby," she says, pulling you down into a hug.

"Do you have a calling to preach?" Zachary questions with an agreeing grin. "That wasn't a speech...that was a sermon."

You chuckle it off and deflect the glory to God.

When Mrs. Harris welcomes you to stay for her birthday dinner, you fix your mouth to decline, but she was only hearing your stomach as she orders you to go wash your hands. Deon leads you to the doorway of the Mia occupied bathroom. Talent runs in the family, because she's french-frying her hair into curls and gossiping on the phone simultaneously, with ease. You don't know the IQ level of the rest of the Harris clan, but you do know that Mia is rocket scientist material and deep space arrogant. She's going into her sophomore year at Louis and is already doing college level work. Her nasty disposition just totally jacks up her soul profile. You're guessing that the Harris kids didn't get their girth from Momma Harris, who is a modest 100 on a wiry 4'11" frame. Minus Zenobia, the offspring average about 220. Mia is 1,680 gallons of skunk funk. They all apparently dipped into Momma Harris' earthy, beauty gene pool.

After she notices you, she twists her face—like she always does when we come mug to mug at school—and clicks her lips as she puts the caller on hold. "Don't take this personally," she urges before she slams the door on your nose. Deon calls her a stupid moose before he guides you to the other restroom upstairs. After Zachary blesses the food with a two hour grace (good grief, the food was about to get cold), you supped with the honorable Harris'.

12

As Professor Larkin methodically drones on about Ibo culture, the class remains robotically receptive while they transcribe the details. There is no room or respect for questions or clarification during his oral dissertation of "The Slave Girl" by Buchi Emecheta. It's half interesting since another dimension of the Motherland is being exposed in vivid story form, and half-insipid because your good G.P.A. is riding on it. The novel is intriguing enough to read outside of school in a leisure setting. However, the only disposable time that you have this summer is the brief trips to the bathroom. The number of white students taking the class still baffles you after a week. What are they trying to prove? Who are they trying to impress? As if they have a deep appetite and open mind for African culture. Even if they ace the class and learn the native tongues of all of Nigeria, their sincerity will always be questionable; they reek of slave master inclinations.

In between jotting down some points and hearing his passionate speech, you drift back to cyber-space, exploring the world wide web, researching diverse topics utilizing the innumerable resources, and even corresponding via e-mail with the cyber soul siblings. You wonder what's the latest on Mumia. As you float in and out of the universe, a gentle tap on the shoulder from above startles you back into class as you retrieve a note from the hand that touched you.

> HI MALCOLM. MY NAME IS FAITH. I NEED TO LEAVE AND I WAS WONDERING IF YOU COULD GIVE ME THE REMAINING NOTES AND THE NEW ASSIGNMENT LATER. THANX. 847 555-4554

You nod as you glimpse back at a bright, ovate-eyed sister with a babyish face and a "Nice hat"—you whisper in admiration of the purple Lakers cap with an extra long bill that she's doming just above her eyebrows.

She smiles and nods as she collects her things and springs out.

Generally, you hate making commitments like that because your penmanship has to be a little neater and your attention has to be honed in on the living exclamation point. There's 15 minutes left and your brain will be hard-pressed to store all of this information. Normally, you filter out most of the rhetoric and recall the bottom line. You accumulate a page and a half of notations (of course, if it was for you only, there would have been about six lines) before he assigns "The Joys of Motherhood" as the next reading assignment. He's not wasting time. Time management in quarters is going to be no minor acclimation, however, it will be mastered.

Although your schedule is too tight to go to the vending machines, you usurp a lunch break like a jacker would steal a Camaro. With a few adjustments and compromises, the reading assignment can be completed by the end of the week. The first three chapters can be knocked out over lunch. Rather than go all the way home and then come back downtown for work, you decide to make do in the Mezzanine. So far, you have only met one person on campus, and that's Bob the busboy who you just exchanged greetings with. Robert Booker reminds you of an old uncle. He confided his age (38) and his plans to start up his own cleaning service at the end of the year. Bob assured you that the campus life will be pleasant, especially since you don't have to adjust to a totally new city. Evanston is a microcosmic, Chicago-ish, melting-pot community with its own ghetto and affluent areas. Of course, he grew up on the rough west side of town. NU has been good to him and he promised that you will have the same sentiments after a year.

A handful of students are refreshening here like African wildlife at a watering hole in the Sahara. You opt for the double cheeseburger, since the seasoning is universal. You really have a taste for fried chicken cooked and spiced right. After placing your tray in a secluded, bright corner, you go back up for a pop and condiments. There are two Caucasian females fraternizing at the drink fountain, so you politely squeeze on the side of one of them and start filling your cup with Hawaiian Punch. It's funny, but when you walked over there, they were speaking the language that you could understand, but all of a sudden, they're murmuring and giggling in what sounds like French.

Picking up on it, but not holding on to it, you fill a small cup with ketchup and start off, when a familiar voice asks, "Aren't you going to satisfy the ladies' curiosity, Malcolm?"

You turn around, and Faith is right below you with her long bill pointing up in your mouth like a microphone. "Excuse me?" you question into the hat.

"These two young ladies who are blocking the ketchup stand were wondering if you are here on a basketball scholarship," she notes, nodding her head towards them. "Since they only speak French, I'm offering my translation services to them at no charge," she states with a sly smile as she balances her tray of fries and polish.

You gaze at them as they wax chagrin red. "They speak English quite well," you observe, handing her your cup of ketchup and proceeding to fill another. You resolved to not even dignify their blatant verbal conspiring, but since Faith has put us all on the spot, you inform them "Yes, I do play basketball, but I also won several merit and academic scholarships to attend here."

Raw eggs slide down their faces as they stutter over a lame explanation that you're not hearing.

"Do you want to copy the notes now?" you query Faith.

She obliges, bidding, "Ill mustard by yitla ill taums mina incha ijbri; Mastardu egrehen ybelete yatafetewal; La moutarde devra faire ressortir le got de votre pied; O ye ki mustard je ke ese re run dada; La mostasa debe resaltar el sabor de tu pie" to the two buffoons as she waves her hands towards the concession stand.

You escort her to your table, pondering what her retort may have been. The French farewell you could pick up based on the lesson you just got, and the Spanish was easily recognizable since three years of classes has you speaking, writing and understanding fluently, but the other tongues have you perplexed. There were at least three distinct sounds that you couldn't identify, and they all had an Afrocentric inflection.

"Question," you state as she urges the query with her eyes. "How many languages did you tell them *'the mustard should bring out the flavor of your foot'*? I understood the Spanish translation, and I assume you said the same thing in the other vernaculars."

"Very good, Malcolm," she compliments. "I told them in Arabic, Amharic, French, Yoruba, and Spanish," she boasts with too much spunk.

"Impressive," you chuckle, placing your drink down. "I think I would rather get cursed out in a language that I can understand rather than getting read in all of those tongues. Thanks for looking out."

"They had it coming," she shoots, adding, "They must be freshmen from a rural town in South Dakota or Iowa or Wyoming where the only images of tall black men are at a theater near you or the NBA on NBC. It was part of their initiation."

"Is there a lot of that on campus?" you question, clarifying, "Racism?"

"That really wasn't a case of racism...stupidity maybe, but they were harmless and ignorant in every sense of the word," she states in a crisp, quick way that almost seems snappy. "Your college experience may or may not include an encounter with a Klansman who moonlights as a college professor, but for the most part, you won't come across anything out of the ordinary. If some poor redneck comes out and calls you a nigger, I wouldn't waste too much sweat on him. It's those closet bigots that have some type of legislative power that we need to be concerned with. And, yes, we have some very intelligent and prejudice potential lawmakers at this school."

You nod and take a seat.

It feels like sunrays are beating against your back as she shadows you, just like her bill shades her eyes. You instinctively turn around to make sure neither she nor your clothes have spontaneously ignited. She just beams while you commence to dig the notes out of your bag. She thanks you as you hand her the two pages. After she settles in, you bow your head, close your eyes, and bless your food without getting her approval. When you finish and look up, she's engrossed in her grace, so you attempt to keep a reverential silence.

"So who were you praying to," you query after she finishes.

"The only God that can actually answer," she shrouds and proceeds to snatch up some fries.

"Does this god have a name?"

She tilts her head back in order to make direct eye contact and announces, "He has many names, and then again, there is none other name under heaven given among men..."

"...whereby we must be saved," you complete. "Wonderful, Counselor, Mighty God..."

"Everlasting Father, Prince of Peace, the blessed and only Potentate..."

"King of kings, and Lord of lords, Root and offspring of David..."

"Bright and Morning Star, Alpha and Omega..."

"the First and the Last, the Beginning and the End..."

"Christ..."

"The Son of the Living God, and That's the only Way to go."

"Ain't that the Truth and the Life."

"JESUS," we both say in unison through mutual laughter as you probe her with your eyes.

"You know...that's never happened to me before."

"You mean how we were able to complete each other like we were like-minded," she says, taking a bite of her pizza.

"Exactly," you emphasize, adding, "like we were part of the same Body."

"and Spirit with the same Hope..."

"with the same Lord, Faith and Baptism..."

"and God the Father," you complete with a tacit chuckle. "That was weird," you state, chomping into your burger. "So what church do you go to?"

Faith is a missionary and the superintendent of the Sunday School at Divine Vine Baptist Church. Second year Pre-med student is her NU classification. However, her undergrad major is—of all things—communications. A sassy, quinlingual M.D.-to-be with the skills to write the bills has an impressive ring to it. Her language skills will be an asset when dealing with foreign patients. She chides you for looking like a first year, fresh-out-of-high school Medill student after observing you examining the building on the second day of class—making sure the number was right—and then coming in with a stoic, strictly serious expression. From what can be seen, her profile is as smooth as butter and—despite not having on any foundation—as clear and evenly-toned as fudge ice cream. Her hair appears to be closely cropped on the sides. Whatever is underneath the hat will remain a mystery for now. She's decked out for a tennis match in her silver-gray sweat pants with the purple NU emblem, and fresh white K-Swiss. Her sub-five four stature makes her attire look like doll accessories.

All three dimensions of this woman (body, soul and spirit) are striking, yet arcane. If there was a single aspect of her that epitomizes the mystery, it is her enigmatic eyes. There's nothing exotic about them: they're black and elliptical with no colorful gimmicks or freaky configuration, and you behold them as if they are 20-karat diamonds. If there is such a thing as a resplendent eclipse, you are staring at two right now. The umbra from the cap doesn't diminish their intensity. Is there a bonfire behind her lenses?

After finishing your lunch, you find yourself gaping dreamily at her as she quickly duplicates the notes. Surprisingly, she doesn't question any of the contents due to bad penmanship. Fluency in five foreign languages and the ability to decipher chicken scratch—what a talent!

Her eyes jump up at you just as she finishes, snagging your gaze, and snaps you back to the present. She giggles and asks, "What are you doing for the rest of the afternoon?" as she hands the notebook back to you.

You check your watch and announce, "I start work in about an hour and a half." You return the query.

"I'm going to probably try and finish the book by midnight," she declares, studying the dining area like it's her first time here. "I guess it would be wise to buy it first, huh?"

"Wise indeed," you agree, rising in unison with her.

She greets Bob on the way to the bookstore, noting that he was the first person she met on campus and that he's a durable friend. When we get to the bookstore, there's only one novel left and there won't be another shipment until next week. By that time, Dr. Larkin would've lectured, tested and moved on to the next book. As you and Faith contemplate the situation at hand, a solution jolts you both as you start "How about..." with her, as we pause to give each other the verbal right of way, starting again like overly courteous drivers at a four-way four-stop intersection, "You can read it first..." we harmonize. Something has to give, otherwise someone is going to come by and snatch the book up, and neither one of us will get any reading done.

"Faith," you start with authority, finishing, "since you were planning to finish it tonight, and I wasn't going to get into it until tomorrow or Thursday, how about we go half and half and you keep it for the first two nights?"

"You sure you don't want to read it first—I don't mind?"

"Look, if I could I would read it with you since we think on the same wavelength," you half-joke, adding, "but since our time tables are different, I'll concede to you."

She hesitantly smiles and verifies, "Are you sure" with her bright eyes.

"It's no big deal. Take it first," you insist. "Besides, I owe you for your translation services."

Finally, just before the quarter ends, she obliges.

After she pays the cashier (she persisted), you drift into the courtyard outside the main entrance and find yourself perched up against the "Rock", listening to her accounts of college life, different challenges and extra curricular activities—which she insists are necessary to stay focused. After her love of the game is disclosed, you couldn't resist challenging her to a one-on-one. You will go easy on her because of her infatuation with the Lakers and *you*: Magic Johnson. It surprises you when she notes that the rules were changed for the Bulls when they played the Lakers in the Finals of '91.

"How so?" you ask.

She pulls you away from the Rock and starts bodying you. "Now tell me that if you're dribbling the ball, that *that's* not a foul."

You agree, but in this case, it's a foul that feels favorable. Although she seems firm and strong like a workout fanatic, she still has a cotton-candy soft sheath that has you contemplating coed b-ball. If she does that when we play, you will give her 20 no-foul calls.

"Notice that when Pippen was doing this to Magic," she says, bumping you for emphasis, insisting, "he wasn't called for a foul once."

"Go figure. That was very insightful. I never thought of that."

"What do you think of Jordan's homer?"

"I'm happy for him. With all of the media mockery he's endured, I hope he hits 50 more before the season is out so he can say 'How do ya like me now.' But in all honesty, I wish he would come back to his real game."

She nods in agreement. "Have you had a tour of the campus yet?" You were about to inform her of the general tour last October, when she informs you that that doesn't really count. "When you have the time, I'll show you all of Evanston."

You nod and smirk your approval.

As it turns out, Faith was born and raised in Evanston, and because her home is a good walk away, she opted against living in the dorms. She works as a community relations specialist at Evanston Community Hospital. Often, she is called upon for her translation services (like she was paged today). Marketing and public relations is her major focus, which contrasts a bit with hard core news writing.

Before you know it, the hour is long gone and you have 20 minutes to cover 10 miles. Hopefully, the traffic is light.

"Did you wonder how I knew your name when I wrote you that note today?"

"Not really," you shake your head as you pop a Bazooka in your mouth that you bought from the school store. "I just figured you picked it up when Dr. Larkin barked at me the first day of class."

"I wasn't present on the first day."

"Well, you could've picked it up from my notebook or something, since you sat right above me. Don't take it personally, but being renown by strangers is nothing out of the ordinary for me. Women, men, boys and girls that I've never seen know much about me, usually because they want something." She silently pleads her innocence as you assure her "No, I'm not putting you in that category. You're cool people, and you almost look familiar."

"Don't you want to know how I knew?"

"I already know."

"Really?" she questions with a skeptical grin.

"Yes," you say confidently. "You pulled it out of my head telepathically, like you pulled the completion of my thoughts out."

She slaps your arm and chuckles.

"So enlighten me. How did you know my name?"

"We'll go with the telepathic rationale."

"Suit yourself," you yield as you glance at your watch.

"Well I guess I'll release you to go to work," she jokes, looking out towards the street.

"You're so kind, master."

"So should I call you tomorrow...with the book?"

"Yeah, that should work," you say, gathering your bag while she gapes expectantly at you. "What?" you ask.

She closes her eyes, puts her hands on her temples and strains, "I'm sorry, Malcolm, but my telepathic frequency is bad and I just can't pull that number out of there."

You shake your head and laugh as you pull out your memo pad and jot down the digits. "By the way, my name is Malcolm Johnson, since we didn't have a formal meeting."

"Faith Blackman," she says, extending her hand. "Nice to meet you Mister Johnson."

"Likewise," you state, joking, "Do you have *faith* in a *black man*?"

She squeezes your hand and asks, "Why did I know a pun was coming?"

"That goes without saying," you note as she walks out to street and you head back towards the University Center.

You scoop up your newspaper and Bible. The page of a visitor came 15 minutes before your scheduled lunch break. Walter okayed the early leave, and since Cynthia is working through hers so she can clock out early, you'll have the time to read to yourself. When you get to the lobby, you realize how taut your face is as a smile spreads across your whole visage, releasing the daily stress. Mitch is standing tall in a crisp black suit, white shirt, burgundy silk tie and black patent leather shoes; Traci is proudly arm-locked to him in a precious pink knee length dress with a pink rose in her hair; Chuck D sports a goofy grin that contrasts well with the gray blazer, black slacks, white shirt and black, tasseled shoes, looking like an usher.

"What up people?" you question as you hug down the line. "Y'all just getting back from job interviews?"

"Not quite," Traci hints, leaving you hanging.

"What's up, CD?" you fish as he looks vulnerable enough to give up the goods. He just continues to smirk as he nods his head towards Mitch.

"Mitch?"

"Man, X" he sighs as he peeks over at the security guard, urging, "can we go somewhere to talk in private?"

You lead them to the cafeteria down the hall as your curiosity snowballs into an abominable monster ready to rip the scoop out of them and dine on it. After sitting them down by the window, you lean up in their faces as your eyes bounce off each of them. "So?" you query.

Mitch and Traci goo-goo at each other and simultaneously announce, "We got married," as they exchange a lip peck.

You almost break the back support of the chair when you fall back with your mouth dropping open into an even bigger grin. Your expression asks, "What", even though you heard them with the ears you cleaned out in the shower this morning.

"We're just coming from my pastor's study," Mitch informs.

"Our pastor's study," Traci corrects, adding, "We're getting ready to go on our honeymoon."

"Yep, we're going to Disney World," Chuck D chides.

"Yes, *we're* going to Disney World," Mitch and Traci affirm as they snuggle up to each other like newlyweds.

You are too surprised and happy to express yourself. "I think I'm going to cry," you half-joke.

"Oh no you don't," Mitch discourages, adding, "I did enough of that at the altar. She thought I was having second thoughts."

"Oh no," you guffaw. "CD, tell me Mitch didn't boohoo. Not Mitch."

"Dawg wept like a bride on her wedding day," he affirms, turning to Traci. "Nothing personal, T."

"Y'all should've told me," you insist. "I would've taken the day off and got dressed up in my Sunday's best."

"It was a last minute thing," Traci assures.

"We decided to do it at 11:59," Mitch confirms. "Tried to call you, but you were all about. Sorry X."

"It's cool," you say with a nod, your grin fatiguing your face.

It is beautiful how they complete each other's sentiments. It reminds you of how you and Faith were speaking today. Not only are they the perfect compliments to each other, but they are the absolute completion of each other. Traci needs someone who can make her laugh, who's not so serious about life, a bit happy-go-lucky and tall. She's going to need to get away from the books once in a while and Mitch is a perfect remedy. Mitch needs a responsible woman that's not going to let him have his way all the time and who can encourage him to stay focused on his studies. Although Mitch is intelligent, he has poor management skills and will only be helped by Traci's talents and her height. Most importantly, it will be good for Brittany.

Of course, she would've grown into an excellent young lady without both parents—as you can attest—but you still feel that two is better than one. It was a mutual decision for them to go to school in Chicago. As opposed to NU, Traci will be enrolled at Columbia, one of the top broadcasting programs in the country. Mitch announced that he'll be playing for Craig Hodges at Chicago State, which translates into first year clock, since the Cougars are hurting for height. Their conference isn't the most competitive, and playing at home with Chuck D will take some of the pressure off. They should be moving into an apartment in Hyde Park within the next few weeks.

You're almost envious of what they have. Of course you're ecstatic for them and wish them the best, but at the same time, you long for that soul connection. There's a lot of love in you to give, but you want it to be reciprocated. You're in love with Cynthia, but it's an unrealistic, unlikely, unrequited love. Cynthia isn't at fault; you're not at fault. It's just one unfair instance in life when two beautiful (at least one beautiful; you're still a work in progress) don't connect like that.

"So where's that fine Momma you've been wet-dreaming over that works here," Chuck asks to your chagrin.

"She's here but she's not taking a lunch today," you abruptly answer as you glance at the Sun-Times. "I wonder what's the latest on OJ," you think aloud, attempting to switch topics.

"I wonder what's the latest on *that* juicy orange over there," CD notes as all heads turn toward the orange clad Cynthia, who's at the Coke machine.

You smile and mention, "That's her," as you go back to the paper.

"*That's* Cynthia," Mitch verifies a little over a whisper to the dismay of his new wife. "Owe," he cries. "I just looked at her," he insists, adding, "and it wasn't a look of lust."

"Dawg, call her over and introduce us," Chuck pleads. You blow him off, but he doesn't move as he shouts, "Cynthia," and turns away as you look up to meet her eyes.

You play it off and gesture for her to come over.

"You got one coming, CD," you mention under your breath as Cynthia seems to hover towards you like a spirit. She's coyly beaming as she makes it over. "Cynthia," you start, almost getting choked up just by looking at her. "These are my friends: Mitch and Traci," you point out, adding, "They just got married."

"Congratulations," she says, extending her hand.

"Thanks," they say in unison as they smile knowingly.

"And I'm Chuck Dawg," CD introduces, extending his hand across you to her. "I'm not married yet," he flirts with her...and with your foot.

"Nice to meet you Chuck *Dawg*—is it?" she verifies with a chuckle.

"Yeah, but you can call me Chuckie the Puppy. RWOOF RWOOF."

Cynthia chuckles, Mitch bites his lip, Traci kicks his shin under the table and you turn bloody red as you bail Cynthia out, reminding them that she's not on break and that they're pretty rigid about the clock.

"I'm sorry for holding you Cynthia," Chuck apologizes.

"That's okay," she assures. "Malcolm, I already have the lines switched so all you have to do is sign on at your desk," she notes.

"Okay," you nod. "I'll see you tomorrow then."

"Okay. Bye-bye," she says in her trademark girlish tone that drives you insane. "Nice meeting you Mitch/Traci...take care, Chuckie Puppy," she says walking away, leaving everyone laughing except you.

"She's a winner, Dawg," Chuck notes.

You just glare at him as Traci rebukes him for hitting on her.

"I was just playing," he pleads. "I wouldn't play you like that, Mal."

You don't even dignify him as you look at the paper like you're reading it. Your ire isn't with him, but with the pining away for Cynthia. Life isn't fair, but you mellow out when Darrin comes within earshot of your crew, which is anywhere in the cafeteria when it comes to Darrin's trumpeting, animated, bloody, Australian accent. Your guests sit in anticipatory silence while he rants about how the "Bloody machine took my money again," as he gives it a Kung Fu kick and storms off. They watch him walk away and turn to you with silent smiles as the laughter collectively oozes out.

"What *was* that," Traci questions.

"That was a bloody psycho," Mitch answers in mock dialect. "He's bloody talking to the bloody machine."

"Call the bloody crazy house," Chuck D interjects, adding, "and bloody bring the bloody morphine."

"You can't modify a verb with an adjective," Traci corrects.

You knew the overuse of the "bloody" adjective was coming the minute Darrin came in. The bloody trip continues for well over 20 minutes as the scene is perpetually parodistic. The topic is off of Darrin, but the blood is still flowing.

"Bring me a bloody Orlando hat from your bloody honeymoon," you demand of the newlyweds.

"Talk to my bloody wife, since she's going to be holding the bloody money."

"That's what I call bloody checked," Chuck D jokes.

"Shut your bloody mouth," Mitch states.

"You have the bloody time," you question Chuck D as we both peer at his watch. He was about to inform you that you have five minutes, when an alarm peals. It brings back memories of the old days of high school fire drills as the bells pierce the building for a good minute before they finally stop.

"Maybe it's a bloody fire," you indicate.

"Should we get in a bloody line and march out?" Traci queries.

"If it is, we're going through this bloody window," Mitch assures, hugging Traci close.

"It's a good thing that we're on the bloody first floor, since you're afraid of heights," Chuck jokes of his lateral vertical. "By the way, you have five bloody minutes," Chuck advises.

You nod as you start collecting your bloody things. Just when you open your mouth to announce the end of recess, the security guard rushes up on us. "Did you pull that alarm?" he questions in an accusery huff as if he was expecting a formal "Yes".

We all look at each other like the toy Robo-cop needs a new battery. "Naw," we all dignify.

"Are you sure?" he fires as he tries to get his breath.

What kind of question is that? "Why would we trip the alarm?" you question his logic. "I work here."

He scrutinizes us as his eyes jump up to the alarm that was just above Chuck D's head and darts away in disgust quicker than he came, without another peep.

"Who does he think we are," Traci asks, breaking the bloody cycle. "As if we don't have anything better to do than pull a bloody fire alarm."

"I didn't like his bloody attitude from the start," Mitch notes. "He acted like he didn't want us to bloody be in here."

"Don't even sweat that bloody fantasy cop," you dismiss as we synchronously rise, just as mister officer wannabe comes rushing back at us with his supervisor and one of the building managers. "Here we bloody go again folks," you warn as they get up to us.

"Look," the supervisor starts, "someone triggered the bogus fire alarm..."

"So what are you bloody saying," you interrupt, your voice, temperature, ire, hair and bloody blood pressure collectively rising with the insinuation.

"I'm asking that one of you just admit that..." the original Robocop starts as Traci cuts him short.

"We already told you that we didn't pull the alarm, so why are you harassing us? Do you harass all of your visitors when something goes wrong or is it a black thing?" she interrogates.

The manager remains mute as the head guard asks, "Do you always go to buildings and play with fire alarms?"

Mitch and Chuck spew a few obscenities as you snap with slob slinging and your volume cranked all the way up: *"LOOK...WE TOLD YOU THAT WE DIDN'T PULL THE BLOODY ALARM. NOW EITHER YOU'RE GOING TO BLOODY ARREST US AND BRING US TO TRIAL OR YOU'RE GOING TO GET OUT OF OUR BLOODY FACES BEFORE I BLOODY YOUR BLOODY NOSE, YOU BLOODY BUFFOON."*

Your illiterate alliteration shocks your friends, but the security folks don't move. Chuck D steps in between you and them and calmly states, "We can squash all of this by reviewing the tapes," as he points up to the camera.

They agree as the manager politely asks you all to follow them to the security office. You have to wait lock-jawed outside with your guests while they review it on the inside. After five minutes the manager comes out and offers a weak apology, indicating that it appears that a little kid pulled the alarm on the second floor. Beavis and Butthead don't emerge from the office as your visitors are dismissed like parolees, without even a minor pardon from the transgressors. You remain in a bloody funk for the rest of the day, and of course you made a bloody stink about the incident to your manager, who sympathized with you and encouraged you to write a letter. If it gets to someone in authority that actually cares, Frick and Frack will wish that you sprayed them with a bloody machine gun.

BJ adjusted the staff meeting to fit your work schedule, which meant that you were up bright and early on your school day off. After critiquing the current issue, we proofread the articles going into the August issue. You are impressed with your article on black sports agents. But then again, you like all of your writings. The interviewing and research fueled your hunger to go to law school and play with the big boys in the boardrooms that negotiate the multi-million dollar contracts. You wish that NU offered the option to study law during your undergrad years—similar to the accelerated Masters program—so you could work out your own deal.

BJ mentioned the Boyz from the Hood charity basketball game coming the following week and suggested a Nick Anderson interview. You jumped on it before he finished announcing it. This gives you the chance to do a little PR writing, which will be a welcome relief to your social commentating. He also announced the CABJ scholarship three days before the deadline. A formal application, three writing samples, three references, transcripts, resume and 500-word essay about why you are interested in a career in journalism and what you would bring to the field are all required.

After the two hour meeting adjourned, you called Nick Anderson's agent to request an exclusive interview and volunteered to fax a formal request with a couple of clips. He promised to get back to you with a date and time. Wasting no time, you contacted a high school teacher and requested a reference letter by Thursday. BJ already promised you one, and your supervisor granted your request for a good word when you went in later that day. You opted on the "Off to the Racist" and Black Agents samples and your first commentary printed in the Sun-Times. After dwelling on your purpose in the field, you finished the essay at 11:50 Wednesday and dropped the completed application with the necessary documentation in the mail a day before the Friday deadline.

By the time the weekend arrives, you feel limp, like a sack of mashed potatoes from all of the running, working, and schooling. However, the call you just received from Nick's agent confirming Saturday, July 23 at 3 p.m. for the interview gives you a surge of life. You will do the exclusive in his suite at the Hyatt Regency a day before the charity game at the Rosemont. He informed you that getting tickets to the event shouldn't be a problem for Nick. As you are entertaining a fantasy of playing, the phone rings.

"Congratulations," the precise, thunderous voice greets.

You freeze. Dad's tone echoes gentle gruffness, among other contradictions. Although his voice inflection is deeper than a black lagoon, it possesses something welcoming, even to none swimmers. "Th-thanks," you stutter. "How are you?"

"Good." Reuben's demeanor dances around curtness to those that don't know better. Rhetoric isn't his forte. If a point is the destination, he wastes no time getting there. "The press indicates that *you're* doing well, but I want to hear it first hand."

You stumble through your account of the senior year, the basketball season, the writing jobs, the college choice, and other details that didn't receive media coverage. For a person that's not very talkative, he is exceptionally attentive, even though you are as articulate as Beavis.

"How is your mother?"

"She's doing well."

"What about your great uncle, Joseph?"

"Pretty good."

"And your Uncle Benjamin?"

"Just fine."

The brusque-likeness gene rears its head. Normally, you can parley until the ear cries for mercy, but Dad strikes fear in your heart like no man. Not a frightful fear, but a reverencing fear reserved for a father. He is not on a godly pedestal, because you don't worship nor praise him. You have an agape love for him, but the other side of that emotion is a reluctant loathe. His ways are more obscure than the Lord's ways. If the perfect heavenly Father can be present in His child's life, speaking often and listening always, how come your earthly father with a body and features like yours can't grace your life? All that you have are pictures, stories and sound-bites. The Lord was merciful to remove his image from your mind that you got when you were a toddler. You resent having the relationship restricted to hearing his voice once every Clipper playoff appearance. Spite should be reserved for a man that forsakes his family for religious reasons. People don't realize that God doesn't advocate cutting family off cold turkey like an object without a soul. He requires total devotion, but He also wants to see the sinner come to repentance, also. Your mother saw something in him, and whenever you face your reflection, you see him. If he sincerely sought to relate with and to you, you would welcome him with love. As it stands, he just wants to...You don't know what the purpose of this shallow call is. You stopped telling your family that he phoned when you entered your third year of high school.

"Well," he starts. "Until the next time, take care."

"Aiight."

As quick as he came like a good idea, he's gone like a lost thought. Now you can sign on to AOL to hang out in the chat rooms.

"How often do you think about Aunt Naomi?" you ask, studying the worn out black and white photos in the family room. Anointed plays on the CD at Uncle JoJo's insistence. For such a contemporary, young group, he seems to really be into them.

Uncle JoJo chuckles and confesses, "A day hasn't passed since the fire that I haven't thought about her, even if it's for a brief moment. And it's rarely a sad memory."

Uncle JoJo's wife, two sons, mother, brother and sister in-law (Dad's parents) were killed when the house was torched during the twilight years of the civil rights movement in 1968. Three generations of Johnson blood was spilled out and dried up with a match. Of course, it was racially motivated. The short story is Reverend John Wallace wanted to buy their dog, Joshua. Reverend Wallace felt that as a white Klan man he had a right to anything in the possession of a black person. Joshua wasn't for sale, so he set the house on fire while they were sleeping. Five lives were lost and countless lives shattered over a damn dog that wasn't even a full breed. Their case got no media play, although it was the talk of the town like other common atrocities. You've seen footage of the German Shepherds being set on black folks by the police; the firemen blasting Negroes with the high powered water hoses; the police beating unarmed, peaceful demonstrators. You know all of the accounts of the martyred civil rights activists. Dr. Martin Luther King was hammered home in every grade in every month besides black history month. You could taste the astringent injustice that was experienced by the generations before you. However, nothing comes close to kindling your prejudice resentment of the white race in America like this story that has been passed down.

It wasn't relayed to stir up animosity, just to educate. Even though the Spirit of God won't allow you to hate, you have willed yourself to bitterness. Wrath is a powerful emotion; an inner boost to your psyche. In the wrong head, it can be fatal. Under the right authority, it can consume obstacles and enemies. While it doesn't compel you to kill or even oppress, it does drive you to excel against the system that allows injustice. You will tell your children this account so that they will not take the black sacrifices for granted. It's one thing to know history as it happened to people who looked like you, but there's a whole different perspective when your blood was victimized. While Uncle Ben never had the opportunity to know his parents or feel the pain of the loss first hand (since he was just weeks old when they were taken away), Dad was 19 when it happened, so you understand what set him off on white folks and—sadly—Christianity, although the Klan's faith was a false form.

Ironically, the Johnson legacy isn't about being submissive to victimization. Contrary, your ancestors made the heat in the hell-hole known as the slave south unbearable for the devil and his imps. Henry Jefferson thought he was going to play Great-great-great-great grandma Mable Mae Johnson like an in-house, sex-for-room-and-board whore. He didn't deem her worthy of getting fucked in the bedroom, so he raped her in the barn. As if the fire would cleanse her of the seed Jefferson sowed into her womb, she gladly embraced the flames of retribution for pinning him to the ground with a pitchfork while he was getting his wind for a second round. That day they both faced their Maker. You look forward to slapping hi-fives with Mother Mable in glory, and you almost wish that it is possible for a saint to descend into hell so you could kill Henry slower one more time. Our oral tradition states that her brother in-law's son—Henry Johnson—shot his "owner" and the whole family (including the dogs) before setting the plantation on fire and fleeing to Canada. Before crossing the border, he cleverly changed his name to John Davis. It's always a treat to fellowship with the Davis side of the family at the Johnson/Davis reunions every three years. Willie "Bone" Johnson—Uncle JoJo's second cousin—ate a shotgun blast from Tommy Foster before he force-fed that shotgun to Tommy. Willie bled to death that night, while Tommy succumbed to his broken neck a week later. Your proud family has a black history that's rarely illustrated in the K-12 school textbooks. You love that defiant dimension of African-Americans that lack the commercial and educational appeal.

You study another photo of your great grandparents and focus in on great Granddad. They say that he was dirt red like his Native American forefathers, although the picture makes him look golden. With the exception of you, all of the Johnson men pulled the sunny, round face from him. Uncle JoJo took a double-dose and walks around looking like the happy face. It seems like Uncle JoJo's father's eyes are focused on something behind the camera. His countenance appears to be as clear as crystal. There is a peace radiating through his intense mask. The suit is blade sharp and the hair is laid back with confidence. If you didn't know better, you would peg him as a Jim Crow era player.

"What was great Granddad like?" you wonder.

"He was a pistol...could move a mountain with his will and snap trees with his quick wit. Made you wish for lashes with an oiled down whip after tongue lashing you. And your father was the same way...and the venomous tongue was passed down to you."

"Dagge, Uncle JoJo," you laugh.

"Now it wasn't always a bad thing to have. As quick as he would shoot some poor soul down with words, he would whisper a word that brought them back to life. Never used it on his own blood."

You nod.

"And yes, he had influence over the ladies," he affirms to your slight delight. "Even without the money, his mouth was rich on charm. Could look at a lady and make up a song about her right then and there."

"So Granddad had some Mack juice," you smile proudly.

"Never misused it though. Was faithful to my mother to the grave. His seed was reserved for her garden, although he had some good words for many women," he notes as he pinches his chin.

"Impressive," you ponder as you close the album. We sit in reflective silence. You never get tired of the oral history lessons. What was so distinguished about our legacy of words? Are we defined by more than a dynasty of defiance? Is there a defining aphorism for our family? "Uncle JoJo, what was the most moving thing your mother ever said to you...that still sticks with you?"

A fiery intensity permeates the pacific glow on his face. The query wasn't offensive, but it strikes a serious cord. He passes the torch of wisdom. "Respect your life," he states with finality. "Respect your life," he repeats. "You know how death follows this family. Satan is eager to take the breath of life from the chosen generation...this family in particular. There is a powerful anointing on the Johnson blood, and the devil hates it with a passion. The less influence we have, the better. If we didn't have mighty, yoke-breaking testimonies, then he wouldn't be worried about us. But we do and he's trying to take us out," he says with a touch of anger as he grits his teeth.

You nod him on.

"My great-granny and granny were midwives. They didn't have the reading skills of a first grader, but they knew the Lord and had spiritual insight that superseded that of a lot of theologians. They always said that during childbirth, death walks across the floor twice with the expectation of taking the new life. If he walks pass a third time, he's taking the mother. Momma explained that for the longest she didn't understand it. She was from the show me state, like me*: how did they know?* When she was in labor with me, she saw death walk across the floor twice, and she wasn't hallucinating either. That's when the Holy Ghost hit her and she started praying like a fearless warrior. You see, death wanted me, but she wasn't going to let him take me. My granny was there and said that she started praying in tongues. Glory Hallelujah! And do you know that death started across the floor a third time? If he couldn't have me, he wanted Momma. But you know what? My granny rebuked that demon like a mad woman. She said he didn't get half way across the floor before he tucked his tail and retreated like the defeated foe that he is. Hallelujah! So respect this life that God has given you, because there's a purpose for it. You have a mission. Don't ever take that for granted."

You match his joyous smile. Profound glee is a potent emotional mix. You hate to add another provocative inquiry to it, but you're rolling. "How did you deal with the losses, Uncle JoJo? Weren't you mad?"

"Still am," he cuts in with a nod before you can get the full question out. "Still am. I probably always will be. But my anger is directed at the main source and not the vessel. I'm fighting mad. Until the Lord calls me home, I'm going to oppose Satan's kingdom with everything that God has given me. If I die fighting, glory be to God. There's no greater honor than Christian martyrdom. *Precious in the sight of the Lord is the death of His saints.* Now I'm not going to sit up here and act like I didn't want to kill the man that set fire to the house. Oh yes, I wanted nothing more than to kill him. I prayed to the Lord to let me have him, but of course you know that He didn't consent to that. Instead of dwelling in a place with so many memories, I came up North. Your parents followed me. Never knew what became of Reverend Wallace: whether he repented or if he died in his sins. Time has given me a perspective on it. The good memories remain and a glorious future awaits once I'm called home. They just happened to go home first. Time is a tricky element. During the season of despair it seems to stand still, but before you know it you're out of it and looking back in victory because you're still here. Look at how quick the five years since

Raymond's home going have passed. So it wasn't how I dealt with it, it was how time dealt with me."

"Do you actually forgive Reverend Wallace?"

"Yep," he says nodding.

You turn away slightly disgusted, but you don't voice it as "Forever Friends" comes on. When you exited the car at the Currency Exchange with Dexter, that song was going off. The title still has a proverbial ring, even after death. Forgiving something that hurts so bad seems so unrealistic. Apparently, he picks up on your struggle.

"Have you come to grips with Kenny Reed?"

"Nope. I still want to shove a stick of dynamite in his mouth and blow him away. I don't dwell on it, but at the mention of his name I have some pretty evil thoughts."

"I've been there. I imagined dragging Reverend through an alligator infested swamp with a belt of pork chops."

You chuckle with him at that creatively wicked idea.

"But when it's all said and done, they were only pawns. With time, your heart will truly forgive him and I will venture to say that you will have compassion for him."

He's right. That part of you that God influences does have a portion of compassion for him. You don't want him to rot in prison and then burn in hell. Salvation is for all, regardless of race or level of sin. Thank God that you don't have the authority to save or condemn, because based on emotions alone, there would be a lot of souls on that eternal barbecue grill down under. Of course, there's that urge that rises up from time to time that wants to torture Kenny to death. God is still working on you. The animosity towards him isn't even your biggest concern. You don't know him. He wasn't close to you in any way, so eventually the rage will be quenched like a match in a sea of ice. However, there's an issue that has a stronger hold on your soul.

"I have some ill feelings towards Dad, I hate to say. Sometimes I wish that I didn't ever speak to him because it's like a mocking tease. He seems like a ghost...a whisper in the dark. I'm not speaking death to him or anything negative—sometimes it seems like he's already dead—but I don't know if I want to hear from him again. How can he go this long without seeing me? Doesn't he realize that I would like to see him? I've told him once, but he danced around the idea, so I never brought it up again. Why doesn't he want to share his pain? It seems like an easy excuse to leave. There's something sadistic about holding on to the hurt and bearing it alone. Like you don't want to let it go. I know. I can feel him. There are serious issues with white folks that I have—not so much for what they've done to me or you all, but the wrath is seductive...inspiring. My determination is magnified when there's opposition, although it would be nice and more productive to work peacefully with them. I'm focused on breaking through, not turning the tables. If it weren't for my negative views, I don't know if I would have the drive that I have. I'm willing to try, and I know the Lord is willing, so it'll be interesting to see my motivation a year from now," you conclude with cool closure.

Uncle JoJo doesn't comment because he knows that you aren't soliciting advice. All you need is an ear to vent in, and God will give the guidance in time.

"So are you ready to conquer the South?"

"Yeah," he exhales. "Hopefully New Orleans will have enough spice to excite my belly." Just before the summer ends, Uncle JoJo hops from southern state to southern state. In addition to New Orleans, Biloxi, Mississippi, Birmingham, Alabama and Little Rock, Arkansas are this year's stops. "After this migration I'm going to hang my horses up for a couple of years," he promises.

"Good idea, 'cause in a couple of years I'm going to send you to the Bahamas."

"Can I get there on a bus?"

"A bus with wings."

"Well then you're not sending me nowhere," he says with a laugh. "The only time I'll fly is when Jesus calls me home. That should be a nice view on the way up."

"I bet it will," you note as "Mighty Long Way" plays to an end.

"A lot of times...it's an unspoken thought...it's an irritation that manifests in a silent critique when you use the name of Jesus in a public setting. Using god in a generic, politically-correct sense is more comfortable. Although I'm not a preacher, I am a Christian, and as the Apostle Paul said 'by the grace of God I am what I am.' I want you all to know that God created you in His image and that He didn't breathe life into you to underachieve. We all have a purpose in life. The duty of man is to fear God and keep His commandments. It is His will for us to

somehow bring glory to Him, no matter how insignificant your purpose may seem. He may put you in the position of chief garbage man so that you can witness and minister to the man eating out of the trash bins; He may allow you to make it to the NBA so that you can be an example to the many viewers that hold you in high esteem. Everything we do is tallied and will be scrutinized. I don't care what you didn't do in the past...look at the present and make the best of it. The penitent thief did and ended up with eternal life. I can testify to new beginnings and second chances. I made some terrible mistakes throughout my life, but the Lord gifted me and brought me to the realization that I have a positive purpose. He could just as easily take us all out, but by His grace and mercy, we're still here. So ask Him to reveal what it is that He has ordained you to do with the precious life He has given you."

You didn't pep-talk them; you preached to them. Your own words increased your faith as they continue to ring inside your head. In practice yesterday you stressed that a mistake is nothing to get down about. It's when you don't play through them when you end up down by 20 points. At first, it seemed like that message sunk in. The Angels matched New Trinity basket-for-basket for the first eight points and were down five at the end of the opening quarter. Then with all they had in them, they tried to stroke you out in the second quarter.

After Trinity got a breakaway dunk, you lost count of the turnovers and the score when they just started giving the ball to the Eagles. Before your eyes they grew feathers, started clucking, fluxed into chicken soup and were sucked up by Trinity. Every trip down—if and when they made it through the light press—an errant pass, a three second violation, an offensive foul (most of the game was offensive), or a missed long-range jumper. On the only fast break opportunity (a three on one), Tate missed a jump shot and threw a temper tantrum as opposed to getting back on defense, while the Eagles played keep away before monster jamming it for a three-point play. True enough, they were tired, but they also had a conniption when you asked them to do laps in practice for endurance. Midway into the third quarter, you stopped yelling and just shook your head as they dropped to 0 and 4 to the tune of 70 to 29. Chris and Terry came to play, but they were really outnumbered 9 to 2 as the Eagles rotated all of their disciplined players.

After the game (which started at 11), you shot home and showered. It is a muggy day, so you wear a white, short-sleeve, button-up shirt, olive green slacks and your tasseled loafers. Making sure you are armed with your recorder, interview questions, writing pad and pen, you set off down Lake Shore Drive. Fifteen minutes credit is what you have when you pull into a parking space under Wacker Drive. You say a quick prayer of thanksgiving and then dash out and up to the Hotel, picking up a little sweat along the way. There's a lot of traffic in the lobby, reminiscent of a convention. After dodging the people, you gleam as you have the reservationist call his room. The line is busy, so she directs you to the house phone down the hall. You waste no time calling. A woman picks up, so you introduce yourself, informing her that you're here to interview Nick Anderson. She informs you that he's on a cruise and asks someone in the background if they know anything about it as you start worrying. Apparently, they don't and now you're getting a bit upset as you insist that you set it up for exactly three. Perhaps she works as his publicist, because she assures you that he'll be back any minute and that you can come on up. The nervous energy and anxiety immediately depart as you gladly accept.

You take a few steps down the corridor in the direction of 2713 when you exit on the 27th floor and the fine young woman is waiting at the door. She introduces herself as April—which you immediately forget due to your professional preoccupation—and Karen is the other woman she was questioning as she welcomes you in. When you take a seat at a small conference table, you notice an individual that resembles Jermaine Dupri chatting with two other dudes on the sofa. The ladies join you for a little small talk, querying your endeavors and commenting on how well the interview should go. Karen's walkie-talkie buzzes during the chat and she verifies Nick is exiting the boat, about ten minutes away.

Dennis Scott walks in as April and Karen continue to graciously host you. You size him up as he goes over to the Dupri clone, or real McCoy (you don't want to sound foolish or seem like a groupie by asking him) and determine that in a shoot-out, *you* would be left standing. You overhear them recalling their night at the Clique as the conversation with the two hostesses' runs its course, giving you the chance to look over your interview notes. When you focus on the Ben Wilson queries, in walks Nick with a black shirt, purple slacks and black walking shoes.

He seriously studies the occupants in the room before his eyes reach you.

"What's up, Malcolm," he greets, flashing a welcoming grin.

"Nothing much," you return, rising to shake hands. Your eyes are parallel to his red-browns, which means that he's either 6'5" or you grew an inch. "How you feeling?"

"Can't complain," he assures as he asks you to hold on a second. He gives Dennis a hug and he ducks into another room. A short while later he emerges and informs you that, "We can do it in here," as he directs you into a large bedroom with a coffee table situated between two chairs.

You set up your stuff while shop talking, teasing him about how others compare your game to his, and going as far as challenging him to a one-on-one during halftime of the Slam-Jam.

"Well, I'm going to turn on the recorder and start this formal interview...is that cool," you verify with a chuckle.

"It's cool."

Of course, you start off with, "How is it after five seasons with the Magic?"

He's animated when he answers that, along with the other preliminary questions. Not that he is frantic, but he relays his answers with the excitement that you imagine that you will have in your rookie season. The thrill is still there for him, which is marvelous. Some athletes seem like they can take or leave their career...like they really don't enjoy it. Nick loves what he does and is having a ball being a ballplayer. You can't help but share in his excitement. He gives you an excellent sound-bite to every general query, vivaciously responding to some of the most redundant queries this side of TV talk-shows. BJ has told you horror stories concerning tacit interviewees lacking personality and a post-junior high vocabulary. And then there are those with the bad attitudes that have a vendetta with the press. They bark out one-word answers and take offense to the simplest questions. Thank God you haven't run into any of that in the infancy of your career.

Nick notes that the transition from forward to shooting guard was hard, since it meant handling the ball more and guarding quicker opponents, but he figures he's one of the top off guards in the league. Jordan, who he keeps in contact with, notes that Nick is among the best and has the potential to be the man. He mentions that his game was patterned after Adrian Dantley's, his toughest opponent is Joe Dumars and—jokingly—Vernon Maxwell is one of the biggest trash talkers in the league. Nothing but praise for the Magic organization comes from his lips when asked about it. The owners are genuinely concerned about the players as people—often going as far as calling to check on them during the off-season to make sure all is well. Bursting with pride, he mentions that he's the answer to the trivia question "Who was the first-ever draft selection of the Magic". If he has the opportunity to play in Chicago as opposed to Orlando, the opportunity would pass. When asked about his feelings concerning Shaq and Penny getting most of the attention on and off court, he assures you that he loves playing with them because they enhance the team and his career. Hinting that they're a Horace Grant or Charles Oakley away from a championship, he credits Indiana with being a better team.

After getting a few more tidbits about his career, the Boyz from the Hood Foundation, and his not-too-personal life, you sit back, eye the diamond studded #25 emblem hanging around his neck and pose the major inquiry: "How much of an inspiration was Ben Wilson to you?"

He leans back, takes a deep breath and with the same zeal, answers: "With Ben—the way his life was taken was a tragedy to us and a lot of other people. I think about him all the time. People know the reason I wear 25. Besides us being teammates in high school, we were best friends—like a brother. We did a whole lot together. He was a role model to me. There's no doubt in my mind that if Ben was still living today he would be in the NBA. There's no doubt in my mind. I did several things because of Ben. I transferred to Simeon because of Ben. I wanted to play with this guy. I went to Illinois not only because of the coaches and the good program, but I went there for Ben because I knew Ben was going there and it's the only place I wanted to be. I wanted to be on the same team with this guy and wherever he was going, I was going with him. He was so special—just a special person; special friend. When I put on my jersey, I tell them it's a part of me—it's a part of Ben. My basketball career is to the memory of Ben Wilson."

13

"A movie won't hurt." The words hang while Cynthia thoroughly measures the prospect of an evening with you in front of the tube. This has to be the two-thousandth proposition. You have been trying to get the May/December hookup since April, and it's already August. According to Malcolm Johnson philosophy, once is enough to be rejected before passing the ball, but it's become an obsession to keep shooting at Cynthia, even if your percentage is 0%. You're like a carriage horse trying to catch the carrot stick. "The Chinese food will be on me; the movie will be on me; the gas will be on me. All you have to do is welcome me in and have a good time," you plead.

"Well..." she starts, twisting her face to decline so she can get out the door.

"How often do you get to watch a movie of your choice? Not often, I know, so why not take advantage of it? I only have a good month off from school to actually live, so why not breathe life into me this evening?" She smiles and closes her eyes. She's off an hour earlier than you today, but you're holding her captive until she consents. "I promise that I'll rinse my mouth with Listerine and use some Right Guard, since I apparently smell like your favorite basketballer that doesn't believe in oral hygiene and bathing."

She chuckles out and insists, "There's nothing wrong with the way you smell."

"That being the case, how about an evening of Chinese and 'The Five Heartbeats'? You haven't seen it and neither have I..." you stop, resolved with the prospect of running a couple of whole courts this evening before trekking to the land of wet dreams.

"Okay," she concedes in a low, yet sure murmur.

"What?" you question to verify it wasn't a hiccup.

"I said yes...I'll pick up the movie on the way home from the store."

The relief and ecstasy induce a gratifying grin. "What time should I arrive?"

"How about eight?"

"We'll be eating Hoy Toy egg rolls and shrimp fried rice to the tune of 'Nights Like This' at 8:15," you eagerly assure as you exhale the built up frustration. It feels like you just dunked the winning basket on Dikembe Mutombo.

Dunk indeed. After further review of the tape, you are called for an offensive foul, the basket is waved off and you lose big by one. Cynthia goes down as the worst date of your short, miserable life. She did nor spoke no wrong. If she started passing gas, turning her eyelids inside out, speaking in thug dialect, and coquettishly purring with everything male, your impression of her will remain perfect. The scrumptious Chinese food gave your taste buds an orgasm; The Five Heartbeats entertained and educated; the conversation flowed like a three on zero fast break; the always luscious Cynthia appealed to you like dripping, chocolate ice-cream on a cone on a humid fourth of July. It was all good, except for two elements: You are slowly killing yourself like a manic-depressive who slits his wrists, and you are tormenting your soul like a spiritual sadomasochist.

Out of frustration and resolve, you rip through your pectoralis major, crack open your sternum, spread your chest apart and walk through the dense wall of taboo like a kamikaze that just got dumped by his wife. After the movie credits roll for the fourth time, since we kept replaying the church scene ("I Feel Like Going On" is her favorite song); after the gastric juices dissolve the fried rice to the point of desiring another meal; after the conversation goes on until you get tired of talking, you face her on the sofa, put your index finger on her lips to hush her up, and somberly splatter her with your heart.

"Right now I can't stand you, because I'm so crazy about you and I know that I can't have you like I want you. My whole mindset is centered on Cynthia, and that's dangerous. However, I know you're harmless, which is one of the many reasons why I want to turn you inside out and upside down. I want to smoke your boots like a potent drug, then suck every succulent inch of you. Since it's more than animal attraction, I want to also seek, discover, explore, flag and cultivate your body, soul and spirit. When I'm in your presence my body salivates, my eyes focus, and I yearn to keep you from anyone else. I'm almost willing to sell my soul to the devil to have you. I'm very fortunate to have fallen in love with an angel, which eliminates the prospect of doing something irrational.

"One of my biggest mistakes was getting close to you and losing control of my feelings. Normally, I would be totally insulted to be rejected because of my age, but with you, I have total respect and understanding. I want to be mad at you for not giving it a try, but when I look at you; when I hear your tender voice, my ire is quenched. I want you more than you will ever know, but at the same time, I couldn't bring myself to possess you if you weren't totally happy and comfortable with me also. This would be much easier if you weren't so damn nice, but I promise you I won't be having another conversation like this with you. Despite your refusal to entertain a relationship with me, I don't think there's anything that I won't do for you. I'm sorry if my boldness has embarrassed you and made you uneasy, but it had to be said. I do pray for the best for you, and although it'll be hard working with you, I still look forward to seeing your bright face everyday."

Her coy eyes are full of lament, which serves as her response. You were expecting a formal hug, but when she embraces you—pressing her breasts against your chest—and then pecks you on the cheek, your entrails turn into mush.

Miraculously, you make it home. Once in, you head straight to the bathroom with the intention of choking your chicken—but decide against it in honor of your oath of sexual abstinence. Instead, you take a three-hour leak, cry a tearless cry, and grow so lightheaded that you think you are being caught up in the rapture. Close. You have the heavenly vision of the ebony rose. The fragrance gives the impression that you are at the florists. Instead of closing up on you, it unfolds like the welcoming wings of a dove to reveal glory.

"What did you mean when you said that the Lord has something else in store for me?" you interrogate, sternly placing your hands on Nicole's shoulders before she could get the door all the way open.

Her startled look demotes to a *'maybe you should go see a head shrink'* expression as she pulls away to the living room. You follow close behind as she queries, "You mean to tell me you came here ringing my bell like a madman at ten o'clock to ask me *that*?" She takes a seat on the sofa, her grin taking up both sides of the couch. "You could've called me."

"I like to talk in person regarding spiritual matters...especially when it concerns my divine love life," you assert expectantly. She grows staid as you tower over her. "C'mon Nicole...who did you see?"

"Why is it that you're so curious about it now?" she questions with an edge. "I revealed this month's ago."

"Every time I start falling in love with someone or whenever I sleep with a woman, I have this dream. When I dreamed it the sixth time I thought the devil had my number, but then I had the seventh this evening—an actual human image—and it was slightly different; it was complete, but I don't understand it."

"What did you see?"

"It was a woman too fine to behold coming out of a blooming rose that changed from gold, to purple, to red, to black, and then to gold, but I couldn't get a good look at her face because her eyes were pure gold. I'm talking sun radiant. And it blinded me," you testify enthusiastically, explaining how you came to yourself—still smelling the roses and seeing spots. The aroma was so strong in the natural that you jumped up and checked in the tub and the linen closet to make sure you were the only one in the bathroom. You then proceed to recount the previous six rose encounters, including the sixth conundrumatic floret that accompanied your wooing of Nicole. "Tell me: what did she look like?"

"I didn't see you with a physical person," she snaps, obviously still coming to grips with the final Word. "God doesn't operate in me like that."

"Well how do you know that the Lord has someone other than you for me? Didn't He show you a vivid image of us?"

"I saw the person's soul...it was intangible and spiritual. And I'm not a fortune-teller. Next thing you'll be asking is the date of your death."

"I know you're not a fortune teller, and I wouldn't want to know the date of my death, but how do you know it wasn't your soul?"

"God has put the mirror in front of my face, so don't you think I would recognize myself?"

You hump your shoulders and shake your head.

"It was a soul of gold that I saw you walking with," she finally reveals, still blindfolding you with a scarf of mysticism.

"So souls are gold?"

"No, the gold is symbolic for purity and deity. The tabernacle—which symbolized the presence of God—was lined in pure gold; the ark—which represented the throne of the Lord—was overlaid with pure gold on the outside and the inside; the Temple that Solomon built was lined and furnished with gold; the mercy seat—or mercy covering—consisted of the cherubim which were made of pure gold. You will be surprised at the total value of the gold that your Bible commentary mentions in the book of Exodus. It's an element that can't be shaken or tainted. This sister has been fire refined and tempted by Satan, but her faith hasn't wavered a bit. She hasn't been perfected, but that's a formality, since God has already declared her righteous. In the midst of the adversity in her life, she praised the Lord. She has something beautiful and sacred to give that very few of us still possess...*a beautiful, gold token.* This is your soul mate...the one God has reserved for you...a true woman of faith. The perfect compliment: saved, sanctified, and Holy Ghost filled."

Deep, but inconclusive, even though you understood her allusion to the mystery woman's virginity. "How come He didn't show me her face?"

"Is that all you think about?"

"No, I just want to be sure. I thought I was in the process of clearer dreams."

"You are. This one started its cycle in that age of obscurity and now it's quite clear."

"Are her eyes going to be gold?" you question like a dupe.

She slaps her forehead and shakes her head as she laughs. "Malcolm," she starts. "You've heard the saying *'the eyes are the window to the soul'*, haven't you?"

You nod.

"The scriptures don't say that verbatim, but it does allude to that."

You look expectantly goofy and she notices it.

"Man—which includes woman, too—is three parts: Spirit, Soul, and Body. We know that though from 1st Thessalonians 5 and 23, which is a reference to believers. The Spirit is the intangible element that allows us to fellowship with and worship God through the Holy Spirit who dwells within, and the Body is the physical vessel of course. We learned that a long time ago, too. So what's the difference between Spirit and Soul? The soul is the seat reserved for God, where the heart and mind reside.

The heart houses the human emotions and desires, while the mind houses our intellect. Now either the Holy Spirit or some other unholy spirit rests in your soul. You were with me when Minister Walker taught that in Sunday School."

It makes sense, but the light hasn't come on yet. She discerns it and continues her dissertation.

"Peter walked on water when he had his eyes on Jesus. His desire was to be with his master. When his focus was drawn to the storms of life, he started to sink. Jesus told the Pharisees—who were bragging about not fornicating—that if they look in lust they are just as guilty. He went on to tell them that if their eyes were causing them to sin, why not pluck them out instead of losing their whole being in hell. The point was the body doesn't cause you to sin, but the soul—your desires. The body is a vessel for the Soul and Spirit. Just like a car won't go anywhere without a driver, the body won't act without the soul.

"The evil eye in Matthew 20:15 refers to an envious heart; the bountiful eye in Proverbs 22:9 refers to a generous soul; the wanton eyes in Isaiah 3:16 are a proud disposition; the lustful eyes mentioned in 2 Peter 2:14 allude to temptation; Psalm 63:1 tells of the soul of David that longs for God, a la Peter. Can you hear what He's saying," she verifies as she nods her head up and points to the sky.

You agree with a smirk.

"When the lights are on in a house, the windows are illuminated, even if there are colorful curtains up. The Spirit is on and in her. Those gold eyes were the glory of God in her soul and the reflection of Christ. You'll know her when it's time. Your Spirit will connect with hers—which is the same Spirit—and there will be no shades of doubt. The Lord has a big blessing for you," she promises. "And you won't be displeased with the way she looks either."

Your smirk spreads across the horizon. Nevertheless, you're still a touch unenlightened. "How are the dreams to be read?"

She sighs and explains that the rose is Jesus—as in the Rose of Sharon—in your heart. The magnificent changing colors represent different stages of His ministry and aspects of his character: gold signifying His deity, purple embracing His kingship, red illustrating His life being sacrificed for sin, black symbolizing His death and burial, and gold signaling His glory.

The closures were the unfavorable reactions to your desire to sin because God wouldn't have any parts in wicked schemes—just as a flower closes up if the sun isn't shining on it and darkness blankets it, your heart grieves and/or grows cold when you quench the Spirit by engaging in some wicked schemes. The aroma of admonition from the Holy Spirit is sweet to the soul, but smarts the heart with a purging fire. The first escapade with Joyce signified the abuse of the beautiful gift of Eros love. While your feelings were sincere, they didn't justify fornication. Your flesh hopped like Shawn Kemp on a pogo stick when you walked in on the Antonette assault, but the stench of culpability charred your lungs and singed your heart. Although you took your eyes off Christ when you clove to Penny in your time of hurt, you were still precious in the sight of God. Instead of going to the source of emotional healing, you induced the infirmity and laid in a bed of affliction. It was the sobering sight of the black petals and the scent of conviction that liquidated the pleasure and the will to seek gratification with Traci. The prickle in your conscience was the catalyst for coming to, pulling out, jumping up and running away.

Knowing Charlotte was equivalent to looking through smoke tinted glass with black sunglasses on: You didn't know what you were into and you got a good whiff of self-deception. Love was the misconception, but secure infatuation was the reality. The thorns of resistance protected Nick, since the sword of the Spirit didn't puncture your heart. The Lord exposed your triple threat temptation—lust of the eye, lust of the flesh, and pride of life—to her, because the rose of prohibition was merely a wall flower to you in that season of heat. You wanted to keep her from anyone else; You wanted to lay like a bear rug with her; You felt that you could, should and would have her because your name is Malcolm Johnson. That was a foul revelation, but you asked for it. The flourishing flower that chaperoned the disparity of not having Cynthia represented your faith, which is blooming in patience and commitment. Along with the glorious vision was the aroma of hope. A bountiful, beautiful harvest is promised to you.

The phone had a certain urgency that comes when it rings after 10:30 p.m. Just as you closed your room door from coming in from Nicole's house, it seemed to jump out of the cradle and into your palm. It was answered on the first-and-a-half ring and you were surprised when Faith hailed how you were doing. There was a personal inflection in her voice that indicated that she wasn't calling to talk about class like she did on the previous occasions (especially since summer school came to a gratifying end anyway). Her inquiry "How are you feeling" was heavily baited with sincerity. You were sure that if you said that you were dying of a broken heart, she would've cut hers out of her chest and given it to you. The conversation stayed on the course of concern and well being as she probed your soul for areas that needed encouragement. You resisted telling her about Cynthia, although you did give her a hint of your anticipation of the woman of your dreams. She just laughed it off as you nebulously grouched about the unknown.

Your heart felt weather-worn from the conception of the impossible dream known as Cynthia to the assurance that there is someone special out there some where some day. Faith's greeting allayed your nerves like a fresh coat of ointment delicately applied by angelic hands on a scar. Although you felt that you needed a good night's sleep and a relaxing afternoon to regroup for the following day's trip to DC, it was soon obvious that what you really lacked was a good conversation. She was an excellent ear and complimentary confabulator up until 1:45 in the morning. It could've gone longer, but since you were going to see her later that day, you opted to rest up. Faith revealed early in the chat that she wanted to know if you wanted to celebrate the end of the semester tomorrow evening. She received movie passes from her job to a special screening of "Fresh", which is due out in another month. Your reply was an indubitable yes.

You agreed to meet her at her house at four, no more, and it's about a stroke past when you exit the car in front of her white frame, two-level house at 825 Colfax. Arrested Development has a way of relaxing your mind. It has to be listened to as a whole, otherwise your mental state would be in the same jacked up condition as a body that stops taking antibiotics before the germs are killed. You and Faith agreed that this isn't a "date", which contradicts your extra effort to groom—going as far as getting a fresh, full-head shave, an hour-long hot bath, and even your Fahrenheit cologne (which you called yourself reserving for that special nose). She emphasized clean casual, so you opted for your black, loose-fitting slacks, seaweed green, button-up short-sleeve shirt, and black, leather bucks. Normally, casual is sweat pants, jumpers and a printed T-shirt, but you were going with the traditional interpretation. The sun is crisp and the temp is supposed to hang around the paradisiacal mid-70's until evening, so you brought your black blazer just in case a slight chill befalls in the evening.

You're as self-assured as a 20-point leading Lakers' team entering the fourth quarter as you ring the doorbell. When Faith opens the door, you forfeit your self-confidence after realizing that you haven't really taken a good look at her as a whole. Her eyes are always enchantably notable; her smile is contagious; her skin is smoother than glass. Every single feature—from her height, guess-a-weight, and loose-fitting attire style—was tallied, but now is the first inventory you take, which explains why it feels like you're beholding a stranger.

She's wearing baggy blue denims by Levi's, which don't conceal the hips that project out from her small waist, climaxing at an angle that mimics capital double D's in a face-off, and arching off into her firm thighs that illustrate the perfect tangency. You didn't know she was hip, because she sure ain't square. Your eyes jump from her eyes to her waist as you take note of the matching denim vest she's wearing over a short, brown, v-neck blouse. A gold, Lara Omega chain with a modest diamond embedded stick cross drapes her slim neck. Her eye level is slightly higher like the evening tide due to her brown ankle boots with buckles on the side just above the 1 1/4 heels. What a sight she is to take in. If there is one attraction of this ball of beauty that stands out, it is reserved for her pea-shaped dome. Her African-grade of hair is closely cut and has your scalp beat by a half inch. She appears to have some conditioner in it that produces black micro curls, which send a craving to your bosom to play in them. Since her head was always covered when you saw her, her hair keeps your eyes above her shoulders. Normally, the more hair on a woman the better, but this is a big exception to that rule. You liked Faith from the start. She was familiar; she was comfortable. If you were going to kick it with a female, Nick, Traci and Faith came to mind. At the moment, you're in a dangerous zone because a libidinous attraction to her snuck up like a thief of hearts on a Valentine's night.

"How are you, Malcolm," she asks through her radiant smile and over the growl of her air conditioner that needs a muffler as she reaches up and wraps her arms around your neck. You reluctantly lean over and embrace her midsection. You weren't prepared for that either and if

Faith isn't careful, she could wind up in a world of forbidden passion and you'll smell the roses.

"With a double portion of faith," you mention as you pull your identical crucifix from beneath your shirt, adding, "I'm doing good with the potential to do better."

"Come in," she insists, holding the screen door open.

You walk in to the welcoming smell of artificial raspberries, quickly analyzing the oil painting of her with gold tinted hair that hangs beside the entrance to the kitchen as you wait for her next instructions. An inspirational gospel tune with a chorus of "More than Enough" by a female vocalist, who you're not familiar with, echoes from one of the upper rooms.

"Have a seat," she commands, gesturing with her arm towards the deep-black, leather sofa and clicking on the TV.

All of the furniture is black (the glass-top end and coffee tables, leather love seat and recliner). There is a Persian rug on the floor with a zebra impression. You're not a furniture appraiser, but you would guess that it's either extremely expensive or covertly counterfeit. Based on your current observation of her, the latter is doubtful. In addition to her portrait, each wall has two exotic works of art. With the soiled state of mind you're in, of course your eyes hone in on the nude, embracing African couple. A vase with some decrepit brown roses in it sits on one of the tables and yanks at your eyes, jacking up the whole ambiance, but you won't joke about them.

"I'll be right with you," she promises as she struts out with the fluidity of a rhyming stanza in a Pulitzer Prize winning poem.

As you scan the living room—paying no attention to the television—your vital signs go back to normal and you adjust your initial lackluster impression to the updated stunning image. Before you can settle into a reposeful mode, the sound of a stampede rushes into the living room. In a blink a four-legged beast too big to be a dog, yet not quite the size of a Clydesdale, comes galloping with a full mouth of foam from behind the doorway toward you. You cringe and throw your arms up to brace for a major collision, when Faith yells, "Beaufort!" The animal is domesticated, because it was a breath away from trampling you when it made a sharp 180 degree'r in response to "Beaufort". Faith sticks her head around the corner as she holds Beaufort, the Shaq of canines, by the collar. "Sorry," she says with a sheepish grin.

"That's okay," you assure, pinching your life by the heal that almost passed before your very eyes.

"You can come on the right side of the couch now," she mentions. You didn't realize that you jumped behind the sofa when Scooby Doo rushed you. "He's much scarier than he looks," she promises.

You reluctantly come from behind the couch, noting, "You're into Great Danes and Dalmatians."

"He's a spotted Great Dane," she clarifies as her smile spreads, confirming, "You know your dogs." She strains to restrain him as she queries, "Do you like dogs?"

Raymond had a dog a long time ago. They say it was mixed with German Shepherd and Collie. You were sure that it was part Wolf/part Demon. The name Damian was descriptive to the detail. Damian didn't like you and he was hell bent on making your life unbearable. Once, when you were helping them carry in a van full of groceries for a church kitchen date, Damian restricted your entrance every trip as if you were a different person. You toiled with a 20-pound watermelon and he had to get Raymond's consent to let you back in. Whenever you and Dexter were over there to play, that dog would eye you as if he was contemplating how to prepare you for consumption: Malcolm a la mode; deep fried and smothered Malcolm; steamed Malcolm with vegetables; barbecue Malcolm with special sauce and minced onions; Malcolm Burger; Malcolm Taco; Chicago style Malcolm Pizza; Tossed Malcolm; Raw Malcolm...Um umph. Damian would actually sit there and salivate buckets. The only thing he ever said to you was GRRRRRRRRR, which is translated "Don't move or your ass is cut grass." The first time he greeted you, you called his bluff and started off away from him. Damian chomped down on your arm and dragged you down the basement stairs. Although you were sad for Raymond when a garbage truck hit Damian, you silently rejoiced the death of the devil. That was your closest encounter with canines up until a minute ago.

Perhaps you're not a man, because dogs are not your best friend by a long shot. You hate dogs, but you politely say, "I have to get used to them...especially if they're big enough to saddle and ride."

She shakes her head and drags Beaufort away.

You silently revel in Faith's promptness in returning. All of the initial excitement has your armpits and back weeping like a possessed statue.

"Do you like to walk," she asks as you rise from the sofa. Your eyebrows jump, answering the question with a question as she just laughs.

The show starts at seven, so she decides to give you the much anticipated campus tour. It dawns on you that her home really *is* within walking distance of the campus. Three convenient blocks to be exact. Northwestern University Press—she points out—is exactly two blocks away at 625 Colfax. The tour starts at Lincoln—cutting through the Patten gym where you unsuccessfully egg her into a game—and as opposed to walking down Sheridan, we stroll down North Campus Drive in view of the Lake, occasionally zipping into the bowels of NU. After floating through the student residence courtyard between Lincoln and Noyes, you reluctantly follow her into the Dellora A. & Lester J. Norris Aquatics Center. "I'm allergic to chlorine," is your facetious excuse for hastening the exit, although she discerns your aquaphobia. She indicates that she was once a lifeguard and that she would rescue you just before you drowned. Mouth-to-mouth with her would be well worth the trip to the Valley of the Shadow of Death. The remainder of the tour stays outside as she feeds you nuggets of personals—periodically interrupting to point out the Seeley G. Mudd Library (you're going to love all three campus libraries), the Technological Institute, the Garrent Evangelical Seminary, the James L. Allen Center, and Cresap Laboratory, among the innumerable attractions—and you reciprocate while bicyclists constantly whiz past us.

It comes as a big surprise that she and Beaufort are the only occupants of the house. You ask about her gold tinted hair that's pictured in the painting, and she informs you that that is a portrait of her deceased mother, who passed three years ago of cancer. You're sorry to hear. Faith spares the details of it, along with her relationship—or lack of—with her estranged elder sister, who's in California. Her father was martyred earlier in her youth on a missionary trip in Nigeria. She notes that militant Muslims butchered him beyond recognition after successfully spreading the Good News to other Muslims in the area. Her losses fueled her drive to practice medicine (cancer research of course) and spread the Gospel. She mentions that she even has some Islamic friends from the Middle East. After a while, she recalls how they tried unsuccessfully to convert her. To your surprise, she states that they have started to open up to the Gospel in the past couple of months. Eventually, you will get her secret. Instead of melancholically musing over her parent's premature departures, she glows about her treasured recollections of both of them.

It's ironic that her father died at the hands of Muslims for the Christian faith and your father is living under the Islamic banner. You barely mention to her how your father's spirit, soul and body are absent (although he's still walking the earth), opting to go into great details about your magnificent mother and *great*, great uncle JoJo. Of course, a discussion on spirituality sprouts from your recollections. After you discuss your three-month trammeling in Islam, you ask about the source of the scar in the middle of her chest. Surprisingly, she doesn't go into a long testimony.

"I had open heart surgery seven years ago," she points out, as she notes the two hours that have passed.

The gait down Sheridan to her house is quicker, and after refreshing, we set out for the show. Thankfully, she agrees with your driving preference. When you hold the door open for her at the theater, she flashes a telling look. Despite her verbal denial of a date and your compliance to that claim, the spirit of liberty laced in the dense, conditioned air of the show hits you and Faith simultaneously. You hold her hand walking down the aisle as if you are chaperoning a toddler across a busy intersection. It isn't vocalized or rebuked, but we both wonder what our hands are doing clasped together. Hand-in-hand, we take a seat and you settle into a comfort zone that accompanies the graduation of the gentle draping of your arm around her shoulder as you get lost in cinema.

"Dexter was shot twice in the chest...both bullets pierced his heart...the doctors say that he died instantly, but the Lord defied medical science and allowed him to live a few moments in my arms," you staggeringly testify.

You freaked out in the theater, and an explanation is only necessary even if she doesn't insist. The playground shooting scene in "Fresh" blew the door off of your replete vault, flashing you back to your two worst nightmares like a Vietnam vet warped into front-line trench mode from watching Rambo. When you cradled Dexter before he exited, God's grace allowed you to tend to him while going into a slight shock. Most of the trauma was suppressed deep into your bosom. You resolved that the painful memories will remain, with the worse being over. The vision of the girl's spasms on the screen mirrored Dexter's twitching leg. A heart attack trotted across your mind first, followed by a sprinting seizure. When Dexter and Raymond rolled off your tongue, you realized that you were hyperventilating. Although Faith figured out what was happening, your reaction managed to scare an inch of hair growth on her head. Surprisingly, she didn't freak out with you. Instead, her oblivion to the spectators augmented as she imperturbably escorted you out. Once out in the fresh, therapeutic, evening air that managed to drop a few degrees, she rubbed your back and crooned you into composure. She must've had the Holy Ghost in her hands, because you waxed calm within ten seconds.

"I would like to say that those moments were a testimonial to his inner strength, but I have a feeling that the Lord was confirming His providence since his last words were in a strange tongue that I couldn't interpret," you ponder as you sip Grape-Strawberry Mystic through a straw. She wisely suggested going to get something to eat, and her recommendation was Cookin With Jazz. You ordered the Lasagna, while she settled on the chicken Caesar's salad and a 7-up. The service was good and brisk, and you were almost finished before you revealed the catalyst to the outburst.

"Maybe it was both," she calmly guesses as she leans forward intently with her hands folded in front of her. "God overruled the laws of nature for many great men...and women. That's what miracles are. And that's why I'm aspiring to be a doctor: to be a vessel of miracles; to be an opponent of death. The memory of my mother keeps me motivated, but my life and career are dedicated to the living God."

You nod and deliberate the point. "I know where you went with that miracle explanation: how Enoch and Elijah didn't see death, even though all have sinned and the wages of sin is death," you verify.

She confirms with a nod.

"How about the several people who died and were resurrected, only to experience physical death again, even though it is appointed for men—and women—to die once, and then the judgment. Personally, I wouldn't want to come back," you concede with a chuckle.

"I know what you mean. I would've been begging God to judge me right then and there and not to send me back."

"When Dex passed, I prayed in my mind for him to get up."

"You're fortunate that prayer wasn't answered, because Dexter might've been upset with you."

"I know that's right. By the way, how many people were resurrected, outside of Jesus?"

She shakes her head and humps her shoulders. "I can name a couple of the documented cases in scripture, but I haven't done an exhaustive search," she declares as you study her expression. "Hmm," she considers as an idea comes to both of you at the same time.

"How about..." you both start, continuing, "Do you want to research it?"

Amazing. Only the omniscient God can sow the same seeds of speculation in separate minds to sprout in the same season. "Do you have a concordance or Bible dictionary," you query.

"I have several biblical reference books, including three dictionaries."

"You want to do it now?"

She guilefully grins and states, "I thought school ended yesterday."

It takes no time to cover the eight blocks to her house. She converted an upstairs room into a cozy study area with three four shelve bookcases full of books, a long banquet table, three rolling chairs, a loveseat and a desk with a PC on top. After skimming her dictionaries, concordance and a couple of Bibles (she has at least ten in that room alone), we compiled an exhaustive, inconclusive list: Elijah raised the Zarephath widow's son (1 Kings 17:22); Elisha raised the Shunem woman's son (2 Kings 4:34-35) and his remains revived another corpse that came in contact with them (2 Kings 13:21); Jesus raised Jairus' daughter (Mark 5:42), the widow's son at Nain (Luke 7:14-15), Lazarus (John 11:43-44), and several saints that rose when Jesus died (Matthew 27:52-53); Peter brought Tabitha back to life (Acts 9:40), and Paul revived Eutychus (Acts 20:10-12).

"The Shunammite woman's son suffered a sunstroke," she observes, like a true physician.

There are a few jokes cracked about the reaction of the witnesses, how the corpse that touched Elisha's bones probably jumped up and scared somebody to death—which still allowed the Grim Reaper to meet his quota—how Eutychus should be a lesson to those who sleep in church and how death got killed at Calvary, since the whole cemetery got up. "Jesus left-jabbed death when He awakened Jairus' daughter, buckled him over with a body shot when He raised the widow's son, floored him with an uppercut when Lazarus got up, delivered a death-blow when he was down after the whole graveyard got up, and stepped on his face when He rose from the grave and ascended to the right hand of the Father. Is Jesus bad or what," you boast.

Luke is her favorite book because he was a physician, historian and theologian who "wrote with a personal touch." She reads mostly from the King James, but she claims that God usually speaks to her through the Amplified. She correctly guesses that Paul is your man, because he went from Christian Prosecutor to Christian Public Defender and wrote in a bold voice.

The digital clock on top of the bookcase rebukes you for being out at midnight. "I guess now is as good a time as any to excuse myself," you offer through a stale pause.

She nods her agreement as we concurrently rise.

"I can just hit the sack since I've done my nightly devotional reading over here."

"Do you always read the scriptures before bed?"

"Religiously," you state, adding, "I like good dreams."

"You dream about the last thing you read?" she questions through a curious countenance.

"Sometimes. However, I'm more concerned about what I say, do and feel as a result of what I see, read or hear," you declare as you take a seat and open her KJ Bible to Genesis 30.

Faith gapes as you passionately launch into the thesis of conceiving what one sees.

"The cattle that saw spots and gave birth to spotted offspring is the biblical illustration; the children in the ghetto that see violence and despair and practice anti-social behavior and see no further than the concrete jungle is the urban example. When the wild designs entered the subconsciousness of the livestock, their imagination produced it because the impression was strong. Poverty breeds mental and moral desolation. When images of blood are saturated into the mind, cold callousness is the resulting psyche. It's not enough for a positive image to flash in their line of vision if the constant conditions are negative. Even the strongest, favorably influenced mind-set can be off-tracked by poisoned soul food.

"I rarely listen to gangster rap because of the angry tone and the catchy beat that often monopolizes my head. Without cogitating drive-by's, I find myself reciting the lyrics three days later. When someone cuts me off, I punch the horn with the passion of pulling a trigger as I spew a few obscenities. The BOX is tube temptation with their promotion of Luke. Whenever I see videos along that line, the urge to sodomize a bitch upsurges with my manhood. The majority of hip-hop is commercialized ignorance, which is as contagious as a plague. On the rare occasions that an artist has a positive lyric, it's more often a hypocritical, politically-correct consolation that is seldom practiced by the lyricist or the listener. Too often, they boast of keeping it real and being positive, but their songs illustrate pride in iniquity by exalting sex, drugs, and violence as *the* way of life, and deitizing money. Even reading news accounts of black-on-black crime fosters the conservative resolution of capital punishment and more jails. Society would have everyone—especially black folks—believe that white folks are so lily perfect living in their celestial suburbs that lack the everyday problems. That's why a lot of okeydoke Negroes take flight from the plight of the hood, even though white folks left the city to get away from them. As it turns out, they want to come back to the city.

"The media is a powerful estate. Think about who's behind the messages that are read, watched and heard in the black community. The messenger will have African-Americans thinking that black men are endangered, and unfortunately, people buy into it. It's a white mind that instructs the colored entertainers how to act. Corporate America dictates what's supposed to be stylish. Why else would brothers wear their pants sagging like leaded Pampers? Negative accounts, visuals and announcements are so prevalent that copycat effects are a natural manifestation to the ignorant. Even the bourgeois think that they're so deep, but they're actually drowning in their own brainwashed state with the rationalization that their intellect is a life jacket and that society is shallow water, since they don't have trouble staying financially afloat.

"Not that I justify someone's actions, even if they only knew negativity, because by the grace of God any rule can be broken—even death: the separation of man from God because of sin. If the Lord can justify us by faith, the least we as African-Americans can do is break the negative thought patterns even in the midst of a desolate ghetto valley. The visual variables would help the process, but it's not a necessity. If you can see it through the eyes of faith, you can conceive it. If you can conceive it, you can do it. For we walk by faith and not by sight. The just live by faith. If a man doesn't have faith, he will see no parts of heaven, because it's impossible to please God without faith and it is by faith that man is saved."

Faith has an awestruck expression as she nods at your point. "Do you have a calling to preach?"

You chuckle. "From the pulpit? Not that I'm aware of, but we all have a commission to spread the Word. It remains to be seen if *Abba* Father will put me in the pulpit though."

"It wouldn't surprise me," she attests with an intent look at you, adding, "You have a way of breaking a thing down with such eloquence that anything short of mass evangelism would be a waste of talent."

You guffaw at the compliment. "Thanks, but I never considered it. Glory to God," you praise as you grow silent and a feeling somewhere in between phileo and Eros blossoms in your bosom like a rose in the morning sun, which puts you in the middle of the thorns. "Listen Faith...I'm not a randy rogue, but I'm conceiving lasciviousness because my eyes are beholding beauty, so I better go. Please don't be insulted."

A slight smile cracks her heedful countenance. "I'm not insulted by your honest restraint. It even sounded like you paid me a compliment in your poetic confession."

You giggle as you clarify your statement. "You're finger-licking gorgeous like caramel cake...Okay."

"That's sweet," she says blushing, adding, "and so are you from this point on, Sweetie."

"It's kinda awkward...I mean I tried to psyche myself into thinking that this isn't a date..."

"It's not," she playfully interrupts.

"Okay, it's not, but it sure feels that way. Sure we haven't known each other that long, but I know you're a joy to be with and I don't want to get too into you if you're not the woman that God has ordained for me as a wife...do you understand where I'm coming from," you ask, not giving her a chance to respond, continuing, "So no more tours, no pet names and I don't ever want to see you again," you joke, rising as if to leave.

She laughs out loud. "You're a joy to be with too, Malcolm, and believe me, I do understand where you're coming from, because I'm coming from the same place. Whether we end up in the same place is up to the Lord. Regardless, I can't lose, because you're a dynamic Christian and person to be around." With that she rises and gives you a gentle, stimulating hug and notes, "You also have the nicest butt I've seen on campus."

That statement reddens your face for the rest of the night.

Altitude is good only when skying on opponents, not in *planes. The trip from Midway was smooth enough, however, as the plane rose to the heavens you sunk to the deepest humility, realizing just how dependent on God you are. Visualizing His hand cradling the aircraft was an instinctive image as you managed to relax in the window seat inside the wing. Ten staff members made the trip, including Dr. Williamson (the advisor) and all six editors. Wally Wilson (his parents need a good flogging for that christening), the sports editor, talked—what else—sports to you for the duration of the flight. If only there was a seat ejection button. Wally would've landed in Ohio somewhere.*

The flight arrived in D.C. just before 11—10 real time—and you were taxied to the Embassy Square and settled in your room by 11:30. Since jet lag was lunch-breaking and our bellies were yearning for company, we decided to get a midnight snack at an all night cafe on Hillyers Place Northwest and 20th Street. If the humidity was any higher, we all would've drowned. The service was brisk for ten midnight orders, arriving before you all could finish the discussion of rats, which was spurred by one sporting an S on its chest and flying across the street, as if coming to the rescue of some law abiding citizen. After biting into the personal pan pizza, you appreciated Chicago style Italian pie and recognized it as the best outside of Italy. While dining, we got a sampling of the natives. Apparently, there was some type of party letting out in the area. Before the stroke of twelve, there were "men" crawling out of cracks in couples like Siamese roaches in a smoke-bombed house. Each of us picked up on the queer action at different points, but collectively we all realized that the scene gave a whole new meaning to the term "Nation's Capital." If it wasn't for the Washington monument—which served as a peculiar phallic backdrop—you would have bet your life that you were in San Francisco.

It seemed like the minute you crawled into bed from praying, it was time to get up and out to the workshops. That hour caught up to us all when it was time to get up. Once at the Sheraton City Centre Hotel, you perked up when you attended your first seminar: "Newspaper Design". Even though the info was geared more towards copy editors and layout people, you ended up with a volume of notes. During intermission, you picked up a couple of cheesy souvenirs and mingled with the other student journalists. To your pleasant surprise, Derrick Baker of N'Digo magapaper accompanied the all black staff of Chicago State University to the predominantly white event. As a commentator/columnist, he rates among the top five that you have read—including yourself—with his superior word knowledge. Whenever you read him, you add two words to your personal lexicon.

The newspaper design workshop actually lasted until four p.m., but you decided to float in on the "Style, Copy Editing, and Diversity" and the "Newsroom Management" Workshops. Before you knew it, the afternoon was climaxing with the opening keynote address and the reception, which the staff unanimously voted to bypass. Although you were worn out when you got back to the hotel, you weren't sleepy, so you, Wally, and Patrick decided to tour the vicinity of Dupont Circle along the way to dinner.

When we pass the chess players in the park, Patrick gives you an oral IQ test by discussing the game and then probing whether you can play or not. As if the only thing you can do is shoot rock.

"Although I can't compete with these big money players," you reason, adding, "I can play a good, casual game."

Patrick doesn't seem impressed, but you aren't trying to move him anyway.

We opt to stroll down Connecticut, since it seems to be alive with businesses and activities. Among the many eateries and attractions that we make an appearance in are Beadazzled: an Afrocentric gift shop that carries artwork, sculptures, jewelry and other ornamental items (when you spot the maracas, you immediately think of Faith and purchase a set for you and her); Kramerbooks & Afterwords: a bookstore/cafe where we browse briefly but don't buy; Dupont Image: a T-shirt and souvenir shop (You can't resist the religious shirt that reads "If Christianity was a crime, would there be enough evidence to convict you?"). People are spilling and hanging out of the Circle and the Underground: a sub-level and bi-level club situated next to each other. You offhandedly peer at the frolickers and keep stepping.

"Did you notice anything strange about that bar?" Wally questions.

"You mean something queer?" Patrick verifies.

"Yeah: there was nothing but men hanging off of each other," you note.

"I didn't realize that homosexuality is the theme of Washington," Wally notes.

"I hear you...I thought San Francisco was queer nation's capital," Patrick says with a chuckle.

"I guess they've gone coast to coast," you joke as we all proceed down Connecticut, window-shopping in the melting pot establishments such as Hong Kong: an Asian gift store with Bruce Lee figurines and other Karate figures, clothing, and art, and The Newsroom: a magazine shop that carries magazines in several African and European tongues, along with other foreign publications.

Tired of walking, we cross the street and opt to dine in Food For Thought. The thick smell of good, greasy food and the riveting sound of live Jazz gives you an endearing hug as we enter the dim, cozy establishment. A hostess leads you to a smoker's section in the center of the crowded restaurant, since there hasn't been a break in Patrick's chain-smoking since we left the hotel. We place our order (the Smokn' Turkey tickles your fancy; Patrick chooses the Whole Brook Trout, and Wally goes with the Chicken Salad melt) and the waitress delivers your drinks in no time. Patrick ordered a Heineken, and even if he wasn't the only one legally allowed to order alcohol, he would've still been alone in drinking liquor.

We settle in and relax as the funky sounds of the pianist, violinist and clarinetist blend some soothing tunes that seem to lull us into a collective musical reverie. Why else don't you go off when Wally makes the asinine suggestion that "Rap artists' should take notes from Jazz and R&B artists' and use their music to promote peace and relaxation as opposed to violence."

Instead of punting him to the second level where the pool players are, you retort in a cool climate, "So can the Heavy Metal and Rock groups that promote drug use and suicide."

That changes his channel, but you want to give Wally's mouth a tranquilizer because he chatters out of tune to the ambiance. He reminds you of a desperate used shoe salesman. All trip it seemed like he was trying too hard to make you comfortable among all of the white people, which set up the perfect tone for him to put his foot in his mouth and for you to put your foot up his butt. Although it isn't the volatile topic for a toe appetizer, he does serve up a subject that has your stomach churning and your leg twitching when your food arrives.

"Do you think that OJ did it?" he asks just before he stuffs his mouth with bird and lettuce. Pat doesn't look at you, but you know his ears are all in your mouth, along with the turkey.

"Nope," you assert with finality.

They silently probe you for the "Why," before Wally gives his commentary. "Don't you think that his record for beating her is incriminating?"

"To me the record could be a biased account. What was *his* story in the incident? If someone was going to judge me according to a record, I would be labeled a woman-beating drug dealer looking for trouble, even though I reflexively hit a woman after she knocked fire from me; I've never sold or used an illegal drug in my life, and I react to trouble when it finds me."

"You have to admit that he looked real suspicious running like that," Pat calmly—but surely—interjects, pausing from the trout.

"It's all about perspective. A brother judges it wise to run from the cops and garner attention when there's the potential to have a confession beaten out of him. With all the camera's on him—which is the checks and balances of the police since the Rodney King incident—they sure weren't going to mistreat him. White America doesn't experience the same police brutality as black people."

They're not satisfied with that.

"I bet there's enough evidence to convict him," Pat notes as he commences to dig in.

You lean forward and ask, "What if there's reasonable doubt—would you still convict if you were on the jury?"

Their impassive expressions say "Yes" as your eyes jump from Wally to Patrick. You got a good look at Wally's mug a long time ago, since he has been in your grill ever since you walked into the office. This marks the first time that you've put Patrick under the microscope. Eyes: unassuming, dull and deep brown; hair: streaky black, slicked back and conservatively straight; countenance: simply stoic. What happens if a negative stimuli is added?

"This is going to sound wrong, but guilty or not, I hope he gets off. I'm not for injustice, but I think that the majority in this society needs to know what injustice feels like. For too many years, the system has favored white people in white-on-black or black-on-white crimes. Until a problem comes to your house, it's only natural for you to be lax, indifferent and uninformed about it.

"Understand this: from the Exodus on, God's people have always been troubled on every side, yet not distressed; perplexed, but not in despair; persecuted, but not forsaken; cast down, but not destroyed. Black folks have suffered like no other people, including the Jews. At least they can blend in with the majority. There's no way for a black man to shed his skin. And take this the way you want, but Cain was cursed, but not persecuted because God put a mark on him; likewise, his descendent Lamech killed someone and it was the same smug attitude that white folks have today that made him say 'If Cain is avenged seven times, then Lamech seventy-seven times', even though he was still under the curse of Cain.

"White people shouldn't assume that because they're not oppressed that they're under God's favor—grace and mercy yes, but not favor. The same reason that Cain wasn't killed is the same reason Caucasians aren't hassled in the United States: because of the visible mark, in your case, the skin tone. And on a different level, if you literally apply the law of reaping the harvest that you sow, white America has a good 400 years of legalized oppression and annihilation coming, so you may get the dark point of view yet."

Your peripheral vision picks up Wally reluctantly nodding an endorsement of the view, but Pat doesn't blink, twitch or blush as you gulp down your Mystic. His hair obediently lays; his lips don't show a hint of a smile or frown, and he remains conspicuously quiet for the remainder of the dinner. The music fills in perfectly for him. You can't help but imagine his same dry disposition if you were snatched by ghosts and dragged through the streets of D.C. Would his response be the same if you reach over the table and backhand slap him? You decide not to test the hypothesis and continue observation.

The fodderish discussion from the time we leave to when we get back to the Embassy Square stays in the safe barrier of the conference. Although the tension lingers like rain forest humidity after a noontime shower when we make it to the hotel, Pat's departure thins it out like an

Arctic cold front. While the doorway to Wally's conscience seems to have a welcome mat, Pat has a no trespassing sign in the front yard to his closed mind, with the threat of prosecution or a shotgun blast to violators. It is still early, but you are way behind on Z's, so you call it a day at 9:30.

After a nine-hour, rejuvenating slumber, you wolf down the continental croissant and orange juice before the rest of the crew crawls out of their rooms. Today's schedule is fragmented into tolerable, 50-minute sessions.

You breeze through your morning classes (Freedom of Information Act: Access to Records On and Off Campus; Insiders' Scoop: Federal Legislation that Affects College Students; Mac Users Roundtable; and Editorial Writing), restricting your notes to a page per clinic. The first hour of lunch is spent chatting with Baker and the Tempo staff before you leave the hotel for a quick dine at J. Sung Dynasty in the Hampshire Hotel. With ten minutes to spare, you phone Faith.

"Can you do me a favor?" you question.

"Sure."

"I need you to check the weather forecast for me."

"The weather forecast?"

"I need to know if there's brimstone and fire in the D.C. outlook, because I feel like Lot in Sodom."

"Really? There are a lot of gays there?"

"Fagedy here; fagedy there; fagedy everywhere. Fat fags; skinny fags; professional fags; thuggish fags; happy fags; sad fags; black fags; white fags. Fagots are crawling around like maggots in a watermelon rind."

"Um," she callously grunts.

"Do you like bike riding," you shift.

"I don't know. It's been years since I've been. Maybe you should get me some training wheels."

"I'm sure you haven't forgotten. It's like...riding a bike."

"It sounds cool, unless I fall."

"Now you know I'm going to have my eyes on you in those biker shorts."

"Is that right?"

"You know it."

"Well...we'll see." She strains to sound excited, but is as convincing as a con man with a speech impediment and bad breath. Getting to her soft, sweet fruit of cordiality feels like scratching through cement.

"I can't wait," you state as the clock mercifully indicates the end of your break. "Listen, I gotta run. I'll try to give you a call when I get back to the hotel."

"Okay. Bye."

You purposely included "try" in the promise as an escape clause. Although her attitude won't be taken personally, you're not in the mood for it. She could have told you that the climate was frigid instead of shivering through the phone call. It was brief anyway. Either speak your mind or don't answer the phone.

The afternoon sessions hobbled like a sprinter with a cast on his leg. After you decided—to your later disappointment—to sit in on the "Sports Writing Clinic" as opposed to the "Diversity on Your Staff and in Your Coverage Workshop", you daydreamed through the "Improving Your Interviewing Skills" and selected the "Headline Writing" class for the purpose of napping. You were conferenced out and—thankfully—the other staff members were, too. When we reached the hotel lobby, Professor Williamson left it to the students' discretion whether to stay for the climax on Sunday or catch an early flight back. The vote was unanimous: ten yeas for flying back; zero nays for staying for more seminars. You were void of the desire to tour D.C. in the 95 humid degrees. With the exception of you and Wally, the staff decided to take advantage of the limited time they had. Missing out on the attractions was a non-factor to your state of mind. Although you planned to see the sights, pictures, postcards and the view from the plane will suffice.

After you shower and slip into your shorts, you sprawl yourself on top of the bed. Wally is surfing through the cable channels before he finally settles on CNN.

"Rough weekend," he comments.

"And to think I thought it was going to be like a mini-vacation."

You both pause and peer at the news, not really paying attention as a foreign correspondent broadcasts a story in Russia.

"I wish I could speak another language," he says wistfully.

"I hear you," you agree, noting, "I have a friend that speaks five languages fluently to my English and Spanish."

"What language were you speaking last night?"

You look at him as your brow wrinkles. "What?"

"I heard you talking in another language in your sleep, and it wasn't Spanish."

Last night you were in the presence of the Lord. Even through your mood shifts today, you still retain the "I'll Fly Away" musical message that accompanied your dream fellowship. The Holy Spirit was moving on and in you, but your eyes couldn't behold Him. Nothing compares to the tingling feeling of the anointing falling on you. There was no prophetic revelation; no vision. Just worship and prayer. However, the dream sinks deeper than your senses. The blessed assuredness of knowing your Source is concerned about you had you oozing with awe. Even when you don't see, hear, or feel Him, you know you're in His care, which is the best place to be. You weren't aware that you made a peep, but you knew your soul was giving Jesus total praise. It's nothing new to you, but the disclosure that you were speaking in the language of angels is a pleasant revelation.

"I only speak and understand English and Spanish," you declare.

"I know I wasn't dreaming," he assures. "It almost sounded like a poem or song...there was a rhythm to what you were saying."

You gaze at him and sit up. "What do you know about speaking in tongues?"

He humps his shoulders and guesses, "I heard that it's the supernatural ability to speak in a language that you didn't know...is that what you were doing...some people say it's demonic."

"Is there a Gideon Bible in that nightstand," you query as the Spirit of God brings some scriptures to your remembrance. Wally pulls it out of the drawer and holds it up. "Turn to first Corinthians 12, 1 through 3, and 10d" you direct. He reads it aloud. You proceed to guide him in Holy Ghost order to first Corinthians 14, 2, 4a, and 22. You reason that a gift from God is not demonic, darkness and light don't fellowship together and blessings and curses shouldn't flow from the same mouth. "How can I curse God when He has put praises on my tongue and worship in my heart," you query, using Balaam from Numbers 22-24 as an illustration of the intent of the natural mouth overruled by divine providence.

Wally indicates that he is Catholic by birth, but admits that he hasn't slept through mass since grammar school. Based on the confession of his mouth, he possesses a commercialized belief of Jesus.

Since prophesy is one of the more vivid channels of communications the Lord uses with you, you note several prophetic scriptures concerning Jesus and when they were fulfilled (How he was: anointed and eternal—Psalm 45:6-7, 102:25-27/Hebrews 1:8-12; born of a virgin—Isaiah 7:14/Luke 1:26-31; declared the Son of God—Psalm 2:7/Matthew 3:17; rejected by His own people—Isaiah 53:3/John 1:11, Luke 23:18; betrayed by a close friend for thirty pieces of silver—Psalm 41:9, Zechariah 11:12/Luke 22:47-48, Matthew 26:14-15; falsely accused and silent to the accusations—Psalm 35:11, Isaiah 53:7/Mark 14:57-58, Mark 15:4-5; crucified with malefactors—Isaiah 53:12/Mark 15:27-28; buried with the rich—Isaiah 53:9/Matthew 27:57-60; resurrected—Psalm 16:10, 49:15/Mark 16:6-7; and ascended—Psalm 68:18/Mark 16:19).

He goes as far as validating the portrait of Michael Angelo as the actual Christ. Normally that type of ignorance steers you to Rage Road, however, he's simply unenlightened, not religiously racist. You replace the blown bulb with a successive series of axiomatic yes/no questions/answers with scriptural references as backup where applicable: Would you agree that Egypt is in Africa? Would you agree that Africans are characterized for their dark—or black—complexion? If Jesus was Caucasian—or white—why would he hide from Herod in Egypt? If I was a fugitive on the run, would it be wise for me to take cover in Bridgeport? With a massive police force, it would be as illogical as you trying to blend in on 51st and State Street. (Wally is the only other area staff member, hailing from Oak Lawn, so he was familiar with Chicago demography.)

He's not speechless and he's not shy. "If Jesus was white, would you worship Him?"

You chuckle. "There was a time not so very long ago that I would have opted to follow a black Anti-Christ to Hell rather than claim a European deity as my Lord and Savior. Since I've had the blindfold removed, His skin-tone doesn't matter," you declare, shooting, "Right back at you: since Jesus appeared to be black, is He still God to you?" as you eye him intently.

"If I'm in need of saving, I'm impartial to the Savior's ethnicity. It wouldn't matter if he had red and green pinstripes and yellow polkadots. But race aside, I'm not sure about Jesus' deity."

That is an allusive answer, but you respect it, and in a strange way, you respect Wally. You can't call him your bosom buddy, but you definitely don't hate him either. He's more tolerable and less phony than most of the white folks you've encountered, and in a strange way, you actually like him. He didn't even come out of the shower smelling like Spot. As simplistic as his response was, it was spiritually profound. While your emphasis was on skin color, his focus was on salvation. Who's schooling who? More dialogue on race and religion is welcome with him, since he's open-minded and harmless. After talking about religion a little while longer, he shifts to—what else—sports, and preaches on athletics for a good two hours.

When he pauses for his second wind, you take the opportunity to succeed in making a courtesy goodnight call to Faith. She sounds as if she had a good nap. When you inform her that you will be catching an early flight, she offers to pick you up from the airport. Your heart and mouth grin as you decline.

Determined to get off soon, you query, "Has God ever left you clueless and curious about a message He gave you", realizing that the obscurity may be answered with an ambiguity.

"All the time. I'm clueless and curious about *Him*. Most of the time I'm at His feet scrubbing them with tears and my coarse hair," she says, eliciting a chuckle from you, continuing, "Other times I'm rising up because He extends His hand to me. But I'm continuing to seek His face. When it's all said and done, I'm ignorant of Him; I'm limited to the revelation and understanding He gives me. As far as knowing Him totally like I want to, I'm clueless and curious still, but I look forward to that glorious day when I will truly know Him. I hope that answers your question, because I know I went around the world and back."

"Truth be told, I really don't know where the question came from or what type of answer I was expecting to hear, but that was very insightful. I guess I was looking for something to mull over in the land of slumber." You notice that Wally is already in dreamland since he doesn't have an audience.

"If you say so."

Yes you do. It was deep. There are divers individuals boasting diverse spiritual gifts. Many men get a taste of prophecy and wax arrogant. The eloquent orators assume that their knowledge and wisdom is innate and self-sustaining, not realizing that if the Lord departed from them, they would be left with empty, meaningless noise. Those who speak in tongues are buried in their insolence. Who can claim to be so tight with God that he can manipulate Him and predict His actions? On some occasions, the Lord has given you and others foreknowledge, but He is still very unpredictable. Jesus was observed for 35 years, yet the loving nature of God surpasses human logic and emotion. How can the passion of Christ be explained when He knew that His Disciples would deny and betray Him? Humanity would've turned. Left up to any other, mankind would still be lost. He's good and He's fair. Based on those known attributes, people could safely say that children won't be killed and the wicked will never have prosperity. However, God doesn't always seem good and life doesn't always seem fair. With all of the biblical literature and revelations given to mankind, everyone is still ignorant to the fullness of Him. The ultimate goal is knowing the Father.

Faith surprised you at the airport anyway (Hallelujah!). After spending the weekend with Wally and company, she hit the spot like an oasis to a desert wanderer. She took you to the Missionary anniversary celebration at her church. Although there wasn't a formal message from a preacher, Chris Bishop Randall and the Company Choir ministered in song. The anointing caved in like an over-pressured roof and the whole place was demolished. Usually emotional services are not your favorite. It's too easy to forget the message when you leave. However, there was a soloist name Shonda Dunlap who could hum better than Joyce, which is saying her mad skills can pay the sad bills. You didn't run around the church or dance in the aisle or shout to the top of your lungs or stand on the pews or clap to the beat, but you were moved like a Corvette under the influence of a lead foot when she sung a song titled "Faith Under Fire," which you and Faith discerned was a word from 1 Peter 1:7. The glory of God was in her voice as you heard from heaven with the lyrical message and the funky piano instrumental. The keyboardist (who you recognized but couldn't place) stroked to a melodic zone worthy of the cherubic chorus. Faith was in tears and still reciting the line "When my faith is under fire; and there's a test for my soul; the outlook isn't dire; He's purifying me like gold" well after the program ended. The understanding that trials strengthen faith hit your spirit flush.

Then your soul started wondering if God was saying something else, realizing that the vague query you posed to Faith while you were in

DC was the subconscious inquiry "Is Faith the woman with the soul of gold?" The question moved to the forefront of your mind. When you dropped her off you felt awkward, yet excited. However, you didn't speak or act on it. It was peculiar how you got up in her face and peered into the stormy black eyes of Faith as if you were going to lock on her lips. Her reaction—or lack thereof—was conspicuous. She didn't push you away, turn her head, jump back, smile, frown, blink, belch or speak. She welcomed you into her personal space without a question, comment, or clarification. Her expression was neutral and knowing, but unfortunately, untelling.

You didn't see her for the rest of the week and barely spoke to her. We originally planned to bike ride on the north side Tuesday, but you had to attend a call meeting for the Testimony staff. After rescheduling for Thursday, she had to call it off for a Sunday school project. During your absence from her, you repetitiously asked the Lord for guidance in the event Faith wasn't the woman of your dreams, because your enchantment superseded the sibling barrier and her presence was torture to your righteous soul.

The season ended the Saturday you were away (Hallelujah!). Never has any team that you've been associated with gone 0-for. If every other team was so much more superior; if the Angels weren't in a position to do better through hustling and work; if the emphasis wasn't so much on individuality and scoring pretty (imitating only the shooting aspect of Jordan's game, while disregarding his hustle and defense) as opposed to team play and unselfishness; if it was because of your inability to coach and teach fundamental basketball, you could accept it without a gripe. Ben said that they played hard and came up two short. For whatever it's worth, we still got a plaque for participating. Terry's and Chris' Christian growth was more than a consolation to a dismal season. Two, young, new souls actually put the game in perspective. They didn't complain or challenge you once. Both were the top two players that made every game and seemed to exercise Christian morals on the court, off of the court and in Sunday school (where they're sitting attentively now as Nick kicks knowledge) more-so than the youngsters that were raised in the church.

Dexter always insisted that a new convert is like an empty cup that's ready to be filled with a savory drink. Raising a kid in the church is all well and good, but too often they're not taught about the ills of the world. Parents sometimes have a tendency of dismissing temptation with an authoritative "Thou Shalt Not" without ever really explaining the ramifications outside of "burning in hell". Several of your peers in the congregation were as curious as Eve and experimented on their own. Instead of sheltering you, Ma allowed you and Dex to observe the negative elements that lead to destruction. Once, she took us to the ward of her hospital for recovering drug and alcohol addicts and even allowed us to sit in on an AA session. Not a pretty sight. Of course, the touchier topic of sex came up and she didn't talk about birds and bees. To this day, you've never heard that fairy tale. All areas were covered, from sexually transmitted diseases to prostitution to pregnancy to parenthood. She even let us talk to a hooker that she befriended in the emergency room after getting stomped by her pimp. Although it was an open discussion, you didn't disclose, question or contribute to the topic.

In bringing the consequences of certain actions home, she also taught us about ministry. While many people make unnecessary mistakes and are often caught in a vicious cycle of falling, she illustrated that we who are strong should administer help when we can. Dexter took to the message well, because he knew more thugs than a New York City hustler. Yesterday you had a chance run-in with JB: James Brock. You were surprised to find out that he is a rap artist shopping his single titled "Baptism of Fire." Unlike Shonda Dunlap's solo that focused on trials and tests, his alluded to the Baptism of the Holy Ghost, which purges believers of bad habits and desires. His stage name is JBC: James B-Rock for Christ and he and his partner (Mark Preston, better known as Mission Possible) gave you a sample of it a cappella. The lyrics were too swift to recall. None-the-less, you could understand every word of the rapid-rhyming stanzas.

At certain times and opportune moods you like rap, but too often the lines are unclear and hard to understand. Usually you're limited to the deep beats and heavy bass, not realizing that you could actually be nodding to devil worshipping music. There is one verse that stuck with you: "My birth is in Your breath; My life is in Your death." That lyric—which recognizes the breath of God being the source of creation of man and the death of Jesus as the source of eternal life through the forgiveness of sin—is worth the price of the CD. After they disclosed that they are called "God's Disciples," in memory of Dexter, you reserved ten copies. As it turns out, shortly after James' conversion, he witnessed to Mark, and he got saved, too. It's amazing how the ministry of Dexter continues although he's not physically present.

When Nick dismisses, you hand her your tithe to put in, and inform Chris and Terry that you're on your way to interview Deon Thomas (Hallelujah!). They express the excitement that you're holding in when you set out for his home on the West Side. Yes, he's your colleague; yes, he's only about five years older than you, but he's made it to the point where countless ballers want to be. For that, you're excited for him. At the call meeting, BJ encouraged you to try to get something on Thomas before he left for the Dallas Mavericks' training camp. You should've thought about that. Tuesday you called his agent, Mark Bartelstein, and he was more than accommodating, promising to talk to him and get back to you. Wednesday morning he called and informed you that Thomas was excited about interviewing with you on Sunday. Wednesday through Friday was spent looking through old articles, researching his career, and preparing the interview.

It takes you no time to make it to his hood, which is in the shadow of Cook County Hospital on Washburn. As you cruise down the avenue, taking note of the glass strewn vacant lots, abandoned houses and overt chop shops, you silently thank the Lord for Deon's success and impending riches. After checking the address once more—making sure of the house—you park and ascend the old wooden stairs of the frame structure. He promptly opens on the first knock and it's apparent that you're in reporter mode, because he looks imposing even though he only has about four inches on you. When you're in player mode, he doesn't look so tall.

"How's it going, Deon," you greet.

"Good," he says, extending a hand and welcoming you in. He takes note of your height and jokes that we could've done the interview over a one-on-one. "Have a seat," he encourages as he leads you into the living room.

His grandmother is obscure in the kitchen. You note the several trophies in the living room as he folds himself up in a love seat across from you. He's right at home in his white T-shirt with the "Above the Rim" logo, black denim shorts, and white socks with no shoes as you small talk him a little about your hoop background before you get his consent to record. You make it a point to always get permission, although it's almost a given. You shoot through the standard, preliminary interview questions (What was the road to the NBA like; What do you expect on the NBA level; Who were your toughest opponents; What was the most memorable moment in your career; Was there a rivalry between you and Juwan Howard; gabba gabba gabba) and he graciously and eloquently answers them all as if he's not tired of hearing them.

Topical sound-bites of the interview stay with you.

On becoming the Illini all-time leading scorer while shooting over 60%: "I knew that it was a possibility that I could do it that game...So that's when I was trying to do it because I knew my grandmother would be down there. While we were in the game, after I made the shot I ran back ready to play defense because I didn't realize what had happened. Everybody was up cheering and I thought that they were cheering because of the basket because I was so zoned out...I just zoned in on the game. So Jerry Hester ran up to me and hugged me. And I was like what are you doing? He was like 'you don't know what you just did, do you?' And I was like 'Awe okay!' That's definitely probably the highest high point of my career."

On Proposition 48: "I studied, that's why I passed it. But once I reflect back on it, I don't think it's fair at all...48 or 42...there are a lot of things that are on those tests—the ACT and the SAT—that you don't get in high school. When I was in high school I never took Chemistry. I didn't go past Geometry. I didn't have all of that other stuff: Trig, Chemistry, Physics. I didn't take any of that. Luckily I had my books to study from...or I probably would've been worse off than what I was. I don't think it's fair at all...they say that it's culturally biased, I would have to agree with that."

On his career aspirations and outside goals: "As long as I can remember I wanted to go into law. Specifically, a Supreme Court Justice, but that takes too long. Hopefully during [my NBA career]...I'm trying to take it [LSAT] before I leave to go to Dallas so I can start applying for law school. I want to take it over the off-season, so by the time I'm done I could just go and start my own law firm."

On being a sports agent: "We definitely need more black sports agents, seeing that the majority of the athletes are black. Not saying that some of the white agents aren't good. My agent is white and he's cool...real good and works real hard. But he can't understand me because he's never had to live the way that I live. I can't expect him to understand that. I can expect him to do his job, because he's definitely going to do his job. And I think that's something that would help benefit some of the other players that are coming up, because I've lived in the ghetto. I still live in the ghetto. There were times when I didn't know what I was going to eat, just like most of the people in the inner city. I've had to live with my skin color for 23 years, so I can understand what a lot of these other athletes are going through. And then on another level a lot of agents take players for their money. Hopefully—if things turn out—I'll have my own money...I won't need anybody else's money, but I would be able to give them some type of insight into what type of business this is and the many faces it can have."

On your boy Bryant Notree and what to look for at Illinois: "I didn't really have a chance to actually sit down and talk to him. I sort of conveyed a few things when he came down on his visit, because I hosted him. I know Bryant's father and his mother. He's going to go to school. That's not a problem. I'm not worried about him. He'll definitely get his grades and he'll definitely graduate."

He credited his brother for "making" him play basketball in high school, Simeon coach Bob Hambric with molding him into a basketball player (since his interest was baseball and he didn't hoop until high school) and Illini assistant coach Jimmy Collins for a successful college career. You were surprised that he hadn't talked to Nick since the draft. When he mentioned his law school aspirations and desire to practice sports law—noting that earning his political science degree was more important than the basketball career—you were almost too inspired to remain professional. Chris Webber and Juwan Howard rate as his toughest rivals because their skills and size mirror his own. Deon confirms that the trash flew when they hit the court together, but that off the court they were tight.

The low-light of his career came in his first year when he had to sit out do to Iowa's tricking. Since Thomas chose Illinois over them, Iowa told the NCAA that the Illini were guilty of illegal recruiting. Deon insisted that he did no wrong and that the animosity towards the Hawkeyes lingered during his first year. Even the polygraph test indicated that Deon was truthful when he claimed innocence. He managed to turn the experience into a positive by developing friendships outside of hooping and maintaining a B G.P.A. To this day Iowa is not in good standing with the public league coaches as a result of their snitching and Thomas not getting the benefit of the doubt. You figure he'll be an interesting addition at power forward to the Mavericks' youth movement, which already boasts Jim Jackson, Popeye Jones and Jamal Mashburn. With Jason Kidd running the point, they're a decent center and two years away from being a title contender on paper.

You peeled your ears and prepared to take written notes when you queried him about Ben Wilson.

"I never met him personally, but I watched him on television during the city championship and when they went down state. I would say that he's one of the greatest players I've ever seen in my life. He would've definitely been an all-star in the NBA. They say he was going to Illinois and that's why Nick got the 25, that's why I wore the 25 and that's why Bryant's going to wear the 25. And then after him, if there's no more Simeon players they better retire that jersey or I'm going to be upset," he says with a chuckle. "He's definitely one of the best players that I've ever seen in my life and he is one of the reasons that my brother wanted me to go to Simeon...because he made some comments about how Hambric helped him and my brother felt that he could help me as well and it proved that he did."

That obeisant hung in the air like a dialogue balloon.

"I'm telling you, Kevin Garnett is the shit," Jayson Reed emphasizes. "He shoots like a 7-foot two-guard."

"That is when he ain't dunking on everybody," Dennis Meachum indicates with an air-tomahawk. "He's the real deal, Mal."

"His game is wicked," Mitch confirms, shaking his head.

"I don't know why he's wasting his time playing high school ball," Chuck D seconds, slapping five's with Jayson.

The fella's went down to Champaign for the Mennega's Back-to-School Shoot-out at Parkland Junior College. Some new kid in town name Kevin Garnett transferred to Farragut from South Carolina to shift the concentration of power to the West Side. He is touted as the top player in the nation, and by early projections, the Admirals should rank as the best team in the country with him joining junior dunkster Ronnie Fields. Jay and Dennis played in the shoot-out and were on the receiving end of a couple of Garnett dunks. So much for a good impression on the Illini. Both are considering Illinois, who were well represented in the stands with Notree, Kiwane Garris, Jerry Gee and

Jerry Hester. According to the news account you're reading, Garnett has the total package: assists, rebounds, scoring, defense, hustle.

They continue to confirm as we chill in Mitch's driveway on the old rusty Cadillac that Mitch crashed up two years ago. Bone Thugs In Harmony thumps from Mitch's boom-box while we break from balling and helping Mitch move some of his things to his Hyde Park apartment. His towering mother is cooking spaghetti for all of us in the kitchen and all five of his sisters are slinking around the house. Ms. Harper and Ms. Dawson will definitely have some tall tales to swap. There's about 13 feet between the two of them. His sisters could make an intimidating squad of centers. They go a statuesque 5'11" to 6'2", and it's not a scrawny height either. These sisters are pleasantly thick. You almost want them to body you up. If Traci were in a lineup with them, it would look like the Sister 6 Gang.

The lips, which all of the Harper offspring possess, are a definite inheritance from Ms. Harper. It's hard to believe that the length of all of that flesh fits in a three-bedroom house and grew up here without limbs hanging out of the windows. It's understandable why Mitch was so into Traci. That's all he grew up with: five older, towering sisters that just adored him to sickness. Even today, they still spoil him. Michelle and Michelin, the 21 year-old twins, play for Northeastern and Valparaso respectively and help him with his game. Twenty-five year-old Mendy is a registered nurse at Cook County and often checks up on the health of her baby brother. Meredith (30) and Melissa (33) are both bankers and the source of Mitch's funds. It's good to see the love between them. The fruit of that love towards Mitch is an unconditional love he has for Traci.

"KG is skinnier than you, Mal, but his game is on," Jay notes.

"...Just like my game, huh," you qualify between sips of Kool-Aid.

You continue to flip through the Sun-Times, taking special note of an article on Ben Wilson by Taylor Bell. Wilson's Mother and two younger brothers are pictured, and the article makes mention of all the crime. It hits you that November will be the ten-year anniversary of his death. Time flies. Of course, you were in school when it happened, but when you got home it was all on the news and in Uncle Ben's countenance. It was as unreal as a dream. That's when the victims of black-on-black violence had a face.

"He be dunking on nigga's left and right," Dennis slips.

They all get silent, because they know what's next.

"What's with this nigga shit?" you question, totally vexed by the magic word and the concept behind it.

"Damn, D...Why you get him started," Mitch chastens.

"My fault, man," he pleads, but it's too late for that.

"What's wrong with brother as opposed...

"TO NIGGER?" Mitch and Chuck D complete.

"Y'all act like y'all don't have no fucking sense of history. It was..."

"NIGGERS THAT WERE ENSLAVED AND RAPED AND LYNCHED FOR 400 YEARS AND COUNTING."

"Gabba Gabba Gabba. Take a chill, X," Mitch urges.

"Chill nothing. Y'all use a word that represents oppression and degradation of black people too lightly. When the white man looks at you..."

"HE SEES A NIGGER."

"...no matter how much education..."

"OR HOW MANY DEGREES, THEY'LL STILL LOOK AT YOU AS A NIGGER."

"I don't understand how the word is a term of endearment for us..."

"EVEN THOUGH WHITE FOLKS STILL USE IT IN A NEGATIVE WAY."

"MITCH," Michelle hollers out, signaling supper and signifying their salvation as we cut the dialogue.

August 30, 1994

Sports Illustrated/Inside Sports/The Sporting News

Dear Sir or Madam:

It was the eve before the first game of the season. Thanksgiving was a day later so there was much to be grateful for. One of the greatest teams ever assembled, with the likes of future all-staters David Knight (now paralyzed), Deon Butler, Erving Small and Orlando Magic

forward Nick Anderson, was starting its much anticipated quest for a repeat.

One of the greatest players to play prep ball was preparing for his swan song. But then it ended before it started. Time stopped. What was everybody doing? Nick was sitting out the first half of the season. Dallas Mavericks' second round pick Deon Thomas was an eighth grader with baseball dreams. Illinois freshman off-guard Bryant Notree was fresh out of first grade. What were you doing, when Ben Wilson was shot dead on the mean streets of Chicago?

That was then, this is now. So what are they doing now—on the ten-year anniversary of the killing? They're keeping the legacy of Number 25. According to Anderson, "I did several things because of Ben. I transferred to Simeon because of Ben. I went to Illinois not only because of the coaches and the good program, but I went there for Ben—because I knew Ben was going there and it's the only place I wanted to be. I wanted to be on the same team with this guy and wherever he was going I was going with him. When I put on my jersey I tell them it's a part of me—it's a part of Ben. My basketball career is to the memory of Ben Wilson."

"They say he was going to Illinois." Thomas reiterates. "That's why Nick got the 25, that's why I wore the 25 and that's why Bryant is going to wear the 25. And then after him if there are no more Simeon players they better retire that jersey."

I had an inspiring encounter with Ben the summer after Simeon won the state championship. He left an everlasting impression on me in my tender age of eight. An uncle of mine is the source of several grammar and high school memories and my basketball perspective will provide much insight.

I propose to write a 2500-3000-word article briefly covering his career and the results of his tragic end. I have already conducted exclusive interviews with Nick Anderson and Deon Thomas and a talk with Simeon coach Bob Hambric is in the works. I also plan to talk to my comrade Bryant Notree, Coach Henson, and a range of players, rivals, teammates and family members who were touched by him in some way.

My writing credentials include articles in the Testament newspaper and a commentary in the Chicago Sun-Times.

I hope that you would be interested in this writing proposal for your publication. Thank you for your time and I look forward to hearing from you soon.

Sincerely,

Malcolm Johnson

Malcolm Johnson

SASE Encl.

14

Although you are realistic in expecting it, you aren't excited, pleased, or prepared. You arrive in your dorm room first. Ben and Uncle JoJo helped you with the moving process. After bringing all of your stuff in (you didn't unload or set your stuff up yet, out of courtesy), they hang around briefly before corporately supplicating the prayer of favor. You wait around for a good hour before getting up to roam the hallways and the perimeter of the building, making note of the minuscule color. By early prognosis, there will be a blackout in the Hinman House. Coming in you knew the ratio is stacked against blacks. We make 12% of the population; 3% on campus. On the way back to your room, you greet a sister with an accounting smile, since she is the fourth African-American you notice.

The door is open when you return, and when you hit the doorway the cultural shock hits you like a well slammed door in the face of a cult member soliciting money on a Saturday morning. At first, your mind tricks you into mistaking this man for a dog, because he is as hairy as a werewolf during a full moon. He's leaning over with his back to you, situating his boxes against the wall as you stand at the entrance. His blue and white, number 25 (your number), Cleveland Cavaliers' tank-top reminds you of the American flag and adds a brick to your wall of ireful isolation that you've been building since your decision to attend NU. Is it too late to change your mind?

"Oh," he says, turning around. "How you doing, dude?" he asks as he removes his beat-up painter's hat and approaches with an outstretched hand. He's a buzzed auburn up top and true blue eyed. Add another brick for the blues.

"Pretty good," you announce through a poker face.

"Levi...Levi Siegel," he introduces with a firm handshake. You place him an inch and a half shorter than you and a couple of out-layers thicker. "Levi like the priestly line and Siegel like the gangster called Bugsy."

You heard him, and you know how to spell Levi Siegel. He gets a brick for being a blabbermouth, a brick for being irritatingly enthusiastic, and a brick just because. Maybe you'll put it to the side in case you need to plant it in his face.

"Malcolm Johnson," you nod.

"I know who you are," he assures.

Your expression asks, "How?"

"I've followed your career. We're going to be teammates," he mentions.

Judging by the cut off blue-jeans shorts, the tired sandals and the Mark Price jersey (who else would be a Cleveland fan besides a native Ohioan), he must be one of the other recruits from Ohio. "You led Central to the Ohio State quarter finals...right?"

"That's me. Ohio is well represented with me and Evan Eschmeyer."

"Okay. I heard about your inside game," you confirm with a nod.

"And I heard that you shoot like a white boy."

People have whispered that before, but it's very unflattering. As if brothers can't shoot. Right now you want to drop the whole wall on his big hammer-head. You know he meant it as a lighthearted, stereotypical joke, but you still hold it against him. "Yeah, brothers can do more than dunk," you assure. You have yet to crack a smile in his presence and you haven't taken your eyes out of his.

He chuckles it off and wisely switches the subject. "So which bed do you want...Just don't choose the one by the window."

"That's the one that I want." That wasn't a plea, but a claim.

"That's cool, dude," he says, shifting his boxes close to his bed. "I'll get out of your way so you can set up your stuff, then I'll get mine together later. I guess you'll take the desk and chest-of-drawers close to your bed."

You don't answer.

"All right," he concludes as he gets the last of his boxes situated to his side. "I'm going to get some breakfast...did you want anything?"

"That's aiight," you decline as you slowly look over your stuff, debating on what to start with.

"Okay. Later dude," he says as he shuts the door behind him.

It's like the cloud moved out of the way of the sun. Maybe you should brick him every time he calls you dude. Good grief.

It takes you no time to set up your computer, hook up your sounds and plug in your video equipment. You boxed the clothes up orderly, so the only thing you had to do was transfer them to the drawers and closet. Within the hour you are settled in with your books neatly on the shelves and your posters and pictures hanging up. You bolt out on your bike because the less you see him, the better. The University doesn't allow freshmen to have cars on campus, so you parked your ride in front of Faith's house.

After finding out Faith is out, you proceed downtown and settle in Burger King for lunch. It takes you all of five minutes to wolf down your Whopper and fries in order to get to your mental food. The recycled Robert Sandifer commentary is unappetizing, so you bypass it to the comics. The story is trite. What makes a story newsworthy? It can't be the age of the offenders and victims. Nor could it be the karma twist. You experienced the story first and second hand more than once. The drama is really an episode with different characters, but for some reason, it's the talk of the day, as if it's the first time for it; as if there's going to be something done about it. Although NU is a microcosm of society, you don't expect to experience drive-by's on campus. For that reason, you can free your head of the threat of a bullet to it.

Chuck D is going to wait for Chicago State to finish the new dorms before moving on campus. He and Mitch started last week and seem to have adjusted. Both noted that it reminds them of high school, with an easier pace and a relaxed atmosphere. Absent was the talk of the babes on campus, which you didn't expect from Mitch anyway. In the past month and a half, he has undergone a radical metamorphosis. He's still as funny and down as ever, but he has a more serious outlook. Traci is prepared to start Columbia in couple of weeks. May the Lord be with her at the school of absurdity. Although the actual honeymoon is over with, they seem to be enjoying each other and the family life. She actually seems to be happy, which makes you happy.

While shopping for a couple of new outfits at the Plaza Wednesday, you ran into Chuck D and Joyce. Although they weren't doing anything outside of talking to each other, a funny air enveloped them as they stood together. Their eyes were as mute as their mouths when you asked, "What's up." According to them, nothing was up, but you couldn't help but think that they were "together."

You like Nick. She enrolled at both Moody Bible Institute (out of her own pocket) and DePaul University (on a partial scholarship), taking two classes each. By all indications, the Spirit has allowed her to pursue her Psychology studies while preparing for and enhancing her ministry. Although she has made the official announcement to Pastor Wells a couple of months ago, she won't start doing any hard core speaking right away. "Despite the inevitability of the harvest, we have to reap and sow in the proper season, otherwise our work will be in vain," she insisted. You're praying hard for her, because she's still a little apprehensive about the revelation of her calling to speak in a public setting. She mentioned that she met a preacher at Moody who recently launched an outreach ministry. Even though she didn't discuss it at length, intrigue overflowed from her announcement.

As you peruse the paper, reading articles from various sections, you find that your eyes are on the words, but the contents are not registering. Faith has a headlock on your concentration. You miss her even though you spoke to her this morning and hung out in Hyde Park with her yesterday, visiting the Museum of Science and Industry, strolling the beach at 57th Street, and peeping the book, art and pet stores on 53rd Street. Questions abound in your skull, so you set the paper down and wax poetically vague:

The path of righteousness isn't smooth
Falls illicit questions of fate
Along the way the soul is bruised
Many detours come with the day
It resembles the road of the fool
But the Way is clear through the eyes of Faith

You stare at it, and after about 20 minutes, the words seem to come to life. Inspiration is like the wind: you don't know where it comes from or where it goes; When it hits you, you move; When it's gone, it's forgotten. If you could bottle it up, you would have a garage full. However, you can't put it on a leash and direct it. Obscurity is not your gift, which is why this stanza-like expression is intriguing. There's a message to you, unlike talking to yourself. You didn't mean to capitalize faith at the end.

"Why are you staring into my eyes?"

"I don't know." And you don't. All you know is that you chased the wind and found yourself at Faith's house. When she opened the door, you got right up in her grill as if to kiss her, and just peered through her soul windows. Surprised by your strange behavior, her eyes bucked open like saucers. If you are seeing something besides her pupils, you don't know.

"Well, can you give me a good two inches please."

You move back as she laughs. "What's so funny?"

"What's so funny?" she repeats, stepping out on the porch. "If you opened your door and I got all up in your face like this," she says, standing as high as she can on her toes and pressing her feather-soft nose against your chin, completing, "wouldn't you laugh or call the police?"

"Okay. You made your point."

"I know you're not crazy, so I laughed," she assures. "So what can I do for you, Malcolm?"

"Marry me so I can move in, or kill my roommate?"

"Uh oh. You got a bad roomy, huh?"

"I don't know how bad he is...I just don't like him."

"Okay."

"Actually, I just came to see you," you confess, noting her rising skin tone and smirk. "I came by an hour ago but you were out. Levi should be getting his stuff organized."

"That's his name?"

You nod.

She smiles.

You smile. "Well, since my mission is complete, I'll leave."

"You're more than welcome to stay...watch a movie or something," she spiels with the urgency of a broke, used-car saleslady.

The glimmer in her eyes has a strong pull and causes a slight hesitation in heart and speech, which is why you lie, "I really need to get back."

Her grin remains but the brightness fades from inside. "Okay," she resolves sorrowfully.

"Okay," you second as you step back reluctantly, feeling like you got from under a blanket on a cold winter night.

Proceeding, you walk out into the elements partially nude and bike it back to your dorm, where Levi is taping a Larry Bird poster just above his desk and just below the image of a tan Jesus, to put the finishing touches on his side. You like Bird, but you figure Levi is trying to make some kind of racial counter.

"You know, dude" he starts as he pulls another poster from the bag and unravels it before you, revealing the Magic shot over McKale in the '85 playoffs—just like the one hanging on your wall. "It wouldn't make since to have two of them up."

You nod in agreement and for the first time flash something in the family of a smirk in his presence as you make a beeline to the bed. The morning high is crash landing. You're too tired to be ornery, so you suspend your wall construction. "Wake me next semester," you half joke as your head hits the pillow.

"You should have seen those people acting a fool, dude."

No this pale, corn-fed hick didn't say *"those people."* It's too early and you're too foul. Not only did you sleep through the afternoon and evening events, but you tossed and turned all night adjusting to this new bed, so it feels like you got no sleep at all. You did intend to go to some of the opening day events, but your coma killed that. To top it off, your neck is cramped. "What did you say?" you grunt.

"I said those people were..."

"Those people?" you cut in. "What do you mean by *those people*?"

He hesitates as his enthusiasm fades. "I mean *those people* that were acting wild at the Dance Party sponsored by the Black Greek Council. I guess I have to qualify it with a disclaimer of broad references based on race, gender or religion. Good grief," he says sarcastically.

"Whatever," you mumble as you rise and head out to the restroom to wash up. It's going to be hard waking up to the smell and sight of him, and you ain't trying to adjust this morning. With no phone line yet, you can't get on-line, so the room is a dead box with an irritatingly ugly white guy in it. The rejection letter from Sports Illustrated that came to Ma's house yesterday is a bug in your butt. How could they not be interested in the ten-year twist to the Ben Wilson story? There is no doubt that you can write a feature just as well—if not better than—their staff writers, especially on that topic. *Screw 'em.* You'll just read their magazine in the stores instead of buying them.

You waste no time in washing up, getting dressed and trekking to Faith's house. She opens the door with puffy, bloodshot eyes, looking like she got TKO'd by a bad dream. Her naturally radiant face is milked of its gleam.

"Hi Malcolm," she greets insecurely.

"What's wrong?"

She closes her eyes and shakes her head gingerly, lying, "Nothing." Her voice borders on hoarse and hurt.

"Faith?"

"I'm fine," she assures unconvincingly as she peers up at you through sagging eyes. "Really."

"You've been crying."

She closes her eyes and nods as she tries to play it off with a forced, quick, half-smirk. "Come in," she resolves. "I didn't mean for you to see me like this," she testifies as you follow her upstairs to her bedroom. The mellow, melancholy sounds of Sade seem to flow through the walls. "I'm sorry, did you want any tea or something?" she asks as she stops just at the top of the steps.

"I'm fine."

We make it to her room where she plops down on the foot of the well-made bed, with one leg folded under her. "Pearls" plays low on the CD after you cut it down. A sunbeam bursts through the curtain on a slight angle and illuminates a large photo album that rests at the head. You gently sit next to her as she gazes straight ahead. After a few anticipatory moments, she takes a deep breath and exhales loudly.

"Today is my mother's birthday," she mentions as she lays back and retrieves the photo album. You put your arm around her and rub her back as she opens it up to the obituary that indicates, "She was born into this world today, and she was born into eternity today" adding, "And I miss her so much," as her body collapses against you and her voice breaks down into a constipated bawl.

You wrap her up in your arms and feel her with your heart. There is power in words. The Word of God spoke the world into existence. Jesus spoke life into Lazarus. It was the spoken words from the multitude that sealed the fate of the Savior. Words have their place, and this isn't one of them. Even though you know how she feels, relating in silence and letting the healing hand of Father Time—the Everlasting Father—is the only way. You allow her to freely weep, and it's a nasty storm. Her whole being seems to burn and quake with grief as an avalanche of tears and dribble pour into your lap. The winds of sorrow seem long, but only blow about five minutes. The precipitation is gone and the thunderous moans subside. We go through the photos, which span her mother's life. There are strong resemblances among family members. Identical twins have different, detectable physical traits. However, you're unable to tell the difference between Faith and her mother, even in some of her mother's later pictures. You can only imagine the eccentricity of seeing your reflection in a casket.

She breaks your grip and lays back. You follow suit, and we gaze at the ceiling for an everlasting instant. Completely composed like a new person, she narrates how her mother was a History professor at NU and her father was a Theologian who schooled her current pastor. "They were the perfect compliment to each other," she mentions. With their background, tracing their roots, diagramming their family tree and determining their genealogy was simple. "Daddy was Yoruba and Momma was Ethiopian—oddly enough for an African imported to America around that time. Her mom was from Ethiopia," she explains. Now her fluency in Amharic and Yoruba (not to mention Arabic, compliments of her father's Iranian friend) is a little more logical. Not that brightness in blackness surprises you, but her parent's background sheds more light on her advanced intellect. Her father had striking features: dense complexion, intense cheekbones, and passionate eyes, which Faith inherited. Faith took the best from two powerful souls.

"I'm sorry Malcolm, I didn't mean for you to see me like this...I know I look ugly," she says with a chuckle. "It's a ritual for me to cry the blues and mope on this day," she resolves.

"Well," you start as you sit up and peer down at her. "Today we're going to break that ritual."

It is hard to believe that in the two years at NU and in her 19 years of life, Faith had never been to the opening week football game or a live game altogether. And a good game it was. Although the Wildcats didn't get the win, she was a never-die cheerleader in the high-scoring, tie game. It was full of drama and she protested that the seven-yard touchdown by Stanford wasn't a touchdown at all. You had to convince her that we couldn't correct the official score of 41-41. She insisted that the television dilutes the excitement of actually being there to measure the speed with her own eyes, cringe at the hits, and observe the whole setting, as opposed to the action in the box. A lack of replays didn't take away from the advantage of the live game.

We dined at Davis Street Fish Market immediately after the game and strolled on over to her traditional spot at the Lake on Lincoln. As opposed to meditating on and wallowing in depression, she chattered jubilantly about this and that, from her door-to-door missionary work to her estranged sister, who she hasn't seen since she put her mother's body back in the earth. It would have been futile to try to slow her down, but your ears were receptive. Her happiness was more important than your commentary. We broke for her house just before sunset. On the way, we picked up "Demolition Man" from Blockbuster and watched it for as long as our eyes stayed open. When you opened your eyes again, your head rested on her soft hip and the sun was rising. We kept going. You ran home to change for church. To your pleasant surprise, Levi was gone when you got into shower. We opted for your church since she hasn't been yet.

Spending time with her felt so natural. At certain points, she felt like your significant, especially when you stepped through the doors of Walk of Faith. There, in all of her worthlessness, stood Penny as you held the door open for Faith. You stuck your chest out like a rooster and put on a territorial, attached air when she took notice of us. When you flashed her a self-confident grin, her face flushed with envy like a fat, pregnant woman without a man at a wedding. Faith unwittingly played the role of your woman by getting intimately close to talk in confidence just before going in. Although you didn't know how we looked together, you imagined that we looked like I, as in 1, as in a husband and wife. Everyone greeted her with warmth after the service, like they were revering Mrs. Johnson. More than a handful of folks pulled you to the side and asked, "Is she your lady?" More surprising than the questions, was your unrehearsed, unforeknown, assured response: "Not yet". Through it all, you didn't miss the residence hall social events or the University sponsored, get acquainted stuff. And you sure didn't miss Levi. Faith was all that mattered at the time, which blotted out the anxiety of a new culture and a higher academic level of competition.

New student week is winding down. Your phone was cut on that Monday morning and you were signed on before noon. For the most part, you've bypassed the daily events in favor of playing on AOL and getting disgusted with the empty, nauseating, slow-motion small-talk from inside the chat rooms. Of course, you attended the mandatory financial aid seminar, which just thrilled you out of your clothes. The New Student Athlete Orientation was pretty informative. They introduced us to the staff and went over rules and policies. You got to joke about turning the athletic program around with some of the other first year jocks, such as full-back Darnell Autry—who came to NU by default, because of his lack of size (he looked pretty stacked to you)—quarter-back D'Wayne Bates (that brother has to have some juice, because black play callers on the gridiron are taboo), and guard Geno Carlisle—who you haven't seen play nor previously met, but you heard his game is tight, and we're supposed to be sharing time at the two spot. We agreed that we may have to let our G.P.A. drop to bring the program to respectability. Medill had a special forum about journalism in the future that you attended, along with the exciting advising and scheduling sessions and the University resources orientations.

Thursday, Faith pried you from the computer to attend the African-American Student Affairs Luncheon, which made your graduation from high school and entrance into college seem like a lateral social move. The juvenile tendencies of giggling at the slightest breeze reminded you of your first year at Louis High. Brothers and sisters flocked to different cliques; the Greeks fronted their fraternities and sororities. Chatter abounded. While Faith stepped away to talk to some of her friends, you tried to strike up a conversation with a reserved female from Philadelphia. Getting her to open up and answer open-ended questions was like mining through a mountain with a spoon. When she did talk, she spoke chalkboard-scratching, irritatingly proper. You were glad when Faith rescued you from that tense silent movie.

During the Greek introduction period, the question of hazing came up. If you were considering pledging, their double-talk would have discouraged you. On one hand, they denounced it in a round-about, superficial way—not outright and not denying doing it—insisting that it's illegal and unnecessary in the 90's, since too many blacks are already beat down. On the other side of their mouth, they assured us that it goes on and an individual has to determine if he wants to go through something harsh to be friends with a group of people. That was a serious slip of tongue. One is supposed to join the organization and not the people, but in other words, if they don't like you, they will smoke your ass for a semester. Mitch is going to pledge Omega, and he can have the purple and gold all to himself, because you haze back.

You give the campus atmosphere three stars, so far. Racially speaking, NU isn't the least bit tense. Most of the returning students have assimilated and socialize based on majors, forming a rainbow coalition. The freshmen appear to stand out in ethnic clusters. Like yourself, there are some that separate themselves and seem uncomfortable with a new environment. While most of your white peers seem to be friendly and liberal-minded, you were restricted to fellowshipping with the non-standoffish campus squirrels, which was a cultural shock in itself. In the 'hood, those thuggish rodents wouldn't let people come within ten yards of them. If you corner them, they'll pull out a Magnum. When you were strolling over to the Norris University Center, a black and a brown one came up and unlaced your Cons, which almost knocked the chip off your shoulder. The campus isn't as overtly whitewashed as you anticipated, which eased your mind slightly. You were geared for confrontation, and it appears that it won't take all of that. Sometimes it takes a small wonder in God's creation for you to appreciate the beauty of the fullness of it and to stop sweating. However, it takes more than friendly rats to set the crooked race record straight.

Levi has hounded you to attend the "fun" extracurricular events. Levi. When you could, you ignored him. If it was unnecessary, you didn't talk to him. If you had to speak, it was brief. You found yourself longing for your room at home. The room with privacy, more space, greater access and the luxury of sitting comfortably nude. You don't know if Mister Siegel is gay or not. You're surprised the gump didn't take the Afro-Lit class with the rest of the counterfeit liberals.

You sign-on to AOL and start reflecting. Maybe it's all in your head and you should stop being standoffish. Perhaps he is sincere. You are ready to let your mind guard down a little, but then "YOU'VE GOT MAIL" chimes from your computer. You click on the icon and read the first piece from a familiar screen name. There are several headers at the top, with commentary promising a big, unpleasant surprise. You're tempted to discard it as a chain e-mail, when you get to subject title. **"NIGGER JOKES"** it screams, compliments of the University of Michigan. You read:

> **Nig-ger (nig'er) n. An African jungle anthropoid ape of the primate family pongidae (superfamily cercopithecoidea). Imported to the United States as slave labor in the late 1700's-1800's, these wild creatures now roam freely while destroying the economic and social infrastructures of the nation.**

Do you know why flies have wings? ***So they can beat the niggers to the watermelons.***

Why did the nig run when his girlfriend said she wanted to give him a blowjob? ***He was afraid it would cancel his unemployment benefits.***

Did you hear about the little nigger boy who had diarrhea? ***He thought he was melting.***

What do you call three niggers sitting in a garden? ***Fertilizer.***

What do you call a nigger with an IQ of 15? ***Gifted.***

Your temp rises ten degrees like helium with each "joke" as you continue.

What's the difference between a pothole and a nigger? ***You'd swerve to avoid a pothole, wouldn't you?***

How do you get twelve nigs in a Volkswagen? ***Toss a welfare check in the back seat.***

What do you call three blacks at a Klan barbeque? ***Charcoal.***

The stupid fuck must've OD'd on phonics, because it's spelled barbecue, not barbeque.

How do you make a nigger nervous? ***Take him to an auction.***

You growl at that one and peer over at an oblivious Levi. It says jokes, but this shit ain't funny.

Did you hear about Evil Kneivel's cousin, Ku Klux Knieval? ***He tried to jump over 50 blacks—With a steamroller.***

Is it Kneivel or Knieval? They need to fire the proofreader.

What do you call 50,000 blacks in the bottom of the sea? ***A good start.***

That one pierces your heart.

Why don't niggers stick their heads out of moving vehicles? ***Their lips catching the wind will beat them to death.***

It would be funny if you said that about Mitch, but you ain't laughing at this cyber-author.

Why does Georgia have blacks and California have earthquakes? ***California had first pick.***

Why do niggers always have sex on their minds? ***Because of the pubic hair on their heads.***

What did the black kid get for Christmas? ***My bike.***

Why do niggers call white people "Honkeys"?

"Enlighten me," you mumble to yourself.

Thats the last sound they hear before we run them over.

This skin-head bastard doesn't even know how to use an apostrophe. And to think he's at a major university.

A nigger, a jew and a spic get shoved off a building at the same time which one hits pavement first?

English is obviously not this Aryan asshole's subject. This is devolution in action. He just set his breed back past crawling on all fours and chewing on raw mammoth meat to a unicell, algae-eating micro-organism that infects warm-blooded animals and withdraws from the sunlight.

Who cares.

You glance over at Levi, not knowing what to think. For all you know it could've been a blue-eyed Jew like him behind it or a part of it.

How do you wipe out 250 ape families? *Blow up Kmart.*

Whats another name for the county jail?

Damn. He still doesn't understand the rule for using an apostrophe. Somebody needs to take him back to obedience school.

The house of apes.

How do you get a nigger to commit suicide? *Toss a bucket of KFC into traffic.*

You don't even like Kentucky Fried Chicken. This stupid motherfucker obviously watched School Daze.

Why do niggers tint their car windows? *They don't—it's the black rubbing off.*

Nigger, your termination is growing near
With my shotgun I invoke my fear
I'll blast you in the legs then blast you in the head
I'll laugh at you nigger till your ass is dead
You grease dripping melon snatchin car jacking fuck
I am near, now you're out of luck
I'll cripple you nigger, then crush your skull
It's so much fun to watch you tremble and fall
You are worth nothing nigger, zero, zip
You should be on the farm, under the whip
Think you're emancipated nigger? Fuck that!
Stupid nigger, you're no better than a jap

Ouch. This caveman is poetic.

I HATE NIGGERS!!!!!!!!!!!!!

Nigger nigger you better beware
I'll shoot your black ass and burn your nigger afro hair
I'll punch you, kick you, and crush your fucking rock hard skull
Then I'll castrate you nigger and make you swallow your balls
I'll tie you up nigger and drag you behind my car
I'll drag your ass forever nigger, far far far
I hate you nigger, your rap and your jive
I'm gonna kill you nigga you will not stay alive
I hate all niggers, the way they behave
Whites are superior beings, NIGGERS ARE SLAVES!!!!!!!
Kill that nigger he's worse than a fag
Blast him in the head with a 44 mag
Kick him punch him and crush that bro
Douse him with gasoline and burn his fro
Hit him with a flashlight and kick him in the head
Just make sure that niggers dead
Big lipped chicken eating melon stealing bast
I can't wait to kill a nigger with a shotgun blast!

You bypass the cyber caricature of a supposed black man and click off without an audible peep as you shout silent obscenities. The contents have your mind smoking. It's hard to believe that an invisible man behind the computer screen has you so worked up that your tongue has all kinds of profanity dripping from it. And this is what's going on at a major university. It could very well be NU. You start wondering how many of the white folks on campus share these sentiments; would these jokes be funny to them? You don't know how to read Levi, so you'll just group him in the same category of distrust with all Caucasians, since he looks just like them.

"You want to go to the Bible Fellowship?" he asks.

Ever since he saw you reading the Word and found out that you are a Christian, he's been dropping self-righteous hints. The campus offers several Christian activities and it seems like he goes to all of them. A Christian tag means nothing to you. The Klan claims Christianity. It was supposed white Christians that reasoned that Africans needed the Word of God and favored slavery. The holier than holy Republicans are extra dedicated to wiping out programs that would fill in the valleys and level off the mountains in America, while adding weight to the burden of black people. What is Christianity without compassion? If they could choose between restoring an African-American caught up in a crime and punishing him, that "nigger" would rot in a jail cell. Claiming the Christian banner is easy, but carrying it is a whole different story.

"So what are you saying—that I need Jesus? I have Jesus," you snap.

He looks at you and lets out an annoying chuckle. "I'm not going to offend you on purpose, but I'm not going to walk on eggshells just because you're bent on measuring every word from my mouth in black and white. If I offend you, rebuke me or kick my butt."

"Don't tempt me," you say, cutting your eyes at him.

"As long as we're going to be living together for the semester, you could try and be a little cordial."

You snicker out loud and declare, "Don't take it personally, but I just don't like you" as you try to read up on Mumia.

"So in other words you have something against white people," he assumes correctly. "The blood of Jesus knocked down the middle wall between Jews and Gentiles; there is no enmity between us; there is neither Greek or Jew, black or white in Christ Jesus. If you call yourself a Christian, you need to free your mind."

"Free my mind?!" you question in disbelief as you spring from your workstation and walk within arms reach of him. "Free my mind? You can't handle a liberated black mind, you soul-less, translucent hypocrite. Free my mind. I oughta arrest my foot up your ass. Don't you *ever* call my Christianity into question," you command, pointing at him.

"Do you think that heaven is going to be segregated?"

"You know what I do know?" you question sternly through clenched teeth as you get eye-to-eye, and peer in. His pupils are stationary as you declare, "The deep blue sea—with its mystery, deceit and danger—will have no parts of heaven. Until your people put forth a real effort to break the cycle of the destruction of my people, you ain't got jack to say to me about heaven. Everything white America touches, it plunders or ravages—and I know *that's* not the loving, Christian way."

We glare for a moment before you turn and walk out without shutting off your computer.

"I was going to walk him all up and down that dorm," you confide.

"Maybe you should take him up on the offer to go to some of the events. He may not be as bad as you make him out to be."

"Why would I go anywhere with him when his very presence irks me?"

"Give it time...you'll get used to him."

"I'm thinking about asking for a room change."

"Why would you go to that extreme?"

"I think Levi is a fag."

"Why don't you ease up off of that word, Malcolm," Faith suggests in a testy tone.

"I'll say what I want to say."

"Sweetie, I know you can say what you want to say. I'm not trying to infringe on your First Amendment right. You're a treat to listen to. I'm just asking you to tone down on the slurs."

Why is the word bothering her? "You're not..."

"No, I'm not a lesbian or bisexual," she snaps. "Don't insult me, because you know better."

"Why is it that you're so bothered by it then? It's just a word."

"It's not a nice word and there are people close to me that go that way. It's along the same lines as nigger, and you know how you feel about that word...especially after that e-mail."

"I beg to differ. As Jeremiah questioned 'can an Ethiopian change his color or a leopard change his spots? If so, then those that do evil without conscience will learn to do good.' Nigger is a skin label; Fag is a sin label, so don't even try to group them together," you demand, adding, "What...are you advocating homosexuality?"

"Let's change the subject, because you're asking a lot of dumb questions," she suggests superciliously as she waves you off.

You don't appreciate that. "Don't blow me off like I'm an idiot. If I was sure I wouldn't have asked. Maybe I should leave since we're getting on each others nerves," you state, starting for the door.

She grabs you by the arm and sugar addresses you. "Listen Sweetie, I don't want to fight you over this or any other irrelevant thing, because I don't think I can win anyway. You have an excellent point. To answer your question, I detest it...I think it's a slap in the face of the natural order of things. The pride that some of them have in it is even more detestable. But I don't condemn them since the Word says all have sinned and Jesus is the Righteous Judge. I'd rather see them repent than burn in hell...they are living souls that are precious in the sight of God. I know you're not condemning them and the word is part of your vernacular, but please don't use it around me," she croons like a seductive, singing gigolo as she reels you in to her chest and embraces you. You can't help but embrace back as it seems like you "won" an argument, but in reality not only did she get the last word, but she defeated you without even fighting.

15

There is no high like the rush of favorable news and the courtship of a good woman. When both are your simultaneous good fortune, a sacrifice is the least. Yesterday Ma dropped off the letter from the Sporting News. It stated that your query letter is intriguing and that they would like to talk to you further concerning the Ben Wilson story. You almost did a backwards flip after reading it thrice. Screaming ecstatically, the adrenaline rush sent you biking around Evanston. When you got back, you were on the phone telling Uncle JoJo, Ben, and Mitch. Of course Faith was the second person to know. She got the news from your mouth. You were so excited that your disdain for Levi paled and you shared the letter with him also. We even discussed the recent shooting of prep hoop star Derrick Mims and how the news' value of athletes is much higher than that of the rest of the population. That wall seems to be crumbling slightly thanks to a little urging by Faith and your burning conscience. Your guard isn't totally down yet, though. And Faith...

We went to her church today. Her minister preached a sermon from Proverbs 31 on the faithful women in Christ. Pastor Coleman honored Deborah (the female judge who accompanied the reluctant Barak into battle), Rahab (the prostitute who helped the spies from Israel) and Abigail (the wife of Nabal who provided sustenance to David and intercession for her wicked husband when he was on the verge of being killed) as heroines of the faith. He also referred to the champions of the New Testament (Pilate's wife, who deemed Jesus righteous; the women at the cross, and the woman who washed the feet of Jesus with her tears and hair). It almost sounded like a Woman's Day message, however, you knew God was commending Faith to you. As with several other times in the past weeks, you stared into her eyes. Unlike the previous occasions, you weren't mute. "Your zeal for Christ makes Faith an appropriate moniker," you mentioned after the altar call. You added, "You epitomize the perfect bride." She was speechless, but the soft gaze she sent you spoke loud and clear, stating that our "ship" is rising with the tide of attraction. We agreed to go to the Ritual (an African-American Theatre Ensemble welcoming program that includes many artful performances). After dropping her off, you headed straight for the bed. You were hurting for a nap since you burned a lot of energy getting excited over the letter.

The program starts at seven and it's about a quarter after six. Faith indicated that she wanted to dress to impress, so you throw on a black collar-less shirt, black slacks, black, leather bucks and a black jacket to complete your eclipsing outfit. After doing a once over, you conclude that a second look isn't necessary. You're razor sharp. The phone rings just as you start for the door. Determined to make a quick conversation, you answer it with an urgent, yet polite, "Hello."

"I heard The Sporting News gave you a play." It's Chuck D.

"Not quite yet, but the letter is promising. I have to call them tomorrow," you clarify, peeking at the clock on the VCR.

"You in there, Dawg."

"I hope so," you note wistfully, trying to set him up for a quick good-bye.

"Guess what happened to me?"

He sounds pacific, so it's definitely good news. "You got a call from the Lakers to try out?"

"Better than that," he assures.

"Well, I don't know what could be better, CD," you claim as you pace over the floor in anticipation of leaving.

"I got saved."

"Saved? From what?" you cluelessly question like a big dupe.

"Saved from death. Jesus saved me."

It hits you like a sucker punch. "Okay. That is excellent," you declare excitedly. "Truly excellent. That just made my week."

"He made my life," he states. "Let me tell you the story, because it's that much more amazing."

You have time for this.

He explains that when you saw him talking to Joyce a few weeks ago in Carson's, something really was up as you suspected. They had been chatting for a couple of hours about this, that, and Jesus. She didn't force the plan down his throat, it just flowed naturally. The unspoken, mutual attraction articulated through their discussion carried over into that night on the phone. Before then, they were hi and bye when they saw each other through you. For two weeks they were inseparable, and that wasn't enough time together, since they had too much to talk about. She invited him to yesterday's musical in which she sung a solo. During the invitation, he boldly walked down the aisle alone and accepted Jesus as his personal Savior. Her shouting didn't freak him out like it usually did when he saw someone get the Holy Ghost. In addition to salvation, he's in love.

"My baptism is in two weeks," he invites, adding, "Our wedding will be announced later."

"You know I'm there, CD. You just don't know how much happier that makes me. I was already having a good day, but now it's like a good week in one day."

"Praise God."

You never imagined him praising God. His speech has even changed. And if you were going to play matchmaker to your boy and an ex-lady, you couldn't have placed a better match. Although Chuck D is known for talking smack about the women he's had, you and Mitch suspect that he ain't had any. He's covertly shy when it comes to women, and he sure ain't aggressive. Joyce is good wife material, even though your feelings for her wore away. You would entrust her with his or anyone's heart, even your own—if you weren't ready to deposit it into the gentle hands of Faith.

"Dreaming In Metaphors" by Seal is blasting in its climax on Faith's stereo. You have to be seeing things. If that's the case, you're not going to blink. At the same time, it's impossible to behold the glorious. "Faith," you enunciate, your mouth gaping open. "Have I seen you in a dream?"

"Onile olo na bi omo oba Afrika," she says, grinning impishly. "That's Yoruba for 'you're as dignified as an African prince.'"

"Faith," you moan, because she has turned your meticulous mind into meandering mush. She's decked out in a deitic gold duster—with the same color configuration you unwittingly spotted her in four months ago—a matching, wrap-around head piece, black stretch-pants and black, string sandals.

"That's how I knew your name during the summer semester. You introduced yourself to me, and although I thought you were irresistibly charming—using those psalm and Song scriptures so cleverly—I wasn't trying to make it that easy for you. I really don't trust my natural instincts, because they're governed by the flesh. The way I look at it, if we're God ordained, it's nothing that I can do to stop us. I got to observe you for a good week. And I took notice of your spirit...the indwelling Holy Spirit. During that time, I prayed for an indication of like yoking for clarification, because I was drooling all over your head like the anointing from where I was sitting. It was quite evident when you queried the origins of the African gods...whether they were in place before or after the first century Church went out into Africa. That was very inquisitive," she compliments, adding, "I knew I wanted to...*fellowship* with you right then and there."

Booyow.

During the program, you replayed her statements no less than a million times while you goggled at her. You literally missed the show due to the entrancing power she yielded over your eyes. With the exception of the sensuous African dance number and the satirical dorm skit that she participated in, the only thing that you caught was the end, when the upper-classmen gave words of wisdom, the African-American Theatre Ensemble passed out the traditional links and they prayed us out. She tells you about it on the way back to her house.

"It still wasn't as good as the show I watched," you flirt.

She cuts you a blushing smile as she sets some herbal tea before you. "Take one last look at it. The next time I wear it will be in February," she says, turning in the outfit.

If only you had a camera. "Kiss From A Rose" by Seal hums low on her stereo as you try to drop your aching smile. You still haven't recovered your verbal skills. She dwells upstairs long enough for your tea to cool down and drink. When she emerges, she's wearing a suave mauve adire cloth, passionate black top and a stealthy grin as she eyes you intently while popping in another tape. Gone are the black pants. Her caramel smooth legs that peek out from a tapering point give the appearance of brown tights. She slides the coffee table to the side for more room. You open your mouth to protest/query, but she puts her finger to her lips and positions herself in a praying position in the middle of the floor facing you. The music starts and so does she. Drums blare gently from the speakers while she gyrates to them. You get to see a show after all. For ten everlasting minutes she dances salaciously intense. She stops simultaneously with the last drumbeat, slowly collapsing like a rose closing up at sundown right at your feet, with her arms supporting herself on your thighs and her head bowed. Your speech demotes another level when she gazes up at you. Your stolid gape is a travesty to your awestruck heart. On impulse, you deliberately stroke her face with the back of your hand. This isn't the first time you've brushed your hand over her tender cheeks. Always petal soft, you feel it in a whole new perspective as you close your eyes and distantly blurt, "Rose of Sharon" in reference to the sound-bite that teetered on your conscious/subconscious borderline ever since Nick referred to it as Jesus.

"How did you know my mother's name? I never told you," she half mumbles in the midst of her faraway bliss.

"Your mother was name Rose?" you verify.

"Sharon."

"I wasn't calling her out on purpose. I didn't even mean to say it, but my mouth speaks what's bubbling in my heart. When I touch you, I think of a Rose. I think of the glory of God as manifest in Jesus Christ: The Rose of Sharon, the most beautiful flower. Just as Jesus was cloaked in purple before he went to the cross, you're royally clad."

Faith shifts slightly and sits up. With her back to you and her head resting on your knee, she dreamily speaks. "You're the deepest thinker...so full of contagious passion, and I'm a passion junkie. It feeds me and gives me growth. Your thoughts give me a high...intoxicate me. You don't realize how a well-spoken thesis mesmerizes me. I never met a man that could hypnotize me with words. How do you cast those spells? You are passion personified...so consuming. A man that stands for Christ, black people and the struggle; that seeks knowledge and spouts wisdom; that feels strong enough to die for a cause, is something too blessed to behold."

That was too much soul vitamins for you to absorb. You were about to give some back, but her light snoring bridles your tongue and prompts you to follow her to her beatitude.

It was only the first day of class and Dr. Feinstein already has you researching the different mediums concerning the coverage of the OJ case. Word is Dr. FrankenEinstein—as he is known—is a dangerous combination of coolness and intensity. He stands about 6'10" and has an olive complexion that reminds you of cucumbers. While he jokingly challenged you to a game for extra credit, he proceeded to load everybody up with assignments. You might as well set up an office in the NU library. Although your computer with the Internet access will cut down on the time in there, the need to retrieve info is inevitable.

After you finished your OJ treasure hunt, you stumbled across a gem while browsing the books in print system. On a whim, you put in Ben Wilson and came up with "to Benji With Love" by Mary Wilson. After scribbling down the catalogue number, you were directed right to it. You wasted no time checking it out. You were finished reading the first two chapters before you reached the courtyard by the Frank Engelhart Memorial Tower just outside of the library. You got so engrossed with the story as you strolled to one of the vacant benches, that the whizzing roller-bladers and bicyclists conceded to go around you like an immovable object.

Already in a reflective state when you start the third chapter, you play with and edit the quoted proverb "Here today gone tomorrow", replacing it with "Here today gone today", as applied to Dexter. The sorrow in your heart starts bubbling up as you lay the book to the side and stare straight ahead at nothing.

"How was class?" the distant voice asks.

You slowly come back to the courtyard and peer up through glazed eyes at Levi the White guy. "It was cool," you announce even cooler as you turn away and take note of all of the socializing, rushing and leisure activity.

"I read that book," he declares, bringing you into a zone of interest.

You flash a glancing nod as you declare, "It's a story that cuts through color to touch a part of everyone's heart...especially mine."

He takes a seat a few feet away. "I know you were like this with Dexter," he says, holding up his crossed fingers in your peripheral line of vision. "How did you handle the idea of Kenny Reed?"

You snicker without a hint of a smile and attest, "I didn't," as you face him. "I dropped him from the same thought as Dexter. All that I heard of him came from a thirdary source that read the paper or saw it on the news. I don't follow him one iota, so I really didn't deal with him."

He pinches his lips into a non-humorous smirk as we pause for him to digest it. "On a different, yet similar, level, I was on the opposite side of the coin," he mentions, looking to the side of you to gather his recollections. "One of my close friends killed a pregnant woman while driving drunk," he testifies.

You urge him on with your eyes.

They were at a house party (where all types of trouble brews) drinking and orgying. There were two carloads of them, and Tommy left in a separate car, while Levi lay knocked out on the floor. Whatever it was that was in the punch, packed a punch. Needless to say, he got re-knocked out by his ol' man when he got home, and suffered the third and most severe KO when he found out about the head-on collision Tommy had. He walked away with only superficial scratches, while the woman and fetus perished. It was big news in Ohio and Tommy was vilified to a devilish degree. With the exception of that one grave mistake, he was a model person. That didn't matter in the ultra-conservative, highly hypocritical town. It hurt Levi to hear his friend's name dipped in venom. At the same time, he ached for the surviving husband and two sons. If the roles were reversed, Levi knew that anything short of a public stoning would've been unacceptable. That's when the process of the yoke of judgment started to break from Levi's neck, and Romans 3:23 was stamped on his heart.

"While he got off without doing any time, I wrestled with the justice of it, which doesn't even speak of the demons Tommy had to battle as a result."

That was interesting, but inconclusive about his nature, so you probe. "Do you support the death penalty?"

He peeks over at you and states, "Absolutely not."

That's unacceptable. He has to explain. "Why?"

"Well, for one thing there's no way for man to judge fairly. In the process of executing the guilty, the innocent will suffer, too. I feel that the Lord is the only Righteous Judge who can decide on life and death. After all, once you die, you go to the real judgment. An eye-for-an-eye doesn't make things right or even. Let them serve time behind bars to think about what they've done and become penitent. And if any one needs to repent and accept Jesus, it's a murderer. The more time they have on their hands, the better the chances for their soul salvation—which is the desire of the Lord."

Even though you share that view, his reasoning sounds like a religiously correct answer from a preschool Sunday school class, so you come to that level in an antagonistic role. "The Apostle Paul states in Romans 13, 1 through 7 that we are subject to human authority, who are ordained by God and are appointed as avengers of evil. First Peter 2, 13 through 16 reinforces the doctrine that the government can punish evil."

"While that is true, it is also true that Romans 6 and 23 states that the wages of sin is death, so theoretically, we all should be executed. However, Jesus said it best that 'he who is without sin should cast the first stone'. I don't think anyone is qualified to pull the switch on the electric chair."

"What about the victim's family that have to deal with the loss?"

"What about the condemned's family that have to deal with a two-fold woe: the victim and their loved one?"

This is getting interestingly educating. "Just as God uses prophets to speak to man, don't you think he can use men to exercise judgment? After all, God's prophets aren't perfect."

"I'm not against the government punishing wrong...I'm against the death penalty. Just as it is God that gives life, it is He who takes it. Otherwise, why would He have prevented Cain from being killed?"

"So you're saying that there's a line to draw in judging?" you verify as a young woman of Oriental descent, who gradually floats just to the side of Levi, seems to take an interest in the discussion.

"Absolutely," he assures.

"Well, tell me this: how do you differentiate between reciprocity and punishment from a divine judgmental perspective? Paul states that God isn't mocked and whatsoever a man soweth that shall he also reap. It was Paul who penned that, and if you recall, he advocated the stoning of Stephen, and he himself ended up being stoned."

The petite Asian woman nods and interjects, "And if you remember, before he was converted on the Damascus Road, he was getting letters to throw the Christians in prison, which is where he ended up on several occasions."

"Reciprocity and punishment," Levi ponders for a moment and addresses it. "Moses was chastised by the Father and was taken home; David got a good whooping by the Lord for the whole Bathsheba ordeal, but he didn't die as a result of having Uriah killed. I believe that punishment and reciprocity are on the same side of the coin, but the other side of suffering has to do with the persecution a believer goes through for Christ's sake. After all, what did Jesus do to deserve suffering? He warned His followers on several occasions that they would be severely persecuted. So my stand is still anti-death penalty."

"Jesus said *'If any man will come after me, let him deny himself, and take up his cross, and follow me,'*" a student with a strong Afrocentric accent quotes, commenting, "We as believers will be baptized with fire, and not in the sense of the Holy Ghost, but of the tribulation Jesus mentions in Mark 10 and 38 and Luke 12 and 50."

We mull over his statement and resume with the topic that branches off into the differences between reaping a harvest from seeds sown, Godly punishment for evil and the trials of Christians. You and the girl, who is armed with her sword and pulls it out to bring out several illustrious scriptures, believes that Paul suffered stoning and imprisonment as a result of putting the early Church through the same. Levi and the deep black brother, who has his Word out to counter, feel that Paul was suffering for Christ and not going through what the Hindu's and Buddhist's refer to as karma. It wasn't so much a debate—although that's where you originally tried to take it—as it is an educating discussion. By the time Faith comes strolling up unexpectantly, we still haven't introduced ourselves.

"Faith this is," you introduce, holding your hand out to the lady.

"Susan Lee," she greets, joking, "as in Bruce Lee."

You turn to the brother sitting on your left and he acquaints, "Charles Quartey, but you can call me Q in order to keep your tongue from getting tied."

"And of course you know Levi. I'm Malcolm," you preface as you shake their hands. Levi greets them also as we drag Faith into the topic by posing the question of Paul to her. "Talk to us Faith."

"That's a good one," she says as she looks down and deeply inhales some inspiration. "Paul wasn't reaping what he had sown. Although he spoke it, he wasn't under that law. Sinners are under that law, which is in their heart—to be differentiated from the Mosaic Law that applied to the Israelites. If you're going to use such a broad interpretation of those isolate verses, that scripture would be in reference to a life of unrighteousness. And you have to figure that a person doesn't always get his just punishment or reward in this lifetime. The parable of the Rich Man and Lazarus is a good illustration of that. A murderer doesn't always reap murder; honest people don't always reap honest wages. If that scripture is to be taken literally, we would all have a dreaded harvest in our future, because I know I've sown some dirt in my short time here," she says as we collectively laugh and agree.

"When it's all said and done, we would reap death in the sense of eternal separation from God if we were going to go with the literal interpretation of Galatians 6 and 7 and Romans 6 and 23."

Levi nods, but doesn't gloat as she backs up his earlier reference.

"To put them in perspective, God punishes His children...they don't always get what they put out...sometimes they do, just as the Lord allowed the deceiving Jacob to be tricked by Laban, but best believe there was only so far Laban could go. David suffered through a violent soap opera reign as a result of the Bathsheba affair. Although the church in America doesn't suffer the same physical trials of the first generation church in the Holy Land and the Middle East, we still have our own tribulations today, which some may suggest is a result of something wrong that we did—like Job's friends assumed—but since Jesus was perfect and suffered, how much more will we as His disciples suffer? If we sow seeds of wickedness and fleshly fulfillment, in this life we may reap a wicked harvest, but surely we—or should we say sinners who are not in righteous standing with God—will reap a body of damnation in the resurrection. To put the verse in it's proper perspective, Paul was making a reference to giving, not a general reference to deeds."

There is no debate. "Amen," Q trumpets in with his deep native-African tone, summing up all of our sentiments as we can feel the presence of the Lord squashing all confusion.

"You're going to have to get up on this," you urge Levi as you rain a jumper through the net from the top that puts you up two-zip. "Not that defense will help you."

You were in good spirits and Levi was talking smack, so we ended up in the Patten Gym after classes. He insisted that not only could he smoke you, but he'll also dunk doing it. The wager is lunch for the game, and the beverages ride on the dunk. Garfield the cat complains about his disdain of Mondays because nothing good happens on them. If only he could've lived your life on yesterday's Monday. It would've made up for all of the heartache and disappointment compiled on his history of the day for him.

The good news. You and Levi were having one of our few, casual, diplomatic conversations a few days after the discussion outside of the library, and the topic shifted to a comparison of the Biblical Jews and the

Blacks in America. Both were in bondage, we agreed. Both were oppressed, we agreed. Both were set free, we agreed. Both are still oppressed, he agreed more strongly than you did, but it was a valid point. You could've gone on a serious tangent about the woes of your folks, but he detailed the differences very eloquently and referenced it with Exodus 12:35-36. "The major differences between the Jews that were freed from the Egyptians and the Blacks that were emancipated in America, is that the Jews had a Promised Land to go to—and they made it—with money to take with them; the Blacks were promised 40-acres and a mule and are still waiting in vain. They didn't have any money when they were set free, so they were set up to lose."

You were impressed, and seconded, "Throughout the 40 years that the Israelites wandered in the desert, God told them not to forget their history and to teach it to their kids. Much of the oral history of blacks is resting at the bottom of the Atlantic Ocean. Slavery stifled it for that 400-year period. Without knowing where we've come from, our destiny is a dismal mystery with the potential to repeat history."

He went on to explain that "That fact alone is the basis for reparations for African-Americans," noting that "2nd Samuel 20 says that there was a famine in the land of Israel because Saul broke the covenant with the Gibeonites that Joshua made 400 years earlier. Numbers 30 indicates that God takes vows seriously. The scriptures don't give an account of when Saul killed them, but God knew it and informed David that the broken promise not to slay them was the reason for His kindled wrath against the Nation of Israel. When David reached out to the Gibeonites to make amends, he let them set the cost of reparations. America needs to truly acknowledge the damage that slavery caused by making some kind of amends. Until then, there will always be racial inequality and tension."

At that moment, your wall came tumbling down, although you've kept a few bricks around just in case you want to bean him with one. His empathy was like a wrecking ball and almost worth as much as the severance pay owed to your ancestors. You wouldn't even wish the black struggle on the white oppressors. That's a level past sadistic. If you had the power, you wouldn't reverse the roles. Above reparations from the United States (which is long overdue), you desire true repentance, which would abolish racism. Understanding is a pivotal step towards racial reconciliation in this country. As it stands, White America is still in denial of the ramifications of slavery. Otherwise, there wouldn't be excess spending on the prison enterprise, while public education is rejected and neglected like a discarded diaper.

Levi suggested that since you, Faith, Susan, and Q all connected as covenant holders, that perhaps a Bible discussion would be good. It sounded like a good idea, so we called everyone else and they confirmed that they had the same vision. Tentatively, we agreed to meet up in a different dorm every other Wednesday.

After going up 6-0, you miss on a drive and Levi rebounds. He backs you down with his 20-pound weight advantage and spins off you. You recover and go for the block, only to be embarrassed. "I'm sure getting dunked on by a white boy was very liberating," he jokes. "I don't know...you may have to put a bag over your face since that's never happened before."

"I've taken off my shades of partiality, so I don't see you as a white boy, but as an albino brother. However, it won't happen again," you vow.

"You know the hole is no place for the famished," he cracks on your toothpick build.

"I just hope you've had your rabies shots, because if you come in here again, it could get bloody," you remark in regards to his hair in excess.

You can't believe he calls your bluff and attempts the same move again. As if lightning strikes twice in the same spot. He cocks the ball back to send it down, but you palm it inches from the rim, sending him back to earth. "NOT IN MY HOUSE," you shout as you stand holding the ball above him.

The great news. You caught up with the managing editor at The Sporting News. He was actually waiting on your call and answered on the first ring. You gave him your angle on the story (which is still strong ten years after the fact), detailed your interviews with Deon Thomas and Nick Anderson, mentioned your connections to key people such as Bryant Notree and an uncle that went to grammar and high school with Wilson, and shared your personal encounter with him at Mendel. He hung on your every word and seemed more excited than you. We verbally agreed on doing the story, although a deadline wasn't set. He said to send him a rough draft and outline as soon as possible. You wasted no time in documenting all of your resources on paper and calling Uncle Ben up for some of his thoughts. He promised to sit down with you soon.

The game is tight 16-14 in favor of you and he has the ball at half-court. You signify, "You need to shear your hands...you look like a lamb."

He pulls up almost at the half-court mark, and pops.

"Love connection," he brags as he runs up cupping his face in his hands. "I wonder what would appear if I connect the dots right now," he ponders in regards to your freckled face. "The NU Wildcat? An Airplane? How about a man that just got eyed? Yesterday I saw the Virgin Mary weeping; today it looks like scribble scrabble."

You have to laugh.

The "I've made it to heaven without dying" news. Faith said that she loved you as her brother; yearned to love you as her lover like no other. "My passion for you is immeasurable," she professed. We snuggled in silence after you dubbed her Rose. Make no mistake about it, your body was fiending for her like a blood-starved vampire in a blood bank. Her flesh ignited, too. If there was a chance for us to slip, that intense moment provided oiled down ice for the occasion. We kept our balance, though. And you can't lie: you were impressed with yourself. However, your own determination isn't to be credited. You have faith in Love and the love of Faith, so fornication would have been as silly as beating the corpse of a nemesis. It was time for you to go when we woke from the catnap, and without announcement or protest, you left. You chilled. She chilled. Sunnight didn't serve as a moment of passion. Monday was a cool confirmation.

The game is tied 30-up and lunch is riding on this last shot. Since there's a score to settle, you dribble from hand to hand as you warn, "Watch my crossover" just as you take it through your legs to the right, only to pat it to the left, getting him reeling back off-balance. You blast off, and like a good dog he doesn't jump as you hammer it down on his head.

"OH!!!" you shout as he rubs his head. "THE SKY IS FALLING—THE SKY IS FALLING!" you tease as the ball rolls to the other end of the court. "Chicken Little, I forgot that you can't fly," you rib some more as you walk up to him to give him a pound. This is such a gratifying victory, that the adrenaline has you ready to run him again. Although in your subconscious you couldn't fathom losing to a white boy, your consciousness was focused on the opponent, not the color. As you reach him, your vision dims and tunnels in while your body moves in slow motion and grows faint. As you open your arms to give a warm hug, the lights fade into a blissful blackness.

"Is Heaven a playground?"

"There's a story in the Bible where the Pharisees and the Sadducees come to Jesus and they say to him 'there was a man and he had five brothers or whatever and he was married to this woman and he died. So his brother picked her up and his brother when he died and so on and so on, until all the brothers were dead.' And they said 'When they get to heaven, who's wife is she going to be?' And Jesus told them 'You do err, because you don't know the scriptures'...because in heaven the scripture says we'll be like the angels: they are non-gender beings and they are being created by God to give praise. And heaven by no means is a boring place. Most people might say 'when we think of heaven we think of getting somewhere where the glory of God is and we gonna sit back and ain't gonna do nothing. Naw...we gonna be busy. I do believe that the abilities and the things that we do down here on earth—everything that we do down here on earth are but a symptom of what we'll be able to do when we get there. And I don't believe that we're doing things down here that don't—or will not have an effect in heaven or do not exist in heaven."

You're in reporter mode without a recorder as Terry Cummings of San Antonio Spurs gives you words of encouragement. It's like a gunfighter at a shoot-out with no pistol. However, it doesn't matter, since for about twenty minutes he sows healing words into your soul, talking about everything except sickness. The discussion goes through life in the NBA and his opinion about role models and Craig Hodges' coaching position at Chicago State and his off court ventures and his positive outlook and his affirmation of being a mentor and the confirmation that all have a calling and the tests' of genuine Christianity. He is deep and passionate. There is so much sincerity in his scriptural quotations, that you know that you have to hear him preach one day. Levi (who is a Pentecostal Christian like Cummings) mentioned that he met him at a fellowship in Milwaukee back when he was with the Bucks. You thank him for taking the time out to call, and he blesses you. Then he's gone, and you're stuck in a grim reality.

The diagnosis: A large tumor on your heart. The prognosis: No more hoops. The treatment: Open heart surgery. The question: Why is it that bad news is always on the heel of positive news and wipes out the good fortune? Ray was killed after graduation. Dexter died during the holiday season. Your grandparents were killed right after the birth of Uncle Ben and the marriage of Dad. You're peeved to the limit, which borders on bitterness. Never will you cross the line and curse God, but you do ask Him "Why". So far, He hasn't given you an answer. Even the scent of Rose only goes so far. She was the first one on the scene—relieving Levi, who yelled for an ambulance to be called after he caught you. Fortunately, you were right up on him so he could keep you from hitting the floor.

A week before your graduation, you woke up at three in the morning to drain the snake. What you thought was a strong case of numbing exhaustion turned out to be the tumor cutting off the blood flow. Just as you made it to the toilet after flicking on the light and pulling your piece out, you were gone. It's almost as if someone simultaneously switched your lights off. Quicker than a blink, you were sitting wedged on the side of the toilet. Even though you put your hand on the wall for balance just before the darkness blanketed you, it amazed you that you didn't damage anything—such as your head or your back—or spill some urine on the floor. You were grateful that no one heard it, and you quickly dismissed it as sleep falling.

This time—unlike the first two blackouts—you didn't regain consciousness immediately. When you woke up, you were looking up at the ceiling of the ambulance with an oxygen mask on your face. You were looking forward to that ham on rye. There's no mistaking your fear. The televised death of Hank Gathers a few years back was one of the most demoralizing scenes to witness. Just last year, Reggie Lewis of the Boston Celtics died on the court. The fool in you is defiant of the prognosis, while the coward in you is reluctant to enter a gym again. Whatever the case, you won't be playing competitive ball again. Ma and Uncle JoJo arrived about an hour after Faith. Nick showed up shortly after, and to your surprise, Mitch came in crying with Chuck D. You had the urge to slap him and laugh for weeping like he was at your funeral. Good grief. It's bittersweet for loved ones to gather during tragedy. While you take notice of how everyone embraces Faith—especially how she and Nick hit it off like old friends—and the potential laugh-fest Levi,

Mitch and Chuck D would've put on, you yearn for solitude so you can hear what God has to say. Instead, everyone goes out of their way to distract you.

"Craig Hodges can still shoot the lights out," Chuck D mentions.

"My Bio-Chemistry instructor is going to be a stubborn mess," Faith predicts.

"Your credit card came," Ma reminds.

"Me and Traci are going to be renting a house out when our lease is up," Mitch notes.

"I may be assigned to teach the women's missionary class after substituting for Deacon Charles and Sister Parsons," Nick hints.

"I can't wait for your Ben Wilson article to come out," Uncle JoJo declares.

Bless their hearts, but they are annoying you to nausea.

"Don't take this personally, but I would rather be alone," you request, shocking them into silence. They peer at you briefly. Ma nods slightly as they file out in a single line without passing any other words. You burn with anger and grit your teeth. Surprisingly, watching them leave makes you feel worse. However, as long as you're going to be miserable, you'd rather not spread it around.

After silently pleading to God for an answer for a good twenty minutes, Nick leads everyone back in claiming, "There's a word from the Lord" as they all surround you.

You're curious, but still seething. "A word?"

"Yes," she declares, pulling a bottle of olive oil from her purse. "The devil is a liar," she proclaims with bold conviction as she anoints your head and chest. Then she anoints the hands of everyone else. "God says He's going to heal you without surgery," she assures through a peaceful simper. That sends a surge of hope through your body as their collective faith is garnered to your bosom. "Faith," she beckons, noting, "The Lord just revealed to me that your healing testimony is what Malcolm's is going to be, and He wants you to lay your hands on his chest, right over his heart."

Faith's eyes bulge slightly as she obliges, speeding up your heart rate noticeably. You could feel the love in her hands.

"Okay Saints, let us all place our hands on the head of Malcolm as Ms. Johnson leads us in the prayer of faith."

Ma is tearing silently as she places her hands on your head first, followed by the rest of them. Before she starts, Faith starts singing "Victory is Mine", and Uncle JoJo follows suit. Without interrupting the glorification of Jesus, Ma launches into a power-packed petition:

"Jesus, my Lord and my God, every good and perfect gift comes from You, for when I asked for a child, You didn't give me a heathen, a pet or a doll; You gave me an anointed son. Just as You remembered Rachel when she was barren and blessed her with Joseph, You remembered me and gave me Malcolm. In her old age, You took away Elizabeth's disgrace and gave her John the Baptist. At 90, You allowed Sarah to give birth to Isaac: the son of promise. 'Is any thing too hard for God,' You asked her. 'There is nothing that God cannot do,' You declared through the angel Gabriel to Mary, backed up by the impregnation of the virgin with Jesus through the Holy Spirit. You gave me your best by giving Yourself as a sacrifice for me; and I gave You my best by giving Malcolm back to You. He is the harvest of the seed of faith that was sown in me; through the rains of adversity and through You—the Sun of Righteousness—he has grown into a vessel of righteousness. For You are the Author and Finisher of our faith; we are heirs of the promises to Abraham. You suffered our punishment; You were wounded for our transgressions; You were bruised for our iniquities; The chastisement of our peace was upon You; And by Your stripes we are healed. Like the Shunammite woman who clung to You for her son, I will not leave You, my Lord, until You put Your healing hands on Malcolm. You gave Hannah a loud song by blessing her with Samuel after she prayed a silent prayer, and You gave me that song when You blessed me with Malcolm. Because Your blessings make me rich and bring me no sorrow, I can sing 'Victory is Mine; Victory is Mine. We have the Victory...'" she chants as everyone joins in.

You've heard Ma pray before, but not like this. She continues to travail with her whole body, soul and spirit, reminding Jehovah of His promises of healing, prosperity and life and that more abundantly. It's not a natural feeling, but your soul could feel the move of faith. Although it doesn't say it verbatim in the scripture, you know it to be true: The effectual fervent prayer of a righteous mother availeth much.

When the Victory praise closes, Nick declares, "The test that you take next week will show no tumor."

16

"How are the grades coming?"

"I'm taking a beating," Traci confides.

The deacons are addressing Chuck D, the lone baptism candidate, about the seriousness of his decision to follow Christ. Everyone is present: Mitch and family, Nick, Deon, your family along with Faith, Joyce, and of course the whole church. Even Levi accompanied you. We managed to get a spot just by the entrance to the stage where we have an unobstructed view of the pool.

"You too?"

"Malcolm, I've never gotten a C in my life. It's like a very bad dream so far."

"A 'C'? It has a nicer ring than DA-DA-DA-DA-DA-DEE," you assure.

You were butchered on that last Biology exam. At the moment, your average is a modest C. And you're not exactly acing the rest of your classes. You're averaging a B-plus in "Editing and Writing the News" and your overall average is around a C-minus. So far, you haven't adjusted. The work isn't necessarily harder; your discipline isn't lacking; the concepts aren't difficult to grasp; Faith isn't a distraction; the article isn't too consuming. Pride is what's killing you, and unfortunately, you're going through a process of humiliation. If good grades didn't come easy (which was usually the case), you studied harder, which always did the trick. All the changes on your end that you could think of, have been covered. When you got your first Statistics test back (a B-minus), you just knew that it was a mistake. Confident that you had aced it, the B bopped your arrogance in the belly. You studied an extra two hours for the next test and waited for the redemptive A. An insulting C was the verdict. That positive medium was so allusive all of a sudden. At first, you were too lax, then you waxed anxious.

"So far I'm smoking all of my classes," Mitch notes, advising, "Try not to study too hard the night before and chill out during the exams."

"Ah shut-up," you and Traci exclaim as the church starts singing "Take Me Out to the Water."

Chuck D rises in his white robe, cap and socks, and treks to the pool just behind the pulpit, where the pastor is waiting. When he steps into the water, our excitement culminates as we flash glancing smiles at each other and hold our breath as he crosses his arms. The preacher raises his right, clothed hand and recites the baptism creed: "Obedience...To the Great Head of Heaven. On the profession of your faith my brother...I'll baptize you...In the name of the Father; In the name of the Son; In the name of the Holy Ghost."

Chuck D is submerged and emerges to the collective rejoicing of the congregation. Surely, CD is full of delectation, although his outward, pokerish appearance remains stationary. Perhaps Joyce rejoices with repetitive shouts of "Hallelujah" and does the Holy Ghost strut because she has emotions and fire for them both.

"She never showed that much happiness when *we* were together," you joke in Faith's ear.

She playfully elbows you and cuts you a rebuking grin.

As Chuck D walks towards the door, he showcases a sanctified smirk as if he dished out a dime of an assist and sticks his fist out to you and Mitch. We oblige with a pound as you greet, "Welcome to the Family" just before he disappears through the door.

Everyone stayed for the whole service. Joyce sang "Be Grateful" on a higher level. Not only did she bring that old spiritual that you love to a new level, but it also seemed like it brought the people to life. Chuck D had an inner glow that permeated his skin. The sanctuary brimmed with love and joy. After a scan of the congregation, you observed that there wasn't a single unclean spirit in the place. The Pastor then proceeded to preach the message from the entire book of Haggai. When he finished reading the text, he could have stopped there. The message was addressing your lack of classroom prosperity. Although you were still active in the church, you neglected your Bible study. As a result, the subjects at school weren't sticking. You vowed right then and there to change that.

After service, we feast in the dining room to cap off a good ol' fashioned Sunday fellowship. The mirth carries over into the drive home. You, Faith and Levi blast a combination of old spirituals and contemporary gospel from the Canton Spirituals and the Mighty Clouds of Joy to Anointed and Yolanda Adams as we cruise down Lake Shore Drive. When we arrive at her house after dropping Levi off, we decide to pay homage to the Chicago Gospel artists by playing their work. For the rest of the afternoon, we let the likes of Mark Hubbard, Albertina Walker,

Reverend Milton Brunson and the Thompson Community Singers, Chicago Mass Choir, and Richard Smallwood minister to us. For edification purposes, we close the afternoon with Beverly Crawford, Dottie Peoples, The Winans and Walter Hawkins. When the last song of "Love Alive II" by Walter Hawkins plays, you state your case for the old style.

"There was mountain moving faith in the tone; a true hope in the music; agape love in the lyrics. It never gets played out, because the anointing supersedes the generations. Some of today's contemporary gospel music is laced with pride and commercialism, as opposed to the Holy Ghost."

"That's true, but some of the contemporaries have a stronger appeal on the younger crowd. You just happen to be unique in your old school advocacy. But know that these are the last days and God has poured out his Spirit and anointed the voices of many young men and daughters."

You flash her a grin of defeat as you shake your head. "I've met my match," you note in regards to debating as you stroke her silky, warm face.

"Yes you have," she seconds as she sows a kiss through your lips and into your heart.

After two weeks of planning and organizing your thoughts, you finally got started on the Ben Wilson feature. You researched that era and got some tips from Ben. What kind of piece would it be without the coach's perspective? Coach Bob Hambric always struck you as a quiet storm. Always cool, you've never seen him with a hair out of place. With the brain surgery he experienced, he took composure to a whole new level. You joked about how you would've sent him to the heart surgeon, too, if you had decided to play for him. Although the interview with him during school hours lasted roughly 45 minutes, you managed to tune out a lot of the dialogue and tack the quotes that mattered to your mental document. When he alluded to a more talented player that entered Simeon at the same time as Ben, you knew he was referring to Sean Wright. Several times you observed him turning Ekersal out. Uncle Ben pointed out that he left after his first year. His face was full and yellow like the moon, and he had emeralds for eyes. At about a compact 6'3"/230, he didn't look like he could hop. It was after he blasted off on you and kept rising in slow motion like a crack-fueled rocket with a vendetta with gravity, that you read the handwriting on his Nikes (which egged, "Fly the Wright Brother: An Unfriendly Sky"), and you realized that he had a "beam me up Scottie" vertical. Calling him the most talented player inside or outside of the NBA that you have personally faced is overly modest, and it's not because he gave you and Mitch a crash-course on dunking in a crowd during Alderman William Beavers' summer tournament. He's definitely Reebok commercial material. To put his game in perspective, if he was in shape, he could seriously challenge Jordan in a one-on-one...and probably win.

The timing of the interview couldn't've be better. Earlier that day you got word that Bryant Notree was declared ineligible to play because some of his high school credits didn't count. It hurt you, although obviously not as much as it hurt him. When you called him, he was too distraught to really talk about it. Sometimes it amazes you how good news and bad news are timed around the same moment, as if competing for emotions. Just last week you read in the Sun-Times how his father, Clarence, received $13,000 in workers' compensation. In 1991, he shielded 30 kids in a school gym and took a bullet, but was denied the money because 'hero' isn't part of the job description. Funerals are expensive and lives are priceless, so the issue stupefied you. However, it's good that they came around and Notree got his due.

It's ironic that you decided to red-shirt. Of course the tests came back negative. When you were tested the first time after the faith healing, the doctors were so perplexed that they almost seemed disappointed. Monday they bombarded your body with cardiovascular exams. As expected, it illustrated the goodness of God. They declared you a top physical specimen. That same day, you got Friday's exams back from all four of your classes. Feinstein and Cooper graded in red, while Ghoolsby and Stone marked in black. Life dealt you a good hand, because you had a straight ace day: spades in FrankenEinstein, hearts in Cooper, clubs in Ghoolsby and diamonds in Stone.

That night you sent up a prayer of thanksgiving and a petition for guidance. You woke up with a divine pat on the back and a perfect peace with the right decision. There is a season for everything, however, 1994-95 isn't yours for basketball. Coach Birdsong was okay with that and referred you to the athletic director. We all met and agreed after 15 minutes that this was the best decision, even though it set the top recruit at NU back for the second straight year. Last year, center Evan Eschmeyer red-shirted, and still has yet to play his first college game. As it turns out, NU's disabled list boasts three of the top freshmen players (you, Geno Carlisle and Evan, not to mention junior Brian Chamberlain) a week away from the start of the season.

As you straddle Beaufort the panting bronco, you mention, "The case of the rare, air-breathing dog-fish was ruled in favor of the Wildcats...ROO ROO ROO" as Faith toys with her CD's.

While you were in the hospital, you peeped out one of the intern's CD-ROM catalogue titled Continuing Medical Education Associates. You jotted down the phone number and ordered one. After it arrived Tuesday, you studied and quizzed Faith about her medical reference needs and placed an order for Dermatology Image Bank, STAT!-Ref Starter Plus, and the ACLS Case Study Simulations CD-ROM, which was delivered today. She's been literally in the screen horsing around with the ACLS for over an hour, while you horse with the horse who you've learned to like.

"As if there was any doubt," she says, barely breaking her concentration from the screen as she glances back and rolls her eyes. "What a waste of time. They oughta make him pay the court costs and then kick him out."

"Give him credit for originality."

"I'll give him credit for being a spoiled, snobbish, white boy. Imagine a black person putting a poodle in a fish tank and calling it a dog-fish to get around the no pets rule."

"Imagine me riding in the dorm on Beaufort and claiming that he's Mister Ed."

She laughs, finally leaning back in the chair. "Malcolm," she says with another chuckle as she rises, steps over to you and clutches you with her head buried in your chest. "I don't know what to say outside of *'I love you.'*"

"That's enough," you insist, embracing her.

"No it's not," she retorts. "Can you take me to Clark and Addison?"

You can take her any place in the continental US right now.

We end up at Fancy Dan's (a clothier only 20 minutes away). The trip was for your pleasure. Dan's has a diverse selection of dress fashions, from silk European suits to African garbs, with no signs of athletic wear. The items sure aren't cheap. You price a tie at $100. And

Faith isn't holding back, either. She picks out three colorful dashikis, a couple of kufis and a deep-plum tunic. While overindulging your body, she seems to bounce joyfully to the beat of an alternative tune overdosed with bass.

"Faith, you don't have to do this," you promise, feeling a little uneasy about a $400 shopping spree at her expense.

"Do you like these things or not?" she snaps.

"I love them, but you don't have to do this because I..."

"Shut up, Malcolm. This is what I was planning to do before you did what you did. Now please accept this without the drama."

You wax chagrinly silent when one of the chic salesmen encourages in a thunderous, authoritative tone, "Never discourage a queen from taking you beyond the baronial treatment," as he winks at Faith.

She blushes slightly as you crinkle your brow up. You try to shake some sense into the word, pulling out your dictionary for verification. The inflexion caused by the suffix almost threw you off, but your guess is correct. "So she's treating me like more than a nobleman," you confirm to him with a smile. "I love when a brother waffles," you confide, perplexing him a bit as he squints his eyes.

He pulls out a dictionary from his breast pocket and queries, "You think I speak evasively" in an offended tone, not offering you a chance to respond as he declares, "I love when a brother's speech lacks solecism."

"What can I say...I'm a journalism major, so I have to be contextually correct."

"Is that right?"

You nod as he seems to glow with that revelation.

"Where are you going to school?"

"I'm in my first semester at Northwestern."

"Excellent," he proclaims. "She said your name is Malcolm?" he verifies, jotting it down.

"Malcolm Johnson."

"My pal Mal...Is this all you will need?" he questions Faith, pointing to the pile of clothes on the counter.

"That's it," she nods.

Another unfamiliar cut comes over the sound-system. When you hear the lyrics *"My birth is in your breath; my life is in your death"* vocalized, "God's Disciples" comes out of your mouth.

"You've heard them?"

"Live a cappella," you proudly state. "I met them when they were real GD's, if you know what I mean."

"More than you think."

He informs you that he showcases the music of up and coming recording artists so that they can possibly get noticed. There is also a hint that he's some kind of talent scout. It was either a slip or insinuation when he stated that he can get a better feel for an artist by hearing it in a neutral setting.

He calls "Veronica" the cashier over and requests, "Give these items to them at 10% over cost and put their names in the system."

Your mouth drops and your speech flees, which indicates that you learned to shut up when someone is hooking you up. The total turns out to be about $150, which means that he has a hell of a mark up and a generous heart. Faith charges it to her VISA and can't thank him enough.

"I assume that you've been in here, because you knew what you wanted and that outfit is something that we started carrying this summer," he guesses correctly of her neutral-toned, loose-fitting pants/shirt outfit. "If you're in need of some fresh attire, continue to look us up and I'll hook you up...your name is in the system for Dan's special discount, per Vic," he promises, pulling out a card from his breast pocket. It turns out that Victor Daniel Hunt is the proprietor.

"Stay strong and keep those grades up," he urges as he gives you a firm handshake. Highly discounted prices on expensive clothing is incentive enough to do just that.

Faith was eager to take you to the Ethio Cafe (an Ethiopian restaurant in the same area). She promises that the spicy food is tailored for your taste buds. You ask her if she can prepare the dishes herself, and she confesses that she can barely pop corn without burning it, admitting that she needs to hone her cooking skills. Six days a week, she eats out. The seventh day is dedicated to fasting.

We sit against the red wall in the murky eatery exploring the atmosphere. The lighting seems crimson tinted. Musical and ethnic artifacts line the four corners, along with historical pictures. Faith ordered the Sambussa appetizer (pastry filled with meat, potatoes, and peppers), Yebeg Wat (Tender lamb chops cooked with hot pepper sauce and blended with home made seasonings), and a strawberry drink. You noticed that while she had no problem pronouncing the things on the menu, you had to point out the Doro Wat (pieces of chicken cooked and gently seasoned with red pepper sauce and a touch of marinated butter). She even had a semi-conversation in Amharic with her Ethiopian waitress friend. They actually taught you how to say God bless you: *Egzi'abehear yebarkesh* to a female; *Egzi'abehear yebarkeh* to a male.

As we soak up the jubilant percussionist flavor that the band saturates the small area with, you pay close attention to the strong hints of Ethiopian blood flowing through Faith. Even if her parents didn't unearth their roots, you could guess her genealogy based on the features. From the skin tone that illustrates the gracious sun, high cheek-bones and naturally outlined eyes, you can understand how King Solomon was inspired to write the "good woman" Proverbs after meeting the Queen of Sheba.

We discuss the impressions that Black Americans have of the Motherland in light of the literary voice of Buchi Emecheta from the literature class over the summer. She understood your misperception of African male/female relationships. You bought into the black-pride belief that they treated each other like royalty. However, we simultaneously point out that there are too many sub-cultures to stigmatize the whole continent. Then Faith spits out a concept straight from the bottom of the sea.

"Do you recall the love scene between Ete Kamba and Nko in 'Double Yoke?'" she questions.

You do.

"Ete freaked out and kicked her to the curb because he didn't see any blood, which in that culture—along with other African and Middle Eastern cultures—was evidence of a woman's virginity. Sex wasn't just a physical act, but a gift that came along with the package known as the bride. The man had to either pay the father of the bride or work for him. Poor Jacob had to work a total of 14 years for his wives. What they paid for was something pure, and they had some bloody sheets—also known as the tokens of her virginity—after the honeymoon for the receipt. Virginity was the worth of a bride, and if there was no blood from the tearing hymen, the book of Deuteronomy states that she was to be stoned," she affirms with a slight smirk.

"From a spiritual standpoint, blood represents life, and in marriage it represents a lifelong covenant. During consummation, the blood seals that covenant because two bodies and souls are becoming one. That's how God built us...not to seek out the pleasure for past-time or game, but to bond."

She takes you with her on that profound lesson and you almost drown. And all along you thought that fornication was wrong because God said "Thou Shalt Not." You're tempted to ask her "If your father were alive and I paid the price for you, would we live happily ever after—according to the law of Moses—or would I have to bury you right after the honeymoon," but you opt against it.

"So you mean to tell me that with all of your privilege and exposure that you've never been to Africa?" you ask as you lightly tug on the tablecloth and tread in less turbulent waters of discussion. "You look like the bountiful harvest of the Motherland."

"This is as close as I've come," she assures with a bashful smirk. "My parents went to teach or do research on several occasions and promised to take me for a vacation. Unfortunately, the promise is buried with them."

You shake your head in disbelief. "That must be the country flag," you guess, pointing to a large banner on the opposite wall.

She nods as the polite waitress sets our drinks before us and scampers off. "I used to be a waitress," she confides as she sips her beverage through the straw.

"I could see myself dropping a tray a day on somebody," you half joke. "They would have to put me behind the hot grill so I could sample all of the food before it is served," you chuckle.

She rolls her eyes at you and claims, "It wasn't all that bad...the tips were where the money was, especially since it was untaxed. That was my spending money, since Momma wasn't trying to raise a Eurocentric, dependant, Black woman."

"I hear you."

"My worse job was at Great America," she says between another short sip.

"Get out of here. Don't tell me: You were one of the cartoon characters?"

She laughs out. "Dagge. Do I look the part?" she questions with amazement.

"Tweetie Bird?" you guess.

"Close. Sylvester."

"Suffering succotash," you cackle irresistibly. "I dought I daw a pudy cat."

She sheepishly smirks and shakes her head as she tosses a napkin at you.

"I'm sure Bugs Bunny and Friends are your favorite people."

"You know it. I can't count the number of times folks came up to me mimicking them. There's nothing like adults making fools out of themselves. The kids were okay for the most part, but the teenagers worked my nerves. I had to literally punch a few that got too touchy with me," she says with disgust.

"I can't imagine you swinging on someone. Sylvester maybe, but not you."

"You have to realize how hot that suit could get in the summer and how ignorant people can get when they fuel up on sugar. Cotton candy, sunshine and a hot suit are a bad mix for me."

"It could've been a Barney outfit. Then you would've really been in trouble. The only thing purple I hate. And what really bugs me is how into it Dexter Junior is. I have to leave the room whenever he's watching him or playing with his stuffed animal. I'm glad you weren't Barney, 'cause you would've really caught it from them."

"Then the kids would've seen an ugly shade of purple. Imagine a smiling dinosaur stomping a hole in some obnoxious adolescent."

The image tickles you. "I had fun at my worse job as a telephone salesman. The work was tedious, no doubt, but once I got to the point where I didn't care—which was when I found out about Penny's child—I took it way too easy to get paid. Two out of three calls I made were personal. Whenever my supervisor would leave his seat, I would buzz his station. Just when he got back, I would hang up. It was like watching a well trained dog," you recall with glee. "The people were much worse than the position. Boss hog John would ask me a question, and do you know he would start up three different conversations with other people as I was answering."

"Needless to say you wouldn't work for him again."

"I would wash windshields just off of the expressway before I worked for him again. That lard-lip fatback had the look of a pedophile. He called himself trying to bond with me in the men's room—talking about *'sometimes a piss feels as good as sex.'* I told that pig to 'go back to your grease pit with that suggestive comment before I flush you down the toilet for sexual insult and then sue you for sexual assault.' He tanned redder and kept his words to himself."

We both buckle over in laughter.

When the food comes, we bless it and eat in relaxed silence. The dishes are spicy to your liking and the tunes continue to mellow your mind. You get lost in the savory moment, concluding that no matter where you are, it's all good if Faith is there. It would be nice to be locked in a closet or trapped on a desert island with her. Her image just brings out a smile in a somber mood. The small talk becomes a big discussion after we finish feeding.

You reach over and rub an old scar buried in her left eyebrow and question, "How did you get this?"

She giggles and states, "At a church picnic, I was horsing around home plate just as the designated hitter was swinging. Can you believe that he used my head for the ball?" she questions in disbelief. "I was actually decapitated and my body kept on running."

The thought makes your body quake. You would gladly take a hit for her. "The closest I've come to that is when I sat on the escalator at Sears and had my behind ripped off. I don't know if you remember back in 1979 when time stopped for a good five seconds...that was when I screamed so loud that the world paused."

"Oh my," she says.

"Believe it or not, the escalator malfunctioned after that. Sorta gives a new meaning to the term 'Buns of Steel'. Needless to say, the doctors had to surgically reattach them. Wanna see the scar?" you question facetiously.

"Malcolm," she blushes, and then frantically insists to your surprise "Yeah, lemme see it," as she playfully goes for your waist.

In the process of catching her wrists, you accidentally brush her miniature breast. We freeze in mid-laughter and just gaze at each other for an uncomfortable moment.

"I'm sorry," you plead, realizing that you crossed a dangerous line. On one hand, you want to absorb her whole body; on the other hand, you don't want to be a vessel of temptation...not on this side of marriage.

"That's okay," she assures, adding, "you haven't violated me."

Maybe not, but it's still uneasy, so you straighten up in your chair and suggest, "Maybe we should get our desserts to go."

She nods her agreement through a chagrin cloud. "It is getting late," she seconds as she waves for the waitress.

Nothing is uttered on the way home. This is the tensest moment you have spent with her. It is unnecessarily unnerving. We did nothing offensive to each other, so we insist. You weren't offended at all, just like she assured she wasn't. Maybe you're wrestling with a religious taboo. Sometimes it seems like your attraction to her is the ambition of the flesh. If that is the case, and it turns out that she is anything less than the favor that God promises in Proverbs 18 and 22, she will go down as the biggest letdown in your life. In the meantime, you're not going to hold back from fear that it won't blossom into wedlock.

When we arrive at Faith's house, you say a quick, silent prayer before walking her to the door. We both stare expectantly, yet dubiously. You break the silence. "Thanks for the outfits and the dinner."

"My pleasure anytime," she insists, bashfully smirking.

You chuckle and ask, "How do you say 'I love you' in Amharic?"

"*Afekereshallo* coming from a female; *Afekerehallo* coming from a male," she affirms as her smile glows with anticipation. "Why?"

"Just asking," you tease. "What about in Yoruba?"

"Mo Feran e yin."

"Arabic?"

"Ana bahabik."

You pause as your heart flutters like a descending dove and your grin waxes warmer than the passion of the infatuated Phoenix. With the sound barrier broken, it's time to demolish the dense wall of touch. You lean down and peck her on the eyebrow scar and proceed to kiss every facial part...except the mouth. Embracing her gently as if trying not to shatter any delicate glass, you put your lips on her lips and sip on the juice of her heart. No physical fluids are swapped; just spiritual. Avoiding the sin of gluttony, you part and promise more to come with your stare. Her unsure gaze questions, "When will we see each other again". You leave nothing for interpretation, audibly assuring, "I have Faith in the morrow," as you fade off.

"I feel sick," you testify, backing into a space while the Take 6 tape plays.

"Don't worry. He'll probably be your easiest interview yet. Y'all will have a lot to agree on and talk about," BJ assures as we exit and start towards the Jacoby Dickens Physical Education & Athletics Center.

"Craig Hodges isn't my concern," you clarify. "Tonight is supposed to be the college inauguration that I've dreamed about, and I'll be here watching in journalistic mode."

"Maybe you should try and play in the celebrity game...bring that scrimmage some baroqueness...flamboyance...flare," he mentions as you discern the meaning of baroque without going to the dictionary. He's good for breaking a big word down.

"That's a thought," you agree as we make it to the entrance.

Two weeks ago, BJ suggested an exclusive interview with Craig Hodges, which was unnecessary since you secretly scheduled a one-on-one talk a week prior. We couldn't agree on a date and time since our schedules constantly conflicted. After Mitch and Chuck D found out that you would be out of action this year, they invited you to the first ever Chicago State Midnight Madness. Why not support your boys since you weren't balling yourself? Hodges agreed to talk after the festivities. Faith insisted that she needed to study, when actually you were sure that she wanted to play with her CD-ROMs. She promised to spend the whole Saturday with you (as if she had a choice). Tomorrow you plan to kidnap her and give her a private birthday party to remember. Since there will be no touching like you are lusting, your creativity is going to have to kick butt to the utmost.

There's a long line that we by-pass after you indicate your press purpose, which is marked down with the security staff at the entrance to the gym. The stands are electrified with the celebrity game being a warm-up away from starting. You spot Mitch and Chuck D at the other end of the court as we make our way down the sideline adjacent to the scorers' table. BJ holds you up so he can rap with Dave "The Jammer" Michaels of 106-Jams. You almost get lost in the excitement as some of the players showcase their game in the crip line. BJ then starts talking to a guy in the stands and urges you over to introduce you to him.

"Mel, I don't know if you've met Malcolm Johnson. He's with the CABJ, too."

You smile and nod your head as Mel stands up to shake your hand. He teases you about being another MJ as he mocks your height. When he asks if you're playing tonight, you urge him, "Don't tempt me" as you explain your assignment and allegiance to Ricky Birdsong. Then, to your slight embarrassment, BJ reveals who you really are by refreshing the guy's memory of some of your infamous, non-basketball headlines. You can only grin as Mel's lady friend detects your chagrin and flashes you a look of pity. After what seems like a couple of days of reminiscing about your Malcolm X days, you bid farewell to them and start toward the end.

Mitch and Chuck D are talking to their women—Traci and Joyce—when you walk up. After you introduce BJ to them, he wanders off to greet some old friends, since he's only a couple of years removed from CSU and several alumni are present. As the announcers go through the introduction of the participants of the celebrity game, you turn your attention to your crew.

"Y'all ready to get it on?" you query.

"I'm good to go," Chuck D swears.

Mitch nods, "Let's do this", as he seems a little preoccupied.

While Chuck D boasts, Mitch pulls you a confidential length away and whispers in your ear "Do you know who that guy is you were talking to," as he nods his head toward the scorers' table.

You peek over and claim, "That's the Jammer: Dave Michaels."

"Not him," he huffs. "The guy that looks like Omar Epps from 'Juice'...in the stands with the babe."

You glance over at Mel, who seems to be blushing as his girlfriend snuggles up to him. "Mel? I just met him, but I remember seeing him at my journalism meetings. He's cool. Why?"

Mitch just stares at you and shakes his head as he leans to your ear. "That's the dude who cleared the party out over on Essex that Christmas," he says. You give him a puzzled look. "The night-train night," he emphasizes, sending you a jolt of enlightenment.

"You mean..."

"That's David's brother. It was *his* parent's house."

"Umm," you say. "So he's a PK."

"Yeah. He was walking up at the same time I was returning from taking Traci home. I hope he doesn't recognize me," Mitch says, visibly flustered. "I don't have time to have someone sweating me tonight."

"Man chill out. He has his hands full with his woman," you assure. It seems like things have gotten chilly between them as the game starts. "Besides, there were so many of y'all, that I'm sure no one stood out, except his idiotic brother."

"I don't know X..."

"Man, go take a laxative before you get out there," you advise, jabbing him in the stomach and rejoining the rest of your friends.

You find the celebrity game too frustrating to watch, because it resembles a pickup game in the park, and you aren't playing. Therefore, you opt to impatiently prance around the gym. When the game ends, you half watch the torturously long Greek step show, which almost goes past midnight and the time the season is supposed to officially start. When the team is ready to come out, you settle down to the right of Traci and Joyce (BJ got lost in the crowd), anticipating your boys' inauguration into college ball. After a ten-second countdown, they come blasting through the banner in express train formation and gel into a lay-up line. Whenever they get the chance, Mitch and Chuck D peek over and wink. When the game starts, they are on opposite teams. Although they aren't dominant, they have contributive statistics and a couple of flashy highlights. After Mitch tip-slams a miss, he hangs on the rim, and when Chuck D releases a no-look alley-oop, he starts back down court, even before the ball reaches the player's hands. When Mitch touches the ball, Traci screams; if Chuck D gets a shot, Joyce hollers. Needless to say, you end up with a left-side headache. When the dizzying paced game ends, Mitch has winner's rights.

As the crowd clears, you spot Hodges taking a picture with Mel and his woman in the hallway, while greeting other fans and signing autographs. You catch his eyes and he assures, "I'll be with you shortly" in between chatting with the admirers. He patiently accommodates all of the well-wishers while you playfully critique Mitch's and Chuck D's game. The crowd dwindles, BJ emerges to inform you that he'll be riding with someone else, and you bade your comrades well, leaving you, Hodges, a few remnants of spectators and the cleaning personnel.

"Right this way," he says as you follow him to his office inside the gymnasium. "Have a seat," he says, rearranging some notes and situating some books in the bookcases that line the wall opposite his desk. All of the press material and basketball literature clutter into several mounds of information and shrink the already tight space into a closet for sitting and talking.

The grin of excitement is still engraved on his face, so you comment, "Your boys look ready to go," when he finally takes a seat at his desk.

"Is it too late to get you enrolled and on the roster?" he jokes.

"Sorry coach, but I'm dancing to the Byrd's Song," you pun, consoling, "My guys Mitch and Chuck D will run the race for you. I don't even think I could keep up with that pace."

"Those are the type of players we have. They're athletic. They're good runners and jumpers and there to contribute," he insists optimistically, stopping short of mentioning the lack of size and a true center, beseeching, "We have to utilize our strength."

You get consent to record and we proceed in like-mind agreement as we touch on several topics out of the boundaries of the court. He affirms his black passion, sending the impression that he's speaking your mind, explaining, "A lot of times what you study is what you become. If you study and you work on athletics, then you're an athlete. I studied the history of our people and our struggle, so that's who I am."

Even though coaching a team that finished 4-23 the previous season is an obvious rebuilding project, he looks at it as an opportunity to interact with and nurture the black community.

Without reservations, he declares that the NCAA is just another branch of the racist system of America—with its restricting Propositions—but at the same time admonishes black folks to take advantage of the opportunities, since we have to play on the "monster's" field. He attributes a two-fold shame to the lack of influential exercise from Black athletes: Jewish control of player contracts (which he insists isn't so bad if the agent is qualified), and black players that don't put their finances to work for their people—which he calls a heavier woe.

"You can go with whoever you want to, but understand that once you get it [money], you gotta hire black folks on some level. They don't have to be your agent...they can run your grocery store; they can run your Laundromat," he qualifies, adding, "Before he [Jordan] signed his last contract, I said 'man why don't you open some of these vacant factories in America, in our community, bring the same means of production that they got in Korea...All the rubber is coming from Africa...you can get the rubber; you can get the machinery. Let's hire some Black folks.' But he said 'who's going to remember me in ten years?'

"'Now my understanding is that you the best player ever. That being the case, if you go to Black people and hire them, white folks going to buy your product, man. You can't tell me white folks ain't going to cross over and get this 'cause you the best. They understand the best. You think that we don't understand the best. But we're also benefiting. We got dollars just like they got dollars, but we think that our dollars don't equate to the power that their dollars equate to.'"

You disagreed with his assessment of Jordan as the best player ever, however, you did insist that his flying icon should replace the one of Jerry West as the NBA trademark. After all, he has taken the NBA to a universal level of appeal that crosses age, gender and racial boundaries and most of the Generation X'ers don't know Jerry West from the Western Conference.

We trip for a couple of pages worth of tape on the blood brother's lack of economical support and their insistence on white women after making it. You jokingly make an oath not to go out like that. John Salley is one of his allies that he names when he mentions the book project that he's working on that documents some of the problems he encountered with the NBA, such as other player's fears of talking to him, because it may be dangerous to their career. His "Operation Unite" organization parallels Nick Anderson's "Boy's in the Hood" foundation in that the purpose is to bring athletes and entertainers to the Black community for economical reasons. The discussion is good and you have more than enough material for an article, but to add bass to the volume, spice to the meat, and attitude to the mood, you steer him to *the* topic.

"What did you do after the repeat?"

He chuckles knowingly and launches into an explanation. "For the first year I thought I was going to play. I never considered not playing any more...not from the standpoint that I knew that one day that I wouldn't play basketball, but at the same time I didn't think it would be that soon because we had just won two championships; I'm 32 years old; best shooter in the game at that time—from the standpoint that I had three 3-point titles back-to-back, two shooting titles. Now...what's up?" he questions in mutual disbelief.

"The million-dollar question that I'm banking on: Were you blackballed out of the league?" you probe like an investigative reporter as you lean forward through his mouth and into his heart.

He takes a deep, ponderous breath and reclines back, as he seems to search the air for the answer. "When I look at all of it, I understand the system and how it works, so I don't get whacked out about it, but I understand from a historical standpoint what has happened. I understand that it's in the realm of possibility that *that* happened. But how will we ever know for certain that it happened? I feel like I have a case against both the player's union and the NBA, because I don't feel like my rights were taken care of the way they should have been by my union. From that standpoint, I thought about possibly suing the league, because I feel like I was discriminated against, but not on a level where race came into it up front, but from a standpoint that I wasn't able to get my skills to the market place compared to how everybody else got their skills there. So for me, I feel like Antitrust Violation, Civil Rights Violations, Constitutional Rights...where if reporters tell me part of the reason that I was not in the league any more is because when I went to the White House I wore an African garment... When we say I got a freedom of expression, do I? Or is it that if I express my freedom, then I will be penalized in what I can do economically?"

You're pissed beyond expression and you don't even try to mask your ire with a smirk of objectivity. If you were a high powered lawyer, you would fight his case to the bloody death. His principle would pay the price. It already has. As it stands, the only thing you can do at the present is write an article for a neighborhood newspaper, which makes your talent feel weak. We conclude the interview by slapping five's and exchanging God-bless-you's before breaking out.

As soon as the morning air slaps your face across the empty parking lot, the day starts bearing down on your eyelids. When you sink into the seat, slumber tempts you right here right now, but it isn't the place or time for snoozing. With maxed bladder urgency, you zoom out of the parking lot, down 95th Street and on to the Dan Ryan. As quick as you enter, you exit on 75th Street and pull into the Walgreen's, where you purchase a grape-strawberry Mystic and a package of Vivarin for a revival test. You ingest the gold-coated pill and gulp down your drink before you get back on the expressway.

Either you're psyched awake or the Vivarin is kicking in with the super-quickness of a turbo-booster. Before you reach 35th Street, your eyes feel strong enough to lift sewer caps, your mind rises to a creative cutting edge, and your awareness broadens to simultaneous hindsight. You chuckle, crank up the volume to the "Night Moods" on V103 and roll the windows down as your bosom seems to tingle with butterflies and your temperature rises like helium. Your heart waggles to "Someday

Is Tonight" by Janet Jackson and the tune seems to croon on behalf of Faith. The car and your mind flow at 100-miles per hour.

Before you know it, you're almost to the end of the line on Lake Shore Drive. The covert cop just ahead in the bushes on the left needs to catch you on a night when the songs on the radio aren't stroking you with the love of Faith. You zip down Sheridan, into Evanston and finally up to the Hinman House. Your legs are revved up, so you bounce to the door and scale the stairs four at a time until you reach your room. You toss your recorder and portfolio on your bed and beeline to the bathroom. It seems like you have a river in your intestines. When you finish flooding the toilet, you hop in your desk chair and garner the juice from your mind into your pen to compose a response on rose printed stationary to the love that Faith unwittingly expressed to you as captured in the song.

How's my favorite flower? So Gold is your favorite color. What an appropriate shade for Faith.

I'm not too cheap to buy a card from the store. It's just that the words in them never speak the authentic emotions behind my sacred door. Those writers haven't looked into the sparkling eyes of a thief of hearts and had their hearts skip a beat when that thief speaks. Besides, I'm a writer, and whatever the card writers can write, I can write better. What a bad case of artists' ego, huh? It's bad enough that you get me too giddy to talk straight. You send those high school freshman feelings surging through me as if it's a first date. I'm sorry to tell you that you will never cramp my creativity. I write from my heart; I write when I'm inspired; I write when the light brings me in from the dark; I write when love ignites my whole being like fire. I happen to be moved by what I see. When I have on my Rose colored glasses, you're black and bold; when I take them off and look through my eyes of Faith, you're too glorious to behold. I hope you like this small token. I would have gotten you something more extravagant, but I didn't want to give you the impression that it is your emotions that I'm stroking. My heart yearns to tell you that "I love you," and this is better than many Words spoken. The four month's that I've known you haven't revealed all of your likes and dislikes. Despite the short time span my level of love has soared to kite heights. I know that it's hard to see at night. But I love Faith, not sight. I realize that I run the risk of getting pricked if I get close and careless. However, the harvest is too bountiful to pass on this destiny

dare. I want to be the sunshine that blossoms you and sends out that honey-sweet soul aroma, so be patient as I learn about you, Rose.
To one the Spirit has given Faith...To another Faith by the same Spirit. To another (wonder-working) Faith by the same (Holy) Spirit...He gives special Faith to another...One and the same Spirit gives faith to one person...
I thank the Holy Spirit daily for the gift of Faith. Not only is this a moment in your life to commemorate, but this is a day of hope for me to celebrate. For I can say that I'm in love with my soul mate. I love you so much that...I decided not to use you as a guinea pig by baking you a cake. I'll come in from the deep end since I can't swim anyway. Happy Birthday Faith "Rose" Blackman and have a blessed date.

You wanted to make love to yourself after penning this. All of that passion put you into a deep sleep, even though the Vivarin was supposed to last at least another hour.

You took that self-made card to Campus Florists, along with the 14-karat gold, rose earrings with matching charm and necklace you bought last weekend, and paid an extra $20 to have a dozen gold roses sent to her at 11. You strategically arrived ten minutes after the deliveryman left. Of course she was still a dewy flower when you walked in. We got dressed in matching Afrocentric gear (you wore your royal dashiki; she wore her deitic caftan). After the crying game, the first stop was Embassy Salon & Day Spa downtown for a cure (pedi and mani) and full body treatment. You weren't foolish enough to do that yourself. Your self-control isn't that strong. Then we went on a little cruise from Navy Pier. Normally boats are not your pleasure, but since she could swim and you hadn't gotten on her bad side, you were sure to be rescued if you got dizzy and fell into the Lake. We proceeded to Army and Lou's on 75th Street and dined on fried chicken, greens, macaroni and cheese and cornbread to the tune of the Jukebox R&B. After dinner, we took in a play at the ETA on 76th and South Chicago. We climaxed the day on her couch holding and kissing and holding and kissing in front of the TV, until Saturnight turned into Sunmorning.

You had enough restraint to know when to pull back, which turned out to be our salvation. She didn't know when to stop. In fact, she didn't know her limit. In the middle of recovering our breath, she sheepishly confided that she had never been defiled with fornication.

The flushing red that waxed over her face didn't diminish her high degree of golden glory that permeated from within the depths of her heart. You truly wanted to become one, but your desire to do it right was slightly stronger. Thank God, because she was the weaker of us. Wisdom normally urges you to leave a potential situation, but you just wanted to be in her presence. We closed our eyes in unison and simultaneously opened them to each other. Her place in your life is almost in perfect focus, but you just want to be sure of the perfect timing.

After breakfast at The International House of Pancakes (you haven't gotten the courage to try and cook for her, yet), we went to service at her church. "Please be Patient With Me" is a simple song that was elongated by the Holy Ghost. You and Faith were on your feet reciting the lyrics with the rest of the church: ***"Please, be patient with me; God is not through with me yet. When God gets through with me, I shall come forth as pure gold."*** *The pastor proceeded to preach a good sermon on the finished Christian, taken from Job 23:10. Afterwards, we lounged around her house for a couple of hours, since the October sun shone with ardency. Surprisingly, you didn't have to pry her from the computer.*

A nap and snack later, she challenges you to the long awaited one-on-one, so we stroll over to the courts in the midst of the Greek Houses on the north end of the campus and go at it. Of course it isn't close, even with you shooting from beyond the arch and playing walk-along defense. You didn't try to go up 16 to 4, but she's having a bad shooting day, and everything you send up is hitting the jackpot, including the no-look hook from half court. "Today isn't your birthday," you inform as she backs you up under the basket. You don't jump and barely extend your arm, but she throws the ball straight into your palm.

"Goal tending!" she shouts. "Play fair, Mal!"

"I have to take advantage of every opportunity that presents itself," you joke, tossing her the ball out of bounds. "16-6. It's too bad you don't have an outside game, otherwise it might be closer."

She frowns at you, dribbles twice and banks it in from the top.

You just look at the basket. "Luck," you insist, passing her the ball. She turns her lip up and repeats her routine, only it rims out. As the ball drops into your hand, you feel her bearing down on you. Instinctively, you protect the ball with your body and your left arm.

Forgetting how short she is, you drop your hand right into her face just as she was coming around. She buckles to the ground. You dug a tear out of her socket with your ring finger, which scares you.

"Are you okay?" you question, kneeling down to her.

"I'm fine," she insists. "Just got poked in the eye."

"I'm sorry Rose," you assure, placing your arm on her back.

"That's okay," she says rubbing.

"Let me see it."

Facing you with both eyes closed tight as she rises, she opens it quickly, before blinking rapidly. With forced determination, she keeps it open for you. You draw back in shock, then lean closer for a better look.

"What?" she questions of your apparently perplexed countenance.

"Your eye..." you mention, trying to grasp an understanding of the mysteriously dazzling pigment. How can you put the glory of God into words?

"What about my eye?" she wonders.

"The sun is in it," you conclude, squinting from the strain placed by its radiance.

Although the center of the Milky Way fell from the sky, that magnificent star remains in her eye. In fact, she possesses twin celestial bodies for eyes. You gasp in awe as she pops out the other Wesley-Jessen chestnut-brown contact—that mysteriously appears smoke-black in her sockets—disclosing her golden eye coloration. Hallowed hazel is the politically correct classification, but you see gold wrought from the fiery hands of the Holy Ghost. God confirms the literal sneak peak of her.

We abandon the bouncing ball and head a few feet east to the lake at Lincoln by the water department, where we park on the rocks overlooking the tranquil, black pool. She insists that she wears them because she hates the stares and comments her eyes get. Although they elicit flattering compliments, the attention is unwelcome. As we talk—pausing for long, nervous periods of time—you don't take your eyes out of Faith's eyes once as you silently rejoice the fulfillment of the dreams. After you testify of the vision, you bottle up your common sense and sail it in the direction of Michigan. On bended knee; with her hands in yours; captivated by her gaze, and your heart helplessly forfeited to her care, you pledge: "I knew you were special a long time ago, yet the Lord has just enlightened me even more; You appeal to my carnal instincts, however we're more than flesh; He called me for a purpose a long time ago, but I can finally answer assuredly 'Here I am Lord'. Words are powerful, however they're impotent without actions. When the Lord speaks, Life happens. God's love is true, backed up by the sacrifice of the only begotten Son. Faith without works is dead. I want to be the Work of Faith, because those two are a coupled unit. I want to be the king that shares his throne with you; I want to be the friend that sees you through; I want to be your servant that stays true; I want us to be of the same gold hue; I want us to be on the same holy cue; I want us to be one-in-two. In the presence of God, as I peer in you, He's in view; together we're renewed; apart we rue. In Faith, I say 'I do.'"

Her eyes buck open and gauze over with tears. She guffaws sheepishly and purposely blinks away from your gaze, stating, "I don't know, Malcolm. This is so sudden." She places her hand over her heart, panting and quickly qualifying, "And that doesn't mean that I don't love you, but..." she pauses.

"But what?" you query, keeping your concentrated eyes on her.

"But it's so *soon*. We haven't known each other that long," she reluctantly reasons.

"How long is the probation period?"

"I don't know...a year...two years. Marriage after four months isn't rational."

"Do you think I'm going on rationale? Do you think I've lost touch with reason?" you question without giving her the opportunity to answer incorrectly. "It is in Faith that I'm pledging my love."

She grows mum as she peers toward the ground. That statement seems to provoke the lake effect breeze, which slices through your chest, sending a chill up your body.

"Through your natural eyes you see a hasty decision, but what do you see through faith—when you close your eyes?"

Her eyelids are peeled back as she gapes through the stationary sheet of mist that covers her lens's, then drop like shutters at the query, sending a swift stream down her face.

"No matter what and when you decide, I'm going to walk in the *perfect* will of God. The answer is *'I do'* whether you say yes now, next year, next millennium or next lifetime. If I have to wait until I'm 90—which I pray you won't make me do—I will just have some well worked patience, my Rose."

17

"When he was a freshman he was a timid kid...I pissed him off and he chased me all the way home almost. We had won the fro-soph tournament and I took his trophy and broke it. I was like *'your punk ass ain't playing'*. It was a guy name Tony Rice, who was another freshman, playing in front of Ben. But Ben would kill—would play well—but Ben would never do it on a consistent basis, so I took his trophy and broke it. And man, you talk about a guy that was pissed...he was crying...chasing me. He didn't catch me until we got on the bus, and then I just explained to him *'You should be playing...you should be playing.'* You could always tell Ben something and he would listen, as far basketball. Especially by me being a year older and I was playing a lot more, he kinda listened to me."

Uncle Ben insisted that a Ben Wilson feature wouldn't be complete without talking to his boy from way back and high school teammate Tim Bankston, who he insists had a game similar to and a touch better than Rod Strickland's. "He put a nasty spin move on Tracy Dildy in the city semifinal that spun him out of bounds," Ben recalled. You were all for it, but finding him was a problem. Ben put the word out to some of his boys from the days and you inquired at Simeon. Coach Hambric hinted that he was managing a nightclub on Racine or Halsted. Through a little sleuthing of his own, Ben got a potential name and phone number. It turned out you were hot on his trail, but he was never in when you called, so finally after a week of messages, Bankston left his pager number. He called you within minutes of the page and gives you an hour of his time. Especially inspiring is his account of Ben's promotion to varsity in his sophomore year.

"Hambric had Bobby Tribble playing the three—on that wing—and they were shooting the ball, and Bobbie couldn't hit the shot consistently. But I had already known that he wanted to move Ben up. And he called him down and the boy must've hit 18 out of 20 shots from this one spot...I'm talking straight flowing: shrooop; shrooop. I was like *'damn, that's the man over there now'*. He really wanted to play varsity. That summer, he played against Lowell [Hamilton] and all of those guys, and really got his confidence."

After recalling some of the triumphs on and off the court, he tickles your ear with his account of the city semifinals against King. The rivalry, which you're familiar with, started with a lot of talk off of the court, but the seed was planted that previous summer, when center Laurent Crawford transferred to King. Bankston confided that Hambric was hot and worried that the whole team had defaulted. You had heard of King Coach Landon Cox's recruiting tactics (You've crossed paths with him several times, but he never tempted you), but Tim is the first to confess to you that he had baited him into transferring. Confirming how much junk Dildy—the former assistant coach at U.I.C.—was spouting, he assured you that he proceeded to light him up and smoke him down. Come to find out, Tim was the man in the state championship game, scoring 25 points against Everett Stephens. He credited Ben with taking a back seat in that game and getting him high off of bravado.

"Thanks for taking the time to talk to me, Tim."

"Any time."

"I'll let you know when the article comes out," you promise as you hang up and head out to the Loop.

The feature is developing. After a week of digging in the sports archives, there were two anecdotal players that surfaced in the equation: Michael Ingram and David Knight. Ingram was the Player of the Year for 1985 and he led his Proviso West team to an early season victory over Simeon. Last night you reached way out across the globe and touched him in Macedonia of the European league for well over an hour. That phone bill is going to hurt. After tracing his steps to the University of Iowa, they referred you to his agent, who gave you his wife's number in Lake County, who gave you his number in Greece. It was five o'clock your time/11 o'clock his time when you caught up with him. He turned out to be a down to earth gentleman, even though he was a world away. Assuring that Ben would have won the award if he had lived, he recalled how touched he was when his mother, Mary Wilson, presented the plaque to him. After discussing a few of the other players of the era that may be able to provide an angle to the story, David Knight's name came up. Turns out that they were JC teammates in Missouri. He mentioned that Mitch Richmond was also on that top ranked team.

That sent you back to the archives for a gem in the mud of details. Knight was the lone senior starter in the memorial season and ended up as an all-state selection. In 1984, Uncle Ben had home delivery of the

Chicago Tribune. Last week he let you peep out the first edition of the story of the shooting. Ben Wilson was still alive when it went to press, as indicated by the headline "Young superstar fights for life." The accompanying picture, however, was off'er than the outdated headline. Uncle Ben indicated that the picture was of Knight, not Wilson. He then showed you a 1989 Sun-Times article that indicated that Knight was gunned down and fighting for his life. The twisted irony is that the headline and picture from 1984 matched the subject for 1989. Although Knight survived, he suffered paralysis from the waist down. You have yet to get Knight's comments, although you have pinpointed his neighborhood (thanks again to Coach Hambric). After pointing you to Lindblom Park, you informed one of the park attendants, who is familiar with Knight, of your story and desire to talk to him. Even though he didn't have a phone number or exact address, he noted that his daughter comes up to the park often, and that he'll see about hooking us up.

As you zip down Lake Shore Drive, you observe how the modest sun is colorizing the atmosphere. The air is crisp and warm, and the breeze that comes through the window is therapeutically smooth as it strokes your dome to the rhythm of the Brand New Heavies' "brother sister" R&B/Jazz tune, which you borrowed from Faith. It takes you no time to swoop in and out of South Loop Florist with your corsage. The Saturday traffic is light, so it takes you all of ten minutes to make it to Uncle JoJo's home from downtown. Just as you pull in front of the house, Whitney Anderson is getting into her black B'mer with—of all people on a day like this—Penny. Whitney looks in your direction but doesn't see you. Ever since you stopped working for Regency, you've been invisible to her. When you get out, she pulls off and stops right beside you.

"Hi Mally Mal," Penny greets sarcastically as you're retrieving your Agbada (robe and pants set) from the back seat.

Determined not to let your grip slip, you casually turn and retort, "Some things in life are stationary: The sun and moon; this big tree in front of the house; the foundation of the earth; God, and last and least, Penny. It's hard to believe that after 23 years your value hasn't appreciated. With inflation variables and all, it's utterly amazing that you have no sense. Just a simple, depreciating cent."

"Oh contrary my love, but I believe my worth is $4,000, compliments of you. Is that correct, Whitney?"

Whitney remains mute.

She thinks that still bothers you. You chuckle it off and shoot back. "$4,000 to get rid of headache incarnate is a small price to pay," you insist. "My head has been clear ever since."

"As usual, your perception is a bit warped. Just as Regency discarded you, I was even more merciless and fired you."

The truth isn't to be debated. When she dropped the load known as Edwin, she referred you to the telemarketing position at Regency Communications, the worst job in the galaxy. You would dig ditches before you took another position like that. In the five month's that you worked there, you totaled two sales. It was all good, until Penny lost her advantage in the game. The mask fell from Whitney's face, revealing a conniving, kissing cousin of Jezebel. She started sniping snide remarks and riding you like a cowgirl. She didn't know your mouth was potently possessed and had to learn the hard way that sowing spit to the wind brings a harvest of venom to the face. Once, a box from BT Publix came in full of copy paper and other office supplies. She spitefully commented in your earshot "I would ask Malcolm to get it, but he's so skinny the weight may break him and he'll be off on disability."

Your repartee: "Show me how it's done, big guy. I know you have the balls to do it." The office fell out as she went from banana yellow to beet red, as in beat down red. You knew from that point on, that you were the working/terminated. They had conspired to fire you the second that you were a minute late from lunch, caught playing Solitaire, making a personal call or any other violation that's collectively committed, but not enforced—sort of like jaywalking or loitering. You were as good as smoked. Her plan was to mentally castrate you on the way out; your scheme was to roast her before your vacation, since that bridge was going up in flames. The inevitable departure prompted you to print out a dated resignation letter for each day you came in. You only had to wait a whole week for the state of the business meeting with John Brenner, the boss hog.

That white-haired buffoon kept emphasizing how hard the sales' position is and how good a job the department was doing and how important we were GABBA GABBA GABBA. The speech had the effect of a tape of waves and other serene sounds that lull people to sleep. You were intoxicated off of indifference and irritability, so without getting recognized, you casually begged, "Spare us the bombastic blow job and give us some more money, you high class corporate hype." John and Whitney were looking like Mr. and Mrs. Lobster. Once you got up stairs, you provoked them some more by taking a nap at your desk on clock. When you opened your eyes, she was there waiting for more punishment. "I must be having a nightmare," you reasoned.

"You're actually dreaming of being terminated for sleeping on the job," she corrected.

"Do you mean I'm fired? I would appreciate simple English so there won't be any misunderstanding. However, you do stand to be corrected," you said, pulling out your resignation with that day's date. "I'm actually terminating you...I mean I'm firing you for blatant stupidity. You are dismissed." She was fuming. You had no regrets whatsoever. To put her whole character in perspective, she neglected to show you and others how to do simple functions, because she wanted to protect her job.

Signifying is one of your favorite hobbies, but it's time-out for going verbal blow-for-blow. A well-measured word can build up or tear down, and since you are gifted with many terms, it is wise to use them to nurture life. You are so blessed, that an improvised beatitude bubbles up from your belly and spills out of your normally venomous mouth like seltzer. "That's okay Penny...you're just a pawn. My fight is with the god of the air that uses us."

She clicks her tongue and reasons, "You couldn't win any way."

"You're right. I can't. But Jesus has already won, and I'm on His team riding the bench most of the time and making the best of my playing time when I get the call."

"I see you've been playing too much basketball," she chuckles.

"Don't worry: I love you, and—most importantly—Jesus loves you too, and there's still time to repent, so be of good cheer," you assure as you start off. "I'll be praying for you. God bless you Whitney."

She's struck speechless. Believe it or not, you were serious. Although your tongue is still sword sharp and your wit is light quick, Love has toned down your attitude towards people that offend you. As opposed to swapping unpleasantries, you're learning to absorb insults like vitamins and dish out blessings like excess cash in a homeless shelter.

Ma is parked at the kitchen table in her flowered dress, with Uncle JoJo and Ben. "You ready? How you feel?" Ben queries humorously as he straightens out his black rose-printed necktie that contrasts well with his ash-hued suit. Uncle JoJo is decked out in a black suit with a black collar-less shirt.

"I'm blessed to have two beautiful flowers: A Lily that only makes my valley a mountain top," you insist, placing the sheer-white lily in Ma's hair—which causes her to bloom red—adding, "and a Rose that adds color to that cloudy mountain top."

"It sounds like he's ready to me," Uncle JoJo comments.

"What about you, Ma?" you query, pecking her on her rosy cheek.

She nods with deceptive resolve.

When you brought the proposal of Faith to her, she rejected it in favor of sight. The two brief meetings with Faith weren't enough to win her over. Although those initial impressions were positive, the marriage of her only son is too big of a step for her. Only the perfect princess will do. You shared your prophetic dreams with her, but she wasn't swayed. While she reasoned Faith may be all of that, she insisted that waiting until college is over with wouldn't hurt. Yes it would. As if you can contain your heat for four, long years. We might as well wait until the new millennium, since four years will bring us to 1998. Good grief. You would be better off holding your breath under water for a day. Ma stated her reservations, and left it at that. You appreciated her insight, but you were walking by Faith. She will be a believer after a while.

If a vote was necessary, you and Faith would be law. Although Ben expressed indifference, citing your happiness is all that matters, Uncle JoJo seemed more excited than you. He's from the old school of romance, when couples married fresh out of grammar school. Enlightened about college life for jocks, he said that it's good for you to marry, since trying to walk in Christian abstinence will be like trying to sit still with fire in your tush. "If you love her and she loves you, do it," he stated. He assured Ma that waiting doesn't always reveal things. "There are many things about a mate that can only be discovered inside of a marriage," he promised, adding, "It's going to take work, dedication and God—in opposite order—for a marriage to last. Since you both have God, the foundation is already set." Ma seemed to seethe in stubborn muteness while he backed you up. Although she's still not for it, she doesn't oppose you.

The two-hour counseling session is scheduled for noon, and if all goes well, Pastor Wells will marry you at 2:00. You did get the robe for a reason, and Faith didn't buy a gown to make a fashion statement. We start out, since it's about 11:30. When you open the door, your stomach drops as if you were taking a nosedive from the top of the Sears tower. You have to rub your eyes to make sure your lens wasn't burned out from looking into the eyes of Faith. You glance back at a smiling Ma, who set you up.

"Aren't you going to give your Aunt Tulip a hug?"

You open the security door and tightly embrace Aunt Tulip...Ma's Sister...Raymond's Mother. "How you doing?" you question sincerely.

It's been two years since you've seen her, and the second time since Raymond's death. A day after we buried her only child, she took flight to Seattle in order to regroup. She insisted that the solitude will do her heart well while she adjusted to life without her gift. Never did she forsake the Lord, though. In fact, her commitment to Him intensified, as she got involved with overseas mission work. The distance and the obligation to spread the Gospel left virtually no space for a closer relationship with us. Superficially, it didn't exist, however, in Spirit it was imposing. The day she left, her face was drained of all signs of life, and her hair was fizzled like wet feathers. Her head hung down to the ground, even when her plane took off.

Time and distance did her well, because her countenance is rainbow bright, her head is confidently raised and her chest is erect with pride. Needless to say, you're not reluctant to smile in her presence, as you have to keep from being overwhelmed with the sorrow of Raymond's untimely death.

"I'm doing good, especially since I have a wedding to go to," she vigorously remarks. "So when do I get to examine the bride to make sure she's suitable for you?"

"Probably after it's too late," you chuckle.

We agreed to go with a little tradition. You haven't seen her since Thursday night—11:59 to be exact—when you kissed her and made a date at the altar. Faith is already inside the church. You immediately spot her Jeep when you pull up. Ben trucked Uncle JoJo and Aunt Tulip in his Blazer, while Ma rode with you. You have exactly five minutes...more than enough time to reassure Ma.

"Well this is it," you note as you turn the ignition off and look at her. She wears a melancholic mask. Deep down she's happy for you, but she's scared. "I can't believe that you're downcast when you're on the verge of coming the closest to having that daughter you always wanted."

"I never said I wanted a daughter," she retorts, cutting you a semi-nasty glance.

"I know Ma...joke," you insist, pausing. "Listen, I know it's kind of spontaneous and I didn't give you a chance to truly evaluate her and all, but you have to trust my judgment."

"99% of the time, I do," she admits, staring straight ahead at the entrance to the church. "It's just that in the affairs of your heart, I have a hard time. This is the most important relationship outside of Christ that you will have, and I just want it to be right."

You nod and qualify/correct that statement with "It is the most important relationship that *we* will have outside of Christ. I know you're too proud to admit that you're a touch jealous, but understand this: If there was a small possibility that my fiancée would get in the way of our relationship, I wouldn't go through with it. While scripture states that I'm supposed to leave my parents and cleave to my wife, it doesn't even hint that you are to be forsaken. When the relationship is Godly and righteous, it won't be necessary to choose between mother and wife, because all will be yielding to each other. I was drawn to Faith because I knew that her personality would be compatible with yours. She will honor you like Ruth honored Naomi in the scriptures. And like Ruth, she will be a strong part of your life whether I'm present or absent. So don't sweat. You're not losing a son: you're gaining a daughter," you assure, sealing that promise with a buss on the cheek.

Animation immediately fills her face. For one of the few times in your life, you've reversed roles and provide blessed equanimity to her.

When you walk into the pastor's study, Faith is almost in stitches as he manages to take the edge off and keep her entertained. If there was any doubt in your mind—which there wasn't—it would've ceased when she rose at your entrance. She *really wears* the sensual, silver-white Iro (wrap around skirt), matching Buba (blouse), Gele (scarf), and Fila (headwrap), which serves as a modest highlighter to her beauty. We decided to go with Yoruba wedding attire, which was her dream that you piggybacked off of. You do—right here, right now—take her for your wife, but you will proceed with the formal program.

After Pastor Wells opens with prayer, he proceeds to go down a mental checklist of queries, scenarios, scriptures and comments. All goes well for the most part. We have an understanding of our scriptural roles in a marriage: You're the head of her and you're supposed to love her as Christ loves the church (you seem to have the worse end of the deal, because sometimes the church can be hard to love); She's supposed to submit to you and we're supposed to submit to each other.

Her concern for breathing room surprises you, although you share the same feelings, since when a writing flow rushes over, you need to go with what you know. Suffocation won't be a problem. Isolation during extreme emotional expressions is her self-proclaimed weakness, while she knocks your confrontational disposition during disagreements. *Confrontational disposition?* Call the wedding off. That sends a chill to your toes and you take offense to that. You agree with her analysis of you, and own up to an occasional blabbermouth, along with clogged ears. You express your displeasure with not ever eating a Faith-cooked meal. Does her mouth drop like a brick, but she can't deny it. Instead, she promises that she will learn how to prepare your favorite dishes. The session ages quickly and we silently rejoice when he gets to the last question to us, after a gauntlet of preparation.

"Why do you want to marry Faith/Malcolm?"

Our answers: "She compliments me, just as Aaron served as the mouthpiece for Moses; *He completes me, as the breath of God brought man to life;* Her gentle spirit is soothing to my fiery emotions; *His passion excites me to action;* I can't contain my desire to lick her up and down; *I want to climb all up and down him;* The Lord showed her to me a long time ago; *The Lord spoke to me through his pen;* She's fine; *He's handsome;* She can hold her own in a cerebral conversation; *He can talk about silly things;* Our spiritual conversations are educating; *We can touch and agree on the Word;* Did I mention that she's fine; *Of course his good looks are a big bonus;* She speaks five languages; *He speaks with Godly wisdom;* She's exciting; *He's charming.*

"Is that all?" he questions us.

We gaze at each other and simultaneously profess, *"I love her/him."*

"That's what I was waiting to hear," he resolves. "Are y'all ready to do this?"

There is just enough room in his office. Instead of having a big ceremony, we opted to only have your immediate family present. Your inner circle didn't even get invited. Thankfully, you were able to get the license early in the week. Faith hesitated at the initial proposition, but when she closed her eyes, she could see us right then and there as opposed to a year or two down the line. You promised her that you wouldn't hold it against her if she wanted to wait, but she was adamant about going through with it, claiming, "Tomorrow isn't promised to us, so let's take advantage of today." And what a beautiful day it is. You purchased an official karat from Diamonds on Wabash the next day, which is formal, temporary, costume jewelry, until you can get the rock she's worthy of.

As you peer into her effulgent eyes, you can literally and figuratively see the glory of God in her. The ceremony is a muffled blur...that is until we get to our extemporaneous vows. That's when the divine seal is stamped on us and we go into a mutual zone.

"I Malcolm Johnson take you Faith Blackman as my wife...*I Faith Blackman take you Malcolm Johnson as my husband...*As the Lord our God blesses me with life, I will be a resource for and a refuge to you...*By the grace of God—Who has given us the Comforter—I will bless you with support and encouragement...*Just as Jesus loved me enough to lay His life down, I lay my life down for you...*As the church is faithful until death, I am faithful to you...*Through fire and ice will I walk for you...*In prosperity and poverty will I be by your side...*In light and darkness will I be true...*In happiness and sadness my love will come through...I am persuaded that neither death...nor life...nor angels...nor principalities...nor powers...nor things present...nor things to come...nor height...nor depth...nor any other creature...shall be able to separate our love"* we recite in unison as Pastor Wells announces us one-in-two and we seal it with a prelude to a passionate merger of souls. Of course, Faith sheds tears, and naturally you collect them. All doubt is erased in Ma's mind concerning Faith. They all witness soul mates incarnate today.

Afterwards, we all dine in the Signature Room on the top of the John Hancock building, which is for their convenience. You and Faith are inebriated with self-adoration. They savor the meal, while we salivate over each other. There is no room for food as we pick over some delicacy that you couldn't name if your marriage depended on it. Once we lose the spectators, we head to our honeymoon suite in the Sheraton.

The silence is deafening; our anticipation is calm. It doesn't dawn on you that we haven't passed many words as you carry her through the door to the Illinois suite. "How you doing?" you query, placing her down on the sofa with crystal handling care and smiling your approval.

She nods her well being, her grin glistening against the neutral tones of the carpet, wallpaper and furniture, bringing color into the dull box.

"You hungry," you small talk.

She shakes her head and continues to glow.

"Reminds me of a studio apartment," you mention, noting the dining room to your left and the living room just to the right. The restrained fury, coupled with your eager reluctance to touch every acre of her elicits...nervousness.

You break her gaze and step over to one of the three floor-to-ceiling picture windows facing south. The cars probe the streets like blood cells in a vein. Directly below is the Chicago River, which looks welcoming. Lake Michigan relaxes to the far left. Like an angel, she appears by your side. She peers down with you. Frozen with consternation, you gaze out in silence as if she's an African goddess.

She gently grabs your hand and murmurs, "I want to go to bed," melting the ice and breathing fire into the inertia.

You urge her to wait in the living room while you prepare the bedroom.

After you finish with the props, you come out and escort her in. She stops and states, "Thank you for saving me and you for this night."

You just grin as we walk eye-in-eye into the bedroom. She doesn't seem to take notice of the candles, which are peppered throughout the room like the decorations of a giant birthday cake. How could she notice if she kept her eyes on you? You answer the gaze with a gaze of your own, and we peer on, signaling the beginning of forever. As we slowly kiss with mutually enlightened eyes, you can't explain how you keep from collapsing. We exist in a state of ecstatic weightlessness. Without breaking eye contact, she methodically peels off your fig leaves with the grace of an amorous phantom, while you delicately slide your hands under her skirt and remove the silk rind from the succulent fruit of heaven in a swift motion. The scarf, blouse and head-wrap seem to fall off with your slight touch. A brisk breath away, we face off for eternity, as if looking at a reflection for the first time. Her crisp body is like an ice sculpture with a heart of molten gold. Her illumination cancels out the candles like the sun drowns out a flashlight beam. All dialogue is restricted to slow-motion body stanzas, shrouded metaphorical facials, and two hearts beating to the same "Our Love" rhythm as we deliberately fuse face first.

The brush of her lips triggers your eyelid switch. Even with them shut, you can still perceive the glow as your arms wrap around her torso like snake-vines, and your hands explore the uncharted hills and pastures of the Promised Land. If it wasn't for the rapturous rising with each covered inch, you would swear that you were petrified with passion. Her limbs bloom and intertwine with yours when you taste-tease her tongue, but you don't let her settle on a grip as you drop to your knees so that you're at chest level. As you plant your fingers into the crease in her back, you engulf her right, cup-cake size breast and gulp it down like a savory morsel of spicy meat, eliciting a sharp cry from her. You figure eight around her nipples in whirlwind fury with your tongue, while she struggles with her breath. She's as tantalizing as a bushel of fresh grapes, and every time you tempt her with a light bite, she quivers and her knees buck. You give her a chance to recover by nibbling on her less-provocative outer thighs, which are flowing with juice beneath the surface.

Just when she thinks she has the wave tamed, you lift her right leg up and place it on your left shoulder. She looks down in fearful reluctance as your gaze tells her to trust you, even to the threshold of the dismal extreme. Without breaking the stare, you gnaw on her inner thigh until it seems like her left leg is going to snap and her stomach is going to detonate. You proceed to munch your way up to the brink of the Garden of Eden. She gasps in dreaded anticipation as you peer at the mellowed fruit of the Tree of Life. It's harvest time, and you rise to reap. As you elevate past her chest and over her marvelous eyes, you gape down at her, gently cradling, lowering and spreading her across the bed of pleasure. Descending in dual cadence, her body tenses up, her face reflects the sting of death, and the sworded cherub provides some resistance to your man, but the Lord calls the guardian of the garden back and blesses your presence as the soul merger consummates. Without seeing the evidence, you know that the covenant is sealed with blood. As you hover over her like a dove, the eyes of Faith shut in zionic bliss while we bask in paradise.

"Just because someone is a baptized, saved, sanctified, Holy Ghost filled believer like yourself that's looking to get married, doesn't mean that they're chosen for you. I believe that the Lord ordains people to be together. Proverb 19 and 14 states," you announce, turning to it. "*'House and riches are the inheritance of fathers: and a prudent wife is from the Lord,'* and Proverb 18 and 22 states that *a man that findeth a wife findeth a good thing that illustrates the favor of God,*" you note as you glance at a flushing Faith.

The discussion topic is right on time: ***"What is it to be Unequally Yoked"***, taken from 2 Corinthians 6:14, with special attention to 1 Corinthians 7. Susan brought Elizabeth Keating: her emerald green-eyed Irish roommate, and Q brought one of his countrymen, Ike Kwarting, and Maria Sanchez, his Mexican Bio-Chemistry classmate. The hosting duties fell on us newlyweds. In light of the funky fresh tragic deaths of so many kids in the area (5-year-old Eric Morris, who was dropped from the 14th floor window by two older kids, and Ruben Bell, who was felled by gunfire), we opened up with a Faith-led intercessory prayer on behalf of the families and perpetrators. Faith prepared fried and baked chicken wings, spaghetti, garlic bread and Kool-Aid, which are the only dishes she knows how to cook edibly well. Just before Levi—the first saint there—arrived, Faith jumped on you in the kitchen and quenched the flame of passion for that moment, although it seems to have rekindled, since she occasionally gropes you on the sly. That's why you're both buzzing with gleeful grins while the Gospel variety tape backdrops.

"What about a reluctant unbeliever that you're burning with passion for?" Maria jokes/questions. "Isn't it better to marry that person?"

"Paul understood the sexual nature of man, that's why he urged believers to marry if they couldn't control themselves, so it seems like that would be the best thing," Susan seconds.

"While Paul advises marriage in that case, he seems to discourage marrying an unbeliever," Elizabeth reasons. "If you're married before you get saved, but your spouse doesn't get saved, he advocates divorce only if the unsaved mate insists."

"He also states that the believer in such a union has a sanctifying effect on the non-believer," Maria notes. "So there is a possibility that the unbelieving spouse will convert as a result of the anointing of the saint."

"And Ruth was considered a Gentile before both of her marriages," Ike says as he takes a swig of Kool-Aid.

"Is a reluctant unbeliever the same as a reluctant believer? What's the difference?" Q puns.

"Paul doesn't leave that area gray, no matter how hot the flesh gets," Faith interjects. "Paul seems to not only discourage marrying outside of the faith in his first letter to the Corinthians, but the scripture that we're discussing is addressing close associations and endearing friendships with unbelievers that result in the adoption of pagan religious practices. Ruth displayed a loyalty to God in the way she lived, and she wasn't trying to drag anyone into idolatry. Take note of how she followed Naomi."

"Does that mean that we are to cut off family members that don't believe?" Levi probes, adding, "That's almost impossible."

"I agree," you say, noting, "I have a friend that's a part of the Nation of Islam, and we can shoot ball together, watch TV, and most of the time have a good discussion about anything. We even teamed up to tutor another guy who was struggling in school, who—coincidentally—joined the Nation."

"I had a chance to talk to some Mormons," Levi testifies. "If I didn't have an open mind about it, the opportunity wouldn't have presented itself."

"I think my point got a little lost," Faith clarifies as she shifts and leans forward. "What I understand Paul to mean is that we are not to partake in what the other religions do...we are not to have an intimate fellowship with them in the name of faith, because it seems like it would be easier for a saint to be misled into darkness than it would be for a heathen to be persuaded to come into the marvelous light. After all, King Solomon was the wisest man ever and Samson was the strongest man ever, yet they were seduced into idolatry.

"Last year I had the displeasure of witnessing the ramifications of a saint yoking up with a pagan in the name of open-mindedness. All three of us were friends and had a lot in common in terms of our struggles, love of African culture and passion for the uplifting of our race. One day over lunch, we started talking about God. That's when we discovered that Joleen was into the Yoruba religion. Now Kathy was intrigued with the novelty of an African religion, but I knew even before Joleen gave us some tidbits, that Yoruba is a very spiritual religion that practices necromancy...unfortunately, it's not a *Holy* Spiritual religion, for Deuteronomy 18 and 11 forbids contacting the dead. I passed on her invitation to a couple of ceremonies and my warnings to Kathy were in vain. To make a long story short, she ended up going to a *babalawo*—which some would call a fortune-teller since they charge a price for a word—and got a pretty accurate reading into her life. She hasn't hearkened to the Lord's voice since."

You nod and second, "And Deuteronomy 13 is a warning of how false prophets can test our faith in God by performing miracles and speaking words that come to pass, yet are not God's prophets. Point well stated, Rose."

"Rose?" Levi questions through a surprised guffaw. "Is that a pet name?"

You redden under their scrutiny as you testify about your near conversion to Islam to qualify your compliment.

"And if you observe Deuteronomy 7, 1 through 5," Susan mentions as we all turn to it and read along as she recites it: "When the Lord thy God shall bring thee into the land whither thou goest to possess it, and hath cast out many nations before thee, the Hittites, and the Girgashites, and the Amorites, and the Canaanites, and the Perizzites, and the Hivites, and the Jebusites, seven nations greater and mightier than thou; And when the Lord thy God shall deliver them before thee; thou shalt smite them, and utterly destroy them; thou shalt make no covenant with them, nor show mercy unto them: Neither shalt thou make marriages with them; thy daughter thou shalt not give unto his son, nor his daughter shalt thou take unto thy son. For they will turn away thy son from following me, that they may serve other gods: so will the anger of the Lord be kindled against you, and destroy thee suddenly. But thus shall ye deal with them; ye shall destroy their altars, and break down their images and cut down their groves, and burn their graven images with fire."

"Oh my," Q gestures.

"Okay, let's rid the campus of paganism and plunder some heathens," Levi motions.

"Some of our fellow students have some good stuff, too," Ike seconds.

"I'm taking all electronic stuff," Maria jests.

"Thank God we wrestle not with flesh and blood under the new covenant, but against principalities, powers, rulers of darkness of this world and spiritual wickedness in high places, because that seems like a gory job," Elizabeth notes.

We all take her literally and collectively thank Jesus.

"We can't physically separate ourselves from the world, especially since Jesus commanded us to spread the gospel, but we don't have to participate in worldly things," Q says as he bites into a chicken wing, pondering, "Where do we draw the line...How do we reach the lost if we don't associate with them? After all, the harvest is great, but the laborers are few, and because of all of the false prophets, it's going to take more than just scripture quoting and track distribution...trust must be earned. Jesus didn't avoid sinners...he ate with tax collectors and rapped—excuse my slang—with prostitutes."

"Turn to John 12:32," Susan directs as she jokingly rushes "It's in the New Testament after Luke." We all read it and she explains, "In our social settings, in the way we live and in our triumphs, we must lift up the name of Jesus and glorify Him in order to earn credibility."

"The key to our social relationships is to stay true and not conform to sinful practices, such as social drinking and casual sex," Faith insists. "We can be militant Christians without being violent. At the same time, don't compromise your faith in order to make people comfortable, because unity isn't the goal if it means that we will all be in a state of collective apostasy. Why please others at the expense of offending God?

"I'm very hospitable to my friends from the Middle East that practice Islam. When they're my invited guests, I'll serve something acceptable to their convictions; when their visit is spontaneous, they know they stand the chance of winding up in hog hell. My diet is not even a minor struggle for them. Just as their dietary restrictions are no secret to me, my Christian liberty is no secret to them. Their main issue is with my belief in Jesus the Christ and Son of God who died, was buried and resurrected, and is ascended. So while my goal is to win them to Christ, I don't let them put me in religious bondage because they're offended when I eat all of the barbecue I can pray a blessing over. They'll be eating fried pork-chop sandwiches and thanking Jesus for them before I change my diet."

We all laugh.

"To take that statement a step further to a conclusion, a lot of other religions are willing to accept doctrines from other faith's as true. Many of them go by the Bible in addition to some other contradictory documents," you attest.

"The Church of Latter Day Saints, for example, with their Book of Mormon, Doctrine and Covenants, and Pearl of Great Price," Levi seconds.

"Exactly, not to mention Islam with the Qur'an. However the Word of God stands alone, and in this day and time, people seem to be moving towards an ecumenical religion for the sake of peace. Jesus said *'Think not that I am come to send peace on earth: I came not to send peace, but a sword.'* Yes, there are those who will say that there's only one god, and while scripture states that there is *'One Body, One Spirit, One Hope, One Lord, One Faith, One Baptism and One God the Father'*, everyone doesn't see Jesus the same Way, for the Word also states that *'the devils also believe [in one God], and tremble.'* That reasoning is an overt illustration of ignorance of God, not just on the part of some Christians, but even to the so-called politically correct spiritual folks that believe in the *'Creator.'* Yes, there is One God, but His name ain't Buddha; it ain't Allah. It's Jesus. If someone says to me 'what's up, man,' man is an informal title towards me as a man, but doesn't illustrate intimacy with me. My name is Malcolm to every culture in this room and abroad, and if someone calls me Buckwheat the Great, they have insulted me; if they call me Magic Johnson or Air Jordan—as endearing as they sound—it shows that they don't know me.

"Compromising Christ to any of them is communing Jesus with Satan. Their very natures are opposite: Jesus is the Truth; Satan is the father of all lies. Jesus is the Life; Satan is a murderer. Jesus is our Advocate, Righteous Judge, and Mediator; Satan is the accuser of the brethren. Jesus is the Lamb of God; Satan is ravaging wolf. So the point is not to have a bourgeois attitude, but to rebuke the devil when he tempts you. It's not the person that we're separating ourselves from, but the hedonistic lifestyle. Jesus ate with the tax collectors—who were on the same spite level in that culture and time as the street drug dealers, politicians or corporate managers of our time and culture—but he didn't serve as an agent for their oppressive system and collect money; Jesus rapped with the prostitute, but he didn't take her to bed or let her seduce him in order to give her the Gospel. And the funny thing is, He didn't start spouting scriptures left and right, but instead, talked to them on their level and schooled them even though they weren't in class. Likewise, we don't have to start spitting scriptures out like a prophet, but our lives should illustrate the scriptures in what we do, say and think, no matter who we're with, what we're doing, and where we are," you conclude with Holy force.

"All right now," Maria says.

"Amen," Q seconds.

"Hallelujah," Susan shouts.

"Preach on, preacher," Elizabeth cheers.

"Praise the Lord," Ike says.

"Let's go kick some satanic butt," Levi encourages.

"There's nothing like a sanctified husband," Faith attests as she pecks your lips and collects the dishes. "Does anybody want any more wings or Kool-Aid?" Everyone declines as she sashays off with your eyes directly on her rear and your mind in the sack with her.

When she turns the corner, you come back to the living room and verify, "Are we all in agreement and understanding?"

They all confirm, however, leave it up to Levi to put it in humorous perspective. "When I make the pro's—God forbid I go to the 76er's—and play against Shawn Bradley, he'll try to block my shot, but I'll dunk on him in the name of Jesus and he'll get the Holy Ghost right then and there and start speaking in tongues."

The level of difficulty in your classes peaked like the erection of a sex-starved honeymooner, and your energy gauge indicates that you were worked like an African-American slave. Although the first week of marriage was gratifying (It took one night for Faith to develop an insatiable appetite, and an hour to twist your head off), it sapped every ounce of juice from you. Faith wasn't sparing anything either, making sure she scraped the remnants of steam from the pit of your being. As a result, staying awake—let alone studying—became a chore, so you've been rolling on Vivarin all week. You're loaded with homework this weekend to go along with the final phase of moving your stuff into your new home. The house is very accommodating. Your personal belongings are scarce, so you won't really be able to take advantage of the abundant expanse. There's enough space for us to stay out of each other's way when necessary and to keep our individuality.

You left Faith on the South side to hang out with Ma, while Ben helps you set things up. Monday you moved all of your smaller items from the dorm. After we got all of the furniture out of the truck and in the house, he ran out to pick up a few sandwiches, leaving you to decide how you're going to situate the stuff. After he left, you popped in a Walter Hawkins "Love Alive I" tape and took advantage of the liberty to blast it. Since you set up an office in a bedroom upstairs next to Faith's office, you had to put the remainder of your furniture in one of the recreation rooms in the basement.

After arranging your chest-of-drawers and bed as orderly in the compact room as possible, you dash up stairs to wash all of the ground in dirt from your hands. All is well and set, and you still have some Vivarin energy left as you take a load off on the living room sofa. You close your eyes and savor the emotions from "Going Up Yonder" while it pours out of the speakers. Midway through the song, you feel a presence in the room, so you open your eyes expectantly. Ben is standing petrified in the doorway with a crinkled forehead and distant gaze. His face quivers slightly before his countenance drops like a landslide and his body breaks down like a human punching bag. The sack of sandwiches slips from his hand as he collapses against the door. Totally surprised, you spring up to embrace him, but he fends you off with a slight shove, refusing to share any parts of his weeping. You retreat back to the wall as his display perplexes you.

When the song concludes, his weeping stops, the tears dry up, and the life seeps back into his face as he sucks in a deep, loud breath, collects the bag and proceeds to the kitchen. You follow him with your eyes until he breaks the sight barrier. You shake your head and follow him into the kitchen, taking a seat at the table. You rarely see him cry, so an explanation is in order. He unbags the food in silence, hands you your lunch and settles on the other side of the table. You take the hint and bless the food, after he looks your way and nods his head down.

Between bites of the remnants of his corn beef, he utters, "Like me, you're not a weeper," as he swallows the last mouthful, adding, "but there is something—even if it's one minute thing—that will bring you to tears. That song does it to me every time, because it brings back so many sad memories...the lyrics epitomize the end of an era...the end of the Ben Wilson era," he attests sentimentally as he sits back in the chair and stretches out. We conversantly peer at each other. "How much time do you have?" he questions.

You recline back. "I have all weekend."

"Go get your recorder and note pad," he suggests, noting, "I got a lot to give you for the article."

You eagerly oblige as we set up in the living room. Without poising a question, he starts, "I was in data processing when the Principle ominously announced *'one of our students has been shot: Ben Wilson...'* That's all I heard," he notes, launching into a weeklong account of that hazy, 24-hour period in his junior year. "Going home he was still alive, and I'm thinking that it wasn't serious and he was going to live and play in the season opener the next day." *Reality can be like a bad dream. He details how he simultaneously read the first edition of the paper about how Ben was struggling for his life and heard the announcement on the radio about his passing. Perhaps it was a mistake.*

"When I walked in the building, the silence confirmed the unbelievable. There was little movement among the hundreds of students, but even less noise. At that moment, there were no enemies at Simeon. Gangsters and Stones were kin-folks." *Of course, the schedule was adjusted. Camera's and media people infested the building, which wasn't unusual for a sports mecca.* "They put together a memorial assembly at the last minute, but it was as perfectly choreographed as a heavenly concert. When the choir sang 'Going Up Yonder', the school collectively broke down. I mean, even the hardest thug was moved by that tune," he declares methodically as he stares straight ahead. "The cornerstone of the story..." he starts and pauses as he coils forward and rests his elbows on his knees. "Would you believe that Mrs. Wilson came up to the school and urged us to be forgiving? Here the loss of her son was funky fresh, and she was giving us encouragement; telling us to show love. I ain't never seen a more profound illustration of strength in the face of despair...*Never.* I know all of the athletes will give the story depth, but Mrs. Wilson will bring the whole thing to life," he declares, peering into your eyes.

He expounds on the Simeon/King rivalry, confirming it began when Laurent Crawford transferred to King from Simeon. Coach Hambric accused Coach Cox of recruiting him, and of course there was a battle of words. It's ironic that Simeon eliminated King in the city semifinals the next season. "Ben promised to *'beat King to death'* during the pre-game pep-rally, and sure enough, it came to pass." *For every Simeon star, King seemed to have an answer. If the Wolverines came out with Andre Battle, the Jaguars retorted with Ephram Winters; Dildy was supposed to be the answer for Bankston; Deon Thomas had a discipline and skill advantage over Rashard Griffin.* "Marcus Liberty was a bad boy, but on his best day, he couldn't touch Ben on his worst. My boy could do it all: post-up, rebound, shoot, dribble, D-up, run, and play within a rigid, half-court system. Liberty was all finesse and effective only in a fast breaking system. No one to date could match the hops of Levertis Robinson...and down low, he could hold his own, but Nick was and is better overall. Even your boy Notree has an edge over Michael Hermon, who has a dangerous game that ain't got no business at Indiana."

Bouncing from era-to-era until the sun sets, he gives you an eyewitness account of the pre-basketball Ben. In grammar school, he could dish out a good football hit, despite his slim stature. You can feel that he was a brother that could skyscrape with the Holy angels, yet, he was lowly enough to look mere mortal men eye-to-eye. His notoriety reached the likes of Magic Johnson, yet he was still down with Ben Johnson. No matter what, he was always real. Still is. "The day after they beat Robeson for the city title, I asked him—like a big fool—why he didn't dunk. He snapped a little and insisted *'I did what I could.'* Not that I was knocking his performance...I was just running my mouth too much, you know," he says, flashing a reminiscent grin.

Four one-hour tapes go by without you querying him. You exchanged comments and urged him on, but you didn't probe him. To wrap it up, you ask, "What is your take on his untimely passing," as you lean into his mouth.

"I believe that God has an ordained mission for everyone. Moses led the children of Israel to the Promised Land, although he didn't enter himself. Then he went to the presence of the Lord. Paul wrote the bulk of the epistles that make up the New Testament and brings an understanding to the Gospel and the new covenant. Then he went to the presence of the Lord. The prophets preached about impending judgment, repentance and the coming of the Lord...many were martyred in the process; the apostles spread the plan of salvation in Jerusalem and

Judea and to the farthest corners of the globe and gave their bodies up for the sake of the Gospel. They, in turn, went into the presence of the Lord.

"Jesus fulfilled the will of the Father before He gave up the ghost. We all have a reason for being here, and if you note when all of those great men and even the great God departed, it was to make way for something bigger and better. Joshua led the children into the Promised Land; the church grew as a result of Jesus sending the Holy Ghost; the church is edified as a result of the preaching of the apostles and prophets. Ben...look at the standard he set for hoopers, and not just on the court. You can't imagine how bad I wanted to see him turn the NBA out. When I was a kid, I aspired to one day go into outer space so I could behold a star. In my naiveté, I thought that I could go up there, capture it and bring it home. To me, Ben was the closest thing to that aspiration. There's nothing like fellowship with a star on earth. Ben reached the ultimate peak and touched a lot of people on the way up.

"When I hear Stevie Wonder's 'I Just Called to Say I Love You', I think of my brother/your father. When I got home that day, I was mourning in my room and listening to that song when he called. Out of the 26 years I've known him, he's never said 'I love you.' He had heard about the tragedy, and when I answered, he said *'I just called to say I love you.'* That incident broke through my brother's wall of emotions and got him to open up a little. At that moment, I stopped crying and I had some peace on a stormy day. This may sound corny, but I believe that Ben was ordained to reach that impossible status, which inspired those after him to reach for the stars. He is an illustration of faith in action."

The recorder cuts off at his period. He saved the pivotal statement for last. He stares at you off the record and chuckles.

"What," you question with an expectant grin.

He shakes his head and explains, "In a crazy way, you resemble BW: same build; similar game; same fiery spirit; same boyish face; and the same bald head."

That statement makes your heart smile like sunshine for the rest of the weekend.

The week was fruitful. All it took was a call to Taylor Bell to get Mary Wilson's number. At first, you were mysteriously reluctant to call. Even though she spoke to Bell in regards to her son, you didn't know how well she would take to you. The reluctance faded quickly when she answered, and within two minutes you had set up a time to talk to her that Friday. Your connection finally came up with a number for David Knight. However, he was harder to catch than the Roadrunner. You seemed to always be a step behind him. Your multi-roles made the week very taxing, too. It was a struggle to keep from using the keyboard as a pillow at work...until you popped a Vivarin.

As you zip down Lake Shore Drive in rout to see Ma, you ponder the twist your life has taken in the last two weeks. Faith makes lovemaking and marriage very gratifying, but at the same time, it's much more complex than mere romance and dating. She's greedy for you and your time, which are both very scarce with work and school and studying and trying to stay in some type of shape and the story and going to the bathroom and eating all vying for your attention. There is not a shade of regret for marrying her so soon. To put her into perspective, if you had to choose between school, your writing career and Faith, you would be an uneducated bum with Faith. It's just that a real honeymoon probably would've given you the opportunity to sap some of her fire. She's like a downer-drug that counters the Vi-high, sending you crash landing into the land of deep slumber. Unfortunately, it seems like the Vivarin is getting weaker and Faith is getting stronger with time.

You pull in front of the house, jump out and silently saunter in. The gleeful chatter of Ma and Faith echo to the front over the muffled sounds of cooking activity. The greens and pressure-cooked chicken give you a dose of hope. When you make it to the doorway, they come to a petrified stop at the counter as they peer stupefied at you. It's obvious that they're plotting to kill you.

"Hello?" you question like Joyce used to do. "Verily I say unto you that one of you shall betray me."

"I'm glad you're here," Ma plays it off. "Now I don't have to take your wife home," she states through a Cheshire grin. She's a terrible, B-rate actress.

"Hey Sweetie. How was work?" Faith questions as she floats over, wraps her arms around you and plants the kiss of death on your lips.

"Faith, betrayest thou husband with a kiss?" you facetiously question, drawing back from her.

"Anyway," she says rolling her eyes as she pulls up to the sink to wash the remaining dishes. "Ma was giving me a few pointers on how to cook for a king."

"Not to mention pointers on how to keep Mal in check," Ma jokes as she proceeds to wrap the chicken in foil.

"What a coincidence: I need to know how to keep the Faith," you note half-jokingly as you gaze at Faith.

"You don't know, you better ask somebody," she advises seductively as she glances out the side of her eyes from the sink.

You can only snicker like an imp as you snatch up a drumstick.

Ma advises you that Penny went into premature labor after taking a tumble down the stairs and gave birth to a girl yesterday. Three months is a lot to make up outside of the womb. Apparently, it's hooked up to a lot of machines, and even the doctors are praying for a miracle. Penny ended up with a concussion and fractured forearm. It pierces your heart like it is your own blood—not your bad blood—and you make a mental note to visit Penny tomorrow. After updating Ma on the article status, your G.P.A., and the other small talk that could've waited, we jet out.

Initially the ride is a bit quiet. Although you are extremely happy to see Faith and Ma bond, you are peeved that you didn't get to talk to her like you wanted to. You are also more than a touch curious about their little chat about you, but you aren't going to go out like the cat. Your desire to be awake goes down with the sun as you let out an obvious yawn.

"Sweetie," she wearily starts as she reclines back in the seat and rests her head on the door panel. "Have you considered giving up the job?"

The Monday after the wedding, we sat down and looked over our financial standing. When it's all said and done, we're standing strong on Faith. She has a savings and checking account balance in excess of $750,000, and some pocket change that's not recorded. That doesn't include the house (that's paid for and appraised at over $300,000), stocks, bonds and other investments. Her net worth clears a million like Jordan clears a deck of cards on the way to the rim. She is adamant about calling it our worth. With the exchanging of vows, your worth multiplied a million-fold. Before we discussed our value, she put you on all of the accounts. You had no prior knowledge before we entered into the covenant. If you had, you might have suggested that she have a *prenuptial agreement made up to assure her that you have no intentions of leeching off of her fortune. The will and death benefits from her parents several policies didn't ease the emotional loss, but it sure made things economically plush. Reading it was a soothing/scathing surprise. You were blanketed with the knowledge of knowing that you didn't have to bring home the bacon, since she already had a pig farm, slaughter house and gourmet chef. That dose of reality served as a kick in the secrets (as the King James Version of the Bible dubs the balls) that knocked the wind out of your bravado and depreciated your pride to grave depth. Sure it shouldn't be an issue, but you couldn't help but feel a little less than the traditional man, since she didn't need you financially. Yeah, you still wear the pants, but she has a closet full of tailor made trousers to slip into if she was in the mood. The idea of living off of her finances made your stomach queasy. She hinted that you should give up the job (like she did the day after she accepted your proposal) to focus more on school and the marriage.*

"Not really," you state, somewhat testy.

"Why not?" she questions nonchalantly.

"Because I haven't," you snap.

She sits up and lets out a loud exasperation that was probably provoked by your waspish response. "Is there a problem with discussing what we agreed to consider?"

"So far it's not," you note as your speed increases from 60 to 70.

She guffaws as you can feel her staring a hole through your thick temple. "What is that supposed to mean?"

"It means that I don't want to talk about it right now."

"So just like that...you just blow me off? I don't think so. I want to resolve it now."

"Okay. We can resolve it," you concede. "I'm not going to quit my job. Discussion over," you declare with finality as you turn on the radio.

She turns the radio off. "So in other words, what's good for the marriage is secondary?"

"I thought we just resolved this." You cut it back on.

"DON'T DO THIS, MALCOLM!" she screams, cutting it off again. "Don't do this," she pleads a touch lower in intensity.

You grit your teeth and accelerate 20 mph more as you inhale some air to cool your inner ire. "I told you that I don't want to give up my job," you reiterate in a calm, deceptive tone that coats your anger. "What else do you want from me, Faith?"

"I want you to get out of that individual mind-set and think in terms of us. We are supposed to be one flesh. What concerns you concerns me, and vice versa. If a choice isn't mutually beneficial, other options need to be discussed."

"Good grief," you exclaim as you take a deep breath and shake your head that is sure to ache before the night is over. "In other words, if my wants are opposed to your wishes, it's selfish? Do I have to abandon all of my individuality so we can merge into this perfectly cohesive unit? Does this marriage ride on whether I quit my job? Fine, I'll quit."

"That's not even ***remotely*** what I said," she clarifies in attitude overdrive as she leans forward to get a better shot at your grill. "Instead of making decisions based on what we feel individually, we should determine what is best for us as a unit. And I happen to know that an addiction to Vivarin isn't expedient for you as an individual and for the Johnson's as a couple."

"Working is necessary for my peace of mind...for my dignity as a man...for my affirmation as the head of the household."

"You're the head whether you work or not, but why work when there are other priorities, such as keeping up in school and adjusting to a new lifestyle?"

"I think I'm doing fine in the above departments, thank you very much."

"I didn't say you weren't."

Our views are crashing into each other like territorial rams. "I'm sorry if you can't understand where I'm coming from, but that's where I stand and I'm not stepping off of it," you close out. You warp up to 105.

For a brief eternity she glares at you before she clicks her lips, exhales some steam and dismisses, "Whatever," as she reclines back like a boulder and acquaints you better with her back. For the rest of the ride she pretends to sleep.

You wonder how long it takes the average newlywed to have that first fight. Regardless of the median, this is too soon and too silly. You also ponder how many more times you are going to have to admit that you are wrong and apologize. If you have to write "I'm sorry, I was wrong" a million times in your blood to keep the bond, you will.

When you come to a stop, you discover that she isn't faking her slumber. It isn't the conflict that tempts you to let her rest. The potential of a passionately laborious night makes it difficult to interrupt her nap.

When you touch her fevered spine, she jumps erect and her eyes buck open as the equilibrium comes rushing back.

"We're home," you announce as she stretches out and sucks in and musters the atmospheric energy in order to collect the food.

After we get all of the dishes in, you dash up stairs and slip out of your casual clothes. After taking a military shower and rinsing your mouth out with Listerine, you slip into your shorts and T-shirt that you will be sleeping in. In your pre-marriage days, you weren't meticulous about showering and brushing your teeth before and after bed. There were two-day periods when you went without a full body scrub-down, and a couple of times when you walked out with unsanctified breath. Faith didn't speak it, but you knew those were necessary hygienic adjustments. When you get back down stairs, Beaufort is towing Faith in.

"You want a late night snack fit for a king?" she probes without a trace of post-war animosity. She put a small pot of greens on the burner and heated the macaroni and chicken in the oven before she set out to walk the dog.

"Since it was prepared by the hands of an angel, how can I say no?" you flatter.

She smirks and flushes over as she shoos Beaufort in the basement. After she ducks in and out of the bathroom to refreshen, we collectively prepare the table in silence. She seems placidly content as you struggle through the dense hush. You can't even make it to the grace with the heavy cloak of guilt, so you shed it.

You hover behind her, place a contrite kiss on her sweet cheek and announce, "I'm sorry for the way I acted on the way home."

She strains her eyes shut and nods as she fills two glasses with punch.

"If it's okay with you, I would like to work until the quarter is over, so I can save up for a special honeymoon gift," you appeal, closing your arms around her and planting your chin on her shoulder. "Is that okay?"

She nods.

"I love you twice as much today as yesterday."

"I love you thrice as much now than a minute ago," she beams. "I hope you like the greens. Ma gave good instructions, but I don't know if they turned out edible for you," she hopes anxiously.

"It already has, because my taste buds are biased toward you," you promise, gently biting her neck, causing her to squint her whole visage and coil up around your face.

She pries your hands apart and squirms out of your grasp, insisting, "There'll be plenty of time for that," as she saunters over to the stove for the dish of macaroni. "Besides, I need you to be well nourished tonight."

"You're just trying to put that marriage weight on me, but it's not going to work," you joke.

She flashes a serious glare your way. With light, measured steps, she stalks up a whisker beneath your mouth and assures, "I wouldn't change a thing about your perfectly chiseled, passionately sculpted body," as she slides her mint-fresh hands under your shirt and slowly presses against you, causing a major merger. Forcing you into the chair, she straddles and comes nose-to-nose with you. With water persistence, she probes the crevices of your outer man, while lulling your inner man into a fantastic trance with her low, dilatory murmurs. "So slim...yet vigorous...You are wonderfully made...the perfect fit for me...not too buffed...your svelte frame is flowing with spirit...I can feel life when I come in contact with you...there's not a moment that I don't want to be completely consumed by you."

You're petrified as her amber, quartz-like eyes give her a possessed appearance. You almost wish for her brown contacts (which she has forsaken ever since that wonderful, revealing night) that veils the power of her gaze. She's dangerous. It's a good thing she launches into your mouth, sending you to Atlantis, because you are getting dizzy. Dinner is surely heavenly.

The stench of the dung factory in the 115th vicinity on the Calumet lingers like a bad day, prompting you to turbo boost while your mind wanders to the sound of Mary J. Blige over the radio. *You finally caught him. He wasn't that outgoing, but considering the ironic circumstance and his lot, David Knight was generous enough to offer a couple of juicy sound-bites. The talk was brief enough to take hand notes. In commenting about the Tribune mix-up, the bitterness seeped out in a small dosage with a curt "I thought it was lame," as his brusqueness about the sad saga hastened the interview. Your heart truly went out to him. As he commented on his relationship with Ben, you sent up a silent, well-received prayer on his behalf. After you got off with him, you phoned UIC coach Bob Hallberg and got Mario Bailey's extension. You knew that he would be a quick, cool interview, because you've crossed paths with him when you were on campus to see Charlotte. Bailey noted that coach Hambric brought the number 25 out of retirement for him to wear for the inauguration of the Ben Wilson gym, and like all of the top players, he kept it when he entered college.*

When Penny answered the phone, it was as if the three years of discord were blotted completely out. Her voice was expectantly bleary, yet gallantly responsive. Instead of visiting, you decided to play it safe—taking a small step to reconciliation. After all, she wasn't doing well physically or mentally. You phoned Ms. Davis first. She informed you that LaChanda passed during the night. Penny initially took it hard, but resolved to let her go back to the Lord. After you expressed your concerns and well wishes, and swapped small talk and lighthearted witticisms, we didn't hesitate to make amends—realizing that time isn't promised to us. She went first in seeking forgiveness for transgressing against you. That was worth a year's pay for slave labor. You repented of the antagonization during our long season of enmity.

Ma's words from 15 minutes ago tarry in your heart. You still were not comfortable living in a mansion and off of a million-dollar savings that you contributed nothing to. Work seemed like a necessity, although the payoff wasn't going to support us. She put it into perspective by noting that salvation by grace is a priceless gift that many feel the need to work for, even though the work makes no difference. Her opinion was neither nay nor yea, but she did urge you to abide in the grace of God and be grateful for the inheritance that came with your God sent wife. At that statement, you felt a ten-ton yoke break off your neck. Uncle JoJo came by and anointed your neck with a confirmation that agreed with the Word of God and with Faith: "'The Earth is the Lord's and the fullness therein'. Not to urge you to be slothful or arrogant, but that money isn't the benefit of her labor, but an inheritance." Faith voiced that same sentiment. Coming from Uncle JoJo—who is an old school workaholic—indicates that dropping the job and investing in the now and morrow is the way of the wise.

Sunday, Faith officially joined Walk of Faith, further strengthening the relationship and reinforcing her devotion to you. While she promised to continue doing mission work in Evanston with Divine Vine, she opted for the Nurses Board at WOF.

Yesterday's Bible study was more entertaining and looser. You and Faith opened our home as the permanent meeting place for the group, since it provided ample space for the growing study. As a compromise, each member will alternate with the food duties, which will make for a diverse bi-weekly menu. As opposed to ordering from Taco Bell, Maria came early and prepared chicken and ground beef Tacos and Nachos (of course), Tinga Poblana (Shredded chicken simmered with smoky and spicy chipotle peppers), Bistec a la Mexicana (Tender chunks of beef simmered with onions, bell pepper and tomatoes), and the best Shish kebobs, with enough beans and rice to feed the multitude. You had to bypass the beans, since you haven't learned to like them in 18 years. We washed it down with virgin Strawberry Margaritas. Señorita Maria could flow in the kitchen. Faith picked up the recipe just as easily as she learns foreign tongues. Next time the catering will fall on Susan.

Bob the busboy came for the first time, along with a broadcasting major who stays in the same dorm as Levi. Timothy acknowledged that he was a non-believer and agreed to put together some clips from some of your favorite horror movies, and sit in on the session with an open mind. If the topic doesn't bring them back, the food will. While the group unanimously denounced Halloween, the tape served as an educational piece to confirm the stance. Maria, who's an education major, expressed a desire to learn how to edit videotapes, so she could incorporate it into her teaching methods. We picked out images from Fright Night, Phantasm II, Dracula and other horror favorites to discuss the Bible's stance on some of the images, names and practices.

You were surprised that several satanic overtones blared out, with the scriptures crying out, such as how vampires kill and drink blood (a violation of Exodus 20:13 and Leviticus 17); turn into ravenous wolves that are the enemies of the Good Shepherd; are repelled by the cross and how the cross only works with faith; the Sun—Light, Bright and Morning Star, Dayspring, Sun of Righteousness—kills them; and how they have no image, while man is in the image of God. It's not to say that you'll never watch scary movies again—because you like the genre—but you will pay closer attention to the messages in them and what God says through His

Word about them. Timothy didn't confess Christ as his Savior, but he did interrogate the group with sincerity, and seemed to lust after the Truth while he contributed some interesting points to the discussion. He promised to come back next week, offering his talents whenever needed.

You exit the Calumet, proceed down Sibley and turn down Dorchester. Today, Chicago got the first sprinkle of snow of the season, and it's not even Thanksgiving. As quickly as it conceived, it died. Here in Dolton, there are a few remnants peppered on the grass like dandruff, but for the most part, it's a cool memory. Slowing down as the numbers get higher, an anticipatory chill dominos down your spine when you pull in front of the house. After going through the formal journalist's checklist, you stare at the house and say a silent prayer. Your steps are jittery while treading up the sidewalk and up to the front door. For the simple task of ringing the bell, you press it methodically as if there was a chance to mess up. The nippy air magnifies your restive shiver. When a man with Deon's girth and a boyish face answers the door, the uneasiness departs.

"I'm here to talk to Mrs. Wilson," you proclaim, sounding just like a reporter.

"Come in," a voice from inside invites as he opens the screen door.

"I'm Malcolm Johnson," you introduce to the usher with an outstretched hand.

"How you doing," he greets with a firm grip. "Anthony," he heralds through a stern expression as he steps to the side for you to enter.

"Pretty good," you assure through your trade grin.

The room warmth is thick and welcoming like an electric blanket on a winter night. Although the lighting is too dim for an automatic camera, the living room sparkles with life and showcases the minor details, such as the textured, loop-piled, sandy carpeting and the natural washed walls. The sour-cinnamon aroma is a balm to your nerves. And Mrs. Wilson... Her posture on the sofa is stately, and her countenance is so magnificent that it spreads your grin and suffuses your bosom.

"How are you Mrs. Wilson?"

"I'm abundantly blessed and highly favored," she regally trumpets with southern charm and royal authority. She has the same skin and voice tone as the afternoon sun. "Have a seat. How are you? Was it hard to find us?" she enunciates with a heavy Mississippi accent.

You oblige and get on your verbal toes to keep up with her spunky spirit. When you spot the white cat endearingly called snowball, you grieve in silence, since you're allergic to feline dandruff. Before you can get into interview mode, she chatters away. Without the traditional opening, you start the recorder right before you comment on the poster-size graduation picture of Ben that hangs over the giant screen television, letting the story flow.

As she passionately and candidly talks about life, Jesus, Ben, and family, she makes smooth transitions from answering the posed questions with recollections of her precious son, to side intimacies that could only come from a mother. Instead of focusing on the two pages of written queries, you mention the memorabilia in the room that are relevant to the article, such as the bronze, original 1983 Air Nikes that rest on the coffee table, and the trophies on a shelf with other family photos.

"It seem like the whole ordeal caught everybody off guard...no one was ready for this..." you state as she confirms.

"I wasn't [ready] either. They say there are seven steps in the grief and mourning process, but I don't think I went through the denial state. I really don't. I think I went through the anger state; I think I went through the bargaining state; I went through most of them, but I always faced reality. And I'm not a person that will point fingers at you: *'He's the cause of it; well if he had done that...I could've done that'* and I do have these thoughts...don't kid yourself. These thoughts visit me and I say *'well Lord, I didn't make this man...You did...'*"

"How did you cope when you got the news?" you question for your own edification.

"Well you see, I love the Lord and I got introduced to Jesus Christ when I was a child. And I have kept this Bible open on a daily basis for a number of years," she concludes, piercing your heart.

"What about your feelings towards the young men that did it?" You're curious. Perhaps she can help purge you of some of your built-up bitterness.

"The anger and the bitterness and the hatred against them? I feel that I have a little more insight than a lot of people because I don't walk by sight, I walk by faith. I'm at the point in my life that I know so many demons. They're real honey...I see that demons or devils caused that incident. It wasn't the boys who actually did it. Their bodies were used to commit the crime, but I don't feel that they feel that they did the right thing today. And I think they have another chance. When I spoke to some young people a couple of months ago, I asked 'What is the greatest gift in your life?' Many of them would say *'my momma and my daddy', 'my grandmomma.'* Those are good answers too, but I'm going to tell you what the greatest gift is: It's life. Your life is your greatest gift...and you must always cherish your life."

Her insight is baffling enough to make you pause and ponder, and she seems to read your mind and address your unvoiced query.

"I got a tape of me and Oprah Winfrey when she was on AM America and she said *'you mean to tell me you don't have any anger'.* I said 'I didn't say that.' Yes I've been through that stage of anger, but I thought it was cruel and it would serve me no profits, so I let it alone because it was destroying me. I said 'sure I felt anger...a lot of it...I felt bitterness...a lot of it, but I had to let it go.' And I said that I would want to see the boys so I could look at them and see how they would feel about what they have done...so maybe they could say to me *'yes, my mind was not my own at the time or something was leading me',* 'cause I know this was a demon spirit...and these boys are not demons—I hope now—and I hope they have shedded that dirty side. And I would like them to know that I care. My kids say that *'you have a problem if you care for them, 'cause I'mma kill 'em when they get out.'* I said that's the devil again. The devil is on his job. I paid when I lost him; now I'll pay again if you go out and take the law in your hands. I said 'don't you think I have suffered enough?'"

Yes you do. "Can I use your bathroom," you request, sniffling.

"Down the hall," she directs, asking, "Are you allergic to my cat?"

"Yep," you confirm as you set out down the hall.

The cat hair isn't bothering you, though, and you don't even have to use the toilet. You quickly shut the door behind you just as your face drops. As you collapse against the sink, you avoid your reflection in the mirror while you weep a dry, silent cry. Your whole body reacts to your sobs. Composing yourself, you ponder, *'does a tree make a sound when it falls in an empty forest? If so, is a cry effective in the healing of the soul if there are no tears?'*

You met Ben for the first and only time in the summer of 1984. Uncle Ben took you to a high school talent show at the former Mendel (currently St. Martin de Porres, where your boy Jerry Gee graduated from). You had turned an old eight the prior week. All was well with you. Break-dancing was in; the A-Team was your favorite show; and you were on your way to second grade. It was also the summer after Simeon won the state championship in basketball. Talk about happy days. After the show, we were shooting the breeze with a couple of his lady friends, when up walks three giants. One of them slapped five's with Uncle Ben and then looked upon you with a contagious grin. That was when you recognized him from television. For the longest time, you thought that TV people were make believe. Never have you seen a star walking around among men. Heaven and earth came together at that moment. It amazed you that someone bigger than life knew the mere molecules that dwelled on the planet. His face was slim like his build and bursting with joy. What made his radiant countenance extra welcoming was the boyish innocence. There was no hair to hide his intentions, just a pure love for a child. It was funny how Ben introduced you to Ben. As you were struck with awe, Ben playfully grabbed you and heaved you up in the air. It was like an elevator ride to Heaven. You kept rising and rising and rising. When you peaked, you were in good hands. It almost seemed like an angel was holding you up to make sure your feet didn't dash the ground. You haven't been that high since, and to this day, you still haven't come down.

You reenter the scene with a professional smile, and continue to hear her out without wrecking the flow with a question. She is already addressing your concerns as they pop up.

"If the Lord chose to let me live—and I could've been gone and I didn't do nothing so wonderful that I need to be sitting up here—I just feel like I oughta be able to lift somebody's spirit, and I do a lot of that. When I was in the church down in Mississippi, my mother used to sing a song *'This little light of mine; I'm going to let it shine; Every where I go, I'm going to let my little light shine.'* Now to me, that's a masterpiece. The Lord gave you a little light. I don't care how many children you have, you gotta let your light shine. If you let your light shine, your kids are going to see it; somebody else's child is going to see it. It's good to teach 'em, but it's good to be an example of what you teach.

"I tell you the devil is so busy. What has happened now that I can't get up and run like I used to, I say things...you see. And sometimes the words that come out are not too wonderful. And the Lord hear me say those things...and the child hear me saying them things. And I realize that I have made a very bad mistake when I let my mouth speak them ugly words. And I give myself a good whooping, honey...I say *'Father in the name of Jesus, I want you to rebuke that lying demon that made me say it...I don't want to say it again...I want to live the life before my children so my children can do something to make me proud and somebody else proud.'* But those are such hard things that we have to keep abreast of that...we are so human—sometimes when you get a little anger, words come out that are not good. And that's why it's so good to charge yourself up with the Bible...and then you go to a Spirit-filled church that can also help—and I just hope that you're in a good church, because I'm telling you God has such a great work ahead of Him 'cause it's so many deceiving, hypocritical people honey, and it starts in the pulpit.

"I listen to Reverend Clay Evans. I've known him for a long long time. And I've known Pastor Richard D. Henton for a while, because you know my children were in his school. And I know a lot of these wonderful ministers. Now I think the Lord is going to be pleased with some of the work that's going on. But I think the Lord is not going to be pleased with a lot of things going on in the pulpit and in the church."

There's no way you could've fished that personal philosophy out with a question. She has every right to be down; to mope; to give up on life...and God, but she hasn't. She has kept the faith.

"So has there been any type of support group for you and others in your situation?"

"They started a meeting for all of the bereaved mothers who had lost their sons to violence and I would go there because they would have it at different hospital settings. So I would go and when I would get there tears would meet me at the door. All the mothers were weeping. And I said 'I don't have any business here.' I cannot focus on the date of death 'cause that's not relevant. All these other beautiful things that this boy has brought in my life? All the joy that this boy has brought in his grades? He was always there to pat you on the back if you needed it and he was there to say *'that's not the way'* if you needed it. I saw a lot of sweet things in him."

You nod as you wonder, "What are some of the beautiful things you remember?"

She jubilantly recalls how he sung "Jeremiah was a Bullfrog" in a grammar school play, a dance contest he was in, and how he used to carry a Raggedy Ann doll when he was a toddler. Then she shifts the focus to his manly traits and advance maturity.

"I was proud that he realized that he had made a baby and he said *'I will not let her carry that load. I will go to the hospital.'* He went and broke the hospital's rules because no kids can come in the hospital in the obstetrics department. He said *'I have a reason to be here because that's part of me in that bed there. I have fathered a child and I want that child to have my name.'* And that child is a millionaire today because of Benji. Now that's a man! The state of Illinois ruled that everything that Benji had would be benefited...except the mother. Mother don't get the checks. When he told me that I said I don't believe this. Nobody has suffered and grieved...I brought him in the world. He said *'Ma'am, that's the law of Illinois. Since your son has acted as an adult saying that he's fathered this child, the offspring of Benji gets the money.'*"

"When did you realize he was something special on the basketball court?"

"He said to me *'I made up my mind...I see what I want to be'* and I think there's a message for other people to know that when you talk about believing in your heart, that's wonderful to believe, but belief must be followed by action. If you believe in something, you oughta follow it up with something other than just saying 'I believe that.' Because I believe that the Lord has died on the cross for me; rose again for me; ascended into heaven for me. I believe that. So even though the doctors at Mayo clinic say I'll never walk, I say that I'm so sorry that that's your diagnosis, because I refuse to accept that. I believe that I will walk again. I don't know when, but I will be trying and you have no idea how many times I will fall. I've been a falling lady because I won't be still and I do as much as I can and I don't let nobody help me.

"So I have some good memories, Honey. I'mma tell you, I will not lay in my bed and worry about what happened because I can't take that back. I don't understand it. I don't understand why my legs don't work, because I'm not one of these little giver-upper people."

Those allergies are bothering you again just as the first hour of tape finishes, so you excuse yourself to the bathroom to bawl once more.

When you return, she begins talking about the rest of her sons, going as far as comparing Curtis—who's pictured in graduation gear on the bookcase—to the other black cat walking around. She notes that unlike Ben—with his fiery spirit—he has a gentle spirit. Jeffery is the studious son who—she claims with pride—is at work. Her oldest—Brumet—made a career out of the army and is on the verge of retiring. Without instigation, she shifts to the ten year legacy and the memorial banquet (unfortunately she won't have it this year) as if she's reading the questions from your list.

"I had so many politicians when I started out. Mister Harold Washington was right there by my side. And then he brought John Stroeger in. All those people came in and raised me a $1,000 on my table. When I had a banquet, I not only had the money from the banquet—'cause my tickets were $50 apiece, so you could very easily count the tables and see how much money I had made, because it was $500 a table...and that meant that I was able to help a lot of children that year.

"Jeffery was not too enthused about it. I said 'honey, I want you to think about what you're doing. Your brother cannot come back, his memory is alive, it's been ten years and somebody needs to realize it's been ten years...'cause a lot of folks don't know how long it's been.' My sister called me up to ball me out...told me *'God is not pleased with your life honey 'cause you making a god out of that boy...and that's why God took him because you made a god out of him. Everybody...worshipping him. Let him die. He dead, let him die.'* I said 'well honey, you haven't lost a child. What would you do if you would lose a son who had made a name for himself at that early age? Wouldn't you want someone to remember that and say something wonderful about him? God understands me and knows that I'm not making a god out of him.' *'Yes you are...you making a god out of him and He not pleased with your life'*...she sanctified and filled with the Holy Ghost and she living above sin. I'm not going to tell that lie. I still have weaknesses; I still have things to overcome."

You are a bit uncomfortable hearing this account, but she takes the edge off by revealing her humorous coping method.

"I listen to the Christian radio station 92.3 and I get Kenneth Hagin and all of these wonderful old preachers that have been teaching the Word. That helps me to sit here and be a woman—and then a hot-blooded, Mississippi-corn-fed woman...do you hear me? Now you know if you're a full-blooded, red-blooded, almost-six-foot-tall woman, would you wanna live a sexless life? Hell naw! No...you wouldn't. I said 'Lawd,

You made me and You know all about me and I know what your Word say.' When you know what the word say you better be careful. I can't get away with something someone else can because God know I know what the Word say. He told me fornicating is wrong and an abomination. That mean you don't lay with no man...I can't do it 'cause it's not my husband...so I had to know that fact and had to talk to the Lord—I said 'I'm depending on You.'"

She goes into one of the lessons she taught Ben, with her job as an illustration.

"You got to be in control. I said 'you're a powerhouse. You are full of power. God done made you beautiful to look at...gave you beautiful, great, big feet like mine...and big hands'—we used to sit up and play with our feet together...me and Benji did. He said *'Momma, you got long feet...look at your foot.'* I said 'yeah, that's the way the Lord made me.' I said 'when you get out of control...Many things have happened to me on my job. When you work in a hospital you have a lot of things to deal with, and I'm the big boss...somebody thought I was wonderful before I got to be. And you got a lot of little people that want to see where you're going, so they try to do little ugly things for you...and I go right in the bathroom.' I say 'scuse me a minute'. I go in there and whisper a little prayer. You hear me? These are my little secrets now. I go in there and whisper me a little prayer. I don't be going in there to use tongues most times. And I come back out...I got recharged, so I don't come out and call you what I oughta call you. I didn't say that. I shoulda called you what you wuz, but I didn't."

You didn't ask about Bobby Knight, but you are amused when she gives you the white-hair, red-sweater bonus.

"I'll never forget when Bobby Knight came to my house. And Bobby Knight will never like me no more on this earth. He will never like me, because I told him 'I have seen you and love games and I'm a sports person. I've trained this boy here—he's a young man now—to be in charge of his actions...his conduct is most important.' Any time you're out of control—I used a jet plane...do you have any idea what the pilot feels like when he takes that plane all the way up; bring it all the way down and then land it? That's a good feeling. I can almost feel it with him...it's such a big joy to take that big plane up and then bring it back down. But do you know that same plane—if you get it out of control—will kill a thousand people.

"I told him 'you're out of control most times. I saw you pick up a chair and throw it. I don't think I want Benji to be around that. I spent my whole life teaching him how to be in control and I've seen you pick up chairs and throw 'em. I've seen you totally out of control and I don't think that's saying a lot for a male.' Honey, that man wanted to kill me, 'cause nobody ever told him that he was out of control. And so what he did, he got another black woman to call me on the phone saying *'I'm calling for Bobby Knight and I just wanted to tell you that my son had an injury playing basketball and it was Mister Knight who's paying his tuition through school and Mister Knight did this.'* I said 'Ma'am, I don't doubt that. I understand there is some good in the worst of us and bad in the best of us. But Bobby Knight is demonstrating with his life what he is: out of control. He's out of control.' Well he hates me honey 'cause I told him he is out of control. He stayed with me three hours after that statement 'that he's out of control'. Both of us had to go to the toilet. I said 'who going first: me or you?'"

"So where was Ben going?"

"I know that Ben was kinda a teacher at heart and he likes things a certain way...he likes to have dignity and professionalism in what he's doing...and I had heard him make some remarks about Joey Meyer. He said *'Joey is just not the kind of leader that's needed for this, and you've got to put your foot down and mean what you say and say what you mean.'* He said *'if I go there, I'm going to have my work cut out, because he lets them folks come in any way they want to.'* He said *'that's never going to happen with me.'* He said *'you're gonna to have to get rid of these earrings in the ear; you're gonna have to get rid of these hats turned all kind of ways...I'm not gonna have that...I'mma clean that up.'* I think that he was so close a friend to the man at Illinois—his assistant coach—Jimmy Collins...Jimmy Collins has been very kind to me and very giving to me. Benji used to date his daughter. I kinda think he might have gone to Illinois. I really thought about that. That would've made me so happy 'cause he wouldn't've been too far from home."

"Has Ben ever taught you a powerful lesson?"

"He documented one of Richard D. Henton's sermons to me and it just made me happy. I told him about those three words...I said 'I'm giving you three words that are very important. One is omnipotent: means all powerful; and one is omniscient: means all intelligent; and one is omnipresent: means He's everywhere you are.' So he said *'I'm going to look them up'*, so he looked them up. He said *'I want you to know I looked up those three omni's.'* I said 'you did?' He said *'well I'm going to tell you the one I love the most.'* I said 'oh, you have a favorite.' He said *'Yeah. I like omnipresence, because it's so comforting to know that where ever I am, God is. That's important to me. I know He's powerful, but it's just the fact that where ever I am, God is.'* He told me *'Momma, you don't have to go to a certain place at a certain time on a certain day to find God. He's where ever you are. You gave me the words...do you know what they mean?'* I said 'yeah.' He said *'You don't act like it 'cause you getting up going to church every Sunday. You're one woman who can lay in bed on some Sunday's. But naw, you've got to go.'* He said *'I want you to think about what you're doing: Are you really serving the Lord, or are you just going to be in your little clique and your little club...to see who got a new suit this week and a new hat and got the fur collar.'* He said *'You all are just a fashion show.'*

Honey, he showed me...he took my words and slapped me in the face with them. When he got through with me, I looked at the whole thing and said 'Lord, I'm going to straighten my life out.' He helped me a lot. I'm telling you, the boy was wonderful. It's so interesting to think about what he might've been if he had lived on. I think he could've been the greatest minister on the planet. And that would've made me happy," she declares, wistfully.

Three well-spent hours are gone and so are the tapes. This wasn't an interview...it was a revival. It is hard to leave her presence, but the physical energy is sapped from you more than her. The Spirit of God works in several ways...on different emotions. Part of you takes a piece of the pain from the loss, which weighs a ton on your heart; Something on the inside of you stirs like lava on speed after she fed you with inspiration to live.

You and Ma are down. She's your best friend. Never have you taken her for granted. However, in this instant, the fullness of the bond between mother and son—between you and Ma—becomes a vivid revelation. That bond is Love; that love is Spirit; and that Spirit never dies. When you walk through the door and float to the kitchen where she's talking on the phone, you utter not a word, but speak loudly as you embrace her as if it will be the last time.

18

Nature has a way of revering the resting soul. Birds recognize the sleeping's vicinity as a no-singing zone, and are forever silenced in the area; squirrels don't gather—as if every day is an Old Testament Sabbath—and remain in a perpetual fast like they're expecting a miracle. Easing down Sunrise Boulevard, your nerves wax calm. When you stop a quarter of the way down Meditation Lane, your feelings are deadened to the idea of the ambiance. Stepping out, you pause, suck in the tonic mist that envelops the atmosphere, and hone in on your friend's bed of peace. You're not looking for any semblance of life in Oak Wood Cemetery.

Dexter would've turned 19 today, and you make the first ritual visit to him. Ms. Lewis opted not to come. She noted that for her, it does nothing to her mood. Just before the funeral, the Lord gave her peace in the matter. She has moved happily on since. This year you have two memorial resting spots to visit. They can't see or hear you. You can't compete with the presence of God on your most glorious day. Why get caught up in the commercialized brainwashing and claim to feel their presence in this rest stop for the body? There's nothing mystical about a cemetery. It reminds you of an empty stage after a play; like costumes without the characters. You feel the cool, damp air on your face and shiver from the wind chill factor. It's just uncannily serene here. After all, the living can't bother the deceased, and the deceased can't bother the living.

Raymond Johnson 1977-1988. Precious in the sight of the Lord is the death of his saints—Psalm 116:15. The scripture in the marble marker has a divine echo that reassures the believers on this side. There's no reason to weep. You don't rejoice, either. The rage was buried with time, however, you anticipate the other side. Once the destiny is realized, anticipation will be dead and buried, and there will be no need to walk by faith. You stroll down a few yards through the Garden of Meditation to Dexter's spot and remain mum as you peer down. You blink to the southeast, where Dexter's fruit resides, and chuckle. More than memories were left behind by Dexter; he left a legacy of life. You scan the other tombstones and ponder the stories behind each one. *What did they do with their lives? Who did they leave behind? How did they die? Did they accomplish everything they set out to do? Were they in the will of God? Where are they now?* The cold truth of the matter is that every one isn't in a pleasant paradise. Some's resting-place is Hell. Determined to sup with the living, you stroll slowly back to the car without uttering a good-bye. Careful not to tread on anyone's last testament, you skim over the writing, but don't register it.

Life is more than shooting rock. There is Faith and school and family and health. And of course, Jesus figures into the equation of life. Lately you've been consumed by the epitome of Chicago basketball. Whenever there's something hoop related—whether it's what to write or what to wear—you think of Ben Wilson. The tedious task of transcribing the hours of interviews and pulling out key quotes is an element that drove you to the graveyard. Two days after your revival with Mrs. Wilson, you had the foundation of the first draft. You needed to come down to a rest. It seemed like you sprung up and couldn't come down. Basketballs were bouncing in your dreams. Perhaps that's why your eyes catch the figure etched into the salmon marker. It's a man in a triple threat stance clutching a basketball. On the opposite side is a goal. *In God's Care. Benji Wilson. Mar 18, 1967. Nov 21, 1984.*

The frosty mist turns into teardrops and the four seasons overcome you like a tidal wave of fire, prompting your mood to spin in a pyramid. A rush of tropical hot air raises your smile and peaks your joy. Only the Lord can order your steps and focus your eyes on something so sacred. Why is the summer the shortest season? Without warning, your countenance drops like an elephant turd. The autumn clutches at your throat with the intentions of breaking your heart in the fall. Just as you bawled a dry cry in Mother Wilson's bathroom, you buckle over in breathless grief and collapse just over him as you struggle to retrieve your wind and composure. An Arctic surge comes in from the north, which kindles your wrath and brings you to your feet. Your temples pulsate with your gritting teeth. He's gone because some punk was proud to pack a pistol. It was the same pride that overcame Lucifer, jacked up the divine order and eventually led to the fall of man. As the drops glaze the stone over, your bitterness sets like the desert sun and gives rise to hope.

"In God's Care," you utter. The concept bounces around in your head and provokes a grin as you promise, "See you when I get there."

You fade off, adding, "I got next" without realizing the magnitude of your words. Ever so subtle were the wheels of a subconscious death wish set in motion, but it is surely rolling your way.

"Do you think they'll give me a toy if I order a Quarter Pounder and a large fry?"

"Nope," Dexter assures. "You haveta order a Happy Meal."

"It's not enough food in a Happy Meal for me," you rationalize.

He humps his shoulders and suggests, "Order two."

"That'll cost too much," you say, asking, "Can I just have your toy?"

He shakes his head as you keep from laughing.

While in the 'hood, you stopped at the church for a planning meeting which included all auxiliaries, and stopped by Angela's house. A month has passed since you've seen them. Surprisingly, Dexter's birthday was remembered, not mourned. There was no formal memorial in the house, for she was already consoled. Instead, the present obligations are focused on. She's making the grade at Roosevelt, and Junior is doing well at Blackstone Preschool. As an incentive to keep up the good work, you decided to treat him to McDonalds.

As you wait patiently in line behind a family of five that's taking a crash course in McDonalds' menu reading, Popeye comes in boisterously messing around with one of the neighborhood runners. He playfully pulls his gat out and whacks him with it. The gold cross that hangs from his neck is bigger than the one that Jesus was nailed to. You take Dexter by the hand and suggest, "Let's go, Buddy," as you ease passed them and through the fragrant wall of weed that surrounds them.

"Shorty," Popeye slurs. His grainy voice grates as if he's been swallowing rusty razor blades and nails and washing them down with pure alcohol. You don't even look when he comes up directly behind you. "Shorty...is that your Shorty?" he asks, coming up to the side of you just when you reach the door. "He looks just like you," he says, playfully punching his face. His lungs must be lined with reefer, because his flapping mouth singes your nasal hairs and gives you a contact high. He slides a bill in Junior's hand, saying, "That's for being down with my Shorty."

You look him in his one eye and order Dexter to "Give the gentleman back his money."

That KO's Popeye's grin as he takes offense. "What's up, Shorty? You think you all that now? You too good for us now that you're at Northwestern? Just because you have it like that and we have to hustle out here doesn't mean you're any better than us. I've known you since you was this high," he says, holding his hand to knee level.

How ironic, since you're an inch taller and a year older. "I didn't say that."

"Why is it that you're turning down my ducks, then?"

You study the patch that covers up the eye socket and the former tear tattoo (a mockery of remorse for killing someone), and boldly explain, "If we were broke to the bone and starving to the point of death, we wouldn't accept your blood money."

His expression drops, his tone darkens and his voice grows even more coarse. "I see you done got turned out with your punk ass. Take your bitch ass on, then."

"Whatever," you blurt, starting out the door again. He follows you out to the car, spewing some more unquotables. When you buckle Dexter in, you turn to face him. "Is all of this necessary?"

"Is it necessary to diss someone that's just trying to survive? Just because I don't have the choices and opportunities that you have doesn't make me a lesser man than you. This is what I have to do. If I didn't do it, someone else would. There's a demand for it, and a black man might as well take advantage of it, or else die."

Your cool is intact, however, you fumble your religion and your clean lexicon as you calmly state, "That's the stalest, stupidest, most-insulting-slap-in-the face, sordid shit I've ever heard in my life...and I've heard some outrageous shit in my days. The Grim Reaper demands lives...just because it's appointed for every man to die doesn't give me the right to help the process along. You might as well have on a white sheet or a swastika tattooed to that big ass dome of yours. A whole generation of our people with much less has made it legitimately. Go wash your face with that bullshit and come correct."

"Does it sound as outrageous as a glock going off in your face, niggah?" he probes, pulling his piece back out.

Now your cool is steamy hot. "Motherfucker, you don't even know what the hell you represent—the Brothers or the struggle—so I ain't scared of you or your gun. If I didn't have reverence for the Lord, I would send you and all these other banal, barbarous, bad-wannabe, base bastards that call themselves surviving, to hell," you growl through clenched teeth as you step closer and crash your head against his forehead. It takes every ounce of restraint in your being to keep from ripping him to pieces. "I know you've used it before...I know you've killed in your lifetime, but I also know that by the mercy of God, the angel of death didn't have your soul earlier this year. Unfortunately, you're too stupid to take heed to the warning and slow down. Instead, you're still walking around trying to be hard, bullying the weak and innocent, but I know you got a chicken heart in your chest pumping honey through your body, and that big, brainless head of yours can't even hide behind your big ol' gun. The next time you flash that gat in front of my godson, you better make sure you blow me to kingdom come, because I'll beat your trite ass to dust and fertilize my lawn with you. Now why don't you crawl your sick, psychedelic, psychopathic, pseudo-gangster black ass back to the pit from whence you came and rot."

He scrunches his mug up into a hideous, intimidating expression, but you don't budge. Seeing that, he tucks his tail, lightly pushes off and turns away.

Your heart hums like it is charged with nitrogen as you regret letting the profane come out of the holy. As vast, profound, and lofty as your vocabulary is, you had to pull out the most disgraceful, debilitating, malignant words. Pristine ears were deflowered by the passion of a trusted elder. Innocent eyes could have been defiled by the benighted bravado of a drug-dealing clown with smeared makeup.

Just when you take a seat behind the wheel, you cringe in discomfort as *the* foot sinks deep into your tush, up through your belly and to your heart, which sends your appetite south. You could force yourself to eat something, but you'll only have indigestion to the tenth power. Taking a deep, labored breath, you close your eyes and lean against the steering wheel. You want to scream and holler, but you've unbecomed enough for the year, and it doesn't make sense to heap more dialogue on the curse pile to repent from.

You lean back, grab your Bible from the back seat, and order, "C'mon," as you exit and stroll back into McDonalds.

Popeye—who's waiting in line with his boy—immediately shoots daggers into you when you step through the door. He gets defensive as you walk purposely towards him. Just as boldly as you cussed him out, you repent.

"I would like to apologize for dissing you like I did. That was my bad," you state in an adjusted vernacular, asking, "Are we cool," as you stick your fist out.

His expression doesn't change, but he nods once and assures, "We aiight," as he pounds your fist.

"Can I pick up your tab?"

"I can handle it," he insists as his boy looks on.

"Please...let me hook you up."

He stares you down for a moment before he consents.

After paying for a meal for three and a half, you carry the tray to the booth seat in the back corner. Dexter blesses the food and we chow without lip service. When we finish, you let him dictate the topic of discussion.

"That must've been rough not playing," Popeye assumes.

"It is rough. I was climbing the walls at first, but it ain't doing anything for me, so I just made the best of the situation. You know I got married."

"Naw, I didn't know that. Go head on, Shorty."

"It allows me to spend time with my wife and focus more on my writing and the books. But it did get to me at first," you indicate. "How come you didn't play after your freshman year?"

He shakes his head and looks down. "Man...my grades killed that noise. I'm trying to get my stuff together and get my GED...play for Kennedy King next year, and who knows."

He was pretty good. Of course, we played the same swing position. His build is similar to yours, with the muscle exception and conditioning factor going to you. In the one official game against each other, you got the best of him by a 12-8 scoring advantage and your team won by 20. "Anything can happen. A lot of big names came out of JC. Go for yours. Maybe I'll see you in the NBA one day."

"Tell the truth, I don't want no parts of the pro's."

"Oh no."

He shakes his head and claims, "It's too restrictive...even for the money. I really want to get into the music industry."

"Really?" you query, then stereotypically suppose, "You're trying to break into the rap game?"

He shakes his head again. "I can play the keyboards and I'm interested in Jazz."

"And I play the drums," his boy—name Reggie—interjects.

Life is full of surprises. He has never taken drum lessons, but he knows how to beat out all types of Gospel tunes. Come to find out, Reggie's grandfather is a preacher. Some Sundays he still plays, but for the most part, he spends his Sabbath in bed resting.

"That's an impressive gift. I wouldn't let it go to waste if I were you."

"My grandfather tells me that all the time."

"He knows what he's talking about. Everybody can't get into music. And especially the keyboards," you note. "I took piano lessons and the piano lessons took me." They laugh at that, although you're serious about them using their gifts. "When people use their talents, more skills are added to it. I remember when the only thing I could do was sky scrap, but pretty soon, I could dunk like the Doc. Before I knew it, I was shooting from the top of the key, back from the free throw line. And I remember I laid off of ballin' for a summer, and would you know that fall it was like I never had game from the start. When I started writing and learning the language, I became skilled at speaking. Educated men run for the dictionary when they talk to me," you mention.

"I know that's right," Popeye seconds. "I'm still trying to figure out what sordid shit is, although I don't think it's nice."

That sets you off a bit, as you have to keep from laughing too hard. "It means low or nasty," you inform. "On the serious side, don't let your blessings waste away. God didn't give it to you for nothing."

"No disrespect, but God don't give a fuck about me and the rest of the hustlers out here," Popeye states.

Opening the Word to Jonah, you knew it would come in handy. After sliding the book over to them to verify chapter four, verses nine through 11, you give a synopsis of the story, using white and black America as an illustration. Pleasingly, Reggie knows his way around the scriptures as you direct them to Luke 19. After you explain that Zaccheus the tax collector was despised like today's street drug dealer, you advise Popeye to try to look past the tragic loss of his eye and focus on God's grace keeping him in the land of the living. Popeye grudgingly reads Matthew 10 and 38 as you shift back to the illustration of God's grace towards Jonah.

The faces say it all when you pause: Dexter—who's been silent through the whole discussion—is well fed, but not satisfied; Reggie is dealing with chastening; and Popeye is fighting the Power. Without pushing, you ask if you could pray with and for them. Reggie nods and Popeye—who doesn't move or murmur—obliges by staying. We all join hands, forming a circle, and you intercede for them, praying mercy, grace, salvation, deliverance and blessings to them. You take note of Popeye's humble mumness and inner reflection in his eye when you hand him your number. Reggie promises to go to church Sunday and to get his act together after you encouraged him to stay in touch. You know your Father and Dexter are smiling.

All was well when you dropped Dexter off and set off for Evanston. When you pass the midway marker downtown, your system has the Vivarin faded and your eyelashes feel as if they have bricks hanging from them. By the time you pull in front of your house, you're functioning in sleep mode. Like a spider can sense when food is in his web, you discern a guest in your home even without seeing, smelling or hearing any evidence. The presence of a stranger in your dwelling doesn't revive you, but you home in on the rear den out of courtesy. As you reach the kitchen, you pick up on Faith's muffled voice. Just before you reach the room, you note the teaching tone she's speaking in. Stopping just in the doorway, you take inventory of the eccentric guest. No doubt, it's a man with very effeminate features: relaxed hair that flows like an oil stream; twinkling eyes neatly framed with black mascara. Did somebody turn the heat up? He brings to mind a pseudo-Michael Jackson. Faith has her Bible out explaining Philipians 1 and 6 to him, so you patiently wait as he looks on intently.

In mid-explanation, she glances up and greets you with "Hey Sweetie...I didn't see you there," as the man seems to tense up slightly. "This is my cousin Shawn" she explains as you step over to him with an extended hand.

"How you doing Shawn?" you question as you peer into his reluctant eyes.

"I'm quite fine—and you?" he snaps with a womanish twang as he gives you his firm, gaunt hand.

"I'm blessed," you note as we all pause.

You feel Faith anticipating your reaction. "Shawn came over to catch up and update," she justifies, adding, "and to get a good Word."

You nod an unnecessary approval and bid, "I'll let y'all finish studying" on cue from the tension.

"I was on my way out..." he assures as you close your eyes and cut him off with a "STOP" hand signal.

"Make yourself at home," you insist, hinting to Faith, "I'm on my way to bed."

"I'll be up there in a sec," she promises, passing an anticipatory gaze at you. We come to a silent agreement that we have a lot to talk about.

"Nice meeting you Shawn," you state with a nod and a fatigued simper as you dismiss yourself.

You bypass the shower, strain to shed your clothes and pop in the mellow sounds of Kim Stratton. Without a prayer, you lay back on the bed to rest before you actually go to sleep. After all, you still have a Statistics exam to prepare for. No sooner than you shut your eyes, you enter the allaying realm of snooze to the tune of "More Than Enough".

The dewy kiss is like a snowflake against your lips, a divine prompt to your soul and the authoritative command "Let there be light", because you revive from the murky slumber and into Faith's glorious golds as she straddles a breath over you. An hour-and-a-half has passed, and it feels like you hibernated for a couple of seasons. We gawk for another season before our faces crack with grins, followed by an abbreviated osculation episode.

You sit with your back against the headboard as she comes up out of her garments and blithely narrates the discussion with her cousin Shawn.

He was notably inquisitive about life, death, and God. While her devotion to God was as blatant as his alternative lifestyle, they tabooishly danced around the topic of salvation and homosexuality after she took the initiative and denounced his lifestyle as a sin—as if he asked—causing a major schism in their bond. After she stated that "There's no salvation without repentance" and he countered with "How can one repent of something that God created him as", the conversation never crossed that line again. The Lord instructed her to show him a message, as opposed to preaching it. Once, her pastor noted that sometimes relatives are not receptive to a lesson from other family members. Although the sincerity is strong, often loving them unconditionally and being prepared to minister to them is all that can be done.

Her seed sprouted after four years. He testified how one of his fellow gaysters—Ricki—was afflicted with AIDS and literally walking—or laying—dead. After a gallant two-year battle, he was reduced to an unconscious heap of skin and bones. Shawn and a couple of the kids kept vigil in his room for a week, saying so long. An "anointed" elder from his former church got wind of his condition. Minister Johnston came and prayed a prayer of healing while laying hands on him. Shawn and the sisterhood thought it was just a wasted religious formality. The next day, Ricki was awake; the next week, he walked out of the hospital. Stranger than the miraculous recovery, was Ricki's behavior. While he joyously praised God and expressed gratitude for all of the support, he seemed to be...ashamed. Every allusion the crew made to the life fell at his feet as he withdrew from them and grew somber at the idea of homosexuality. There was no mistaking: he was a changed person. From the way he talked to his gestures—or lack of—there was a new spirit in him. They didn't confront or question him, because they already knew that he was shunning the life. All he seemed to talk about was the goodness of Jesus, which made them a bit uncomfortable.

Several weeks and pounds later, Shawn did pay him a visit with the purpose of getting to the bottom of things. Richard—who he insisted on being called—was a physical specimen in a short amount of time and the doctors said there was no sign of the disease. He claimed that the desire to have a man was dead, cremated and scattered in the sea of forgiveness, insisting that the Lord delivered him from that sinful lifestyle, and homosexuality isn't even a temptation. At first, Shawn rebuked him with the same argument that "God made us this way", but Richard's riposte "God created us, not the sin, which has it's source in Satan," sent Shawn reeling out in tears, doubt and frustration. That was two months ago, and he was finally seeking God for answers and starting to recognize that homosexuality is a sin. Just before he left, he prayed the sinner's prayer of faith and walked out a child of the King.

"The prayer of the righteous availeth much, because I've been praying for his salvation forever, without ceasing," she says with a chuckle, shaking her head. "You should've seen the way he used to dress," she notes as she hangs the last of the laundry up. "Ironically, he's the mediator between me and my sister, Deborah. He says that she says that she loves me, even though her line still has my number blocked. Oh well."

You grin dreamily at her as you rise and gravitate towards her. When she turns around, she runs out of personal space as you peer down at her and wrap your arms around her so tight that your hands stretch to your back. The gold and purple rose that you hold in each hand reach up to mirror her face while your creativity oozes out of your mouth:

"You're the I's in my pride
the vessel where my heart abides
The fruit of my harvest
where my mind is at rest
My Faith in action
my soul's satisfaction."

She claims the roses with a giggle and wonders, "Where did you learn to flow so poetically," as we part.

You gaze down and advise, "Wait here" while you retrieve your minder.

"Read the entry from December 24," you order, opening it up and handing it to her.

"Although Black is beautiful, there are some ugly shades.
The hue is always in the negative light though.
Shadows consume each other. The reflection of luminosity.
First there was black. The source of white. The source of sight.
When illumination infiltrates the dark, blackness leaves faster than the speed of light.
But what happens when you snuff out the light?
White light is replaced by total blackness and you shall see no evil," she concludes with a questioning glance, gathering, "There was a lot of anger in it."

You nod as you explain how your pen scribed the venom from your heart the day of Dexter's home going service.

Dexter was a deft poet. He had a psalmist's anointing. Often he could extemporize stanzas like they were simple sentences. Except for the few notes he penned to Angela, he rarely documented them, because "They were documented in heaven." His talent amazed you, since he loathed writing and wasn't all that particular about speaking. A couple of years ago, we attended an open mic at the Green Mill on Broadway and Lawrence. At the time, you thought slamming was exclusive hoop lingo. To put his poetry slam in dunk perspective, it was a 360-degree windmill from the free-throw line. The bar was dim, like the weeping dawn. Poets danced around euphemisms for fucking, breathed life into inanimate, despicable objects such as dog shit, brought glory to lasciviousness, humorized death, and twisted simplicity into complexity. While the patrons got intoxicated from the booze and smokes, Dexter soothed them into sobriety and spiritually seduced them. When he spoke, dusk turned to day. Whereas the naked eyes could make out silhouettes prior to his stanzas, the glory made minute details such as hair color vivid (In a lounge no doubt). His glow canceled out the stage spotlight. The mostly white revelers in the cramped quarters didn't know what hit them.

The title was "Voices", and it was a melange of preaching, spiritual warfare, psalms and proverbs. It was sea deep, yet Simon-says simple. He theatrically described the subtle, persistent voice of temptation. The account was so real that it was almost like the voice echoed in your mind. Like a trained theologian on a mission, he made a smooth transition to the voice of Faith. Good Lord, if only he had recorded it. The audience didn't know that he had just made agape love to them. Perhaps you will never see the manifestation of the seminal stanzas, but there will be a bountiful harvest of righteousness.

You ate, slept and lived to communicate orally and in writing. Commentating was your forte. Word power fascinates you to no end. Early on, you discovered that letter sequence can be the difference between God and dog. You were a step away from envying his lyrical ability. If your life was riding on your bardic output, you would be in the presence of God. When you held Dexter in the waning moments of his life, his anointing somehow rubbed off on you. It almost seems like you got a double poetical portion, which is a minute dimension of his sundry gifts. You wonder what else did he will off to you. Surely it wasn't patience, which you are lacking like a BeBe Kid lacks discipline.

"Last night, I dreamed that a part of me went with the Lord. The rest of me watched as I was totally consumed by Him. It hurt at first, because I thought that I had surrendered my whole self to Him already. Then He beckoned for me to come. That was all well and good, except the sea was between us, and you know that I float like an anchor.

Anyhow, I stepped out on faith—no pun intended, Rose—and do you know I was walking on the water? I've learned that faith is tested, and that water went crazy stupid on me. Tidal waves were all around me; there was even a waterspout. I tell you though, I kept my eyes on Jesus and kept stepping as my soul sang "Order My Steps in Your Word". None of the drama got my attention. I was determined to go through that storm. But then things got calm and I lost focus. That's when a whirlpool started sucking me under. In the past, I would will myself awake, but last night I cried out *'Lord, save me'*, and you know He extended His hand.

"I see a lot of me in Peter: I needed to be rescued from drowning—just like Peter; I denied Jesus for a season—just like Peter; I was encouraged after I took a spiritual behind-kicking—just like Peter; I have a foul mouth at times—just like Peter, and I struggle with racial prejudice—just like Peter. My soul is committed, but the flesh is weak. I'm hurting for some restraint on my tongue," you say wistfully as you recall how you cussed Popeye out.

As an aspiring lawyer, you're gifted with a stubborn, contrary spirit. With your tenacity and determination, you pursue evidence to support your belief. When it's all laid out, you end up with volumes of supporting documentation. At that point, you have a tendency to assault your opponent with prosecuting propaganda...even if you're wrong. Just the proper ingredients for a career in law. Fortunately, when it comes to the Gospel, your stance is on the Truth. Unfortunately, your means of witnessing may not be necessary. There's a strong possibility that your verbal victories over Khalid came at the cost of alienating him from Christ even more. You're learning that if the words from your mouth don't compel people to come to Jesus, they're just sensational sound-waves on a breeze of bad breath.

She rubs your back as she confesses her "weak timing" when it comes to sensitive topics with her loved one's. "A lot of times my message is correct, but it's usually out of season for the receiver."

For a moment, we ponder our problems while laying sprawled out on the bed with "Rich in Jesus Name" saturating our souls. Then the Spirit hits you with a K and Faith with an O, for a simultaneous KnockOut as we gaze knowingly at each other. She proclaims, "Whatsoever ye shall bind on earth shall be bound in heaven: and whatsoever ye shall loose on earth shall be loosed in heaven..." and you second, "If two of you shall agree on earth as touching any thing that they shall ask, it shall be done for them of my Father which is in heaven," with a guffaw. We waste no time dropping to our knees and praying for a no cussing mouth and in season speeches. Then we touch...and bind up together...and loose love.

"Joy—Joy—Joy, that girl she brings me joy," you croon like a crying crab along with BlackStreet, while Faith occupies your mental TV. The law of gravity is coming down hard on your eyelids, but you rebel by singing while coasting down Stoney Island on your way to the expressway. Although your mouth is keeping up with the beat, your head is bobbing to the sound of the Rock-a-bye-baby lullaby.

BJ is as busy a man as you. Mel (Duffus David the Party Man's brother) and his girlfriend, Cherelle, were at BJ's place to put together a commentary in regards to her father's shooting death. The story barely made the press, and the killers are still out and about, as if taking someone out is the norm. You could tell she was still distraught over it, so you gladly stayed for victory prayer after he finished writing it. You've been there and could actually feel her in full effect. Since the hour was late and you were tired, you didn't worry about him editing your article. Just before you stepped out, he dropped a bomb of good cheer: You won the CABJ scholarship. Not only did you win, but also you won the $2,500 Max Robinson Award, which is the highest award that you didn't even know existed. You were under the impression that they were all for $1,000.

While you were on this side of town, you paid Nick a quick visit, since it had been a couple of weeks since we've talked. Nick is always overflowing with inspiration and good news. Her grades are good at both institutions, even though she struggled in Elements of Bible Study. She insisted that exploring the different study methods was a humbling adjustment for her. Her friendship with Deon is on the verge of drifting into a relationship. He's doing well at his job at Jewels Food Store, but spiritually struggling ever since his dad had recently reappeared on the scene after a few years of a vagabondic existence. After shooting through the small talk, she bombed you with "I delivered my first evangelistic message at a home for troubled youths." You were pleasantly shocked. Nine souls accepted Christ after hearing the message spoken by her. She insisted that it wasn't planned. When Elder

Lamont called her up to testify, she went into a twenty-minute zone that covered the Gospel message and her own trials in her young life. Her excitement was communicable and had you wondering about the fullness of your own calling, and whether it would include any preaching. It was clear that the inhibitive yoke that rested on her neck was broken by holy boldness.

After the Statistics test you crammed all night for, you popped another Vivarin before putting the final touches on the Ben Wilson first draft and sending it off. When you mailed that burden to Missouri, you were due to start work in ten minutes. You flew down the clear Lake Shore Drive and managed to make it in five minutes after your start time. You wished you didn't commit to chairing the Walk of Faith Anniversary, because as much as you tried, you couldn't divide yourself into three parts, delegating the different tasks to the other two parts. You tried hard to do it, but the Lord wasn't having it.

Thank God that the school paper has allowed you to do a couple of player perspective pieces, even though your view has been of a regular fan, since you ain't seeing no action. Judging by the prayer request of Wally, it's a good thing you're not a full-time participant. Family, academic and emotional struggles had him wishing for death. He informed you that he has no peace, an abundance of stress, and an insatiable desire for fulfillment. You noted that fulfillment comes only from knowing Jesus. Without selling him a fantasy, you said that there will still be problems, but Christ will make them easier to deal with while going through, around or over them. He pondered it before confessing his belief. However, he didn't know what to do. That's when you prayed the sinner's prayer of faith with him and took it upon yourself to mentor him. You provided him with an NIV study Bible, and the time for the Bible Study in your home. Amazingly, you could feel the limitless love of God flowing through your soul, because you're naturally disdainful of white folks. Although some racial scars remain, you were able to embrace him as a colorless brother with all of your heart. It's interesting what a little wall demolition can do for a point of view. And Faith...Mercy.

The night before, you were trying to write the Craig Hodges feature, but she wasn't trying to be denied. You found out that the sex drive of a new bride is as powerful as a space shuttle. So insatiable is her fire, that you would rather take your chances standing in the path of molten lava. She gently massaged your scalp, which sent all types of libido buzzing through you. Her hands on your head peaked you in that instance. Your excitement put her in a feeding frenzy. She ended up pinning you down and tying you up in some kind of freestyle wrestling move that you couldn't resist or break. It happened in record time, but it was...awesome. Faith discovered inner passion that you didn't know you had. And she would've run you back, except your piece and mind went limp. What kind of statutes are on the books concerning the rape of a husband?

You're not going to make it to the holidays with the job. There is no other choice but to resign yesterday, as in today is your unofficial last day. There's nothing like an uncooperative body. Your mind wants it on; your body wants off. The brisk, wintery wind that rushes through the window does nothing for your alertness. Your consciousness sputters in and out like an old rusty Ford that's hurting for a tune up. With each surge of anxiety that perks you up for a moment, comes a stronger shove of exhaustion that weighs your awareness down. As you exit Lake Shore Drive on Sheridan, it dawns on you that you can actually slumber with your eyes wide open. With your vision defiantly on the road, the blinders of fatigue close in, making your peripheral sight null and void. All of the headlights blur and the darkness blankets you. As the atmosphere gets dim, you can feel yourself nodding forward. You're not asleep, and your eyes are not closed, but in a deceitful blink, you are out of it. Whether the black sheet flashed your face for a second or covered it for a minute, you couldn't tell. All you know is that when the lights brighten up, you have a mouth full of steering wheel and an upside down point of view of the buckled up hood of your ride in front of the windshield as Digable Planets blasts in through the speakers.

A look of urgent disappointment registers on Faith's face when she bursts through the door, so you beat her to the lecture. "I'm going to officially quit tomorrow," you assure, holding the ice pack up to your 40-stitched upper lip. "And if it'll make you happy, I'll check into Vivarin Anonymous, too."

She barrels into you head first (like you did to the Volvo) and squeezes you like a hungry Python constricts a pig. She kisses you on the cheek so hard that it feels like she's biting for blood. When she releases, she examines you through glazed eyes. The water falls and she embraces you again as her body bucks against your chest with the successive sobs. She can barely blurt out a breathless "If I lose you, I'd die."

What a heart stopper and tearjerker. You pat her back and assure, "I'm okay Rose" as you contemplate the reality of the near-premature separation. Decapitation is more appealing, because you can't even begin to imagine living without her either.

If the accident was measured in poetic terms, it was an uncensored, Ghetto Boys' rap. The picture reminded you of twisted and balled up aluminum foil. Thankfully, no one was in any of the three parked cars. Somehow, you swerved and flipped the car over before sliding into the others. When you hit the Volvo flush on the license plate, it knocked the Jeep Cherokee in front of it into the Buick Skylark onto the curve. Of course, your car is damned and burning in hell. Although the floor was pressed in and the dashboard was adjusted forward, the steering wheel didn't knock your heart out of your back. Technically, you should've been killed, instantly. Perhaps you were, because you only remember waking up. You escaped with a fat lip, bruised shoulder, slight limp and high blood pressure. The paramedics were surprised to find you outside of the vehicle when they arrived, figuring that you had to either be a bystander, ghost or the miraculously pieced-back man that was peeled out. Standing two feet from the scene, you whimpered and wished in vain for tears while your heart muted and you struggled to feel the nerves in your body, when you should've been thanking God.

As you hobble through the door with the aid of Faith, you ponder how you're going to tell Ma. The sun is rising when you make it to the bedroom. It takes all of two seconds for you to pass out into a dreamless, zionic slumber. At the midway point of life and death, you hear Faith squaring things away with the insurance companies. When you come all the way around, it feels like you have jumper cables hooked up to your lips, so you waste no time in popping the 800mg of Ibuprofen.

"You shouldn't take that on an empty stomach," Faith warns.

You ignore her, not to be rude, but you're hurting and out of it and the proud owner of a foul mood and a fat mouth.

"I told your mother already," she says.

You nod. "What did she say?" you mumble with difficulty.

"She just wanted to know that you are okay."

You shake your head as you reach for the phone. Ma picks up on the first ring. "Hey Ma," you greet dejectedly.

"How are you?"

"Not too good. I totaled the car. I'm really sorry."

"Sorry for what?"

"You worked the whole year saving for it..." you start as she cuts you off.

"I spent nine months making you and 18 years raising you, so stop sweating. That's what insurance is for," she assures. "Malcolm, I'm disappointed in your perspective: God granted you grace to walk away from a major accident with a few bruises and you're concerned about something that is easy to replace. Just think if you didn't make it, all of the people whose lives' would've been devastated. Now stop worrying about insignificant things and give thanks to God."

You take heed to her command and sigh. "Ma."

"Yes."

"I love you."

"I love you, too."

Faith served you well. After our intimate Thanksgiving meal, we went to Ma's house to feast. Then she dragged you to the theater to see Hoop Dreams. With your focus being on Ben and the game itself, the last thing you needed was another basketball nightmare...or movie. The game is not serious enough to have several screenplays centered around it. That was your thought going in a day after getting a somewhat discouraging response to the first draft that you sent in. The editor noted that there was too much recycled focus on the past, and that the bigger story was in the present scheme of things. With that, over a third of the article was cut out and all of your creative wind was knocked out of your heart. It didn't help that the letter came on the ten-year anniversary of Ben's tragic death. Dinner was good though. After watching the long, savory documentary that brought back a lot of pleasant and painful memories, your good mood was resurrected. A day after you spoke to Ms. Wilson, you interviewed Jeffrey—Ben's younger brother—over the phone. When he commented that Ben's life story should be put into film version, it didn't mean anything. But when you saw Hoop Dreams, you could see where he was going with it. And you could see where your article is going. Then you had your own pleasant dream, only to wake up to a bad day.

"It seems so unfair that dirt sticks to clean, white garments," you reflect, studying a blatant atmospheric stain on your white tank top.

Faith glances over at you sitting sprawled out in a posture that would raise the blood pressure of a chiropractor. She turns back to the stove where she's flipping hot cakes and frying swine. The aroma alone fills you as you anticipate a greasy, tasty breakfast. Even though your body responds to the scent, your mind is churning in a funky dumpster.

"Setting high goals seems vain and dangerous, since the higher you go, the deeper the fall," you muse to yourself. "Birthdays and funerals appear to be joined together in holy matrimony...what a perfect match."

Faith stays focused on the stove while you continue to ruminate about nothing and everything.

"Why is it that a curse is always sandwiched between the blessings of bread? I dream vivid dreams, only to wake up to bleary realities."

Faith freezes to a halt, cuts the stove off and sits directly across from you in a patient silence. Her peer urges you to let it all out, so you lean forward and oblige.

"Fear is the opposite of faith, and I hate to tell you, but I'm scared. Faith moves me, while fear tries to paralyze me. With an increase of faith, comes a bigger challenge, and Lord knows I've had some tests. I have you, so my faith has gone to a higher level, but the future scares me. I fear what's ahead. It's not myself that I'm worried about. Bring on a battalion of demons and I'll cut 'em down like blades of dry grass. I'm concerned about things happening to the people that mean so much to me: You, Ma, Uncle JoJo, Ben, Nick and my boys. You see, when good things come my way, I lose people. Outside of Jesus, you're the best thing that has happened to me, and I'm afraid to be happy. It's like when the rain falls, the weeds come."

She reaches across the table and gently clasps your hands.

"The Lord spoke to me last night, Rose...in a dream."

She closes her eyes nodding, and adds, "And you spoke to Him."

Her knowledge perplexes you. "You heard me?"

"Yep."

"What did I say?"

"I can translate it, but I can't repeat it."

Your brow crinkles as you shift your head back.

"You were speaking in a Hebrew tongue, which is a language that I haven't learned. The Spirit gave me momentary discernment."

"Deep," you chuckle.

"Not as deep as sleep-walking."

"What?" you question, tilting your head to the side like a dog trying to comprehend a new sound.

"Sweetie," she starts with a giggle. "You got up seven times during the night. The last time, you stepped out on the porch—in the sleet, with only your purple pajama bottoms—worshiping the Lord. Imagine if it had been a routine night. You would've been as bare as a newborn. Your steps were so light and sure, that it seemed like angels were holding you up as you paced on a cloud."

You lean back in the chair and focus on the replay on the wall. As vivid as it was, there was nothing to see. You couldn't see the day before you, let alone the morrow. The intense blackness was brilliant and embracing. It wasn't hard to recognize the crisp, still voice that beckoned you to *"Follow Me."* That theme was as elementary as basic math, yet as complex as Calculus. Weren't you already following Him? What exactly did He want? Where did He want you to go? Was your living in vain up to that point? You had no vision. There was neither a person nor a path to follow. It hurt your heart.

Follow Me
From the Valley of Transgression
Across the Sea of Tribulation
Through the Season of Affliction
There is a Pacific Garden
That eyes have not seen
Follow Me

That was the chorus of the new song that still rings in your ears. It surely wasn't a product of your creative mind, because that's not your rhyme scheme.

"What did I say...the translation?"

"What came out of your mouth is not important," she assures. "What's important is what came out of the Lord's mouth."

You encourage her to reveal it with your nod.

"The Lord says, ***'Behold, I am doing a new thing; now it springs forth; do you not perceive and know it, and will you not give heed to it? I will even make a way in the wilderness and rivers in the desert.'***

"The Lord says, ***'Herald and preach the Word! Keep your sense of urgency (stand by, be at hand and ready, whether the opportunity seems to be favorable or unfavorable, whether it is convenient or inconvenient, whether it be welcome or unwelcome, you as preacher of the Word are to show people in what way their lives are wrong) and convince them, rebuking and correcting, warning and urging and encouraging them, being unflagging and inexhaustible in patience and teaching.'***

"The Lord says, ***'The steps of a [good] man are directed and established of the Lord, when He delights in his way [and He busies Himself with his every step].'***

"I like this one, Lord," she chuckles as she closes her eyes. "The Lord says, ***'For we walk by faith [that is, we regulate our lives and conduct ourselves by our conviction or belief respecting man's relationship to God and divine things, with trust and holy fervor; thus we walk] not by sight or appearance.'***

"Sweetie, don't be afraid, for the Lord is with you always," she assures, adding, "and so am I."

19

"All I know is that when I read that it's easier for a camel to go through the eye of a needle than for a rich man to enter the kingdom of God, I prayed for poverty," you half jest, adding, "but then my Pastor explained that in order for a camel to go through the gait next to the main gait in Jerusalem, that he had to kneel and almost crawl, which is almost an image or sign of humility."

"It's like Agur's prayer to be neither rich nor poor, so that he wouldn't forget the Lord or be tempted to steal and bring shame upon the name of the Lord," Elizabeth reinforces.

Maria adds, "Jesus didn't have anything against his people having wealth...after all, his disciple, Joseph was loaded."

Finals ended and vacation officially started Friday. The Bible study decided to have one more discussion that we had been building up to: the figures of speech in the scriptures. Anthropomorphisms are probably the biggest misunderstandings and craftiest weapons of false religions. Like the Nation of Islam, the Mormon Church teaches that God is a man with a physical body. The primary verses that they use to support the argument are found in 2 Corinthians 3:18 and 1 John 3:2, with Exodus 33:20-23 as evidence. Never mind Jesus' words "God is Spirit and those who worship him must worship him in Spirit and in Truth." Levi indicated that the Church of Latter Day Saints didn't favor colored folks (so of course their god is a white man), noting that up until 1978, they didn't allow blacks to be "priests".

While Wally couldn't make it (you did have several biblical discussions with him to explain the doctrine of repentance, salvation, and true faith, and we had casual conversations about race, journalism, music, and—of course—sports), Timothy confessed a belief and hope in Christ two weeks ago and was baptized at Faith's former church today, since he's originally a native North-sider. All are in favor of applying for official club status with the University, possibly next fall. Some of the functions would be outreach efforts, teaching and some type of feeding and/or tutoring ministry in conjunction and alliance with churches that have that type of ministry, but lack the talent and participation to supply certain needs outside of the plan of salvation. The possibilities are unlimited with the way we were able to reduce a racially and religiously diverse group down to the least common denominator: Jesus.

Q and Ike catered our last semester supper, treating us to seemingly the whole menu. They didn't even attempt to play chef, opting instead to pick up the meal from Ofie: a West African Restaurant on Sheridan Road. We filled up on Gold Coast Shrimp, Tsire (West African version of shish kebob containing beef and lamb), Kaza Sabongari (Cornish hens with special spices), Coconut Jollof Rice (a chicken and rice dish), Niger Stew (tomato based stew with goat meat), and the Bukom Special (Deep fried fish, which is a Ghanaian favorite). The flavor of West Africa had us longing for the Motherland. Instead of giving Faith a kitchen lesson, they started teaching her Twi (one of the Ghanaian languages). Not only did our spiritual appetites get a diverse serving of edibles this quarter, but also our natural bellies were delighted with some exotic dishes. Of course, Susan prepared the traditional fried rice (with shrimp, chicken, pork, and beef), beef Chop Suey and chicken Egg Rolls, in addition to vegetable Egg Foo Young, roast pork Chow Mein, and shrimp Chow Mee Fun. She was a cooking machine that day and filled us with the traditionally light servings. For financial rewards and the satisfaction of her clients, Susan might want to consider changing her major from engineering to cooking. The chef duties will fall on Levi when the new quarter starts, since we ran out of Wednesdays. He promised us a big, pleasant surprise.

Although we haven't come up with a name, Susan planted an interesting concept in us by accounting a congregation from Japan that went about spreading the Word throughout China in the face of intense communist governmental opposition, which resulted in imprisonment or death. They earned the nickname "Kamikaze's for Christ". Not that they went about over-zealously force-feeding the Word to the unwilling. She noted that they peacefully congregated and willingly gave up their bodies to be destroyed. We agreed that fellowship together is good, but the real work is reaching those on the other side of salvation. After recalling Dexter's efforts and results, there was no reluctance to go to the 'hood and bring the Gospel.

After Faith dismisses us with prayer, we collectively embrace and go our ways. You follow Levi to his dorm to shoot the breeze and help him get packed. It is nice not to have to go through the drama of interstate traveling home, although you *do* plan to take a long trip. With the help of Ma (good ol' clutch-winning Ma), you are on your way to the Gorrie Islands in Africa. You promised to sign your scholarship money over, but she just waved you off and said, "Don't worry about it." You're going to pay her back anyway.

"Geno should be punching the clock often, with the roster receding like the morning tide and all," you mention of your fellow first-year teammate Geno Carlisle, who's in the midst of an exodus of squad members. You're curious to see how good we will be next year when you and Evan Eschmeyer return.

"I'm surprised he bounced back from the arthroscopic knee surgery so soon. These knees can be too stubborn to my liking," Levi notes, patting his legs.

"Even though his dribbling gets on Coach's last good nerve—which ain't a good thing—he should even see some time at the two."

"He does dribble like Curly Neal on speed...gets on my nerves, too."

After packing up a few things, Levi turns on the news, which is broadcasting the scandal that we're discussing. Yesterday, shooting guard Dion Lee, along with running back Dennis Lundy, were caught up in a gambling probe. While Lundy's season is over with and he didn't play in his last game, Lee is suspended for six games. It didn't seem like a big deal with you, but it was a serious violation of NCAA, Northwestern, and team policies.

"Makes me cringe at the lunch wager we made in our 1-on-1," Levi testifies as he lays back on the bed.

"I won't tell if you won't," you second, parking on his desk.

"It would be a different thing if they were fixing games," Levi reasons as it is announced that the findings don't indicate it.

"You never know."

He agrees with a pause while the report continues. As the account comes to an end—leaving several unanswered questions—Levi listlessly confesses, "I used to fix games back home."

You glance over at him for a hint of humor, but he keeps his solemn gaze on the TV.

"Did it twice. Never got caught. Holiday tournament games that featured the state's best. Me and a couple of teammates hooked up with a small-time bookie who let us in on some of the action. As long as we won, we didn't have to put up nothing but points, which was our specialty anyway. The rewards were sweet—I won't lie and say that they weren't. It wasn't a matter of if we would win, but how many points we would score. When the game was out of reach, I insisted on staying in—you know, the bench-clearing, waterboy-mascot minutes. I didn't know the consequences of it until a friend from another school ended up committing suicide. It was big news and a trail led to the bookie. As it turns out, he was playing several opposing players against each other. When Jason Thomas lost and kept choking—which sunk him deeper in debt—the bookie set him up to lose big. He told Jason not to let the score get above 50. I almost scored that by myself, since he told me to at least get to 75. We ended up with 86, and my stats ended up splattered with Jason's blood. Needless to say, I didn't deal that way again, but I still bet on games with friends...just lunches though. I used to put up $50, $100—as much as $500 on some of the college and pro games. Simple bets among friends that we couldn't control the outcome in, and the outcome wouldn't control us. Gambling was my vice grip, and I still have to be cautious not to get carried away with those lunch wagers," he says, adding, "I only hope they're not the fall guys of something big, because I know how complex it can be."

You nod your understanding. That was never a weakness, and you were never enticed to make it your business. Small wagers among your boys is all. Now you know not to tempt Levi—even with a bet for a cup of water.

"Let me tell you about this dream I had a week ago," you insist. *God called you out with 1st Peter 2 and 9:* ***But ye are a chosen generation, a royal priesthood, a holy nation, a peculiar people; that ye should show forth the praises of him who hath called you out of darkness into his marvelous light.*** *You liked that, because he showed you you and your family among them. But then He dropped a bomb on you from Proverbs 30, 11 through 14:* ***There is a generation that curseth their father, and doth not bless their mother. There is a generation that are pure in their own eyes, and yet is not washed from their filthiness. There is a generation, O how lofty are their eyes! And their eyelids are lifted up. There is a generation, whose teeth are as swords, and their jaw teeth as knives, to devour the poor from off the earth, and the needy from among men.*** *It made you uneasy, because He showed you preaching the Gospel to that generation of gangsters, whores, perverts, drug dealers, revelers and reprobates, trying to bring them to the chosen generation. And the* *eerie element was the faces. The whole multitude looked like Kenny Reed.*

"Sounds like a calling to me," Levi notes.

"I always told you that our generation as a whole—my race in particular—is going to hell by the freight-train loads. We won't even see a lot of our peers in heaven. The drugs, drive-by's, killings, ignorance, gangs, irresponsible parents and anger makes this the hell raising generation...not Generation X."

"I can only share your woe, my brother, which makes my cross that much more excruciating. The nation of Israel—my nation—is in perpetual denial of Jesus; they missed the ship of Zion and there will be too many of my fellow Jews swimming in the Lake of Fire. Imagine every generation from the nation—with the exception of a small remnant—stumbling over Christ the solid Rock...stumbling all the way to Hell, which will make the Holocaust seem like Heaven to them. Sometimes I long for the Great Tribulation, so that my people can wake up. It's ironic that after ages of persecution, the greatest genocidal movement will open Israel's heart to Jesus. In the meantime, I'm going to continue to try and spread the Gospel to my brothers, because that's my purpose for being here. And you have to stand up and bring the Good News to your generation who're in denial of Christ, because He chose you this season for that very reason. Imagine being minorities among our own people. That grieves me to the point of death."

You nod your agreement and wonder, "I don't know why He would—if that's what He did—choose me to bring the Gospel to them. I guess since I took note of the need, He called me on my observation. Good grief."

"It's plain to me and the other Bible study members that you're the unofficial leader, even though it's an open forum. When an issue comes up in the class, the anointing usually falls on you. Your boldness and knowledge is head and shoulders above the other members, not to mention your widespread appeal."

"Appeal?" you guffaw with amazement. "I still have too many issues to deal with before I can effectively lead. How can I speak a Word in love when I have so much animosity? I'm liable to curse them quicker than I bless them. Shoot, I haven't fully forgiven people that have wronged me, and although you're down with me like a blue-eyed brother on the struggle, I'm not yet color-blind."

"You still have color issues because color is still an issue. There's no gray area in America. When it's all said and done, we all have issues that God is correcting, but until your change comes, wait on the Lord...wait as in waiter—as in serve Him with what He's given you. In the process, He'll kill the flesh," he assures. "Listen: Over the summer, you took a stand like very few would have the courage to take. How many hoopers would turn down an invitation from Nike to play in a tournament crawling with agents and scouts? The potential to make good connections and build a speaking relationship with the high rollers was great. There was even a possibility that a door to future endorsements could've been open. You knew that. But not only did you turn them down, but you also spoke out against them. No one that you could see had your back on that issue, but that didn't deter you."

You nod as you recall the event.

"In terms of the strength of the stand, Moses relinquishing his Egyptian birthrights of luxury and pleasure to suffer with his brothers, and Rosa Parks' refusal to move despite the consequences, come to mind when I think action-statements. You blasted Nike about the Apartheid issue; you knocked them for benefiting from the black culture, yet refusing to invest in the community; and you even called the name—Nike—in question, noting that Jesus is the only God of victory...defeating death, sin and Satan on the cross to live, die and rise undefeated. That was powerful," he states passionately.

"I didn't even know people outside of Chicago could see me standing," you chuckle with humility.

"You were too tall to miss. And you know what? You had a brother from Ohio standing with you in his Gospel of peace shoes, 'cause I refused to attend after I heard your position," he says as he holds his fist out.

You smile and pound him, stating, "It's good to know I got a brother helping to hold up the blood stained banner."

"So I say again: Your faith in action can move the masses."

You chuckle. "And I say that you just came up with a name for the study group."

He grins as he ponders, "Faith in Action...I like. It's a done deal: You'll be a Moses to a people and I'll be a Joshua, if necessary."

You shake your head in agreement and mull over that comment in silence. Not that it's a confirmation (not that it's not, either), but you're enlightened like a light bulb. If it is a calling, you have to go with His perfect timing, because even though the vision came last week, it's not necessarily coming to pass at the moment.

As we stare at the television, a late breaking story indicates that fugitive Reuben Johnson was shot and killed in a police confrontation in downstate Eldorado. The sound of the details go in and out of your ears, leaving residual gloom as Levi utters, "I hope he was saved." You agree with a silent grunt. It sticks on your mind like dirt on tape, but it doesn't register on your heart. Emotions can be a poor gauge of a person's well being. Nothing manifests as pain, which to the naked eye would seem like cold-hearted callousness. You don't blink; your heart doesn't race; your blood pressure doesn't rise; your eyes don't well up. Make no mistake about it: you're critically wounded, and when you come around, it's going to hurt like hell-and-a-half. For the longest time you prepared for this moment. Although your heart is under anesthesia, you experience a slight swelling in your chest that dissipates with the flow of blood. The blunt of the blow isn't apparent and your countenance must be an enigmatic blank as you announce, "Later dude" and exit. Levi has you saying "dude."

"My father is dead" is a melancholy melody that grates against your heart. The pain is throbbing. When you dwell on it, the ache rises up; when you focus on other things, there is no feeling. Numb is an understated cliché. The acidic reality is percolating from your mind and into your bosom. You're concerned about his soul salvation. Did he call on the name of Jesus before he passed? There's no way that you can bring him from that mysterious, other side. You've accepted his death. Truthfully, you accepted it years before he gave up the ghost. This is a closure for you. Faith has been a perfect manifestation of grace: an ear to listen to your thoughts; a mouth as a vessel for the voice of reason; space when you needed solitude; and company during the despairing moods. It seems like death is always on your heals. *"I pray that God takes me before He takes you, because to live without you would be like an eternal death,"* you wished to Faith.

The memorial service at Gatlings seemed...stolid. Just a handful of relatives showed up. You're glad the media didn't connect you to him. Not that you're ashamed to be identified as his only son. It's just that you don't want to have to send someone to the dentist for saying more about him than needs to be said. Dad's only written request was to be cremated immediately after death. Ben didn't voice an objection, but you could tell that he wanted to hold on to something tangible. He didn't cry in your presence, but his whole air wept in silence. From a natural standpoint, Dad was closer to you, but spiritually, he and Ben were thicker than ketchup. There was much more history and intimacy between them. Never in your life have you seen Ben without a mouthful of humor or wisdom...until today.

Ma's reaction matches yours, although her soul couldn't hold the water when she first got the news. When you got home from Levi's, she was weeping on the phone with Faith because your heart concerned her. After she discerned your collected presence, she fed off of your strength. We talked briefly and laughed a little before we closed out with "I love you" just before you were about to release your water.

Uncle JoJo lost his oldest "son", so naturally he is devastated. You couldn't measure it by his behavior. His powerful character hasn't missed a beat. Instead of being comforted, he has managed to keep everyone else upbeat. What you really want him to do is go into his praying closet and leave his burdens with the Lord. That's the unwritten theme of your life, which was captured in your unnatural composure during the whole ordeal. In this dark, cold season of despair, for the first time in your short life, you take notice of the wings of Love encompassing your heart.

> ***Jesus, Hallelujah does You no justice. Against the odds, You created me. What words can I render to the Word? For singling me out of a great cloud of prospects; For blessing my life with a plethora of saints who enrich and edify my soul, thank You, Lord. You have guided me around the storm of Ray's passing; lifted me over the mountain of Dexter's homegoing; taken me through the flood of the fear of my dependence on and place in You. When my attention was on a god contrary to You and I followed the crescent to Damnation Drive, You redirected my focus on the cross and ordered my steps back to the Path of Righteousness. Father, You have given me a testimony; You have endowed me with a talent to communicate; You have emboldened me to stand on my faith. My God, I want to be just like You when I grow up. Resolve the race issues in my life. I don't want to be color-blind;***

I want to be able to appreciate the beauty and diversity of Your top creation. Help me to see people through Your loving eyes, so that my witness will be laced with love, for I hear Your summons to visit the prisons. You have given me the talent and commission to tutor those who are now incarcerated and prepare them for abundant life, for You have ordained them to be set free. Lord, I'm willing, and You're able. By the power of Your Word, it is so. What's my next step? Take my faith to another level. Your vessel is waiting to be filled. December 15, 1994.

"My pal, Mal," the voice trumpets from over Tupac's "Shed so Many Tears", bursting your thought balloon as you wander towards Harold's Chicken on 79th and Essex.

You turn around as the grinning African clothier approaches you. You smirk as you grab his name from the air. "What's up, Victor," you greet just when his moniker comes back.

"Nothing much," he says, slapping your hand into a clasp and embracing you firmly. "How the grades coming? You got any new words for me?" he jokes/queries.

"I got straight aces, but I can't school you with any new words today. Try Reader's Digest." He has a jubilant spirit that just rubs off and has its way with anyone around.

"Where do you think RD gets their challenges from?" he quizzes in jest (you think). "I'm glad to hear you're doing work up at NU. You almost have me inspired to go back to school."

"Just building positive images and destroying negative myths," you declare as you peek at all of the transactions taking place at the drive through pharmacy on the corner.

"I hear you, little brother," he confirms, taking note of the action, too. "Where's that fine lady of yours? I know you're treating her right, 'cause she was sho nuff treating you right."

"My wife is getting the queen's treatment," you announce.

"Is that right? You married her, huh?"

"What can I say and what can I do when a good woman comes along, but marry her?"

He nods as he misses a beat in reflection. "I'm trying to make amends myself, because a good wife is more precious than jewels," he assures wistfully.

"I agree with Proverbs 31 and 10."

"A Bible scholar, too...you got it going on little brother."

"I'm just growing in grace."

"I hear you. I'm finding my way back to the Lord myself, so pray for me."

Your heart smiles. "Sure thing, Victor."

"And pray that I can make amends with that beautiful woman that I messed up with."

"You got it."

"You been in the store lately?"

"I'll be in there tomorrow for a couple of outfits to take with me to the Mother Land."

"Is that right?"

You nod.

"Well, just mention my name first, then your name, and you'll get the hook up."

"You know I will," you promise, scrunching up under the Hawk's pressure.

"Well, I'm not going to keep you, since you're trying to get your bird...and I don't want to keep mine waiting, so look me up sometimes little brother," he says as he starts back to his Pathfinder.

"I got you," you assure, starting off...just when someone yells, "Aiight Folks!"

You should be conditioned to take cover when you hear that, but it's almost a background noise. There is nothing startling about the clap of a firecracker. Like the back-play of an M-80, the fizz of the live fuse bearing down on you pierces the air. Your senses are shocked and your reflexes are delayed, just like the slow motion projectile. There is time to think about the present; dwell on the past; ponder the future. TSN will be editing the final draft; Faith promised you a surprise when you get home; You earned straight A's. This time last year you were on the verge of a serious religious rebellion; Dexter took your advice and bought junior the Sega Genesis basketball for Christmas; Charlotte was your woman. You're not taking any prisoners next season; After your basketball career, you'll go to law school; We leave for the Motherland Monday.

Your back is the point where the sound runs out of real estate. The combustion that rips into your spine—slicing you in two—sends shockwaves throughout your body as the gust of pressurized steam picks you up like a dry leaf in a cyclone and floats you in the air as if you were swimming. While you feel the angry fire eating away your flesh, nerves, and bones; as you come crash-sliding on the pavement; as you quiver in agony on the ground, you go into auto-prayer. Nothing elaborate and long as you force your eyes shut. Just a breathless, repetitive, "Jesus" while nature allows you to slip into the pacifying shock. The pain dims in quenched wick fashion and your consciousness fades like a sunray in the twilight.

20

"There's nothing like a forced fast," you note, scooping up the remnants of the Doro Wat from the Styrofoam carryout plate. Faith clutches your free hand for dear life and scrutinizes your every blink, as if you are going to disintegrate. The notoriety of hospital food being as tasteless as a Def Comedy Jam comedian didn't prepare you for the cuisine fit for the damned. Coupled with the cableless television, it seems like this heavenly sterile, virgin-white institution discourages staying. "No diet is as effective as hospital confinement."

Ma overtly coerces her mouth to smirk at your stale humor, as if she had a gun to her teeth.

Mitch gazes at the floor like it's chastising him.

Nick looks depleted of hope.

Chuck D uncomfortably observes your feasting with the knowing expression that you're consuming cyanide.

Levi sits mum, as if his First Amendment Rights are revoked.

Uncle Ben and Deon peer out of the window at the micro flakes that are racing towards the west.

Uncle JoJo measures his fragile words, consoling, "I can run out and get you a second helping" as the sincerity almost spills over his eyelids.

"That's okay," you assure, glancing at an unknown show on the television. "I'll run out and get it myself," you chuckle, prompting all eyes to behold you.

You grow solemnly silent as you ponder this pitiful scene. Faith strokes your hand, which would normally soothe you, but with a room full of dismal mannequins, it grows more annoying than a rash. You snatch your hand away and request, "Can you tell the nurse to bring my jumpers, so I can hop up out of here?" No reaction. "Somebody shoot me, because y'all are as bland as hospital food." Not a laugh or a stir. You drop your head and pray, "Lord, when I wake up from this nightmare, please let this valley of dry bones be restored to life" as you blink into the blissful black.

Your eyes pop open from sleep exhaustion to the welcoming whites. "Good grief...all of these teeth. I feel like I'm in a dentist's nightmare. Tone it down before I give y'all a root canal."

"Better than one of those mad alliterations," Nick notes as you drop your mouth and chuckle.

"I'm saying. He starts off slow, low and methodical," Faith describes. "Then he gets hot, faster and complicated."

"Half the words he uses are foreign to the average John Dawg," Chuck D pitches.

You can't believe they're ganging up on you.

"Sounds like he's rapping," Mitch says as you cover your head with the pillow.

The phone rings and you plead, "Somebody answer that, please," while you remain buried.

"Now you know it ain't for nobody in here but you," Ma reasons.

"Good grief," you say coming up from under the pillow and answering, "Hello."

"As-Salaam-Alaikum."

"Wa-Alaikum-Salaam."

"How you doing black man?"

You can't lie and be phony. In a course of a day, your mood can rise a level above hell to an empyrean of joy, and then some of the swings in between. "Some moments are better than other's, but I'm living one minute at a time, Khalid, and that's a blessing in itself."

"I hear you. I just wanted you to know that I'll be praying for you, and the real God will somehow get the answer," he assures.

That doesn't fade you a bit, but you still don't back down from a challenge. You're nice in informing him that if you walk again, Jesus got the message; if you don't, Jesus still got the message.

"You heard that Kenny is studying with the Nation." His reminder/announcement is a boast laced with indemnity.

"Yeah, I heard," is all you can utter.

You want to inform him that Kenny has a stronger chance of making the pilgrimage to Mecca than earning a seat in the heavens by studying the doctrine of death, however, incivility is unnecessary. His soul going to hell from a jail cell brings you no satisfaction whatsoever. Grief gripped your heart like a bear hug when you read the small excerpt in the paper. In a strange way, it stung worse than Dexter's soul ripping from his body and sliding through your fingers. Somehow, the burden of guilt weighed you down like two tons of tort.

When you get off the phone, they're still in festive-overdrive mode, which is a touch annoying in your state, but beats the hell out of the funeral tone.

"Dude..." Levi starts as Chuck D cuts him off.

"Eh man, you're gonna have to drop the dude. How many times do I have to tell you? Call 'em Dawg."

"Dog..." he tries, with too much proper enunciation.

"DAWG," Chuck emphasizes. "D-A-W-G: DAWG. RWOOF!"

"Okay. Dawg...you know, I forgot what I was going to say."

"Now I can teach you how to say Snake: Ssssssnnnnnaake," Ben jokes.

"Don't think you're getting out of the trip to Africa," Faith clarifies. "I expect you to be ready tomorrow at three sharp."

"Now you know he's in no condition to travel," Uncle JoJo defends. "I'll go in his place."

"I thought you were afraid of flying," Ben questions.

"I agreed to put him under before he boards," Ma notes.

"Save some for me," you dryly joke. "What did you get for Christmas, Nick? And don't give me an ethereal answer, either. Give me some tangible details."

"Well, I really didn't get much of anything. A few clothes...cards...another Bible of course...some CD's," she concludes, P.S.ing, "and some jewelry," as she holds up her ring while gleaming at Deon.

Your eyebrows and smile jump. "Get out of here...Deon?"

Deon is muted and crimson.

She nods once as she beams away.

"Santa dropped the same thing down my chimney," Joyce notes, holding up her carat finger and pecking Chuck D.

You forget about your misfortune for that moment as the collective joy spreads in the room. With all of the marriage talk, you happen to catch Faith smiling at you. You return the knowing grin while everyone continues to feast on the beatitude.

The Lord lets the sun shine on the good and the bad and He sends rain to the garden of the wicked and the garden of the righteous. God's grace is

evident when I wake up to another day, especially since I deserve to enter into an eternal sleep. I recognize that grace and thank Jesus for every moment in my life. However, there are times when I desire to manipulate His providence. If I was at the helm of divine authority, Ben Wilson would have survived the shooting ten years ago and gone on to take the NBA by storm; my two closest friends—Raymond and Dexter—would not have been felled by the same gun violence. With my finite mind, I don't understand the fullness of His purposes in such tragedies.

While interviewing, researching, and writing this article, I took note of the many lives Ben Wilson positively influenced on his way back to God. In reflection, I could understand why God called him home: He had fulfilled his purpose in this life. For some, it takes longer, while others never dance in tune to His music. It is in that light that I am able to put my recent paralysis into perspective. I can't say that I know why it happened to me, but I know that He allowed me to survive for a reason. If I had my say in the matter, I would have gone into His glorious presence.

My friend Bryant Notree of Illinois dropped an interesting soundbite in my inner ear that has given me the courage to press on. "God only tests the best" was his answer to the trials of life. I believe that even in the midst of a tragic cycle of gun violence, there is a message in the life of Ben. Ben understood that he was called to raise the standard on and off the court. And he did that. He made it to the top and didn't fall from grace. Not many can say that. With the time that we have, let us give love and honor the talent that God has blessed us with in order to live out His perfect will. It is that legacy of Hope that I will incorporate into my daily walk, for we walk by faith and not by sight.

"Well," you say with finality as you hand Faith the longhand sheet. "This is it." You talked to the editor at TSN and agreed to do a side commentary about your tragedy. He promised that he would give you editorial authority on it, meaning that it will appear as you write it.

She takes it and kisses you on the forehead as she continues to stroke your chest. "Do you think that once you get out you can give me a rematch on the court?"

You smirk.

Faith is not in denial. The doctor's outlook is myopic. What you see is how it is in laymen's terms. The wheelchair will be a permanent part of you. However, through the eyes of Faith, there is no wheelchair. It's just you and her. She insists that the Lord told her that this is only a test. She promised you that although she's willing, it won't be necessary to devote her medical school focus on neurological studies. Some days you believe her without a shadow of a doubt, while on those same days you wish that He would not only tell you that, but also bring it to pass. But then that would take the element of faith out. She informed you that Levi flew back to Dayton after flying back here when he heard of the shooting. All of your Faith N Action comrades have been in constant prayer. Sometimes when you don't feel the effects of God's hand, it's good to know that it's there. And at your suggestion, the group will be called Faith N Action.

Her hand strokes lower and lower until...Nothing. That area has been a point of concern. What if you're not able to produce? You don't even want her to stick around to swap saliva. She already informed you that she's not going anywhere. Whatever. Apparently she can read the concern in your heart, because she kisses your lips and whispers, "Continue to look through the eyes of Faith" as she gently brushes her nails over your scalp. Her touch charges your blood and orders your soldier of fortune to salute the queen of wet dreams. It's amazing how her touch gets a rise out of you. You liken it to the breath of God giving life to man.

She grins mischievously at you and promises, "You have a lot of quality time to make up."

"Afekerehallo," you reaffirm.

"Emi na Feran e yun," she returns.

Your coy smirk reflects the hope in your heart as you close your eyes and enjoy your foreplay to heaven.

Dear Brother Reed,

That's the only way I can address you because—yes—we are brothers of the human race; descended from a single seed. Like all of Adam's children, we have fallen short of perfection. There's no need in measuring our follies on a scale of morality, because when it's all said

and done we're all made of dirt—which is evident every time I take off a white shirt.

And we're brothers in a racial sense. We face the same struggles in this country; shared the same dreams; ate at the same Mickey D's; abide in the same social class; and played at the same parks. You're probably a Lakers fan like me. However, the brotherhood is a three dimensional fraternity. The last one is a matter of choice. When it's all said and done, it's the only thing that matters in this life: entering into the covenant of the blood of Jesus. I have many blood brothers that look like me; act like me; speak like me; sleep like me. Then I have many more blood brothers of different shades, from white to red to yellow to brown.

I'm not going to be phony with you. Losing Dexter was like the amputation of a limb. The sun forever lost a touch of it's luster that day. I lost a lot of blood that day. Bitterness set in and sucked me into a resolve to give up; to not care whether people live or die; to wish for death. I didn't think that the hurt would stop; that I would be able to look at brothers the same way again. And yes, I hated you for it. I wanted you cast into hell. And I wanted you to pay rent there, too. At the mention of your name I envisioned cross-bones and a skull.

As usual, time and the healing hands of the Lord have worked wonders. My whole perception of that day has changed forever. Now when I look at the situation, I realize that Dexter is not lost at all. As a matter of fact, his accommodations are much better than ours.

You would've been down with Dexter if you got a chance to know him. There wasn't a man that he disliked. He was blessed with a touch of God's vision, which allowed him to see men as more than just muddy mortals, but as sweet souls. By grace I can finally see that aspect of man...I can call you a brother from the heart.

I don't know if you've taken any oaths or recited any creeds, but I dare you—I beseech you—to invite Jesus into your heart. You can pray without ceasing 24/7/365; you can fast until you wither up and turn into dust; you can give all of your goods to the poor and offer your body to be burned to measure your sincerity, but all of that will not atone for your sins. Make no mistake about it: Every knee shall bow and every tongue must confess that Jesus Christ is Lord—either on this side of consciousness or on the other side of the grave. Jesus paid your debt even before you were born and knew you were in debt, but it's up to you to

take advantage of the grace, mercy and love of God. Adam committed Spiritual suicide when he bit the forbidden fruit, and we all inherited that same death.

Don't be played: God the Father is Spirit, not man. A man will not be omnipresent. And if a man is not omnipresent, he will not be omniscient. And if a man isn't omniscient, he will not be omnipotent. Since man is physical and visible, there would be no need to have faith in God if he was a man. That's as ridiculous as having faith that your team will win after they romped over the opponent.

My God lowered His level and lived in a body. That didn't stop Him from being God, though. By taking on a body, He not only provided a living illustration for us, but by his life he defeated sin, by his death he defeated Satan and by his resurrection he defeated death.

Just as mankind was conquered when Adam slipped, mankind has victory through Jesus. Just as the Spirit of God left Adam and mankind because of sin, the Spirit of God dwells within us because of the Righteousness of Jesus.

The newspaper stories can't be retracted; history can't be erased; the facts can't be removed. However, when I look at you and when I hear of you, I don't see and think murderer, I see and think brother. I don't hold you accountable for what happened in the past. More importantly, once you're down with Christ, God doesn't even remember what you did and He sees you as a son; a brother and a friend.

The work of the Nation is commendable; their discipline is admirable. But when it's all said and done, it means nothing in the case of salvation. God is holy, perfect, pure, sinless. The Father can't dwell with sinful man and man can't dwell with the Holy Father. Even if your goodness outweighed your wickedness, just a touch of unrighteousness is too much to approach God with. After all, according to human logic, Adam didn't do anything so morally wrong that would warrant the death penalty. Salvation is based on who you know, not what you do. I'm here to tell you that Jesus' recommendation will take you into the eternal presence of the Father.

The Christian creed concerning salvation is summed up in what is called the Romans Road: All have sinned and fallen short of the glory of God—Romans 3:23; The wages of sin is death but the gift of God is eternal life—Romans 6:23; God showed His love in this: when we were sinners he sent His son to die for us—Romans 5:8; If you confess with your mouth and believe in your heart that Jesus is Lord and God raised him from death you will be saved. It is with the heart that you believe and are justified and it is with the mouth that your confession is made into salvation—Romans 10:9-10. That reinforces the Gospel message of John 3:16: God loved us so, that He gave His only son to be sacrificed, and whoever believes in Jesus, will not die without hope, but have eternal life. As long as your heart pumps blood and words remain in your mouth, Jesus is willing and waiting to save you.

Your affiliation with the Brothers brought with it a bad reputation, even if you didn't earn it. Consequently, players had to give you your due. It was by works that you got respect among your people. It was by those same works that you ended up in prison. That quarter moon and five point star tattooed on your chest and on the other side of your ear was an outward sign that you weren't your own. As a result, red was your color.

When you're affiliated with Christ, you will have a reputation. While salvation is a gift, rewards come from works, and God didn't call us not to work. The works of the Spirit will not earn you respect from the world, but best believe it will go a long way in setting others free. I'm not going to play you: people will cross you once they find out you're a follower of Christ. Christianity is more than wearing a cross. It's about the covenant in your heart that seals your salvation. And yes, red is still the color of significance. Jesus donned a red robe, which was symbolic of the sin that he bore in and on himself; the blood that he shed that washed away our sins and put us right with God.

Although the use of my legs are gone for a season, I will continue to stand in the gap for you. There's more to talk about, and I'm willing. The enclosed N.I.V. study Bible should help in your understanding of God's Word. I will be writing you in a couple of months at the latest. If you feel comfortable in calling, my number is (847) 555-4554. In the meantime, I pray that the grace of our Lord will be with you, preserving you until you accept the plan of salvation, and keeping you for His glory and honor.

In the name of Jesus,

Malcolm Johnson

Epilogue

For I walk by faith, not by sight. But what if I can walk no more? Is my faith gone?

You don't have an answer, and to top it off, you're creatively crippled—to add a pun to the tragedy. You close your journal and let it lay on the side of you as you look up into white space. Your spirit has fallen into a ditch. Illinois just smoked the Wildcats 82-55. Notree had an okay game, but what disturbed you more than not being out there making some kind of difference to the outcome, was the reception the NU fans gave your boy. When he got in the game and every time he touched the ball, they chanted, "Eighth Grade Science" in reference to the grammar school credit that counted towards his eligibility. You are lying through your thoughts. It didn't disturb you; it pissed you off. Your mood gives some consolation in not playing.

Khalid called you, excited about the soon-to-be-open Salaam restaurant on 79th Street, just east of Halsted. He was mute on the issue of the charges against Qubilah Shabazz, the second-oldest daughter of Malcolm X. Last week, she allegedly tried to hire a hit man to take Louis Farrakhan out. It's a sad, intriguing topic that Brian is having a problem digesting. As a result, he is starting to question his faith.

The Ben Wilson article ran this week, and from all indications, it was well received. You only glanced at the finished copy. After all, you trusted it was in perfect order. All of the research has you fatigued on the topic, and on journalism in general. The winter quarter started for Faith and the rest of the NU students. They allowed you this and any other quarter off to adjust. It should only take a couple of month's to get used to your handicap.

Technically, the shock was over two weeks ago, and you've been out of critical condition long enough to mentally move on. The bullet from Hook shattered a vertebra and sent your nervous system to a nursing home. Of course the doctors want to sound as positive as possible. Maybe they will come up with some treatment to heal paralysis in ten—twenty—thirty years, but medical history isn't on your side. Since patience isn't your forte, time is going to be another Goliath-like foe. Uncle JoJo says, "All things are possible if you only believe." And you believe that, but why put God to the test? It will definitely take a miracle. The healing process starts with acceptance. Gone are the days of dunking in a crowd. The NBA is a non-option. You ain't ever going to walk again. Now you have to get over the spiritual shock.

A sweltering tear scorches a path down the left side of your face as you look expressionless out of the window. Crying is a liberating gift of the Spirit that you've tapped into lately. Slowly, but surely, all of your hang-ups and issues that are compressed deep in your heart are oozing out without hurting anyone. You're graduating to a level of restraint. A small stimulus of stupidity would set your mouth to spewing in the past. If one got sprayed with obscenities, you would repent later. Those days are passing fast. Before the shooting, it would take a poke in the eye from the hands of the brisk, Windy-City Hawk for you to shed a tear. Now you have nothing else to do. You already miss the good ol' days when your pride wouldn't let you cry, no matter how much pain you were in. Although the bullet didn't kill you, it killed your pride. Maybe that's a good thing. Pride can be a heavy burden, and you feel like the burden has been lifted.

Now you shed emotional tears. Tears from within the deepest crevices of your heart. Tears of happiness. You could be dead or in a coma or paralyzed from the neck down. Tears of sadness. Some of your dreams did die. Tears of madness. It was a black man you knew and played ball with in the park that pulled the trigger. Tears of frustration. You didn't have a choice between life and death, and if you did, you would have chosen the later, so you could be reunited with Dexter and Raymond, and finally hook up with Ben Wilson for a game of Heavenly Hoops. Tears of gratitude. Victor didn't get hit, although the bullet had his name on it. Tears of fear. For the first time in your life, your destiny is so unclear. Tears of confusion. The Word says that God will never leave you nor forsake you, but you feel all alone right now. It'll be hard to go looking for Him, since you'll be confined to a wheelchair. What if He's on a mountaintop? How does He expect you to roll up there?

Hallelujah anyhow. God is great, but you still have questions that your mind voices to Him: *'How did I manage to get out of the presence of Your grace?' 'What did I do wrong?'* The questions echo against the wall of your head so long and so swift that it becomes a serene hum, which lulls you into an empyreanic trance. As darkness gives way to light, you hear the soft sounds of instruments blending "Never Alone" into the tranquillity. Then, like noticing a picture that's always been hanging on your living room wall for the first time, the Lord makes His voice heard in a whisper: ***"You have not sinned, but that the works of God should be made manifest in you."***

If you had been listening for it, you would have missed it; it was at a pitch that cannot be picked up with the natural ears. But it was louder than an atomic bomb, crisper than a dry whip, and clearer than Windexed crystal. The anointing is as gentle as a gossamer Comforter, yet as sure as a Sword through the heart, as the Holy Ghost ushers you into the presence of God. Your soul shouts, "Holy Holy Holy" in the spiritual and natural realm, although you neither know nor care if anyone else can hear you. As the glory of God becomes more consuming with your closer fellowship, you can feel the Spirit all on and in you; you can feel...your legs...in the physical! Instead of rephrasing your first foolish query, "Lord, why did You leave me like that", you let your Spirit touch and confirm with the Living Word. *"Never Alone, I don't have to worry 'cause, I'm never alone. He walks beside me, all the Way; He guides my footsteps, every day."*

The lyrics are quickening. Walk is a critical, operative, action Word. With that revelation, you open your mouth to beg His pardon for wishing for death in the face of adversity, but you feel anointed hands on your head, which sends power throughout your body; like pure gold in the sanctifying fire; like instant glorification after sudden death. "What are you doing, Lord?" you hear yourself ask.

"See," He answers as a vision comes before your eyes. You are not only walking, but also excelling on the court—in future tense—beyond NU. It becomes clear that the Spirit is making love to you and impregnating you with a testimony. ***"I have come to give you Life and that more abundantly."***

With His Word in your heart; in His presence; with your natural lids shut and through your open eyes of faith, you stand...and give praise: "Holy Holy Holy."

Order Form

Name:____

Address:______________________________________

City/State/Zip:_________________________________

Phone:_______________________________________

___ copies of Eyes of Faith	$15.00 each	$__________
___ copies of Shades of Black	$14.00 each	$__________
Please add $2.00 per book for postage and handling		$__________
Illinois residents please add 8.75% sales tax		$__________
Total amount enclosed:		$__________

Make checks or money orders payable to “Terrance Johnson”, then send it along with this order form to the following address:

7-Fold Publishing
7732 S. Cottage Grove
Box 121
Chicago, IL. 60619